Love is the Answer

Published by Brolga Publishing Pty Ltd
ABN 46 063 962 443
PO Box 12544
A'Beckett St
Melbourne, VIC, 8006
Australia

email: markzocchi@brolgapublishing.com.au

All rights reserved. No part of this publication may be reproduced, stored in a retrieval system or transmitted in any form or by any means electronic, mechanical, photocopying, recording or otherwise without prior permission from the publisher.

Copyright © 2013 Tracy Madden

National Library of Australia Cataloguing-in-Publication entry
Author: Madden, Tracy,
Title: Love is the answer
ISBN: 9781922175304 (paperback)
Dewey Number: A823.4

Printed in Indonesia
Cover design by Chameleon Print Design
Typesetting by Wanissa Somsuphangsri

BE PUBLISHED

Publish Through a Successful Publisher. National Distribution, Macmillan & International Distribution to the United Kingdom, North America. Sales Representation to South East Asia
Email: markzocchi@brolgapublishing.com.au

Love is the Answer

Tracy Madden

Dedication

To my first born grandson, Hunter Gordon Madden. Three and a half years ago you came into this world bringing insurmountable love into my life, enriching it beyond all belief in a way I could never have expected.

Through your eyes I have seen the world anew, with wonder, awe, enthrallment and excitement. You take me to places where imagination knows no bounds. Mystical rainbows now have colours I had never seen, caterpillars on the pavement are placed there for us to discover, the wind rustles the tree tops for our eyes only, and yes we can spend twenty minutes talking about why a leaf is the colour it is, or about how interesting a rock is we have found in the park, conversations that simply must be had.

You are my wonderful excuse to spend the day playing, something I had forgotten I loved so much. Why it took 53 years for me to take up the air guitar is beyond me, as I am so damn good at it. I dance with you like I have danced with no one before.

Finally, I have a mini wing man who loves my juices, smoothies, and super foods, listens to my stories about how good they are for us, loves doing our special yoga, and welcomes loving the day with me.

Thank you my gorgeous man, I cannot wait to see what new things your little brother Baby Boston Bear will teach me. You are both Gracy's greatest treasures.

Chapter 1

First a confession... I interviewed my husband's mistress for him. You might ask yourself *how could I?* Well I didn't bloody-well know, did I?

It's not what you think. I interviewed her for a position. Not that type of position, a position with our company. I thought she was a dream.

I thought she could replace me in the business perfectly. I just didn't expect her to replace me everywhere else as well.

Today was not a good day. Today was a doona day. Today I shed tears. Today I ate too much chocolate. Today I got angry. And today, I finally walked away.

On second thoughts, perhaps today was a great day.

*

One last time, I cast my eyes around our warehouse home, the decor uncompromising and modern, with free standing units and open chrome shelving, never my idea of how a home should look. *So...* it had come to this.

My eyes settled on a small crystal bird sitting atop of a gardening book, *Field of Dreams*. I thought of how the book had been *allowed*, as it was personally signed by the author, a so-called friend of Davis's. The crystal bird had been a gift from Davis in happier times. My mind went to the look on Davis's face as he had repeatedly moved the bird to my bedside table, out of range of viewing. He abhorred clutter, always telling me I had bowerbird tendencies.

For a few brief seconds, my hand hovered as I toyed with the idea of taking it with me. However, much like my old life, I no longer wanted it.

My eyes settled on the contemporary chandelier hanging

over the dining table. Really, how could you miss it? Six sheets of silver coated paper, it was truly ridiculous, looking more like an old fashioned flying machine. I wondered what our friends had thought.

And then something made me walk down the hall towards the master bedroom, a room I had vacated many months earlier, preferring the guest room. Hesitating at the door, I glanced around as if I was looking for something. Without knowing why, I walked over to what used to be my side of the immaculately made up sleek modular bed, and slipping my hand under the cool charcoal coloured top sheet, I reefed it back. Using both hands, I mussed the bottom sheet, and then pulled the pillow on an angle.

Standing back, I surveyed my handiwork. I may have been evacuating my home, walking away from my business, my life, and unwittingly giving *her* my husband, however I sure as hell wanted *her* to know some things *had* belonged to me. In fact, there was a half-eaten sandwich still on the kitchen bench. I wondered if she wanted that as well.

Dusting my hands, I walked back along the hallway. I paused outside another bedroom door. It was closed. My hand went to the knob. I hesitated, before wisely walking on. The nursery I had been readying was now packed up and in storage. The room was empty, much like my heart.

Seeing my coffee mug on the kitchen bench, I automatically picked it up, taking it to the sink to rinse. Running the tap, I reached for the sponge to wipe the tell-tale lipstick mark from the rim, when with mild satisfaction I left it on the drainer, lipstick mark and all.

With a snort of indignation, I shook my head at the memory of Davis many months earlier, during our one and only counselling session. In response to a question from the counsellor, his answer had been that he didn't like the way I drank my coffee. Apparently he found it annoying when he saw the lipstick marks still on the rim of mugs after they had come out of the dishwasher.

Really! I wanted to shout to him now. *Tell someone who cares!*

Picking up my keys from the spotless plexiglass study desk, I stared out through the huge pane of glass at the top of the stairs. To the left, my eyes settled atop the massive Moreton Bay Fig trees at Davies Park. Each Saturday, those same trees canopied the famed West End markets. Although Davis used to tease me that many years earlier, the park had been owned by his family, and that is where his name originated from, I used to think of them as *my* markets. Now nothing seemed like mine. I felt misplaced, uncertain of where I belonged.

Turning to the right, I took in the impressive view of Brisbane city's skyline. Davis called it *the money shot*. I recalled the excitement we felt when we moved here. With a view like that we thought we'd had it made.

Exhaling heavily, I headed down the steel staircase, my purple suede Stella McCartney heels loud on each tread.

Halfway down, I caught my reflection in the huge round mirror from Space furniture, a mirror we had shopped for together to celebrate our first anniversary. How many times had I checked myself from this position one last time before heading out? Although, for the past eight months I had refrained, not liking what I saw. My normally filled out heart shaped face, had become a leaner version of its former self, the shadows under my eyes, smudges that didn't erase. For goodness sake, I was only 34.

Although I may have recently been *terra incognita*, when I glanced across, I noticed there was a small measure of the real me returning, and although I saw relief on my face, my middle finger went to a small frown line embedded between my brows. I could not remember that being there a year ago.

Continuing the last few steps, my eyes cast down to the harsh pigmented concrete flooring spreading across the first floor entry. I could not help but be reminded of the amount of arguments we'd had over this floor, me wanting something welcoming and homely, Davis insisting on keeping the industrial look.

I glanced back the way I had come. This was it! We had shared hopes, dreams, sorrows, thoughts and memories, and now it was over. I exhaled, waiting for something to rear up. Nothing!

The thing was my new life was not apparent yet. I had to believe it would come to me.

*

Ten long weeks ago, which now seemed like eons away, my mother Bea, handed me a small blue card. Silently, I read: *Do you want to free up your body, heart and mind from years of old patterns and baggage? Are you ready to create a healthier, happier, more harmonious way of living?* I remembered looking at my mother. She shrugged, dusted her hands together, climbed into her white seventies Peugeot cabriolet and roared off down the street, without a backward glance.

I recalled watching her drive away, her brightly hued scarf billowing in the wind as if waving to me. Had she been wiping her hands of me, or simply feeling it was my choice? It was the same when my sister had her wrist tattooed. Bea had handed her a card and said, 'No doubt this will come in handy.'

The card had the name of a doctor who specialised in laser tattoo removal. Bea loathed tattoos, but she never bought the subject up again. She had done her job, much the same as handing me the card that day. I will say, she was not wrong.

I studied the blue card, turning it over, reading the therapist's name, Emerald Green. *Pleeeease! What type of name was that?*

However, I guessed if my rather unconventional mother was going to recommend someone, they certainly were going to be out in left field.

Emerald Green turned out to be a small wiry woman, dressed in army fatigues and a navy singlet top. She wore her shaved head well. However, like my mother, I was unsure of the tattoos on her wrists and foot.

Although not at first, I very soon came to love her piercingly beautiful green eyes and open honest face. While we were much the same size, I felt quite diminished beside her.

Emerald Green was clear on two things. In fact they were so non-negotiable that I was asked to sign a contract to agree to them. Firstly, I had to journal three pages each morning, and secondly, I had to take myself on a date each week.

'What are you talking about?' I had asked, regarding the later. And then I spoke very clearly, as if the poor woman was hard of hearing. 'I am living on own. I'm with myself all the time.'

She of the piercing green eyes nodded, pulled her tanned bare feet up and sat cross legged on the chair. 'Did you and your husband ever attend couples therapy?'

'Yes once… after the horse had well and truly bolted. Obviously it did not one ounce of bloody good.' I'm not saying I did not have attitude that day, and my tone was undoubtedly direct. 'What on earth has that got to do with it?'

'Did the therapist ask you how much quality time you spent together?' She joined her hands in front of her chest as if in prayer. 'Not just being in the same house, but proper quality time?'

Puzzled, I had nodded.

'Well it's the same thing Peach. You have to take *you* on a date each week. Something that impresses *you*. Don't take anyone else. Think of all the things you could do if you had the time.'

Obviously, the look of complete bafflement on my face became clear to her, because she threw her hands in the air, and began making suggestions. 'Think Peach... walk on the beach, sit under a tree, ride the City Cats up and down the Brisbane River, attend the ballet, walk through Southbank and sit on Kodak Beach, browse art at Goma, visit the museum, the State Library,' she rapid fired, 'see a foreign film, volunteer at the RSPCA. These are meant to be *your* things... you'll think up something. The point is find out who *you* are. It's time to defrag, time to just BE.' She gave me a determined stare. 'Do you understand?'

I nodded and left thinking I would not return for the following appointment in three weeks. I knew eventually I did want to date someone, just not me.

To test her out though, I began to journal the three pages each morning. After all, what else did I have to do? The first week, I wrote cynical things such as: *I have nothing bloody to say! Here I am again, booooring. This is wasting my time. Blah, blah, blah... bloody blah... Happy now Emerald Green?*

Then something changed. I began to write about my feelings. I could not write fast enough. And the time flew. Each morning, I would write the last word on the third page, then raise my head as if only a few minutes had passed. I had bursts of tears and bursts of laughter. There were times when a certain giddiness overtook me, accompanied by a sudden loss. And I have to admit, there were ghastly moments when I felt like an accident victim walking away from a crash.

I returned for visit number two with the green eyed therapist.

'Welcome back,' she had said, as if she had guessed my thoughts three weeks earlier. She hugged me tightly, surprising me. 'What did you do on your dates?'

Sheepishly, I said, 'I saw an Italian movie at the Palace cinemas in James Street. I took a long walk along Sunshine Beach. Plus I sat in New Farm Park among the roses, with a coffee and a Dello Mano brownie and read a book for two entire hours. To be honest, I cannot remember the last time I did something as frivolous as that. It was sheer bliss.'

'Congratulations. You are getting to know *you* again,' she had said. With her once again barefooted and cross legged, and me sitting primly on my chair, legs crossed, hands in my lap, we spent the next 90 minutes speaking to a pink crystal on the floor. In the third person! No I's or me's allowed. Depending on how you looked at it, it was either very interesting, or very odd!

By my third visit many changes and shifts in attitude had begun. Firstly, I hugged Emerald Green as warmly as she hugged me. Secondly, I began to uncover certain likes, such as I required nature, nature, nature; and dislikes such as the sound of the television, social networking - a necessary tool for my former business life, and probably every single thing about Davis. *What a relief.*

I soon realised I had blurred my uniqueness with overwork, underplay and under sleep, and living someone else's dream.

After my fourth visit with Emerald Green, (I never thought of her as just Emerald, although she did tell me she had been christened Emily Green), I had this sudden epiphany that I needed to leave the warehouse behind. It was part of my old life. As part of the settlement, I offered it back to Davis. There was tension and relief in my decision. Months of depression had eased, even though my new life was uncertain, I had thoughts I would spend time at my father's chateau in Provence.

I weeded through my belongings, old papers and my extensive wardrobe. Emerald Green had said I may have the impulse to dress differently. This had not occurred. And although her shaved head suited her, it would not me, nor was I into army fatigues. I still loved feminine clothes and that was not about to change, crossroad or no crossroad.

Bea suggested I come to her home. As I am in need of maternal guidance, I have accepted with pleasure, knowing full well there will be no maternal guidance. Although she will be there for at least a week, after that she is heading away on an artist's retreat to Byron Bay and requires someone to feed her dog. I have taken her up on the offer until I decide on my travel plans.

*

I slid the heavy iron door of the warehouse shut. It clanged with its usual metallic sound, giving a sense of finality. Briefly, I rested my forehead against it. I told myself that it was the last time my petite 157centimetre frame would ever have to wrestle with that door again. From day one, it had never liked me, always jamming in the tracks and making me drag it, using my entire body weight, almost pulling my arms out of their sockets. Was it any wonder I constantly had neck and shoulder problems? Wiggling my shoulders, I rolled my neck, reminding myself of the positives, as I was attempting to do more often these days.

Davis loved the door, said it gave the warehouse a sense of history. It made people wonder what was behind.

Swooping my flouncy Alannah Hill skirt under my legs, I slammed the car door and backed out of the driveway. I raised the back of my hand to my face and wiped a lone tear. Farewell, *adieu, auf wiedersehen,* goodbye. I attempted to busy myself thinking of my favourite childhood movie, "The Sound of Music". With grim determination, I refused to look in the rear view mirror.

Heading up Boundary Road, I felt a sense of leaving everything I knew behind, and although I had a hollow feeling in my stomach from nerves, I could not lie, there was also the slightest tinge of excitement. On the right, I farewelled my regulars - the convenience store on the corner, my nail bar, the Swiss Gourmet Deli and The Avid Reader bookstore. On the left, Jam Jar - my coffee haven, and Charlie and Liz's Fruit.

The eclectic and dynamic suburb of West End was extremely popular with young professional couples, just like us, looking for a lifestyle close to the city. It was a suburb known for its strong local identity, high street cafes, ethnic restaurants, interesting bookshops and proud local communities. The positive vibe was palpable and the people friendly. Although only three kilometres from the city, I had always felt as if we were somewhat separated from the rat race of the CBD.

Driving along Vulture Street, I raised my left hand and mouthed a silent goodbye to Southbank Parklands. It had been our favourite training spot. Three mornings a week, rain, hail or shine, we would run from home and meet up with our trainer at a designated meeting spot, under the curling steel columns of the magenta bougainvillea covered arbour.

The sight of that arbour had always bought me a feeling of happiness. However, I now wondered if I would ever be able to roam through the parklands without thinking of my former life with some regret.

The fact was, counselling aside, I *was* still getting used to my marriage being over. Part of me was afraid that I never would. He had been my best friend, my business partner, my partner in life. Together we were going to conquer the world. Well, that's what he used to tell me. I guess though, we could only conquer the world if I continued to dream his dreams, and not bother to have any of my own.

As little girls we were told we could have it all. Our feminist foremothers said so and even our mothers agreed, suggesting we could be loving wives, caring mothers and kick-arse bosses if we wanted. We could, they whispered, be *superwomen*.

So, I had this perfect life all set up. I wanted to find a partner of equal footing, one who made the good times doubly good and made the bad times better.

Davis was it. We had met at university. There were the three of us, Davis, Marty and me, the three musketeers. Even back then we had a business plan. While we studied, both of the boys worked for Davis's mother, Eileen, in her real estate business.

I, on the other hand, worked at a prestige cupcake shop. They weren't just any old cupcakes. They were glamorous, melt-in-the-mouth, special occasion cupcakes. I thrived on the creativity, and the nurturing of making edible love for people. I stayed on until I graduated from the University of Queensland with honours. I had a secret dream of one day owning my own cupcake emporium.

However, somewhere along the line I became side tracked. Davis had ideas and they sounded so big and grand, and mine sounded small and pathetic. I had to weigh it up: cupcakes or three million dollar properties. Hmmm? How many cupcakes would I have to sell to add up to three million dollars?

Before I knew it, Davis had me wanting his dream. That's

what happened to Marty as well. We went along with what Davis wanted. We opened a real estate business. He said it was time for some young guns to get into the industry.

Davis said the inner city suburb of West End would be our niche market, that it was about to hit its straps. He had done his research and felt that although it had originally been one of the poorer suburbs of Brisbane, the cottages that housed the working class and migrants all those years ago, were fast becoming coveted pieces of real estate.

It wasn't the way I had seen my life going, however Davis painted a picture so perfect, how could I resist? The boys knew I had a great business head. They said they needed me. Well, Davis did.

We all want to be wanted, and I was no different.

When I look back on those heady days, I remember nothing but the best. I had loved both of the boys. Physically they were quite similar. In fact, with their blonde hair and blue eyes, they could pass for brothers. However Davis was the one for me. He had charisma, passion and energy enough for all of us. Tall, broad shouldered, slim hipped.

Davis had the power, and power is a very seductive thing. He revved us up and got the dream going. Back in those early days we worked our butts off. No one kept track of the hours, we just did it. We had an absolute blast.

There was little time for seeing other people, but when we got the chance we did.

Who am I kidding? I barely saw anyone, however I pretended I did.

The boys saw plenty.

After a couple of years we moved our business to larger premises right on a prominent corner in Montague Road, where we had phenomenal signage, with our name, *Address*, blazoned across the front. Our staff continued to grow. We were going somewhere. The boys bought in the sales and I grew the business.

The thing about being a passionate person is that they have their highs and lows. I always knew when it was my job to placate Davis. Marty would give me a look that said: *Get in there and do something, Peach.* At first I loved the power. *I could pacify Davis Riding.* Now you had to hand it to me *that* was pretty clever. To be honest, it was only in the last year or so that I really saw those highs and lows for what they truly were... tantrums! And tantrums aren't all that attractive. However, I didn't care.

They didn't stop me loving Davis. I loved him. Totally!

It took years for Davis to wise up to the fact. Marty caught on first. I loved him too, but differently. I loved *him* like a brother, a mate, a best friend. Not like I loved Davis. But Marty was a great salesman and excellent businessman, and was also incredibly insightful and sensitive. Somewhere along the way he let me know that he had picked up on my feelings for Davis. However, we both said nothing. Marty goes down as being one of those few friends that you take with you throughout your life. On the female side of things, he did pretty well himself, there was no shortage of girls lined up and I certainly understood why.

We'd had the business for about five years when finally Davis and I became a couple. Six months earlier, I had caught him studying me with an unusual look on his face. It was as if for the very first time, he had seen saw me as a woman and not only as a business partner. Because let's face it, with Davis, the business *always* came first. Unfortunately around that time, I also noticed Davis and Marty becoming snappy and argumentative with each other. It was a first in many ways.

I still shudder when I think back to a particular Friday night in the office. We'd had a gruelling week. We had been uncertain if a particular buyer, who we had spent months getting over the line, would settle on an extremely lucrative property. There we were, just the three of us, having a few drinks, when I came on to Davis. Glass of *pinot noir* in one hand, the other hand clutching a cheque with a sizable deposit scrawled across it. I pranced around gleefully waving the cheque at the boys. As Davis attempted to playfully take it from me, I quickly put it behind my back. As he leant closer, I went up on tiptoes and kissed his lips. Briefly!

I caught the look of fear in his eyes.

It was one of the most embarrassing moments of my life. Marty coughed and quickly began searching his desk for some miscellaneous nothing. While Davis told me, and he did it nicely, that he didn't want to spoil what we had. I agreed wholeheartedly, laughing it off, saying, 'God only knows what the hell I was thinking. Totally bad idea! The absolute worst! Quite funny really.'

I asked if he'd spiked my drink, as I slung my bag over my shoulder and then left laughing, glass of *pinot noir* still in hand.

Pausing long enough to leave the glass on the footpath, I laughed all the way home in the cab. I'll point out at this point we had parted company, so I don't know who the hell I was trying to kid, as I sure as heck knew the cabbie couldn't have cared less.

Looking at myself in the mirror in the elevator in my apartment building, I continued to laugh, shaking my head at myself, nervously playing with my hair, wrapping it around and around my index finger. A habit left over from childhood. In hindsight, I think I may have been a tad hysterical and at one stage imagined slapping myself. However, it really doesn't work when you do it yourself. I've tried before.

Entering my apartment, I kicked off my fire engine red patent, bejewelled Mui Mui heels and then, dramatically leaning against the door, I cried with embarrassment and through my rantings told myself that it was because I didn't have long legs. That was definitely it. My legs were the problem.

To my utter dismay, somewhere around the age of 15, I realised I was never going to have long legs and I was always going to be curvy. I think a good description would be small but voluptuous, with my fantastic breasts... yes I do say so myself... svelte waist, curvy hips and rounded bottom. And can I tell you, I rather like the way I look. If I had lived in the 1940s, I would have been perfect movie star material. A bit short, however perfect, none the less.

And look, I make the most of it. With my well styled expensive suits I liked to wear low cut shirts and blouses to show off my assets.

I was well known for it. There were even times, when Davis, propped on the edge of my desk, would say to me, 'Seriously Frenchy, we need to pull out the big guns for this client... can you flash your tits a bit!'

He was the only person in the world who called me Frenchy, as most people were unaware, that my biological father was French. Davis, with his voice low, would literally breathe it, never failing to send shivers up my spine, so sexy was it.

Being vertically challenged meant that I had fallen in love with heels. They gave me confidence, made me feel taller, thinner, like I wasn't going to slip through the cracks of life, and that something fantastic was going to happen to me. Men turned to look at me. Hell, I turned to look at me.

They were such a weakness of mine. Jimmy Choo, Louboutin, Manolo Blahnik, Ralph Lauren, Chanel, Sergio Rossi and Roberto Cavalli's were all friends of mine, paired beautifully, sitting on the custom designed shelves in my wardrobe. It wasn't actually a wardrobe, but the second bedroom in my apartment turned into a walk-in-robe. The boys often joked that my investment portfolio needed to include my terribly expensive, designer, killer shoes.

I kept thinking that in the right pair of shoes, everything would be alright.

Well moving right along... six months later precisely, there we were on another Friday night, jammed in along the onyx bar at the Cru Bar, among a sea of suits in navy and various shades of grey, and over his *pinot grigio*, Davis was crying on my shoulder after another blonde five foot ten... yes they were all tall and blonde... who had left him for greener pastures. Hang on, I lie, there had to be a couple of five elevens and even a six footer thrown in there – bloody Amazonian!

Anyway the thing was, on that particular night, although I was giving him the lip service he required, I didn't know why he was so upset. He didn't really spend that much time with any of his girlfriends. Truth be known, they were trophies for him. And I was bored stiff with hearing about them. Glassy eyed, I wondered how long I could stare at the Baccarat crystal chandelier, nodding my head, without him noticing, that *Hello, I'm not bloody interested.*

Elbow on the bar and propping his chin on his hand, out of Davis's mouth came the words, 'Frenchy... why can't I find someone just like you?' And then while I absorbed this bit of information, he lent closer. Narrowing his eyes, and with his wine smelling sweet breath cool on my face, he whispered, '*What* are we doing Peach? You know you're the one.'

At the time, I had just taken a mouthful of my *sauvignon*

blanc, and I was so surprised, I sprayed it all over him. I mean literally. All over him. In his eyes, his face, down the front of his crisp white, double cuffed, business shirt, and violet pin striped tie. Did I happen to mention he was an impeccable dresser? I grabbed a white cloth napkin and with trembling hands busily attempted to blot the wine.

In my mind, I wanted to yell at him, "What do you mean I'm the one? I'm a five foot two, brunette. If you wanted someone like me, you've been bloody well looking in the wrong direction." And then there was the other part of me, that felt all warm and fantastic, because how long had I been waiting for this?

So there we were at the bar, and finally after all these years, he has noticed me. He has said he wants someone like me. *Like me!* He has said I am the one. *The one!* Yes, I know I am repeating myself, but I could not believe it was actually happening, so every time I think of that night, I go over every detail, twice!

Reaching out, Davis touched my hair, delicately playing with one of my dark perfectly blow dried waves.

I didn't look directly at him, just continued to fuss with the napkin and made a sound in the back of my throat, attempting a light hearted laugh, however it came out all wrong.

Gently, he took my busy hands in his, holding them quiet. I let out a deep breath and looked at him. I mean *really* looked at him and I saw it. *He actually loved me.*

I wanted to do that Sally Field thing where, at the Oscars, she had yelled, '*You like me, you really like me*', but thought it a tad obvious and inappropriate.

And then he lent down and kissed my lips. Slowly. My God, how long had I wondered how that would be? Baby, he did not disappoint. I lost myself totally. Time stood still.

Pulling away, he looked at me once more and then kissed me again, longer this time. And look, there was absolutely no argument from me. And he knew it. Because at some stage I realised I had my hands in his hair, and I may have moaned.

Over his shoulder, I briefly spotted the smile on Marty's face. I could tell he was genuinely pleased for me... for us. I blushed and thought my world could not be any more perfect. In fact, I remember later thinking that I wanted to have a group hug with him as well.

And for some time, life went on like that. I had my apartment. Davis had his. In personal matters he didn't like to rush things. Business was different.

We were so loved up.

I once asked Davis about his reaction to my kiss six months prior. He explained that Marty, sensing his feelings earlier, had read him the riot act and told him he had to be absolutely certain.

Anyway Marty seemed pleased for us. And it appeared as if it was forever going to be us three musketeers, in between Marty's girlfriends of course.

I remembered it being nothing new when Davis dragged his feet on the two of us living together, however finally he got sick and tired of going between apartments. Mind you, it only took him another three years.

We had listed a superb modern apartment in a renovated warehouse building with lots of glass and glamour, not far from work. It provided the lifestyle that Davis craved. He felt it was the way we should be living and would look good for the business, for us to be a united front.

Now, you would think that I would have jumped at the chance and of course I wanted to. But I wanted it to be because of us, not because of the business. Up until this point of time I had been an independent woman. I could have actually bought that warehouse on my own if I'd chosen to. For that matter, so could he.

Although, I was thinking different thoughts, I was thinking about the future. And by that I did not mean how much capital gain we would have on the property. Shame on me I know! Davis had recently had his thirtieth birthday and I was coming up to mine. At some stage, I did want a family.

The thing that did it in the end was when his brother Steve asked me to go to a PR conference with him to Paris. Months before, Steve booked the conference and paid for his partner, Thomas, to attend all of the dinners and partners' events. Because of the economic decline, Thomas decided that it wasn't timely for him to be gallivanting all over Europe and needed to stay put in his hair salon, keeping an eye on his staff and his clients.

Steve didn't want to go without Thomas, however having an alliance with a worldwide public relations company meant he had to attend a certain amount of conferences per year to stay in the association.

Plus, he could not get his money back on what he had already paid, and, if he was going to go to Europe, he sure as heck did not wish to go for five days only. I didn't even have to think twice when he asked.

Anyway, Davis and I were in the middle of something. The something was I didn't want to move in with him unless we were going to go forward in our relationship. In fact, if he didn't see us moving forward, I didn't see us having a future. Obviously, this affected us in more ways than one.

I told him we needed time apart and I needed time to think. Time away was exactly what I required.

I loved Steve almost as much as I loved Davis. In fact these days, I do love Steve more. And if you had to pick someone to shop with in Europe then Steve would be it.

Steve was like a Staffordshire bull terrier: short, solid muscle, fiercely loyal, a loving family member, but ruthlessly tough and he knew when to stand up for his own territory. In his words: *He took no shit!* His wardrobe consisted of well-cut jeans and cowboy boots. He never walked anywhere but strode with sexy confidence... gay or not. He headed Brisbane's top lifestyle public relations company and did wonders for our business. Thanks to him, barely a week went by that one or another of us was not in a publication.

When Davis and I finally got together and Steve found out, he had thrown his arms around me and yelled, 'Bout bloody time. I was beginning to wonder if he was the poof!'

I loved Thomas equally as much. Although his uber-luxe hair salon, *Groove,* had quite a celebrity clientele, he still managed to keep all of our tresses styled as well.

Anyway *Groove* thrived. Whether it was imported beers, or the best herbal tea, or organic coffee and handmade biscuits, alongside the massage chairs and huge plasmas fitted throughout, he was a one man PR team for his own business. Personally, I would pay big money just to have him shampoo and condition my hair. There was something about those big powerful hands cradling my head and giving me the best scalp massage, it was positively erotic. I could moan now even thinking about it.

So back to the trip to Europe... yes I had to go. To be honest I was feeling a little down. Very down in fact. As much as I was excited about the trip to Paris, I knew that I had to do a lot of thinking while I was there.

To lift my mood I had set up appointments with Chanel, Lanvin and Dior. The House of Guerlain awaited my precious skin. Plus I could not miss the opportunity to visit Laduree for possibly the best macaroons and their simply unforgettable thick hot chocolate.

While Steve was at his conference I would have time on my own, a good thing, and when he was finished, we'd play, another good thing!

*

I changed lanes on the Story Bridge, heading towards my mother's at New Farm. Although it was only a matter of kilometres as the crow flew, as I crossed the Brisbane River, I felt torn between leaving my old life and beginning a new one.

New Farm was not a love of Davis's, and I could never quite fathom why. Maybe it had something to do with the fact that if we lost a buyer to West End, it was often because they had gone to New Farm. Davis used to say that the *New Farmians* thought they were better than us. I don't believe the *New Farmians* gave it any such thought.

As I veered right at the end of the bridge, I was once again confronted by the huge sign someone had painted that said: *The more you think about it the bigger it gets.* What I couldn't help think, and not for the first time, was that every time I saw that sign it reminded me exactly of what I wanted to forget. *Blast it!*

I turned into Brunswick Street and pulled to a stop at the red light. With a French manicured finger tapping my top lip, for the millionth time, I wondered if there had been any way I could have fought harder. Who was I kidding? The relationship had been exhausted. We had spent long enough throwing the blame back and forth. Finally, it was time to exorcise all and move on.

It was unlike me, because usually I held onto things even after they were broken. As a child, I'd had a teddy called Fella.

Even after both of his arms, and then legs, had fallen off, I'd treasured him and taken him everywhere.

'Come on Peach,' my dad, Johnny, had insisted, attempting to prise my little fingers off him. 'Surely it's time to put Fella to rest.' However, I could not part with him.

'I don't care if he's broken,' I had argued, through my tears.

However, my marriage was more than broken. It was shattered into little pieces. One minute I had been young in love and planning a family, the next I was nearing mid-thirties and on my own. Where had my life gone?

Slowing the car, I passed Montgomery's on the left hand side of the road. I played the game that if there was a car park out front, I would stop for a well needed coffee and have a chat with Chilli, my dear friend and one of the owners. However if there wasn't, I was meant to head straight to my mother's. With disappointment, I noticed Montgomery's was as per usual busy, so I continued on. At the next set of traffic lights I checked my rear-view mirror, and saw a car pull away directly out front. However, as like other things, it was far too late.

Minutes later, I pulled into Bea's driveway. Checking my eyes in the mirror, I jumped when my phone rang.

It was Marty. He was running late to pick me up.

'Don't worry,' I told him. 'I think I'll walk down to the New Farm shops, pick up a couple of travel books from Mary Ryans, and have a coffee while I wait. Pick me up when you're ready.'

I didn't miss the concern in his voice when he asked if I was okay.

'Mmmm... just left the warehouse for the last time, that's all. I'll be fine,' I lied.

Chapter 2

Briskly stirring the satiny smooth latte on the table in front of me, regardless of my mood, I couldn't help but revel in its pervasive aroma. I took a tentative sip, testing the temperature, and relaxed visibly. Making an effort to remove the world-has-come-to-an-end look from my face, I sat further back in the chair.

The New Farm Deli owner placed a *cannoli,* a favourite Italian sweet, on the table in front of me. 'How are you Bella?'

I wondered if he too like the rest of the world, knew about my failed marriage, or was simply being polite. I attempted a smile and shrugged. 'Fine thanks Vince.' And then as an afterthought added, 'Maria good?' It was as much conversation as I could attempt.

Within our West End community, personal and professional, my humiliation had been great. There were days when I did not want to leave the house. Sometimes I had come over to New Farm to shop, grateful for the anonymity.

I flicked my long blow-styled locks behind one ear and absentmindedly fiddled with one of my earrings. The numbness I had felt since leaving was beginning to scare me. Shouldn't I be crying, weeping and wailing? Yet I didn't feel like hysterics. I felt devoid of everything

Swallowing hard, I attempted to distract myself. I smoothed my skirt, crossed my legs, and examined my impossibly high, black toe-peepers, bought all that time ago on the trip with Steve to Paris in a quaint little shop in *rue St Honore*. I had always loved the fact that as I walked the green sole could be seen from behind. Today, I was almost mesmerised by them, flexing my calf first one way and then the other.

The day I had bought them, I had been playing a game with myself. Again, if I found the right pair of shoes, everything in the world would be alright. I told myself later, they were definitely the right pair of shoes. Funny, I had chosen to wear them today.

*

Davis's proposal, when it came, was always going to be our special little story, the one that we would bring out and tell our grandchildren. Steve and I had spent four days in London and were on day three in Paris for his conference. Tired after a day shopping, I casually lingered in the restaurant downstairs in the *Hotel Meurice.* The tea was wonderful, a refreshing blend of green tea and Moroccan mint, scented with bergamot. I must admit, it wasn't just the shopping that had made me tired, my heart was heavy as well, and it took energy to put on a brave face each day, after I had spent the night crying into my pillow.

Steve called earlier to say that he would return to the hotel later than expected. Tonight we were free from the conference and I was looking forward to some fun, anything to take my mind off Davis. Even though I had said I was determined that if he didn't want our relationship to move forward, it was over for us, in my heart I knew I would be devastated.

On our arrival at the hotel there had been a dozen red roses waiting in my room from him. But I didn't call. What could I say? *Thank you for the roses and it's okay that after all of this time you're not sure about me.* The day before, a silver cake stand with delicate scented rose macaroons awaited me. Yes, from Davis. They *almost* had me at first bite, and although I faltered, I still didn't call.

After I had drained the last of the tea from the silver teapot, with heavy feet and equally as heavy heart, I wearily crossed the grand foyer and made my way to my room. Immediately upon opening the door, my spirits lifted as my shopping, entailing different carrier bags with designer names emblazoned on the sides, had been placed by the concierge upon the pink brocade chair, in front of the ivory silk draped window overlooking the *rue de Rivoli*.

Kicking off my hot pink patent Pradas, I undid the gold buttons on my cream coloured Burberry trench coat and hung it in the wardrobe. As I closed the mirrored door, something on the bronze silk bedcover caught my eye. Another carrier bag! I swung around. It was not just any carrier bag, but a legendary Loius Vuitton carrier bag. I stopped in my tracks, narrowing my eyes. Surely it must be a mistake. Perhaps the concierge had delivered it to the wrong room.

Stealthily, I crept over to it, as if it might bite. I surveyed it for a few moments and then lifted the edge of the bag, peering inside. There sat the bag of my dreams... the gold mirror bag. I had been raving about this bag for months. Only this morning, I had visited the flagship store on the *Champs Elysee,* hoping that it was still available, only to be told that the last one had been sold earlier. This had to be it! *Oh bother...*

Seconds later, I picked the phone up, and dialled the concierge. '*Bonjour*, it is Peach Avanel speaking. I believe there has been an error. There is a shopping bag in my room that does not belong to me. I think it must have been delivered by mistake... Oh! ... Is that right? ... Are you sure? ... *Really? Merci boucoup.*'

I hung the phone up. I couldn't believe it. The concierge said that he had delivered it personally. The next moment the phone rang startling me. It was the concierge again. He told me that there *had* been an error, and asked if I could bring the bag downstairs.

I took the Louis Vuitton carrier bag, my room key and my mobile phone, in case Steve should ring, and lethargically retraced my steps from only minutes before, thinking that really if there was an error, the concierge should rectify it, not me.

Crossing the grand foyer, once again I admired the luxuriousness and beauty of the colour scheme, a harmony of beige marble, accented superbly by tones of red and black.

'*Oui Mademoiselle* Avanel, have you opened the bag yet?' the concierge asked, his voice heavily accented.

'Well no, as it's not mine. I did look inside but that's all. I assure you...'

Firmly, he held his hand up. 'Perhaps we should look together to make sure all is well.'

'But I assure you, I haven't touched it.'

'*Oui Mademoiselle.*' Removing the gold handbag from its wrappings, and placing it on the desk between us, he admired it. 'It is *tres magnifique.*'

'*Oui*, it is very beautiful,' I agreed.

'Would you like to try holding it for a moment?'

I opened my eyes wide at him. 'I don't think so...' my tone carried an air of humour.

He smiled and narrowed his eyes at me. 'Really *Mademoiselle,* you should, just to see how it looks.' He pushed the bag towards me.

I glanced around, uncertain of his strange behaviour. I took the bag and placed it over my arm briefly. 'Very nice!' I returned it to the desk top.

'Ah *Mademoiselle,* you must have a better look. It suits you. Take it to over to the bar and look in the mirror there. The lighting will be better. You should see how *tres beau* you look.'

'No really...'

'You must! You must! Come along, I will come with you.'

Before I had time to say more, I was handed the bag once again, and escorted across the marble foyer into the spectacular Bar 228. It was impossible not to admire the work of the world renowned designer Phillipe Starck.

Lavish tobacco toned leather chairs, highlighted by the sparkle of rare crystal decanters, all to a backdrop of warm timber detailing, made me feel as if I had been transported into the finest gentlemen's club. This was the perfect place for drinks with Steve later that night.

The barman came towards us, a single glass of champagne on his tray. '*Mademoiselle*,' he offered.

Bewildered, certain there must be some mistake, I put my hands out and began to laugh. 'Look I'm not sure what's going on here, but this isn't my bag, and I didn't order any champagne.'

'But you must,' the concierge said, pulling out a chair and pressing me into it. 'You must sit here while I sort it out.'

Before I had time to protest, with a level of importance, he strode off. I glanced at both the bag, still on my arm, and the glass of champagne on the table in front of me. Completely baffled, I glanced around. *What* was going on? The poor man was definitely rather odd. I placed the bag on the table and studied it. Someone was lucky. My phone rang and I jumped in fright.

'Do you like it?' was all he said.

The moment I heard his voice, I felt the tears well in my eyes. '*Davis?* Did you do this? Is this from you?' However my heart felt heavy. It wasn't gifts I wanted.

'Open it.'

'Davis please... you're making this harder.' My chin quivered. 'It's not flowers or macaroons or handbags I want. Please don't do this...'

'Open it.'

I exhaled heavily.

'I said to open it,' he insisted.

For a moment I sat doing nothing and then with the phone tucked up to my ear, I reached out, took the bag onto my lap and unzipped it. Inside was a small black velvet bag. As if bitten, I rapidly pulled my hand away and placed it to my mouth. 'What is it?' I murmured.

'Have a look.'

I slid the drawstring open. Inside sat a ring box. My hands began to shake and emotion overtook me. 'Davis...'

'Stop crying and open it.'

I nearly dropped the phone, and once again tucked it tightly under my ear. 'No, I can't.'

'Frenchy... open it.'

With trembling hands I opened the black box and there sat a stunning princess cut sparkling engagement ring.

'Davis...' I sobbed, too overcome to say more.

'Peach Avanel, will you marry me?'

'Yes, yes I will...'

'Stop crying, you've got mascara running down your face. You need a tissue.'

'What...?' Shaking my head, I jumped up from the seat and spun around. Davis was standing in the doorway. I gave a cry that sounded as if it had been torn from my heart and threw myself into his arms. They closed around me hard and strong.

I guess I wasn't surprised that this was happening, although I was surprised at the way Davis had planned it. Any woman being presented with a beautiful diamond ring, as a girl you squeal with delight, you say you can't believe it, but of course you can, it is exactly what you had hoped for.

Davis told me he knew he needed me the moment I flew out of Brisbane. He stayed with me two nights, and then was gone again.

We married eighteen months after that. I wanted a September wedding, but Davis said the following March was better. After all what was six months? I wanted something small and intimate. Davis wanted half the suburb there. He said it was good for business to have as many clients as possible.

However, my wedding day surpassed all that any girl could dream of: the romantic Vera Wang dress, the champagne toasts, the promise of time alone with Davis cruising the Maldives on our luxurious honeymoon. Although Davis was terribly handsome in his Hugo Boss tuxedo, I felt like the day didn't belong to us alone.

I wanted children straight away but Davis said he wanted me to himself for a while longer. Three years after we were married, I finally put my foot down. I told him it was now or never. He agreed.

I wish my body had agreed. Somewhere along the line it forgot what it was meant to do.

*

Shaking my head, I was instantly jolted out of my reverie by the sound of a tiny voice. 'But Mummy I want a baby chino.' As if waking from a sleep, I blinked and glanced around the surrounding tables. Tables spilled out from the inside eating area under an awning onto the pavement, where customers, just like me, perched to watch the passing trade.

'Emma sit up here and wait for Daddy to come,' the blonde, blue eyed mother gently coaxed.

'But Mummy...' the little voice rose higher.

'Emma,' the mother's voice was firm. 'Daddy won't be long. You can eat your sultanas while you wait.' Snapping open the hot pink Tupperware container, she handed it to the little girl who was dark haired and appeared to be of Chinese decent. I wondered about the father.

Holding the coffee cup to my lips with both hands, I sipped slowly, watching.

A tall fair haired man, dressed smartly in business attire, crept up behind the tiny girl and then hoisted her into the air up onto his shoulders, among squeals of delight.

'Come on Miss Em,' he said. 'Come inside and help me order coffee and treaties.'

I noticed the mother's face as she watched her husband and child go into the deli, a child who I gathered was adopted. I wondered about it, the mother's look was one of satisfaction. To have denied her the right to be a mother would have been criminal. And not for the first time, I pondered whether motherhood was a right or a gift. Suddenly I was reminded of my looming childlessness. Whenever it came upon me, like it did at that moment, it hit me in the pit of my stomach and I literally felt ill. I knew I was still in mourning. Not only mourning the person who I had thought was the love of my life, but also mourning the loss of my perfect dream, the expectation of becoming a mother soon, something I had been planning and dreaming of for years.

With some effort, I attempted to change my thoughts, knowing that thinking about my desire for children did me no good whatsoever. Emerald Green and I were still to work on that one. I had told her I was not ready. She had said soon. *Soon* was looming.

No amount of effort to re-direct my thoughts helped and I was reminded of those early days of finding out about Davis's affair and the huge realisation that I was not headed towards motherhood. There were many nights where I lay in bed feeling pain that was bigger than my body. A huge circle of pain encompassing not just me but vibrating through the air around me as well. My crying scared me. It was instantaneous and loud. I could not contain the sound. I would get out of bed and roam around, trying new places to sleep, another bedroom, one of the lounges. And then I would sleep a little again, only to repeat the performance a short time later.

*

Two women parked their loaded trolleys in front of my table before they entered the delicatessen. Earlier, I had chosen a table right at the end, pushed up against the window. Although out of the way, it seemed perfect to people watch. The two trolleys appeared to be filled with display paraphernalia, creating a wall that couldn't have hemmed me in any further if it was made from besser blocks.

I was miffed the two women had given me so little regard. Coughing, I attempted to attract their attention. However, as they were already inside joining the take away coffee queue, it did me no good whatsoever. Noisily, I slid my chair back, hoping the sound would show my plight. They did not even turn around.

To make it worse, while they waited for the coffees, the two women leant against the trolleys, and in voices that resembled fingernails on a chalkboard, loudly discussed the issues they had with a work colleague.

'... and so I told her, if she didn't *friggin'* get real...' came from the teased redheaded, her eyes rimmed in purple liner, lipstick in the corners of her mouth.

Not for the first time I had the feeling of being invisible. It hadn't seemed all that long ago that I was a well-known business identity around town. And now...

I glanced around to see if anyone else thought my predicament odd. However, the problem was I could barely see anyone else. My desolation returned and hung off me like a heavy cloak.

For an instant, I wondered if I could be the type of person who would down an entire bottle of sleeping pills. However, as I was on my third cup of coffee that day, I realised there was a good possibility that I would struggle to close my eyes. *Blast!*

Resting my chin on my hand, I exhaled heavily and stared down at the bottom of my now empty cup, thoughts playing out in my mind, replaying scenes from the past.

*

The moment I heard her voice, I knew it was her. I had forgotten how charming Felicity Best could be.

The tall striking blonde sailed towards me. 'Helloooo darling! How are you?' she sang as she air-kissed my cheek. Four of the first five minutes of meeting after nearly fifteen years, we conducted that catch up dance in which you move from subject to subject, leaping great chasms of time, while still in shock over the unexpected meeting.

Her hair was swept up in a platinum blonde Marilyn Monroe do, and her smile was pure Hollywood. A cloud of expensive perfume wafted around her. Even at that hour of the morning, she was wearing a blazing sapphire blue silk dress that rippled as she moved. I could tell that she was aware she had attracted nearly every pair of male eyes within cooee distance.

Images flashed into my mind of Felicity Best at school; on the netball court with her long tanned legs; sitting in the middle of a group of gobsmacked girls while she handed out snippets of her glamorous weekends. She was the queen. God, we all loved her. God, we were envious.

And even after all this time, and my own success, I felt

that same feeling of inadequacy come upon me again, as I stood there in my leggings and singlet top, waiting in line for a vegetable juice at some ungodly hour of the morning. Davis was away speaking at a conference, and rather than wash that bloody juicer yet again, I had stopped off after a session with my personal trainer to buy one.

Who was I kidding? The morning hadn't begun well and I was going straight for an iced chocolate mocha – a mixture of eighty percent pure chocolate, vanilla ice cream, espresso coffee and chocolate shavings. The mood I was in, if I could have taken it intravenously, I would have.

Twenty minutes earlier, my period had reared its ugly head once again. Another month had passed with no luck. I could not explain my complete disappointment and frustration. I held myself together at the trainers, and waited until I got in the car. Down the road, I pulled over, rested my head on the steering wheel and cried. I was feeling less of a woman every month and I cursed myself that we had waited so long.

The emotional journey was absolutely exhausting.

By the time I arrived at the juice bar in the James Street markets, I knew I wasn't a pretty sight. Actually, I didn't care how I looked, I wanted that iced chocolate badly.

Of all days, there was Felicity Best, looking like sunshine after the rain, still as gorgeous as the last time I had seen her. When you have legs that long, you always look gorgeous.

Afterwards, I called into my mother's.

'I ran into Felicity Best earlier. Do you remember her from school?'

I watched Bea as she sat in front of her old fashioned dressing table, wildly piling her blonde hair on top of her head and expertly wrapping a signature colourful silk scarf around it. Next to the mirrored jewellery tray, a cut crystal rose bowl held the hugest bunch of overblown white roses, their fragrance filling the room.

'Which one was she?' Bea asked, absentmindedly riffling through her lipstick drawer, finally finding the perfect shade of red. She turned to me. 'Darling, you should try this colour, it would give you a lift.' She began to fill in her lips and then turned to me, eyes narrowed. 'You mean the girl whose father was a barrister?'

'No, Felicity Best, her father was an author.'

'Oh of course,' said Bea. 'Jack Best's daughter.' Watching herself in the mirror, she paused while a small smile played about her lips. She played with her hair. Then she remembered something else. 'The tall girl with the bleached blonde hair and the long legs? The one you all wanted to be?'

There was a moment's silence while I registered this uncharacteristic insightfulness. I shrugged. 'I'm not sure what you mean.' But I did know what she meant. It's not often you want someone else's life. Back at school, I'd have given anything to be Felicity Best. She was our free one, our wild one, the one that got away.

From the dressing table, I picked up a bottle of Youth Dew, Bea's signature fragrance. Removing the lid, I inhaled it directly from the bottle. Didn't matter where in the world I was, the moment I smelt it, I thought of her. I spritzed my wrists.

'Still the only one in the world is she?' Bea asked, mascara wand mid-air, not taking her eyes from my face in the mirror.

'What do you mean?' There was silence.

'*Oh darling...* I do know you all thought she was the coolest girl at school. The one all the boys liked, and she knew it.' She paused for effect and then turned to look directly at me. 'If I remember correctly, she was mean to you. Flavour of the month one minute until someone better came along. Always wanting what everyone else had. I do remember the tears.' She turned back towards the mirror.

Nonchalantly, I waved my hand at her. 'I hardly remember that stuff. It was too long ago. But it was good to see her. She's been living in London for the last ten years as a business development manager for a publishing group. Sounds like she has been rather successful.'

'What's she doing back here then?'

I shrugged. 'It seems her love life has been rather turbulent.'

Bea raised her brows, which I wasn't sure if it was in response to what I'd said, or if it helped her pencil them in.

I sat on her bed, and without looking at her, explained, 'She's terribly qualified. I'm thinking of offering her a job.'

Bea spun around again. 'Do you think that's wise?'

'Look Bea, I'm never going to fall pregnant the rate I'm going. I need to take some pressure off. I want to take six months away from the business.'

'And what has Davis said about that?' she asked, looking down as she slid a huge aquamarine cocktail ring on the middle finger of her left hand.

I shrugged. 'He's been a bit funny, but I promised him I'd find someone to fill my shoes, and I have a strong feeling Felicity could be the one.'

'Go steady darling.' And then with a spritz of her perfume she was done. 'And look, do take this lipstick, it could be just the thing you need.'

She glided across the room, our deep and meaningful over. My mother's vanity and her meticulous attention to the details of her own appearance had always struck me as incongruous in a woman who lived such an alternative lifestyle and bordered on being a hippy. However, she rarely left the house without lipstick, mascara and perfume, often stating, 'Just because you're different doesn't mean you can't look pretty.'

Later that day, Felicity phoned me. The old Felicity never phoned me. Years ago, I had always been the one who rang her, and then I'd walk over to her home to find someone else there. I remember feeling in the way and very much on the outer. But that was then.

Now, I set up a time for an interview. I had a feeling she could be the one.

She was.

Chapter 3

My entire life I had craved conventionality. Up until now that was how I had lived, because I wanted a different life to what I'd had as a child.

It wasn't as if I hadn't had a good childhood, as far as childhoods went, it was great. However it *wasn't* conventional, and all every kid wants is to be normal. They want to fit the mould.

It was a common occurrence for my parents to return home from one of Dad's clubs as the garbage men began their morning shifts. Still in the clothes from the evening before, propped at the kitchen table, mug of tea in front of him, Dad would pull both of us up onto his knees and kiss the top of our heads. After breakfast, he'd drop us off at kindergarten or school, and then they would both sleep until it was time to pick us up again. Following dinner that night, they would flee back out into the club scene.

We were never neglected. We always had Aunt Honey with us. Although she wasn't a real aunty, we loved her like she was. These days they're called nannies. But to us, Aunt Honey was more of a grandmotherly figure. She smelt of Lux soap and freshly baked cakes. She was always cooking, and when Lou and I came home from school there was the smell of fresh bread in the air, and there were tins full of Victorian sponges and butterfly cakes. Those big bosoms of hers were perfect for snuggling into and she had a constant soothing word or a cuddle for us.

She was the only one my mother would listen too. Many a time, Aunt Honey would scold her for some thing or another and chase her from the kitchen with a tea towel. However, my mother would laugh and later kiss Aunt Honey on the cheek.

I once overheard my mother telling my dad, Johnny, that the poor darling relied on us as much as we relied on her. Apparently, she was a widow, and her children weren't much chop. At the time I remembered wondering what *much chop* was.

However the part of my childhood I most clung to was Lou and I spending small pockets of time with Nan and Pop on the farm at Dover in South Tasmania. Our mother never came with us. She said she didn't do the cold!

Although Pop was retired and my uncles ran the orchard, Pop still spent his days tending the garden. Despite the harsh conditions he was determined to have his spring garden every year. I was never far from his side, unless I was with Nan at her old Singer sewing machine, or cooking in her kitchen. Hours went by, while I watched Nan sew my Barbie doll's new wardrobe, or with her pottering around the kitchen, stewing the apples and peaches that fell from the trees, and brewing jams and marmalades, which at morning tea time, Pop would generously spoon on homemade scones. In hindsight, I realised that I relished watching the way Nan did things in the kitchen, and Pop in the garden. If it's true that one's passions are handed down through those that are passionate, then I know where my love of life, and stewed peaches and jam, was first nurtured.

And then as we got slightly older, many holidays were spent picking and packing apples at the farm. I cannot tell you how much I looked forward to this. Lou and I thought we were very important standing alongside the packers at they placed the apples into bags and then into larger crates, which were then taken to the packing shed by tractor, with us running gleefully behind. Once sorted by size, the apples were packed into boxes and stored in the cold room until the trucks took them to the ships in Hobart. I still remember the wooden boxes my uncles used to make for the apples. And can see the top layer of apples individually wrapped in purple and green tissue paper. I even remember with some pride pasting the brightly coloured labels on.

These days my cousins are the ones running the farm. Once a year we still wait for our crate of apples to arrive. Even after all of this time, Granny Smiths are my mother's favourite, and when they arrive, she cooks up a storm of apple pies. It is the most I ever saw her in the kitchen.

My mother had always been and still was a bit out there. Artists have a way of being out there. It wasn't what I wished for. She wore caftans, cheesecloth, masses of bracelets, and was spoken about. As both an artist and a singer, along with her pug dog Piggy, she cut a well-known figure in our area. She used to say that if it was good enough for Marie Antoinette and Empress Josephine to have a pug, then it was good enough for her.

Although I knew I was loved and there was plenty of laughter, the thing was, I always felt like the grownup. My parents were the kids. Even now, I sometimes feel as if I'm raising them.

I remember at five being so frustrated by my parents, I yelled at them, 'You're not the parents I want, and I'm going to get myself adopted.' Charming you might say, although, it was exactly how I felt.

To this day, I still remember the shocked look on their faces. As elegant as ever, Bea put her lacquered scarlet fingertips to her equally red glossed lips, drew deeply on her cigarette, turned her head on a slight angle, blew a plume of smoke in the air, and then in a calm voice spoke.

'*Daaar-ling*,' she said, dragging the word out. 'We're terribly sorry that we're not the parents you wanted, but we do love you.' Although her gaze held mine, I still noticed her trembling hands, giving away that she was not as confident as her voice sounded.

That particular phrase of my mother's became her favourite catchcry whenever she found me all too difficult to deal with.

I had stood there, arms folded across my chest, tears rivering down my cheeks. Dad opened his arms, and even though I wanted to stay angry, I fell into them.

I can't remember a time when my dad, Johnny Lynch, hadn't been there for me. Although I called him Johnny, one day that changed.

Lou was almost four, and I was six. It was the first time I had ever heard my mother and Johnny argue. It had gone on for a couple of days. And then one morning my mother came into my bedroom. For a few moments she stood at my window gazing out. Her eyes were puffy and red rimmed, an unusual sight for my vibrant mother. As she inhaled on her cigarette, there was the tell-tale nervous sign of her fingers trembling. I have never to this day seen anyone who looks as sophisticated as my mother did smoking. Taking one last drag, she threw the butt out of the window and exhaled slowly through those beautiful scarlet lips.

Without looking directly at me, she perched herself on the side of my bed, crossed her elegant legs, and explained in a voice, throaty with cigarette smoke, that later that day there was to be a visitor. That was nothing new, our house seemed to be constantly filled with people coming and going.

However, my mother went on to explain that it was my papa who was coming to see me, all the way from France. I couldn't actually take it in. How could I have two dads? I was very quiet and wished to be left alone to deal with this bit of information. Minutes went by before there was a tap on the door and Johnny crept into my room. Kneeling beside my bed, he took my hands in his. Playing with my fingers, he looked at me and explained that he knew that this was difficult for me to understand, however I mustn't worry as no matter what, he would always be my dad, and then he hugged me tight, kissing the top of my head.

I was scared you see. What if this man who was meant to be my father tried to take me back to France with him? I explained my fear to Johnny, and he told me that even though Alexandre was my father, he, Johnny, was my dad and he would never let that happen unless I wanted to go. I asked him if he was sure, and he said *abso-bloody-lutley*! I knew then he was certain. It was a favourite terminology of his. For many years I thought I might find it in the dictionary. From that moment on though, I never called Johnny anything else but Dad.

For the next few hours you could have cut the air with a knife, the tension palpable between my mother and Johnny, as they waited for the visit from my papa. When the car pulled up, my mother looked through the venetian blinds, ran her hands over her long colourful caftan, checked her lipstick one last time, and the headed out to welcome him. Lou and I were told to wait inside. With a face that looked like thunder, Johnny headed out the back to the garage.

Lou and I threw ourselves onto the aqua faux leather cushions on the cane lounge, and cautiously peered through the venetian blinds. We watched as our mother, who did indeed look beautiful with a colourful scarf tied around her head, and huge gold hoops through her ears, elegantly made her way to the man who climbed out of the taxi. They embraced. To me, it appeared that they embraced far longer than was probably necessary. I remember seeing him kiss my mother on both cheeks.

Beside me, Lou, in a small voice, asked who he was meant to be again. Swallowing, I told her it was my papa. The look on her face told me that she had no idea what a papa was, so I explained it was a father. For a minute she was quiet while we continued watching as our mother laughed, perhaps a little too loudly, and ran her hands over her headscarf smoothing it at the back. She kept tilting her head to the side and using her eyes in a way that I didn't understand at the time.

Lou's next words were how come I had two fathers. Nervously, I shrugged. I had once asked my mother why she and I shared the same surname Avanel, but Lou and Johnny were both Lynch. She simply told me that sometimes that's how it worked in families and it was not a big deal. I guess at that age, that's all I needed to know. It did become more of a big deal as I grew older and it became more obvious. After all, Lou was long limbed like Johnny and blonde like our mother. I, on the other hand, was always one of the shortest in the class and a honey chestnut. Some people call it non-descript… I like to call it honey chestnut. And, as I reached puberty I had generous breasts and curvy hips. Some things have never changed.

After that first visit from Papa, my mother often commented that I was very much like his mother Helena. Generally she said that after we'd had a row. I never did get to meet my paternal grandmother.

Eventually my mother bought my father inside to meet me. Lou and I scrambled off the lounge and even though we were much the same height, Lou stood slightly behind me, slipping her hand into mine. I squeezed it tightly. It didn't matter how tall she was, she was still my little sister.

There was a part of me that registered my mother was actually trying to impress this man. That's what totally pissed Johnny off. Even at six, I could see that.

Papa wasn't nearly as tall as Johnny, and spoke with a heavy accent. However, the thing that shocked me most was that he was so much older than my mother and Johnny. Twenty years to be precise. In hindsight, I do realise that he was terribly charming, and if you thought Johnny was somewhat stylish, then he had nothing on this man. But back then, I thought him just different. And kids don't like different. Kneeling in front of me, he took me by my arms and kissed both of my cheeks. Quietly he said my name, Peach, but it sounded like *Pesch*.

It pleased me that he spoke to Lou as well, although she stayed pretty much behind me most of the time. Although, at one stage she became bored and sat upside down on a cane saucer-chair, swinging herself around and around until she fell off, knocking her head on the timber coffee table and creating a ruckus. That was Lou for you, always the centre of attention.

Alerted by her cries, Johnny eventually came back inside and leant against the door frame, arms folded across his chest, his body language speaking volumes. Lou clutched at one of his legs. Johnny simply nodded as Papa walked towards him and extended his hand. For a minute, it didn't look as if Johnny was going to reciprocate. Without changing the look on his face, slowly he looked Alexandre up and down, before he put his hand out. It was clear to me that he, for one, was not interested in being charmed.

Plans were made for Papa to take me to lunch the next day, and something I was most grateful for was that he asked Lou if she wished to come as well. However Lou, still with a tear stained face, and busy doing that double-hump-sniff, shook her head no. With my eyes, I begged her to come, however luckily my mother intervened and said that she would join us. That was the good part. I really had no intention of seeing this man on my own, papa or no papa.

The bad part was that this made Johnny mad as hell. Much later that evening, I heard my mother telling Johnny she had no choice and she must do it for me. I didn't see Papa for a long time after that. And the thing was, it never seemed to be the same between Johnny and my mother again. I believe Johnny realised that Alexandre was always going to be the love of her life and he paled in comparison.

Years later, I asked my mother why she never married Johnny. She told me that he had never actually asked. It was obvious to me that he didn't wish to be hurt by her rejection, so he settled for what he had.

Just around the time I finished high school, my mother moved out of our Kangaroo Point home and into a house at New Farm, directly across the river. She said it was important for her to have her own space in which to be creative.

Lou and I stayed with Johnny. It was our home. Johnny had been the best father and had provided for us in a way that was better than most. His first club was always *the one* though, and no other had been as lucrative since. Often he had dabbled in other things, once going into business with his brother Terry in the tree loping business. It was called, *The Lynch Mob*. Johnny thought the name was hilarious and continuously reminded us how funny it was. He would say, 'Get it, The Lynch Mob! Johnny and Terry Lynch!' And roar with laughter again, before saying, 'Abso-bloody-lutely fantastic!' Although he was unconventional, he was a good dad.

As the years went by, my mother eventually gave me enough information to explain what had happened between her and

Papa. The youngest child of Nan and Pop, and bored with life on the farm in Tasmania, my mother had craved more, and waited for the day to spread her wings and travel.

Originally, the sun drew her to Provence and then as an artist, the colours captured her as it had captured the imagination of many artists over the centuries. She said that Renoir, Van Gogh, Cezanne and Matisse were all, at some point during their illustrious careers, inspired by its light, vivid colours and spectacular scenery. My twenty year old mother was no different.

She drank it in. Thirstily, she painted like she had never before. Never had she been so happy in life. She told me she felt as if she had come home.

One afternoon, while sitting at a cafe in a little square in the town of *Vence*, enjoying a splendid cup of coffee, the most beautiful man she had ever laid eyes on strode around the corner.

'He was dressed in a terribly elegant grey suit,' she told me. 'His hair was rather long, he had a glass of wine in one hand and a cigarette in the other. He lifted his glass to toast me and I was a goner. You know when you see a handsome man and you go weak at the knees or feel your heart race?' I nodded and she continued, 'Well this was that – 10,000 times over. I swear to God, it was one of those moments where you know this person will play a role in your life. He was 40 years old, had huge brown eyes and a divine body, perhaps slightly shorter than I was used to, although that didn't stop me. I fell into a passive state of contented bliss. He was so damn gorgeous.'

Anyway, the short story of it was, he was an antique dealer and his family chateau was close by. He was the only son, therefore the chateau belonged to him, although his mother still lived there with him. He had been in a relationship with a woman called Sophie for the previous 13 years before meeting my mother. Not much was said about her. When my mother came on the scene, Sophie was forgotten about, and within eight weeks my parents married. I was born eight months later.

My mother told me that Alexandre chose my name. He said that I looked like a beautiful Peach. She said initially they were very happy. Nothing could have burst her bubble. However from the start, Alexandre's mother Helene, the doyenne of the chateau, had not warmed to my mother. Later, things became a lot worse when my mother realised that Alexandre was still seeing Sophie with the encouragement of his mother. He didn't see it as much as a problem as my mother did, explaining simply that he was French.

My mother, living at the chateau in the countryside, and married to a man who was not about to change his womanising ways, fled to London with an 18 month old me in tow. There she met up with a friend of a friend. You guessed it... Johnny! He was bowled over by my mother's beauty.

Only in London briefly, Johnny was looking at clubs and was soon heading back to Australia to open his own in Brisbane. Weighing it up at the time, it seemed like a good option for my mother. Brisbane was by no means the big city of Sydney or Melbourne, however, it sure as hell beat Tasmania. It was a place she could be a big fish in a small pond.

Her catholic parents were already upset with her. Firstly, for marrying in a hurry to a man she barely knew, and secondly, for leaving her husband with the same speed.

My mother and Johnny came back to Brisbane with me in tow. Before long Alexandre attempted to woo her back. She once confided in me that she had decided to pack us both up and return to France. However on that very day she found out she was pregnant with Lou, so she did the only thing she could. She stayed. She said it was a good decision. I was grateful that she said that.

But you see, Alexandre really had a hold on her. Although she did love Johnny, Alexandre was like a magnetic force that drew her to him.

After that initial visit with him when I was only six, I didn't see him again for years. Although I did at some stage realise that he sent generous cheques to my mother, cheques that paid for my private schooling. In turn, I was encouraged to write letters about my life to him.

One day, not long after my mother had found her own house to live in, I popped around after school to see if I'd left a particular book there. I had taken the ferry across the river and then walked. Surprisingly, Alexandre was there. He and my mother were both at the kitchen table, dressed in robes, wine glass in hand, sharing the same cigarette. It was only three-thirty in the afternoon. You see where I'm coming from.

This was the second time I had ever seen the man. Although there had been many generous offers for me to visit France, I had never really wished to. I kind of thought it would upset Johnny, so I had declined every one of them.

Well, for a 17 year old girl it was embarrassing to say the least. Alexandre didn't stay long and returned to France not long after that. I didn't see him again. However, I had promised that when my studies were over, I would finally go and spend time in Provence at the chateau.

For the next few years my mother went to France annually and stayed a couple of months each time. It was now easier for her to do so, since Papa's mother had passed on. Of course, there was always a valid reason why I could not join her.

When I was in the middle of my exams during my final

year at university, my mother told me Alexandre was unwell and wished us both to visit. I should have gone with her, but I didn't want to have to re-sit my exams. It was too important to me. I told her I would go later.

Alexandre passed away from lung cancer. Not for one minute had I understood that he was so ill. I never saw my mother smoke again.

*

I checked my watch. The loaded trolleys and little family of three long gone. Exhaling heavily, I leant back in the chair and looked around, hoping that Marty would not be too much longer. I watched, as a woman from the next table excused herself, taking a packet of cigarettes from her pocket. Standing over beyond the post boxes, she took one out of the packet, lit it and inhaled. Something about the way she did it reminded me of my mother all those years ago.

The entire time, I watched her face, and realised for the very first time, that there seemed to be nothing else in the world that could bring you down that quick, and give you that look of absolute satisfaction in such a short time. It was a look of satisfaction I had seen time and time again on my mother's face. Enviously, I wish that I had something that could give me that satisfaction right now, if only briefly.

I had smoked momentarily. Like most teenagers, I had started up because everyone else did. The super popular girls made a point of getting caught in the school toilets, upping their schoolyard cred. I persisted long enough to know I hated it. I was never one of the cool girls at school. And the way I felt right now, it seemed as if some things never change.

Chapter 4

From the passenger seat I glanced across at Marty. 'Apparently the house is hidden from the road. Turn right at the roundabout. It still doesn't make sense why the lawyer called me.'

'Tell me what he said again?' he asked, his tone as intrigued as mine.

'His name is John Scott. He said poor old Mr Carmody had passed away. There doesn't appear to be any children. Mr Carmody had a recent will drawn up where it was stated that I must have first option on the house. It's totally baffled me. Anyway, I explained that although I had been in the real estate industry for some years, I was taking a break from it for now. However, John Scott said that he had strict instructions I was to look at it first and then get back to him.' Pointing, I indicated for Marty to turn left. 'To be honest, my curiosity has gotten the better of me. So thanks for coming with me.'

'Thanks for thinking of me. I'm keen to list it.' He looked sideways at me. 'Davis will be on the warpath when he knows you gave the listing to me.'

'He would have to be bloody kidding wouldn't he?' The anger was strong in my voice. My face turned to the window. I tucked a long dark curl behind one ear.

I felt Marty's glance. 'Who would have thought?' was all he said, his tone full of irony.

I gave a wry smile. Who would have thought indeed? The three musketeers no longer existed. Three months before Davis and I had separated, Davis had come home one evening, thrown his keys on the stainless steel kitchen bench, and with his hands on his hips, told me Marty was out.

'Out of what?' I asked. Apron clad, I proudly lifted from the oven the large stainless steel baking dish heavy with my latest culinary creation, beef wellington.

'The business! We're on our own now.' He didn't look at me, but I knew his face looked like thunder. 'I've been on the phone to the lawyers all afternoon. The papers are being drawn up. He wants to open his own agency.' His voice filled with rage. 'He's gotten too big for his boots.' His fist came down and slammed the kitchen bench. 'If he wants war, I'll give him war.'

To say I was shocked was an understatement. I stood rooted to the spot, oven mitts on my hands. 'Davis? What are you talking about? You must be joking?' However, I could tell by the anger he wore on his face it was no joke. Baffled, I asked, 'How long has this been going on for?'

'For God's sake Peach, he's been trying to undermine us for years.' Loosening his tie, he stalked off towards the bedroom, his long legs like a giraffe. Without turning, he shot over his shoulder, 'Look I don't want to talk about it anymore. It's done.' From behind, I saw his hands cut the air like a knife.

Throwing the oven mitts on the bench, I hurried after him. He was standing in the robe taking off his trousers. In frustration, he flung them on the bed. They slipped to the floor.

I hovered in the doorway. 'Davis... I don't understand... he is your best friend... *our* best friend.'

'Not anymore.' He brushed past me and went back to the kitchen, snatching a Corona from the fridge. He opened it roughly, spilling some on the floor. He left it. His behaviour was so out of character I didn't know what to make of it. He took a lime from the fruit bowl, slammed it down on the stainless steel bench, pulled the largest knife from the block, and angrily hacked a slice, pushing it into the neck of the bottle, before retreating to the terrace. I watched as he stood with his back to me, one hand on the railing, the other throwing back the beer. He looked as if any moment he might hurl the entire bottle at the wall opposite. I could not think of a time when I'd seen him like this.

Davis was such a perfectionist. Ever since we had moved into the warehouse, he'd been over the top about the housekeeping. *Anal*, might be a better word. Everything had a place. The newly laid light-coloured timber flooring was incredibly soft, and rather than offend our guests, Davis bought six pairs of white towelling slippers to keep just inside the front door, so our female visitors wouldn't mark the floor with their heels. He kept bringing home different mops for the cleaners to use. Trialling them first, giving them a ranking out of ten. It drove me crazy. It annoyed me more, when I turned the tap on in the evening to get a drink of water, and he'd comment that he'd already wiped the sink down and now there were water marks.

'Davis, it's a sink,' I'd say, and shake my head in frustration at his *analness,* if there was such a word.

Marty broke into my thoughts. 'So tell me again how you know this Mr Carmody?'

I shrugged. 'I really didn't know him that well. Sometimes I'd see him when I shopped at New Farm. Poor old guy was in a wheel chair. He'd had one leg removed from the knee down.' I glanced across at Marty and caught his grimace. 'He used to sit outside The Deli most afternoons, having a coffee, watching the world go by, and attempting to have a bit of a chat with anyone with a keen ear. Occasionally, I'd see him struggling to roll himself up the ramp, so I'd give him a hand. To be honest, at first I always thought he looked a bit cranky, but surprisingly, when he spoke he had a wonderfully melodious voice. The more I got to know him, I realised he was extremely articulate. Apparently, he'd been a notable landscape architect in his former years.' And then I smiled to myself. 'And, after a while, I realised he was a bit of a joker as well.'

Marty glanced at me. 'How do you mean?'

'I remember once asking how he was. Instantly, he grabbed at his heart, looking concerned. Startled, I leant closer and asked if something was wrong. "No, the day could not be any more perfect now that I have set eyes upon the beauty of you," he said.' I shook my head in mirth. 'Another time, he said that his doctor had only given him a short time to live. Obviously I was shocked and when he saw my face he said best not to waste any time, we should have coffee immediately, and then he laughed.'

'Sounds like a flirt to me.' Marty chuckled. 'How old do you think he was?'

I shrugged. 'I don't know. Perhaps in his late eighties, early nineties.'

'Cheeky old codger. Sounds like he did a good job of staying in his own house for as long as he did.'

'No, he didn't. The house has been closed up for a couple of years now. Mr Carmody was in one of the aged care facilities in the area, although he never gave up hope that one day he would be able to return. He told me the hardest thing of all was giving away his dog Wilbur, when he went into the facility. I met Wilbur a couple of times, tied to his master's wheelchair. He was a beautiful blonde labrador with huge dark eyes that appeared to say so much. He looked as if he understood what was going to happen to him and was scared and sad. When Mr Carmody told me, it really bothered me and I cried. I told him I would try to find a way to take Wilbur for him, but when he knew we lived in a warehouse, he said that it would be unfair to Wilbur, that he was used to a large garden. Apparently, Wilbur went up the coast to a friend of his. So although it was good the dog had a home, it meant Mr Carmody couldn't see him. You could tell he was heartbroken. In fact, it was as if he went downhill after that.'

'So has it been a few years since you've seen the old guy?'

'No... I continued to see him at the shops, up until about six months ago.' I laughed lightly. 'He'd tell me that he'd escaped from the facility. Truth be known, they were probably glad to have a reprieve from him for a short time. I gathered he was a demanding patient.' I smiled and shook my head. 'Anyway, he'd wheel himself up to the shops and wheel himself home. One afternoon after work when I had raced over to pick up some of that Italian ham that Davis used to like, Mr Carmody told me that it was *Happy Hour* back at the facility, but no one was ever bloody happy, so he preferred to chat to his friends at the shops.' I laughed again.

'How come you shopped over at New Farm so much when you lived at West End?'

I glanced over at him and indicated with my hand to turn right at the roundabout. 'In the beginning it was almost quicker for me to come across to do my shopping, than to stop and talk to every man and his dog at West End. As delightful as our clientele was, being so well known in the area meant the smallest tasks took forever. And then in the last year, it was simply because I could not face those very same people.' My face blushed at the way I had felt.

Marty gave me a fleeting look. 'I understand. Speaking of dogs, you've always loved them, why haven't you had one of your own?'

I rolled my eyes to the heavens with frustration. 'Because Davis said *no*, that's bloody why.' Neither of us spoke for a minute and then I continued. 'Also with the hours we worked, it wouldn't have been fair.' I thought for a few seconds. 'Funny, but I have always wanted a dog. I remember begging Bea and Johnny. All we ended up with was a guinea pig called Harriet. Johnny said it would teach us the responsibility of taking on a pet. Harriet was such a lovely little thing, with funny little teeth that munched noisily on celery. Quite clever really, she reacted to my voice, and to the sound of the fridge door. For a while I even pretended she was a small dog.' I paused. 'Funny thing was though, when Bea left us and moved to New Farm, the first thing she did was get a pug. I never could work that one out.'

I was quiet for few minutes thinking of one of the "dates" Emerald Green had insisted I take myself on. Fifty kilometres north of Brisbane was Marcoola Beach, a secluded broad expanse of white sand that I had not visited in over 20 years. It bought back fond memories of childhood holidays with our Uncle Terry. It reminded me that some things never change. However, on that particular "date" day, as I walked along, I'd caught sight of a pretty little redhead in the distance, running after two French bull dogs, one black, and one white with a black face. The dogs dodged and weaved the waves one minute, and the next they tore up the beach. The curvy redhead took off after them and the closer she got the faster they ran from her. The little dogs reminded me of circus clowns. However, what I loved most was the joy they appeared to bring to their owner. The look on her face was priceless, and the way she laughingly called to them delightful. I decided then and there that no matter what my future held, I would have dogs. Maybe I'd become a crazy dog lady and have a whole heap. Perhaps that was my destiny. Denied as a child, and later by Davis, I would one day make up for it.

Shaking my head to clear it, I changed the subject. 'I'm not sure why Mr Carmody wanted me to see his house. He once told me he had seen an article about *Address* in the local paper, and after that he was always asking about the property market. I did try to explain to John Scott that I was taking a break from the industry, however he said he must proceed as instructed. Anyway, it'll probably be a good listing for you. Sounds like a fairly large property.' I pointed. 'It's down here on the right. It must be the one that's hidden from the road by the trees.'

Tucked away in a quiet tree-lined street, and only minutes from the city centre, Marty's black BMW, a twin to mine and a triplet to Davis's, slowed to a halt near the end. A large blossoming poinciana in front of an ivy covered imposing stone fence shielded the house from the road. Climbing from the car, I was aware of something I had not experienced in a long time, and briefly had trouble putting my finger on. I glanced around. And then I recognized it. It was silence. Fleetingly, it was punctuated by birdsong. Immediately it registered to me as a sound of tranquillity.

A feeling of awe crept upon me. I handed Marty the key to the wrought iron gate. The back of the gate had been boarded up, so we were unable to see through. Marty fiddled with the key for a while, before it finally turned in the rusty lock. He then had to lift up one side of the heavy gate so he could push it open far enough for us to slip through, as it had dropped through age and lack of use. It was just as well he was with me, as I wasn't sure if I would have managed on my own.

Once inside, I was able to see that although many years of neglect had taken its toll, there was something mysterious and beautiful about this property.

Stepping with care, my eyes swept from side to side, taking it all in, relishing the solitude and peace. Aside from two late flowering jacarandas, magenta coloured bougainvillea had taken hold of nearly the entire front garden. Trust bougainvillea, I thought. It always liked a good neglect. My eyes travelled up, following a couple of stately palms which shot skywards like elegant umbrellas.

We crunched our way up the weed infested, curved, gravelled driveway. The call of a whipbird snapped through the tallest branches. A butterfly fluttered over to me, escorting me as if in welcome. Perfuming the breeze, a row of unruly crepe myrtles stood like untidy soldiers either side of the drive. A few metres further along an old stone fountain of substantial proportions came into view. I could almost hear the faint sound of water trickling. Our footsteps disturbed pigeons drinking rainwater from the fountain, and in a flurry they flew away, giving us a fright at the same time.

Gravel crunched underfoot. A few more paces and the wonderful perfume of star jasmine added to the superb fragrance this garden had so far produced. Birdsong was loud in our ears. Surveying my surroundings, it was difficult to believe that I was merely a half dozen blocks or so from the bustling cosmopolitan heart of New Farm, and only minutes by car from the city centre. Instead, it felt like we had been whisked off to some far away fantasy country garden.

Already I felt drawn in. Mesmerised, I wanted to see more. The path divided. To the right, the wide driveway led to a garage, with some sort of storeroom behind. To the left, the path edged by agapanthuses, narrowed and curved around towards the house. Two broad plinths with oversized antique urns welcomed us to a gravelled forecourt, giving the first glimpse of the house. My first thoughts upon seeing the sandstone house nestled amid this fairy-tale-like garden, were that the house might easily be made from gingerbread. Up until then, both of us had been quiet with our own thoughts. However, right at that moment I made a little '*Oooh*,' sound.

'Wow!' said Marty in a hushed tone, as if to speak any louder would be irreverent.

I nodded my head, too busy examining the front of the house to speak. From there it appeared square in shape, but with a bay window projecting slightly at the front, and a sweeping wrap around veranda. To my knowledgeable eye, I believed the house to be built around the end of the nineteenth century. Original decorative cast iron balustrades, posts and valances were still in place, but were in need of much work to return to their former glory. The hipped roofline and detailed fretwork still very evident, as well as three stone chimneys and a wrought iron roof feature. The silver corrugated iron roof, possibly newer than the house, was covered in mould and grime and in desperate need of a high powered hose to reveal what condition lay beneath.

Climbing high on the front wall of the house was a rose vine covered in wonderful clusters of rosy pink blooms. Entwined with it was an orange scented rose whose flowers were so dark to be almost magenta. Neither rose appeared to have thorns. They trailed and bobbed and threw a halo of blooms around the front door as they clambered up the stone walls. Instantly, I was reminded of a conversation I'd had with Mr Carmody, about how I missed a garden at the warehouse and would one day be keen to see how green my thumb was. I smiled at the thought.

However, it was only as we ascended the six stone steps to the veranda that the full magnificence of the house's river view was revealed through a window to the side.

While Marty fiddled with the rigid lock on the front door,

I turned and surveyed the garden directly in front. A generous space had been devoted to this part of the property. I glimpsed through the overgrowth, the relics of a large ornamental pond was on a direct axis from the front door. A nineteenth century cast iron bench graced one end. Even with the neglect, I was able to see the formality of the front garden. Further ahead, following the same line of axis, I noticed a sundial and the remnants of a rose garden. Shafts of sunlight magically appeared like spotlights showcasing certain key pieces of the garden and once again I noted my butterfly escort, or its twin, fluttering around me.

Everyone has their own idea of heaven. Some see it as a place of spiritual reward. However, for me, right at that moment, it was this garden.

'Coming?' Marty asked, interrupting my thoughts.

Turning, I nodded and followed him. I placed a hand to my nose, to cover the smell of old and neglect. A wide entrance hallway greeted us, with sizable rooms off to either side, but with dubious décor and old-fashioned fittings, all rather sadly neglected. However, most of the rooms were filled with light and well proportioned. I was immediately taken with the house, along with its solid walls, high ceilings and ideal layout, although, the dark kitchen at the back of the house left a lot to be desired.

An aged lace curtain hung ethereally and silent in front of a small window. There was a tiny tear in the bottom right hand corner, the light spilling through, illuminating an otherwise dim space. I stared mesmerised. The hole in the curtain was in the loose shape of a heart.

I walked towards it and peered through the heart shaped hole to the garden below. The view from the window was spectacular, overlooking the entire back garden. Impatient to see more, I swept the curtain back, and noticed that through a corridor of trees, a perfect snapshot of the Brisbane River was revealed. I watched as a lone kayaker headed for shore after crossing the wake left behind by a jet ski. Just then one of the iconic City Cat ferries came into view.

Brisbane River was the heart of Brisbane and the ferries made it an inexpensive and fun way to access the city and riverside suburbs, from Breakfast Creek right up to the Queensland University at St Lucia, where I had studied. Recently on one of my weekly dates with myself, I had ridden one of the Cats from one end to the other, marvelling at a city I had grown up in, but had never taken the time to explore.

Marty's low whistle brought my thoughts back to the present. 'What a find.' He came and stood beside me, he too mesmerised by the river view, the trees framing the vision of bobbing yachts. 'If only some of those trees were lopped, that view would be opened right up.'

He began to explore further, assessing the house with a professional eye. He turned to me, arms folded across his chest. 'What are your thoughts Peach?'

'I'm not sure what to say. Something like this doesn't become available often.' How well I knew. In all of my experience in real estate in the inner city, I had never seen anything come onto the market such as this. In fact, the entire time Davis and I had been trying to have a family, I had kept my eye out for a house like this, something to raise a family in. Heck, I would have settled for something a quarter as good as this and still been deliriously happy.

I was at the window. From out the front I had realised that the land dropped away behind, however I had no idea the house did as well. It was huge.

I began wandering and found a door at the end of a minor

passageway off the kitchen. With some difficulty, I wrenched it open to find a courtyard. It was an extremely large, walled courtyard - sun filled, ventilated and watered by the recent rain. Large stone pavers had been laid in a grid pattern and in between, pretty native violets grew rampant. It was only as I stepped into it, I was able to see how big it actually was.

'Come look,' I called to Marty, my voice excited. 'This must have been the herb and vegetable garden for the kitchen. Isn't it wonderful? You never see anything like this in the city.' There was nothing left of the herbs, but the citrus trees were abundant - lemons, Tahitian limes, cumquats, dwarf oranges and mandarins. The dwarf orange tree hung heavily with fruit, giving such a lovely burst of colour and fragrance. Mostly the pumpkins had taken over, smothering other plants and even escaping over the fence.

As we went deeper into the house I noticed that every downstairs room opened onto its own garden terrace. The ornate extravagance of the garden was key to every bedroom in the house.

Fleetingly, I wondered what had happened to Mr Carmody's furniture, as the house was completely bare.

At that moment though, the garden seemed to take precedence. We wandered down to the terraced back garden to explore further. With every step, more surprising plants, shapes and colours came into view. The most eye catching display of cascading purple wisteria flowers tumbled down the face of a stone retaining wall, rendering me breathless in awe. Wisteria blossoms for only such a short time that I knew we were in luck to see such a show, as it is one of those plants that are mostly bare vines for the better part of the year.

The garden seemed to consist of a series of rooms unfolding one after another, linked by paths and stepping stones, making it a joy to explore.

Something was stirring in me as we wandered about. We followed a flagstone pathway where shadows and light danced about on the ground. I imagined little heart shapes among them.

We arrived at a set of stairs. On either side sat two huge urns. We took the steps and found ourselves at the pool. The large turquoise tiled rectangular swimming pool was derelict, the bottom full of green slimy water, with one large palm frond floating lost at sea. At one end was a sandstone fountain in the shape of a classical head that in its day would have spurted water into the pool, but now looked dry and lonely. Behind, a row of eight pencil pines awkwardly reached skyward.

We wandered further into the back garden where lilly pillys, gardenias, azaleas, flowering oleanders and overgrown bougainvillea grew rampantly. In the far left hand corner we found a small olive grove. I picked one of the deep green-grey lance shaped leaves with the silvery white underside, a smile forming on my lips.

'What?' Marty asked.

'Olive trees are a symbol of peace.'

Marty nodded with interest. Silently we both continued on our discovery.

Finally, Marty spoke. 'Your Mr Carmody had a spectacular garden in its time.'

Nodding, I began to wonder about Mr Carmody and what he must have left behind. But *why* me? *Why* did he think I should have first look at the house. Not much more than an acquaintance really. He had told me he liked my smile. That was good, because in the last year there were days when I thought my life had turned to utter shit, and I didn't think I would ever smile again.

However, already I knew. This house and garden needed me. Or if I was truthful... I needed it.

Serendipity can play a large part in the real estate game, something I knew first hand. The house had found me. But what was I going to do with it? Yesterday when I received the call from the lawyer, if you had asked me if I would be interested in buying this house, or any other house today, the answer would have been an emphatic 'No.'

With my arms folded across my chest, I turned and looked up at the house once again. Surprisingly, I noticed an upstairs window above the kitchen area. I wondered what was up there. I was sure I hadn't seen a staircase. But what I did see was, beyond the house's derelict state, was the house of my dreams.

If I put my real estate hat on, I would have had to admit that this property covered three important criterions: privacy, peace and quiet, plus an intimate connection to the river. It was the perfect mix of city and country.

'What are you thinking?' Marty asked.

I looked at him. 'I'm thinking I want it!'

He blinked. 'What?' He stared at me in disbelief.

I exhaled heavily. 'I want it. It's as simple as that.'

'But we haven't even looked at the rest of the house yet,' he spluttered.

'I know. I've just noticed there's an attic. But what does it matter? It's not as if I'm going to change my mind because it doesn't have enough wardrobe space, or not enough bathrooms. I think I'm meant to have it.'

Marty scratched his head and let out a low whistle. 'Phew Peach, what the heck are you going to do with a house like this?'

'I don't know, but I am going to find out…'

Chapter 5

Marty started the car and then looked across at me. 'You want me to drop you at your mother's?'

I nodded. I didn't need to remind myself that I didn't have a life. Well not yet anyway! It was funny, but it had taken my sessions with Emerald Green to realise I was still living Davis's life by staying in the house. I guess I had been hanging onto it. But why? *He* wasn't coming back, that was abundantly clear. He now had the long legged, blonde. Something I could never be.

Anyway, I couldn't have a dog and there was no room for my books. I should rephrase that, there was plenty of room, although it had never been the look that Davis had wanted. Minimalistic, you know, one of those interiors where the owners look as if they don't have any belongings. Even a toothbrush looked out of place. And there wasn't even a garden, only three cacti in pots on a small terrace, overlooking rooftops.

Taking myself off to the rose garden in New Farm Park for a personal date had shown me exactly what I had been missing and perhaps yearning for, for years.

Once Davis moved out, I had found myself rattling around our home with only the ghost of my marriage for company. I felt like a stranger in my own life, picking objects up and placing them down as if I had never seen them before. As I looked around, my old life seemed to rebuke me in the form of artwork, mirrors, pieces of furniture that although we had selected together, had never reflected who I was.

Once I made the decision two weeks ago, to offer the warehouse back to Davis, I had wanted to be out of there as quickly as possible.

I had emailed Davis and told him I would be gone by the weekend. In return, came a reply with a single cross on it. How ironic! Was he sending me a kiss or crossing me out? Funny, but I didn't even have any qualms about Felicity Best living in my home. She could have it.

Deliberately changing my thought process, I broke the silence. 'I've decided on a new car.'

'What?' Marty glanced across at me, eyebrows raised.

I gave him a look. 'I can no longer drive around in a car that has *Address* blazoned across the back. I want it gone.'

'Then change the number plates. Surely that would be easier.'

'Nope,' I said quite smugly. 'I've decided on one of those little Fiat 500 Abarths.'

Marty spat out a laugh. 'You're kidding! A Fiat Bambino?'

'The grown up version. It's quite a little pocket rocket. It's amazing how much you can personally customise them. I've chosen a red …'

Marty laughed interrupting me, 'You'll look like Speedy Gonzales!'

I ignored him. '… and they let me pick the seat coverings, and whether I wanted a black steering wheel or a white one. I chose the black with red stitching. And I've selected a white speed stripe as a trim! For a tiny car, it's terribly stylish. The alloy wheels are trimmed with a touch of red, and the side mirrors are black. You should see them, they look like cute little ears sticking out.' The thought of it made me smile, however I caught Marty shaking his head, a look of humour on his face.

'Look Marty, it's a bit of fun. I feel I deserve that after everything I've gone through. After all, it will only be me driving around in it. Before…' I swallowed, 'before everything happened we were looking at upgrading to a family car, a BMW four wheel drive… or perhaps it was *me* that was looking.' I rested my chin on my hand, glancing out the window. And then I turned back. 'Anyway I don't know what I'll be doing, so if I want to travel, it's not too big to keep in someone's garage. It'll be zippy, a bit of fun for a change. And it's so cute… you'll see.' Pleased with myself, I folded my arms across my chest. 'The Abarth is to a Fiat, like the AMG is to a Mercedes.'

'Then get yourself the Mercedes AMG coupe. You can afford it. It doesn't have ears, it has wings.'

Good naturedly, I slapped his arm. 'Stop it!' He was such a teaser.

He ducked. 'Never pick me up in it, okay? We'll look like Noddy and Big Ears.'

I let out a peel of laughter. 'I am not even going to ask you which one I am… but come on admit it… it's a cheeky little car.'

'I'll have to see it to believe it,' he told me. I could see he enjoyed our good natured bantering, something we had both missed.

We were quiet for a few seconds and then I glanced over at him. 'You know Marty… I'm not sure I've ever had the chance to thank you.'

He shot me a puzzled look. 'What for?'

'I think you know.' I exhaled. 'It's why you left *Address*, isn't it?'

He nodded although didn't look at me. His voice was soft. 'Peach what could I do?' He shook his head. 'Look we both knew Davis was ruthless, but at what cost? This time he had gone too far. I asked him to either stop or at least be honest with you. That's why we argued. He told me to butt out. And he banked on the fact that I would never tell you. He was bloody right.' He paused. 'You know I hated that bitch the minute she came on board.'

I laughed, enjoying hearing him voice those words. 'Marty...'

'Well think about it. If she hadn't come, we'd all still be together. And Davis might be a pain the butt, but he would have been our pain in the butt.'

'Believe me, I have been thinking about it and I have come to the realisation that that's not entirely true. I wish it was so I could blame it all on her. But... the truth is... if it wasn't her, it would have been someone else, or something else.'

His tone carried a cynical edge. 'You're charitable.'

'No... just finally coming to my senses. Come on, we both knew he was the most selfish person that walked this earth. But,' I shrugged, 'call me crazy, I loved him.'

'We both did. He was like a brother to me. We had some phenomenal times. I hate to admit it, but there are times I still miss him. Still miss the good side of him…'

'Hmm ... I'm not going to go that far. I'm not that charitable today. But Marty, thank you for standing up for me.'

He sighed. 'I should have told you the truth that day when you came to see me after Davis and I had the bust up. I couldn't look you in the eye. I knew how much you loved him and I couldn't be the one to tell you. I hoped that he'd come to his senses and maybe you'd never have to know.'

'Well that wouldn't have been exactly right either. But I don't blame you.' After I had found out about Davis's affair, I was angry with Marty as well, because I wondered how long he had been covering for Davis. Numerous times Marty had phoned, but I hadn't taken his calls.

In the last few months, I had come to the conclusion that Marty had been in a no win situation. The firm stand he had taken had cost him dearly, personally and professionally.

The car slowed to a halt outside Bea's house. Leaning

across, I offered Marty my cheek.

'You know I love you babe,' he said.

'I know and I am always going to love you too sweetie. I hated not talking to you.'

'Yeah it was the pits.' And the look he gave me told me what an ordeal he too had been through.

I flashed him my mournful look. 'I'm sorry.'

Fondly, he pulled one of my perfectly blow dried curls. 'What are you going to do about that house?'

I climbed out of the car. 'God only knows? Leave it with me. You'll be the first to know. I need some thinking time.' Strangely enough, even after all of these months, I still wasn't out of the habit of wanting to share every new event with Davis. However, that certainly was not about to happen.

*

'It's me,' I called, slinging my laptop bag onto Bea's French oak kitchen table. I needed to check my emails. Davis and I were doing our property settlement. Anyone who thinks the divorce is difficult is kidding themself. That's a piece of paper, over in a day. It's the property settlement that was a pain in the butt, to put it mildly.

Filling the air was the smell of an artist at work. For me it was the smell of years gone by, the smell of our childhood home; a mix of acrylic paints, turpentine, canvases and artist paraphernalia. It was the smell of Bea.

Flicking the switch on the kettle, I called out to her in her downstairs studio, 'I'm making tea.'

She was painting more often lately. She had an exhibition coming up in a couple of months, which was why she was heading to Byron Bay. She said the serenity helped. I had been treading carefully while staying with her. I was aware she liked her own space and needed the quiet to be creative. Her work was intensely vibrant in colour, applied by a palette knife, giving a rich deep impasto finish, with striking textured effects to give a three dimensional result that made the paint pop right off the canvas.

I was searching the tall glass fronted pantry when she came in. Turning to face her, it still sometimes took me by surprise how beautiful she was. For a woman nearing her mid-fifties, her free spirited allure had kept her face pretty. Plus she wore her individual style well. Although dressed in her signature white, an exotic piece of colourful fabric was wound around her head like a turban. Tendrils of blonde hair escaped and framed her expressive face, still lit by brilliantly blue eyes. Chunky bangles and rings accessorised her wrists and hands. Tucked into her headscarf was a hibiscus, picked from the garden earlier. It amused me that she wore white so often when painting. However, she reassured me she covered herself in a smock while doing so. A white smock.

I smiled. 'I can't find any normal tea, just these flower power ones - rose petal, dandelion, and rosehip and echinacea.'

Wrists jangling, she poked around. 'I think there should be a new box in there somewhere. And the others are not flower power teas darling, they're very healing. There is some wonderful passionflower tea in here as well.' She turned to face me, giving me a look. 'It would be perfect for you at the moment, excellent for nervous tension and anxiety.'

Gracefully, she perched herself on the edge of a rattan Antoinette chair, wiping her face with the back of her hand, smudging her forehead with a crimson hue. Once again, her bangles jangled, and I relished the sound of this constant comfort. She was like a kitten, you could find her anywhere in the house, simply by the ting of her jewellery.

Ignoring her reference to the state of my mind, I made a

mental note to visit the shops later. An unconventional person, Bea had always struggled with the simplest of domestic chores. Well, it was her house, and she could live as she pleased. I readied two white mugs and placed some chocolate *biscotti* on a plate as we sat in her kitchen in companionable silence.

My laptop beeped that an email had come through. I glanced at it. It was from Davis's email address. Hopefully, it would be the finalisation of our settlement. I opened the email and within seconds could feel the steam coming from my ears. I wanted to pick up the bloody laptop and hurl it across the room. I balled my hands into fists and almost began hyperventilating. 'Oh my God, oh my God, oh my God...'

'Peach, what is wrong?' The look of fright on Bea's face said that I was scaring her.

I could barely speak I was so angry. With shaking hands, I spun the laptop around and pointed, 'Read...' I put my hands to my face and kept them there. The email wasn't from Davis it was from that cow, Felicity.

Moving to the other side of the kitchen, I distanced myself from the laptop as if it was poison. I watched Bea's face as she read.

Dear Peach, I believe you need to positively reinforce the situation and you will find happiness too. Only going through my own separation last year, I do have empathy for you, however it is your bitterness that makes this a distressing situation. Our careers are an integral part of our being and I strongly urge you to find something new to fill your days. Davis and I are far too busy working hard to be constantly interrupted by your demands on the settlement. When Davis has more time he will get to it. I don't believe you know the pressure we are under running this business. Obviously you have no time-management skills, therefore you need to utilise your time more effectively. Felicity.

I watched as Bea's eyebrows shot higher by the second. I put a hand to my stomach feeling like I might throw up.

'Hmmmm,' was all Bea said, her jaw clenched, her eyebrows still scarily high. For seconds we watched each other, both unable to speak.

'I have only one word for you,' she said. 'Karma!' And she nodded her head firmly. I know she wanted to say *I told you so*. I was reminded of that first day when I had mentioned Felicity Best's name to her and her reaction. She had been right. I had been tunnel visioned, almost oblivious to everything else but the thought of having a baby.

'Really Peach, if Davis is letting that little upstart handle his affairs, then he is a bigger idiot than I always thought he was.' Matter-of-factly, she handed me two tissues.

It was no surprise to me that my mother didn't like Davis. I had always sensed it. And then since our separation, she had not exactly held back, telling me she had consistently found him ruthless, and as much as there was a charming side to him, she had always thought he was one to watch. Apparently, mothers seem to know these things.

'I truly understand what it feels like to want to murder someone,' she muttered, her arms elegantly folded across her chest.

I sniffed. 'Erectile dysfunction would probably make me quite happy.'

'Hummp,' Bea snorted. Shaking her head she returned to the laptop, picking it up and taking it into the living room. As she came back in, she closed the glass panelled art deco doors and then slapped her hands together as if removing something distasteful from them. 'We'll deal with that later.' Opening the top cupboard she pulled out delicate white and gold porcelain cups.

Catching the look on my face, she explained. 'It makes such a difference to drink tea out of the right cup. Plus, I think we need something pretty to look at to distract ourselves.' She set a small plate of dates down between us. 'Drink your passion-flower tea darling. I daresay you need it now more than ever.' However, she didn't sit down. She stayed standing looking out the backdoor, down into the garden, not saying a word.

*

With my head pounding, I laid down in Bea's guestroom. I pulled back the off-white coverlet and thirty thousand cushions in all shades of purples, mauves and lilacs, and rested my head against the cool pillow. Once again I was rocked by sorrow. I wanted my illusions back. I wanted to pretend it had never happened. I did not want the trauma of searching for another life. In my mind I keep saying *poor me, poor me, poor me.* I thought of Emerald Green and knew she'd want to slap the bejesus out of me for feeling so sorry for myself.

In a bid to stop my wallowing, I turned my attention to one of Bea's paintings opposite, in hues of magentas, purples and gold. I reminded myself, as Emerald Green would have advised, that right this moment, I was okay. But then again, she never liked it when I used the word, *okay*. She said it was a blanket word for covering all sorts of squirmy feelings. All right then, right this moment I was... and I fumbled around for the correct feeling... and then it hit me. Right this moment I was *bloody pissed off*. And *that's okay Emerald Green!*

For the thousandth time I asked myself how I could have been so dumb. How I had let Davis make every decision about my life, until I was living a life that resembled no part of who I was, not one iota. I exhaled heavily. Recently, during my therapy, there had been moments of clarity, when it dawned on me Davis may have done me the biggest favour of my life. But if that was so, then why, oh why, was I feeling so horrible. Once again, depression and loneliness welled.

Finally, I climbed out of bed, and went into the downward dog pose, my favourite yoga position, stretching my spine and rejuvenating my emotionally drained body, mentally thanking Emerald Green for also introducing me to yoga. My eyes, exhausted from crying, felt like they might literally pop out of my head in this position. However, I heard the voice of my yoga instructor... *feel this position making space in your spine. Can you feel it...?*

No... but I am bloody trying, I wanted to yell. Lacing up my joggers, I headed out, hopeful a brisk walk would render some sense into me. I began to walk faster and faster, wishing I could move fast enough to outrun my own unhappiness.

I headed towards New Farm Park, a park I had now begun, once again, to enjoy. As children, thanks to Johnny, we had been frequent visitors to the playground, and although it'd had many upgrades, the swings still had the ability to bring back fond memories.

With a determined swing of my arms, I rounded the jacaranda lined ring-road until I caught sight of the playground. Instantly, my mind was invited into fantasies of years gone by and I felt my mood lift. Pausing to take it in, I watched, still amazed at the impressive tree-house-walk that wound through the roots of massive mature fig trees, incorporating their trunks and low hanging branches. The climbing net, looking like a huge spider's web, had not been there when I was a child. The real estate agent in me instantly noting that it would have excellent city views from the top

With a smile, I watched as a young mother pushed her little girl on a swing, while a round faced baby brother, sucked furiously on his green dummy, from the safety of his pram.

'Higher Mummy, higher Mummy,' the girl squealed with delight. And then my mood fell again. As if in protective mode, I folded my arms against my chest. I knew that this was what I was missing. This… *normalcy*! I was nearing my thirty-fifth birthday and was single, but more painfully, childless. All of those years I had spent working in the corporate world had come around and bitten me, rendering me alone.

'Cry, let it out,' Emerald Green had said. 'No pain, no gain.' But there was *too* much pain and I wondered if I let it out, would I ever be able to stop. Surreptitiously, I wiped at my face, hoping no one would see my grief. Unable to punish myself further, I walked on, my thoughts drifting to only the year before.

*

Felicity had been with us for some months, and I was going in to the office less and less. I had felt my decision to hire her had been excellent. The truth was, I had outgrown the job, and I was well overdue for the position as a mother.

For the first time, I was spending huge chunks of time at home, nesting and loving every minute of it. Wonderful culinary feasts were prepared, we entertained lavishly, and I loved the fact that I didn't have to be superwoman, and for the first time could be a homemaker. I couldn't believe I was having those thoughts, however I was. I was also having thoughts of never returning to the corporate world, or at least, not for some time.

I didn't voice my feelings to many, as it seemed disloyal as a woman, to not want it all. After all, I had been Telstra Young Business Woman of the Year only a couple of years earlier. However, my feelings had changed. At this stage of my life, I wanted a traditional relationship, where the man went to work and earned the money, and I stayed at home, cooking and having babies. Odd, I know.

Nearly a year went by while pregnancy eluded me. In desperation, I had begged Davis for the two of us to take a holiday. He kept putting me off, saying that the timing wasn't right. Finally, he gave in. I was ecstatic. I checked my ovulation dates and booked accordingly.

There we were in one of the Small Luxury Hotels of the World at Blanket Bay in New Zealand, and my husband had turned into an adrenaline junkie. If he wasn't bungy jumping, he was parasailing, jet boating, mountain hiking, heli-skiing and canyoning. I was exhausted just watching him and felt that we were wasting our precious small window of ovulation in the most romantic of stone lodges on Lake Wakatipu. At one point, Davis had even suggested that we cut short our stay in the lodge and hike to Milford Sound. I told him that was not going to get me pregnant, and began to wonder if he knew exactly how it was done. Sure I wanted him to have fun, but I wanted him to have fun with me.

Although he was on a high, it seemed as if our days were filled with adventure, and every night he was exhausted. One night he even said, *'For God's sake Peach, I've had it.'* I should have taken that as a hint, silly me, however so tunnel visioned was I with my biological clock ticking away rapidly, I needed a sledge hammer to hit me over the head to get it.

Anyway that was my first tip off. Second one, the next night, New Year's Eve. Mid our eight course degustation, the mystical sound of bagpipes drifted into the dining room, drawing us and the other guests out onto the stone terrace. Spellbound, we listened to the unique harmonics, as the bagpiper played *Amazing Grace*, stirring all sorts of emotions in me. Shivering, I wrapped my arms tighter around myself and stepped in closer to the man in my life, thinking we were the luckiest people on earth to be in these surroundings.

'Are you cold?' he asked. 'I'll get your jacket.' I smiled at my chivalrous hero, telling him to be quick. I didn't want him to miss any part of this evening.

When the bagpiper had finished, the other couples returned inside, however Davis still hadn't returned. Surprised, I went in search of him. I walked through the drawing room, passing the mammoth stone fireplace, thinking maybe he'd become waylaid there. I continued up the huge staircase and along the hallway to our room. The door was ajar.

I glanced around at our empty luxurious suite, noticing once again the sumptuous furnishings and elegant rug, the schist stone walls, and the timber beams. I made a mental note that the next day, there was to be no more activities. A day in this room was required. Earlier, we must have left the French doors ajar. We could not get enough of the view of the spectacular lake and the snow-capped mountains. They looked so close that it was as if we just stretched our hands out, we could touch them. I crossed the room to secure the door and with surprise noticed Davis's tall shadowy figure in the darkness leaning against the balcony rail. He had his back to me. I went to call out, but noticed he had his phone to his ear.

Listening, I strained wondering who he would be talking to at that time of night. Davis didn't say much at first, he just seemed to be listening. Then he said, 'Yes, okay then. I need time.' And then he paused again and after listening, he chuckled. 'You're very persuasive. You know that, don't you? Yes, I know, I know. I feel the same way.' It wasn't so much what he said, it was the tone of voice he used.

For what seemed to be an eternity, I didn't move. My heart hammered in my chest so loudly, I was sure he could hear it as well. Feeling desperately ill, I put a hand out to the wall as the cold hand of fear clutched at my heart.

Silently running back the way I had come, I returned to the dining room, terrified my face would give me away to the other guests. Within minutes Davis followed suit, minus my jacket. I didn't ask where it was, there was no need. And I didn't know how I was going to get through the next four courses. With my hands clutched together under the table, I kept thinking I was going to throw up. Rapidly, I blinked back tears. Looking at the man I loved, I wanted to beg him not to do this to me. He was my best friend, my lover, my life, the father of our unmade babies.

I watched anxiously as Davis drank from his wine glass, oblivious to my state of mind. And then the crushing blow hit me. I thought maybe I had gotten away with it, like when you kick your toe and for that first moment there's nothing, and then the pain hits you. It hit me, like a sledge hammer hurting in a place I didn't know I had.

Two weeks earlier, a staff Christmas party at our home. I was busy topping Atlantic salmon slices with my homemade chilli jam. Felicity was propped on a stool chatting to me, firstly saying that I had the most awesome life. I was *so lucky*. She even commented on my black and white striped apron with hot pink ties. It was one of those back handed compliments. 'How… Stepford Wife-ish of you,' she cooed, batting her lashes, throwing her head back and laughing. 'You look very…' she searched for the word, 'cute!'

She then went on to tell me that *Address* was the best thing that had ever happened to her, every now and then elegantly recrossing her long tanned legs. The aquamarine mini dress she was wearing riding sky high. Her pretty blonde hair was in waves around her face. A brand new Louis Vuitton clutch on her lap. I remembered thinking could this girl get any more beautiful?

Davis had come in looking for something in one of the kitchen drawers. I noticed the way Felicity turned side on and over a bare tanned shoulder, flashed her eyes at him. I remembered pausing, hands clad in oven mitts, with the kitchen tray in my hand, stunned, and thinking she was a tad obvious. I had this sudden urge to say, '*Excuse me dear, but I am in the room. Do you mind?*' But so taken aback was I, that I didn't say a word. Party noises drifted inside from the terrace.

Davis appeared oblivious. He placed his wine glass on the monolithic stainless steel kitchen bench, and rifling through the cutlery drawer he asked me where the gas refill was for the wine opener. There was a feeling, and I couldn't put my finger on it. Something was trying to make itself known to me, but I didn't want to know. I bent to place the salmon into the oven, but still aware, with my back to them, I glanced at the mirrored splashback. I saw Felicity pick up Davis's glass and seductively drink from it, the entire time her eyes on him. He took it from her, his hand touching hers. Smiling, he put the glass to his lips, where hers had been. Holding her eyes, there was a look flowing between them that no psychiatrist would need to glimpse to decode.

The intimacy of their pose took my breath away. I felt it deep in my gut. My face flushed. I spun around and looked at Davis directly. He caught my look although nervously glanced away. Casually, Felicity slid off the stool and sashayed through the house and out onto the terrace, proudly swinging her new Louis Vuitton handbag, a gift from an admirer she had told me earlier.

Just at that moment the doorbell chimed, heralding the arrival of another guest, leaving us no time to talk. The next morning when I bought it up, Davis waved it away reminding me how inebriated staff became at Christmas parties, and it was the one time of year when bad behaviour just had to be excused. He said it was normal for people to either love or hate the boss, generally the latter.

I honestly accepted his explanation. I wanted to. My focus was on getting pregnant. We had our romantic holiday all planned and nothing was going to get in the way, although, something about Felicity's handbag kept seeping in to my consciousness, making me uncomfortable.

However now I knew, Felicity Best the girl who had everything, now even had my husband. Well I had fed her to him very nicely. *Stupid me!* And the handbag… I came to realise that was his calling card.

*

Lost in thought, I walked on until I had reached Oxlade Drive. I skirted down the side of the Merthyr Road Bowls Club and out onto the walkway that ran along the banks of the Brisbane River. I hadn't realised New Farm was quite so liveable. Davis had always been so dismissive of it. However, it was similar to West End in the fact that they were both cosmopolitan, inner city suburbs, gracing the river.

Continuing along the riverside path, I paused briefly to allow a mother duck to pass as she protectively ushered her little family across the path. With delight, I watched as one by one they gracefully slid into the water. Not too much further along, I came to the Sydney Street City Cat terminal.

For years I'd often said when I had more time, I'd ride one of the City Cats from beginning to end. Well now, because of Emerald Green's insistence on my personal weekly dates, I had done it. It's interesting how you live and work in a city and mostly you never see what tourists see. Over the last couple of months, I had seen more of Brisbane than I had perhaps ever seen. And I had loved it.

In gaining awareness about myself and my values, I was fast losing the false sense of self I had been sustaining, and gradually I was meeting the truth, and finally I was meeting me. Where it was going to lead me, I still had no idea. However I was slowly becoming okay with that. Sorry Emerald Green, I was slowly becoming *comfortable* with that.

My mind ticking over, I headed up Sydney Street, and before I knew it I realised I was heading towards Frank Carmody's house as if on auto pilot. Although I had been coming to my mother's house for years I had never been to this part of New Farm. Now it intrigued me. I still couldn't see much from the footpath, so I leant heavily against the gate, attempting to make a crack I could peer through, to no avail. It was locked – lock, stock and barrel. I could have brought the keys with me, however I hadn't planned on walking this far.

From under the sturdy knotted branch of a massive Moreton Bay Fig tree, with more than a little interest, I admired the shady street, lined with the mature trees. The view of the neighbour's mulberry tree soothed me, evoking memories of the huge mulberry tree in my childhood backyard at Johnny's house. It had been the centre of many activities. There Lou and I had perched for hours in its branches eating an endless supply of the messy berries.

Most of the neighbouring houses were in the Queenslander style and definitely more modest than Mr Carmody's. Directly opposite, I noticed a large, white, rather handsome cat saunter out of a track of some sort which was positioned between two homes. I hadn't noticed the track earlier with Marty. Flanked heavily by trees, you would almost have to know it was there to see it. It must have led from the street below.

The cat nonchalantly continued across the road and then sauntered into some overgrowth right beside Mr Carmody's eastern boundary. There appeared to be another track, which must have led down to the river, so unkempt I imagined it was inaccessible to all except those who knew about it.

Bea belonged to the New Farm Historical Society and occasionally told us interesting titbits, some harder to believe than others. Originally, the suburb of New Farm had been a huge farm. When the farmer divided the land to sell, he put easements in place so he could lead his oxen down to the river. Some of those easements still stood in place today, although there was, of course, not one oxen to be found. Some property owners saw no need to have the "Oxen Easement" clause removed from their title deeds, and every now and then they came up again. Perhaps that was what the track had been.

Hesitantly, I took a few steps towards the track. However, just then the white cat came bolting out, hackles raised, looking like he had seen a ghost, and scaring the living daylights out of me. Hastily stepping back, with one hand to my chest, I watched as he took off back across the road and disappeared into the overgrowth. Heart still pounding, I spun around as a bike shot out of the trees behind me.

Once again I jumped back, my hand to my thumping chest, crying out in fright.

By the look on the rider's face, it appeared I had startled him.

Instantly he stopped, propping himself on one leg, turning to me. 'I am sorry,' he said. 'I wasn't expecting anyone.' He removed his sunglasses. And in that instant there was a flash of energy, almost a recognition.

Narrowing my eyes, I took another step back. 'It's… it's fine. No problem.' With my arms folded in front of me, I ran my hands up and down my goosebumpy arms, wracking my brain to see if I remembered meeting him before now. However, nothing came to me.

Curiously, I watched as he continued across the road and disappeared down the unkempt track opposite, the same one the white cat had vanished into. I daresay this was not the first time the rider had used the track, leaving me to wonder if it posed a security issue.

I turned my attention back to the house. Although I could barely see a thing in the late afternoon light, a wonderful sense of peace washed over me. There was something enchanting about this house. I walked back to Bea's home somewhat slower than I had headed out.

It was almost dark when I arrived back at Bea's. I was pleasantly surprised to see Lou getting out of her car with her two children, Lakshmi four, and Bob two. I remember when she was born, Bea saying, 'Lakshmi? It sounds like the name of some exotic food. What sort of name is that for a child?'

And although I agreed with my mother, I could not help but wonder if my nan had said the same thing to her about my name. 'Peach? It's a piece of fruit. What sort of name is that for a child?'

Lou had explained she wanted her baby to be named after the Hindu goddess of fortune and prosperity. She wanted her child to be the embodiment of beauty, grace and charm. That was Lou for you. By the time she got to Bob, she chose his name because she liked it - go figure.

'Aunty Peach, Aunty Peach,' Lakshmi called.

'Hello darling, what are you doing here?' I cuddled the small blonde replica of Lou, kissing the top of her head before doing the same to Bob. I took in Lou's face and instantly knew something was wrong.

'Go surprise Bea-Bea, she's in her studio,' I urged the children, using their pet name for their grandmother.

Lakshmi ran off with Bob in tow. I frowned. 'What's up Lou?'

Wearing cut off denims and scuffed camel suede boots, she plonked herself down on the bottom step and crossed her long legs with a look on her face that said the world had come to an end. She was a gorgeous tall blonde, with a perfect lithe body - we still didn't look anything like sisters. And I was still her protector. Some things never change.

She signed theatrically. 'It's Mitch.' She shrugged and looked forlorn, looking very much like Lakshmi at that moment.

'Darling, what is it this week? Let me guess. He can't decide between his X Box and his bong?' Lou and Mitch were often on a break and every few weeks it was something different.

Ignoring my comment Lou spoke. 'He doesn't pay any attention to me. I could be chopped liver for all he cares.' And then she cupped both of her hands around her small breasts, her face lighting up. 'I'm thinking of having a boob job.'

'Right!' I said. 'And *that* will fix all of your problems?' I sat down beside her. '*Lou,* how about finding a guy with a car to begin with? A job would also be good! Not to mention a wallet. One with credit cards in preferably.'

Lou had had her fair share of dating guys who were hot but generally hopeless. However, Mitch was the one she had decided to have children with.

'You could do so much better. You are worth more…'

She cocked her head to the side, blue eyes wide, and looked at me, brushing her long hair behind one ear.

I read her mind in a flash. Crossing my arms in front of myself, I looked away. 'I know, don't go there. I'm the last one who should be giving advice when it comes to relationships.'

Lou exhaled heavily and then wailed, 'He never wants sex. It's not fair.' She pouted. 'I'm thinking either a boob job or an affair.'

'Lou,' I admonished. 'Don't say that stuff. You don't mean it.'

'It's okay for you. You've got the best boobs around...'

Wearily, I shook my head. 'May I remind you they're obviously not the answer to everything.' I paused and exhaled heavily. I was in no mood for one of her tirades. Everyone knew Lou was a drama queen. So much so, her jersey in year 12 had it stamped across the back.

'Look, you're just going to have to forgive me, if I'm not that understanding today. The way I feel, I may never have sex again. The man I thought I'd spend the rest of my life with is with someone else. So, *you* not having sex very often certainly does not stir any sympathy from me.' I looked at her, shaking my head with frustration. '*Lou, Lou, Lou* it's time to grow up.'

I noted the shocked look on her face. For the first time in my life, I felt not one ounce of guilt, however I leant down and kissed the top of her head, before turning on my heels and taking the steps two at a time.

The next morning, before I left the house for my appointment with Mr Carmody's lawyer, I went in search of my mother to say goodbye. I could hear the sound of her voice coming from her studio downstairs. It sounded as if she was on the phone to Johnny. God love them, they were still the best of friends. We were an odd family. Johnny's latest wife Patrice, she was number three, came along to every family gathering whether Johnny was coming or not. My mother told Johnny if he ever left Patrice, she would have her, she loved her that much. See, I told you... odd family.

Halfway down the stairs I stopped in my tracks. I could

hear Bea talking. 'She seems to be doing better. Johnny, *honestly*, I always thought Peach would be our stable one. But really, it's quite the opposite. Look at Lou. I know we don't love Mitch, but who would have thought she'd be so sensible and secure? You can't pick them can you? Quite frankly, I'm not sure what Peach is going to do with her life. It's all rather depressing. Of course I am hopeful she will head to Provence and spend some time there. You know she has to do it Johnny. She has been running away from it for years. Yes… I'll give her your love. Give mine to Patrice.'

I raised my eyes to the heavens. Invisible again. Lou, *the sensible one*! Was my mother kidding? I left the house in a huff. My sister had only been seeing Mitch for three months when she fell pregnant. Right from the beginning their relationship appeared to be fraught with difficulties, with Lou often returning home to either Bea or Johnny, but that didn't stop her falling pregnant with Bob, saying that she wanted more than one child, and therefore thought they should have the same father. Mitch was probably a nice guy, however it might have helped if he worked slightly more often. And now Lou was thinking of either having breast implants or an affair? Lou was stable alright!

The only thing giving me an ounce of pleasure at the moment was my new car. I pulled into the smallest parking spot out the front of Montgomery's in Brunswick Street, where I was to meet John Scott to return Mr Carmody's keys. My friend Chilli was co-owner of the restaurant with her son. I don't know what I would have done without her words of wisdom these past ten months.

There was the lingering aroma of coffee and bacon in the air. Montgomery's was already full and the busy hum of conversation greeted me. For a few seconds, I watched as Chilli crossed through the restaurant to me. I noticed how many patrons looked up and smiled at her as she passed. Briefly, she stopped, a warm greeting for first this one, and then another. Catching her eye, I winked and waved, indicating I already had a table as I had already spotted John Scott seated on one of the white leather studded banquettes. The lounge made quite a statement sitting against the backdrop of an ebony wall adorned with two enormous sparkling Venetian mirrors.

Sitting very upright, glasses on the end of his nose, Mr Scott was busy perusing paperwork, giving me a chance to observe him.

I hazarded a guess that he was perhaps in his early sixties. Dressed in a double breasted suit and pale blue silk tie and pocket square, he appeared a rather formal man, his silver handlebar moustache making him more so. Snapping a folder shut, he stood and pulled out the chair opposite for me. Yesterday, I had felt he was a man of little emotion, however today I observed that he gave a fleeting look of admiration at my attire.

I had never been a trousers girl, legs not long enough. Instead, I have always opted for a far more feminine look, and today I wore my favourite Alannah Hill red silk tiered skirt, with a red and white polka dotted ruffled blouse, along with my secret weapon, shiny nude patent leather heels. Nude heels helped the legs to look longer. I flicked my long dark curls behind one ear. The swishing of my silk skirt was audible as I sat, placing my monogrammed Louis Vuitton handbag on the chair next to me.

Mr Scott gestured to the waiter for two coffees. I must say I was a little disappointed we didn't order anything to eat, as it almost seemed sacrilegious to be at Montgomery's and not order their delicious fare. However, I was most grateful for the bite sized shortbread that escorted the fragrant brew. Mr Scott appeared to be a man who wasted no time on pleasantries, getting down to the task at hand.

'Right,' he briskly stated, clasping his hands together on the table in front of him. 'I believe you've seen Mr Carmody's property.' He glanced at me over the top of his glasses. 'What is your opinion?' He was direct, I'll give him that.

With my elbows on the table, I leant forward, resting my chin on my hands. I could feel my face light up. 'I truly love it, and let me tell you, I'd love to buy it myself. However, I'm astute enough to realise that the price would be well out of my reach. Such a pity. A girl can dream though.' I flashed him a smile.

I had tossed and turned all night over Mr Carmody's property. I was realistic enough to know that I would never be able to afford something of that scale in the New Farm area. I was reminded of a couple of years ago, when a developer showed us a presentation of apartments he was seeking council approval for, in Hastings Street Noosa Heads, a small but very sought after prestigious holiday destination, an hour and a half north of Brisbane.

There were a dozen of us in the meeting. As soon as I saw the artist's impressions, I instantly made an audible sound of lust. Surprised, all heads turned to look at me. I *wanted* one of those apartments. I *wanted* the ocean at my door. I *wanted* the life that went with it. And I *wanted* to be one of the people that lived that type of life. However, the price tag was exorbitant. So, realistically I got over my wanting. Yesterday, I had felt like that about Mr Carmody's property. And just like the Noosa apartment, I'll eventually get over it.

Mr Scott tapped his fingers on the table top. 'And what is it that you would do with a property of that size if you owned such a thing Mrs Riding?'

I laughed. 'Oh don't worry, I've given that heaps of thought and I have so many ideas, I wouldn't know where to begin.' However, that did not stop me. 'The garden is *truly* spectacular. It must have been a paradise in its day.' I glanced at him, but he wasn't the best conversationalist. 'That house and garden needs to be filled with people. It has so much to offer. One thought I had, was an inner city B&B, but with old fashioned charm. I'd call it Carmody House.' I began to warm to the idea once again. 'Sounds nice doesn't it?' And this time I got a curt smile from him. 'Or I even thought about running cooking classes from the house, using produce grown in the kitchen garden supplemented by the numerable gourmet outlets in the area. It's one of those properties that could have many uses, and could bring pleasure to many people. Even weddings in the garden, I can see them now!

With my hands in my lap, I leant back in my chair smiling, watching Mr Scott's face. Momentarily, he appeared amused. His long pale slender hands once again clasped together on the table in front of him. Hands that looked like they had never done a manual day's work in their life.

Briefly, he looked down and then he looked up at me again. 'And you would have a dog?'

I sat up in my chair, looking surprised at his line of questioning. I spluttered, 'Sure... of course... a couple of dogs.' I felt my face light up again. 'Actually, I love dogs. I'm sorry to say my former husband was not so keen, but that's about to change as soon as I get myself settled. In fact, there are going to be many changes. Anyway, I have a list, and dog is on the top...' I stopped. I knew I was rambling, however as Mr Scott was very quiet, I was filling in the pauses, as I had a habit of doing.

'So, you didn't see it as a family home?' he asked, brow furrowed, looking over the top of his reading glasses, making it sound as if there should be a correct answer.

'Oh absolutely, for someone else I could not think of a better place to raise a growing family. It would be idyllic. But...' and I glanced down at my hands in my lap and swallowed. 'Just not for me...' My face clouded over, my pain returning where I thought it had eased. I cleared my throat and attempted to move on. 'I'm sure ...'

Mr Scott cut me off. 'Perhaps one day?'

I blinked a couple of times and swallowed again, unsure if he was asking me, or offering words of comfort.

'Perhaps one day Mr Scott.' In a far more business-like manner, I moved on. 'I'm sure you remember me saying that I am no longer in the real estate industry, and while I am flattered that Mr Carmody thought I might like to market the property for him, yesterday I took a former colleague with me to view it.' I looked directly at Mr Scott. He said nothing. I pulled Marty's business card from my bag and slid it across the table. 'As Mr Carmody appeared to trust my judgement, I'm happy to oversee Marty Edwards and will endeavour to make sure we do the right thing for Mr Carmody's family.'

He glanced briefly at the card, but left it where it lay on the table. He reminded me of a headmaster, and I, feeling once again like a school girl, had become nervous of my answers, hoping to respond correctly. John Scott's hands were now joined together as if in prayer, at his chin. 'So your living arrangements at the moment are?'

'*Oh?*' I was rather taken aback. He was an unusual man, his line of questioning odd. 'I'm staying with my mother here at New Farm for the short term.' I didn't feel it necessary to explain my plans for travel.

'And then you wish to...?'

I gave an ironic laugh. 'Mr Scott... I'm...' For a few seconds I was lost for words. 'I'm trying to make a new life.' There I'd said it. 'A new career, a new home, a new everything.'

He leant forward. 'Yes I see.' Squinting at me, he looked as if he did see. He exhaled heavily and if it was possible, sat even more upright. 'Mr Carmody spoke highly of you.'

I slowly nodded, smiling, grateful for the compliment. He scratched at his temple. Patiently, I waited.

He opened a folder and studied it for a few minutes. Murmuring to himself, he then glanced back at me. 'So, if you were to purchase the property, what do you think a fair price would be?'

I put a hand up. 'Mr Scott, I don't think you understand! As much as I *love* the property, I am not in a position to be able to buy a property of that calibre. I wish I was, but I'm not.'

'Right... hmmm,' he said slowly, and then pushed a piece of paper towards me. 'What do you think about this figure?'

I looked at the sum. 'What...?' I frowned. 'I'm sorry but I'm not following you? Are we talking about the same property?'

'Yes we are. Perhaps I should explain further.' He straightened his glasses on his nose. 'That price comes with a condition. You may not find it agreeable and you are within your rights to say so. For quite some time Mr Carmody knew he was not long for this world. As I have handled his affairs for many years, and as he had no family, he asked me if I would act as executor of his affairs.'

'No family at all?'

'No. His ex-wife was an American lass and that is where she now resides. Mr Carmody was an only child and he had no children. His loves were his dog and his garden.' He looked at me.

I nodded. 'Yes, I met Wilbur the labrador. I told Mr Carmody, I would gladly take Wilbur for him, but unfortunately our home at the time was unsuitable. I believe he went to an old friend of Mr Carmody's. I know how traumatised he was by it. It was terribly sad.'

'That is correct, but it was never meant to be long term.' He cleared his throat. 'Now, Mr Carmody was most grateful that you kindly made that offer. He was moved by your generosity.' He exhaled. 'Which leads me to this next point. Mr Carmody left strict instructions that if you were to purchase the house, at what we shall call a special price, then he has one wish.'

Baffled, I looked at him closely.

'The dog comes with the house.'

I gave a small laugh. 'Mr Scott, as soon as I get myself settled I will gladly take Wilbur. It would be a pleasure.'

Mr Scott leant back in his chair. 'I see Mr Carmody was right about you. He said you were a generous person. The thing is he wants you to have the house. But he also wants to assist a struggling business. Perhaps you have heard of it. It's called Silverback Acres.'

I shook my head.

'It's a sanctuary in Tasmania for old dogs whose owners have had to go into care. The people that run it are a retired couple and are self-funded. Mr Carmody has bequeathed the money from the sale of the house to Silverback Acres. Although he was impressed with the sanctuary, he thought Tasmania would be too cold for Wilbur.'

'I'm still not quite following. If Mr Carmody wanted to assist Silverback Acres then surely he would want top dollar for his property. The price you've mentioned is about a fifth of what that property is worth.'

'Yes, but you've missed one important thing.' He paused briefly. 'He wants the dog to spend his old age on his property.'

'Oh I see.' I leant back in my chair. Mr Scott sat quietly. I looked at my hands while I thought, and then I looked up. 'I would have gladly taken Wilbur for him you know.'

'I do know Mrs Riding.' And he pushed the papers towards me. I looked at them, but did nothing. Mr Scott sensing my hesitation raised his eyebrows in question.

'Mr Scott, I have been in the real estate industry for many years. I know paying this small amount of money for that property does not seem right.'

'I wouldn't call one million dollars a small amount of money.'

'I think you know what I mean.'

He nodded. 'Mr Carmody said you were honourable. I have a question. Can you afford this sum, because I can work something out for you?'

I blinked rapidly and held my hands out. 'That's not it. I can afford it. It's just that...'

'Let me help you here Mrs Riding. Mr Carmody wishes to bequeath one million dollars to Silverback Acres. He wishes Wilbur to live out his life on the property he loved. He thinks highly of you.' He paused watching my face. 'I know this is a lot to take in. Why don't you give yourself a few days to think it over and get back to me?'

Chapter 6

With her arms folded, head on an angle, Bea stood back and surveyed her latest canvas. 'So tell me how you feel?' she asked, her attention still on the artwork.

'Mother,' I said with mock seriousness, my eyes averted, investigating a small table filled with a mecca of paints, sketch pads, picture frames and paper weights. 'That's so unlike you. *Tell me how you feel.* You've either been taking a course in psychology, or watching far too much midday television.' I gave her a look.

In turn, she flashed me the briefest of glances over her shoulder. Narrowing her eyes, she indicated the canvas, her bangles jangling. 'More vermillion up here don't you think.' She turned back to me.

I had used sarcasm to hide my wild ride of emotions. I picked up a tube of midnight blue paint, closely examining it. Bea leant across and removed it from my fingers. Arms folded, she looked at me for an answer.

I shrugged. 'I feel numb one moment, and the next I'm overcome with emotions I didn't know I had. By Davis's email earlier it looks like the settlement is all but done. I have to sign a couple of documents and that's it.' I cut my hands through the air. 'We're over.' And there was that odd feeling again, one of nothingness. We might as well have been discussing a stranger.

Typical of Bea, she swiped her hands together as if dusting them off. 'Well, that's that then.' I was unsure if she meant my marriage or the painting. She leant against the bench. 'Actually, when I asked how you felt, I was referring to the house you've been talking about. I think I have an idea how you feel about the other. What's your gut feeling here? Is this a house you *really* want?' She wiped her vermillion stained hands on an old hand towel.

'Yes I do. I think... no... I know it's a life I want. I've surprised even myself. From the moment I walked through that gate, I felt an immediate connection to it. I really can't tell you what happened... I walked in there and said *this is it.*'

There was no denying the feeling of peace, like a floaty gossamer cloak that had settled over me. I looked at my mother. 'Bea it's hard to explain. It was as if I belonged. Everything that had happened in my life, had led me to that point.'

She sighed. 'I understand, that can happen in life, with people and places.' She smiled wistfully and I knew her thoughts were of Papa. And then her blue eyes continued to regard me. 'Peach you always had that *pleaser* gene that I was worried about. You did things because you thought you should, rather than follow your heart. You've done it all your life and I saw you do it time and time again with Davis. However, this time it seems as if you are following your heart.'

I shrugged and gave a small smile, feeling she was right. 'Not to mention the phenomenal price. I can't get my head around it.'

'You must do whatever makes your heart sing,' she said, flopping onto a cushion strewed, cream calico day bed, next to the loudly snoring Josephine, Bea's latest in a long succession of pugs. Poor Josephine still snored loudly, even though she'd had an operation on her nasal passages, such is the problem with flat faced dogs.

For a person that used vibrant colour every day in her paintings, Bea's colour palette for her home was whites and creams, even down here in her studio. She said it allowed her a tranquil blank canvas with which to showcase her spectacular artwork.

I put both of my hands up. 'Hang on, it's not that easy.' I perched myself on a stool opposite her and folded my arms across my chest.

Reclining, Bea raised her eyebrows in question, and shrugged her shoulders. She was never one to think too hard about anything. She went with how she felt, although there was no doubt in my mind my mother was a very strong woman.

I explained further. 'It might be a phenomenal purchase price, but I do have to consider the extensive renovations, then furnishing it, plus bringing that huge garden back to its former glory. I am going to need decent money to do it justice. That's really my problem here. I would prefer to keep some of my interests invested to keep them working for me.' I shrugged.

We both sat quiet, contemplative, and then I continued. 'But Bea you should see it.' And my voice warmed to the idea once again. 'There's something so wonderful about it. The garden reminds me of Enid Blyton's *Magic Far Away Tree*. It has dreamlike qualities like an enchanted forest. I did know Mr Carmody was a landscape architect, although I can't remember giving it much thought. He has left a wonderful legacy behind. That place is crying out to be filled with people. I've been giving thought to a few ideas, but the one that keeps coming to mind is a luxurious inner city B&B.'

I began to visualise, describing it to Bea as I went. 'Imagine coming up that drive, and seeing the house for the first time; a mix of contemporary and antique furniture, and fabulous, luxurious comfort; peace and quiet guaranteed, but only minutes from the cafe precinct and city centre,' my voice began to race, 'stunning gardens with beautifully maintained flowerbeds; a kitchen garden; breakfast on the terrace with views of the river; and relaxation by the pool.' And then I came back to reality. 'However, I'll have to do my figures. It might be one big dream. As I said earlier, this is going to cost serious money.' Thoughtfully, I tapped my fingertips on my top lip.

Reclining in resplendent comfort, Bea draped an arm over the back of the chair. 'Do you know anything at all about running a B&B darling?'

'Nope, but I intend to learn. After all, I do know about running a business, and at the end of the day, it's another business. Plus Mum...' there was that *Mum* word I used whenever I was stressed or needed comfort. I roamed over to the French doors and looked out to the back garden. 'Plus I have to work out what to do with my life.' Neither of us said anything for a few moments, and then with my eyes still on the garden, I continued. 'I really thought I would have been a mum by now.'

Shrugging, I turned and looked at Bea. She looked thoughtful. I watched her face. Rising from the chaise, she beckoned. 'Come with me.'

Taking a green tasselled key from the drawer of a small French dresser, she unlocked the large storeroom next to her studio. Pushing the door open, her hand reached for the light switch as she gestured me in front of her.

'*What...?*' I was taken aback, my eyes blinking in disbelief. And then with mouth agape, I stared. It was an Aladdin's Cave crammed full of French antiques. My eyes lit up as they scanned the tightly packed room, making out a Louis XV style console, half a dozen ornate mirrors, two commodes, a sideboard, a pair of wing back chairs, and what appeared to be a Napoleonic chandelier.

With a flourish of her hand, Bea gestured. 'Some things of your father's he thought you may want some day. Each of these treasured pieces he selected for you on my last trip to France.' Her hand smoothed over the worn patina of an armoire, her face now alive with memories. 'When I came home after… after that sad time…' I knew she was referring to my father's death, '… I mentioned that there were some antique pieces of his being shipped, for whenever you wanted them. And then when you moved into the warehouse I asked again. Remember?'

I did remember Bea asking, and I distinctly remembered Davis taking me aside, firmly stating that we didn't want anything *old*, only new shiny modern stuff for us.

I glanced around once more. I had thought this room was full of art supplies and old canvases. My eyes settled on a console where atop it sat a pair of gilded candle holders, highly decorated and forming branches of flowers, next to them a clock in marble, gold and bronze.

'Oh,' I gasped. 'Look at this gilding.' My hand smoothed over the gold work on the clock.

'I believe that's called ormolu,' Bea explained.

'Oh,' I repeated, too overwhelmed to talk.

Bea began to move the console forward and I obligingly helped. Wedged in behind were a pair of cast iron urns covered in an off white coating, showing a few rusty marks of the time. However, behind them was the piece I loved the most. A roll-top desk. Lovingly, I ran my hands over it. 'Oh Mum, look.'

'If I remember correctly that piece is circa 1780 Paris. It still has its original marble top.'

'Mmmm,' I answered, busy rolling up the top to reveal a large writing pad and eight smaller drawers inside. 'Oh my goodness.'

'Will this help?' Bea asked.

I looked around the room. 'What, for Mr Carmody's

house? Mum it would be magnificent... perfect... what can I say?'

'Well I daresay your papa would be very pleased.' And Bea's face showed it. 'Finally he has done something right.'

*

We adjourned upstairs to the living room, where I nestled into the corner of one of the cream damask sofas. Placing my feet upon a plump cushion, I enjoyed the fading sunlight sparkling through a giant crepe myrtle tree outside the front door. Every March, Bea would fill our home at Kangaroo Point with huge vases of the heliotrope coloured crepe myrtle blooms cut from the trees in our garden there.

I glanced around Bea's living room. Filled with romantic talismans - painted crosses, wooden hearts, keys strung on the end of rosary beads, the words *armour* embroidered on one of the cushions – it was the perfect Bea room.

The quiet was punctuated by the squeals of children playing in neighbouring yards. I liked the sound of it. Across from me, Bea, her eyes alive with excitement, spoke more of Papa than she had in my entire life. Or maybe it was just that I was ready to hear.

'Your papa had a law degree when he first started out working with the best auctioneers in Lille and Paris. At 24, he became the youngest dealer in Chinoiserie for the European Biennale. His first shop was in Chartres and was opened solely on weekends catering to the Parisians who would make sabbaticals to their stately country homes. Weekdays, he spent passionately scouring antique markets and sourcing irreplaceable pieces from some of France's most expensive private homes.' She smiled. 'He was passionate, intelligent and hardworking. You're much like him Peach. Perhaps you have more of him, than me.'

I smiled at her. 'But what of the chateau?'

'Yes, the chateau and your grandmother, Helene, the doyenne of the family.' Her voice still held an edge of dislike, even after all of this time. 'When your grandfather passed away, your papa's older brother Philippe inherited the chateau.'

I narrowed my eyes in disbelief. 'I didn't know there was an older brother.'

'Yes, but when your papa was in his late thirties, Philippe, along with his wife and young son, were killed in a car accident. Of course, as was the done thing, your papa went home to run the family chateau, although he never gave up his involvement and love of antiques.'

'Did he want to return to the chateau?'

'Hmmm… I'm not sure that he had a choice, however from what I understand it was not entirely bad, as he had been coming and going for many years and seeing someone in the next town. Plus I believe his mother thought it was time he settled down.'

I narrowed my eyes. 'Helene didn't like you, did she?'

'No, not at all. It was awful for me at the time, but I understand now.'

'How so?'

'Well she was a widow, and then her oldest son, daughter-in-law and grandchild tragically die. The younger son, she thinks will settle down at the chateau with a woman she likes… instead I turn up. A young inexperienced, flighty foreigner. In hindsight, she was right about me.'

I raised my eyebrows in a questioning look.

'Well I didn't stay, did I? And I was as bored out in the country as I had been in Tasmania. At that age, I really wasn't interested in some old chateau. Of course I loved Alexandre.' She glanced down at her hands. 'Very, very much.'

'But what about Dad, you loved him as well, didn't you?'

'Yes, but differently. Of course I loved Johnny, in fact I still do, but more like a favourite sibling. It's not hard to love someone who is a genuinely good guy and loves you. He adored you girls and we had a good life. And let's face it, Johnny is a great character, quite a larrikin, everyone loves him. The difference was, I was in love with Alexandre. Always was and always will be. From the moment we met, we could not deny the powerful force between us. For many years, I regretted leaving France so quickly and not giving him a second chance. However as I got older, I realised that although he loved me, he was always going to be a charmer with the women.' She clucked her tongue. 'Typical of so many Frenchmen. They are so charismatic and so terribly seductive.' Bea played with her hair in a girlish way and pulled her legs up underneath herself. 'They get into your blood and you can think of nothing else. The thing about them is that they genuinely love beautiful women. Almost worship them, in fact.'

My tone was droll. 'I'm not sure that's an excuse. Don't all men?' I drummed my fingers on the arm of the chair.

'Yes and no. If you asked all men they would say they did, but men like your papa make it an art form. They let you know that they *appreciate* the beauty, they *cherish* it, and it makes them who they are. *Their* masculinity makes *you* all the more feminine. There is a magnetism about them. The way they speak of beautiful women, you feel it is an honour they have picked you. And you understand that they just can't help themselves but enjoy the beauty of others.'

My voice held a certain edge, my recent past rising up to haunt me. 'I'm not sure I understand. Surely it's not something you can forgive?'

'I tell you, with maturity, I would forgive Alexandre everything. And I did. He was, and is, the love of my life.'

I realised we were speaking of something else. 'I'm not sure I could ever forgive Davis,' I said quietly, absentmindedly playing with a silk tassel on a cream and gold brocade cushion.

Bea shrugged. 'Who knows? The thing is, sex is a much more powerful thing for a woman than a man. Men can be spasmodic. For a woman, it is deep and meaningful. Anyway, I think the way *you are* right now, if that's what Davis wanted, you would forgive him in a heartbeat.'

Giving my head a shake, I looked at her, screwing my nose up. 'Why do you say that?'

'Because it shows. But you know...' and she paused, her eyes narrowing, while she carefully chose her words. 'I know you loved Davis, but I'm not sure he is the love of your life. I think you are still to find him.'

I shrugged, unsure if she was right.

'I know you don't believe me right now, but I want to ask you something.' She paused briefly. 'Can you tell me he bought the best out in you?'

'He certainly did in the business. We made a fantastic team,' I said proudly, as much for myself as for her. I needed to remember that not everything had been bad, that there were times when we were phenomenal together.

'That's a little different. That's called being a good boss or a good business partner. But what about who *you* are Peach, the real *you*, your dreams and what you want out of life. Did he enhance those things for you? Have you lived the life you wanted?'

Touché, she and I both knew I had not. I sat back. 'Did Papa for you?' I asked boldly.

'Absolutely! When I was with him, my paintings were never better. He made me feel I could live the way I wanted, and be the best me. I didn't have to pretend to be something I wasn't. I was fulfilled. I was a better me. More me... if that makes sense.'

There was a part of me that understood what she was saying, but there was a huge part of me that wondered how she could have loved him so much, when he could never be faithful to her.

It appeared as if she read my mind. 'Relationships are very private things, Peach. People work out what works best for them. It may seem odd to others, but that's how it goes. I always knew I was the love of his life. He married no other. However, I had made choices, and had to stick with them. And mind you, I was never sorry for those choices.' She smiled and I knew she meant Lou and me. She continued. 'He respected that, and always looked after me very well. You too for that matter.'

I nodded. After all, he had paid my school fees for Brisbane's best private girls' school, then my university fees. When he passed away I received a nice sum of money. He had been extremely generous. Plus I always knew I could have gone to Provence whenever I wanted, although I just could not do that to Johnny. While I was quietly thinking, Bea stood up and went into her bedroom. Returning a few minutes later, she stood in the doorway. I caught the look on her face.

'What?' I asked.

'I know I haven't always been the parent you wanted Peach, but I do love you.'

'For God's sake Bea, not this again,' I said, a frustrated edge to my voice.

She let out a breath. 'When your papa died he left a large amount of money to me. I would never have had all of this.' She waved her hands around her home. 'He also left enough money to look after me for the rest of my life. He also left a fairly substantial amount of money to you.'

'Yes I know. The money you gave us on our wedding day. It irks the hell out of me now, as I realise that it's being used in the property settlement. Davis bloody-well doesn't deserve half of it.'

'Well, to be honest, there was more than the $200,000 I gave you back then.' She walked over to where I sat, handing me a piece of paper.

It was a bank statement. Mouth opened, I looked back up at Bea. She nodded. I looked back down and scanned the statement. The figure in the closing balance column was just over three million dollars. 'What's this?' I couldn't grasp it.

'It's what Papa left to you. We discussed it and he made me promise not to give it to you until the time was right. I really hesitated on your wedding day. On one hand I felt it was the right thing to do, but on the other I never felt right about Davis. Funny that! Anyway, I've had it in an interest bearing deposit account all this time. Next time it matures, which, as luck would have it, is in about 30 days, instead of rolling it over, I can cash it, and deposit it into your account.'

I closed my eyes, attempting to fathom what she was saying. 'Hang on a minute. Are you telling me, this money is mine? Just like that. *Oh by the way, here's a cool three mil. Meant to give it to you a while ago.*'

Bea plopped back down on the couch opposite. 'I am. You'll have to trust me with the timing. I know I haven't always gotten everything...' I leapt off my chair and ran to her, throwing my arms around her. 'You got this right Mum. I can't believe it.'

From the look on her face, I could see she was pleased.

'I can buy the Carmody property and do what I want with

it. This was all meant to be.' I began to laugh and jumped up, dancing around, flicking my silk skirt around my thighs. 'Oh my God,' I shrieked, 'imagine if you'd given it to me sooner and now I had to divide it up with Davis. Bea you *really* got this right... really, really right. I can bring Wilbur home.'

'Peach... one more thing...'

I halted my dancing and spun to look at her, wondering what else there could be.

'It's time for you to go to the chateau,' she said with an air of firmness.

'Of course, of course.' I would have promised her anything at that point. I had never visited the chateau, even though I had been close many years earlier. My plan, at the time, had been to enjoy my time with Steve in Paris, and then head to Provence on my own. But when Davis proposed, that idea flew out the window and I returned home with Steve into the arms of my fiancé.

'We'll both go directly after my exhibition. I know it would be timely to go now, while you're in limbo, but I need a few months. I want to show you your father's house. It's your history Peach.'

I nodded my head, shrugging at the same time, unused to Bea being so parental. 'Whatever!'

'And my advice to you,' Bea continued on with her unexpected words of wisdom. 'Is to get those settlement papers with Davis signed pretty quick smart. Then move on the Carmody property after that.'

'Good advice.' I leant down to kiss her proffered cheek. As I stood up, I straightened my skirt which had twisted to the side.

'Look at you Peach, your skirt is swimming on you.'

'I know, I know, I know!' I said still dancing around. 'Yep, try as hard as I might to lose a kilo or two for years and then my skanky assed husband goes off with a blonde tart, to put it politely, and guess what, I've lost four kilos. I should market it.' Bea shook her head at me while I continued with my tirade. 'You know, a few weeks before I found out about him and... Davis pinched the top of my thigh and said, *Ooh got some wobbly bits here. We really should watch that, shouldn't we.* Condescending bastard.' I threw myself in among the cushions on the lounge.

'He always was Peach. You just didn't see it.'

I brushed my hair out of my eyes. 'Or chose not to.' From my vantage point I could see straight out the front door and now noticed how late it had gotten. I looked at my watch. 'Marty is coming by to take me to dinner. Do you want to join us?'

Bea cocked her head to the side and raised her brows. 'Oh... I see... Marty?'

I waved a hand at her and shook my head. 'It's nothing like that.'

'Really?'

'Really Bea. He will always be just a friend.'

'Mmmm.'

Chapter 7

Slowly and languidly I drifted back to consciousness, deliciously stretching. It was so quiet here, last night I had slept the sleep of the dead. With my eyes still closed, I snuggled further into the warmth pressed against my back, enjoying the feel of another person. And then quickly one eye snapped open. From the mattress on the floor, I saw the early morning light creeping through the window. *Where was I?* Instantly the other eye opened. I blinked rapidly. Turning, I hurriedly pulled away from the sleeping body.

'*No you don't.* Up,' I commanded, pushing with my foot. 'No Wilbur, I'm sorry, but dogs do not sleep on beds, much less with their heads on the pillow. Come on... off.' I attempted to shoo the sleepy labrador off my mattress with some difficulty, as his body weight appeared to be not much less than mine. His dark brown eyes looked at me and for a minute I softened, stroking his blonde head. 'Yes, I know. You don't understand where your master is, do you?' He cocked his head to the side and looked at me, clearly attempting to decipher what I had said.

'Don't worry boy, I'm at a bit of a loose end too. This is all new to me, but we're family now.' I ruffled his fur.

With a deep snuffle, his heavy tail hit the floor once with a thud, as if that was as much joy as he could muster. However, I felt it was a promising sign. We had officially been friends for less than 24 hours.

*

Yesterday, with some measure of excitement, I had wiped my feet on the front door mat, weathered and worn with age, and turned the key in the stiff lock, ready to begin my new life in my new home. Breathing through my mouth, even the stale air did nothing to dampen my excitement. Dropping my bags in the hallway with haste, I walked towards the window with the heart hole curtain. Reefing it back, I was rewarded as sunlight cascaded into the once dark kitchen. Walking around, I had flung open every window, letting light and air flood through the home, as once again, I began exploring my new domain.

John Scott had allowed me free access for some time. On my second visit, I had found the staircase to the attic. There was a door to the left of the entry, which I had originally thought to be a cupboard. Upon opening it, a staircase, softly illuminated by an ethereal amber glow from a stained glass window above, was revealed.

Timidly, I had trod each step lightly, up towards a small landing with a door on either side. On the left, was a small dark grimy room lined with shelves. At first glance I was dismayed. I shoved aside the dark curtain. Mr Carmody had been damn keen on awful heavy old drapes. Natural light lit up the room. With some resistance, I opened the small attic window, and delighted in the breeze that instantly hit my face. At second glance, I could see that if I stripped the room bare, and painted it white, it really could be a lovely room, although somewhat small. For what purpose I was uncertain.

Next, I explored the room to the right. As I opened the door, magically I was greeted by a sizeable sunlit room filled with small lost planets of golden drifting dust motes. The side wall was dominated by a marble fireplace, much the same as the one in the formal area downstairs. Stroking the marble mantle, and feeling the thick caked dust I pulled my hand away. The room's ceiling sloped towards the front of the house where, to my pleasure, a huge window overlooked the entire front garden.

The room had to be at least nine metres wide. By the time I had taken in the view from the back windows, my mind began to tick over and excitement was building. Already I could see it once completed. This was indeed the icing on the cake.

Glancing around, I had taken in the remnants of old newspapers and cardboard boxes, and realised that in recent years Mr Carmody must have used it as a storeroom. However, for me, it would make the perfect bedroom.

There were times I still had to pinch myself that this house and garden were mine. Lost in thought, standing at the back window in the kitchen, entranced by the view, the sound of a car on the gravel came to me.

From the front door, I saw the battered old EH Holden utility pull to a stop. I guessed the driver to be Wilbur's recent carer, old Alex Smith. Sitting tall in the passenger seat, Wilbur had given a yelp and bounded from the car, running in circles, foraging around, sniffing.

Laughing with delight, I greeted Alex. 'Would you like to come in for a cup of tea? I have a kettle and some tea bags but not much else. The truck comes tomorrow with my things.'

It was a hot day, and Alex was wearing well-worn navy stubbies. He was a weathered man, his face heavily wrinkled and craggy, the skin on his knees falling down a bit. Briefly, he lifted an Akubra that had definitely seen better days. 'No thanks luv,' his gravelly voice said.

His response surprised me as Alex had been a carpenter back in his day, and not only worked on the house but had forged a lifelong friendship with Mr Carmody. When I had called him about Wilbur returning home, we had spent ages talking about how the house had been in former years. Perhaps he wanted to keep his memories as he remembered them from the past. After all, the house was rather sad at the moment.

Leaning against the utility, he licked his dry bottom lip as he stuck a Tally-ho paper to it. He pulled out a pouch of tobacco and began to roll a scrawny cigarette. Taking his time, he put the cigarette to his lips, holding it between his index finger and thumb. I noticed his scrutiny of the house. A long plume of smoke escaped his lips.

'A glass of water then perhaps?' I offered.

'Never have me water straight luv. I figure if it can rust iron, I don't want to see what it'll do to me insides.' He must have missed the look of surprise on my face as he continued. 'Got to get back up to Cooroy. Traffic'll be heavy this time of day.' He squinted at me through the haze of his cigarette smoke. 'As I said on the phone luv, we're ready to go to our little place at Donnybrook. Good spot for fishin'. Always saw meself finishin' off me days there. We were just holding out 'til we had Wilbur sorted. Wasn't really sure what we were going to do.'

Climbing back in the car, cigarette still in his mouth, he muttered through the open window, 'I'll miss the old mutt though, but he belongs here. Frank'd be happy.' He lifted his hat once more. 'You take care luv.'

I waved as Alex's car disappeared around the curve of the gravel driveway. At the sound of Wilbur's bark, I spun around in time to see the white cat I had seen on the very first day, bound across the yard, Wilbur hot on his heels, before the cat managed to scale the fence. Looking very happy with himself, Wilbur stood at the base of the fence and gave a few good natured woofs. I wondered if these two were old friends.

'Haha, you'll have your work cut out for you keeping Whitie out,' I called to the dog. 'I daresay he's had complete run of this place while you were gone.'

In a frenzy of excitement, Wilbur began to dash around

the garden. He went from one tree to another, from one place to another, madly sniffing, nearly turning himself inside out with excitement. I knew what he was doing. He was searching, searching for Frank Carmody. I wasn't sure if he remembered me, as we'd only met briefly a couple of times at the shops. I stood on the front veranda and watched as the dog bounded through the house, exploring every room. A few times he dashed into the laundry, but then ran straight back out again.

With pride, I took the new, shiny stainless steel water bowl into the laundry and filled it. Next time Wilbur came in, he made for the laundry once again. This time he drank furiously from the cool bowl, the registration tag on his collar hitting against the metal with a ting. Like a proud mother, I stood watching his every move as if the dog was a genius. We were forging our lives together and these were firsts for us.

And then, back out the front door he went. With my one folding director's chair pulled up at the window, I busied myself ringing the tradesmen I had lined up for the next few days. My wish was to retain the historic elements of the house, but put a contemporary spin on the place, like making over a glamorous old lady.

Not one moment had been wasted during settlement time. Once the documents were signed, I'd had a one month intensive shopping period sourcing antique doors to be used throughout the house, antique beams that would be installed in the main living area, and adding to my cache, six exquisite seventeenth century *torchiers* for lighting, and many more decorative objects.

Next, on the advice of John Scott, I engaged a draftsman who was well versed in the council requirements for a house of this genre, to draw up plans for the renovations. He put me in contact with a certifier who would do on-site approvals.

My first move was to change the proportions of the internal spaces, knocking out the walls of the smaller rooms, upsizing doorways and removing doors altogether in some areas to create open thresholds. The house pivoted around the great main room with a lovely high ceiling. Pushing the room out into a former chamfered bay window, extending the glass to the floor and adding a deck, would enable me to capture the view to connect the spectacular garden and river below.

Not surprisingly, the kitchen was, and would be the heart of the home.

John Scott, who I had originally thought formidable, had been quite different once the contract had been signed. His help and wealth of information regarding the property was invaluable, his interest and friendly, although always formal manner, endearing. He had gone to great lengths to supply me with a list of people who Mr Carmody had formerly relied upon.

Brownie who had maintained the garden a few years prior was starting in two days' time, although I was certain one man would not be enough. On the phone he had explained that he would happily come out of retirement for Mr Carmody's garden. I had the feeling he was more of a maintenance man, even though I envisioned the garden needed a complete makeover first.

A bevy of tradespeople were about to descend upon the property, turning the old house into a luxurious B&B. Anyway, that was my plan. In the last few months, I had researched B&Bs and knew exactly how I wanted Carmody House to be.

For me hospitality was about being generous - the magnificent surroundings, the food I would present, and the time and effort that would go into planning day trips. I wanted my guests to experience all the best things that New Farm had to offer – the cafes, the little local gourmet shops, the river walks, transport via the City Cat ferries, the spectacular New Farm Park, the local markets and more.

Running a cooking school, where I took my guests to the markets before returning to a magnificent kitchen to cook up a storm, intrigued me, and was an idea that had taken up residence in my mind, refusing to budge. I had always cooked from the heart and with passion, right back to those first cupcake days. It delighted me no end, to imagine creating special dining experiences: enormous breakfasts, gourmet hampers, summertime garden lunches. However, I may have been jumping ahead of myself. I needed to open the B&B first. Papa's money had given me the luxury of time. I could do things properly and take one step at a time, and I also had my trip to France with Bea in a few months, so it was imperative I be well organised.

With much thought, I had decided to co-ordinate the renovation work myself. I knew it would be a challenging project, however I was up for it. My settlement with Davis had been finalised a few months ago. He had tried to talk to me once or twice since but I hadn't taken his calls. What was there to say?

*

I finished my phone conversation with John Scott and checked my watch. Where was that dog? He seemed to have been gone for a long time. With my arms folded, I tapped an index finger on my top lip, a habit that used to annoy the hell out of Davis. *Big deal* was the thought that crossed my mind now.

I shook my head. Good God, I had just gotten the dog, I could hardly lose him. What would Mr Carmody think of me? My feet crunched over the gravel driveway as I went to check the front gate was locked. Not for the first time, I realised that heels were going to be a problem. As second nature as they were to me, they certainly weren't compatible with gravel paths.

Sometime later, after combing most of the garden, I spotted Wilbur right at the bottom of the garden, under the haunting horizontal limbs of a Chinese Weeping Elm. He was sitting beside an aged teak garden bench facing the river.

I called to him, and although he turned his head to me, he then looked back towards the river. I called to him a few more times, however he refused to budge.

Making my way down, I was determined to buy proper garden shoes the first chance I had. Wilbur gave me the courtesy of a brief look as I approached. I had never seen a dog's eyes look sadder. Spreading out the skirt of my colourful jersey Charlie Brown dress, I sat on the bench. It was a very peaceful place.

'Is this where the two of you used to sit?' I asked, stroking his head. 'Hmmm?' I spoke, as if expecting him to answer. In that twilight hour, I talked to him, attempting to reassure him with my voice. I felt terribly sorry for the poor dog, after all how could he know what was going on.

At one point, in the distance, I saw the white cat stalking around the garden. 'Look Wilbur,' I whispered. 'Whitie's back.' However the dog took not one ounce of notice.

As dusk loomed, the heat of the day still clung in the air. I could hear birds gathering for the night and the gentle sound of the lapping of the river. The male cicada buzzed their song, their mating call. While the bustle of the cosmopolitan New Farm shops were less than a kilometre away, this little pocket of land felt secluded, and a bit like my own little secret. My throat ached with the beauty of it all, and I knew this was my home.

It was nearly dark and I began busily slapping, first this way and then that, at a few pesky mosquitoes. However, I still could not entice the poor dog to budge. He appeared to be on a vigil. Attempting to bribe him, I promised a bone if he came up with me. All I received in return was a blank look.

'Now you're being silly,' I told him. 'We can't sit here all night. You should come up with me.' I turned to go, hopeful he would follow. No such luck. With some hesitation to leave him, I explained, 'Five minutes, okay? I'll give you five minutes more and them you have to come up.'

In the blue spangled dusk, I made my way across the wide expansive grassy area, around the pool, and up the terraces, following the path around the side of the house, delighting that at this hour all of the white roses magically gleamed.

It was dark by the time I reached the front door and I had to fumble to find light switches inside. I left the door ajar, hopeful the dog would follow. I was concerned about my dog raising skills, not something I had given thought to before.

It was so quiet here. No sound of traffic from outside the front door, no buses belching toxic clouds as I was well used to, just the sound of peace. Although I could still smell dust and old, when I glanced around I found myself unexpectedly filled with a buoyant sensation that took me a moment to recognise as excitement.

The house had an old soul from its history and had that indescribable quietness which bought me a wonderful sense of peace. I felt as though I was custodian of the property, and would add layers of memory to the place. I knew it would be a privilege to live here.

The sadness, hurt and betrayal I had felt, and the huge sense of loss, had not suddenly evaporated, although I had begun to notice a certain equilibrium returning. For the first time in many years, I was going to be on my own and what's more, strangely enough, I was looking forward to it.

Briefly, I paused at the back window in time to catch a perfectly positioned big yellow moon above the Story Bridge. Striking a match to a Jo Malone vintage gardenia candle, the air was filled with femininity, just how I wished my home to be from now on. Roaming from room to room, I was enthralled with my purchase. There were so many elements of the house, however it wasn't just about looks, it was the way it made me feel. From the kitchen window, I noticed with delight how the city lights twinkled behind the massive gum trees.

It was some time later before Wilbur returned.

'Well hello.' I jumped to attention and followed him into the laundry, where he devoured the dinner that I had so recently placed in his bowl. With a look that gave nothing away, he collapsed on the timber hallway floor, one brown eye opened, watching as I poured over the new plans for remodelling the house.

Every now and then I paused and chatted to him, attempting to make him feel welcome. 'I think you're going to like this place when it's finished. It's going to be a new start for us Wilbur. In fact, I think I'll even have a picture of you on the website. After all, this is your home.' He closed both eyes.

Goodness, even the dog found me boring. What was happening to me? If I wasn't invisible, I was boring.

'Give me a chance?' I asked, patting his head, as I readied myself for bed. I was rewarded with one half opened eye. It closed just as quickly. I left the bedroom door open and hopped under the covers on my mattress on the floor. I said a silent thankyou to Johnny for dropping the mattress of the day before.

In a fatherly fashion, he had walked through the house, checking the doors, making sure they were sturdy and lockable, attempting to be handy. He was too well dressed to ever be handy, but I loved him for it all the same. When he left he kissed the end of my nose.

'Abso-bloody-lutely phenomenal Peach. I'm pleased for you sweetheart.'

I blinked rapidly. Tears still never far away, even these days.

Johnny hugged me and kissed the top of my head, murmuring, 'Ahhh Peachy. Your dad loves you. You know that, right?' He always told me he loved me and I loved that about him. And then, as if I was still a teenager, he attempted to press fifty dollars into my hand. 'Buy yourself something nice,' he said, as he usually did.

'Dad no, I'm fine,' I insisted pushing it back.

It would probably be some time before Bea ventured over, even though it was in her neck of the woods. 'I'll leave you to it,' she had said, as I kissed her cheek, when leaving earlier. I was uncertain if she meant to the unpacking, or life on my own.

Years ago, I had overheard her speaking to someone regarding Lou's rebelliousness at school. 'I don't like to intrude on the school. It's not my style,' she had said. 'I'll leave her behaviour to them.' I remembered thinking that Lou was such a handful, I bet the school wanted to leave her behaviour to Bea. She had also said the same thing, whenever I asked why she didn't ever do canteen duty or volunteer at the school. 'Not my style *darling*,' she'd say. 'I'll leave it to them.'

Who? I'd wanted to ask. Teachers? Other parents?

Looking back, it was as if she was half in, half out of our lives. I think we accepted it, knowing she was different. She once told me, some women are mothers and some are lovers. 'I am a lover,' she had explained. I wondered how I was supposed to take that comment in a positive light, seeing I was only 12 at the time.

However, for all of those things that I could either choose to see as shortcomings, or just as Bea being Bea, she had certainly come through when she withheld Papa's money until the timing was perfect. She had given my best interest thought, and acted wisely. It was very motherly of her, and I liked that.

*

Cup of coffee in hand, I padded over to the window in my Peter Alexander pink ruffled short nightie and fluffy slippers with the kitten heel, and watched as the early morning light brought the garden to life. My garden, I reminded myself with pleasure.

It was nice to wake up to the sound of birds. For many years, my norm had been listening to Davis in the bathroom, giving himself a pep talk for the day, telling himself how good he was, how many sales he would achieve that day, and how he was the *Top Gun*. All the while he looked at himself in the mirror admiringly, examining himself first this way and then that. He'd flex his muscles, and when he was satisfied that all was good, he'd slap his hand on his abs in a sign of approval.

Thinking about it now, I almost gagged, wondering why it had taken so long to irritate the hell out of me.

I glanced over at Wilbur. I must admit it was nice to wake up beside such a quiet sleeping companion.

'Come on boy. Let's go for a walk around the garden before the truck comes. We've got a big day ahead and then the boys are bringing dinner for us. You'll like them and I think they just might like you.' I patted his blonde head and I was sure those black lips smiled, if only briefly.

*

'More champagne babe?' Steve asked, filling my glass without waiting for an answer.

From behind me, Thomas began kneading my exhausted

neck muscles with those wonderfully powerful hands of his. I rolled my neck. '*Mmmm,*' I moaned. 'Don't stop.'

'*Darling* please tell me this is not going to be the new you? Your hair is ghastly. Let me organise a blow-dry for you tomorrow with Carmen. You know you love her big Texan blow dries. Treat yourself, *please*,' Thomas begged.

I laughed and swept my long dark curls up into a ponytail. 'Thomas I've spent all day with the movers and tradespeople. I promise you this is not the new me.' Swinging myself around, I placed my legs over the side of the armchair.

'Well what time is Marty coming? You mustn't let yourself slip,' Thomas admonished, taking a sip of champagne.

'Just leave her be, Thom,' Steve chided over his shoulder, as he continued to investigate the house further. 'I love this *armoire*,' his voice came from the next room, his boots loud on the naked wooden floorboards. 'I'm taking a walk outside before it gets dark. Wilbur's coming with me.' I heard the sound of the heavy front door close.

With folded arms, Thomas turned to me and demanded, '*Well*, what time?'

'He'll be here shortly. He's picking up dinner from Sitar for us. And Thomas I need to remind you…' I enunciated clearly, 'he is just a friend.'

Thomas waved a hand at me. '*Darling*, both Steve and I love Marty. Steve just won't admit it yet. He's in a tough spot. He's struggling to be loyal to Davis on any level. He may be his brother, but God knows, he's behaving like a horse's arse.'

I laughed at his honesty. 'That's putting it mildly.'

'Truly he is. But what can you do? He's been led around by his dick… Sorry darling, that didn't help did it?'

I hardly needed reminding. I shook my head, my heart sinking rapidly. 'Thom, I don't think it's just that. I think it's his ambition as well. But he's gone too far. I've been thinking about it, and I know this all began when I wanted to step back from the business, when I stopped making it my first priority and decided that I wanted to spend more time at home and have a baby. God, we know how driven Davis is. To be honest I think he and... I'd rather not say her name... are cut from the same cloth. They suit each other perfectly. They're both completely ruthless and they deserve one another. I'm sorry to say it has taken distance for me to see him clearly, and now I wonder how I could not have seen it before.'

'Oh *darling...*' he said, patting my knee. 'I feel just dreadful for you.'

'Yes I know, but it's even more than that.' Standing, I walked over to the window and then I spun around. 'If he wasn't happy, I wish he could have told me, been honest. It's the lying that I hate the most. I think he got to a stage where it just rolled off his tongue, and he no longer knew what the truth was, and what was a lie.'

Thomas shook his head with disgust. 'Tell me you've at least heard from *the dragon?*' and he drew inverted commas in the air.

I smiled at his terminology for my ex mother-in-law, Eileen. 'Not a word.' I shrugged. 'I know you've had a few run-ins, but I've always gotten on fairly well with her.' Now that I was reminded, I was rather miffed. 'You'd think I was the one who'd run off with someone else, not the other way around.'

Thomas flapped his hands around. 'She's hopeless darling. I think she'd like to call, but some people just don't know what to do at times like these. You and I made such great outlaws together, now...' He threw himself back on the couch with typical Thomas theatrical style.

I attempted to change the subject. 'I'm ravenous. Hope

Marty's not too much longer.' I caught Thomas's look. 'Thomas, *stop it*. You're hopeless. He is truly a good friend and he's been invaluable over the past few months. It's been great having someone to share my ideas with. But that's all.'

'Well my dear, all I'm going to say is, I believe it's about bloody time you made up a shopping list of exactly what you want in a man, because it may just bloody-well be under your nose. Now where the heck is that champagne bottle? A man is not a camel.'

*

The house was in far too much disarray to have dined inside, and as it had been a spectacular early evening, I had suggested we spread our Indian feast upon the front steps and gaze at the garden. I had even found the brand new white damask tablecloth, crystal champagne flutes and candlesticks, all of which, among other things, I had purchased last month for my new home. As I had set up the formal picnic, I had seen all three males give each other the "she's crazy" eye, however it did not deter.

After dinner, Steve, the gadget guru, attempted to set up a small TV in the kitchen. One by one, the other two males had drifted from the front steps to assist. Even Wilbur appeared to have offered his help as one minute he had been beside me and the next he was in the kitchen.

Finally, realising I had been deserted, and with the sound of good natured jesting coming from inside, I joined them in the kitchen and began to rummage around to find four new mugs for instant coffee. I was hanging out for the new coffee machine to arrive.

'Truly Steve, don't worry too much. I have never really been a TV person,' I told him over my shoulder, as I searched a large box labelled "new kitchen things" for the sugar bowl.

'I'm almost there,' he told me, fixated on his task, while the three of us watched on.

Finally, Thomas had had enough. 'Take me home gorgeous or loose me forever.' He draped himself over Steve's back.

With the remote control pointed at the TV and not taking one bit of notice of Thomas's dramatic behaviour, Steve muttered, 'One more sec. I'm almost done.'

'I'm simply *exhausted*,' Thomas exaggerated, while Marty and I shared a fleeting smile. Pouting with impatience, Thomas roamed off, only to be heard seconds later shrieking. 'Oh my God. Nooooooo! Peach!'

I quickly followed Marty and Steve towards Thomas's cries. In unison, both men came to a direct halt at the front door and began laughing.

'What?' I demanded, pushing past them, unable to see what they were laughing at. And then, I too stopped in my tracks.

There stood Wilbur, frozen to the spot, guilt written right across his face, in amongst the Indian picnic, the remnants of dahl around his mouth, the tandoori lamb container now licked scrupulously clean, a new crystal wine glass on its side. All that remained of our dinner was a few pieces of well licked, but obviously not liked, onion in the bowl that had held the leftover fish boona, a dish full of spices, garlic, and ginger, slathered in a thick onion sauce.

I groaned. 'Will it make him sick?' I looked between the three men for an answer.

Through his laughing, Steve shrugged. 'I'm not sure, but I sure as heck would not want to be around him tomorrow. For that matter, Thomas we're out of here now.' And then all three men began to laugh once again and Wilbur took it as his cue to bound down the steps and off into the darkness.

I must have looked worried, because Marty attempted to reassure me. 'He's probably gone to eat some grass…'

'What on earth for?' I interrupted.

'It will help him to throw up.'

'Oh no…' I put a hand to my chest. 'I should have cleaned it up immediately. I didn't even think of him. '

'Come on, I'll help you clean up and then we'll check on him.' Marty began to carry dishes inside.

'You guys go,' I shooed Steve and Thomas.

Steve kissed the side of my cheek, taking both of my hands. 'Peachy... take care lovey, we'll speak soon. Let me know when you want to start the PR for this joint. I think you're onto a winner. Got to get this tired boy home or he'll miss his beauty sleep.'

Thomas bent to kiss me. 'Get your sexy arse in to the salon soon. I'm going to have to keep an eye on you now that you're living off the land.'

I gave him a flat measured look. 'Thom I'm two kilometres from the city centre. I'm hardly going to turn into Granny Clampett.'

He began to laugh. 'Perhaps not Granny, but Elly May more than likely.' And then he lent in closer and whispered. 'We're doing up that list Miss.' He looked down the hallway towards the kitchen and then gave me a wink. I slapped him on the shoulder.

I could hear the two of them laughing as they headed down the driveway. Bending to pick up the new white damask tablecloth, I frowned at the red curry footprints courtesy of Wilbur. And then I glanced around into the darkness and wondered where the poor dog had taken himself off to. I guessed it was time I became friendly with the local vet.

Chapter 8

Thomas took the tail-comb from Carmen. 'I'll finish Peach off thanks babe.' He swept the hair on the crown of my head forward and held up a section. '*So*,' he said peering over my shoulder, 'what's happening with that list?'

Waving the blank piece of paper, I eyed him in the mirror. '*Nothing!* I'm not ready for a list.'

'Oh yes you are sweetie. Now be a good girl and write. Another coffee will help you out.' Waving his hand at one of the young assistants, he indicated my empty cup. Vigorously, he began back combing a section of my hair, briefly glancing at me in the mirror. 'My one-thirty has just cancelled, so I've got all the time in the world and you're not leaving until that list is done.'

'Thomas please don't, I'm not in the mood.' I was having a flat day. It happened like that sometimes. Emerald Green had said it was normal. Two steps forward, one back.

'Think about it like this.' He paused. 'It's a shopping list.' He waved a hand at my indignant face. 'Don't look at me like that. If you needed an evening gown, you'd hardly come home with a pair denim shorts, now would you? I mean the shorts might be a bit cheeky and fun for a while, but they're not suitable for a formal occasion. Same thing! I mean how are you going to know, if you don't plan for it?'

I grimaced. He pulled my hair.

'*Ow*,' I yelled, grabbing at my locks.

'Down girl, you're scaring my clients.'

I flashed my eyes in frustration at him.

Thomas took no notice. 'Let's start with tall, dark and handsome. Although, I can see you with a blonde.'

I couldn't keep the acerbic tone out of my voice. 'Well gee, I've already had tall, blonde and handsome and look where that got me.'

'Pfft.' He pretended to think. 'Perhaps it's someone we already know?' Cocking his head, he not so subtly eyed me in the mirror.

I ignored him.

That didn't deter him. 'Successful, hardworking, manly, nice... I mean it could be someone right under your nose... let's say... I don't know... Marty perhaps?'

'No, it definitely could not be Marty.' I spun around in the chair. 'Look Thomas, he is a friend. Let me spell it out to you f-r-i-e-n-d. Get it, friend. What's wrong with you? Simply because he is single and I am single is not enough. Let it go.'

Unfazed, Thomas spun the chair around so I was facing the mirror once again. 'It's just that back in the early days we always wondered which one you'd choose.' He smoothed the crown of my head.

'It was never a choice between the two of them. I honestly was in love with Davis.' Frustrated beyond belief, I wondered why we were even having this conversation.

'*Mmmm*,' he said, pursing his lips in distaste. 'Come on... tell Uncle Thomas what you want then.'

I exhaled heavily, suddenly exhausted by this ridiculous conversation. Attempting to simplify it, I said, 'I want someone who likes dogs. No... not *likes* dogs, *loves* them. Is that alright with you?'

'Mmmm. Good start. And?'

I rolled my eyes. 'And... and must have integrity,' I said, my exasperation with him building.

'Good, write that down.'

'Right,' I huffed and scribbled across the paper. Eyebrows

raised, I glanced at him in the mirror. *'Happy?'*

'Yes, keep writing. You have to be clear about it. Make sure you put male. The last bloody thing you want is finding a female with all the qualities you're looking for. We've got enough homos in the family already honey.' He didn't miss the look on my face. 'Okay, okay, give me more information.'

I shook my head. 'God, I don't know... someone who is secure enough in their own skin, not to constantly have to ring their own bell. Humble... that's the word!' I was completely frustrated now, and not only with Thomas. 'And someone who wants to have a family and thinks that it is a priority.' I wrote *family man*. 'And truly, there was nothing wrong with him being such a hard worker... I have a bit of that in me as well... but for God's sake there has to be a balance.' Hastily I scribbled the word *balance*.

'And,' I raised my voice slightly, 'not so *bloody* selfish.' I spat out selfish with utter distaste. In large letters, I scrawled *selfless*. 'And someone who can be the man in the relationship.' My voice rose. 'I mean, stuff this equality shit, I want to be the woman. Is that too much to ask?' My hand slapped at the glass bench in front of me. 'If I need time off to fall pregnant or give birth, I don't want to feel like I'm letting the team down. I'm meant to be a kick arse boss, loving wife, gourmet chef, look phenomenal all the time, fall pregnant in my non-existent spare time, obviously all by myself, exercise my pelvic floor muscles and run a home.'

I sat fuming for a few moments. Thomas was silent. I glanced around noting the rather busy salon had also fallen quiet, and a few heads had turned my way.

Thomas shrugged. 'Phew *babe*, you needed to get that one off your chest.' A cloud of hairspray assailed me.

'Mmmm,' I murmured, feeling a little sheepish, retying

the red polka dot scarf at my neck.

Thomas took the piece of paper that I'd scribbled on. 'It's a start.' He folded it and handed it back to me. 'Keep this in your wallet and add to it from time to time. After all, you know what you don't want.' Removing the cape, he gave my shoulders an affectionate squeeze. 'You're terribly tight.'

'I've had a headache for days.' I checked the mirror for the tell-tale dark circles under my eyes. Only yesterday, I had felt as if my head was going to blow off my shoulders. Today, it was fractionally better, although only just.

Thomas gave me a look of concern and began kneading my taut neck muscles. 'Have you booked an appointment with Chang?'

Moaning with relief at his touch, I shrugged. 'No, I know I should.'

'He's the best acupuncturist around, you know that.' And then he couldn't help himself. 'And he's bloody hot.' Leaning over my shoulder he lowered his voice. 'I can't believe he's not gay.'

I cocked an eyebrow at him in the mirror. 'You're terrible Thom. In case you've forgotten, you have a partner.'

'I know, I know. But can't a man dream. Have you seen that smooth olive skin? It's practically indecent. Every time I see him, I want to stroke him. I'm told he gets it from his Thai mother. Dad's an Aussie, big guy, just like Chang.' And then he folded his arms across his chest, and narrowed his eyes. 'Come to think of it... hasn't he always liked you?'

'Oh God... I don't know.' My blush gave away the fact I actually did know. He wasn't exactly my type, whatever that was, but, and this is a huge but, he was *terribly, terribly* good looking. I felt the colour in my cheeks rise again.

'Hmmm Miss I-don't-know, I think you do know.' He

looked knowingly at me. 'You'd have very good looking children.'

I flashed him a look. 'Of course, and then my name would be Mrs Peach Chang. Nice ring to it,' I added sarcastically. 'It sounds like iced tea! And come to think of it,' I frowned, 'is Chang his first name or his last? A few months ago I was having coffee with Dad at Campos and we ran into him. I had absolutely no idea how to introduce him.'

Thomas folded his arms thoughtfully, pursed his lips and watched his reflection in the mirror, something I noted he often did. 'Hmmm… just Chang,'

'No one is just anything, unless you're Oprah.'

'Well smarty pants, you do know who I'm talking about when I say Chang. You never say, "Chang who?" And listen, I haven't heard you mention your dad in ages. Is he well?'

'Abso-bloody-lutely.'

He laughed. 'That cracks me up.' And then his voice sobered. 'But on a serious note, I am going to see if Chang has an available appointment this afternoon. And listen, he may not be the evening gown, but he certainly would be a great pair of shorts.' And he spun on his heels before I had a chance to swipe at him.

*

'*No* a smidge lower Chang,' my muffled voice said. I knew lying like this was messing up my new blow dry but who the hell cared. '*That's the spot. Yes. You've got it. Yes,*' I breathed, '*Yes, yes, yes put it in.*'

Chang's sensitive hands pressed on my upper back once more. 'And here?'

'*Yes,*' my eager voice said. '*Yes, yes…* that's it,' I moaned.

He flicked another needle. 'And I bet just here?' His knowing fingers pressed my back feeling for tension.

'*Yes.*' I popped my head up for a second, careful not to move too much in case I upset one of the needles. 'You really know your stuff.'

I heard the smile in his voice. 'I trained in Japan with blind monks. It's all in the touch. My fingers are *very* sensitive.' I felt him flick another needle, already the pain in my head lessening.

'Mmmm they sure are.' Allowing myself to give thought to my earlier conversation with Thomas, I sighed heavily.

'By the sound of that, I think your liver is low in qi.'

That wasn't all that was low in qi, however I felt it prudent not to mention it.

*

I pulled the car into the driveway, just in time to see a blond tail disappearing down that laneway next to the house. I had stressed to all of the tradespeople to be extra careful with the gate. The lock was so impossible, often it was left ajar. I had taken to tying it with a strap, but occasionally it was still left open.

I fumed to myself. I was going to have to do something about it, sooner rather than later. I couldn't keep the poor dog tied up all day. I was quite sure that wasn't what Mr Carmody had in mind for Wilbur.

Hurriedly, I stepped from my little car which I had now christened Bambino, and rather unladylike, I hollered to Wilbur. In my teetering nude patent-leather Christian Laboutin heels, I made a mad dash over to the laneway, however I need not have hurried. A few metres along, Wilbur was being restrained by the tall cyclist who I had noticed took this route regularly. He had a firm grip on Wilbur's new red collar.

'Is this the Wilbur you're looking for?' he asked, ruffling the dog's head. Once again, I noted his bright white teeth, and now closer, his olive skin. Of average height, but considerably broad shouldered, he carried a strong air of masculinity about him. I can't say it did not cross my mind that there was something incredibly attractive about this man.

Walking towards them, I tutted loudly and shook my head at the dog. 'That's him, I'm afraid. He's turned into an escape artist.' I took Wilbur's collar. 'Thank you for your help.' I began to walk back towards the car, leading Wilbur beside me. I turned back. 'Does the track go down to the river?' I asked.

'It does. But it's narrow and rather secluded.'

'Really?'

'Yes. I used to come here when I was a child,' he explained, walking along beside me, while he pushed his bike.

'Oh, right.' I nodded, letting go of Wilbur's collar as we neared the front gate. On the loose again, Wilbur took advantage of my open car door and jumped in.

I rushed over. 'No Wilbur, bad dog. Out!' He took no notice, so I began to beg. 'Please Wilbur, be a good boy. Hop out of my car.' Thinking it was a game, Wilbur climbed over the front red leather seats and into the back of the car, no mean feat for such a large dog in such a small area.

'Wilbur,' I cried. 'You're making a mess on Bambino's upholstery.' I don't know why I thought it, but it went through my mind that it was just as well it wasn't one of the BMWs, as Davis would have had kittens at seeing the large dog in one of our cars. His fleet, as he called them, were his pride and joy. I noted how at times, my mind simply went to him out of sheer habit. I shook my head.

Rather awkwardly in my pencil-cut skirt, I knelt on the front seat, beseeching the dog to remove himself. However, Wilbur stayed put, smiling more than he had in the last few weeks.

'Can I be of assistance?'

Still kneeling, I turned to see the cyclist, one of his brows quirked, a small smile playing at the edge of his mouth. A rather nice mouth, I decided. I was uncertain if his display of humour was directed towards Bambino, or the predicament I was now in.

Frustrated, and with some effort, I backed out of the car, shrugged and folded my arms. 'I am turning out to be the worst dog owner possible. I'm not sure I'm cut out for this.'

Still with his helmet on, he leant in the car. Pointing, he commanded, 'OUT!'

With that tone of voice, I would have obeyed as well. Wilbur leapt from the car, and with his tail between his legs, disappeared inside the front gate.

'Thank you. I'm quite new at this. The adoption was not that long ago.'

'I see.' There was that brief smile again, but it was as if he was unused to it, and before I knew it, it had disappeared. 'Respect takes time.'

'The car I mean. The car is rather new,' I attempted a joke, and laughed at myself, but then exhaled heavily. 'No seriously, I've been thinking I need a dog trainer.'

'Good idea. They'll have you in shape before you know it,' he said, his face unreadable.

I laughed. *'Touché!* Very funny.'

And then, he laughed. I think he surprised himself as well. 'Simple concise instructions are all you need. A dog is a pack animal and needs a leader. One or two clear words spoken firmly and he'll get the drift.'

'Well thank you, once again...'

Before I could finish, I heard the gardener cry out, '*BAD DOG! WILBUR, DOWN!*' And then his voice rose even further. 'Will you bleedin' well get off?'

In a flash, I took off down the gravel driveway, once again struggling in my fitted skirt and heels. I knew I must have looked ridiculous attempting to run on my toes. Halfway along, poor old Brownie was crouched on the ground on all fours with Wilbur on his back. Wilbur's front paws were bracing the man's shoulders, and he was nibbling at his ears. The dog looked to be having a wonderful game.

I shrieked. 'NO WILBUR, OFF.' Awkwardly, I ran to them and grabbed hold of Wilbur's collar, and with strength I didn't know I had, hoisted him off the older gent. The cyclist was one step behind me and helped Brownie to his feet, dusting him off. Meanwhile, Wilbur spotted a couple of inquisitive black and white honeyeaters feeding in the lower leaves of the murraya hedge and instantly distracted, shot off after them.

'Brownie, I'm terribly sorry. Are you okay?' I asked, holding the older gent's elbow. He looked feeble enough without the dog doing him any harm. I brushed a leaf off his shirt sleeve.

Brownie, too, brushed down the front of his overalls, looking for damage. 'I'm fine Mrs Riding. That dog's quite some weight, isn't he? I was busy crouching getting the nutgrass out of the gravel and before I knew it, the dratted dog leapt onto me. He very nearly winded me.'

'Perhaps you should sit down,' the cyclist suggested, picking Brownie's hat up off the ground, and giving it a brush off before handing it to him.

'No, no, I'm fine. Just gave me a bit of a fright more than anything. Mr Carmody always had labs, but this one seems a bit more mischievous than the others, and that's saying something.' He glanced at his elbow, checking to see if it was alright. 'Anyway Mrs Riding, I was about to pack up, so I might be off. I'll put these tools away in the potting shed.'

'How about you sit and have a cup of tea first?' I offered. 'I was about to have one.'

'I think I'll call it a day, if you don't mind.'

I watched as he walked back down the driveway towards the house. Wilbur, bored with his game with the birds, ran over to him. The old man waved him away. 'Go on, git out of here.' But his tone was friendly. From high above in one of the gum trees, a kookaburra cackled as if in derision. I turned to thank the cyclist yet again.

Standing a few metres away, he was examining the garden. When he turned to me, I caught the admiration in his ark eyes. 'It's all still here,' he said, his voice so quiet, I struggled to hear what he had said.

I watched his face, noting that his deep-set dark eyes were surrounded by long, dark lashes. But what struck me most was not the colour, though it was rich and velvety, but their expression. They were filled with something I could not put my finger on, a sadness perhaps.

'You know the garden?' I asked, surprise in my voice.

'Yes, I spent time here as a boy.' His face appeared animated as he glanced around. 'My father was the head gardener here for twelve years.'

'*Really?* Here... twelve years... I would love to chat with him and see what he remembers.'

He paused for a few seconds. 'I'm afraid he passed away years ago.'

'Oh, I'm sorry.' I was unsure of what else to say.

He shrugged, and was quiet for a few moments more, but continued to observe the garden. 'I forgot how spectacular the Lagerstroemia Indica was here.'

'I'm sorry? The what?' I gave him a questioning look.

There was the slightest look of amusement on his face. 'The hedge,' he indicated.

'Oh the Crepe Myrtle?'

Nodding, he walked over and peered through a gap. 'The rose garden. Yes I remember it.' He turned to me. 'My father was obsessed with them.' He gave a small laugh. 'He'd say they had delicate but wise little faces.' A pensive look crossed his face and I felt he was sorry for sharing so much information.

'Would you like to have a further look around?' I asked, intrigued by someone who actually had seen the garden in its heyday.

'Yes... I would.' He removed his helmet and with surprise I noted his closely shaven hair, so short I guessed it to be a number one blade. A haircut like that could go either way. You could either look like a thug, or very attractive. Let's just say he didn't look like a thug, but really how was I to know. Luckily for him he had olive skin and a good shaped head, two of the requirements for men who wished to wear their hair that short.

Helmetless, I was able to guess his age as a well preserved perhaps mid thirty something. Hmmm... previously, because of his fit physicality, I had thought him much younger than me. I observed him checking his watch and as he did his sleeve rose up and I noticed the bottom half of a brand new tattoo, on a particularly well-muscled bicep. It appeared to be the bottom half of some letters, however in those few brief seconds I was unable to read it. I guessed it to be only recent by the brightness of the colours and the fact it actually did look rather sore. I was not partial to tattoos.

'Actually,' he said, 'I didn't realise the time. It's late.'

'Of course,' I said, however the way my mind worked, I

couldn't help but wonder what he was late for. 'Perhaps another time.' Suddenly, I was glad it had turned out as it had. His face appeared to say more than what he actually did. He was one of those men who was saving his words.

He turned to walk away, and then turned back. 'I might have a few pictures. I'd have to find them.'

'Thank you,' was all I said, now, odd for me, saving my own words. Silently, I watched his retreating figure, thinking he had to do more than ride a bike to get those guns. A heck of a lot more.

As I walked back to my car, I glanced down at my shoes and saw the damage the pebbles had done to the heels. Annoyed, I tutted loudly. Smoothing my skirt I climbed back into the car, and suddenly felt rather ridiculous. With my purple patterned silk georgette shirt, this was my corporate wardrobe, and somehow it no longer seemed to fit. I checked my hair in the mirror on the visor. Mmmm, for the first time, I contemplated if the big blow-dry was appropriate for my new life.

And then I thought of Emerald Green, and how she had said perhaps I might find my clothes no longer suited. Out of everything she had said, that was the one thing I had been most disbelieving of. Now, I pondered the fact that perhaps she had been right! But I was always going to love my heels.

*

I held the sketches of the gate out to the blacksmith. 'I like the curly bits here. And that's where I'd like the letters spelling Carmody House to begin. I should imagine the pedestrian gate to be just here.'

'Would you like a remote control?'

'Of course.' I nodded. 'Do you think you can have the quote back to me as soon as possible?'

'Sure. Do you want flat bar or round steel?'

'Um… I'm not sure. Can I think about it for a few minutes while you measure up?' I roamed across the road to visualise it from there. I had on my new rose covered Hunter gumboots, a gift from Steve and Thomas. The boys had said that now I was woman of the land, I needed proper shoe attire to go with it. I wore them with a white shirt, the collar up, and a denim skirt. For the first time in many years, I was leaving my curly hair to do what it wished. I was over the glamorous blow dry. Against his better judgement, Thomas had styled it to a curly bob, which when dry shot up to just below my shoulders. I had insisted on attempting to return it to its former honey chestnut colour. I was beginning to like this more casual me. It gave me a feeling of freedom, one of lightness. And I had surprised myself and taken to gardening.

During my adolescence and early twenties, I had given little thought to gardening. In fact, none at all! My interests had been my career, fashion and travel when I could find the time to squeeze it in. I had taken the gardens surrounding me for granted, and had little understanding of the knowledge, creativity and tireless effort that went into them. Now my evenings were spent pouring over gardening books, earmarking pages with ideas I liked. The garden had become my new best friend.

The infrastructure I was undertaking on the house included plumbing, electrical upgrades plus a security system starting with the gate. The appropriate trucks were lined up opposite.

From my position across the road, I watched as Brownie slowly and methodically mowed the grassy nature strip. I knew I was going to have to come to a decision about him. At the rate he was going, it would be ten years before the garden was in order. I pushed it to the back of my mind.

Thoughtfully, I tapped my upper lip with my fingernail and stared at the place my new gate would go. 'Flat bar or round? Flat bar or round?' I repeated out aloud, as I noticed I'd begun to do more and more.

'Round for the uprights and flat bar for any decorative work,' a quiet voice said from behind me. I turned quickly to see the cyclist. 'I do take it you're talking about a new gate?' he asked, standing astride his bike, gesturing to the blacksmith's truck parked opposite.

'Actually I am,' I said, almost too stunned to say more, the sound of Brownie's lawnmower so loud, I hadn't heard the cyclist approach. It unnerved me. I looked sideways at him. 'What is this? Are you a mind reader?' More and more, I had noticed him on his bike and his avid interest in the property, or at least that's what I hoped, and that he wasn't casing the joint.

I had found being a woman living on my own encouraged my already vivid imagination to often go into overdrive. Thoughts came to me that would never have entered my head in the past. Just the other night as I prepared for bed, I heard a story on the late night news where a woman came home disturbing an intruder. She was murdered in her own home. I swear I spent the entire night sleeping with one eye open. Although I must say having Wilbur did give me a measure of comfort.

My thoughts were interrupted by the cyclist. 'You've undertaken quite a huge project?'

'Did you know Frank Carmody well?' I found myself wanting to question him.

'Yes, in the earlier years when my father was alive… and then,' he paused, 'and then our paths crossed quite a few times after that. The last was here about eight years ago when he took me on another tour of the garden. I still remember its magnificence. Frank was a very clever man. He's left a wonderful legacy behind. That's the thing with gardens...' he drifted off.

Intrigued by him, I once again attempted to guess how old he was and when his last visit would have been. Physically, he was in great shape, and his olive skin and dark eyes gave an air of health about him. However, there was something about his eyes that I just couldn't put my finger on. Usually, I was excellent at reading people. He was a hard one to pick.

He interrupted my reverie, his eyes on the blacksmith opposite. 'The gate will be galvanised?'

'Ah... yeah... sure!' I was pensive for a few minutes and then turned to him, my eyes narrowing. 'And that is?'

'A zinc coating to protect the steel from corrosion.' He nodded at the blacksmith. 'He should have taken that into consideration, or perhaps your husband has already told him.'

'No husband, just me,' I said, without giving it much thought, and then wished I hadn't. 'I'll certainly mention it to the blacksmith. Thank you.'

I took a few steps towards the road when he called out to me. 'I have some photos.'

I stopped in my tracks, now pleasantly surprised. 'You do? Of here?'

He held an envelope out to me.

'Oh... thank you. I'll take a quick look so you can have them back.'

'No, keep them. They're yours. I have copies.'

I looked at this mysterious cyclist, who had kindly taken the time to unearth these photos, and wondered not for the first time, at his lifestyle that he could go bike riding whenever he wished. Although, the day was getting on, most people would still be at work.

My guard down, I offered, 'You're welcome to take a look around the garden today if you wish.'

He checked his watch. It went through my mind that perhaps he was a shift worker.

'Sure, I should have time. Thank you.' We crossed the broad carpet of neatly mown lawn, and he propped his bike against the front fence as Brownie turned the mower off.

'I'll have that cup of tea now Mrs Riding, if you don't mind?' Brownie called to me.

'No problem Brownie.' Horrified at the Wilbur incident, I was continuously making tea for the old gent, who liked a chat at the same time. I'd made a rod for my own back with that one.

The cyclist glanced at me. 'I can roam around on my own, if you like.'

'Of course.' It was what I'd hoped for.

*

Once I might have considered looking out over the same view each day as boring, however from the kitchen window I had begun to constantly note the changing details of the garden. Washing up the teacups in the make do kitchen sink, I glanced out the same window, a couple of times catching sight of the cyclist with Wilbur, the overfriendly escort. Occasionally, the man went down on his haunches to study a plant. I noticed him push palm fronds aside authoritatively, looking as if he knew what he was doing. Once or twice he scraped at the soil and then pushed it back, shaking his head. Bending, he cupped a flower face, turning to see it more clearly. He took his time, and if his body language was anything to go by, he appeared to appreciate the garden as much as I did.

A voice called from the front door. It was the electrician,

Pete. I checked the time. It was now after four. How typical of him to come so late. Pete kept odd working hours, however Marty, Davis and I had been using him for years at work and at home, and had become used to his peculiar hours. We had been known to go to bed and leave him working, telling him to let himself out when he was finished. However last night, now on my own, I shooed him out at eleven. 'Time to go home to Julie,' I said. 'Come back tomorrow. I need my beauty sleep. Try to come a little earlier tomorrow hey?'

I flicked the switch on the kettle once again. I knew he would want coffee. I honestly wondered if these guys would expect tea or coffee from a male project manager. Somehow I doubted it, however, anything to keep them on side. Last Friday afternoon, I had even gone to the Brunswick Hotel drive through and bought a carton of beer, a tip from Marty. He said it kept everyone happy and keen to return Monday morning.

I followed the sound of Pete's voice still booming from the front door. 'Sorry I'm late Peach,' he called. 'You'll never guess where I've been?' His voice sounded animated. '*Davis's*. Let me tell you, there's trouble in paradise brewing over there.' He laughed. 'You'll never believe…'

I put one of my hands up. 'Not another word Peter.' My voice sounded sharper than I intended, and without meaning to I noticed I had used his full name. 'I am not interested.' The last thing I needed was a setback. Hearing about Davis's life kept me in limbo, instead of moving forward as I had been doing lately.

'You're going to want to hear this one.'

'No, I am not.' My voice sounded determined. I reached the front door to see the cyclist standing legs astride, hands low on his hips, surveying the gravel forecourt, just in front.

I did hope he hadn't heard what had been said. But then I caught the forlorn look on Pete's face. If there's one thing he loved, it was gossip. My voice softened. 'I've put the kettle on Pete, coffee will be ready in a minute. And... I'm sorry,' I called out the front door, 'but I don't know your name...'

'Phil... Phil Hunter.' Walking towards me, he offered a decisive handshake and a brief smile, reminding me once again of his dazzling white teeth. Although he was friendly, I felt the smile did not make it as far as his eyes. It was as if he was holding back and was unsure of what happiness felt like. There was something there, a huge sadness, perhaps a troubled past.

'Peach Riding,' I smiled. 'Phil would you like a coffee?' I caught him checking the time once again. 'You can have it while you finish your tour?' It was the least I could do after he had brought those photos for me, which I still hadn't had the time to look at.

He looked indecisive for a moment. 'Sure.'

'Come in and I'll show you the kitchen garden.' I caught his look as he saw my furniture piled in one of the front rooms with drop sheets covering it. 'I haven't been here long,' I explained. 'I'm still adjusting.'

He paused at the doorway to the room. 'Change takes time. This is a special place. You will be very happy here.' He spoke as if he was predicting my future. Although he seemed a man of few words, he said what had to be said and that was that.

'You'll have to excuse my make do kitchen, the new one is being manufactured as we speak.'

As a work station was required, the Louis desk Papa had left to me, took pride of place, although I continuously draped an old pink floral flannelette sheet over it, to protect it from building debris and dust. This had become my favourite place to sit. At night, I loved being able to look across the water to the view and the reflections. By day, I loved seeing the garden below.

Phil glanced around and appeared to be studying the renovations to date. 'Very wise,' he said nodding his head. 'Brings the garden in.'

I poured coffee into a mug and handed it to him, pushing the glass sugar bowl his way. 'What do you do Phil?'

He hesitated, while he tentatively sipped at the hot brew. Then he looked steadily and replied, 'I'm between things at the moment.'

'I'm sorry, it's just that I've been frantically looking for someone to help with the garden, and I saw you from the window, you appear to know your stuff. You're not... I mean... you wouldn't consider...?'

'I don't think I'd have the time.' He took another sip, glancing down at his coffee.

'Of course. If you happen to know of anyone...' Uncomfortable now, I drifted off. 'Anyway, come this way.' I was keen to show him the kitchen garden. I led the way through the laundry, but the door was jammed. I pushed as hard as I could but it didn't budge. 'The rain we've had lately,' I explained.

'Let me,' he suggested. Phil put his shoulder into it and the door freely opened out. I saw the reaction on his face and his eyes lit up at the sight of the garden. 'I remember now.' He walked around, hands on his hips, touching the leaves of different species. 'Much to do, eh?' But he looked thrilled.

He continued exploring and I stood watching. His obvious enjoyment intrigued me. And then he shared a memory. 'Frank had a distinct style of dividing larger gardens into a series of garden rooms, creating mystery and enticement.' And then as an afterthought he added. 'In here your plantings should be staggered. Plant little and often, that will be the key.

You'll need pea straw mulch around the basses of all the plants to suppress weeds, provide nutrition and retain moisture. And don't forget the worm castings.' For a minute he paused, his eyes narrowing as if remembering something. And then without looking at me he continued in a quieter voice. 'Gardens certainly have a spiritual value. Flowers, herbs and vegetables nourish the soul as well as the body.'

Before I had a chance to respond, he glanced at his watch yet again, and looked startled. 'I'm sorry, I've lost track of time.'

He appeared hurried and I walked him back to the front door. 'I meant to say,' he said, turning to me, as if an afterthought. 'There was another photo but I couldn't seem to put my hand on it. It had my father and Frank Carmody standing together in the garden. I'll keep looking.'

'That's very kind, thank you. Perhaps when you find it, you'll finish off your tour of the garden,' I said stepping out onto the front veranda. The heat of the day was still coming out of the ground in waves, the scent from the roses and jasmine hung heavily in the air.

I needed to shower. Marty was taking me to dinner.

Chapter 9

From the formal lounge slash library, the smell of freshly baked cupcakes wafted in from the kitchen. My earlier love affair with them had returned. Each day found me experimenting with ingredients, fixated on embellishing them with icing crafted butterflies. The fact was I had no shortage of guinea pigs, the tradesmen happily obliging, some even giving my artistic work a score out of ten. It usually only varied by half a point or so.

With paying guests in mind, I held a picture of cake stands of varying heights lining the kitchen bench. All were filled with an assortment of different flavoured cakes, each adorned with their signature icing, some with butterflies, and some simply embellished with a cursive *CH,* Carmody House's new logo.

Beside them was the place for my impressive new commercial Gaggenau coffee machine, which I was expecting any day. I made a mental note to book in for the barista class. No point in having a hi-tech piece of machinery and not using it to its full advantage.

Crouched on my haunches in the front room, I peeled the tape off a packing box filled with books. I had promised myself everything would stay sealed until the house was finished. However, I could not help myself, keen to find a book I had been given years before. This box, along with ten others like it, had been packed away in our storage room at the warehouse. I had always been a voracious reader and it had been disturbing not to have my books around me.

There was no point in unpacking them yet, as the custom bookshelves were not yet installed. I had shown the furniture craftsman a picture of Elton John's library in his country home. He was under strict instructions to copy the joinery to the very last detailed pilaster.

Facing north, the library was a welcome suntrap. The French doors perfectly framing the spectacular Sapphire Dragon tree outside. Deciduous, already the tree had begun to drop its leaves. By the time winter well and truly arrived, the sun would be able to stream in through the library windows, making it an all the more inviting place to read. Although, I was keen to see it in September as Brownie had told me that the tree would explode into a myriad of mauve bell-shaped flowers. Obviously that was what Mr Carmody had in mind when he had planted it. Once again, I mentally thanked him for his wonderful design and planting selection.

I turned my attention back to the task at hand. Davis had always insisted that we didn't have anywhere for my books. It wasn't the look we were after. However, that didn't stop me buying more and burying them around the warehouse.

I'd had an obsession with books for as long as I could remember: the look, the smell and the feel of them – in hardback, paperback, special and limited editions. At school, being well-read was one of the highest compliments anyone could have paid me, and then at university I stockpiled textbooks and non-fiction, in the hope that their contents would magically work their way into my brain and onto my essays by osmosis. When I purchased my first apartment, textbooks and glossy coffee table books were a way of showcasing who I was and who I wanted to be. Sadly, when Davis and I merged our lives, there wasn't room for many of them.

However, on the floor of the library, as I pulled out one old friend after another, my heart warmed at the sight of them, many of whom I'd had wild passionate affairs with.

I unearthed a stack of journals in which I had sketched, glued photos, and written down ideas of my dream home many years earlier. The addictive smell of the leather covers enticed me to open them. Briefly, I flicked through, exciting myself with my earlier ideas, as if I had predicted that one day I would live in a home such as Carmody House.

I stacked them neatly on the floor, keen to have a thorough look later. Finally, I found what I was looking for. It was a CWA cookbook. My hand smoothed across the worn cover. With pleasure, I leafed through it, knowing my nan's hands had touched the very same pages. She had told me it had been her bible, sending it when Davis and I had become engaged.

The book was a record of life in a gentler age, when women of all ages enjoyed homemade baking together, and drank from pretty china cups on embroidered tablecloths. Its practical hints ranged from chemical-free cleaning, so useful for today's way of life, to how to tan your own sheepskins... not so useful.

Smiling wistfully, I couldn't help but think that back then people loved each other forever. Or at least Nan and Pop did. Now the hectic way we lived meant suddenly, if we weren't needed anymore, we were out.

A few hours earlier, frustrated by the lack of speed Brownie was showing, I had launched myself into the garden, determined to work something out, a way to get on top of it. I did not need reminding that it needed far more than an elderly gardener; it required a team of people.

I had spent the past two hours attacking the kikuyu that had been rampantly marching though the place, its runners up and over the edges of all the garden beds. It appeared as if I had barely made a dent. And then I had remembered Nan's book. Distracted by the thought of actually being able to grow produce to make my own homemade jams, preserves, pickles and chutneys, I had taken a break from the unruly grass and come inside, pleased to escape the scorching day, if only briefly.

On the way in, I had passed Pete. Surprise, surprise, he had actually turned up at a respectable hour. He was leaving to pick up some specialised cabling and I realised that it was a rarity to have the place to myself during daylight hours with so many tradespeople coming and going, but today they had all left earlier than usual.

Kicking off my gumboots, in my sock feet, I made a pot of tea and begun to rifle through the boxes, itching to put my hands on that particular book. Wilbur had followed and was now slumbering peacefully beside me.

As I sat with the book in my lap, I noticed a small piece of paper sticking out, yellow with age. It was a copy of *The Women's Weekly* Quick Mix Christmas Cake, the bottom left hand corner dated November 1982. Bless my nan. I guess that had been a hint at my former hectic corporate lifestyle. I decided right then and there that there would not be any quick mix Christmas cake for me. I would take the time to soak my fruit weeks in advance, much the same as I had seen Nan do. Although I remembered her using sherry, I would use port.

I wished to God I had taken Davis's Grandfather Port he had so treasured. I remembered once using a tablespoon in a recipe and him hitting the roof about the cost. My retort had been that if it was good enough for him, it was good enough to use in the dessert for our guests to share.

And then my hand went to my mouth, covering a smirk as a memory surfaced. I wondered what Davis's reaction had been when he had noticed that he was short at least a dozen bottles of his precious Grange Hermitage. What can I say? Those first few months had been difficult. I might have enjoyed a glass or two… or perhaps three… home alone as I was.

Davis's own behaviour had left him nowhere to go with this. And I had not heard a word! But imagining his reaction gave me the slightest amount of pleasure. Who am I kidding? I loved it!

With the CWA book on my lap and lost in a world of thought, in a heartbeat I was bought back to reality as my eyes caught a movement on the veranda outside the open French door. In a micro second, prickles ran all the way up my spine, until every hair on my body stood on end. My heart hammered so loudly, I felt as if I might have a heart attack. Blood pounded to the top of my head and my mind began yelling, *SNAKE, SNAKE, SNAKE*, as if the word was physically hitting my brain. The only thing that came out of my mouth was 'UGGGGHHH!'

Outside on the patio, a huge snake was slithering at quite a speed towards the open door. I *hated* snakes.

Upsetting my teacup, I lunged for the handle of the French door, pulling it towards me just in time. But the snake didn't stop. It rammed its head against the door as if it had every right to be there, in fact, had been there many times before, perhaps even had a nest somewhere inside. Terrified, I yelled and stomped my feet at the determined reptile, not appearing to deter it, although waking Wilbur. He couldn't fathom what was going on, however he began to bark.

Petrified, I backed away, uncertain of what to do. I grabbed at Wilbur's collar and pulled him with me, taking off for the front door. There had to be *someone* around, *somewhere*. Without even taking the time to put my gumboots on, at a speed I didn't know I had, I continued across the front porch, down the half dozen steps and around the curved driveway, begging for Pete to return.

Stumbling across the gravel in record time, with nothing more than socks on my feet, I held Wilbur's collar firmly, not wanting to release him in case he confronted the snake. It didn't bear thinking about. For the first time, I was grateful to see the gate had been left ajar. On the footpath, I frantically looked up and down, praying to see one of the work trucks that had been incessantly parked out front for months on end, returning.

The back view of Phil Hunter on his bike heading down the laneway opposite was a godsend.

'*Phil*,' I screeched and then took off after him, running faster than I thought possible. I'm not sure what Wilbur thought was going on, but he kept up with me. 'Phil stop, please!' I wailed, stumbling in my socks. He continued on. I gave it all I could, screeching, 'PHIL! HELP!'

Halting, he straddled his bike and turned. Briefly, I caught the look of bafflement on his face. He removed his sunglasses, and narrowed his eyes in question as he peered back at me. Gasping for breath, I caught up to him, steadying myself by holding the handlebars of the bike. 'S… snake,' I heaved, putting a hand to my chest, attempting to get air in my lungs. 'Big brown snake on side patio.' And then I doubled over, breathless.

His dark eyes opened wide and he gave a decisive nod. He turned his bike towards my house but then turned back to me. 'You keep hold of Wilbur.'

As much as I didn't want to, I followed, my fingers clamped around Wilbur's collar like a vice. As I rounded the bend of the driveway, I saw Phil's discarded bike laying on its side on the gravel forecourt, one wheel finally coming to a halt. His helmet wasn't far away. With trepidation, I made my way up the front stairs. I knew that Wilbur's lead was just inside the front door. Tentatively, I reached for it, and secured the dog. He seemed to sense we had to be quiet.

With one hand still firmly holding his collar, the other held the lead. Tiptoeing, I ventured inside, looking for Phil through the windows. Halfway along the hallway I felt the prickle of the cobblers pegs in my socks. Quietly, I peeled each sock off, leaving them where they fell to the ground.

I spied Phil on the side porch. He was deathly still, his hands on his hips, his eyes the only thing moving. On seeing me, he slowly raised a finger to his lips. And then stealthily he began to creep around, pushing the plants that lined the porch aside, peering around them. With Wilbur in tow, and heart still hammering, I crept through each room, looking out the windows to see if I could see the intruder.

I made my way to the laundry and noticed that as usual the bottom half of the dormer window was open. Due to the damp, I had been having trouble with the laundry door jamming, making it impossible to open. Until it was replaced, I took every opportunity I could to let fresh air in the room. Shivering, I ran my hands up my arms. The laundry wall jutted out and although the door only led to the kitchen garden courtyard, the window came off the side porch.

I heard Phil's soft voice call to me. 'Peach... where are you? I can see an open window here which it may have gone through. It may be the laundry.'

There was an instantaneous prickly sensation as adrenaline washed over me in tidal waves, pounding to the top of my head. Once again, I thought I was having a heart attack, my heart hammering so loudly in my chest it physically hurt. With both hands gripping the door handle, I put my shoulder against the door, and finding the strength of ten men, heaved, swinging the door out in such a hurry, I went with it, falling to my knees, Wilbur on his lead tangling up with me.

Clambering to my feet as quickly as I could, I put as much distance between myself and the laundry as possible, which was difficult as even though it was a large courtyard, it was walled. Quick as a flash, I mounted the garden bed and stood with my back against the stone wall, my knees slightly bent, ready for anything. With one hand to my chest, I gasped for air. Wilbur's lead was now wrapped tightly around my other wrist, biting into it, although I did not notice. My eyes darted around. In my entire life, I do not believe I had ever been so scared.

I watched the laundry door until I saw Phil's tall body frame it. Slowly he once again placed a finger to his lips, and then began to search the small room. He gestured to me. 'You can come in. I think it's safe. It doesn't look like it's in here.'

Rapidly, I shook my head. '*No, you have to find it.* I will not be able to sleep at night if you don't. In fact, I'll never be able to step foot inside again.'

He held a hand towards me. 'I understand, but you're in a walled courtyard and there's no other way out except through here.'

I glanced up at the top of the wall behind me, attempting to figure out how I could possibly scale it successfully, run down the front drive and never return. I mean, I'd tried this house, garden thing. It didn't work out, not everything has to.

Phil persisted. 'Come on Peach. Come inside. I'll have a thorough search. You can't stay there among the pumpkins all day.'

I actually thought I could. I mean if I wanted to I could… and I wanted to. Wilbur barked, bringing me back to reality. I edged my back away from the wall. 'You're sure it's not in the laundry?' I asked, climbing out of the garden.

His voice was firm. 'Yes.'

He stood aside for me as I stepped back inside. 'Y... you lead the way,' I told him, following as close as I could without actually touching him. Although, at that point, I wondered if he would mind piggy backing me. I wasn't that heavy and after the break-up, I'd lost those few kilos which made me lighter again. I considered how I could climb up on his back... he might have had to bend down.

In the kitchen, he stopped abruptly and I ran into him.

'Sorry,' I whispered, watching as his eyes scanned the room. Silently, he held a hand up. 'I'll check everywhere.'

He began poking around the cupboards looking under things. I stood in the middle of the room, eyes darting around, briefly resting on the cupcakes. One of my hands clutched the front of my shirt, the other still attached to Wilbur's lead. He too stood alert. As time went on, I relaxed slightly. Tentatively, I walked down the hall and back towards the front room where I had been when I first saw the snake.

Hesitantly, I stepped closer to the French doors, and then a little closer again, until my nose was practically pushed against it, my breath making a soft mist on the glass. I peered out, scanning the side porch and the garden surrounding. A mesmerising movement caught my eye and there outside, but right up against the glass, the snake slithered along.

The cry in my throat froze and then it rose up and spilled out like hot lava from a volcano, and I screamed, '*IT'S HERE! SNAKE, SNAKE, SNAKE!*' I bolted from the room, dragging a nervous Wilbur, running smack bang into Phil, and in the bedlam kicking my little toe so hard on the door jamb, I knew straightaway it was broken. But my fear of the snake was stronger than the pain, although that didn't stop me from crying out in agony.

Phil turned in circles. 'Where? Where?'

From the hallway, I pointed outside the door. In two steps he had the door open and stood hands on hips looking at the reptile. I saw him glance around for assistance of some kind.

'Don't let it get away,' I yelled. I could just picture the snake heading towards the climbing curtain of ivy on the side wall, where we'd never find it. If that happened, I knew I'd have to leave immediately, never to return.

I watched as in those few brief seconds, Phil debated what to do. And then, looking on in absolute horror I saw him reach down and grab the snake by the head, clamping its mouth shut. Within a split second, the snake rapidly coiled itself around his arm, its tail flicking aggressively. I had never seen anything so terrifying.

Phil looked at me. I screamed hysterically, and without having a rationale thought, ran over and locked the glass door, terrified he'd bring it inside. I began to cry, hysterically. *'I'm sorry, I'm sorry, I am so sorry,'* I told him, from the other side of the door. 'I'll get my phone. I'll get help.'

Right at that moment I heard the sound of Pete's truck coming up the gravel driveway. I headed for the front door and before Pete even had time to stop, I waved him down. He took one look at my face and leapt from the truck.

'QUICK,' I yelled. 'We need help.' I pointed. 'Big brown snake on side patio.' I didn't want to waste time on unnecessary words. Pete ran around the back of his truck, opened it and reached inside. He pulled out a rifle.

'What...?' I asked, blinking in disbelief.

'We may need something else mate. It has wrapped itself around my arm.' As cool as a cucumber, Phil had wandered around the front of the house. I backed away as quickly as I could, dragging poor Wilbur with me.

'Do you have anything else?' he asked Pete, as if someone producing a firearm was common.

'You never know what you might find in some of these old ceilings, and under houses,' Pete explained. I visualised him shooting a ceiling to pieces while the customer stood below. He pushed the gun back into the truck and then took another look at the reptile, narrowing his eyes. 'I suppose *you'd* like to take it off somewhere and relocate it.'

I watched Phil deliberate. 'I would. However, I'm not sure I'm going to be able to get this big guy off my arm successfully to do that. I hate to do this, but I'm not sure we have a choice. Do you have a knife?'

I was waiting any moment for Pete to say in typical Crocodile Dundee fashion. *Do I have a knife!* And pull a dagger from the truck. Instead, I turned away, shuddering, thinking I might throw up.

Discreetly the dead snake was disposed of in Pete's truck. Kindly, he said that he'd take it away somewhere immediately, sensing my distress at even the thought of a dead snake still being around.

Suddenly, the pain in my toe began to make itself known to me in the hugest of ways, the throbbing hitting my brain in waves. I released Wilbur who ran to Phil, expecting more excitement. Tentatively, I limped over to the front steps, grimacing with the agony. Lowering myself down, I examined my injury. The top of my foot was already purple where the muscle had been reefed so furiously, it had been pulled out of place. A couple of tears escaped and rolled down my cheeks. Surreptitiously, I wiped at them with the back of my hand.

Shaking my head, I looked at Phil. 'I am *so sorry* Phil. I behaved abysmally. I really don't know what to say.'

He cast an amused eye over me and to my surprise, laughed

out loud. 'You're good under pressure, I'll give you that.'

Shaking my head again, I put it in my hands, disgusted at how out of control I had been.

'Hmmm your Virginian creeper is showcasing itself beautifully.'

'Huh?' I looked up at him, wondering what on earth he was on about. I guess he was attempting to give me time to compose myself. Unable to understand, I screwed my face up, and followed his glance over to the garage. 'Yeah, of course,' I sniffed. To be honest, I really couldn't have given a hoot about the Virginian creeper or whatever it was called.

'It's always the last to bud in spring, but it's the first to turn a rich scarlet in autumn.'

'Hmm,' I said with very little interest, which I'm guessing he picked up on. Touching my toe, I winced.

'You need ice,' he stated.

I glanced up. 'What?' He was studying my foot and I could tell he wasn't looking at my latest Shellac colour.

'Ice for the swelling. Pain killers as well.'

I nodded, relieved he was talking about my foot, and not the snake or the *bloody* Virginian creeper. I have never been more embarrassed about my behaviour. I sniffed, uncertain if I was crying because of my toe, my bad behaviour, the shock of the snake, or all three.

'Are you able to walk?' he asked.

Nodding, I attempted to stand, although now the pain barrier was too high. I winced audibly and sat back down.

'Here, I'll help,' he said.

Without putting the injured foot down, I awkwardly stood and took his arm, crying out as I did. In a flash he swooped me up in his arms and carried me inside, the afternoon surreal enough without this as well. He placed me on the makeshift kitchen bench beside a bowl of slender brown *beurre bosc* pears, the most elegant and decorative thing in the room at this point of time, other than my artistically iced cupcakes.

'Ice?' he asked.

I indicated the new twin door refrigerator. Glancing around for something, he took the tea towel and filled it with ice and then gently pressed it to my foot. I winced and hurriedly pulled back, but then tentatively let him rest the cold pack on it, unable to withhold the audible signs of pain. Embarrassing audible signs of pain!

'Pain killers?' he asked.

I motioned to a basket on the counter. Rifling through, he found the box, popped two out of the foil casing and filled a glass with water.

'Swallow,' he said. I did as I was told, feeling utterly drained by the events. But the tears that had been close for so long now, poured out, rivering down my cheeks and I couldn't hold back. I saw the look on Phil's face. All this was far more than he had bargained for when he went for a ride this afternoon.

'I'm sorry.' I sniffed, wiping at my nose with the back of my hand. 'But I've just decided that I never want to go into that garden again. And I was really enjoying it,' I wailed. I caught myself, and attempted to calm down, taking few breaths and putting a hand on my chest. 'The thing is,' I wiped at my face with my sleeve, 'Brownie is far too slow.' I knew I was beginning to ramble, but was so overwrought, I was unable to stop myself. 'The garden is beyond him, and I've no idea who to ring or what to do.' My voice broke once again. '*It's all too much.* I've called people and they've said they'd give me a quote, but two have been no shows and the other one, I didn't think was right. But to top it off, I've got snakes. I'll never cope. I'm not a snake person.'

'I noticed,' was all he said. He walked back over to the basket on the bench and found the box of tissues, handing me two.

'Thank you,' I said in a wobbly voice, blowing my nose. 'Do you want a cake?'

He wore a look of bafflement. 'Sorry?'

Sniffing heavily, I indicated the cakes piled high on the stand.

I was rewarded with the briefest of smiles and he shook his head. 'Look a lot of Brisbane backyards have snakes, but you rarely see them. No doubt with all the work going on, it's been stirred up.'

'I didn't like it,' I said in a small voice.

'That was obvious.' His tone was dry. 'Although that one was a bit feisty, generally speaking, snakes don't come after you. They're as scared of you as you are them. I think your visitor was possibly looking for somewhere to curl up for the winter. More than likely you will never see another one.'

'Are you sure? Because sometimes my sister's children stay over and I'd never forgive myself...'

He shrugged. 'I can't promise it, but I can promise you they will be few and far between. It's really not something you'll have to keep thinking about. Although the sooner you get that undergrowth cut back the better.'

I gave one of those double sniffs, feeling better. Phil looked at his watch and raised his eyebrows as if in alarm. Before he could say anything, Pete's voice bellowed from the front door. 'Look who the cat dragged in.' I heard footsteps on the hallway floor and Marty popped his head around the corner.

I was so relieved to see him I began to cry once again. '*Marty!*' I put my arms out to him. 'It's been the worst afternoon. This huge snake tried to get in. It was pushing its head against the door, literally head-butting it. And you know how I feel about snakes.' I hiccupped. 'And Phil picked it up and it wrapped around him, and then Pete had a gun and a knife, and I broke my toe and it's killing me.' And the tears continued.

Marty laughed and put his arms around me. 'Oh you're a funny girl. Pete rang me and said you'd had a bit of a fright, so I thought I'd come by and see if you were okay.'

'Look at my toe,' I sniffed.

Marty bent down and examined my foot, making sufficient sympathetic sounds, attempting to placate me. He brushed his lips across the top of my head and then reached for a cupcake. Biting into it, he nodded his head in approval.

'I'll be off,' Phil said.

Marty turned as if noticing Phil for the first time. 'Err yeah, thanks mate. Do we owe you anything for your trouble?' He reached for his wallet.

'No... of course not.' Phil looked uncomfortable. I cringed that Marty had made him feel that way.

From my perch on the kitchen bench, I thanked him. 'Phil thank you so much. I truly don't know what I would have done without you. You were an absolute lifesaver.' From beside me I took two patty cakes and swiftly wrapped them in a napkin. 'Please take these,' I insisted, pushing them towards him.

I think it was more to please me than anything else, however he took my proffering, and then made a hasty exit.

'Tough bloke that one,' said Pete from the doorway.

Chapter 10

For the past hour I had been delighting in a new catalogue. No, it was not the *Victoria's Secret* catalogue or even *Anne Fontaine*, instead it was a gardening catalogue giving details of new roses being released. Brownie told me I had room for three new rose varieties. It was hard to choose. I loved them all, deep red, rose pink, apricot, cream and even sunshine yellow. The main criteria for me was that it must have a scent.

Of late, I had begun to hear the sounds of nature, more than the busy thoughts in my head. And indeed the progress of the garden was a mirror of the progress of me. Although my upbringing had been Anglican, I had never really taken to religion. Now, my daily tending of the gardens at Carmody House had become my spiritual practice.

Pushing my chair back away from the Louis desk, I stretched my arms above my head.

The evening after the snake incident, I had phoned Johnny. I hoped that from his brief tree lopping days he would have a few contacts who could come and clear some of the undergrowth.

'Abso-bloody-lutely,' had been his answer. A crew of three had spent the last two weeks removing undergrowth and scrappy planting. I was now feeling somewhat better about outside. All around the house had been cleaned up. Although it didn't solve all my problems, it was a start. What I needed now was someone with vision of how the garden had been and how it could be again. Brownie was making inroads although they were slow.

I glanced at the picture on my desk that I'd found in my letterbox last week. Obviously Phil Hunter must have left it for me. I say obviously because one of the men in the picture was the spitting image of him, however he had a full head of dark hair. I looked at Phil's father's dark eyes. They were hauntingly similar to Phil's. He was standing beside a much younger Mr Carmody. An old red wheelbarrow and some brightly glazed pots were in the background. Mr Carmody was broad but slight like a swimmer, and tall, not resembling the man I had come to know in the wheelchair. The early photograph of the property showed a garden of splendour. It was a world away.

'I saw that fellah the other day,' Pete, from the top of a ladder, broke into my reverie.

'Sorry?' I asked, turning to look up at him. His eyes were now on the ceiling and he busied himself with a screwdriver, connecting low voltage lighting and their adapters to the wiring. Already in place were the French style black enamelled pendant lamps, hovering above where the new kitchen bench would go.

Pete glanced down and gestured to my desk. 'The guy in the picture.'

'Do you mean Phil?' I asked.

He nodded. 'That's him. You know... Snake Man.'

'This isn't him. It's a picture of his father. He was a gardener here at one point. There is a great likeness though, isn't there, although he appears not to be as tall as Phil, plus he has more hair. I daresay, he might be of similar age to Phil at present.' I studied the photo once again. 'Anyway where did you see him?' I asked, my curiosity aroused now.

Pete removed the screwdriver from between his lips. 'Saw him maintaining a rather impressive garden on a big house up on Tenerife hill. I was about to give him a blast with my horn, but just then the owner of the house, an elderly lady, pulled in and got out and began giving him instructions on what she wanted done.' He placed the screwdriver back in his mouth and used both hands to connect the adaptor to the light.

'Right,' I nodded. 'I sensed he had something to do with gardens. Mmmm, I guess he took after his father.' I thought for a minute. 'I've got a bottle of wine here for him, to thank him for his help. But on second thoughts, he'd probably appreciate a carton of beer. Neither of which, I might point out, would fit on his bike.' Ever since the snake incident, I had been keeping a lookout for him, checking the letterbox around the time I expected him to ride past, to no avail.

'If you see him again will you let me know?' If you wanted to find something out, you left it to Pete. He loved other people's business.

'Sure,' he said, his eyes on the ceiling. 'I've got a client on the hill at the moment. I normally go there before I come here. Might see him then.'

Sliding the chair away from the desk, I walked across to the massive window overlooking the back garden, down to the river. I wondered to myself how Pete's other client lucked out and had him at decent hours, whereas I got the late shift, sometimes far too late.

*

'Please take it,' I insisted, pushing the bottle of red wine into Phil's hands. 'You were a life saver that day.' I had pulled my car into the driveway when I had seen Phil coming out of the laneway on his bike. 'I'm afraid I didn't behave in a terribly helpful manner, so if you accept this wine I will feel enormously better.' I paused for a minute. 'Oh you do drink, don't you?'

'Of course, it's just rather unnecessary, plus...' Still straddling his bike, he waved his hands encompassing it.

'Bit hard to ride with a bottle of wine?'

'Something like that.'

'Well, it seems I have a lot to be thanking you for. I found that photo you left in my letterbox. I must say it was an eye opener seeing Mr Carmody when he was much younger. I can only imagine his immense frustration at his limitations after his surgery, and then being wheelchair bound. Looking at that photo helped me to gain a better understanding of him.' And then I had a thought. 'You never did finish looking around the garden. Do you have time now? There's something I want to show you. I have an idea and I'd like to get your thoughts, as you're the only one who seems to have any idea of what the garden was like before.'

Propping his bike against the fence, Phil removed his helmet and gloves, and followed me.

'I see you've done a bit of clearing,' he said.

I turned. 'Yes, some men my father knew. They're almost finished.'

'They've been a tad ruthless,' he said, shrugging, as if he was still making up his mind if it was a problem or not.

'Oh... too much... you think?'

'Just keep your eye on them. Make sure they don't take it back any further.'

'Of course.'

And then I saw him examining a creeper with much interest. He gave a light chuckle. 'This is a rare one. I should have known Frank would have fostered this.'

'Oh?'

'Aristolochia prevenosa. It's the food plant for the caterpillars of the Richmond Birdwing butterfly. Once they were common in Brisbane. Unfortunately now they are under threat of distinction.'

'Oh?' I said once again. This was all new territory to me.

'What do the butterflies look like? I'll keep a look out.'

'They have a bright yellow thorax with a big red spot. The males have iridescent green and yellow wings.'

'Well I'd best keep the clearers away from the… umm… *aristotles…* or whatever,' and I caught the slightest flicker of amusement cross his face, although it went no further. 'I'd love it if we encouraged those Richmonds. They sound spectacular.

'Now, let me show you my surprise garden.' The walled garden was the *piece de resistance.* A place all of my own that I could sit in perfect peace and quiet. Already I could see an abundance of pretty flowers, imagining their wonderful fragrances.

With difficulty hiding my excitement, I led Phil around the left-hand side of the house, the winding pathway carpeted by subtle miniature violets, leading to where I had made the most delightful discovery.

Not for the first time, I fondly recalled the Enid Blyton books Aunt Honey had read to us, and the effect that they must have had on me. In fact, it had been many, many years since I had even thought of them, but now all I could think of were my two all-time favourites, *The Enchanted Garden* and *The Magic Faraway Tree.*

Crazy as if may sound, it had taken me some time to work out this stone wall was not the wall of the enclosed kitchen garden, but of another garden that long ago would have been private. It appeared that in its day, two sides would have been enclosed by a hedge and the remnants of some of the bushes still stood. A disused fountain and water rill were offset by a bed of unkempt box.

Proudly, with my arms folded, I turned to look at Phil. I watched his face and saw it change as a look crossed it.

For a while he said nothing, and then he placed both of his hands on the back of his head, linking his fingers. Seconds passed and I watched as he surveyed the scene. Once again I wondered at his age.

He turned to me and briefly I saw something in his dark eyes, as if he had a memory of here. Although fleeting, I liked that every now and then he let me into his thoughts by the look on his face, but the second I saw it, it was gone again.

Taking large strides he paced the garden out, not saying anything while he did. For a few moments he quietly examined the hedge that looked as if it had seen better days. With an authoritive air he snapped one of the twigs. I saw a look of surprise cross his face.

'Hmmm… these lilly pillies can be cut back as surprisingly there is still life there.' He gestured to a rather desperate looking few. 'Although those ones are too far gone and will need to be replaced.' Once again he stood with his hands low on his hips, glancing around. 'It would be sacrilegious not to take this garden back to its former glory.'

He had used the exact words I had so often espoused. 'Right.' I had my hand up to my brow shading it from the late afternoon sun. This man's knowledge surprised me.

Nodding his head, Phil was quiet again as he studied the fountain. Going down on one knee, he felt around the base. I watched the expressions on his face, aware his mind was working. When he found what he was looking for, a look of satisfaction showed, and he stood once again.

'It's fixable.'

'Right!' I said once more, as if I knew exactly how to fix it myself.

Slowly he nodded, exhaling. 'Water adds movement, sound and emotion to a garden.'

Pursing my lips, and with a look of agreement on my face, I too nodded, feeling like I was in a horticulture class. I wondered if he was telling me or reminding himself.

Crouching, Phil poked his fingers into the soil, loosening it. He ran some through his fingers and then stood, shading his eyes with his hands and glancing around. Once more he nodded. 'There is a good feeling here.'

I liked the simplicity of his words. It was enough. With his hands once again on his hips and his eyes taking in the space, he continued his study of the area. Patiently, I waited.

And then he explained in his quietly spoken voice. 'This was Frank's wife's garden. The one time I saw it, it was very pretty. I remember my father telling me that once she left, Frank told them just to leave it be.' For a few moments he was quiet once again with his thoughts, and then he turned to me. 'I like the idea of a garden being a paradise. The Islamic notion of walking into a walled garden and suddenly feeling as if you've been taken away somewhere, is very appealing.'

'Mmmm.' I glanced around, enjoying the garden all the more, and feeling rather pleased with myself for owning it. A smile played around the edges of my lips, as I enthusiastically asked Phil's opinion. 'I was thinking I'd love to plant a cherry tree here. What are your thoughts?' The notion of the dark red heart shaped fruit being a focus, conjured up all sorts of wonderful visions, and of course, gave me my own Magic Faraway Tree.

'I believe you'd be hard pressed to have luck with it. For a start, they do not do well in climates such as this. The summers are too long and hot. And although it would guarantee a huge bird population flocking to the garden, birds have been known to strip a cherry tree in less than an hour. So you would more than likely have to net it and then you'd lose the feeling you're after.'

This was the most I had ever heard this man speak. However, today he was parting with a few more words than usual. I almost cheered him on.

Exhaling heavily, he narrowed his eyes. 'It was, and can be again, a visually exciting space – good for the soul and pleasing to the eye. I believe a degree of formality is needed. You would need to select your planting wisely. Over there,' he indicated, 'I'd recommend a row of mature pleached Manchurian pear trees. I can see...'

I interrupted. 'Pleached?'

'The lower branches are removed and the higher ones are trimmed to create a canopy...'

I cut in. 'You seem to know a fair bit about gardens.' Watching his face, I put a hand up to shade my mine.

'Enough,' was all he said, glancing away, and I saw a closure in his face, as if the shutters had come down.

I had strained my ears to hear him. 'I'm sorry?'

He turned back to me, hands on his hips. 'I know enough.'

I found myself nodding, as if knowing enough was a good answer. There was something about this man that intrigued me. Where the next question came from I was unsure. 'Phil I am looking for someone to take over the huge job of bringing this garden back to its earlier magnificence. To be honest, I'm rather in awe of the planning and execution of it. By any chance, do you know of anyone... or would you be able to assist... or oversee? I'd be agreeable to anything.'

I didn't miss the look of discomfort that crossed his face. He rubbed his hands together as he attempted to explain. 'Look, I... I haven't been doing anything for quite some time. I'm sort of trying to work myself out, not really looking for anything.' He paused. 'I've been... I'm between things.'

I could see I had stepped on tender ground. I wasn't sure why I had asked again. Although I must say, I liked the way his face looked when he remembered what the garden had been like.

I attempted to be flippant, shrugging. 'Sure I understand... I thought you may know someone. And Pete, my electrician, said he'd seen you maintaining a garden up on the hill, so I thought... perhaps you were looking for more work... You know this is the kind of place where you really want to do justice.'

'I understand. It's just... I'm not sure what I could offer.' He ran a hand over his almost non-existent hair as if smoothing it. I'd noticed him doing that before. Without looking at me, he spoke. 'I don't really have the time...'

'Of course, of course...' I held up a hand. 'I'm sure you have a lot of other work on.'

'It's not that...' He glanced away, and I could see he had difficulty in explaining. 'I'm sort of... not keen on working too many hours at the moment.'

'Oh... sure. No problem.' Although I barely knew this man, already he appeared quite a paradox. He seemed to have great knowledge, but on the other hand didn't want to work. Something didn't stack up. And the other thing was, I didn't like lazy people. Call it judgemental if you like, but they just didn't appeal to me.

I felt a sense of discomfort between us, and I was sorry I had pushed him on the work front. In silence, we walked back the way we had come. As Phil turned to leave, he appeared to be struggling with something. 'Perhaps... I'll have to have a look... maybe I could spare a few hours.'

I knew well that the garden certainly required far more than a few hours. 'It's fine Phil. I understand.'

'No... I mean... I may be able to offer something. Even if I get you going and then get someone appropriate to take it over.' And then he rushed on. 'I'm not sure how long I'm staying. I'll give it some thought.'

'Okay.' I nodded slowly.

'I'll come tomorrow and look around.'

'Okay,' I repeated, hoping I hadn't made a mistake.

*

'You'd think Wilbur was an old pro at this,' Lou flung over her shoulder, as she snapped with her camera. 'And now,' she instructed her children, 'one over here with the crimson azaleas behind you, and a glimpse of the river in the background. Bob darling, just move slightly in front of Lakshmi. Lakshmi help him. No Bob we don't need Wilbur in all of them. Just leave him be.'

I placed the afternoon tea tray on the cast iron table under the white wisteria covered arbour. Calling to Wilbur, I tossed him a doggy treat. Taking a moment, I sat down on the teak garden seat which was flanked either side by two Anduze pots shaped in the classical style. Blissfully relaxing, I crossed my legs. From this pretty perch, I was able to appreciate the house.

Admiring the climbing roses that trellised around the front, the suddenness and intensity of their blossoming bought me a delightful surprise. Sighing with pleasure, I glanced around taking in the beauty of the rest of the front garden. I liked Phil's suggestion of replanting the Anduze pots with English Box clipped into a dome. He appeared to have an eye for detail. It was exactly what this place required.

For a while my eyes followed the children at play, unaware their mother was snapping away at them. Lately, I had come to realise that there was no greater pleasure then watching them explore the garden. It seemed to bring them such joy.

And I cannot lie, they were not the only ones.

Smiling with a sense of satisfaction, I called to Lou. 'Teatime when you're ready.'

With her camera still around her neck, she flopped down on a chair opposite me, the tinkling from her wrists reminding me of our mother, although Lou's tinkling came from some pretty wicked looking cuffs and some mighty looking knuckledusters. The girl had a distinct style all of her own.

Dolling out pink and white iced biscuits to the children, with mild concern, I kept my eyes upon them as they skipped through the hedges, Lakshmi's blonde ponytail flying out behind as she weaved in and out. Wilbur, excited by the children cocked his leg, and marked his territory on nearly every tree within cooee distance.

Catching the look of unease that crossed my face, Lou straightened her back. 'Are you still worried about snakes? Should I call them back?'

'I'm not as worried as I was. Now that it's cooler weather they're probably all hibernating. We'll keep our eyes on them though.' I passed her a mug of tea. 'Phil said the chance of me ever seeing another one was slim. But all the same...'

'Phil?'

'New gardener... or something.' I chewed on my bottom lip. 'Not sure if I made the right decision there but I'll let you know.'

Lou glanced around. Her face wore the look of satisfaction. 'God, this is a kid's paradise, or for that matter... adult's paradise. You could turn it into something like the Playboy Mansion. You know all of those cool pool parties they have. Adults only... how I would love that.'

'Yuk Lou, you're all talk,' I told her, wrinkling my nose and pulling my legs up onto the bench, and wrapping my arms around them. 'I couldn't think of anything worse.'

She flashed me a look. 'A girl can dream can't she?'

Shaking my head, I placed both of my hands around the mug of hot tea, relishing the beautiful time of day. Earlier, I had helped the children make *tussie mussies*, small old fashioned posies. It had become their favourite pastime whenever they spent time with me.

Together we had cut long sprigs of rosemary, lavender, and curly parsley along with small fragrant roses and tied them together with pretty curling ribbon. It had fast become a habit for them to always take something home from Carmody House's abundant garden, either something pretty or something edible. The children had even begun to leave a change of clothes with me, so we could get outside, get our hands into the earth, and get truly dirty. More than once, I had pondered on the delight something so simple could bring.

Dreamily I turned to Lou. 'How's it going over at Dad's?' Lou and the children were at Johnny's once again. This time it appeared final.

Lou shrugged. 'Dad's offered to pay for me to do a photography course. You know,' she said, sitting up taller, 'I am going to do it this time.' Strangely enough, I believed her.

'It's always been your thing.' I could barely remember a time when she hadn't had a camera in her hand, or her pocket, or looped around her neck. Her first one had been a present from Johnny, a little black Instamatic, back when people shot on film. Many years ago, when our parents saw how enthused she was, they allowed her to convert her walk-in-robe into a darkroom. Of course, that was long before she found boys and marijuana. In recent years one of her counsellors had suggested that her picture taking was a strategy of removing herself from what was going on around her and viewing life as a spectator.

Thoughtfully, Lou nodded. 'I do find it therapeutic you know. I love the entire process from taking pictures, to printing in the dark room. Dad's let me set up one at his house now.' She paused for a few seconds. 'Did I tell you I took my portfolio into that guy down on the corner of James Street? He appeared to think I was a natural.' With infectious enthusiasm, she continued. 'He told me to get out there and do it. So I've been photographing everything, people mostly.'

I had never seen her more determined. I watched her face. Was it possible she was finally growing up? Alleluia!

Lou continued on dreamily. 'Most of the people have their backs to the camera, but there's something about them that I find intensely interesting.' Smiling, she shrugged. 'The way they're walking or standing, what they're wearing or what they're doing.' She narrowed her eyes. 'There's a sort of beauty in their everyday moments.' And then her voice changed, as if she was coming out of the trance she was in. 'I think the course will give me the confidence I need. Plus I've got to do it for the kids Peach. Dad's spoken to Aunt Honey and she is going to help out with them.'

Thoughts of wonderful afternoon teas, with Victorian sponges fresh from the oven, smelling like heaven and oozing with rich raspberry jam, along with generous bosomy hugs, with soothing words of comfort came to mind. 'How perfect, I can't think of anyone better. How is the old darling?'

'As grandmotherly as ever, and let's face it, the kids could do with a bit of that.' We both smiled in agreement, and then her face clouded over. 'I know I've left it late, but finally I've realised there's only one thing wrong with kids from a broken home...'

'And that is?' I asked.

'Living in a broken home one more day.'

I looked at her thoughtfully and realised she wasn't just talking about her children. 'Is… is that what you think we did?' I took a sip of tea, my eyes fixed on her over the rim of the mug.

Glancing away, she shrugged. 'At times, and then at other times I think we had the best childhood any kids could have.'

I had never been brave enough to discuss this openly with Lou before, instead I took it upon myself to protect her.

'I think…' she said, 'you and I had different experiences.'

I was puzzled. 'How do you mean?'

'Well, although we both had Bea, she loved your father more than she loved mine. And I wanted her to love my father more.'

A slight tone of indignation crept into my voice. 'I did too, you know. I mean, Alexandre was Alexandre, but Johnny's always been my dad as well.'

'Yes, of course, of course, and he is,' she rushed on, realising she had offended me. 'It's just that once Alexandre came back on the scene nothing was ever the same, and I was always worried Bea would leave, and eventually she did.'

'But sweetie, we were much older by then,' I said gently, however I knew exactly what she meant. I had felt the same way. Plus we had both decided to stay with Johnny. I had seen it as our choice.

'Do you know, just after she moved over here to New Farm, I was almost expelled from school…'

I interrupted, laughing, 'Oh I remember all right!'

She looked sideways at me, but continued. 'You were always Miss Perfect and so studious. It was your last year of high school. I had just turned 15 and was so angry. I had such attitude with everyone. I used to test Bea to see if she loved me enough. I mean, I always felt she loved *you* more because *you* were the almighty Alexandre's daughter, but I was just Johnny's. Good old bloody Johnny.'

'*Lou...*' A feeling of sadness filled my chest. I ached for her.

'It's how I felt.' Shrugging she glanced away. I could not help but notice the rapid flutter of her eyelids before she turned back to me. 'Bea was always buying me things. Later she'd say how ungrateful I was. And I probably was, because I didn't want those things, I wanted her. And I knew it was Alexandre's money paying for it anyway, so it meant nothing to me. Easy come, easy go. But her love and attention… that's all I actually wanted. I began to do all sorts of stuff. Deliberately not taking my lunch to school became frequent. Then ringing her and demanding she bring me something to eat. It was a test. If she turned up, she loved me. Or I'd end up at a friend's house on the other side of town, and then ring her and tell her Dad couldn't pick me up and she had to come immediately. It took me years to get over being angry. Particularly once she began going backwards and forwards to France to visit Alexandre. One minute she was away, and then she'd return and expect to tell me how to behave. I used to think that the week before she couldn't have given a rat's arse, and then the next week she was laying down the law. I couldn't help but feel she chose Alexandre over us.'

'To be fair, she wasn't exactly a laying-down-the-law sort really, was she?'

Lou shrugged again. 'I think you know what I mean.' We were both silent for a minute and then she continued. 'Anyway you were always the strong one. You always coped. It hasn't been that easy for me.'

'I think you're being strong now. I really do. And I'm not as tough as I look. I've had my days of sheer hell.' I felt my throat close over and I swallowed hard to stop the tears. With an attempt at humour, I continued. 'There were days when it was somewhere between the second chunky Kit Kat and the fourth soy latte before I realised I may have needed some help.' And then I became serious once again. 'But I'm coming through the other side, and you will too.'

Lou nodded. For a while the two of us sat in companionable silence, finishing our tea and enjoying the peace of the garden. And then I changed the subject. 'Now listen, there's something I wanted to talk to you about. It may take a little pressure off.' I paused momentarily. 'I want to pay for the kid's education. It's the least I can do.' I caught the look of surprise on her face. I'd never been sure if she'd known Papa had paid for her education along with mine. Plus I'd kept the exact amount of money I'd inherited from Papa a secret. But I wanted to pay it on.

I nodded my head towards the children. 'Knowledge is power, and those two are going to be powerful sources to be reckoned with.'

Her face was shocked. 'Peach, you don't have to.'

'I want to.' I shrugged. 'The rate I'm going, it doesn't look like I'll have any children of my own. Don't deny me this.'

'Oh Peach, you always look after me.' She came across to the bench and hugged me.

'Yes, but sweetie, it's time to grow up and be responsible. No more bad decisions.' I looked at her and laughed. 'Well, not so many okay?'

'It's okay for you, you've always been clever and applied yourself. It doesn't come that easy to me.'

'Well it's time,' I said firmly, sounding like her parent, as I had always done.

I watched as Lou's eyes took in the house. 'It's true what I said earlier Peach, this house and garden would make the most perfect family home. Imagine being a child and growing up here.'

'Don't remind me sweetie. I honestly think that's not going to be for me. My biological clock has been ticking uncontrollably for years, and it's fast running out, and there's not a damn thing I can do about it. That's why I'm turning the house into a luxurious B&B. I need to focus on something else or I'll go crazy. Anyway, with my business background, I know I can do this and do it well. And I'm looking forward to the challenges it will bring.'

'You say it all so simply.'

'I might sound that way, but it's killing me inside. But what else am I to do? I have to move on. I wasn't as lucky as you to have those two munchkins to take with me.' I glanced over at the crouching figures of Lakshmi and Bob, who were threading fallen hot pink azalea flowers through Wilbur's collar.

'What about Marty? What's happening there? You've been seeing an awful lot of him.'

'Mmmm… I know no one believes me,' my voice carried a frustrated edge, 'but *he is* just a good friend. A really good friend.' I pulled at the long leaf of a spider lilly and ran it through my fingers. Both of us watched as the children led a patient Wilbur around the garden on his lead.

'Don't go too far,' Lou called after them, 'Stay where we can see you.' She turned back to me. 'Really? Are you sure? You know Peach, take it from me, guys don't want to be good friends.'

I shrugged. 'We've never even kissed. We have a lot of history but we don't have that type of relationship.'

'Are you kidding?' Lou squealed. 'God I would have ravished that gorgeous body long ago. What's wrong with you woman?'

My tone carried an air of annoyance and sarcasm. 'It's pretty simple… I'm not in love with him Lou.'

I caught the look of impatience on her face, as she shot back at me, 'I'm not sure what love's got to do with it, but I believe *like* helps a lot and lust is essential. So anytime you don't want him honey, send him my way. I've always thought he was hot.' And with a flick of her wrist, she gave me a look.

Surprised, I looked at her. '*Really?* I set you guys up years ago.' Loving both of them as I did, I had thought that they could have been good for each other, however one date later and Lou told me in no uncertain terms, he was too straight for her. Marty had simply said she was kooky. I agreed with him, and smiled at the memory of it now.

Lou broke into my thoughts. 'Yeah, I know, I know. He's not my type. I was only joking.'

I couldn't help myself. 'What… tall, good-looking, hardworking, nice guy… no I see why he wouldn't be your type.' We both laughed.

Lou poked her tongue out at me. 'Well, you said you don't think he's yours.'

'No, he is my type. There's just not that… *thing* there. Well I don't think there is anyway.'

We both looked up as we heard the kids squeal out with laughter. From where we sat in the arbour, the familiar slightly lanky physique of Marty came around the corner with Bob on his shoulders, and Lakshmi in his arms. Bob had his hands wrapped around Marty's eyes and although we knew he could see, he pretended not to, much to the children's delight and was stumbling about.

The moment I had seen him, my heart skipped a beat. I thought he was Davis, the two of them similar in so many ways, and with his face half covered by Bob's little hands, even more so. Also, quite unlike himself, Marty's hair was much longer at the moment and curling on his collar, just like Davis's used to.

I clenched my hands to stop them shaking. One minute I was excited about the day and confident with where I was going, the next I was a blithering mess. I hated having these feelings. They unsettled me for days. Just when I thought I was getting a handle on it, something would happen and I'd be a crying mess yet again. Standing up, I downed the last of my tea a little quicker than planned and noticed Lou watching me.

'I didn't realise it had gotten so late. I'm sorry I'm not ready Marty. Lou will look after you while I quickly change. There are Coronas in the fridge and limes in the fruit bowl.'

Tonight we were going to the Lyric theatre to see a play.

*

From under the shower, I reminded myself I had to push that Phil Hunter for his tax file number. Pleasingly, he had been quite a few times now. Although a little spasmodic with his hours, I still had to sort out payment. I'd mentioned it already, attempting to work out what rate I should pay him. He wasn't exactly much help and it frustrated me. The man obviously had no interest in money. I would speak to him again tomorrow and sort it out once and for all.

With nothing more on than my navy bra and panties, both trimmed in latte lace, I stood in front of the mirror. Reaching for my Pierucci navy dress, I stepped into it and then spent an inordinate amount of time doing up the finicky buttons. Wrapping the belt around once and then back to the front, I tied it into an expert bow. Still in disorganised chaos, I riffled through a drawer and pulled out a black silk pouch. Removing the trio of silver necklaces, I fastened the clasp at the back of my neck. I took some notes and a credit card from my wallet and placed them into the side pocket of a small silver evening bag, and then I searched through the side zipper looking for some coins just in case. I pulled out a piece of paper. Uncertain of what it was, I unfolded it. It was, *The List.*

I read through – integrity, family man, balanced, selfless, centred, has to be the man. Mmmm, it did sound like someone I knew. But was there a spark there? I felt I should have known that without wondering. Also, I needed those feelings about Davis that kept rearing their ugly head to be over. The conversation I'd had earlier with Lou had unsettled me. In different ways we were both victims of our childhood.

The unresolved pain of Bea and Johnny's separation had fuelled a hunger in me for the perfect relationship, and the perfect *happy ever after*. On the face of it all, the idea of being completed by one man had appeared deeply romantic to me. I thought if I'd had that, I would have had it all, and I could not let it go. However for Davis, my fantasy weighed down our relationship with expectations that he could never live up to. It only worked if I continued to be the person he needed, the person that completed him.

At that moment, it struck me that that person no longer existed. A weight lifted from my shoulders. Strength had come when I had been forced by adversity, and I was discovering my life was something I was in charge of. I did like that feeling.

Maybe I needed to make some more decisions. This business with Marty was silly. I think we both knew it, both grasping at the past.

I was not immune to the idea that somewhere in the universe there was a person who was just right for me, someone who would respond to all the things that were important to me, and with whom I could share my life. It was something that I had begun to ponder on more and more. In spite of Bea and Johnny, in spite of Davis, I had always lived my life as if all things were possible. Surely this could be as well.

Standing, I turned for one last glance in the mirror. I smoothed my hands over my dress and then walked down the stairs and briefly stood at the front door. From there I had a perfect view of Lou and the children and Marty. I stopped in my tracks. Lou with her long legs crossed, her blonde head thrown back, was the perfect picture. Peals of laughter rang out. Marty stood watching her, his legs apart and his hands in the front pockets of his pants. He wore the look of delight. They seemed like quite the little family. And that… stirred no emotion in me whatsoever.

Chapter 11

The sky was sapphire blue, not a cloud to be seen. After four eventful days in Paris catching up with old friends of Bea's, we had boarded the TGV fast train at the bustling Gare de Lyon, and headed south to Avignon, happy to sit back and watch the spectacular scenery go by.

Two and a half hours later, with some difficulty, we dragged our heavy suitcases from the upstairs level of the train, concerned it would pull out of the station before we had time to disembark. On the platform below with our bags piled around us, courtesy of far too much Parisian shopping, we wondered how we were going to get our luggage any further. It was with some relief when we were welcomed by Louis, the chateau's driver. Instantly he took charge of our weighty cases. Mine, I was embarrassed to admit was the heavier.

'I 'ave no English,' he told us, which was of course not a problem for my mother, and be damned if I was going to let it be one for me.

'*Bonjour* Louis,' I cried, thrilled to speak my schoolgirl French to him, my eyes darting around, wondering if after all of these years, anything would appear familiar.

With Bea's exhibition behind her, she had uncharacteristically insisted it was now time for me to see the family chateau. Even though I was right in the middle of the renovations, she told me that as in the past, there would always be some excuse. She was right.

The chateau was now owned by Henri from a neighbouring property. The two properties had been merged to form a larger wine address, with my father's chateau often used for special events. We had timed our visit well, as only last week,

Hermes had taken it over for a photographic shoot.

Bea knew Henri well. She explained that although he was younger than my father, he often reminded her of him. I was unsure how I felt about that.

Sitting beside my mother in the back of the car, I had never seen her like she was. She appeared as taut as a finely strung violin, with her hands tightly clasped in her lap. Although to me she had never looked more beautiful. Not for the first time of late, I pondered how our twenty year age gap appeared to be narrowing. Her hair was loose and falling down her back in shiny blond curls, her erect posture from her many years of dancing an advantage. Her blue eyes drank in the view from the car window, as if it was the first time she had witnessed such scenes. I wondered at her thoughts, knowing that for her, this was the first trip back to France since Papa had died.

Suddenly, she turned to me, her eyes flashing. 'You know, when I was growing up, I knew there were two things I had to do. One, be an artist in France, and two, wear lots of berets.' She laughed, and I caught her mood. To me, it was as if by that one sentence, she was summing up her childhood years.

France was in the full throws of spring. The trees were all in leaf and undulating fields of vines shimmered in their first leaves in the gentle golden light. As we snaked through the gently, hilly, narrow roads and tiny picturesque villages, we passed many vineyards on either side, with their long rows of thick stalks and green leaves, rows of fragrant lavender, and fields of gnarled olive trees.

With a feeling of unexpected joy, my face pressed to the car window, I inhaled the lavender fragranced breeze, watching the most spectacular scenic landscapes, none more beautiful than the delicate powder puff blossoms that fell from the fruit trees, as if confetti. I pointed to the roses growing in abundance at the end of each row of vines.

'Yes,' Bea nodded, explaining, 'They are planted to stop the ploughing oxen from nibbling vines as they turn to start the next row.'

As the road narrowed, the car slowed. I was sure only one car could manage at a time, however I soon realised that cars coming in the opposite direction were not afraid of the tight squeeze. They barrelled along at breakneck speed, their engines roaring. In comparison, Louis appeared more courteous. Although Bea seemed undeterred, I could not help but hold my breath each time, until they passed, turning to look after them, as if a miracle had occurred that we had missed each other.

I spun back around in my seat as we passed a romantically dilapidated structure, appearing to be in the first throws of a renovation. Three men dressed in work overalls casually leant against a wall, cigarettes to their lips. Feeling knowledgeable on some small level, I wondered if they were smoking *Gauloises*, the French cigarettes that I always thought sounded terribly romantic. However the thing that I noticed most was the causal manner of the men. In that glimpse, it appeared they were in no rush, a little different from my own project at home, where daily a dozen men or so swarmed over the property.

It was different here. Life had a go slow feeling about it. I smiled, feeling my excitement continue to bubble up inside. Even when a slim mean dog on a chain barked sharply at the car, it did not deter my jubilant mood. *'Bonjour un chien!'* I called out the window waving, laughter still in my voice. As I glanced back the dog appeared to pause, perhaps stunned by my pathetic French. I did not care, and only laughed again.

After some time, we turned into a gravelled driveway that

wound its way through fields of olive trees. Finally, the car swept up the long curved driveway beneath an ancient avenue of massive plane trees, my eyes glued to the window, not wanting to miss a thing.

As we merged from the shadows, I caught my first glimpse of my father's chateau. Knowing I had left as a baby, although still hoping to have some memory of it, I felt a mix of awe, nervousness and excitement all well up. The car circled the gravelled driveway, and drew to a halt. From there, I was afforded full view of the chateau and its steep scalloped edged terracotta roof, rich cream limestone, and ornate black balconies. It appeared that duck egg blue shutters protected all of the windows and doors from the penetrating Provincial sun.

Instantly, I knew that this was the exact recipe I needed to finish Carmody House. Hungrily, my eyes scanned every detail, delighting in the manicured garden, with colours so beautiful it made me think of an impressionist painting.

Laughing with enchantment, I climbed from the car, as a pair of pugs charged out the grand entry doors, distracting me, both jumping up at once. I laughed with delight, so used to Bea's long line of pugs.

'*Arreter, arreter,*' a charismatic, heavily accented voice commanded the dogs to stop. The man did not have to speak again, as both dogs instantly obeyed, although continued to greet us with snuffles and wet noses.

I turned with delight to our host, a man perhaps in his early fifties, who came towards us, his arms stretched out. His attractiveness hit me instantly.

'*Bonjour belle dames.*' His tanned face creased about his blue eyes, where the crow's feet were already long and deep. 'Bea it has been too long.' This man appeared to be aging in exquisite taste and had the kind of smile that radiated instant warmth, warmth I was attracted to. His French accent was so delicious, I almost declared myself available and ready to elope at a moment's notice.

With anticipation, I watched as he held my mother at arm's length studying her, before kissing both of her cheeks, giving me a chance to study him. He was handsome. Handsome as hell. His body language carried an air of self-confidence, and his clothes, a black opened neck shirt and suit, were impeccable.

And then he turned to me, smiling broadly, his blue eyes, beneath a full head of steel grey hair that curled on his collar, appraising me. 'Ahhh, Peach! You are a beautiful woman. Beautiful! But 'ow could I be surprised. You are your mother's daughter. *Non!*' Taking my hand, he drew me in. And may I say, I was very pleased to be drawn in, as it was not so much what he said, but the way he said it. I inhaled the wonderful masculine fragrance of wood, leather and tobacco, with a touch of fruitiness. It did not escape me that my body reacted to the delectability of him, understanding for the first time how arousing pheromones really were.

Feeling all floaty, and warm in places that had not been warm for some time, I realised I was blushing. Wondering what had come over me, I then felt myself batt my eyes at him. As if reading my mind, he gave me a look, and instantly I felt our energies connect. I gave a sharp intake of breath. By the look on his face, I realised he had not been immune to it. He kissed my hand, which I realised he was still holding, and the feeling of warmth travelled all the way up my arm. Okay, so he was not only handsome, but charming as well. *Ooh la la!*

He ushered us in though a fragrant rose covered stone archway, in through the huge timber entry doors, into my father's house. The house I had lived in for the first twelve months of my life. As I followed him across the square flagstone floored hall, dominated by a sweeping stone staircase, and a giant fireplace full of neatly-cut logs piled one on top of another, my head turned looking from side to side. On the mantelpiece, ancient bottles of wine were lined up on display. My eyes darted taking in details, searching for something, perhaps some familiarity.

There was a distinct fragrance in the air. I inhaled deeply, smelling a combination of beeswax, linseed oil, freshly cut flowers and lavender. I found it comforting and wondered if perhaps it held memories for me.

Henri escorted us through the high ceilinged drawing room. The long crimson drapes framed French doors that opened onto a wide stone balustrade terrace, where a table had been laid with blue and white linen and gleaming glassware and china in preparation for us. Our bags had already been whisked away to our rooms.

'It is warm here in the sun,' Henri told us. The pugs followed, trotting off to noisily sniff the borders and cock their legs against the balustrade.

Henri had come from a meeting and apologised for his formal attire. I was very happy with his attire. In fact, I silently wished he be so well dressed for the entirety of our stay.

The sound of the running water from a nearby fountain was both cool and tranquil. I took the first deep breath I had taken in a long time. This visit was timely. Forget the yoga, I should have come here sooner. The pugs stretched out languidly at Henri's feet in the sunshine. Briefly, the thought crossed my mind that I would be happy doing the same. With some difficulty, I tore my attention away from Henri and glanced around, drinking in the details. Beyond the spacious lawn, dry stone walls and fragrant lavender beds gave way to fields of shimmering olives.

For a while, I was quiet with my thoughts, thinking how different my life could have been had I had grown up here.

The chilled champagne, a welcome delight, was served with a tiny dish of rustic olives, and a small farmhouse goat's cheese. It was extremely difficult not to feel swept away in such superb surroundings.

Bea was beaming and chatty, and I watched intently as I saw a side of her I had never seen. Soon Henri was insisting he show us around the vineyard. Bea, obviously having seen it many times, declined gracefully, floating off for a siesta. Now in his shirtsleeves, Henri escorted me around the grounds. I followed him down the wide stone steps to the garden, where, as he opened an old iron gate, it whined on its rusty ancient hinges. He ushered me ahead of him. Together we strolled the property.

Henri explained how the large pebbles found in the local soil, stored up the heat of the day and gave the vines the energy they needed to reach their full potential. With Henri's gentle guidance, he educated me on *terroir*... flavours that correspond to the time and place... vintage, acidity, growth, aroma and colour. He promised by the end of my sojourn, those words would roll off my tongue as if they were my everyday vocabulary.

Eventually, as we walked around the properties, Henri told me about his early years growing up in the area, and the rich French heritage that was the heart of his life. He explained that my father had been like an older brother to him. After a couple of hours, I felt I knew more about Henri than I did my own father. It was an uncomfortable thought. Why had I waited so long to come? I knew Emerald Green would say that I was here now because I was meant to be here. I held that thought.

We wandered back through a series of five *potages*, and with Henri as my expert guide, I was filled with ideas for my kitchen garden at Carmody House. On our return to the chateau the shadows fell long, and the aroma of *Boefe en Daube* wafting from the kitchen, sent my already heightened senses into overdrive.

The day was full and exciting like no other I had experienced. With clarity, I was able to grasp exactly how my mother must have felt all those years ago coming to this beautiful place in the world, where the light was so beautiful, and revered by so many, and then meeting my father. If he was anything like Henri, I now had no doubt why she fell so heavily. I would have as well.

That night we dined at one end of a huge nineteenth century hunting table. I pictured my mother here many years earlier, this being a norm for her. For me, it was surreal.

The food, as anticipated, was delicious. The beef was bought to the table in an earthenware cocotte, still bubbling and steaming. The conversation flowed freely backwards and forwards across the table. We relived every moment since our arrival, telling tales, embellishing incidents, and savouring the intense moments of the day. As the evening progressed, the wine flowed more freely, and Henri talked with passion of the wine industry. Flickering candles, glowing ambers, and delicious food made a perfect end to my first day in Provence.

Petit dejeuner, breakfast the next day was a lingering affair. We sat in the garden, the fresh air suffused with birdsong, eating crusty bread with lavender honey, and drinking strong coffee with hot milk.

Earlier, as I had peered through the shutters of my bedroom, an enormous boudoir, which I had been told was my late grandmother's, I spotted Bea, clad only in a long white voile nightdress, leaving her bare footprints on the dewy grass. The scent of newly cut grass and sweet smelling shrubs rose up in the air. I watched as Bea draped a white shawl around her shoulders.

Surreptitiously I gazed, unable to tear my eyes away, wondering at her thoughts. Sitting on a teak garden bench, with a curtain of classic pencil pines behind, with youthful energy she pulled her knees up, and wrapped her arms loosely around them, pensively resting her chin. After a while, she rose to her feet and began to pick a small posy of lavender.

I continued to watch as Henri came across the stone terrace and greeted her, kissing her on both cheeks. He offered his arm and together they continued on her exploration of the garden, occasionally her throwing her head back in laughter while he patted her hand. With him in a crispy cream coloured shirt, khaki chinos, tan leather belt and shoes, and a cashmere sweater thrown loosely around his shoulders, alongside my mother's night attire, they made quite a pair, and there appeared to be a genuine fondness between them.

I sat on the edge of the four-poster iron bed, which was draped in white linen, and, not for the first time in twenty four hours, realised I knew so little about my mother.

By the time I came down for breakfast Bea was already dressed in a long white caftan, and waiting for me in the garden, a white rose tucked behind one ear.

I kissed her proffered cheek, noting that she was different in these surrounds, more the lady of the house.

'I see why you were drawn here,' I told her, pulling my chair out, the iron legs noisy on the stone pavers.

Exhaling in a relaxed manner, she nodded. 'It is impossible to visit here and not be swept away by its magnificent beauty.'

With a contentment I had never seen on her face, she glanced around.

'I saw you out here earlier.'

'Yes,' she turned back to me, her face glowing lively. 'Your papa was quite a gardener, and most mornings he picked a posy of flowers for me. The garden has more of him in it than anywhere else.' She smiled wistfully at the thought of him, and her face radiated love. Once again, I was reminded that she was still a beautiful woman and looked nothing of her years.

I kept watching her face, as she continued. 'I wish he were here now. Everything is bursting into flower – and the fragrances, it has never smelt more delicious.'

However, I knew there was more to her wanting him than for the garden.

We were interrupted, as steaming bowls of *cafe crème* were poured by Francoise the housekeeper.

'I didn't know he liked gardening.' But then again I really didn't know much about my papa either. Bea shrugged reflectively, her face showing she'd had the same thought as me.

'What's Henri's story?' I asked, changing the subject, taking a bite of the crusty bread slathered with the fragrant honey. I nodded my head, and rolled my eyes in appreciation of how something so simple could taste so fantastic.

'Henri?' My mother laughed, and pushed a blond strand of hair behind her ear. 'Henri is a rather beautiful man. Is he not?'

'Yes... he is rather good looking,' I said, thinking that was the understatement of the year. With both hands, I placed the coffee cup to my lips, and sipped the hot liquid, hoping it would hide the transparency of my face.

Bea didn't appear to notice. 'He reminds me a little of

your papa, one of those delicious creatures that make women swoon simply being around them.'

I raised my brows in question at her. 'Oh?' Fully knowing exactly what she was talking about.

Bea batted her hand at me. 'Don't look at me like that. Henri is like a brother to me. I see the attraction that other women feel, however he truly is a wonderful friend. He was good to Papa as well.'

I nodded, thoughtful for a few moments. 'Is he married?'

Now it was Bea's turn to raise her perfect brows in question at me. I shook my head as if dismissing her. She explained anyway. 'Yes as a matter of fact, to the tall buxom blonde Michelle, quite good looking in her day, however perhaps a little matronly and formidable now. She lives in Nice and he lives here. As far as I know they have not divorced, although they have not lived together for many, many years. They have three grown sons and a couple of grandchildren. Perhaps it's too much trouble to get a divorce, especially as Michelle is still involved in the business and comes up from time to time. They appear very respectful when they are together.' Bea shrugged.

'It sounds quite lonely though?'

Bea laughed, her fingers tapping the white clothed table. 'I think Henri does quite well for himself and I'm not sure about Michelle, although there are stories that she has a secret lover. Perhaps he is married?' Once again, she shrugged her shoulders. 'Who knows?' She took in the look on my face. 'Don't be like that darling, relationships are every private. You'd be surprised how many people already have everything worked out, they just don't wish to broadcast it to the world for everyone to judge them.'

'I don't like the sound of it, that's all.'

'I know. You're the incurable romantic. One great love all your life.'

'You can talk. Anyway, I am hoping that's not going to be the case, or I'm going to be pretty damn lonely,' I told her wryly, thinking she was rather blunt.

She waved a hand at me. 'Yes, but darling I have a strong feeling you haven't found him yet. He's still out there.' Absentmindedly, she waved her hand behind her towards a tottering old gentleman, slowly wheeling a wheelbarrow laden with rakes and gardening tools. It appeared far too heavy for him, and I wondered if I should offer to help.

'Well I hope that's not him. I'd like someone with a bit more life thank you,' I said indicating the man over her shoulder.

She turned her head, her face lighting up. 'It's Pierre,' she said, excited at seeing him. 'Oh Pierre...' she called. She stood and hastened her step towards the aging gardener.

'*Madame Avanel...*'

I watched, noting the joy on the old gent's face at seeing my mother. I glanced around me. This was my mother's home. Funny, but we don't always stop to think about our parents being more than simply that. We forget that they have identities beyond us. And even though Bea had always been a free spirit, I still hadn't taken the time to give her life too much thought outside our little circle.

*

'Louis has the car ready to take you ladies wherever you wish to go,' Henri explained, with a flourish of his hands. Difficult as it was to tear ourselves away from the beautiful food, there was much to explore, and many calories to burn in order to make room for the next delectable French meal.

With his razor-sharp tailoring, I decided Henri's style was

one of a mature Ralph Lauren catalogue model. Hmmm… My fingers twitched and I realised that my hand, as if a life of its own, wished to reach out and stroke his cashmere sweater. Soft and precious, cashmere's appeal had always been undeniable to me. However, I held myself in check, wondering what on earth was going on with me.

'Thank you Henri, but I may stay in today,' Bea told him. I knew she felt my father's presence at the chateau and was loath to spend time away from it.

I stood up and smoothed the skirt of my sundress. 'That sounds lovely thankyou Henri. I think I will take the opportunity to explore a little further afield.'

He gave a nod. 'I will tell Louis to be ready for you shortly. You may need a light jacket.'

I skipped up the stone staircase and along the corridor to my room. Here at the chateau, I had the feeling I had escaped my former life and entered another world. Upon entering, I noticed my bed had already been made, the traditional snowy *Marseilles* quilt pulled up and smoothed flat, the rounded corners of the hem, not touching the floor.

As if reading my mind, the look was *exactly* the way I had pictured the guests' beds at Carmody house. I wondered if it was possible that some small memory of them existed for me from when I was a baby and that was the reason I was drawn to them.

Inspired by the beautiful white needlework for which *Marseilles* and the surrounding Provence region are known, the distinctive style involved creating intricate raised patterns, by stuffing shapes in between two pieces of cotton. I would have loved to take five home in my luggage, but knew after my Parisian shopping and the train debacle, that would not be possible.

I found the cardigan I was searching for in the *armoir*. The ribbon rullet on it shaped into pretty bows. My dress reminded me of spring. Square necked and fitting beautifully over my breasts, it showed off my waist, and then flared out into a full skirt. It was my Grace Kelly dress. Although my toe-peeper wedges were rather glamorous, they were still comfortable enough for exploring.

Spritzing my wrists and cleavage with one of the Annick Goutal fragrances I had purchased in Paris, I replaced the fluted beribboned bottle back on the antique mirrored tray on top of the dresser. With a refresh of my lipstick, I slung a soft calfskin handbag over my shoulder, and placed my cardigan inside.

On the gravel forecourt, I was surprised to see Henri waiting in a vintage Aston Martin Roadster.

'Waiting for a hot date?' I called.

He let out a burst of surprised laughter. 'I believe that is you Madame,' he quipped, climbing out and coming around to the passenger side.

'Oh... I thought Louis was...'

'He was,' he held the car door open for me. 'But I 'ave sent him on other errands. As I 'ave to pick a parcel up in Cannes, I thought you might enjoy the scenic trip, and I could do with the company. We will be gone most of the day, so I'ave instructed Francoise to inform your mother.'

He took a baseball cap from the glove compartment and pulled it on as we roared off under the shadows of the massive plane trees, down the driveway.

Feeling that tell-tale rush of excitement that accompanies the start of something memorable, I asked, 'I hope I'm not holding you up from your work?' I tucked my billowing hair behind my ears.

'Not at all.' He glanced at me. 'I do 'ave one small errand and it gives me a chance to appreciate some of the reasons I live in this part of the world. Sometimes we forget.' He indicated the rolling patchwork sea of greens either side of the road, so many different shades, and each one more deeper, brighter or dazzling than the one next to it.

'Just beautiful.' I grabbed at my hair once again.

'It is annoying you, *non?*' he asked, indicating my hair.

'A little.'

Frowning, he glanced over at me. 'I will put the top up.'

'No, please don't. I love it.' I had to admit the sensation was exhilarating.

'*D'accord.*' He nodded smiling. 'I thought after Cannes we might stop off at the village of Mougins for lunch at one of my favourite restaurants with the best view of the *Cote D'azur.*'

The valley was trilling with cicadas. And once again either side of the road were lined with vineyards – long rows of stalks and green leaves.

Henri was an excellent guide and time flew as we talked for much of the picturesque journey. My head went from side to side, admiring the exceptionally beautiful scenery of oceans of lavender and red poppies colouring the fields, punctuated by the sight and the subtle fragrance of cypresses, parasol pines and plane trees. The region, a treasure trove of wonderful monuments and idyllic countryside, was as if it had been laid out by an artist planning his next painting.

Henri explained that it was a tradition in Provence for landlords to plant three Cypress trees near the entrance to their property to welcome guests for a drink, a meal or bed. Loving the idea, I wondered how I could do this at Carmody House.

Passing through a small village I laughed and pointed at a large black snuffling pig tethered to a stake in front of a shop.

'I like your laugh,' Henri told me, his tanned face creasing around his eyes. 'It makes you an even more beautiful woman, if that is possible,' his voice low and sexy, his eyes catching mine for a little longer than necessary.

'Oh,' I said, blushing, however I sat a little higher in the seat, stealing another glance at him.

He was watching me with an amused expression on his face.

*

In Cannes, we drove along the palm lined famed promenade, *La Croisette*, the street awash with beautiful people. Excited, I asked Henri if I could walk along the Mediterranean seashore while I waited for him to conduct his business at the Hotel Martinez.

Returning to our designated meeting place a little earlier than expected, I sat under the shady terrace of an open air restaurant, sipping coffee at a corner table, watching the world go by, mesmerised by the yachts and the beautiful sea opposite, thinking I could possibly live in this part of the world forever. I realised that I probably sounded very much like my mother many years earlier.

When Henri returned, he explained that it was imperative for us to make one more stop before we drove to Mougins for lunch. A few blocks further along the boulevard, Henri slowed the car.

'We are 'ere,' he told me, his hand gesturing at the pink marble facade of the Hermes store and its elegantly decorated window. 'You 'ave 'eard of Hermes, I'm sure?' he asked, not waiting for an answer, and coming around to my side of the car to open the door.

'Of course.' I mean, did I know Hermes? Hello, I knew their scarves were precious collectables although up until this moment I had never owned one. However, that had never deterred me from lusting after them.

With his hand in the small of my back, Henri escorted me though the black framed glass door. Tables and chairs were scattered about where clients browsed through catalogues. With my head turning in every direction, I quickly realised that I could easily purchase every possible item to make this luxury brand part of my life, from teacups to bath towels, to wrist cuffs to handbags. Henri ushered me towards the silk wares, while customers busied themselves in front of mirrors.

'We need a *carre*... a ...' Hesitating, Henri touched his head, 'a scarf... for your 'air for the return journey.' He continued with an air of embellishment. 'A beautiful French luxury renowned around the world for their excellence in workmanship. A must for a beautiful woman.' With a wave of his hand he summoned an assistant. 'Something to go with Madame's dress, *s'il vous plait!*'

From the glass topped cabinet, the sales assistant presented the spectacular squares of colourful silk, each one more beautiful than the last. With a flick of her wrist she unfurled them across the counter, watching Henri's face for his approval.

Of course it was exciting, although in the back of my mind I was wondering how much this was going to cost me.

'I think this one,' Henri decided. '*Le jeune.*' His tanned hand held it up to my face. He nodded. '*Parfait!*' he said, handing the yellow scarf with flowers in hues of purples and greens to the assistant.

'Of course,' was all I could say. The selection so magnificent, I would have been unable to make a decision anyway. The scarf was placed in the legendary orange box, tied with a chocolate monogramed ribbon, and placed it in the Hermes carrier bag. The price had not been mentioned. I fumbled for my credit card.

'*Non, non* Peach, allow me please,' Henri insisted, stilling my hand and holding my gaze, once again a little longer than was necessary.

Overwhelmed, I put my hand up. 'Goodness me, Henri no... I cannot allow it.'

'Pffft,' he said dismissing me. He leant in closer. I felt his warm breath on my neck, as once again I inhaled the masculine fragrances of tobacco, wood, leather and something else decidedly fruity, his aftershave, powerful and seductive. He purred, 'Beautiful things for a beautiful woman. It will bring me great pleasure. Please do not deny me.' The vibration of his tone sent shivers up my spine, as his blue eyes held mine. I was electrified by his presence as if he was spring incarnate, coaxing my winter branches into blossom.

Henri took the bag from the assistant, and I realised the woman had barely said a word. Henri had been the only one talking. With a slight bow of his head, he presented me with the carrier bag. '*Avec plaisir,*' was all he said.

I must admit, it certainly had been *pleasurable* for me, although I took a fraction longer than was necessary in accepting it. '*Merci* Henri.'

With his hand in the small of my back, Henri escorted me to the car. I couldn't help feel that there was now something different in my walk. I glanced back briefly to the assistant, however she was already assisting the next client.

In the car, with nervous fingers, I wrapped the scarf around my hair and tied it around my neck at the front. Feeling rather glamorous, I glanced at Henri for his approval.

I flashed my eyes at him and joked, 'Grace Kelly or Audrey Hepburn?'

'*Non, non*. Much more beautiful,' and he took one of my hands and kissed it.

'Henri, you... flirt.' I had almost said the word *old*, however at the last second held back, not wishing to offend such a gorgeous man. I was having the most wonderfully delicious day. The weight of the past year lifted from my shoulders. There was that feeling of escapism once again.

'As I said, I am French. I say 'ow I feel,' he told me, blue eyes unwavering, one hand on the gearstick, the other on the leather steering wheel. It did not escape me that the car had the same fragrance as Henri's aftershave. Notes of leather, wood, tobacco and yes there is was, the hint of blueberries that had intoxicated my senses.

For a split second, I too held his gaze, and then I hastily placed my Roberto Cavalli sunglasses on and crossed my legs. 'And now to Mougins?' I caught his surreptitious look as he glanced at my legs. His look was one of appreciation. And it was perhaps the merest suggestion of a possibility.

'*D'accord*, Mougins.' Henri pulled his cap back down on his head and roared off down the street. I settled into my seat, placing my hands in my lap and exhaled heavily. My thoughts turned to my mother. Finally, I was able to completely understand the seduction of not only Papa, but also Provence. At twenty years of age, it would have been hard for her to have been immune, as I, at the present time was struggling. Hmmm...

To be desired is extremely arousing. A side of me I hadn't felt or seen in the longest time was emerging. It was one I had forgotten had existed. Rejection rocks your confidence. However, right at that moment, I felt attractive because someone of value was finding me attractive. I felt desirable because, I was being desired by such a beautiful man. I felt more of a woman than I had in a long time. I was visible. And that affected every cell in my body: the way I walked, the way I sat, the way I moved, the way I thought... everything.

A little over ten minutes later, Henri slowed the car as we entered the charming town of Mougins. The small medieval village was without a doubt the most wonderful surprise. Instantly, I was seduced by the colourful flowers bordering narrow lanes. Perched from a height of 260 metres, the panoramic sea view was breathtaking. Set amongst pine, olive and cypress trees, it was an artist colony with dozens of studios and galleries, and precisely restored stone cottages with picturesque doorways, and beautifully designed window frames. Wherever I looked, the detail delighted me.

Henri's restaurant had a sense of informal luxury, the waiters greeting him with courteous familiarity.

'The service is excellent, plus they are *tres* discreet.' He whispered over my shoulder while seating me, his breath tickling the back of my neck. Briefly I closed my eyes and put a hand to my chest.

'Oh, do we need to be discreet Henri?' I asked teasing him, attempting to lighten the moment, but all the same, wondering how many other girls he had bought here.

'That's entirely up to you *mon cherie*,' he replied, holding my gaze. I challenged his scrutiny. He threw his head back and laughed a little too loudly.

I sat through lunch feeling radiant, knowing Henri had noticed. Although I must say, Henri was not only wonderful company, he was the perfect gentleman.

However, my downfall was the decadent dessert of intensely flavoured spiced, black chocolate truffle, with salt-caramel ice cream. My tastebuds were not the only part of me that was already stimulated by the *fois gras* terrine and scallops *meuniere*. So by the time I placed the first spoonful of salty caramel ice cream into my mouth, it slipped down my throat with a blissful sigh, and my tastebuds finally went into overdrive and sang to me, *Oh caramel, how much do I love thee, let me count the salty ways.*

Watching me rhapsodise, Henri appeared delighted, and gave a rich velvety laugh. 'This afternoon *mon cherie,* on our return we will drive through Grasse, the perfume capital of the world.'

I nodded, busy taking tiny spoonfuls of the delectable combination into my mouth, savouring, and allowing it to drape over my tongue, filling my mouth with a silky milky feeling in a positively obscene way. Although I had only partaken in two delightfully chilled glasses of champagne, I felt drunk on food, France and Henri. Not necessarily in that order.

I watched as Henri's fingers seductively played with the stem of his champagne flute, slowly and rhythmically stroking it up and down, up and down. Lowering his voice, his delicious French accent was now all the more so. 'Did you know Chanel is one of the few perfume companies to 'ave its own flower fields in Grasse? The local people transform the beautiful coloured petals into subtle and delicate perfume, with love and passion.'

'Love and passion,' I repeated softly as if in a trance, nodding, watching the sensual curve of his lips as he spoke, his story sounding to me, not just of perfume, but of sensuality.

'In every bottle there are moments of passion, love affairs 'ad, and adventures shared.' His glance held mine. 'But long before a spritz of perfume reaches your delicate skin,' he explained, his fingers reaching out and delicately stroking the inside of my wrist of the hand not holding the spoon, 'the fragrance creation begins with a flower. For Chanel No 5, those flowers are May Rose and Jasmine. Twice a year, those flowers are 'arvested in Grasse, and the scent of every bottle begins with them.'

My eyes were mesmerised by his fingers. Swallowing, I glanced from my wrist up to his face, my spoon perched mid-air above the crystal dish.

Speaking slowly, as if disclosing an intimate detail, he continued. 'It is a sensual fragrance...' He emphasised the word sensual in such a way, I caught myself before I moaned audibly. He continued, '... with notes of ylang ylang...' and now his voice had a certain rhythm to it that quickened, 'amber, iris, patchouli, neroli, sandalwood and,' he touched his fingers to his lips and inhaled languidly, 'vanilla.'

'*Oh*,' was all I said, perhaps a little too breathlessly.

'Mmmm.' His murmuring voice sending shivers up my spine and I hung off every word as he continued, '*Tres elegant*, an intoxicating floral blend, perfectly capturing the essence of a woman.'

I put a hand to my chest, breathing deeply.

'Did you enjoy?' he asked, noticing my empty dish.

'*Oh yes*,' I said, placing my spoon into the dish and flopping back in the chair. '*Yes*.'

*

Henri slipped a hand beneath my hair at the back of my neck and pulled me to him, pressing his lips to mine. I didn't pull away. I wanted this. His arms closed around me, strong and hard. His mouth was so soft, his kiss as passionate as I'd thought it would be. Eagerly, I parted my lips letting him in, drinking him in. I wound my arms around his waist inside his linen jacket, feeling his surprisingly firm body beneath his shirt. My stomach swam with pleasure as he ran his tongue down my neck. His hands reached under my skirt.

I was far from home. I felt reckless and very desirable, my body reminding me so.

Intoxicated by the manliness of him, combined with the

scents of France, I forgot everything. I was in a fantasy world where only Henri and I resided.

He didn't attempt to take me the few feet to the bed. Instead with passionate urgency, he swung me around so that my back was against the door, and then as I moaned in need, pressing my face into his neck and knotting my fingers tightly in his hair. Seconds later in an orgasm of exploding intensity, he took me where I stood.

Breathing heavily, I drifted back to consciousness. I opened my eyes and with surprise, blinked a few times against the light, glancing around the bedroom. I arched my back and exhaled, disappointed to have woken from such an intense dream. For a few minutes I just lay there. Stretching my arms out, my hands smoothed the pressed linen embroidered sheets, smelling fresh from the provincial sun. My body throbbed with deliciousness, a feeling I hadn't felt in the longest time. Putting my arms over my head, I snuggled into the feather pillows. Turning on my side, I pulled my legs up and wrapped my arms around them.

Spending the week with Henri had been a wonderful elixir, but I knew Henri was not what I wanted... some things are better left as a fantasy. However, there was no denying that there was something special about this place, which was just what I had needed. It awakened senses like nowhere else I'd been.

As tempting as it was, I knew I did not need to walk the same path as my mother. I had a life in Australia waiting for me. A life I had chosen. And I was not about to give my heart to another man and live his dream.

Languidly, I got out of bed, and padded across the parquet floor over to the *fleur de lis* patterned chaise, and rifled through my wallet to find 'the list'. Yes, that list that Thomas had bullied me into writing. At that moment, I finally comprehended its true value. I also realised I needed to give serious thought to what was going on between Marty and me. And the truth of it was there was nothing, not one damn thing. I knew it and I knew he knew it. Both of us were trying to hang onto something from our past, a past we had both loved at the time, but neither of us were those people any more. We owed ourselves so much more.

Looking at the list now, I realised how incomplete it was. I knew the more time I spent getting to know and remember who I was, the list would be a work in progress.

With fond thoughts of Henri, I smiled and jotted a few words across the paper, *je ne sais quoi* – that certain something, indescribable quality. That was a requirement for me.

*

Louis held the car door open for me.

'I'm not sure how long I'll stay,' Bea told me, pulling a shawl around her shoulders to ward off the early morning chill.

'I know, but I have to go Mum, Thomas has his hands full minding Wilbur and it's not his job to oversee the plumbers. Not to mention, there'll be a barrage of tradesmen knocking on my door in a few days' time.' I kissed her cheek. She wrapped her arms around me. I liked the person she was here. She seemed more motherly.

It was Henri's turn. 'Peach you will be forever welcome, this will always be your 'ome... it was a promise I made your papa.' He held me tight and kissed my cheek, speaking softly for my ears. 'We could have been so good together *mon cherie*. What am I to do?'

I laughed, and kissed his cheek, looking up at him. 'Henri, I know you'll survive... but thank you. I mean it, thank you.' I squeezed his hands and looked into those gorgeous blue eyes. Dressed in my new French fit white jeans and black scalloped top, I climbed into the car before I could change my mind.

Through the window, he handed me a small beautifully wrapped parcel. 'Something for later,' he said, his voice quiet.

As the car circled the drive, I lifted my hand and watched as Henri offered his arm to my mother. I could have fallen in love this week, but instead I'd fallen in lust. It was time to go before it became too difficult.

I opened the wrapping paper and smiled. A bottle of Chanel No 5. *C'est parfait!*

Chapter 12

The rain had ceased, and the pale moon shone its light in through the French doors. Thomas and I were curled up on the sofa, sharing the remains of the bottle of red we'd had with the special dinner he had prepared upon my return. Wilbur lay contentedly on the floor beside us. While I had been away Thomas had unearthed my sound system and linked his ipod to it. The sound track to *As Good As it Gets* played softly in the background.

'You're such a romantic Thom,' I nudged him with my toe.

'There's something about this place.' Lazily, he stretched. 'I've been content here.'

With a start of surprise, I realised I had as well. My time in Provence had been wonderful, however it had bought me to the conclusion that I had to clarify my relationship with Marty. I loved him, but I loved him like a brother. I'd always known that. And I admired him enormously, but I wasn't attracted to him. Such a great guy, however for me he did not have that... *je ne sais quoi*, I now knew was so important to me.

Thomas broke into my thoughts. 'Time for me to go lovey.' Kissing my forehead, he climbed over the top of me and slid his feet into his chocolate leather moccasins. 'Steve will be back from his conference in the morning.'

'You missed him sweetie?' I asked, turning on my side and languidly stretching my arms above my head.

'Yep, it can get a bit lonely at home when he's not there, so it was a nice change of scenery staying here and minding old Wilbur.' He yawned. 'He's my friend now. Aren't you buddy?' He ruffled Wilbur's fur.

'You know I appreciate it,' I told him from my curled up

position on the couch, the jetlag beginning to set in. 'Thanks for picking me up.' I arched my back.

'No probs. Thought Wilbur would want to see you the minute you were back. Now that we've bonded we're going to have to have plenty of play dates.' He slung a leather duffle bag over his shoulder. I caught the look on his face as he eyed me carefully.

'What?' I asked, lazily wrapping one of my curls around a finger.

He scrutinised me. 'There's something different about you Peach.'

Exhaling heavily, I languidly closed my eyes at him. 'Like what?'

'Hmmm. I've been thinking it since you first stepped off that plane. I don't know... you're moving differently, more relaxed, a bit of something... sexiness... in your step. And look at your hair. It's... wild. I'd say you've got that just fucked look written all over you.'

'*Thom,*' I moaned, opening one eye. 'Go away.' I batted a hand at him.

He perched himself back on the edge of the couch. 'Do tell Uncle Thom.'

'There's nothing to tell.'

He looked sideways at me. 'I know that's not true.'

I gave a thoughtful pause. 'What can I say...? I had a very erotic experience... but no sex.'

'Sounds bloody boring.'

I laughed. 'See, I told you I had nothing to tell. Other than, I think I found a little bit of me that's been missing for the longest time.'

Cocking his head to the side, he raised an eyebrow at me. 'It suits you.' He paused. 'Are you expecting Marty?' he asked with an air of obviousness.

Acting as if I had no idea of what he meant, I glanced at my watch. 'Hope he gets here soon, I'm pooped. Those awards ceremonies can go half the night.'

'Hey listen, I'm sorry about the toilet situation. I really thought the plumber meant just one of them, I didn't realise all three were going to be out of action. He seemed to think the fact that you were away would be perfect timing.'

Rolling my eyes, I shook my head. 'Have you been using that disgusting builders' portaloo?'

'*Disgusting* is the word. But it's only been for today.'

'Look I'm not even going to think about it tonight.' And then I threw my legs over the side of the couch. 'On second thoughts, I'll walk you out and make a pit stop while I'm at it.'

'Piss stop or pit stop?' Thomas teased.

I ignored him. At the front door, I slipped my feet into my gumboots, the grounds in more of a mess than ever since the renovation work had begun, the rain not helping.

'That gardener bloke's been here a bit.'

'Brownie?'

'No, the other one. Pete calls him *Snake Man*.'

'Oh?'

'Mmm, it seemed every time I stepped outside he was here.'

'Really, I have to say I'm surprised. I had to twist his arm to come at all. He was only going to come one day a week, and the odd extra day here and there.'

'Works like a bloody Trojan.' He glanced sideways at me. 'What's his story? He's *very* good looking you know. The strong, silent type. Reminds me of Daniel Day Lewis in the Last of the Mohicans. He could almost be a Native American, you know. I can just see him in a buckskin breechcloth and leggings.'

'Hmmm, been having a little fantasy, have you? He's actually *nothing like* Daniel Day Lewis!' Typical Thomas, always attempting to drag everyone into his fantasies.

Thomas pouted. 'Darling, there's nothing wrong with looking. Anyway, I was only wondering about him.'

'To be honest, I'm not sure about him. He's different isn't he? He seems to be,' I drew inverted commas in the air, '*between things*. Whatever that's meant to mean? Sounds to me like he's missing a chunk of his life, so I'm not sure...'

Thomas stopped and looked at me. 'Where do you think he's been?'

I shrugged. We had reached the portaloo and I paused outside the door. 'Your guess is as good as mine. However, it's always a little odd when someone's *between things* and doesn't appear to have a recent past.'

With an even more over-active imagination than me, his mouth dropped open and he leant in closer, his voice almost a whisper. 'I get it... you think he's been in jail.'

'*No*, I'm not saying that... it's just... odd.' I folded my arms across my chest, wishing Thomas hadn't voiced something I had wondered about. Hearing someone else think the same thing, made it more of a possibility.

Thomas was on a roll. 'Do you really think he should be around here? I mean what if the guy's got a record or something? With the house being set back from the road and the thick garden at front, no one would...'

Prickles ran up my spine. 'Stop, stop, stop. You're scaring me. Look, I get a good feeling from him. I'm honestly not worried. Whatever his story is, it's his.'

'Peach, I'm not sure I like this. And it certainly does not sound like you.'

'Promise me you won't say anything to anyone. I mean we

don't really know. It was just something he said that's all.'

'You promise me you'll find out a bit more about him, or I will tell someone. Okay?'

'Okay! Okay!'

'Right, well quickly get in there and pee will you, I can't stand being near the bloody thing. It offends me.'

*

I woke with a fright. Disorientated, I couldn't figure out where I was for a few seconds, but the sight of Wilbur racing for the front door reminded me. I glanced at the time, just after ten. And then I heard the gentle tap on the door once again and Wilbur began barking.

For the second time that night, I wearily climbed off the sofa, and through a series of yawns, made my way to the front door. I took hold of Wilbur's collar and, mindful of the conversation Thomas and I had shared, called out. 'Is that you Marty?'

'Are you expecting someone else? George Clooney perhaps?'

Bleary eyed, I fumbled far longer than necessary with the finicky lock, eventually opening the door. Sleepily, I stood on tiptoes, turning my head slightly for him to kiss my cheek. Inhaling his cigarette perfume, I wrinkled my nose.

'The weary traveller returns.' He slid his arm around my waist in a way that was far too intimate for my liking.

'You've got that right,' I told him, slipping away and leading him back to the kitchen. 'Coffee?'

'Looks like you've had some wine,' he said taking in the empty bottle on the kitchen bench.

'Looks like you have too,' I told him pointedly.

'Don't be like that.' Draping his pin-striped jacket over a chair, he plonked himself down on the sofa, loosened his tie and kicked off his shoes. Wilbur settled at his feet.

I almost told him to make himself at home, although realised it would sound sarcastic. Maybe I meant to, however I refrained. Inwardly, I groaned. My bed was beckoning. I don't care which end of the plane you fly, France is a hell of a long way away, and *plane* and *sleep* do not go together.

And then I noticed the shirt he was wearing. Really how could I miss it? Davis had the same one. In the past, it had been quite a joke the way the two of them had such similar style, even occasionally buying the same clothes. I had always liked that shirt on Davis because of the French cuff. I glanced at Marty's pink and green cat's eye cufflinks, and noted they were the ones we had given him for his thirtieth birthday. That was back in the day when we were the three musketeers. It seemed a million years ago.

What was I doing rehashing all this stuff, particularly on the heels of my return from Provence? I guess, as unfair as it may sound, it was the sight of Marty that took me back there.

'What's the verdict?' he asked.

Leaning against the kitchen bench, I shook my head, 'Huh?'

'*Wine?*'

'You didn't drive here, did you?' I asked, taking a bottle from the refrigerator.

'God no. Taxi.' He patted the sofa. '*Come here.*'

'You're a bit tanked, Marty.'

'Come here,' he repeated, slurring slightly, patting the lounge once more as if that somehow made it more inviting.

Handing him the wine, I exhaled heavily and sat down next to him. He pulled me closer. Annoyed, I wiggled free. 'Marty!'

'*What?*' he was indignant.

I knew I sounded like a bitch. 'Nothing... it's just that I'm tired, you're... tired. Let's just sit here and listen to the music.' Thomas had left his ipod behind and the soundtrack was still playing.

'Don't you want to tell me about your trip?' He took a mouthful of wine, leaving a burgundy smudge on his lips. 'I did miss you, you know.'

Automatically, my fingers went out and wiped at the stain. 'Did you?' I gave a weary smile.

His hand grabbed at mine. I realised that he'd had more to drink than I'd originally thought. I slid my hand away. 'Lay back Marty.' I pressed him down on the couch. He didn't need much encouragement. I slipped a cushion under his head. 'Looks like you've had a long day. I'll make coffee,' I said, standing, prising the wine glass from his fingers and placing it on the floor.

Once again, he grabbed at my hand. 'Peach you always look after me. You know that don't you?'

'Yes sweetie.' I patted his hand. That was something I did know. But I feared it was because I loved him, just like I loved Thomas, like a brother.

The kettle had just begun to boil, when I heard the first snuffled snore. Thank God. I switched the kettle off, tossed a blanket over Marty and turned off the light.

Climbing the stairs, and pulling on a ruffled pink nightie was as much as I could muster. I was asleep almost before my head hit the pillow.

The distant call of crows awakened me just as the dawning sun cast its rays through the branches of a jacaranda tree outside my bedroom window and across my bed. Instantly, I was reminded of my bladder.

Although I had woken a couple of hours earlier, there was

no way I was going out in the dark to use that horrible porta-loo. Blast that plumber. In the early morning light, I peered through the window. Hours earlier, I had heard the rain, however it appeared to have cleared to a spectacular day although the ground still looked pretty sodden.

I glanced around for my dressing gown, but due to the fact I was still living in utter chaos, nothing was where I expected it to be. My suitcase lay open on the bedroom floor. On top was my pretty lemon cardigan with ribbon rullet bows. I slipped my arms into the three quarter sleeves, and struggled to tie the ribbons across my breasts, and then gave up, the desperation to pee greater. I padded down the steps to the front door.

There was a scrabbling on the timber floor, as Wilbur alerted to my sounds woke to join me on the toilet trip. As I opened the door, he pushed in front of me and shot around the side of the house. I pushed my feet into my gumboots, and with arms folded across my chest, traipsed through the mess to the builder's toilet. The sound of twigs breaking caused me to glance over my shoulder. No doubt it was those pesky crows. I heard it again. I craned my neck once more, folding my arms even tighter, an uncomfortable feeling creeping up my spine. 'Wilbur, what are you doing?' I called, glancing around.

Holding my breath, I stepped up into the smelly cubicle. The stench so great I kept the door slightly ajar.

It was very difficult at that hour, with the state of oblivion I was in, attempting to hold my nightie up, get my panties down and not touch a thing in sight, let alone hold my breath. However, somehow I managed. Having trouble keeping my eyes open, I pulled my panties up. I could hear a crow fusing about in a nearby tree broadcasting to all and sundry. Then I heard the sound of Wilbur approaching. 'Wait for me,' I called.

I pushed the door fully open and as I jumped down off the step got one hell of a fright to see someone merely a metre away.

'Ahhh...' I put a hand to my thumping heart. 'God Phil, you gave me the fright of my life,' I chastised. However, in the early morning light, I could see he felt much the same way. I was quite certain he was not expecting me to be in the portaloo.

'I am sorry I didn't know you were back.' For a few moments neither of us spoke and then he explained. 'I love the early mornings best.' I watched as his face settled into a look of solemnity, his eyes on the early morning sun rising behind the gum trees. 'I love the transience of it. The moment you appreciate it it's gone.'

Glancing around, I nodded my head. 'Of course...' I pulled my gaping cardigan across my breasts, mindful of the conversation I had shared with Thomas the night before, and mindful of the fact I was wearing a very short nightie, with a tiny cardigan and gumboots. I must have looked ridiculous.

I half turned towards the portaloo. 'Toilets aren't working,' I said by way of explanation.

He nodded slowly. 'I thought I'd take advantage of the quiet to go over a few plans I've sketched.'

'Oh?' I eyed the rolled up paper under his arm. I couldn't work this man out. He was quite a paradox. One minute he didn't want to work, then would work, but not too many hours. Next, he takes it upon himself to draw up plans, in his own time. *And*, as Thomas pointed out last night, he was working far more than I had been expecting.

'Peach,' Marty's voice called out.

Relieved, I turned. I had almost forgotten he had slept on the lounge. Striding towards me, jacket thrown over his arm, unbuttoned shirt brimming with chest hair, he looked rather dishevelled. Thomas would have called him deliciously dishevelled.

'Taxi's on its way. I've got an early morning breakfast meeting to get ready for. Call you later babe.' He leant down and pecked me on the lips. I was so taken aback with his uncharacteristic display of intimacy, I blinked rapidly and looked sideways at him. He winked at me, nodded at Phil and trudged down the driveway.

Once again, I folded my arms firmly across my chest. 'Well,' I said, 'I'd best get dressed and then phone the plumber. Would you like a coffee?' I asked as if it was perfectly normal for me to be roaming around the garden dressed as I was.

'You look like you've got your hands full. I'm fine thank you.' He deliberately kept his eyes on the garden, which I must say I was most grateful for. And then he continued, 'I'd like to show you the plans. I won't hang around too long this morning, although I can come back later today.'

'Wonderful.' I smiled, sounding a tad too cheerful. 'Well, I must get on with my day.' Every time I spoke to this man, I sounded like a prissy school teacher, an old maid one at that. Squaring my shoulders, I headed back the way I had come, calling to Wilbur as I went, feeling utterly ridiculous in my attire, however not enough to stop my mind ticking over. He wasn't going to hang around too long this morning? How on earth was this going to work? Although, hadn't I said he could do as little or as much as he wished? I did hope I hadn't made a stupid decision. Maybe he was on a prison work release program. No… that couldn't be it… I'm sure they would have checked with me. But wait a minute. He'd told me from the start, he'd never be able to come on a Friday. At first, I'd thought he had meant he worked for someone else on a Friday, or perhaps he wanted to have a long weekend every weekend. But something in the way he had said it, now made me think differently. He probably had to see his parole officer. Whenever someone doesn't appear to have a recent past, there's a good reason for it. I'd already ruled out sickness. Although he had that faraway look in his eyes, he did look healthy. Hard to tell. It was probably a good thing he had seen Marty leaving early this morning. Good for him to know there was a man around. I really wished Thomas hadn't been so damn concerned. I hardly needed anyone else's vivid imagination. Mine was quite enough.

Mounting the front couple of stone steps, I grabbed for the back hem of my nightie, wishing to lengthen it, only to realise, with absolute dismay and extreme embarrassment, that in the chaos of attempting to straddle the *bloody* toilet and not touch a thing in sight, it was now caught up in the elastic of my knickers, the pink ones covered with white hearts, trimmed with ruffles, *and* the image of a Paul Frank monkey right in the middle of the backside. *Good one Peach!* I don't believe my face has ever burned so red.

Ten minutes later, I headed back out, a bag in my hand. I was sure Bea would not mind if I semi moved in while she was away. You cannot, let me repeat that, *cannot* live without a bloody toilet. Period.

*

'What do you mean, there's no way you can get it off the truck?' I asked, knowing my voice was tinged with impatience, frustration growing by the second. I eyed the extremely large spotted gum timber bench still on the back of the truck, looking less likely by the second that it would be unloaded today. 'Didn't Al organise you to deliver it?'

The big raw boned man gave a lopsided grin and opened

his arms wide, assailing me with the worst body odour my nose had ever inhaled. Tactfully, I stepped back and placed my hand delicately up to my nose as if in thought.

'Lady, we have delivered it, but I was told there would be another five men here to help. Me mate and me aren't work horses. Don't know how you think we could possibly lift it. I don't care if it is in three pieces, it *aint* coming off the truck with just us. And we don't have all day. We've got other jobs to get to.'

'Hang on, hang on,' I attempted to placate him, at the same time wondering how this man ate solids with only a few teeth left in his mouth. 'Give me a minute to ring the craftsman. He said it would be heavy and you may need a hand, but *nothing* was said about five men to help. Plus I thought he would be here to help.' I fumed. Of course Brownie was somewhere around, although I very much doubted he'd be of help.

As I headed inside to find my phone, I wondered what time Pete would grace us with his presence. Still, one man would hardly make a difference. On a daily basis, this house was teeming with tradesmen, although it appeared every time I needed one of them, they were nowhere to be found. I dialled the furniture craftsman's number. It went immediately to his message bank. *Bugger!* And then I heard Phil's voice from outside.

Phone to my ear, I pushed redial while I returned back to the front steps, and watched as Phil seemed to appease the men.

He appeared to give it thought, quietly studying the huge timber pieces, glancing at the delivery men, and then scratching his head.

And then he came over to me. 'You know, a small crane

should do the trick to get it off the truck. We can take it from there.'

Feeling myself frowning as I listened to Al's recorded message once again, I had no idea what to do. I pressed end. 'Hmmm… a small crane you say?'

'It's your best option. There's a guy I can ring for you. He owes me a couple of favours. It might cost you three hundred dollars though?'

Hopefully, it would cost Al the three hundred dollars! What on earth was that man thinking, sending it with no way to get it off the truck? He should have at least called me. I thought for a few seconds, and then saw one of the delivery men look at his watch. 'We don't got all day lady,' he said stepping closer. My nose would never survive another onslaught.

I turned to Phil. 'Okay, sure.' I nodded. 'Ring him.' I would take it up with Al later.

Dialling his phone, Phil walked a small distance away and all I heard was, 'Lennie you old bugger, how…' I raised my eyebrows. God who was he calling? Probably some other ex-con. Stop it, I told myself. Just stop.

Hearing his voice drop, surreptitiously I could not help but concentrate on what he was saying, all the while looking the other way. All I could make out was, 'I want out…' before Phil walked further out of earshot.

Startled, my mind went into overdrive. What did he want *out* from? Do not even think about it Peach. Get the table off the truck and stop with all the suspicions. He could quite possibly want out from the Ten Pin bowling team. Phew… yes that could be it. Or it could be… it could be a million things.

Within a few minutes, it was all organised. Lennie, Phil's friend, would be here within the hour. Phil suggested it might be a good idea if I gave the impatient delivery men a carton of beer for their trouble. I raised my eyebrows in question, and nearly suggested a spa voucher, but thought I might sound like a right bitch if I voiced it.

I called to Wilbur, taking him with me to keep him out of mischief. As I slowly backed down the driveway, I heard Phil call out to me. Stopping, I put the window down. 'What? Don't tell me, a kilo of prawns for each of them as well?' My tone sounded a trifle sarcastic.

He smiled good-naturedly, something I had rarely seen. 'I didn't want to mention it in front of the delivery guys, but Lennie suggested, two fifty cash otherwise it's three hundred. I've got some cash on me so I can cover it for you if you want.'

'No thanks... It's fine.' I looked over my shoulder and squeezed the accelerator. And then Thomas came to mind and I remembered his warning. My foot slammed on the brake. Through the open window I called out to Phil. 'I'll organise it at the bottle shop. I never carry cash. *Never!*' Last thing I was going to do, was admit to having cash on me. I wondered if I knew what I had been getting myself into.

Looking in the rear view mirror as I backed out, my eyes fleetingly returned to where Phil continued to stand, his legs apart, arms folded, watching us. Even from that distance, I could have sworn a look of humour crossed his face.

'Apparently we're amusing him,' I explained to Wilbur with mild annoyance. Wilbur was sitting up rather tall in the passenger seat, mouth open and a smile from ear to ear. And then I gave a small chuckle. 'I guess the two of us must look pretty damn funny in this little car. It's a cutie though, aren't you my little Bambino.' I gave the steering wheel a couple of fond taps.

*

Upon my return, the small crane was already in place on the

crowded gravel forecourt. Pete followed me up the driveway and took the carton of beer from my car, always glad to be part of some drama. Phil was on the back of the truck and with the crane operator's side kick, attaching ropes to the first of the three pieces. The two delivery guys leant against the railing on the front veranda.

With my hand securing Wilbur's collar, I stood at a distance and watched as Phil leapt from the truck and waited on the veranda for the first piece. Blinking with astonishment, I noticed my front door had been removed from its hinges. Beside me, I heard Pete mutter, 'Bloody hell.'

My sentiments exactly.

And then the first piece effortlessly swung into the air and across the few metres to where Phil's outstretched arms steadied it. I caught sight of the tattoo on his well-muscled bicep once again, although from that distance I still couldn't make out what it said.

As Phil yelled instructions to Lennie, I realised I had not been able to drag my eyes away from the definition of his muscles, and if truth be told, it had nothing to do with reading his tattoo. I gave my head a shake.

With Phil guiding it, the huge piece of timber was lowered onto a squat trolley with sturdy wheels. He gave Lennie the thumbs up and the ropes were loosened. With Phil's help the first piece was taken along the hallway and into the kitchen. I couldn't help myself, I had to follow, with Pete and Wilbur close at my heels.

'Well, you might have it in here, but how in the bloody hell are we meant to fit it together?' the more outspoken of the two delivery men asked.

'Piece of cake,' answered Phil, not looking at him. The second and third piece followed suit. My constant thought was how long would it take for the offensive body odour to disappear from my home.

Once all three pieces were in the kitchen, Phil returned outside.

'Bloody hell, my wife wouldn't like the look of this,' the charming delivery man announced.

'*Really?*' was all I said. I couldn't help but wonder what she thought of his lack of teeth, and what exactly her thoughts were on his body odour.

'Yep, my wife has good taste. Nothing but the best for her.'

'*Really?*' I repeated once again, this time accompanied by a huge smile.

I was answered with a large productive clearing of the delivery man's throat. He leant out the window and spat a huge globule of phlegm. By this point I was ready to throw up. With a hand on my stomach, I looked at Pete, my eyes wide.

And then I heard the beeping of the crane as it backed down the driveway. When Phil came back in, I raised my eyebrows at him in question. He waved a hand at me. 'It's all done.'

'I'll fix you later,' I told him.

'Sure,' he said, his mind elsewhere. He eyed the two delivery men. 'Right, which of you two blokes is the strongest? I'm going to need a hand. Here Bazza, you look like you're the one mate,' he tossed one of the straps he was carrying, which I presumed he must have found in their truck, towards my friend, now better known as Bazza. Who would have guessed?

Phil demonstrated to Bazza how it should be done. 'If we put them over our shoulders like this, wrap them around our hands and brace ourselves, it'll be a piece of cake.'

'You don't have to tell me how to do it,' Bazza growled. 'I've done this more times than you've had hot dinners.'

'Good on you mate,' was all Phil said. He turned to Pete. 'Can you and Nev,' he glanced at Bazza's offsider, 'hold this part in place and steady us if we need it?'

'Can I help?' I asked, noting that Bazza and Nev seemed a little more willing to assist knowing they had a carton of coldies to take home.

'Sure,' Phil turned to me. 'Can you check to make sure we've got it lined up properly?'

'Right,' I said, glad to be able to do something, Bazza's body odour no longer the only odour in the room, the testosterone now overpowering as well.

It all happened quicker than I thought, and before I knew it, the two delivery men were out the door, and I breathed a sigh of relief as I heard their truck leave. I was glad I knew exactly where the oil burner was, as I had unpacked the box it was in only yesterday. I filled the top with water, sprinkled in some drops of lemongrass and lit it. I glanced at Pete. 'That should deodorise the room pretty quick smart.'

'MacGyver did a pretty good job.' With his head he indicated Phil, who had disappeared outside.

I wrinkled my brow, '*Huh?*'

'MacGyver... Phil.'

I snuffed. 'What?'

'Don't you remember the eighties action man series MacGyver? Well Phil is a lot like him. Resolves every situation quickly using not much more than duct tape and a Swiss army knife.'

'Ha,' I laughed. 'He is a bit like that, I suppose.' I was glad Pete felt that way, as it took away the nagging doubts I had, and cleared Thomas's thoughts from my mind.

My hand smoothed across my new kitchen bench. I stood back and looked at it. It was well worth the wait.

'It's a beauty,' Phil said from the doorway. He glanced at his watch. 'I'll put the front door back on, but I'm afraid I have to take off straight after that.'

'No problem. Thank you for your help.' I raised my eyebrows.

'What?' he asked.

'It's all I seem to do... thank you. It seems so feeble. You keep coming to the rescue.'

'It's all in a day's work.' Phil turned his head and looked down the hallway. 'You've got a visitor.' He nodded to someone.

Marty called to me. 'Good lord, Peach, someone's stolen your front door.'

I laughed. 'I'm in the kitchen Marty. Come and see my new kitchen bench.'

*

Wanting somewhere safe and familiar for a chat with Marty, I had chosen Claret House Winebar and Restaurant, a little gem tucked away in the ground floor level of the London Woolstore building. It used to be a favourite haunt for the three of us. Wednesday evenings were their famous "Roast Night" and many Sunday afternoons we had lazily grazed on cheese platters, washed down with good reds.

It was a mood lifter type of place and I was hopeful that the laid back vibe and homely feel would put Marty at ease. I wanted us on neutral territory.

As if it had been a week since my last visit, I was greeted by the owners Lili and Chewie with much friendly banter. I was ashamed I had been avoiding such lovely people for so long.

Pleasingly, I noted we had a table closest to the edge of the decking, nestled behind a hedge. I felt quite sick thinking about the conversation I was about to have with Marty, however I could not put it off any longer. Even though he hadn't arrived, I wasted no time ordering a drink, anything to keep my nerves at bay.

The minute he sat down I began to waffle. 'Do you remember their Paris mash?' Without giving him time to answer, I carried on. 'It only has two ingredients, potatoes and lashings of butter. I don't care how many calories it has, I want an extra serving. I've dreamt of nothing else in the last few days. And I am going to have the chicken pot pie. What about you? You used to love the pork sliders…'

'That was Davis.'

'No that was you… wasn't it?' I felt my face flush.

'Chicken pot pie for me as well.' And he snapped the menu shut.

All through dinner, I attempted to keep a bright, light hearted look on my face. However the effort of doing so, when I felt the opposite meant it was now wearing thin. Eventually, I couldn't eat one more mouthful, even of the Paris mash, heavenly though it was. I could feel Marty's watchful eyes on me. He could read me like an open book.

'You okay?'

I shook my head. 'Nope.' I slid my chair around beside him, catching the look of surprise on his face. Wiping his mouth on the cloth napkin, he threw it on the table and pushed his chair back. Our backs to the restaurant, the hedge afforded us some privacy.

I knew it was now or never, and I hoped I'd be forgiven for what I was about to do. I took one of his hands, and I saw him look at me in wonder. Squeezing his hand, I leant forward and kissed him. It was incredibly brief.

I felt him pull up with a start but then lean in closer. His other hand went up to the back of my head.

I could not do it again, although I did keep a grip of his hand. I felt sheepish and embarrassed for him, and for me. I glanced down at my lap.

'I'm sorry,' I said, my voice small. Without wanting to, I ventured a look at his face. I could tell he was confused. 'I am sorry Marty. But be honest… did you feel anything?'

I could see the puzzlement on his face, as he attempted to talk, his tone slightly indignant. 'Hang on… give me a chance?'

I spoke quickly, hoping to ease his discomfort. 'No, be honest. There was nothing, was there? I mean… I know we both love each other, but I know we love each other like best friends, like family.'

By the look on his face right at that moment, I was not sure he was following. His brow furrowed and he wore a look of complete bamboozlement. However, it did not stop him from attempting to pull me closer.

I wriggled out of his embrace. 'Sweetie… don't. We go back too far.' Feeling unkind, I linked my arm through his, feeling his body stiffen. 'We've been playing around as if there's something between us. But the fact is, there isn't. Well, not romantically anyway. And both of us deserve so much more.' I tried looking at him, but he wouldn't make eye contact with me. 'I know you don't want to hear this…' I put my hand on his knee. 'I *do* love you, but I love you like a brother. *I really do*. And that's important, because that way I can have you in my life forever. And I know you love me exactly the same way.' He still would not look at me. 'Come on Marty, you know there weren't any sparks.' He said nothing, so I shook his knee. 'Come on, say something.'

Using the heels of his palms, he rubbed at his eyes. When he took his hands away he looked weary, but I could tell he knew. Perhaps he had known all along. He shrugged, and put his hands up in a *whatever* motion. And then he glanced away. When he spoke his voice was not much more than a mumble. 'We weren't exactly going out you know.'

I refrained from giving a snuff that wanted to escape. 'Of course. I know.' That was a male for you. Next thing you know he'd say the reason he had called everyday was that he felt sorry for me. I pushed on. 'I don't want to tie you up any longer and stop you going out with anyone else.'

He nodded, and we sat there for some time, neither of us knowing exactly what to do next.

My hands rubbed up and down on the arms of the chair, willing a brainwave to come to me, to make everything easier. 'Would I be selfish if I asked you to still be my best friend?' my voice was small. I felt him shrug. I could see he wasn't interested in talking any further.

'Marty, what would I do without you?' I attempted to take his hand again, but he pulled away.

He stood up. 'Listen, I've got an early meeting tomorrow. I probably should head off.' He began to get his wallet out.

'Please don't. This one's mine.'

He didn't argue. I looked up at him wistfully, 'Marty, *I'm sorry...*'

He flinched. 'Hey... don't worry about it. No harm done.'

But I could tell I had hurt him, or at least embarrassed him.

'I'll call you tomorrow,' I called to his retreating figure in the dark.

Without turning around, he waved back at me and mumbled something I couldn't decipher. As he walked around in front of the hedge, I stood, my voice louder now. 'The next day then, because I want to tell you about someone who thinks you're the hottest thing since sliced bread.' He kept walking and my voice got louder. 'She wants to ravage your sexy body.' And then I glanced around to see if any of the others diners had heard me, before I looked back at him. In the dark, I saw him pause briefly. He didn't turn around.

'Bye,' my voice was loud.

He didn't answer.

Five minutes later from the safety of my car, I dialled Lou's number.

Chapter 13

'No Wilbur, you stay here. That's a good boy. I'll be back later.' Covering the look of surprise on my face, and acting as if it was perfectly normal to be hopping into a red Holden one tonne ute that appeared to have been in a time warp, with bucket seats and wind up windows, I looked across to Phil in the driver's seat.

'Right,' I said, uncertain of anything else to say, giving him a brief smile. Next thing, I'd bring out my old maid lingo and say, 'We're off!'

Placing my soft calfskin bag on the black rubber mat on the floor, it did not escape me how impeccably clean the car was. It was immaculate as if it had barely been driven. Smoothing the skirt on my white cotton embroidered dress, showcasing my now tanned legs, I glanced around.

'I didn't realise you had a car?' I commented, as I pulled the seatbelt around me and secured it. But then again, I didn't realise a lot about Phil. I was fast learning the man was a paradox. Just when I thought I'd worked him out, he surprised me yet again.

A raise of his eyebrows was as much of an answer as he was prepared to give. Putting the gearstick into reverse, he then looked over his shoulder as he backed down the driveway. The first few times I had seen Phil on the bike, he had mostly had his helmet on. Once he had begun working at Carmody House, part of his daily uniform, aside from a black polo shirt with the collar up, knee length khaki shorts, and dark brown Blundstone work boots, was a well-worn beige akubra, with a leather strap pulling in the sides giving him the look of a cowboy.

However, for the first time today, without his hat, I noticed that his ever so slightly longer buzz cut, appeared to have a small patch of silver grey at the front. Dressed in camouflage cargoes, a fitted V-neck white tee, and black Havaianas with metallic trim, I thought to myself that if I had seen him out, I may not have recognised him.

I was struck by the fact he was a man who wore causal well. And once again, it went through my mind that he had to be doing a damn sight more than riding a bike, to be in the condition he was in.

When he stretched out his left arm on the steering wheel, his sleeve rose up a couple of centimetres. Briefly, I glimpsed the tattoo on his well-shaped bicep. There were four letters in cursive writing. I tilted my head to get a better look. The last three letters were more obvious, 'O-V-E'... *Mmmm?* Narrowing my eyes to see the first letter, I silently mouthed the letter *L. Ahhh.* My lips moved to form the word *LOVE.* And then I caught his eye.

I gave a quick smile. 'Nice tattoo,' I said, unsure what else to say, even though much like my mother tattoos had never been my thing.

He nodded. I placed my hands in my lap, and settled in for the drive, expecting minimal conversation. Yesterday, when Phil suggested we take a run to the nursery to look at the Fairy Magnolias, I had expected we would go in Bambino, even though I thought we may be a tad squashed. However, Phil had tactfully suggested a larger car would be required to load some plants in, and he would pick me up.

Glancing around the car, I couldn't help but notice that there was nothing in it to suggest it belonged to someone. The usual things: coins in the ashtray, business cards in the console, the odd half eaten packet of mints, not even a speck of lint. Nothing! I wondered if it was his or someone else's, although didn't think it prudent to bring it up again. Questions seemed to be met with monosyllable answers.

Hmmm... and then my heart sped up and my mind went into overdrive. *What if...* what if the car was stolen? Why oh why did I keep thinking these thoughts about this man? I couldn't help it but when someone didn't stack up, I knew there had to be a reason for it.

Davis used to tease me good naturedly when I would make an assumption about a client, telling me to turn my overactive imagination down a few notches. However, I know he loved hearing my theories. I suffered a fair amount of ribbing when I decided buyers Klaudia and Anja Meyer, a mother and daughter were part of the witness protection program.

Davis was propped on a desk, arms folded, challenging me, although he did not hide his smirk. 'Then why did they openly buy the property Peach? Surely the people who set these things up would have done that for them?'

'Oh you mean the property that had built in security on every door and window, plus greater than average privacy from the street? Not odd in itself, but I am sorry,' I had stared him down, my arms now folded across my chest. 'When the 25 year old daughter tells me she was born and educated here, in a voice with a stronger German accent than her mother, all the while peering out from behind that thick luscious hair, which come on... just has to be a wig... and she doesn't appear to have had a job outside the home since finishing school, you do not have to be Einstein to work out that something doesn't add up.'

'Yes Sherlock Holmes!' He shook his head. 'You crack me up Frenchy.'

'I'm so glad you find me amusing. Have you ever wondered

that since we sold them that property two years ago, we have seen them at least a dozen times out and about, however never once on their own.' I eyed him. 'That is odd, therefore I am sticking to my theory. witness protection program.'

Whether or not I had been right about Klaudia and Anja Meyer, I could not deny that Phil was a enigma. He was turning out to be invaluable at the house, a damn hard worker who really knew his stuff. From all appearances he was enjoying the work. I had noticed a certain something in his face that had begun to soften. However, he remained a closed book, careful with how much he gave away. But I guess, if you were going to steal a car, it would hardly be an early model ute in immaculate condition… or would it?

Mentally, I made a list of what I knew about him to date. He was *between things*, hadn't planned on being in Brisbane for too long, wasn't money motivated, plus could only work certain times, as he appeared to have to check in somewhere. By now, I knew to never ask him to work on a Friday although, he could occasionally be seen on weekends finishing off a task. Go figure!

Pete still referred to him as MacGyver. The thing was, as much as I knew little about Phil, he didn't appear to have the aura of someone who was dangerous, quite the opposite in fact.

Years ago, Lou had briefly dated a guy who we all had misgivings about. All, except her. His life didn't stack up either. He was missing a sizable chunk of his recent past. I gleaned enough to know he hadn't been unwell. Something made me wonder if he had been in prison. Anyway, Lou wouldn't have a bar of it. Soon after, they broke up and four months later, there was a picture of him in the newspaper. I still remember the shivers running up and down my spine when I saw his face, with a name I did not recognise underneath. The article said he was a drug runner in and out of Bali and had served time before on drug related charges. The authorities had been watching him for some time.

Lou had thought she had known him. But how well do you know anyone? Phil's voice broke into my thoughts.

'Chandler first,' he said.

'Sorry?'

'We'll head to the Chandler Nursery first. I called earlier to make sure they had some sizable Fairy Magnolia Blushes in stock…'

'I love that name,' I interrupted. 'Fairy Magnolia Blushes, so pretty. You instantly conjure up the blush colour.'

'They're the right specimens for that hedge in the private garden. They're quick growing, reaching somewhere between nine to twelve feet and have evergreen dark foliage. You're right about the colour, they start off as a lilac pink, and later in the season age to white. Along with the lavender, that's going to be one fragrant garden.'

'Great.' I nodded. That was quite a bit of information from him in one go. *Well done*, I wanted say.

I was sure he was right about the Fairy Magnolias. He appeared to have been on the right track with everything else. It had been my suggestion to plant the lavender, a little reminder of Provence.

It was a spectacular day with not a cloud in the sky as we sped over the Story Bridge. Proudly, I stared out the window across the water, looking for the brief sight of my garden, as its triangular point met the Brisbane River. There stood the familiar fig tree and a few palms shooting skywards. That tiny glimpse made me feel blessed. It really was quite beautiful and had turned into my slice of heaven.

Smiling, I turned to Phil. 'So you feel the need to be reminded?' And then quick as a flash, I wished I could take the words back.

He wrinkled his brow at me in misunderstanding.

I shrugged. 'Your... tattoo. You need to be reminded to love...' my voice trailed off.

He looked straight ahead and I had to strain my ears. 'Sometimes.'

'Of course, I mean... I understand. Everyone does at some time.' Right that moment, I wished to be anywhere another than in that car. He wasn't making this easy. I was just trying to make conversation. I wasn't the Spanish Inquisition. I let out a huge breath. 'I guess you noticed Marty's not around much these days,' I explained, attempting to be inclusive.

He glanced at me, giving a curt nod. 'I had.'

'It was never going to work. I love him too much as a friend. We go a long way back, you know.' I glanced over at him with a smile, unable to stop my nervous rambling. 'We were in partnership, my ex-husband, Marty and I. In the settlement, I kept Marty as a friend, and Davis, my husband... I mean my *ex*-husband got the blonde, long legged, bimbo.' I attempted a joke, but was only rewarded with a look, however at least his face had softened.

With my eyes focused on the road ahead, I saw nothing. My hands clasped together in my lap, I was remembering. And as the pain of it resurfaced, I was reminded that this never did me any good, however it didn't stop me sharing the information. 'She was more "into the business",' I said drawing inverted commas in the air. 'I mean, kill me for wanting a baby. For most people that's the next step, but with Davis... *nooo*... the business always came first.' Exhaling heavily, I paused and neither of us spoke, and then I said quietly, 'He wasn't ready to be a father.' I glanced down at my hands. And then, I was unsure if I was speaking to Phil or myself, 'It just wasn't my time.' I felt him glance at me.

Attempting to lift my voice, I said, 'Anyway I am well and truly over it.' Looking down, I smoothed my hands over the skirt of my sundress as if removing it of wrinkles.

'I noticed,' was all he said, but he said it with humour. I gave him a brief smile, however was quiet for the rest of the trip.

*

In the car park, Phil told me to go ahead. At the entrance, I turned to see him carefully spreading a rubber mat over the floor of the polished hardwood timber tray on the back of the ute. I had glanced in the back earlier, thinking it too looked like something a craftsman had made. With a raise of my brows in wonder, I continued on.

I had come to find that nurseries were interesting places. The air was filled with the perfume of jasmine, daphne and sweet peas, along with the unmistakeable delicious aroma of brewing coffee and just baked bread wafting from the gardener's cafe. Already the queue for freshly baked croissants was long, and the wait for lattes was even longer, however the delay gave me the opportunity to browse.

Locals relaxed in the outdoor cafe or roamed the rows, while children shrieked and darted in and out. The nursery had a family feel about it and was a happy place. After I had selected the Fairy Magnolia Blushes, I left Phil to organise the delivery. As if by osmosis, I was drawn across the nursery to the organic vegetables. Edible marigolds bobbed amongst the rainbow chard, staked broad beans and tomatoes heaved on their stalks, and notes of basil and rosemary wafted on the breeze.

By the time Phil caught up with me, not only did he have a trolley in tow, so did I.

'I know you've already ordered seeds, but can I get a head start with some of these punnets of young plants?' I asked without waiting for an answer. 'What do you think of these tomatoes plants?' I was really enjoying the feeling of sharing my ideas for the garden with him.

Phil gave one of his characteristic decisive nods. I had worked out he sometimes used them instead of words. However, he did surprise me by continuing. 'I'll lash some bamboo canes together to make tripods for them.'

I felt my face light up. 'Oh… I like that. Thank you.' My fingers glanced over some of the greenery I had collected. 'I think we need to freshen some of the herbs. And look at this ginger. Isn't it wonderful? And the galangal, perfect for my curries.' My voice carried an air of excitement. The more I saw, the more I wanted. Who knew this would have bought me such excitement.

'Sure. I'll load them.' Phil glanced at his watch. 'I'll probably have time to plant some of them when we get back. I've organised manure and worm casings, which we'll mix with Brownie's compost to create a rich organic fertiliser. The magnolias will be delivered first thing Monday morning, but we can take the lavender and these jasmines now.' Phil's fingers gently smoothed over the dark glossy leaves in his trolley. 'I prefer this species, Trachelospermum jasminoides. I'm not as fond of the variegated leaf. Your thoughts?'

'Absolutely! I am loving the sound of this garden. It's going to be so fragrant.' Happily, I glanced around. 'I'll see if the lattes are ready. No sugar right?' I threw over my shoulder as I almost skipped off.

*

Waiting in line for the coffee, I was in a world of my own, as my mind went from one thing to another. I reminded myself to ask Phil if we could plant some edible petals. They would really brighten the area as well. Perhaps nasturtiums or marigolds? Actually, I remembered some time back him telling me that marigolds planted in a vegetable garden kept the pests at bay, so they'd be perfect.

When I had suggested lavender, Phil had said anything to attract bees was a good thing, without bees the world food chain would quickly dry up. In a rare moment of verboseness, he had told me about a variety of stingless bees, and suggested I might be interested in cultivating them. At the time, I was unsure, however the more I thought about it the more I liked the sound of them.

Anyway if I was thinking of encouraging the bees, regardless of if they were mine or not, it was probably a good thing to add fragrant alyssums, as well as little daisies and geraniums. My mind was bursting with plans, the garden was bringing me so much joy.

Finally, with a coffee cup in each hand, I added flowering chives to the list in my mind. A smile on my lips, I turned from the busy queue. Isn't it funny how one minute you can be so happy and the next completely devastated? Actually make that a microsecond not a minute, because that was all it took for me to stop dead in my tracks.

Only later would it come to me that in those first few seconds it was as if a bomb had gone off, a bomb in my brain, the silence so deafening. People were still talking, children playing, the coffee machine whooshing… but I heard nothing.

Time stood still, and I was uncertain of how I actually held the coffees and did not collapse dead on the floor. Kill me now, was all I could think. Only metres away, at a small white table, Davis was staring at me, with a look of bewilderment and discomfort clearly written across his face. He was not alone. In the moment I had turned and seen them, I had seen far more than I ever wanted to see.

For what felt like an eternity, we all looked at each other. Davis stood, the cast iron chair loud on the stone tiles. Details crammed my brain. His hair was too long. There were new lines etched deeply around his eyes. Weariness draped over him like a heavy cloak. The vibrancy he usually wore, now no longer evident. His green striped Paul and Gun shirt, a gift from me, was not as crisply ironed as he liked his shirts to be. I wanted to tell him that his shorts didn't match. Even then it penetrated my brain that his standards were slipping.

'Peach...' he said, coughing uncomfortably as his eyes had trouble meeting mine.

I glanced down at the coffees wondering how on earth I could disappear into thin air. I noticed one of them had pooled a little on the lid, a funny thing to notice at a time like that. And then I realised that my knees had turned to jelly. I bit my lower lip and begged for the ground to open up and swallow me. Odd thoughts careened through my mind. Really, how was it possible Davis was sitting here at 10.30 on a Saturday morning? I mean, didn't he have open houses to show? Saturday was a big business day.

My mind rambled to keep me from looking at Felicity and seeing the truth. *Please, I do not want to know. Do not register, do not register,* my mind begged. But there was no escaping it.

And then she stood, and even in her far-too-elegant-for-a-nursery shoes, I noticed her ankles were swollen. I did not want to look any higher. But my eyes were disloyal to me, and deliberately followed the lines of her dress as it unmistakably outlined a baby bump. *Oh... my... God... No!*

With her head cocked to the side, and wearing a look that would freeze nitrogen, almost deliberately one of her hands went to her stomach.

I hoped the sound I made wasn't audible. A terrible feeling of desolation rose in my stomach. A hot sweat washed over me, my hands trembled. There was perspiration above my top lip, and I felt as if I could dry retch. All three of us stood still. I knew I must move aside for the other patrons. Hesitantly, I took a step forward. Davis put a hand out to me. Like a vice, Felicity reached out and grabbed at his arm, her face even more glacial.

Behind Felicity I saw Phil walking towards me, the look on his face odd. In a few strides he was beside me, placing a reassuring hand into the small of my back and I felt I could breathe again, if only slightly.

I looked up at him.

With one eyebrow raised, he said loudly, 'Darling, the car is loaded. Here let me take those coffees.' With one hand somehow balancing both takeaway cups, and the other in the middle of my back, Phil steered me away, past the shade loving plants, through the gift store, out the front entrance and over to the car. Without a word, he opened the passenger door and put a hand under my elbow and assisted me getting in. He pulled the seatbelt forward, crossed it in front of me, and clicked it in place, as if I was a child.

My hand fumbled in my bag, until I found what I was looking for. I wished I had a hand grenade, one that I could pull the pin out with my teeth and hurl it back in there… instead my fingers curled around a small glass bottle of Rescue Remedy. By the time Phil had roared out the front gate, I had put three drops under my tongue. I said not a word for the next twenty minutes. And then by way of explanation, in a quiet voice, a hand nervously rubbing my neck, I explained, 'That was my ex-husband and… and…'

'I gathered that.' Phil didn't look at me, but his tone was kind. We travelled the rest of the way in silence. Every now and then I felt his glance on me. The journey seemed endless. Both coffees sat untouched wedged into the middle console.

Feeling very small and insignificant, my hands clasped together firmly in my lap, I rested my head on the passenger window, desperate to close my eyes. My mind went to Emerald Green. How many times had we role-played the scenario of what I would do if I ran into *them* together? I had decided that I would act as if *she* did not exist. As if *she* was thin air. As if I hadn't even seen her.

From the first moment of finding out about Davis's affair with *her*, I had not spoken, nor seen her again. I had told Davis to tell her to keep away from me. If she saw me, to walk on the other side of the street, that *she* was the type of woman you warned other women about. It was abundantly clear why she did not appear to have any female friends. The only contact I'd had with her was that email she had sent when I was staying at Bea's.

But today I had seen her. I could not pretend she did not exist. I often wondered if she knew or cared about the pain she had caused in my life. Occasionally, I had toyed with the idea of writing her a letter. Emerald Green had said it was an acceptable thing to do. But we both knew it would mean nothing to a woman like that. Not one thing.

However, the scenario Emerald Green and I had *never* discussed was me seeing *her* pregnant with my husband's child.

With frustration, I wondered what else the universe wanted to throw at me. Well-meaning friends had uttered clichés like *what doesn't kill you makes you stronger*. Was I not strong enough yet? Other friends had felt that because Davis and I had not had a child, it somehow lessened the relationship. As if he was more of a boyfriend rather than my husband: the man who had shared my adult life, my dreams, and hopes for the future.

The same people had said, 'Well it's just as well you didn't have children with him'. Didn't they get that at my age I desperately wanted children, that now I saw myself getting older, with no man on the horizon, I had to begin all over again, meeting the right person, dating, finding out if he even wanted children, and then doing it all in the right order. Didn't they get that I looked at their children with longing. No… they thought I was lucky we didn't have any!

Once in the driveway, Phil began to unload the plants. As I had found in the past, shock always sent me into a state of exhaustion. Keeping myself awake for the trip home had been difficult.

I walked around the back of the car and pointed towards the house. Wilbur sensing my mood, for once wasn't jumping all over me.

Phil nodded.

And then I turned back to him. I closed my eyes briefly. 'Phil… thank you.' I felt as if my voice was not my own. There was a lone tear under the bottom lashes of one eye. Even through my pain, it registered that this man had pretended for me, and I was grateful.

'No problem.' However, he had his back to me, and was stacking the plants to one side. 'I'll hose these and then if it's okay I'll plant the herbs.' His voice was quiet.

I nodded. As I turned to go, I noticed a box of marigolds. With a barely perceptible shrug, feeling that Phil had read my mind, I made the tiniest noise of 'Huh.' I think only the first letter came out.

Wilbur followed me. I knew I had to lay down before I collapsed. I pulled my dress over my head. My eyes were so heavy, I could not keep them open. With only my bra and panties, I fell into bed and pulled the covers over my head, attempting to block out… life. I felt every pulse in my body, even the ones in my lips were resounding.

It seemed like only minutes had passed, and I resurfaced to a hammering in my head. It felt like a truck had parked itself on my forehead. And then I realised that someone was also hammering on the front door. I wondered if I could stay huddled under the doona, however I heard Wilbur barking. I grimaced as the knocking persisted, as if each sound was a physical blow to me. I put my feet over the bed and slipped them into pink fluffy slippers. Halfway down the stairs, I turned around and returned to the bedroom to put my dress back on.

Feet shuffling, I walked heavily down the stairs towards the door, as if I was wearing a suit of armour, and not my new white embroidered-anglais sundress, which only this morning I had thought showed off my healthy tan.

I placed a hand to my back, feeling one hundred years old. With all the manual labour I had been throwing myself into, I had lost a couple more kilos and had adopted a more casual way of dressing. My hair, no longer blow-dried and styled within an inch of its life, was left to its own curly devices at my shoulders, although I could not help myself, a small Chelsea de Luca crystal clip secured my fringe to one side.

'*Oh,*' I said, putting a hand to my forehead and closing my eyes. '*It's you.*' I sighed heavily, and leant against the front door to keep myself in an upright position. Wilbur sniffed disdainfully at our visitor.

'Please go away Davis. I have *nothing* to say to you…' The effort of speaking to him exhausting, wearily, I attempted to close the door. He put a hand up to stop me, and I saw the look on his face. Once again, I saw that worry was etched deeply around his eyes. Eyes that looked tired and much older than when I had last seen him.

I wondered who one earth this man was, this stranger at my door. Was I married to him for all of those years? Had I known him since we were teenagers? And how could I have wanted so badly to have babies with him when he could discard me so easily? I shook my head to clear it. Hot angry tears pricked at the back of my eyelids. *Damn you, damn you, damn you.*

Briefly, Davis eyed Wilbur as if deciding how friendly he was. 'Peach, *please… don't.* I need to speak to you. I have tried.' He ran a hand through his unruly hair and then awkwardly shoved his hands in his short's pockets.

I continued to look at him, searching for recognition of the man I once knew.

'You look good Peach. I almost didn't recognise you. You've done something to your hair. You look more relaxed, more casual… younger in fact.' From his position at the doorstep he glanced around appreciatively, although I caught the tone of surprise in his voice. 'My God you've done well… how did you afford…?'

His brow furrowed and I cut him off, acting as if he hadn't spoken, narrowing my eyes. In a low voice, I asked, '*What* really happened Davis? *What?*' Protectively, I folded my arms in front of myself.

He shrugged. 'Things changed. I can't put it into words.' He shook his head. 'You stopped caring about the business as much, and I needed…'

'*YOU* needed...' I yelled. '*YOU* needed... It was always about what *YOU* needed. Well now *YOU* seem to have everything you need. So just... go away.'

He put his hands up to placate me. 'No, please... let me talk.' He glanced down at Wilbur. Wilbur gave a short woof as if to let him know he was on tender ground.

With my hands covering my ears, I turned on my heels and stumbled towards the kitchen. Later, it would come to me that I wished I could have been a tad more graceful. Davis followed me.

'*WHAT?* I yelled, turning to him, taken back by the fact he was openly and admiringly touching my newly painted latte coloured hallway walls. 'What could there possibly be to say?' And then I noticed I was crying, and wondered if I had been all along. When I next spoke, my voice was low and I looked directly into his eyes. 'Davis, I would *never* have done to you, what you did to me. *Never!*

Davis put a steadying hand out to me. 'Frenchy...' he said, his voice affectionate.

It gave me the creeps. I flinched and roughly pulled my arm away. '*Don't you dare,*' I said, dropping my head. Rivers of tears cursed down my face. Using the back of my hand, I wiped at them. My back was up against the kitchen bench. Placing one hand to my mouth, I sobbed loudly, scaring even myself. I looked back up at Davis. He looked alarmed. So did Wilbur. Ears back, he was standing guard at my feet.

'I didn't mean to hurt you Peach.'

'No... well you have done the best *FUCKING* job you could have.'

'Peach...'

My voice rose again. '*Even a baby?* Wasn't the rest enough? I mean... she got the *bloody handbag.*' My hand came down hard on the kitchen bench. 'But a baby as well?' I put my hands up to the heaven as if beseeching it. 'That … person… she has my husband, my house, my business and now a baby. That was the one thing I wanted.' I was uncontrollable. 'And you… you… you… didn't even want to be a father,' I spluttered. 'Well not with me anyway.'

And then it dawned on me by the look on his face that he still didn't want to be a father. I glared at him, the sight of him repulsive. 'What are you doing here Davis? What do you want with me? Don't tell me you were worried about me, because if you were, you've had long enough to come around before this.'

'I tried, but you didn't take my calls.' He glanced around, and even through the turmoil, I could see he was doing a professional appraisal. He just could not help himself.

My brain wasn't quite registering something. And then I saw that there was something seriously wrong with this picture. On the kitchen bench sat a stack of cookbooks, pages earmarked with new recipes. To the left was a bunch of unruly herbs pinched into a small white ceramic jug sitting atop three gardening books, my vegetable bible *Vegetables from Amaranth to Zucchini* in pride of place. Above the stove was my collection of antique French *confit* pots. To the right hung two small vintage pieces of art I had stumbled upon at a flea market. Beside the sink, a flowery cup and teapot mimicked the real blooms I had scattered throughout the house in vases, the lavender perfuming the entire house. Over the laundry door handle draped Wilbur's lead. *And…* Wilbur was standing guard at my feet.

This was the life I had created, and immediately I saw what was wrong, what was bothering me. It was *Davis*. I had created a picture that he did not fit. In fact, he would have hated every one of the things I had chosen. However, they were more me than anything else had ever been.

He turned back to me and with slight hesitation asked, 'I was wondering about your boyfriend…'

'*What!*' I snapped. With distaste, I narrowed my eyes at him, my back still pressed against the kitchen bench. 'What are you doing here now?' I said through gritted teeth.

He put a hand out. 'Frenchy… you look great…'

'*Will you stop that*,' I spat out.

'Look it's a bloody mess. I've stuffed up.' Leaning forward he spread his hands wide on the kitchen bench. 'Frenchy, the thing is, you mean more to me now that we've had some time apart. You're the only person that I've ever felt really knew me…'

For the second time in a matter of seconds I was gobsmacked. 'What?' I spluttered, astounded at his utter selfishness.

'The second time around can be so much sweeter than the first,' he said.

And then the top of my head nearly blew off. '*Davis… GET OUT*,' I screamed, my eyes literally popping out of my head. I pointed at the front door. 'Just. Get. Out.' Wilbur began to bark, and I grabbed at his collar and hung onto him, catching sight of the look on Davis's face. I had rattled him. He had never seen me so unhinged. And then my tirade continued, 'You are the most self-centred human being who has ever walked this earth. I cannot believe I was married to you. What did you think? You'd come around here and I'd help sort things out like I always have in the past? You have a baby coming into this world that you are responsible for, you moron. Now GO.' I glared at him. 'Go. And for God's sake… GROW UP.'

I turned my back on him. He attempted to talk but I held my hands up. 'Go,' I said, this time much more quietly. I used a voice he understood, because I heard his footsteps retreating back down the hallway.

Halfway down he stopped and turned. 'Peach, I am sorry. I never meant to hurt you like this. If I could take it back I would. If we could both go back…'

I didn't turn around, but stood rigidly rooted to the spot. A small part of me registered that I had never heard that man apologise before. After a few seconds I heard him leave. And then I cried, huge howls of anguish. I stuffed my hand into my mouth when I realised I was scaring Wilbur. There was an aching in my heart so horrendous, I placed one hand there in an attempt to soothe it, the other covered my mouth. I rocked back and forth, crying in silent torment. Wilbur sat at my feet, looking at me with worried eyes, every now and then whimpering and placing his wet nose on my leg.

After what felt like an eternity, I went to the fridge and surveyed the contents. Reaching behind the marinating lamb shanks, a recipe my friend Chilli had passed onto me, I pulled out a bottle of crisp white *pinot grigio*. I toyed briefly with the idea of swigging it straight from the bottle, however, even at time like this a sense of decorum overrode. Deftly, I removed the screw cap and filled a wine glass to the absolute brim.

At the window, I sat in my Louis chair and put the glass to my lips. With a worried look, Wilbur settled at my feet.

I had always wanted to be a big drinker. Drinkers knew how to drown their sorrows, something I had never accomplished. Well, it was never too late to begin. My stomach growled, letting me know there had been very little food or liquid in it today. However, I ignored it and ploughed on.

I was three quarters of the way through my drink when I

heard a gentle tapping. I glanced down the hallway towards the front door, but realised with some surprise it was coming from the laundry. With a start, I saw Phil. He was carrying a cardboard box filled with dozens of empty herb pots. I stared at him. Gesturing towards the kitchen garden, he spoke. 'I've planted the herbs. They're well watered.'

I had no doubt they were very well watered, however I kept looking at him, knowing full well he would have heard every word that was said earlier. Instead of speaking, I nosily cried some more, and stood to fill my wine glass.

He didn't move and I could see I was worrying him, but there was not a thing I could say. So I poured him a glass and pushed it across the kitchen bench. He didn't take it, although he didn't say no either. I sat back down in my chair and swivelled around to face the window. Nursing my glass, I rested my feet on the edge of the desk. I heard footsteps as he went out the front door and then some time later I heard him return. I was almost through my third glass of wine, wishing for numbness against the pain.

I heard the sound of the kitchen tap running, and realised Phil was filling the kettle. I kept looking out the window. I felt like the muscles in my face had fallen and had set in concrete. I didn't think they would ever return to where they should be again. Silently, as if draining an internal well, tears kept coming. I wiped at my cheeks and saw mascara on the back of my hand. I imagined I must have been a very attractive sight to look at, but didn't care. I took another gulp of wine. All I could think of was how heavy my eyelids were.

And then a handful of tissues were placed in front of me. I didn't even look up and was unable to stop my chin from quivering. Nothing was said. I heard cupboards being opened and still I said nothing. Eventually a cup of coffee was placed beside the tissues. I looked at the strong brew and shuddered at the thought of mixing it with the wine in my near-empty stomach. I felt my stomach heave. Almost tripping over Wilbur, I bolted for the bathroom, holding my hands to my mouth as I ran.

My stomach convulsed giving up far more than I would have thought possible. Hugging the toilet bowl to me, I was now kneeling on the cool black and white checkerboard tiles, attempting to hold my hair back from my face. Even at this point, I was still crying, loudly. Involuntarily, I retched and leant forward. A hand pulled my hair away from my face, and held it back for me, while I placed my head in the toilet once again. I heard Phil gently shooing Wilbur from the bathroom. A wet face washer was placed on the back of my neck. Its sudden coolness was comforting.

'Thank you,' I said, my voice small, as I tore toilet paper off the roll to wipe my mouth. I lay down on the cool tiles and threw one arm across my face to cover it. 'I'm fine,' I said from behind my arm. 'I think I have a stomach bug.'

'I can see that,' Phil said, his tone dry.

Retching once more, I quickly sat up and reached for the toilet bowl yet again. When I was done, I slid back down to the floor. On my side, I curled into a ball. 'He even gave her a Louis Vuitton handbag,' I said, as my voice broke, another wave of grief engulfing me. 'That was our thing.' My words sounding incomprehensible, even to me. Although, it did not stop me from continuing. 'That's what he did when he proposed to me. But now it means nothing.' I said this as if her having the bag was far more painful than her having his baby.

'Come on.' I felt Phil attempting to help me up.

With eyes still closed against the world, I gave him no assistance whatsoever. I wanted to be left where I was. 'I can't,' was all I said, so soft I'm surprised he heard me. '*I can't... I can't stand, I can't go on, I can't face the world, I can't, I can't I can't!*'

Phil picked me up and carried me to the couch. I turned away. He went into the laundry and returned with a bucket and towel, quietly placing them beside me. Wilbur flopped heavily alongside the couch, his tail thumping on the floor a few times.

'I'll be fine,' I said, uncertain if I was talking to Wilbur or Phil. I sniffed, wishing to be left alone.

'You will,' Phil softly answered for both of them. 'I'll make tea and then leave you in peace.'

'No, you don't have to.' I was unsure if I was talking about the tea or being left in peace. I gave a double sniff, sounding very sorry for myself.

'I know, but I will anyway.' I still didn't know if he meant the tea or being left in peace.

Once again I closed my eyes, attempting to shut out the nightmare of what had just happened... in fact what had happened over the last couple of hours. After a few minutes, I heard Phil place a cup down beside me. I heard him walk about on the timber flooring and then he returned with a quilt. Gently, he placed it over me. I feigned sleep to cover my humiliation. A man I knew absolutely nothing about had heard and seen me at my lowest point.

Wilbur's tail gave another thud on the timber floor.

Chapter 14

It was incredibly bizarre, but I felt strangely uplifted.

It could have been that the first thing I saw through my puffy eyes, as the first rays of spring sunlight bled through the edges of the blinds, were Wilbur's concerned dark eyes staring straight at me, his blonde head resting on the edge of my mattress, leaving an imprint on the white damask Moss River sheet, a noise of affection coming from the back of his throat.

Or it could have been the stroll around the property, my own veritable wonderland, Wilbur at my side, the sky still umber at that early hour, our footsteps leaving imprints on the dewy grass.

The garden was in full bloom. White, yellow, pink and orange ranunculus, all poked their pretty little heads up, smiling. I found myself smiling back at them.

As I passed the indigo blue hyacinths, my breath was taken away by their beauty, and I was reminded of how ingenious nature was. The bold hedge of purple hydrangeas, their flowers heavy in the early sun, sleepily nodded to me as if in greeting. Banks of lavender thrusted their lilac flowers towards the sky, filling my nostrils with their heady scent.

Everywhere I turned, vivid jewel-like shades of ruby and amber, amethyst and jade swam before me. I stood marvelling at the cleverness of the white daphne, their pink tips looking as if someone had individually hand-dipped their edges in paint.

I became quite dizzy with the flood of colour and scent that assaulted me from every direction, but then clarity of thought swept through my mind, and looking around I felt nothing but pride. It was as if I needed to be reminded this morning. These were my flowers! Along with my olive grove, my private garden, my kitchen garden, my house, my dog, and my new life. Wrapping my pale pink silk gown around me a little tighter, I breathed it in. At the first sound of the cackle of my new resident kookaburra, I was reminded of the magpies I often heard in the evenings, and the serenity this place bought to me.

With a sense of smugness that they had not let me down this morning, I called a greeting to the wild ducks who had begun to frequent the garden of late, along with the usual parrots and frogs.

My eyes went to the old weatherboard garden shed, prettily gracing the east boundary, minding its own business. Up until now, there had been much to do elsewhere, and I had taken little notice. However, this morning I could not help but be drawn to its magical qualities. In a trance, I watched as with a flurry of emerald coloured wings, four lorikeets perched atop the gable roof line, their blue heads nodding in unison, as if in approval of me.

My voice was soft. 'Thank you.'

Over my shoulder, I spotted the lone kayaker out on the river. Seeing him so regularly at his time, I had begun to think of him as my kayaker, and this morning I waved, hopeful he had seen me.

A neon coloured butterfly, with wings pulsing together like a spectacular crepe paper heart, began to hover around my head and then fluttered towards the garden shed, drawing my eyes to the side walls covered in Boston ivy. Something I had not noticed before that moment. My attention moved on with the butterfly as it flittered in and out around the trailing passionfruit vine, and then returned to me, magically circling, before once again fluttering over to the shed. 'It's okay,' I said to it. 'I see it.'

It could have been all of those magical things that had given me such a sense of gratitude that day. Plus, the eight o'clock yoga class certainly helped as well. The first I'd been to in many months. The room full of slim blonde yoginis moving like synchronised swimmers through a vinyasa series: cobra, downward dog, then finishing in chair pose. Too many years of wearing heels, that pulled at my calves and meant I struggled to keep up. However, I was reminded to be non-judgemental of myself and listen to my body. I felt I needed the fluidity of the movement. My mind needed the breath.

Breathe, I told myself, as the instructor guided us to eagle pose. 'Extend your arms out to the side. Find your hips, knees bent, wrap your left leg around your right, and hold your hands in prayer position in front of your heart.' *Breathe*. 'Try to find your balance with a sense of movement rather than trying to hold on.' *Breathe*. 'Release and come back to standing.' *Breathe*.

It could have been the powerful words she spoke that resonated with me... *find your balance... hold on... release... come back... heart.*

Or it could have been after standing under the shower for 35 minutes last night, unable to get out, the two dozen cupcakes I'd then gone on to make, the hard icing butterflies my best to date. Go figure!

What can I say? There had been a significant change! Quite frankly, even I was astonished at my calmness and clarity of thought today.

I'd had a serious talk with Wilbur the evening before explaining that if I didn't smile for a few days, it had nothing to do with him. I had simply run out of smiles for the time being. He had sat forlornly with his head cocked to the side, looking as miserable as I felt. Our little talk had weighed heavily on my conscious, and now I wished I hadn't disturbed him.

Driving home from yoga, my thoughts were on firing up the Gaggenau, my statement coffee machine, and making a rich strong brew. I might have to taste test one of the cupcakes as well. After all I didn't have my bevy of tradesmen coming today to help out. Someone had to do it!

I noticed that my mind kept returning to my garden shed. That this morning of all mornings, I was meant to see it. There was a purpose for it, which up until now I had not been ready for. Goodness, I was beginning to sound like Emerald Green.

At times I saw no end to the work that had to be done, however as I drove Bambino up the driveway, all I saw was beauty. Steve and Thomas's steel grey Cayenne was out the front and I knew they must be wandering somewhere.

I found Steve perched on the front stone steps, Whitie not far away sunning himself, the familiar sight of that cat never failing to amuse me.

'Hey hottie,' Steve called. I noticed when he kissed my cheek, he hugged me, holding me tighter than usual. It was no effort to return the hug, and at the same time inhale his signature fragrance of John Varatos Vintage aftershave. I glanced around looking for Thomas.

Steve inclined his head. 'He's taken Wilbur down to the river.'

With a level of suspicion, I eyed him. 'Now, what brings me this pleasure?' I hadn't been expecting the boys, and I could tell by the look on his face something was up. He followed me down the hallway and into the kitchen, his boots loud on the timber floorboards.

'The latte-toned walls look great,' he complimented, glancing around at the latest additions. 'And I like the way you've picked out the architectural mouldings in that vanilla hue.'

I have to say, there is nothing like a gay male for noticing the details. Nodding, I busied myself putting fresh De Bella coffee beans into the shiny stainless steel appliance. I made no attempt at small talk as I could clearly see what Steve was doing.

The machine expertly whirled, as it ground then brewed the coffee, and the delicious aroma quickly filled the air with a fragrance of comfort, deliciousness and luxury. I breathed it in. Sitting on the sofa opposite, Steve, one hand draped along the back, was now quiet as he observed me.

After chargrilling three pieces of sourdough, I selected three of my home grown tomatoes from the bowl on the kitchen bench. With pride, I briefly held one to my nose, a practice that was fast becoming a habit, and inhaled. Zingy and fragrant, I could smell the sweetness right through the skin.

Pulling a resin handled knife from the wooden knife block, deftly I sliced, arranging the juicy reds on the toast. Adding freshly torn basil, next I dolloped spoonfulls of labne, fresh from the farmer's markets early yesterday morning, which now seemed a lifetime ago.

I handed a piece to Steve. Eating, he busied himself looking out of the window, pretending to be taken with a view he had now seen dozens of times. Although I could hardly blame him, I too got lost in thought with the sight of it. Silently, I took three cupcakes and displayed them prettily on a plate and pushed them across the bench.

Coffee cup in hand, I perched on the edge of a stool. I slowly stirred the satiny mixture, then tapped the spoon a couple of times on the edge of the cup. Watching Steve's face, I put the spoon to my lips before placing it back on the saucer.

As if the cupcakes were the sole reason for his visit, Steve examined one of them far longer than necessary, even turning the plate and looking at it from another angle. 'Peach I have never seen anyone ice cakes as you do. You're quite the artist, you know. I like the way you use the silver cachous on the wings.'

Still I said nothing, knowing that was not the reason for his visit.

Feeling my eyes upon him, but avoiding them, he propped himself on a stool opposite, one boot clad foot resting on the stool rung, fingers randomly tapping on the bench. He took a sip of coffee and then swallowed hard. 'Davis called…' He cleared his throat, and took another sip, looking at me over the rim of the cup.

'Uh-huh?' I folded my arms across my chest, and eyed him.

Pointedly, he eyed me back. 'He was worried about you.'

'Nice of him,' I said quickly, glancing away.

'Yeah, I know.' His voice softened. 'Are you okay?' And then without giving me a chance to answer, he rushed on. 'Honey we only found out about the baby a few weeks back. God knows we had absolutely no bloody idea how to tell you. Thomas has been nagging me for weeks, telling me we had to do something.' He paused and tapped the bench. 'To be honest, we didn't know what the hell to do. I mean we couldn't make it go away. And you had told us not to disclose any information about Davis and… that you never wanted to hear another bloody word.'

Heavily, I exhaled. 'I know.' Shaking my head, I looked at him. 'And I know that's unfair to you. He is your brother. And this is your nephew or niece.'

He held the palms of his hands up to me, his voice flat. 'But under the circumstances…'

'Yep... I know, I know.' For a moment I was pensive, attempting to find the right words. Dropping my head, I looked at the floor, taking the deepest of breaths. 'I can't tell you how I felt when I saw her.' I glanced at him. 'I think that moment in time will stay with me forever.' Shivering, I shook my head attempting to erase the memory of how gutted I had felt such a short time earlier. 'But... what can I do? It's not your fault Steve. Nor is it your responsibility to tell me. You have a loyalty to your brother and I understand that.'

His fingers gave another tap on the bench. 'And I have a loyalty to you.'

I smiled grimly. 'Thanks sweetie.'

'I can't help think how excited we would have been had this been you.'

'*No*,' I put my hand up. '*Please... please don't Steve... I just can't* go there.'

'Well let's put it this way... it's bloody hard trying to be happy when it's her.'

I gave an ever so brief smile. 'You can say it that way if you like.' Gathering my thoughts, I was silent, and then I attempted to explain. 'I realise that some minute part of me was holding back. I think maybe I wondered what I would do if he ever wanted me back. On some level I hoped he would... and I was never really sure of what I would do. I mean, I hoped I'd slam the door in his face. But I didn't really know. So in my mind there was this sort of limbo... you know when you've loved someone for such a large chunk of your life, it is filled with moments that are amazing; some that are less than fine; and then there are some that are downright ugly. However,' and I shrugged, 'this morning I woke and thought... *phew* that's it. It's *really* over. And guess what? If I'm totally honest, there was some sort of relief, because I actually love the life I am living now, and he wouldn't fit in.'

I waved my arms around me. 'This is everything I've ever wanted. *This* is the real me. And do I want to share it with someone? You bet you. But he better be one hell of a guy. And this time, his dream had better match mine or I *aint* doing it again.' I cut the air with my hands.

'Daresay you need to add that to your list,' a voice said from behind me.

I snuffed. 'Damn right I will.' Turning, I offered my cheek to Thomas. 'You two have a good walk?'

'Yep, Wilbur showed me all the secret spots. He's my buddy.' Thomas patted Wilbur's blonde head, and then glanced over at the tiered tray of cupcakes. '*Oooh* I daresay we're just in time. I always love the way you decorate them. They're like little works of art.'

'Do you really think so?' I asked.

'Of course! Haven't I always said that?' he said, taking a bite out of one of them.

Dismissing the cupcake talk, Steve clapped his hands together. 'Right, what's the schedule here? When am I going to be ramping up the PR for this joint? I want to begin your campaign three months out. We'll need to be in all of the major publications.' I knew this was a far more comfortable topic than the earlier one for Steve.

'Down boy, there's no hurry. I'm just enjoying the process.'

*

The sun was warming the earth, flowers were waiting to be picked, and if I listened hard enough, the sound of a neighbour's radio could be softly heard, gently reminding me that I was not on some rural property as I so often felt, but smack bang in the middle of suburbia in a somewhat large Brisbane backyard.

My protective clothing consisted of a large denim shirt buttoned to the neck, black leggings, a leopard print scarf covering my hair, and a huge pair of sunglasses. Leaning over, I dragged a dusty old box filled with empty terracotta pots backwards out of the shed and over to the fence. Huffing and puffing, it did not escape me that from that angle, it was quite obvious that my legs were becoming trimmer and trimmer almost daily. I am not sure if I ever remembered seeing them so thin. With a gumboot clad foot, I pushed the box the last few inches, swatting at a couple of daddy long legs with my pink rubber gloved hand.

Standing, I put a hand to my lower back and surveyed the scene in front of me. Old paint cans were stacked to one side. Original spare roof tiles needed binning. A large piece of trellis had required real muscle power to move, however I found where there was a will there was a way. Actually, I had felt as if I had the strength of ten men when I had dragged, pushed and pulled it all the way to the fence. Varying sizes of old plastic and terracotta pots, some garden tools that looked defunct, a box of rusty old nuts, bolts and screws, a couple of old hoses, and some irrigation stuff, all could go.

The rest, try as I might, I could not move and would need help. Curls had escaped from my scarf and hung around my hot face, annoying me. Using the back of a gloved hand I wiped at my face, entering the shed again.

With French doors across two sides, it was really quite light filled, and rather wasted storing old junk. Now that I could actually move around inside, I picked up a straw broom and began swiping at some cobwebs.

Wilbur's friendly bark alerted me, and broom held mid-air, I briefly paused before I heard Phil's voice calling. '*Hellooo.*'

'I'm in the shed, Phil,' I called. It was unusual for him to come by on a Sunday. I continued clearing cobwebs, attempting to look busy, anything other than looking him in the face after yesterday's debacle. It was one of my less than finer moments. Probably dropped by to make sure I was still upright or something like that.

Although mind you, after a month of asking him for his tax file number, he had asked me to make out his pay to a boys' school, up on the Sunshine Coast hinterland. It baffled me, but he said he was a man of meagre wants and the school was needy. For some months, each week I still handed him his payslip and inquired if he was still certain about the arrangement.

Over my shoulder, I asked, 'Did you leave something behind?'

Studying my handwork, he ignored my question. 'Looks like you've been busy.'

I nodded, turning the corners of my mouth up ever so slightly. Folding my arms in front of me, I explained. 'I'm turning it into an art studio for myself.'

'You're an artist?'

'Actually, I'm not sure.' I shrugged.

Slowly, he nodded. 'I see.'

By the look of confusion on his face, I could tell he didn't. To be honest, nor did I. I realised that it wasn't baking the cupcakes I loved, it was artistically decorating them. Who would have thought? Never in my wildest dreams did I think I had anything of my mother in me. Lately, I had realised I had been so busy choosing a different path to her, perhaps I had denied who I really was.

'What are you doing with this other stuff?'

'It's too heavy. I think most of it needs dumping. But I'm not too sure what to do with those bed frames.' Removing my rubber gloves, I tossed them on the ground.

'I might know someone who could take them away. I'll organise a skip to be placed down here and we can toss this lot into it.' He nodded at the heavily congested passionfruit vine that had taken hold of the shed, attempting to smother the Boston ivy. 'Better prune that while we're down here. I'll mention it to Brownie.'

Once Phil had come on board, Brownie had felt displaced for all of five seconds. Phil had a way of making suggestions to him, which left Brownie thinking he had come up with the idea first. Plus, it was plainly obvious the older gent quite liked the younger one.

He broke into my thoughts. 'Did you remember about the boys coming later in the week?'

I tapped the side of my head. '*Oh...* is that when it is? I wasn't sure. But... I guess it's still fine.'

'A couple of the older ones can move this lot. The rest I'll get onto planting, mulching and fertilising. Thanks for allowing them this opportunity. It'll be good for them.'

'No problem.' I scratched at the top of my head, realising that this was what had bought him here today. He obviously needed to be certain that I was still *au fait* with it.

A few weeks earlier, Phil had asked if instead of hiring extra labourers, would I allow him to bring a group of boys in from a special school he helped at. I gathered he was talking about the school his pay check went to. By the sound of things, these boys had troubled pasts with rebelliousness and aggression, however through the school's program they were learning to control themselves. Although Phil didn't give too much away, he made it sound as if he volunteered regularly. I was grateful for the way the garden was coming on, so I had agreed on the spot. Meanwhile, I had hoped I hadn't acted rashly.

Phil broke into my reverie. 'They're good boys. They need some positive opportunities to boost their self-esteem. Mostly they have learning difficulties, which in the past has led to truancy and breaking school rules. Little by little they're getting there…' he drifted off.

'How many are coming?' I asked, attempting to sound casual.

'All twelve.'

'Twelve!' I expected maybe half a dozen at best. I rubbed a hand across my forehead in apprehension. God what was I getting myself into?

Phil must have sensed my uneasiness. 'As I said they're good kids. They just need a break.'

'Of course, of course. What time shall I expect them?'

'The bus will pick them up straight after meditation, so I'd say around nine.'

'Meditation!'

He caught the look of puzzlement on my face, and explained, 'Amongst other things, it helps with their physical relaxation and mental alertness. They are taught how to become masters of their minds rather than slaves to it.'

'Oh… I see.'

Phil must have suspected I didn't, because he continued to explain. 'Research has found that when such a practice is established in the childhood years, the rewards are truly remarkable, particularly for those young people with debilitating hyperactivity.'

I couldn't fault someone who championed the boys so well. One day's work was the least I could offer.

With a casual voice, I asked, 'Is this the school I send your wages to?' I had to be careful as Phil kept his cards close to his chest, and I didn't wish to pry for fear of losing him. He had already mentioned more than once, he was unsure how long he would be in town. I was well aware any minute our loose arrangement could halt.

'It is,' was all he said on the subject, before moving on. 'I'll pull those two bed frames out, so you can see what's behind. It'll make it easier later in the week for the boys.'

'Here, let me help you.' I wedged myself between a bedframe and the dusty glass French doors, attempting to lift the back end of one of the beds.

'Hey careful,' Phil warned, his voice sounding alert. 'Quick step back, it looks like a redback spider.' He pointed to a messy cobweb glinting in the afternoon sunlight on the lower edge of the window frame. He glanced around looking for something to kill it with.

'Hang on.' I lifted my right foot and my gumboot came down heavy and squashed the spider on the concrete floor. I wiped my boot along the ground, dislodging the now flat creature. I caught the look of surprise on Phil's face.

'I'm not scared of everything you know.'

There was a barely perceptible snort, and an amused flicker in his eyes. 'Really?'

Despite the fact that I rolled my eyes with derision, I explained, 'Best to be careful though. I have always found in the past that whenever I find one redback, there is another close by.'

I saw him glance around cautiously. Hmmm... so I had found his Achilles heel. *Touché.* I kept to myself the fact that earlier I had jumped back cautiously every time I had moved anything because I had been terrified of waking a sleeping snake. With an inflated sense of bravado, industriously, I continued to help Phil with the heavier pieces, finding strength I didn't know I had.

For the next hour and a half we worked side by side in companionable silence, lifting, hoisting, pulling, dragging and sorting the rubbish into piles outside near the fence. I was aware that this was not what I had hired Phil to do although he didn't appear to mind, and I certainly didn't mind the help, or the company. Once or twice, I noticed him shooting me admiring glances, and I liked it when he told me that for someone my size I was particularly strong.

Probing around the rubbish I had bought out earlier, Phil found a whiteboard propped against the fence. Taking his time studying it, he held it up.

I nodded. 'Looks like Mr Carmody used it for weekly tasks and yearly projects.' One column was headed with the word, *Always*, and the other *Wish List*. In the *Always* list, there was mowing, spraying, weeding, and standard tasks. In the *Wish List* was, brick edge the drive and extra wires for the honeysuckle on the eastern fence. It appeared that Mr Carmody was constantly making himself known to us.

Phil's voice was soft and thoughtful. 'My father used to do these boards up at our home. He must have gotten the idea from Frank.'

'Or Mr Carmody from him.'

'Perhaps.' His eyes were still on the whiteboard and he was thoughtful for a few seconds. And then he picked up a piece of irrigation I had placed in a pile earlier. 'Need this to repair a sprinkler down near the olive trees. I'll do it now.'

Removing my rubber gloves, I slapped them together and then wiped at my forehead with the back of my hand. 'I'll make coffee.' I sensed he needed a few minutes alone.

Surprising me with a definite nod, Phil took the sprinkler part and headed towards the river. Although most other tradesmen took me up on the offer of coffee, tea and cupcakes, Phil had not. I was unsure even of what he had for lunch. Although he appeared to get on well with everyone, he also appeared to keep to himself, and often I saw him leaving at lunch time, arriving back an hour later. I actually wondered if he had to report to someone at a particular time. The man was an enigma. However, it was easier for me to accept him rather than question him.

I was grateful for whatever time he was able to give.

Chapter 15

Phil drained the last of his coffee and placed his mug on the front veranda railing. I noticed the habitual glance of his watch.

'That's good coffee,' he said, using the back of his hand to wipe at the corners of his mouth. 'Thursday will be a big day for the boys. Hopefully, they'll cover most of the spring tasks I've got planned for them in one day.'

'I can't interest you in a cupcake?'

His hand hovered and then he pulled back. 'No... thank you.'

I caught his hesitation. 'Take it with you?'

'Thanks. You do a great job with the icing.' He gave the delayed smile that I was beginning to get used. It made me think that perhaps the smile sometimes surprised him. Perhaps he was unused to feeling happy.

'So everyone says.' I smiled briefly, before my face became more solemn. Busily, wrapping the cake in a napkin, I swallowed uncomfortably, and then cleared my throat. I turned to face him. 'Phil... yesterday was one of those less than finer moments for me.'

His voice held a serious tone. 'Life can be filled with less than finer moments.' He shrugged. 'We all have 'em.' I watched as he dropped his gaze briefly, his index fingernail scratching at the paint work on the railing. And then he placed his hand on his hips, and turned, his eyes narrowing, looking at something in the far off distance.

'Well...' I coughed. 'I'm rather embarrassed by my behaviour.'

Turning back to me, he dragged both of his hands through

his hair and stood with his hands locked at the back of his neck. 'Don't be. I daresay under the circumstances, it was warranted.'

'Thank you. But I assure you the hysterics are over.'

I saw the gentle upturn of the corners of his mouth, and I caught the look of amusement in his dark eyes. 'Now that would be a shame. I was quite getting used to them.'

Smiling grimly, I shook my head.

His voice was kind. 'You seem a lot better today.'

'I am… thank you.' I put my hands out, and spoke with an air of authority. 'I'm moving forward.'

He nodded. 'That's all a person can do. I mean… what's the alternative?'

I attempted to lighten the moment. 'My dad always says… "There are plenty of people in the graveyard who would love to have your problems." No doubt he's right!' I gave a light hearted laugh, but was unsure if he understood my joke. I moved on. 'Anyway, I hope you'll accept my apology. My whole life bared open to you like that. I feel… quite ridiculous.'

'No need.' He glanced at his watch. 'I've got to go.' Turning, he took a couple of steps, and then faltered. I watched with interest. Scratching his head, he turned back to me. 'My…' swallowing, he hesitated, and it was as if whatever he was about to say he changed his mind. 'We all have stuff. Shit happens. It sort of sums it up.' He paused and I saw the pain in his eyes. 'Believe you me, in the last couple of years, I have had many less than finer moments. Your little blowout was nothing.' He strode off down the driveway, my eyes following him.

*

From the kitchen, I heard the sound of crystal clinking in the library, as a gentle breeze stirred the newly installed chandelier, reminding me of its glamorous presence, making me feel as if perhaps I could be somewhere in Venice.

Since the installation last week, I had stood at the library door umpteen times admiring my latest acquisition, although for some odd reason, somewhere around mid-day yesterday it had managed to slip my mind. Today the entire house and garden had spoken to me, reminding me of the life I had now created.

'Helloo… anybody home?' From the front door, Lou's voice rang out loud and clear. It was accompanied by the excited voices of Lakshmi and Bob, and some good natured woofing from Wilbur.

'I'm in the kitchen,' I called, as with some concentration as if creating a masterpiece, I positioned the last white snapdragon into a tall slender vase and placed it in the middle of the new twelve seater, custom made, stained oak and metal table. The willowy flowers, an old fashioned favourite, arranged *en masse*, looked spectacular, and very much in proportion to the table.

As I stood back to admire my creation, the afternoon light filled the kitchen, catching the jewel-coloured lead lights from some of the windows, splashing a kaleidoscope of colour across the walls. With a renewed sense of contentment, I smiled a thank you.

When I had first come, all of the rooms had been painted so many different ghastly colours, I had barely noticed the lead lights. However, once the new paint job had begun, each window became a thing of beauty. All that was left was the new one I had now commissioned for above the front door, the cursive letters spelling out Carmody House.

As the crystal stirred once again, I heard Lou's footsteps pause at the library door.

'Oh Mummy, look,' Lakshmi breathed.

Lou gave a low whistle. 'Impressive!'

'You like?' I asked, as she admiringly glanced around, slinging her oversized handbag onto the table. For a few seconds, she removed a shoe and ran her foot, complete with glossy black varnished toenails, over the Aubusson rug which was now under the table, in sheer appreciation, before she wasted no time in asking, 'Are you hiding some secret hot lover?' Folding her arms, her feline eyes, smudged in black kohl, stared at me demanding an answer.

'What on earth are you talking about?' I asked, as I fired up the Gaggenau for the hundredth time that day. I was becoming quite an expert.

'That *hottie* that held the gate open for us on the way in.'

'Oh you mean Phil, the gardener. He's been here for months. You must have seen him around. '

'Hmmm, the gardener.' Raising her eyebrows, she swept her long blonde hair over to one side, and plonked herself down on one of the stools at the spotted gum kitchen bench. She cocked her head. 'He could be boyfriend material for you! What do you know about him?'

'Nothing,' I said drily, from inside the walk in pantry, still enjoying the novelty of it, my eyes casting an admiring glance over the stack of white china to one side, the other, glass jars filled with every conceivable thing. I reached for the plastic Peter Rabbit plates I kept especially for the children.

'Now you take these out to the front steps,' I told them, 'But don't share any with Wilbur.'

'What do you mean?' Lou asked.

'He's getting too fat. I think the painters share their lunch.'

'*No...* I mean about the gardener. You must know something or you wouldn't have hired him. I know you, you're like a truffle hound, sniffing out precious delicacies.'

'Ha-ha Miss Smartie. Truly I don't know anything.' She was right, generally I prided myself on my razor sharp intuition. I was thoughtful. 'That's a lie… his father was Mr Carmody's gardener for quite some years, so Phil has memories of how the garden was years ago. Plus he has extensive knowledge of plants and gardens and construction, now that I think about it. The transformation over the last few months has been unbelievable. I truly don't know what I would have done without him. He was exactly what the garden needed.' Reminding myself, I walked over to the huge pane of glass on the rear wall, and my eyes followed the garden down as far as the river bank, taking in the vibrant hues of nature at its best.

And then I turned. '*But* he doesn't do a regular day's work. He comes and goes all over the place, however I did know that when I employed him. He's not motivated by money. He's *between things*,' I drew inverted commas in the air. 'Doesn't know how long he'll be in town for. Never mentions anyone else, so I presume he's a loner, and, he volunteers at a school for troubled boys.' My voice carried a sarcastic edge, 'Now, altruism may well and truly be an aphrodisiac… but the rest aint doing it for me. Your thoughts?'

'Smart arse!' From across the monolithic island bench, Lou looked down her nose at me.

'You want coffee or not?' I asked drily.

She propped her chin on her hand. 'Surely he has mentioned his recent past?' She looked directly at me, making a point. 'I mean to say,' and she imitated my voice. '*Whenever someone doesn't have recent past, there is trouble.*'

With a cocked eyebrow, I gave her a look. 'He's not saying and I'm not asking.'

'Mmm living dangerously for a while are we? This guy

comes at all hours of the day and night. Sometimes you are the only one here, and he knows it.' She glanced about, her voice now almost a whisper. 'No one would hear you scream.'

'LOU! SHUT UP!' Between her and Thom, let alone my own imaginings, I was becoming a nervous wreck about this guy, and if truth be told he really hadn't given me reason to be, even though… I still didn't know anything about him.

She laughed. 'I'm teasing. But that's exactly what you'd say to me. You did in fact.'

Grudgingly, I shook my head. '*Touché…*'

Lakshmi, with Bob behind her waving a stick, came running in to see what the commotion was. Pulling Bob up onto my lap, I nuzzled his warm moist neck. 'I could eat you,' I said laughing, loving the sweaty baby smell of him. And then I tickled him, surreptitiously taking the stick away, handing it over to his mother who hid it under the couch.

Wilbur roamed in and plonked himself down on the floor, his collar filled with bunches of mauve bell-shaped flowers that the children had busily attached. I wondered what he thought of his new life.

Once I had Bob calmly settled on my lap, I couldn't help but ask Lou, 'So, to what do I owe this pleasure?'

'What, a sister can't visit?'

I flashed her a look letting her know I knew it was more than that.

'Two things,' she said before pausing. With my head tilted to the side, I gave her the eye, as I sensed an air of nervousness about her. She proceeded cautiously. 'Thomas phoned this morning…'

'Oh did he now? Well I'm fine.' But I glanced away. Bob wriggled to be put down and I obliged.

Lou put a hand out across the bench to me. 'Really? It

must have been an awful shock.'

Shrugging, I sighed, not wishing to talk about it anymore. She narrowed her eyes. 'Are you sure you're okay?'

I nodded. 'I can't say I was immediately upon seeing... *her*... but this morning when I woke... there was a change. I can't put it into words. This place. I feel such gratitude for it. There's something about it, I don't know, some kind of greater purpose.' Shrugging, I lowered my voice. 'Anyway, he's such a drop-kick you know. It helps knowing that.' I looked over at her, attempting a smile. 'It was the push I needed to change my name back to Avanel. Sounds a hell of a lot better than Rider anyway. And your second reason?'

'Well, you won't believe it, but this morning I also heard the weirdest thing. Quite odd in fact, so I had to come straight over to see if you'd lost your marbles.'

I picked up on the change of tone in her voice. '*What?*' I asked, my eyes wide.

'I overheard Dad on the phone to Bea. She told him that you were turning a garden shed or something into an art studio. She asked him to give you a hand.' She laughed. 'You know Dad, he kept saying *abso-bloody-lutely!* Anyway, I knew that either they had to be wrong, or you'd gone stark raving mad.' She gave me a look, waiting for an answer.

I shrugged, laughing to myself. Firstly, I had only called Bea about my idea this morning. I could have told her I was turning my house into a brothel and she would have said... *that's nice darling...* however I tell her about the garden shed and she rings Dad immediately. And secondly, I couldn't believe Bea had asked him to help. I was making over an entire bloody house and an enormous garden, and they offer to help with the garden shed. But that was my family for you.

Sheepishly, I looked at the ground. 'It's only an idea,' I said slowly, and then I looked at her for approval. 'Everyone nurtures the idea of doing something creative in a tranquil haven. I'm just exploring ideas, that's all.'

Lou's voice carried a baffled tone. 'But you've *never* shown the slightest inclination. Quite the opposite in fact.'

Once again, I shrugged, explaining, 'It's this place. For some reason, this morning I looked at that shed and all I could think of was creativity.' Suddenly other thoughts flooded my mind. 'I'm not saying I wouldn't love to hear the pitter-patter of little feet, but,' and I smiled at Lakshmi and Bob who were lying on their tummies on the ground beside Wilbur, stroking him from head to toe, 'these guys might be it. So meanwhile… I'm going to find out exactly who I am right down to the last brushstroke.' I lowered my voice in a conspiratorially way. 'You know, you and I were so busy not being Bea, we chose a totally different path. Bea was not the conventional mother that we both craved, but she did love us, and has made us who we are. Surely as mature women we should embrace that?'

Begrudgingly, Lou nodded thoughtfully. 'I know what you mean. I've been so busy bucking the system, I've worn myself out.' She continued, 'But you can't suddenly say *I'm going to paint*, and paint. Can you?'

Shrugging, I pushed the plate of cupcakes towards her. 'In case you didn't notice, I've been inspired by butterflies for the longest time, creating them on cupcakes since I was a teenager. And the first day I came here one welcomed me. They've been fluttering around me since I arrived. I think they've been trying to tell me something. I can't put it into words, however this morning it made sense. It's time to do something much grander. I've already thought about my first exhibition…'

Gobsmacked, Lou could not help but interrupt. '*Exhibi-*

tion? My God, you are really serious?'

'Yes, I am. I'm going to call it *The Butterfly Effect*! Butterflies are the ultimate symbol of transformation…'

'And what… you think that's you?'

'God only knows. I'm just saying what popped into my head this morning.' I really did think it was me, but that was my business. 'Anyway, they are such tragic beauties, they only live a few short days on this earth, and that's what I want to capture. It will be a reminder to live our days as butterflies do – as if it was our last.'

'Well you'd better get painting then,' Lou said matter-of-factly. 'If you say you're going to do it, you will. But a word of warning… I think there's a scary movie with that title.'

I fobbed her off. 'I dunno love. I only thought about it this morning. It may be called something else entirely.'

However, I was already picturing enormous canvases featuring an overwhelming intensity of colour. I guess I wasn't too different from my mother after all.

'But Peach…?'

'What?'

'Where the heck are you going to find the time, with running the B&B?'

Then I changed the subject, needing to voice my grievance. 'I am so annoyed with the council. It has been one hold up after another on that back decking. Just the other day, I read an article that said Brisbane's council approvals are happening much quicker. It stated that if something hadn't been approved over a certain period of time, then it was deemed permitted. I cheered for joy. That was until I phoned them and they explained that they had followed the book to the letter T. Do you know they phoned me right in the last hour of the last day and requested another 28 days to make their decision? Each time they said they would approve it, but they needed more time. This has gone on four times. The water tanks are meant to be hidden beneath the deck, but meanwhile it is delaying the opening.' I took a deep breath. 'Hence giving myself something else to do, my new art studio, while I wait to get this place finished.' I didn't add that Papa's money had given me the luxury of time.

Lou wrinkled her brow at me. 'What… you didn't feel you had enough to do before?'

'Yes of course,' I waved a hand at her. 'But there is so much to me, so much bursting to come out. I'm really enjoying it. And…' I paused. 'The next guy who comes into my life had better appreciate my qualities and the lifestyle I wish to lead or I'm not going there.'

'*Touché*,' Lou said, but I was already heading for the stairs to my bedroom to add a few more qualities to 'the list'.

Chapter 16

There had been no chance of a sleep in as I had been awake since the crack of dawn listening to tweets, chirps and the calls of honeyeaters, cockatoos, magpies and sparrows. However, I was still startled when I realised that Phil and the boys had arrived earlier than expected and I was still in my nightie. It was the sound of the gravel crunching that alerted me. Wilbur, lying beside the bed, could not get up fast enough, his claws scrabbling on the floor as he hastened down the steps to the front door, where he began to whimper. Surreptitiously, I glanced out the dormer window.

With a finger to his lips Phil motioned the boys around the side of the house and down towards the river. The motley crew were simply just boys: some short, some tall, downy hair, skinny ankles, dimpled cheeks, shy downcast eyes, oversized shorts, the oldest looking no more than fourteen.

I overheard one say, '*Scuse* me Phil, do you have a tissue?', while wiping his nose on the back of his sleeve. Once again, Phil placed a finger to his lips, and then pulled a wad out of his pocket, as if this was a norm for him. I spied another man bringing up the rear. I guessed him to be in his forties, although he was youthfully dressed in a T-shirt, cargo shorts and joggers. From my position at the window, he appeared to give off a healthy and fit demeanour. Phil, as per usual was dressed as he always did for work, black polo, khaki shorts, chocolate coloured blundstone boots and a beige akubra.

Intensely interested, I moved to the back window which had spectacular views over the garden and beyond, waiting to see if Phil's entourage came into view again. Not a cloud in the sky, spring was well and truly upon us. The blossoms of many deciduous trees provided a spectacular display, and lush new growth could be seen in every hue, from brilliant chartreuse to the softest aquamarine.

Phil and the boys came back into vision as they descended the stone steps. I watched as Phil pointed things of interest out to them on the way. Unable to draw myself away, I began to dress, my fingers busy doing the buttons up on a khaki coloured shirt dress, rolling the cuffs back, standing the collar up.

They stopped at the lawn area near the pool, where Phil directed them to place their backpacks under the huge flowering jacaranda. He sat on the grass and the boys formed a semi-circle around him. I counted eleven, wondering where the twelfth was.

My hands riffled around in the scarf drawer, settling on a leopard print one. Hastily, I folded it into a long band, and tied it around my hair, attempting to keep the curls off my face. Wilbur's whimper turned into a whine. Rapidly, I buckled a black patient belt at my waist and took the stairs, letting the impatient dog out. At the front door, I slid my feet into leopard print flats, and made my way down to the group. As I rounded the house I came across the painters, their scaffolding high against the outside of the house.

'Hope we didn't wake you,' John called down to me. 'We've been here since sparrows fart. Once we're done here, we've got the shutters to do and that'll be nearly it.'

I waved back. 'Not at all. Don't know what I'd do without you, John. You've become part of the furniture.' I smiled up at him. 'I'm hopeful the shutters will arrive later in the week. How did you go with the duck egg blue I wanted?'

He gave me the thumbs up. 'Done!' he said. 'Will show you the colour chart later.'

'Well don't be in too much of a hurry to finish.' With my

fingers crossed behind my back, I flashed my eyes in an attempt to cajole him into more work. 'I'm thinking that lovely little timber shed over on the east boundary might need a coat or two. You'd have time wouldn't you?'

He raised his eyebrows in question. 'Whatever love, you let me know.' He nodded down towards the bottom of the garden. 'Phil has bought the boys.' With some level of surprise, I realised he had spoken as if he knew all about them. And then he continued, 'We'll keep our eyes on them for you.'

It had not gone unnoticed by me, how most of the tradespeople appeared to be quite fond of Phil. Often deferring to him when they wanted to know something.

Giving John a wave, I skipped across the flagstones, admiring the random plantings of the purple echiums between the gaps. As like the rest of the garden, this area had a colour theme. Lining the path were thymus, alyssums and aquilegias in various shades of lilac, purple, blue and mauve. And then the garden leading to the pool was heavily planted with agapanthus. Their purple ball like flowers striking when massed as they were. Once you stepped out into the clearing, the huge jacaranda tree came into view showcasing its beautiful colour as only a jacaranda can do. The entire thing was not only pretty, but soothing as well.

As I neared, I saw that Phil had his eyes closed and was deep in thought. I stopped nearby at the bottom of the stone steps, and crept behind a huge cycad in an Italianate urn. Peering from behind the huge prickly fronds, I felt like a voyeur, but could not tear my eyes away. I strained my ears to hear.

Gently, softly, he led them into a meditation. 'Backs straight, eyes closed. Breathe… You're doing well. Return your thoughts to peace, to calm, to love. Remember if you can master your mind, you will never be its slave. Breathe. Repeat in your mind…'

Even my breath slowed, and I felt calm listening to him.

Ten minutes later he opened his eyes and smiled at the boys sitting around him. 'You guys did really well. Well done Byron,' and he shook the boy's hand. 'You managed to maintain your silence for the entire time.'

Byron's face lit up, obviously happy that Phil had singled him out for praise. 'I did good, didn't I?'

Phil laughed, and the perfect white teeth and the dark eyes sparkled. 'You did good mate!'

The control I was used to seeing had disappeared as his smooth tanned face burst open like a sunflower. My observation had been that mostly Phil didn't like to hear himself talk, however it was plainly obvious, that others liked to hear him.

From the polite nods he gave to the boys, to his considered responses to questions he had undoubtedly answered many times, to the delight that lit his eyes as he spoke, it was clear that he was more than comfortable in this position, and I noticed the boys were paying rapt attention to what he had to say.

'Remember boys, you have only 86,400 precious seconds a day to spend how you choose. Let's choose to spend them wisely. The only person you are destined to become, is the person *you* decide to be.' And then he winked at them. I noticed that it not only bought a smile to the boys' faces, but to mine as well.

I watched while he continued to busy himself, handing each boy a sheet of paper instructing them on the day's tasks. He explained that there would be rewards given at the end of the day, and those rewards would go towards the merit board at school. The entire time his voice was gentle and he was smiling. His eyes were focused on the faces of the boys and I could see he was connecting with each of them.

I saw one of the boys, a sandy haired, round faced fellow, elbow another. 'Ya 'ear that?' he said. His smile said it all. And I couldn't help but wonder about those boys? What was their story? And for that matter… *what was Phil's?*

'There's more to our Phil than meets the eye.' I jumped as Brownie spoke right beside me, so engrossed in the scene in front of me I did not hear him approach. However, before I had time to answer, he left me, his step a little quicker than usual, and approached the group.

As Phil introduced him to the other gent, Brownie stood tall with his hands behind his back. With an air of authority, which I had failed to see in the past, he looked at each boy carefully, while Phil spoke.

'Boys, I'd like you to meet Mr Browne. Mr Browne served in the Australian Army as a Colonel. I'm sure you'll agree he could teach us a thing or two.'

My eyes were popping out of my head. *Brownie, a colonel? Well, I never.* There was a murmuring from the boys. Phil asked them for silence. I noticed that Brownie was beaming.

Phil continued, 'After that Mr Browne worked at a boy's school as a marshal. So… he is well used to people your age. Please give him the respect he deserves.' Phil eyed each of the boys. 'Luke, Nigel and Ben, please stand and go with Mr Browne. You'll be starting with the shed. By the time you're finished we will meet for morning tea back here under this tree.'

He looked up at me as if he knew I had been standing behind the cycad the entire time. I realised that this man did not miss much.

'Boys, before you go, please say good morning to Ms Avanel. Ms Avanel has given us all a wonderful opportunity here today, so we shall be *respectful and courteous.*' He spoke as if reminding them. 'And as I explained earlier, there will be no reason for *anyone* to go into the house. There is a toilet at the back of the garage, should you need to use it. This area here is where we shall have our morning tea and lunch. *Is that clear?* Phil's voice had the quality of being gentle, although firm at the same time. I could tell by the looks on the boy's faces that they appeared to like him. One of them, short, chubby, fluffy brown hair, took every opportunity to touch Phil's shoulder, or stand next to him.

A chorus of 'Yes Phil,' rang out, as the boys clambered to their feet.

'Peach, I'd like to introduce you to Frank…' before Phil could get any further, a small fracas broke out, and he instantly stepped in. It appeared one of the boys had lost the piece of paper Phil had given him and he thought that one of the others had taken it.

Although Frank was now explaining that he taught maths, English, physical education and yoga, my attention was drawn to watching how Phil handled the disturbance.

'Well that's quite a combination,' was as much of a response I could give Frank, all the while glancing over at Phil, my mind ticking away. The piece of paper had been found, folded small in the boy's shirt pocket. I watched while the boy, Simon it seemed, was encouraged by Phil, to shake Henry's hand and tell him he was mistaken.

'He's fantastic with the boys. I don't know what we'd do without him. I don't know what the boys would do without him,' Frank explained, noticing that I could not drag my eyes away.

I nodded, uncertain of what to think. And then I asked, 'Frank, I was under the impression there were to be twelve boys. Was one unwell?'

'No,' he exhaled heavily. 'Max was sent home with his grandfather again today.'

Puzzled, I looked at him.

'Max has only been with us for six months. He's still at that settling in stage. Not every day is a good day. But there are more good days now than bad. When he came to us, he hadn't lived at home since he was eight and had been in seven different foster homes. Last year his mother had another baby and he couldn't figure out how that baby could live with her, but he couldn't. Thank goodness his grandparents finally took him in. They're good people, but they're struggling. However, when Max rang and asked if he could join our school...'

'Max rang?'

'Yes that's part of our deal. The boys must want to come. We do the deal with them.'

I nodded thoughtfully. This was another world to me. 'You were saying?'

'We asked his grandfather to be his safety net. We knew Max would take time to settle. So we asked the old man to wait in the car each day for the first hour or two. If Max plays up, he goes home. We have to show that bad behaviour cannot be tolerated. However, we ask that he returns the next day. We need to let him know we care. And let's put it this way, it is happening less and less.' Frank smiled, and I could see his job was greatly rewarding.

I turned back to the boys. They were just that... boys.

As soon as the eight boys and the two men returned to the top of the garden in front of the house, I went in search of Brownie. I was concerned that this would be more than he could handle.

From a ladder at the side of the shed, he appeared to be keeping a sharp eye on his three, while he thinned the passionfruit vine. One of the boys, a smaller boy who looked to be the youngest of the group, I guessed around eleven, stood below and picked up the cuttings, depositing them in the skip. Meanwhile the other two, who were larger boys, lifted and hoisted the rubbish into the skip at Brownie's direction. Every now and then he encouraged them by saying, 'Good lads, now see that pile there…'

He climbed down the ladder to speak with me, brushing his hands off on his overalls. 'All well, Mrs Riding?' I did not bother to correct Brownie on my name change.

'Yes,' I replied, but took the opportunity while the young boy was over at the skip to say, 'Brownie, I had no idea you were a marshal at the school. I'm sorry, I thought you'd told me you were the gardener.'

'To tell the truth Mrs Riding I was. But I saw how those marshals handled things, and sometimes I had to do a bit *meself*. You know, you've got to show them whose boss, or they have it all over you.'

'I understand,' I said smiling, as he climbed back up the ladder. 'I'll see you at morning tea then Brownie.'

'You will. We have those patty cakes of yours do we?'

'We do.'

As I passed the two older boys, I heard one of them saying to the other, 'Simon said that the old codger used to be a sniper in the war. Poor bloody Lukey. Hope he doesn't shoot 'im.' He glanced over his shoulder at the younger boy picking up Brownie's trimmings.

'Bloody 'ell Ben. Don't turn ya back.'

Wiping the smile off my face, I glanced back to Brownie. He called to the young boy, 'Good lad Luke. You're doing a bloomin' marvellous job.'

*

Feeling that it was indeed a spectacular day, I could not help but notice how buoyant I was feeling. And, not only was the cloudless sky, indigo blue, but everywhere I looked bulbs were exploding from the ground. I could smell the earth warming along with the weather. It was a perfect time of year. Earlier, it had amused me when poor old Wilbur had been swooped upon by a cheeky magpie. By the look on the poor dog's face, he wasn't too amused.

Navigating the steps and long walk ahead, I trod carefully, walking slowly, balancing the wooden tray with the huge pitcher of icy cold homemade lemonade. I'd already placed the cakes on a table under the tree. Phil had told me they'd bring their own morning tea and lunch, however the effect these boys had on me was that I just wanted to spoil them.

As I neared the stone steps I saw one of the boys sitting at the top, nursing his arm and silently crying. He sat hunched and facing away from me. He wiped at his face with the back of his sleeve of an extremely over washed black T-shirt that was now a dull grey.

'Can I help?' I asked, balancing the tray as best I could.

Grimacing he held out his arm, showing three raised red lumps. 'Wasp stings,' he said, sniffing. He rubbed at them. '*Oww…*' and screwed up his grubby, freckly face again, giving a triple sniff. 'I'll be okay,' he said, but I could see he was shaking. My heart went out to him.

'What's happening here,' Phil's voice came from behind. 'Matty I told you not to leave the group.'

He sniffed again. 'Frank said I could go to the toilet and I thought you'd be down here by now so…' he blubbered, putting his head on his chest and holding out his arm.

Hunkering down on his haunches, Phil examined his arm, speaking gently. 'They got you good mate.' He rubbed the boy's back. 'Come on… take some nice slow breaths.' Taking his wallet from his trouser pocket, he opened it and took out a credit card.

Still standing with the tray, I wondered what the heck he was doing.

'Stand back boys. Give him room.' Using the edge of the card, Phil drew it firmly across the skin. 'Got it,' he said. 'The sting is out.'

'Hang on a second.' I turned to Frank. 'Can you hold this please?' I asked, handing him the tray.

Quickly I untied my scarf letting my hair fall forward. With a spoon, I fished out half a dozen ice cubes from the lemonade. Placing them in the scarf, I handed it to Phil. 'This might help. I'll head back up to the house and get some Panadol and see if I've got some sting cream.' Over my shoulder, I called, 'There are patty cakes under the jacaranda for morning tea.'

'Peach?' Phil called.

I stopped and turned, 'Yes.'

'Actually a piece of aloe vera from the kitchen garden would work a treat.'

'Right!'

Five minutes later, as I rounded the bottom step I took in the view of my garden, and thought how much my life had changed. The pretty carpet of fallen jacaranda was littered with tired boys' bodies, cooling off on the grass, drinking homemade lemonade, made from the abundance of lemons from my kitchen garden, and eating cupcakes. Wilbur lay in amongst them, enjoying the extra attention he was receiving. Brownie walked around topping the boy's drinks up, as if this was his daily ritual. I could see Phil off to one side speaking slowly and rhythmically to Matty. I stopped to allow them the privacy they needed, giving me the chance to observe them.

There was no denying Phil was excellent with these boys.

Keeping eye contact with Matty, Phil had his hand on the boy's chest. 'We'll breathe together. That's it, nice and slowly. The ice is helping isn't it? Good. Bring your breath down. And again.' Glancing up, he caught my eye.

Removing two Panadols from the packet, he handed them to the boy. 'Here we go mate.' Snapping the aloe vera in half, he pressed the gel from inside, and with his index and middle fingers carefully smoothed it onto the stings. At first, Matty pulled away but then he appeared to trust Phil enough to let him spread it.

I placed a cold wet face washer on the back of the boy's clammy neck. 'Anything I can do to help Matty?' I touched his bony back and briefly felt him stiffen. I pulled my hand away, glancing at Phil to see if he had noticed. Kindly, he winked at me and shared a brief smile. I nodded and moved away, unsure of what to do now.

Earlier, I had surreptitiously watched from behind the French doors in the library, as Phil and one of the much younger boys crossed through the white garden. Phil appeared to be extolling the virtues of nature. Pausing, he had put out a hand and delicately cupped the head of a white hydrangea, explaining something. The boy nodded eagerly, appearing glad to be the soul receiver of Phil's attention. And then gently with his fingertips, Phil began to coax a bug onto his hand. He crouched and the two heads bent together to study it. I watched as the boy's face lit up in wonderment before he put out a finger as if to touch, but then pulled his hand away. Gently, Phil placed it back on a leaf. As they continued on, Phil's voice reached me as he patiently explained the names of all of the plants in the white garden: camellias, lilies, fuchsias, hyacinths and dogwoods.

My reverie was interrupted by the boy who Phil had praised

for sitting still through the meditation. 'Me mum'd luv these miss,' he said.

'Would you like to take one home to her?'

'Nah. Not sure when I'll see her next.'

'Oh…' I was thoughtful for a few seconds. 'Perhaps you could take one anyway for later.'

'Bloody awesome.'

'Byron,' Frank admonished in a pleasant tone. 'Manners please.'

'Sorry… Miss.'

I smiled at the boy. With my arms folded, I turned and surveyed the raggedy bunch. They just wanted to be loved like every other child their age. I watched as Phil pulled Frank aside and spoke quietly to him, every now and then nodding towards Matty.

'Excuse me Phil,' I said. 'But can I be of some help with Matty? Perhaps he should come up to the house with me.' I watched as Phil looked at Frank. At first, Frank didn't say anything, but then he shrugged and nodded his head. He walked over to the boys and gathered them into the semi-circle, leaving us alone.

Running both of his hands through his hair, Phil stood with his hands clasped at the back of his neck. 'Peach, this exercise with the boys was not meant to put you out.'

'It hasn't. I'm truly grateful for the work they're getting done.' My face softened. 'They look like good kids, Phil.'

He raised his eyes to the sky, and gave a hint of a smile. 'That's a bit of a stretch, even on a good day. But… they deserve better…' he shrugged.

'I've got some things to do in the kitchen. Matty can help.'

He narrowed his eyes. 'Are you sure?'

'Yes, of course. It's the least I can do.'

'Really, you've done more than enough. This is a fantastic opportunity for them. It's important for them to see that people trust them. And then to do physical work in nature, well it's wonderful. And not to mention morning tea. You know it was unnecessary, but thank you.'

'Well, they seemed to like it.'

'They loved it. It's not often someone goes to that much trouble for them. They're not used to it. It means a lot. Thank you.' He touched my arm in earnest. We both looked where his hand rested, and then he gently pulled it away.

*

The kitchen garden, now fully productive, was supplying an assortment of vegetables and fruit on a daily basis. It gave me the kind of satisfaction where I'd catch myself standing back, placing my hands on my hips, gazing with pride. And then I'd shake myself, feeling silly because without thinking about it I was mirroring Phil.

I liked how the seasons offered me ideas. Earlier, while watering, the luxuriant basil had drawn my attention. It seemed to be telling me that it was going to be a pesto making day.

With tongs, I removed small glass jars from the top shelf of dishwasher. I had put them through the rinse cycle to sterilise them. Careful not to touch them with my hands, I placed them on a clean tea towel and was about to spoon in the brilliant green mixture.

'Matty, I'll press the mixture down really well, and then you follow me and cover it with a good half centimetre of that beautiful olive oil.' Removing the cork from the Joseph's First Run Extra Virgin Olive Oil, I pushed it across the bench to him.

'Thought it was a bottle of wine,' he said in wonderment.

I smiled. 'It is in a wine bottle, but look at the lovely green colour. It's like nectar.'

'Hmmm… nectar,' he repeated, but looked a little uncertain as to what nectar might be.

For a minute, we worked in silence. I watched the young boy's face, the tip of his tongue protruding at the corner of his mouth in concentration.

'Great job Matty. And you did a fantastic job with that roast tomato sauce as well. Make sure you take that container with you.' I pointed to the small plastic take away food container on the end of the kitchen bench.

My tomato crop had been a marvel to me. The Black Krims a favourite. Not a day went by without me eating them in some manner. However, I was peeved to notice the coriander had already run to seed, a reminder that nature was indeed in control. I smiled to myself when I realised I was beginning to use Phil's terminologies.

As an exercise, I had planted a single gooseberry bush. I had high hopes of making gooseberry pies, but when I had mentioned this to Phil, he had explained that perhaps Brisbane was not the correct climate for gooseberries. We would have to wait and see. However, there was still my token blueberry bush. My hope was for a handful of berries each day to add to my breakfast smoothie. Phil had warned that I would need to net the bush as it was irresistible to the birds. There was much to know.

Hands clad in oven mitts, red checked tea towel thrown over my shoulder, I removed the freshly baked cupcakes from the oven, the smell heavenly. With pride, Matty finished lining up the small glass jars across the bench, while I readied the ingredients for the icing.

'And now we need four cups of icing sugar,' I instructed. 'And just a few drops of this blue colouring. Go slowly. Perfect! You could get a job making these any day of the week.'

Plugging in the hand held electric beaters, I handed them to him. 'Keep them low in the bowl. That's it. Well done.'

'I wouldn't mind being a chef. But me mum's boyfriend says it's a job for pansies.'

'Really? Well perhaps he doesn't know any fantastic chefs. You know Matty, if you have a passion for something, you can be anything you want. Don't let someone tell you otherwise.'

A beautiful smile lit his face, deeply softening, and instantly endearing. 'That's what Phil always says.'

It was hard for me to imagine this was a troubled boy.

'Well he's very wise. I'd listen to him. I'll pour this lemon juice in for you. You keep beating.' Surreptitiously, I glanced at the boy. 'So you boys like Phil, do you?'

'*Yeah*, he's a top bloke.'

Nodding to myself, I repeated. 'He *is* a top bloke.' I paused, and when I next spoke, I didn't know if I was talking to Matty or myself. 'He seems to know a lot of stuff.'

'He sure does.'

'I see all's well in here then.' At the sound of Phil's voice, I turned to see him leaning against the door frame, his gaze fixed on me, his shirt sleeves tight around his biceps, the veins on his forearms standing out.

I was caught so much by surprise, that for a long moment I held his gaze. Something about the intensity of his look caused colour to rise in my cheeks. 'How long have you been there for?'

'Long enough,' he said, and then paused, his gaze still upon me. 'All of the boy's will want to be stung by wasps if this is what they end up doing.'

'Peach and me...'

'Ms Avanel and I!' Phil nicely corrected.

'Sorry... Ms Avanel and me are making cupcakes for us

boys to eat on the bus on the way back to school. She's going to show me how to decorate them with butterflies.'

'She's very good at that.' And over the top of Matty's head, he winked at me for the second time that day, and mouthed a silent thank you. Warmly, I smiled in return, turning to wash my hands at the sink, feeling the warmth of happiness spread around me. But then I heard Matty give out a loud laugh.

'Ah-hum,' Phil cleared his throat.

As I turned around to face Phil, my eyes wide in question, I saw him give Matty a stern look, with a quick shake of his head.

Phil pointed. 'You've got a floury hand print on the back of your skirt,' he told me.

Twisting this way and that, I found the offending print and using the tea towel brushed at my left buttock.

'Boys this age laugh at everything,' he said by way of explanation.

'Hmmm…' was all I said, feeling a tad silly.

*

From the front steps, I watched as the boys finished with an acknowledgment session, where each boy acknowledged the virtue of another. 'I would like to acknowledge Mikey for helping me when I couldn't carry that log.' 'I would like to acknowledge Byron for digging the holes for me to put the plants into…'

It was pleasing to be reminded of how easy one can be happy. Joining them to wait for the bus, I looked around, and noticed that the boys were exhausted, not only from their manual labour, but also the effort of their good behaviour. Bored, they begin to mess about and wrestle each other. I watched as unwittingly, Lukey pushed Nigel against the fence. It wasn't a big thing.

However, Nigel hurt his leg, and his pride. To my shock, he pushed the smaller boy in the face. I felt the anger, and it scared me.

'*Boys no…*' I shrieked.

Oblivious to me, for a second Lukey cowered, but then he retaliated, as he leapt onto Nigel's back amid a flurry of punches. 'You fuckin' prick.'

In less than a second, Phil burst between the two of them, grabbing Lukey by the back of the shirt and one arm. The powerful physicality of him overwhelming me, but not enough for me to miss the bulging muscles of his biceps. With a mixture of fright and awe, I watched as he easily hauled Lukey off to the side of the garage.

With less ease, Frank dragged Nigel off in the other direction. Brownie came forward and eyed the rest of the boys. My heart pounding, I stood shocked, unsure where to look.

From beside me, Matty assured me, 'It's awight Miss!'

Nodding, I smiled nervously at him, scratching at the back of my hand. I had been about to ask him to come any time to bake with me, although now I was uneasy about the entire thing. What really upset me was how adept these boys were at fighting, and how quick something could blow up. And for the first time reality dawned on me, and I realised what a gamble today had been. Phil's speed and strength at separating the boys was something else I could not get my head around. This was something he was used to… and good at.

Twenty minutes later, the boys were seated on the bus, Lukey in the front seat, Nigel in the back. Before Frank got on board, he had a quiet word to Phil. He then climbed in and the door closed. I waved to them. On one hand, glad the day was over, on the other, rather sad. A discomfort fell over me, which I could not place.

I began to walk towards the front steps. Phil fell in step with me. 'You just have to get one of them out of the way,' he said.

I didn't look at him, and was quiet for a minute, unsure of what to say. 'I'll make coffee.'

He glanced at his watch, and for the hundredth time, I wondered who he had to check in with. Without knowing why, my tone carried an edge. 'Am I keeping you?'

'No, no of course not.' However, I caught the note of uncertainty in his answer. He appeared unclear as to why I had attitude, he was not alone.

And then I felt uncomfortable, because there was no need for me to offend him, he was attempting to do something wonderful today. Although once again, the nagging thought crossed my mind, that I knew *absolutely* nothing about this man. Not one bloody thing! And it went against my better judgement. Plus I had allowed him to bring eleven difficult, to put it mildly, boys to my home. Who the *hell* was he? Attempting to think clearly, I gave my head a shake. Unsettlement washed over me. I feared that I had deliberately asked for trouble. Lou had been right. It was very unlike me.

He must have felt he owed me something, because all he said was, 'Coffee would be good.' Then he slipped an iPhone from his pocket and walked out of earshot.

And there was that damn paradox again. Annoyance reared up in me. The man could not work normal hours, was not interested in money but could still afford an iPhone, so typical of society today.

In no particular rush some minutes later, I returned to the front veranda with three coffees, unsure where Brownie had taken himself off to.

Phil was seated on the top step, leaning forward, his hands

were joined as if in thought. Wilbur was lying on the ground with his head resting on one of Phil's feet. Anger rose in me, and for one brief second I wanted to tell Wilbur he was a traitor. He was *my* dog. We know nothing of this man. He is just passing through. Don't get too attached, he could be gone at any moment. I deliberately gave Wilbur a stern look, however he avoided eye contact with me.

Without looking at me Phil began to speak. 'I feel I connect with these kids because I have experienced some of what they are going through.' Briefly he turned to me, accepting the coffee mug. 'Except I had the good fortune of having someone care deeply enough about me to save me from myself. They don't have that good fortune.' He blew on the hot liquid and took a tentative sip.

Silently I slowly nodded at him, wondering what exactly he had experienced that these boys had, and not liking my thoughts. I sat on the next step. We sat that way for the next few minutes, hands around the mugs, the warmth comforting. There was much to say, much to ask, but I said nothing. I sensed that he was unsettled by my silence and was waiting for me to say something.

Looking straight ahead, I began. 'Phil,' I cleared my throat, 'I feel I should know…'

But annoyingly, we were interrupted by Brownie. 'There you both are. Coffee would certainly hit the spot, thank you.' He raised his mug. 'It went well Phil.' His voice was full of enthusiasm. 'They're not a bad bunch, but you've got to have eyes in the back of your bloomin' head. I'll say that much.' The old man looked happy and his step had more spring in it than I had seen the entire time he had been at Carmody House. 'You let me know if I can help out again. It's the least I can do.'

I did not miss the camaraderie between the two men. And I was reminded of the way the painter had spoken earlier of Phil. With apparent ease on Phil's behalf, everyone appeared to like him. In fact, they treated him like he was the expert on everything, constantly deferring to him. And then, with surprise, I realised I too had been doing the same. Blast this man!

Brownie appeared not to have noticed that he was the only one talking. 'I've got that fungicide that you suggested for the botrytis on the roses. I'll get onto it tomorrow, its best to remove any infected tissue first.'

Standing, Phil nodded but said little.

Chapter 17

Nearly two weeks later, ready for bed earlier than usual and dressed in my white embroidered silk pyjamas, I stepped out onto the front terrace. My head was aching and I pressed my fingers to my throbbing temples. Wilbur followed and collapsed at my feet. The heat of the day was still coming out of the ground in waves. The scent of rose and jasmine hung heavily in the air. Something had unravelled in me, and I needed to clear my head to sort it out.

The clear night sky was pricked with dozens of stars. A gentle breeze ruffled at my night attire and stirred the tree tops. Gazing into the darkness, I was reminded that Phil had suggested an upgrade of the outdoor lighting system, to highlight key plants and pathways. Just another thing that needed consideration. My thoughts went to a place, where months ago I had decided not to contemplate. What if he never came back again? Who would finish what he had started? How would anyone else know my garden like he did? Questions tumbled out.

In my former business life I had always maintained that everyone was replaceable. However, right then, I felt that Phil was linked so strongly to the garden, no-one else could possibly have the vision he had.

Even at that time of night, the garden beckoned. I strolled around the side of the house, stepping carefully in my Jimmy Choo slippers, making my way down to the river.

At the top of the stone steps that led to the grassy area, my foot slipped on a piece of rock covered in moss. No harm was done. I knew I should have changed into my gumboots, as my slippers had no grip whatsoever. I made a mental note to mention the moss to Brownie.

With care, I meandered down, finally finding a seat on the teak bench where the Brisbane River was merely a stone's throw away. With a small degree of pleasure, I noted that to the backdrop of a deepening blue velvet sky, the lights on the Story Bridge were shining like diamonds. With one hand resting on Wilbur's furry head, my eyes transfixed by the lights, my mind began to wander.

I had not seen Phil since the day the boys had come. Earlier that afternoon, I had had come across Brownie in the lower garden raking up the last of the old winter leaves. He had placed an old tarpaulin on the ground, and was piling the leaves upon, before dragging the entire thing to higher ground for disposal. I had asked him if he knew when we were to expect Phil next.

The old gent appeared as puzzled as I was, scratching the top of his head, contemplating his answer. 'It's got me baffled,' he had said. 'But of course, I've got all the spring chores to get on with so it's no matter to me, Mrs Riding, ah… I mean Mrs Avanel… although I do like the lad around. He seems to know his bloomin' stuff alright.'

I felt for Brownie, who was struggling with my name change, as it was much the same for me. I didn't bother to correct him on the Missus part. And try as hard as I might, he appeared to have no intention of calling me by my first name.

He continued. 'Anyway, I have my work cut out for me. I've got to finish off the mulching, plus it's time for the spring slow release fertiliser, and the lawn food. And I nearly forgot, Phil mentioned to me the other week that the tomatoes in the kitchen garden need staking to encourage optimal growth. I'd best get onto that.' He picked up the rake once again, but then turned back to me, and with a knowing voice said, 'I gather there's a bit to *our* Phil, but we can't be complainin' can we Mrs Riding… Mrs Avanel… he does such a bloomin' good job.'

I was missing Phil in a way that surprised me. I began to worry that I might have a crush on him, and what did that mean? I told myself that it was natural, after all he was handsome, rugged, capable, a good listener, knowledgeable… I could have gone on. And what was a crush after all? It didn't have to mean anything.

A sudden cool breeze caught me unaware, and with my arms folded across my chest, I made my way back up to the house. I thought of Brownie's words. He wasn't *our* Phil. He was… if anything… a Phil that obviously belonged somewhere else. He was *passing through* Phil. And *I* had best remember that.

About to close the front door, I noticed that the background hum from the traffic on the Story Bridge had faded, as Carmody House settled for the evening.

*

Absentmindedly, Johnny picked up the Mercedes Melbourne Cup invitation I had left on the kitchen bench. 'Hmmm, this looks good honey. The Mercedes tent at Eagle Farm hey?' He let out a low whistle. 'Some people have the life.'

Nodding, I didn't comment. Last year, I had sold a house to one of Mercedes top salesmen. He had been courting me with different models to test drive ever since, knowing I had sold the BMW and had replaced it with *a toy* as he had called Bambino.

'You are going aren't you? You don't want people to think you've disappeared off the face of the earth. You've got to be in it to win it honey.'

Smiling at his euphemism, I shrugged.

'I think you're forgetting something. You have this place

to promote. Don't let all your contacts go beside the wayside. You've worked too hard for that.'

I knew he was right. Although only a few kilometres as the crow flew, my new life was a million kilometres away from my past. 'Not sure I have someone to take Dad.' I placed my elbows on the kitchen bench, and rested my chin on my hands. 'You wanna be my date?'

'*Abso-bloody-lutely* honey. You just let me know.' He leant across and kissed my forehead. 'Now where the bloody hell do you want all of these canvases your mother sent over?' He shook his head. 'I don't know… that woman still has the capacity to make me jump when she speaks.'

'Somehow I don't think you mind.'

*

'For God's sake, I've been looking everywhere for you. Where the heck have you been?' All blonde hair and skinny legs encased in ecru ankle length skinny jeans and leopard print boots, Lou had such a way with words.

Removing my floral gumboots at the front door, I kissed her cheek. 'Nice to see you too little sister. I've been down in the garden shed, my new art studio.' Ignoring the brief shake of her head, I continued, 'The painters have finished putting the last coat of White On White, it's such a clean bluey white, it looks beautiful.' I beckoned her inside. 'Anyway, what brings you all the way out to the country?' I asked, glancing at her over my shoulder.

'Ha bloody ha… you're quite the comedian,' she said, giving me a look. 'Just finished a shoot at the new Taste down in James Street for a PR promo.' And she flopped on the couch.

'Ah… so you're getting more work? Good for you.'

'Yep, and Steve has been sending heaps my way. I'm so glad you kept him in the marriage settlement. Actually, I think you may have married the wrong brother.'

One of my brows shot up as if on its own accord. 'You think? Not too sure Steve would have been the right brother either darling. Fantastic to travel and shop with, but I kinda think it stops right there.'

'Which brings me to the reason for my visit!'

Sighing heavily, I crossed my arms, knowing there was something to come. 'What is it this time?'

'There is no way you're taking Dad to that Melbourne Cup do.' Noting my pained expression, she put her hands up. 'And I'm not going to argue about it. We're finding you a date. It's not normal for someone to be on her own as long as you've been.' She screwed her face up. 'Aren't you the slightest bit horny?'

'Lou!' I spluttered. 'You're terrible.'

'You have to be. I only say what's true. How long has it been?'

'LOU!' I shrieked. 'What the hell is wrong with *you?*'

'I think we might ask that about you sis. You don't have to lie to me. I know there's been no one since Davis…'

'What would you know? Mind your own bloody business,' I squealed. 'I've had plenty…'

She shut me up with a wave of her hand. 'Sure, sure… But, if you keep shrieking like that, it will be everyone else's business.' Lazily, she stood. 'Let's go through all your Facebook friends and see if there's anyone there.' She parked herself in front of my Louis desk, opened my laptop and flexed her fingers as if she was about to play the piano, flashing me a mischievous smile. 'If we can't find anyone among your friends, we'll go through mine.'

I rolled my eyes, and nudged her with my hip. 'You can talk. You're not exactly seeing anyone.' And then I caught her smug look.

'Marty?' I asked, my eyes popping.

Wiggling in her chair, she looked coy. 'Let's say we're talking.'

'Ah-huh so my Sunday lunches have finally paid off?'

'Might have.' And she glanced at me sideways. 'Are you absolutely positive you don't mind?'

'Absolutely positive.' I felt a certain radiance of happiness float up and my mood lightened. 'Listen sweetie... I'm not going to that Melbourne Cup do anyway. Davis will probably be in the BMW marquee next door. And... I just don't want to.'

From her place at my desk, she scratched at her head. 'Peach, you didn't do anything wrong. He may, or he may not be there. You need to show up looking hot... with someone hot, and show that you have moved on. And you need to do it for what you're creating here. It's business Peach.'

I narrowed my eyes as her insightfulness. She shrugged. 'Marty's teaching me a thing or two. And he said you have always been extremely professional and now is not the time to change.' She waved a hand at me. 'I'll start typing and you get the wine.'

Just the thought of dating made me sick to my stomach. I didn't have to be Einstein to work out that at my age the stakes were now much higher. If I were to date someone it would be with purpose. I would be looking for a life partner, my equal, and a good dad for hopefully future children. I felt it futile to waste time on a succession of unsuitable men. Plus, the last thing I wanted was to be propelled back into the dating world, where let's face it, I had practically no experience. I attempted to stall. 'Don't you need to get home to the kids?'

'They're at their fathers. The wine?' she commanded.

Two hours later, I might admit we were a tad tipsy. 'Oh

my God… not Alex Band. He was in my grade at St Josephs. I'll never forget him telling me that even though I might have thought I was good looking, really I had hair likes a rat's bum.' With a huff, I viciously sliced a piece of oozy Brie from the wedge, and popped it in my mouth.

'Think it might be time you got over it? He's bloody good looking.'

'*Never!* Not if he was the last man on earth.'

'Okay, okay, what about Lionel Washington?'

'*Nooooo* way.' Getting comfortable, I tucked my legs up under myself. 'Lionel went to St Josephs as well, but he was five years older. I remember buying my first jam donut from the school canteen. I can still see myself carrying it with two hands out in front, like I was carrying gold. Remember, Bea was a stickler for carob and dried apricots and stuff at home, so a jam donut was a pretty big deal. I'll never forget *that* Lionel Washington racing past me and sticking his dirty finger right in the middle. He pulled it out covered in jam and licked it. I threw the donut in the bin after that. So, do I want to take him to the Mercedes tent, for fantastic champagne and food? No, I do not.'

'I think we could give him the benefit of the doubt that his manners have improved since then. After all, it appears he is something of a high powered tax accountant now.'

'Boring!' I blinked. 'Next.'

'Guy Osborne…'

'Read a little further.' I huffed and folded my arms. 'Married with five children.'

'Oops! Fergus King?'

'Fergus… always thought it sounded like a dog's name. No Ferguses thank you.' I lay back on the couch, throwing my legs over the arm.

'Peach, you have to pick someone. You're being difficult.'

Sitting up, I leant over her shoulder, I pointed. 'Let me see that guy. He looks nice.'

'Nope you can't ask him.'

'Why? Oh my God *noooo*,' I shrieked. 'Not him *too*. Lou how many guys have you slept with?'

'Now you sound like Mitch. He was always badgering me about it.' She caught my look as I raised my brows at her. 'I always told him I'd tell him on my deathbed. I'd be 102 and I'd yell out 137 or 162 or something equally as stupid. That would shock the pants of him.'

'Darling if you were 102, he'd more than likely not be there. And to be honest, it hardly appears to matter now. You're not with him anymore.'

Lou flashed her eyes at me. 'So it might have tortured him, but now he will *never* know.'

*

The morning was grey and blustery, storm clouds were brewing from the west. Unusual for Brisbane, there had been a record amount of rain in the past six months. For the previous seven years, we had talked of nothing but drought, and just when we thought it would never rain again, it now appeared relentless. With muttered promises that we wouldn't complain, as the dam filled, one by one we weakened, with me finally breaking my silence, irritated beyond belief with the holdup of my renovations, not only by the council but by the weather as well. Although, I had to admit, it was doing wonders for my new plants and grass.

The background hum of the ride-on mower ceased. I gathered Brownie had been taking advantage of the lull before the storm. Crossing the floor of the lower guest room, I threw open the French doors, and welcomed the smell of freshly cut grass into the room. The sound of gently trickling water from a French urn nearby added to the serene ambiance in this part of the house.

With outstretched arms, I flicked the white sheet in the air, and watched as it slowly settled over the large bed. Pleasingly, my hands smoothed over the cool damask fabric, making perfect hospital corners. Earlier that day, all the Celestial Dream King beds arrived along with the Parker and Morgan king sized feather pillows, although, in my bedroom at the top of the house, I was still on a mattress on the floor, awaiting my French bed.

The Moss River damask sheets had been freshly laundered and ironed a few days earlier, and I was now making up one of the beds, in the only fully completed guestroom. I knew it was far too early, but I wanted to see how the room looked when dressed. Luxurious sheets were an indulgence I enjoyed and I knew it was the experience I wished for my guests. For the first time in a while, my mind went to Davis and how he had insisted on charcoal coloured sheets.

With a touch of satisfaction, I spoke out aloud. 'Only white sheets for me now.' I glanced at the slumbering Wilbur. He opened an eye, as if to say he could hardly care less. Poor dog had appeared lost in the last two weeks and had become my shadow wherever I went. I sensed that he was missing Phil as well. 'Better get used to it boy. He may not be coming back,' I told him.

Plumping the feather pillows, I placed them against the cream coloured upholstered headboard and then adjusted the silk cushions.

Draping a duck egg blue cashmere throw across the bottom of the bed, I stood back to survey my handiwork. I had been lucky enough to source snowy Marcella bedspreads, and although Henri offered to have them sent from Provence, I had saved him the worry.

'Well, what do you think Wilbur?' I asked. He gave me his *I am a boy dog* look, *not interested in textiles and stuff.*

And then out of the blue, he jumped up and took off through the open French doors. 'Glad it had that effect on you,' I called after him, my voice dry. 'I do hope it has a slightly better one on paying guests.'

Shaking my head, I turned and glanced through the doorway and into the Calcutta marbled ensuite. Other than luxurious linens, dreamy beds and quality fit outs, when completed, no two rooms would be alike. That particular bathroom boasted a striking black bath, with gold clawed feet as the centrepiece. Above it hung a decadent black chandelier. This was the spa suite. The white Calcutta marble with the grey vein gave the bathroom an opulent look. In the vanity cupboard, once again I ran my fingers over the oversized Egyptian cotton white fluffy towels and robes, and took the time to inhale the beautiful fragrance of the L'Occitane bath and body products.

The sound of Wilbur's playful bark bought me out of my reverie. Walking across the room, I tilted the duck egg blue shutter blades so I could see the lower garden. Narrowing my eyes, my heart gave a thud as I watched Brownie help Phil with a cage-type of contraption, Wilbur gleefully escorting them.

Hurriedly, I dashed out the French doors, across the newly laid herringbone travertine flagging and took a short cut down to the lower garden, leaping from paver to paver, keen to see what they were doing. Heads bent, Phil and Brownie were assembling an A-frame structure with a rectangular timber framework attached. Brownie was uncoiling a roll of chicken wire, while Phil had already begun nailing it in place.

'What do you have here?' I asked, a trifle breathless, pushing back the sleeves of my orange cowl neck jumper.

Phil glanced back at me, and nodded. His eyes crinkled, so I guess he smiled. It was a bit hard to tell with nails protruding from between his lips.

Finally, he spoke. 'Your chicken coup.'

'*Oh*,' I said surprised.

Crouching, he pulled a hammer from the tool bag at his waist. With one deft blow he drew a nail into the frame. 'Yep, the Isa Browns are coming this afternoon.' He must have taken my silence as a negative. Pausing, he turned, glancing at me from under his Akubra. 'You did remember?'

'I didn't realise it was this week. But it's fine… it's great,' I assured him. Life had been so chaotic of late, the very last thing I had thought of was the hens. I had been unsure if Phil had ever intended returning to Carmody House, much less organising chickens. And chickens… what on earth was I going to feed them?

Briefly, my mind flashed to a memory of Lou and me on one of our holidays to Nan's and Pop's farm in Tasmania. Being the eldest, it was always my job to collect the eggs for breakfast. I was always terrified about putting my hands under the big fluffed-up chooks. And that feeling returned to me now. *Bloody hell!*

Phil's voice cut into my thoughts. 'Just remember they're eating machines. They'll pick clean a lamb roast, love fish scraps even spaghetti bolognese. And they'll free range with the run.' He gave a couple more adroit blows with his hammer.

I refrained from mentioning that it seemed highly unlikely as I only cooked for one that I'd have such things as lamb roast or left over spaghetti bolognese on a regular basis. I wondered how they'd feel about my jams, relishes and pickles, as that is what I had been stockpiling!

'One of these bloomin' wheels feels loose,' Brownie cut in with. 'I'll need the big red tool box in the garage.'

Phil continued attaching the chicken wire, and like a prize goose, I continued to stand there, arms folded across my chest, watching. It frustrated me that it was such a typical scenario where the female wished to speak, however the male pretended not to notice. Wilbur stood beside me gazing at Phil with such a rapt look in his face, I nudged him with my foot, and wrinkled my brow at him. It did not deter him at all.

And then expectantly, Phil turned to me and cocked a brow in question, before turning back to the business at hand.

I swallowed, and for some reason stood a little more upright. 'Um… well… Phil, I know we have a very loose arrangement, but I wasn't exactly sure you were returning. And I mean…' I put my hands out, lacking something better to say. How had I run a business with fifteen staff and won business management awards, when right this moment I was stumbling over my words?

Before I could say more, he cut me off.

'Bugger,' he spat out, throwing his hammer down and swinging around to face me, his face looking like thunder.

'Oh!' Taking me off guard, I took a step back, and fired from the hip, my tone of voice startling even me. 'Look Phil, this is normally how businesses are run. People start and finish at certain times on certain days.' Without drawing breath I continued, knowing I sounded prissy. 'Now I understand you are between things,' I drew inverted commas in the air, 'and don't think for one minute I don't appreciate every little thing you have done here, because I truly do, but I need to know when you are coming, and not wondering if you're ever going to turn up again. I get that you aren't money motivated, and don't want to work too many hours, obviously have no commitments unlike most, but I have…' Coming up for air, I noticed that although his eyes were boring into mine, he had stuck his thumb in his mouth and his brow was wrinkled. I paused. 'Are… are you okay?'

Slowly, he nodded. 'Whacked it with the hammer.' With the back of his hand, he pushed at the brim of his hat. Narrowing his eyes at me, he asked, 'You were saying?'

'Um.' I placed a hand on my chest. When he had thrown the hammer down, I had thought he had been sounding off at me. 'Um… can I get you something?'

'No it's fine. It's not the first and it won't be the last.' He flicked his hand a few times, and then rested both hands low on his hips, although I was sure his thumb would still be hurting. He stood there for few seconds, looking like he was summing up the situation.

I read his body language loud and clear, taking in his powerful pose: legs apart, hips forward, hands resting on them making him appear bigger, direct eye contact.

He narrowed his eyes. 'Peach I believe I told you last month there was a period of time coming up where I needed a couple of weeks off and I would make sure everything was organised.'

Wearily, I shook my head, and then scratched at an eyebrow. 'Ah… did you… I don't remember… look… forget it… it's just that…'

'It was when we discussed the boys coming. I said to you they'd get a mountain of small jobs done which would free me up.'

'Oh… did you? I sort of remember about the freeing up part but not the two week part.' I put my hands up. 'Look its fine. I just didn't remember, okay?'

For a minute neither of us spoke, Phil stood looking at me, his eyes narrowed. I was thinking to myself how I appeared to be rather forgetful of late, and I was grateful he didn't mention it.

Nodding his head towards the coop, he spoke as if dismissing me. 'The chooks will be here soon and I'd like to get this finished.'

I sighed heavily. It did not go unnoticed by him.

Once again he pushed at the brim of his hat. 'I can see you'd like to have a chat with me?'

Oh you think, I wanted to say. Instead I nodded, knowing I hadn't handled the situation in a very professional manner.

'The girls will be here any moment.'

I was about to ask *what bloody girls*, when he must have read my face.

'The hens,' he said clearly, as if speaking to someone who understood little. Yes… that would be me.

'Right,' I said, I mean of course I understood when he called them the girls, it just threw me for a few seconds.

With the eventual opening of the B&B, chickens had been an obvious choice to supply daily fresh organic eggs for the kitchen. At the same time I'd be able to recycle kitchen scraps and produce high quality fertiliser for the garden.

A noticeable silence went on for some minutes, as with arms folded, I stood and observed, thinking what to say next.

'The coop looks good,' I spoke to his back.

He didn't look at me. 'Mmmm.'

'Did you buy it in pieces like that?'

'Nope,' he said, with one final smack of the hammer, and then turned to me. 'Made it myself.'

'Really?' I asked with obvious surprise.

'Yes,' and I saw a slight smile playing at the corners of his mouth, as he cocked his head to the side. 'During the time I had off.'

'Oh,' I said in a trifle too prissy tone, avoiding his eyes. 'You did a great job.' I continued to study it. 'It's a bit of a penthouse isn't it?' I said attempting to lighten my tone.

'Yep, there's a ladder for them to get to the laying area upstairs, and a decent run to keep them happy. It would be best faced north, so they can get plenty of sun. I've put wheels on, so it can be moved all over the yard.'

To demonstrate, he picked up the coop, and began to roll it on the wheels, his back to me. Mesmerised, by the ease and grace of his movements, I was struck by the smooth skin on the back of his neck, the side curve of his jaw, his strong hands, and his powerful shoulders outlined through his black shirt.

Feeling chastised, I quietly said, 'You did a great job.'

'Thank you,' he said just as quietly, without turning around, his calmness evident.

*

'I hadn't thought of names.' Thoughtfully, I tapped my top lip with my index finger. 'Right, what about Rose, Lavender, Ivy, Daffodil and…?'

'Daisy,' Phil chimed in.

Surprised, I glanced at him. 'Daisy… love it! That one there,' I pointed. 'She can be Daisy.' Once the chickens had actually arrived, I was really quiet pleased, and my mood had lifted, as had Phil's.

Marvelling at the coup, and attempting to show it to the new chooks, I ran my hand along the side of it. 'And look here ladies, this is your new…' I snatched my hand away quickly. 'Ooh… splinter!'

Holding my hand close, I scrutinised it, attempting to see the minute piece of lodged timber. I ran a finger nail across it.

'Damn it,' I said.

'Here let me see.' Phil took my hand, and held it up close to his face. It bought back memories of being child and absolutely hating when Johnny attempted to remove a splinter. Generally he hurt me more than the intruding object.

Tentatively, holding my offending hand by the wrist, I too kept my eyes on it, worried Phil would pull out a needle and probe around, much as Johnny had. Both of our heads bent, transfixed on the unwanted bit of timber, I exhaled, realising I had been holding my breath. I could feel Phil's breath on my cheek. I also realised something else. He smelt very nice. It was a deep rich fragrance, manly and rugged. Briefly, I closed my eyes and inhaled the musky sandalwood and spicy scent mixed with the smell of clean warm skin. The perfect manliness of him was so intoxicating it almost made my head spin.

It was at that time, I realised one other thing… I missed the fragrance of a man.

Seconds dragged on as we continued to stand ever so still, while Phil examined my hand, and happily I continued to inhale the pure smell of him, when suddenly using the fingernail tips of his thumb and index finger, he gently pulled the offender out. Feeling his eyes on me, I glanced up at him. We said nothing, but he continued to hold my hand close.

'*Aunty Peach, Aunty Peach!*'

Blinking, I stepped back, and swung around. 'Darlings, what are you doing here?' I called with surprise, as Lakshmi and Bob flew down the stone steps and across the grass, Lakshmi holding Bob's hand with some authority.

'Mummy said we could see the chickens,' Lakshmi told me, a trifle breathlessly. 'Didn't she Bob?' As was her habit of speaking for him, he nodded, but smiled all the same. She put her hands on his shoulders and slightly pushed him ahead of her, although shyly he attempted to hang back.

'You can come a little closer,' Phil instructed.

'I don't believe you've formally met my niece and nephew,' I said, resting a hand on each of their blonde heads. 'This pretty girl is Lakshmi.' Bashful now, Lakshmi cast her eyes down, and then looked up smiling. I continued, 'And this gorgeous hunk of a little boy is Mr Bob. Children, this is Mr Hunter.'

Still on his haunches, Phil smiled, pushing his akubra back on his head. 'They can call me Phil. So Lakshmi, you have a beautiful Hindu name.' His response surprised me, as mostly people screwed their face up in misunderstanding, and asked for it to be repeated.

He continued, 'Do you know what your name means?'

'Ummm yes, Mummy says it means goddess of everything good.' One of her white sneakers bashfully kicked at the grass.

Phil burst into a startled laugh, the sound surprising me. 'It does indeed... and Mr Bob, by the looks of things a big boy like you just might be helpful with these new chooks. What do you think?'

Turning to me, Lakshmi pointed, 'What's that one's name?' Her little back was upright, the same posture as her mother.

'Daisy,' I said, looking at Phil over the top her head for confirmation, as at this stage they all looked similar. Surprisingly, at only 18 weeks they appeared to be healthy, large and friendly.

'And that one?' Lakshmi continued.

'Um I think that one's Rose... no, no Lavender. That's Rose over there. And that gorgeous lady is Ivy and that one who looks like she's doing a yoga pose is Miss Daffodil.'

The children laughed, their shyness in front of Phil fast disappearing. Holding his still chubby baby hands in front of himself, Bob attempted to pick a chicken up to no avail.

Clucking, the chooks backed away, side stepping every time he came closer.

'What do they eat?' Lakshmi continued with her questions.

'I was just about to tell your aunt.' Phil turned to me. 'There's a huge bag of good quality pellets in the back of the garage. As I said earlier, you can feed them leftovers, but for quality eggs, a high protein diet works best.'

'Right,' I said nodding my head. I was still getting my head around the chooks. Although I had agreed to them, now they were here, I was wondering if I had bitten off more than I could chew. 'Lakshmi, Bob, step back, don't get too close just yet. We don't know their temperament.'

'I think you'll generally find them very gentle and affectionate,' Phil reassured.

'Really? Hmmm...'

'Uh-huh, and it won't be long before you're collecting those large brown eggs.'

'Of course, of course,' I rapidly nodded to cover my uncertainty, although when I realised I had my arms crossed in front of me. I dropped them to my sides.

'It's probably best if they're kept in the run for the first month or so until they become accustomed to it. After that, they can free range.'

'What do they drink?' Lakshmi asked, looping her hands together and jumping around.

'Lakshmi darling that's more than enough questions,' I gently admonished, running my fingers through her blonde ponytail.

'That's a good question Lakshmi. Fresh water at all times,' and then Phil looked at me. 'Basic rule – if you wouldn't drink it – change it!'

'Got it!' I turned to the children. 'Where's Mummy?'

'She said to tell you she was putting the kettle on.'

'Okay then, come on, up we go,' I said, taking Bob's hand.

'*Nooo*,' he wailed, pulling his hand out of mine. 'Bob wants chickens.'

'They're fine with me,' Phil cut in, obviously keen to stop Bob's ruckus. Bob was rather like his mother when it came to fuss.

'Yes, we want to stay,' Lakshmi chimed in. 'We can help. Can't we Bob?'

'Bob help,' was all he said, turning his attention back to the chooks. Squatting on his baby haunches, he began clucking to them.

I glanced at Phil.

He nodded, 'They can stay. You should probably put some antiseptic on your hand anyway. I can watch the children while I finish up here.'

'Are you sure? I won't be long.'

He gave me a wave. Dismissed, I happily walked across the grass, listening as Lakshmi continued with her questions. I heard Phil explain, 'They'll scratch around, dig up seeds, eat weeds and leave behind their natural fertiliser. Do you know what fertiliser...?'

Shaking my head, I wondered about that man. That extremely nice smelling man. *Stop it,* I told myself. *Stop it now.* I gave myself a pep talk. *Remember your golden rule. Never mix business with pleasure. Goodness me, you were firm about it at the agency. Pity your ex-husband didn't take that rule into consideration. The minute something goes wrong, you're down a staff member. Yes and it wasn't meant to be me, but there you have it!* Why the heck was I thinking of that right now.

My thoughts returned to Phil. He appeared to have a way with children. First the boys and now Lou's two. On the stone steps I hastened my pace, counting as I went, the mossy step catching my eye once again. Since coming to Carmody House I hadn't had a personal training session, however I was slimmer and in far better condition than before. No doubt the new lifestyle suited me.

Attempting to shift my thoughts away from the splinter incident and the closeness, not to mention the fragrance of Phil, I visualised how good these stairs were for my legs and butt. I'd heard that if you visualised the muscle as you exercised, it did far more than just working them. Focus more, I told myself. Think about what that muscle looks like right now. It's flexing and coming back. Firming! Ah good. I touched a hand to my right buttock cheek. Buns of steel. I laughed to myself. Hardly, but I could keep trying.

I hoped to have had time to chat with Phil that afternoon. I felt extremely uncomfortable about the way it had gone earlier. Not my best moment of communication. I really needed to know how long he intended staying, and if I should have a contingency plan for when he left. At some point he had mentioned that his time was almost up. I remember at the time wondering if that was how long his parole was. Parole… I laughed at myself and how I let my overactive imagination run away with me sometimes. But really… what else could it be? I scratched at the side of my head, passing through what I now called the blue garden. The agapanthuses looked amazing massed the way they were. The sight of them always made me feel happy. There was something about that blue, purple colour that did it. Hmmm… what was I thinking… yes the parole…

And BOOM it hit me. *The children*! Hastily, I swung around, my feet doing triple time on the way back down, my heart hammering in my chest. *What had I been thinking?* Oh my God, do not let me faint with fright and not make it back to them. My irresponsibility shamed me.

Rounding the corner, I bounded down the last of the stairs, the large expanse of grass in front of me. Bob was holding one of the chooks in his chubby arms with Phil standing over the top of him. I couldn't see Lakshmi anywhere. My knees went weak and I thought I may stumble, I put a hand to my mouth. I had been gone a few minutes, no more...

Lakshmi came out of the hen house, full of smiles. 'You should have a look inside Bob.' Her high voice floated to me. 'You'll fit better than me. They even have an upstairs, they're lucky chooks.'

By the time I reached them I was so breathless I almost needed to double over to catch my breath, however I refrained from doing so. I felt clammy all over, and I could feel the perspiration above my upper lip. Putting a hand to my chest, I attempted to talk, avoiding Phil's yes. When I spoke my mouth was dry. 'Guys... guys... your mum wants you.'

Frowning, Lakshmi halted, quickly folding her arms across her chest. I saw the small stamp of her foot in disapproval.

'*Nooo*,' Bob wailed. 'Bob want chooks.' To the dismay of the chicken he was holding, his little arms tightened.

I swallowed, wondering how I was going to handle it. I glanced at Phil. He was very still. His eyes locked on mine, and from the look in them, I knew immediately he was confused by my attitude. But then a look passed across his face, and I gathered he had guessed what I was thinking.

He kept his gaze on my face. 'I think the chickens need to have a sleep. You can come back later.'

'Good thinking. Come along then.' I attempted to gather the children as if they were the chooks.

'*Noooo*, Bob wants chooks,' Bob howled, as I attempted to

remove the chicken from his grasp.

'Come on Bob, don't you want one of Aunty Peach's cupcakes?' I cajoled in a voice that was not my own.

Phil went down on his knees in front of Bob, making eye contact with him. 'The chicken needs to have a sleep, just like you do sometimes. You can come back later.' Gently he removed the startled chicken from Bob's tight grasp.

'Thank you,' I said, in a trifle too prudish tone. 'I shouldn't have left them, the river is so close and everything...' Which of course was the truth.

'I understand, absolutely...' However with his hands on his hips, he glanced away.

'Good,' I nodded feeling my face taut. 'Right, we'll pop up... and we'll come back down later.' Yes, that made sense. *Bloody hell!*

I took both of the children's hands and led them back the way I had come.

Lakshmi turned. 'Bye Phil. We'll be back soon.'

Bob echoed. 'Bye Phil. Soon,' he said in his baby voice.

'Good,' Phil answered, but I saw him exhale heavily and turn his back.

On the walk back up to the house, my mind was busy. Firstly, I should not have left the children, it was too close to the river. What on earth was I thinking? That intimacy over the splinter had thrown me. Bloody hell, what the heck was wrong with me. Some mother I would make! And where the heck was *their* mother? Bloody irresponsible of her. Plus another situation handled badly on my behalf. However, the circumstance with the children and Phil clearly outlined the fact that I was naive and needed to know more about the man who was spending so much time on my property.

*

'Lou where have you been?' I knew my voice sounded snappy.

With her back to me, and perched at my desk, her fingers tapped away at my laptop. Briefly, she held a hand up. 'I was watching you all from up here. One sec.'

I raised my brows in irritation. 'Come along children, time to wash your hands.' I was beginning to think I sounded more and more like Nanny McPhee. Or maybe that's how an old maiden aunt spoke. Now that was an uplifting thought. Thirty-five, single, no children, loves gardening, has chooks. Hmmm... I'm sure I sounded tempting these days.

Lifting Bob, I pumped soap into his hands, and the fragrance of geranium and orange rose in the air. Those little chubby hands always amazed me with their cleverness. I held them to my lips and kissed them, much to his delight. Tilting him backwards in my arms, I began kissing under his neck and nuzzling my nose in.

His baby laugh rang out loud in the tiled room, instantly lifting my mood.

'Bob want cake.'

'Come on then Mr Bob,' I said taking his hand and leading him back to the kitchen. Ahead of us, Lakshmi was filling her mother in on the chickens. Lou continued typing for a few more seconds and then she snapped my laptop closed and turned to us. I have to say, I did wonder what on earth she was doing on my computer, but before I had the chance to ask, she spoke.

'Right ... chickens hey?' For the next few minutes she gave her attention to the children as they excitedly talked.

Once I had them settled up at the kitchen bench, baby lattes and cupcakes in front of them, from her viewing spot at the kitchen window, Lou turned to me and repeated. 'Right... chickens hey?' There was a quizzical tone to her voice, and it matched the look on her face.

'What?' I asked, wrinkling my brow.

Lou folded her arms. 'Peach,' she let out a deep breath. 'Aren't you taking this farmer girl thing a bit far?' She caught my look. 'I mean, one minute you're business women of the year, your social life and wardrobe is the envy of all, the next you're becoming a recluse, wearing gumboots all day, growing green stuff and mothering chooks.' Before I had a chance to answer, she glanced out the window. 'Mind you, Farmer Joe looks pretty damn hot!'

Annoyed, I snapped, 'Cut it out Lou!' surprising even myself. I turned my attention to the children. 'Do you guys want to play with Wilbur, but don't let him out of the laundry yet. We don't want him chasing the chickens.' I closed the laundry door after them.

Slumping against a kitchen cupboard, I said. 'I'm trying to get this B&B up and running. The bloody council are holding me up everywhere I turn. The weather is driving me nuts. Where the bloody hell is the sunshine we are so used to? Of course I'm wearing gumboots everywhere. I'm doing my best, okay!' I caught her raised brows.

'Sorry,' was all she said.

Neither of us spoke for a minute, and then she said, 'You're sensitive aren't you.'

'Hmmm.' Firing up the Gaggenau once again, I breathed in the blissful aroma of coffee. 'Sit,' I commanded Lou, still perched at the window. I could tell she was watching Phil. She was *bloody* hopeless.

She held her coffee cup up to her lips with two hands. 'You don't seem to be in a rush to open though.'

I shrugged. 'There isn't any rush. I want Carmody House to be perfect. It takes time. I've got time.' I perched myself on a stool. 'And strangely enough, I am enjoying it Lou. But ...' and I glanced across at her over the top of my coffee mug, 'am I becoming a bore?'

'Not at all! Just... I don't know... you don't seem interested in anything you used to. It seems odd.'

I glanced away gathering my thoughts. 'It's funny,' I said selecting my words. 'I don't miss certain things that I used to love.' I narrowed my eyes in thought. 'I used to love the buzz of activity, the rush as a deal closed, deadlines, corporate events, and being around loads of people all the time. I don't miss it one iota.' I shrugged. 'It's as if it was someone else's life. But here...' I smiled wistfully.

'Well that's all well and good, but you do have to keep your networking up for when this business opens, you know.'

I narrowed my eyes. Marty was definitely having a good effect on her.

'I agree.' Steve had been in my ear regarding the PR as well. I was on his mailing list for functions nearly every week. Over the past year, I had declined all. However, I knew what they were all saying was right. Business was business.

'Good. So who are you taking to the Melbourne Cup do?'

I grimaced. 'Oh leave off Lou. I'm not going. I know Davis will be there. It was the highlight of the year for him.'

A smug look of satisfaction washed over her face. She leant forward. 'What if I told you, I heard on the grapevine he might not.' Her fingers tapped the table.

Laughing derisively, and getting off my stool, I asked, 'What could *possibly* make Davis Riding miss such a wonderful opportunity to network a function like that?'

'Ummm... baby scan.'

'Oh!' Glancing towards the window, absentmindedly I nibbled a quick on my index finger. I looked at Lou. 'That's ridiculous. Appointments such as those can be changed at the drop of a hat.' I turned back to the view, pretending even to myself, that I wasn't really looking at Phil from that distance, and wondering what the heck his story was.

'Not if the doctor "someone",' and she drew inverted commas in the air, 'is demanding as the only one good enough, is away, and that date is his first available appointment upon his return. And let me tell you, there's someone else not too happy.'

Shrugging, I turned my attention back to her. 'His problem!' However I knew my lips looked prissy. Lou called them cat's bum whenever she saw me do it, although she kindly refrained from mentioning it just then.

Instead, she cocked her head on the side. 'So ... who are you taking?' and then she rushed on. 'You could go with Marty, but that will get everyone talking again...'

I gave her a look. 'Plus *you're* going with him?'

She looked questioningly at me, and gave slight shrug.

'Mother dear,' was all I said. It appeared to me that my family had gotten together and decided that I needed to find a date. Even Bea had been sequestered to speak with me, as quite out of character, she had called earlier to say she would be dropping by tomorrow. She wasn't the kind to simply call in. Sometimes it appeared months went by without a visit. I knew something was up.

'Truth be told Lou, there's not a man on earth I'm interested in.'

'Really, because you haven't taken your eyes off Farmer Joe down there.' She nodded towards the window.

My voice rose with irritation. 'Will you stop calling him that! And I am not interested in him. Just curious, that's all. But more importantly, I am watching those storm clouds, to see which way they're heading.'

'Before Dad left this morning, he said they were going to head north and that Brisbane wouldn't see a drop of rain.'

'Did he now? Sometimes I forget he's a meteorologist,' I retorted sarcastically, shaking my head.

'I know, I know,' Lou laughed. 'He always thinks he knows far more about the weather than what the forecasters say. In fact, I'd forgotten until recent times, how he gives the TV weathermen cheek, talking back to them, telling them they know *abso-bloody- lutely nothing!*

In spite of how annoyed I had been feeling, I laughed at Johnny. 'My God, is he still doing that?'

'Yes, he is. Oh I nearly forgot, he told me tell you there's going to be a king tide tonight at midnight. Plus they're letting water out of the dam today, so to be careful.'

'And I'm supposed to do what?' Wrinkling my brow, I walked back over to the kitchen bench, picked up my coffee mug and perched myself on a stool.

Lou shrugged. 'I don't know. Watch it, I guess.'

Shaking my head, I took a sip. Suddenly, I remembered something. Keen to move to a safer subject, I asked, 'What were you doing on my computer earlier?' And then I caught the sheepish look on her face.

'What?' I asked. Avoiding my glance, she kept her silence.

'Lou?' My eyes bored into her.

'I was finding you a date.'

'WHAT?' I yelled, my eyes literally popping out of my head. Turning my head as the laundry door opened, I saw little Lakshmi's face. I attempted a laugh. 'It's okay sweetie. I couldn't hear what Mummy was saying, and I yelled a bit.'

'Can we take Wilbur for a walk?' she asked.

'Hmmm… later… okay.'

'Lakshmi… in about five minutes?' Lou cut in. 'Keep playing with him in the laundry for now, and I'll call you in five minutes.' She pulled the door closed and turned to me. 'Don't yell okay?'

With my arms folded, I shook my head at her, whispering in a furious tone, 'What do you want me to say? What have you done Lou?'

Casually, she walked over to my desk, opened the laptop, typed in something and then turned it towards me.

With my arms still folded, I read: *Dinner for Six!* 'What is this?' I asked, the blood beginning to pound in my ears.

Lou put a hand up. 'Hear me out first.' When I didn't respond, she continued. 'Everyone's worried you're becoming a bit of recluse…'

Before she could say more, with my frustration apparent, I asked, 'What are you going on about? Do I look unhappy, or have I let myself go? What is it?'

'Quite the opposite,' she placated. 'In fact we all agree you've never looked better. However you are very tunnel visioned…'

'What's new?' I snapped again.

'Peach!' Lou frowned. I exhaled with gusto and sat down heavily on the arm of a chair. When had our relationship reversed? For the entirety of Lou's life I had looked after her, helping her through one disaster after another, and now here she was attempting to organise my life. I said nothing, waiting for her to talk.

'I pretended to be you and now you're a member. I've put your name down for a dinner next Saturday night at Vine.' Before I could open my mouth, she rushed on. 'There will be three men and two other ladies. At best you'll meet someone nice. At worst you'll have dinner in a nearby restaurant you love.'

Still I was quiet, unsure of whether to blow up or just walk away.

She took my silence as a good thing. It was as if she was cajoling Bob to eat his vegetables, the way she spoke. 'You only have to go once, and you just might like it.'

'Lou, Lou, Lou.' I exhaled heavily, quite exhausted by the entire thing. 'I have one question? Will it get you off my back? Because that would be the only thing that could possibly make this worthwhile.' And then as an afterthought I added, 'Lucky for you, I just so happen to like Vine.'

Clapping her hands enthusiastically, Lou danced around. 'Great! It's a 7.30 start. The age bracket is between 32 and 42. They are probably all likeminded. You'll have fun!'

No, I would not, however I would go under duress, simply so she would leave me alone. Before more could be said, the laundry door opened.

'Please Mummy, can we take Wilbur now?' Lakshmi asked.

I don't know who was the happiest for the subject to be changed, Lou or me, however as I reached the door, Wilbur dashed past and made a bee line for the open front door.

'The chickens… he'll get the chickens,' I cried, taking off after him. Lakshmi was hot on my heels, so Lou swooped Bob up under her arm and followed us.

Puffing and panting and hollering Wilbur's name repeatedly, I yelled ahead to Phil attempting to warn him. From that distance, I saw Phil head him off grabbing him by the collar, speaking sternly. He waved at me. 'It's okay,' he called. I bent over attempting to catch my breath. Within a matter of seconds, the others had caught up, throwing themselves down on the grass beside me, laughing hysterically, the children acting as if it was the most fun they'd had in ages.

Lou laughed the hardest. 'We must have looked so funny,

all running in single file like that chasing Wilbur.'

I laughed with her. 'It's not that funny. It's the second time today I have run up and down here. Can you imagine how sore my muscles are going to be tomorrow?'

'And that's why you look so good.' And she propped herself up on an elbow and smiled at me.

'Crawler,' I said, never able to stay angry with her for long.

Chapter 18

It was dinner time before it dawned on me that I hadn't seen Wilbur for some time. After Lou and the children had left, I had begun sorting my library. The ebony shelving trimmed with pilasters had been installed the day before. And now, many of my favourite books were lovingly arranged on the shelves.

Happily, I inhaled their special scent. Seeing them in their new home reminded me of the enormous pleasure they had all given me in the past. On tippy toes, I reached up and touched my battered old copy of *War and Peace*, my badge of honour.

As I glanced around at the books still piled on the newly laid French oak parquetry flooring, I reminded myself not to spend too much time reacquainting myself with each book, or the remaining ones would never find their home.

The time had well and truly gotten away from me, and with some surprise, I noticed that it had become dark outside, much earlier than normal for this time of day. On my way from the room, I glanced with pleasure at the new glassed in wine cellar. Another of Phil's suggestions.

My original plan had been to use the small storeroom. Rather unimaginative of me, I know. Phil had pointed out that rather than trying to hide the cellar away, placing it here on show would create quite a sensory input for my guests. I could not deny he had been right, and not for the first time, I was reminded that he was a man who was always coming up with great ideas. I liked his way of thinking.

With Wilbur's whereabouts concerning me, torch in hand, I walked out to the front gate to check it was latched, calling his name as I went.

From the library, I had heard the howl of the wind, but was

so engrossed in the task at hand, had taken no notice. Now it wildly whipped my hair about my face, taking me by some surprise at the actual ferocity of it.

There was a feeling in the air, and although I could not put my finger on it, I found it disconcerting. The back of my neck prickled. Placing a hand to it, with the other, I shone the torch in front of me, my eyes darting, wondering what was unsettling me.

Twigs snapped, leaves rustled, trees swayed as if reaching out for me. Shivering, I pulled away uncomfortably, folding my arms across my chest, awkwardly still attempting to hold the torch. Looking up at the sky, I could just make out a sliver of moon shining its pale light out from behind a high veil of cloud, but then it was gone again, and my surroundings were cast in darkness.

Other than the snake scenario, for the first time since coming to Carmody House, I felt a little unsure of the garden. To the west, I saw a flash of lightening.

Obviously Johnny had been wrong with his prediction of the storm missing Brisbane. Though no doubt, with living on the edge of the Brisbane River, and the letting go of water from the Wivenhoe Dam, I should have listened to the weather report earlier. I then thought about what Johnny had said about the king tide and wondered if the river would come into the garden.

It was times such as these that my sense of bravado left me. I wasn't meant to know everything, nor did I really want to. A man would know this stuff.

Before leaving the house to look for Wilbur, I had called Lou to see if she remembered seeing Wilbur on her way to the car.

'Pop Dad on will you?'

'I told you earlier he and Patrice left for Fiji this morning.' Her voice carried an impatient edge to it. 'What's wrong with you tonight Peach? You seem rather forgetful.'

'Whenever the wind howls like this, it gets under my skin. I feel like a dog, ears back, tail between my legs.' Gripping my forearms, I had shivered.

Lou laughed. However, the fact was that was how I felt. If I could hide under a bed, with my face buried between my paws, I would have gladly.

Regardless, none of this was helping me to find Wilbur, and I realised I had not seen him since we had chased him down to the back garden.

With my gumboot clad feet, I trod carefully in the dark, keeping a keen eye out, shining the torch not only in front of me, but to either side as well. There were times when the thought of that snake still rattled me. It didn't pay to become too complacent.

As I rounded the house, I caught another flash of lightning, so rather than going any further, I hurriedly dashed inside and secured all the windows. And then the rain came, bucketing down, making it impossible to see further than a metre from any window. I stayed put.

By ten pm I was beside myself with worry, every now and then going to the front door, loudly calling Wilbur's name. Normally, the only time he wasn't my shadow was when he was Phil's.

That afternoon Lou and the children had stayed on, and although I had been hopeful to have had a chat with Phil, it never eventuated. Once the thought had taken up residence in my mind that perhaps it was negligent of me not to know more about him, particularly with Lakshmi and Bob around, I knew I had to sort it out as quickly as possible. In my former business life, without fail, I had checked out every staff member's previous employers. Tomorrow I would talk to him. I would put it off no longer.

Once again, I looked at Wilbur's untouched bowl in the laundry. Where was he?

Not wishing to miss the sound of him at the front door, I showered quickly, and put on my white silk pyjamas, the first things my hand touched in the drawer. Normally I loved the comfort of the fabric against my skin, but in such a state of concern, I took absolutely no notice, as I scurried back down the stairs, to the front door to call him once again, hearing the tone of fright in my voice.

Although late, I decided against turning the kitchen light off, and curled up on the new butterscotch velvet chesterfield lounge, hugging a huge goose feather cushion to my chest. My mind kept going to Wilbur. Determined to think of other things, once again Phil popped into my thoughts.

In a micro second, my fervid imagination went into top gear, coming up with every possible scenario of what his past could possibly be. *Maybe* he was part of a witness protection program? Or *perhaps* he had been in jail after all, and that's why he had that number one buzzcut? But what crime could he have committed? *Ah-huh...* he was probably on home detention? *That was it!* And that was why he always had to leave at a certain time. *Hmmm...* I felt it unlikely he'd been in an accident and lost his memory. After all, he knew too much stuff. I *was* forgetting about the troubled boys though. *What was that about? Okay...* maybe that was community service. That was it. That *had* to be it.

I played out every scenario, frame by frame. I tell you, my imagination was so damn good I should have written fiction for a living.

By eleven it was still bucketing down, and if possible, sounded even heavier. My overcharged mind had exhausted me, not to mention added to my already jangled nerves. And then the hugest crack of thunder hit, and the kitchen light went out. Quick as a flash, I pulled my legs up under me, my arms wrapping tightly around my knees. For a few moments, I sat frozen to the spot, my heart hammering in my chest. I just wished I knew where Wilbur was.

I spun around as the back windows rattled and shook in their frames. The rain pelting so heavily on the glass, for a moment I thought it was hail.

The wind was now a constant howl and really unnerving. Even though Brisbane was not known for having cyclones, this had to be one. And then some part of me registered, it was not only the sound of the wind, but also the sound of an animal howling. I wondered if I was imaging it. Keeping as still as humanly possible, and barely breathing, I strained my ears to see if I could hear it again. And then it came.

Oh my God! In a split second I was off the lounge on my feet. In the darkness, my nervous hands outstretched, I fumbled around for the torch I had earlier left on the kitchen bench, knocking over a coffee mug and spilling the dregs across and onto the floor.

My hands reached for the dishcloth, and then I heard a loud thud on the side veranda. Once again I froze, the racing pulse in my neck the only part of me moving. I stood for what felt like eons although was possibly only seconds, before I tentatively made my way to the library, my hands clasping the unlit torch like a weapon, not game enough to turn it on yet, in case there was someone outside who could see in.

Sidestepping the piles of books on the floor, I approached the window, surreptitiously peering out. Squinting, I barely saw a thing. I placed my hands against the glass, almost touching my nose to the window. My heart slowed a fraction. It appeared that both of the cane chairs had slid across the veranda and one had crashed up against the French door. *Phew!*

I wished there was someone I could call. But pray tell who would venture out in this weather.

And then I suddenly remembered the chooks as well. *The bloody chooks!* I shouldn't have said that, because they were possibly as nervous as I was, poor little things. However, that fact did not stop me rolling my eyes and cursing.

Grabbing an umbrella from the forged iron hallway stand, I went to the front door, opening it a crack. The wind pushed hard against it. For a second I closed it again, and then I opened it, slipped out and pulled it closed behind me. And then I heard the howl again, and I knew it be Wilbur.

'I'm coming Wilbur, I'm coming,' I called loudly, dashing down the front steps, attempting to put the umbrella up as I went, tucking the torch under one arm as I did. My thoughts had been to check the fuse box around the side of the house first, however when I heard that last howl, I knew I had to get to Wilbur.

Almost instantly, I knew I should have put my trusty gumboots on, however it was one of those times, when I argued with myself that it would take more time to go back, when the truth of the matter was my leopard print Jimmy Choo slippers slowed me down. Using my toes, I clutched them to my feet, as I hurriedly crunched over gravel, and then along the flagstone pathways, wet branches, like tentacles, clinging to me.

I was almost at the stone steps when my pink frilly umbrella blew inside out, the wire frame distorting, the fabric tearing from it. For a few seconds, with some difficulty, I awkwardly argued with it, and then with frustration tossed it aside. What did it matter? I was drenched though anyway. I glanced down at my white silk pyjamas and cursed yet again. What the hell was I doing outside in such useless clothing?

Thoughts of snakes crossed my mind once again. Every hair on my body stood up, the back of my neck prickling, right up to the top of my head. Shinning the torch from side to side I shivered, and not from the cold. Did this type of weather encourage them to move around? Probably not! But then again, here I was moving around outside, and that sure as heck was not normal for a human being in these conditions. What if I stumbled upon a nest of Copper Heads? Or what if the river came up so high it washed me away. *What if…*

Another crack of thunder sent me scurrying forward, but with fright I pulled up short as a branch from a gum tree crashed down and fell in the blue garden, right on top of the bed of agapanthuses. I needed to get out of here quick. Flashing the torch around, I saw how my peaceful garden had now become so angry and tortured. Mother Nature was not happy.

When the next bolt of lightning lit up the sky, I was astounded to see that in the distance the river had risen and was cutting across the bottom of the garden. The brief glimpse I saw showed me it was travelling at an extreme rate of knots.

I scratched at the top of my head, my wet curls feeling a like a nest, a piece of twig entangled. Where the heck was Wilbur? Clutching the torch to my chest, I bent forward and wailed his name as loudly as I could. '*WILBUR!*'

And then I thought I heard someone call my name. Snapping my neck, I spun around and then froze, legs apart, feet bracing the ground, my eyes the only thing moving. I couldn't see a thing. Hurriedly, I zigzagged the beam of the torch up the path. And then as the lightning lit up the sky once more, I caught sight of a man standing on the path above, his white t-shirt glowing in the lightning strike. I felt myself make an audible squeak of fright. It took only seconds for me to register it was Phil. *What the hell was he doing here, creeping around at night in the middle of a storm? Bloody hell! I knew there was something about him…*

Quickly, I trod back on the stairs, my right foot slipping in the wet. I felt myself tumble backwards, and with flailing arms, screamed out. With a heavy thud I hit the wet grass, knocking the wind out of me, something I had only ever experienced once in my life when I was about seven years of age, and had fallen out of a mango tree. That horrific feeling came back to me, as I tried to breathe but only felt pain, the rain pelting down on me. Phil was beside me in seconds, his face a mask of concern. With difficulty, I attempted to mouth to him, that I couldn't breathe, that fact scaring me far more than him at that moment. I put a hand to my chest and tried taking small gasps of air to no avail.

Phil's voice was steady but commanding. 'You're winded, don't panic. It'll take ten or twenty seconds. We need to sit you up because you'll need less oxygen there than on your back.' Easily he raised me, placing my back against the wet stacked stone wall.

His voice was loud over the storm. 'Put your arms above your head,' he instructed, assisting me. 'You'll be able to take in more air.'

With closed eyes, stiffly I raised my arms, taking a shuddering breath as I did. I felt something cold and sticky on my face. Briefly, I brushed at it with the back of my hand to no avail. Still crouched in front of me, Phil reached out and picked a leaf off my wet face, continuing to watch me. The storm raged on around us. His face wore the look of something… I was uncertain.

He was making a point of taking long slow breaths, watching me, encouraging me to breathe along with him. I did so for a minute, and then I caught him glancing around with concern at the havoc the storm was wrecking upon the garden.

Abruptly, he turned back to me. 'What on earth are you doing out here?' he asked, his voice loud over the storm, his hands futilely wiping the rain from his face. 'Lucky you're wearing white, or I would probably never have seen you fall.'

At first my voice wavered however it became louder the more I spoke. 'What the HELL are you doing here at this time of night Phil?' My eyes bored into his. I refrained from adding that I would never have fallen, had he not given me such a fright. However, I also knew my slippers were far from suitable, plus I had noticed moss on the steps a few days earlier and done nothing about it.

He scratched at his head, raising his voice to make himself heard over the ruckus. 'This afternoon I locked Wilbur in your shed.'

'What?' I yelled, screwing my face up in misunderstanding, knowing I had attitude. 'What the heck for?'

'You let him out when I was settling the chickens,' he yelled back at me. He wiped at his face again.

'Oh!' I was quiet for a few seconds. 'You could have called,' I said pointedly, unsure if he had my number, as I certainly did not have his. Both of us turned towards the shed as we heard Wilbur howl once again.

Glancing around with concern as another crack of lighting lit up the sky, Phil, his voice authoritive and loud, said, 'I am not going to argue with you. Can you stand?' But already he had hold of one of my elbows, encouraging me. 'We shouldn't stay here any longer. This storm is a ripper!'

I brushed at my sodden pyjamas, feeling leaves and mud

on them. I ignored the fact they were now rather transparent, as there was not a thing I could do. Miraculously, I could see the torch close by. I reached for it.

'Come on,' Phil guided. 'Let's make a dash to the shed.'

'I can't find my slippers,' I yelled back, shinning the torch all around.

'What?' he called, screwing his face up in misunderstanding. Knowing that it would have been impossible to navigate the now mine-field terrain without shoes, I shone the torch on my bare feet.

He must have had the same thought as me, as for all of five seconds he looked around on the ground, found one sodden bedraggled slipper, handed it to me and then with one foul swoop, bent and lifted me, one arm around my shoulders, the other under my knees.

'Put me down,' I yelled, batting him with the slipper.

'Bloody hell, would you just shut up.'

'What?' indignantly I yelled, my eyes almost popping out of their sockets, stunned by the tone he had taken.

His answering tone was precise and loud. 'I am not going to argue!' and he literally dumped me rather unceremoniously. 'Come on then.'

With one slipper, I began to hobble after him. But suddenly, I cried out as I stood heavily on a small pine cone. *Shit, shit, bugger, bugger!* I desperately wanted to hop around on one foot although the rest of my body would not let me. By now, I just wanted to cry. I saw Phil glance around. Even in the dark, I knew I must have looked a sorry sight. Feeling deflated, I let out a breath, and even though he could not see it, he obviously felt it. If I could have, I would have sunk to the ground and stayed there.

Instead, Phil came back and once more swooped me up.

His tone was firm. 'Not one single word or you are going over my shoulder,' was all he muttered, not looking at me, but picking his way across the grassy area, now littered in debris. I felt myself flush and I buttoned my lip, his wet T-shirt sticking to me, his bare arms feeling firm. I shone the torch in front of us. It was the least I could do. And I sniffed, just once, swallowing heavily and blinking rapidly.

In that second, a huge palm frond fell in front of us, and I felt Phil slip. He went down on one knee. In an instant, my hands went up around his neck as I grasped him tighter to stop myself being flung on the ground. He clutched me to him. Mumbling something, he righted himself, hoisting me a little higher. My lone slipper fell off.

'Are you okay?' I asked. Still not looking at me, he nodded, rain trickling down his grim face.

As we reached the shed, he lowered me slightly so I could turn the side door handle. In an instant Wilbur was all over us. Phil put me down.

'It's okay boy,' I crouched, hugging the excited dog. 'I wondered where you were. You silly, silly boy.'

Wilbur began to make noises in the back of his throat as if he was attempting to explain. He then disappeared out the door. Hobbling over, I watched his outline as barely a metre from the door, he cocked his leg for the longest wee imaginable, and then dashed back to me.

With my hand on Wilbur's head, I heard the sound of Phil checking the light switch to no avail.

The noise of the rain on the tin roof was deafening. 'The power went out,' I explained loudly, shining the torch around the shed. On the floor were a few of the painters' drop sheets and an A-frame ladder they had left behind. Against one wall were six blank canvases, courtesy of Bea.

From behind me Phil spoke. 'I think most of New Farm is the same. I'd better check on the chickens and turn the coop around. You wait here.'

'The river has cut across the bottom of the garden,' I warned. 'It won't come up as far as the coop, will it?' I was concerned for the safety of the chooks.

His voice came from the darkness near the door. 'I can't imagine it. But I'll have a look.'

'Phil…'

'What?'

'Be careful.'

Although, I think he heard me over the din, he didn't answer. I watched as his silhouette left. Wilbur attempted to go with him. 'No Wilbur, stay,' I heard Phil firmly command.

Wilbur's paws tap tapped across the concrete floor to me. He nuzzled my hand.

'You silly boy, you missed dinner,' I told him. 'You must be hungry.' I continued speaking to him, more to comfort myself than anything else. Once again, I shone the torch around the shed. What was I to do here?

As I attempted to walk, the sole of my foot throbbed. Leaning against the wall to brace myself, I shone the torch on the offending foot examining it. No major damage, some broken skin, and no doubt, a nasty bruise.

I hobbled over to the French doors and with my hands pressed against the glass, I attempted to see if I could see anything of the river, or of Phil for that matter, to no avail. For some time, I stood motionless watching, as the relentless storm continued to rage outside, the gale force winds tearing at my garden, a branch suddenly being flung only a metre from where I stood inside the door. In fright, I jumped back. Before I had time to think further, there was a loud crash on the roof as a branch or a tree smashed into it. With no time for thought, I instantly went into a crouch position, sheltering my head with my hands, expecting the ceiling to fall in on me. After a minute, I furtively shone the torch over the ceiling. It was with relief I found it intact.

Wilbur at my side, nudged me with his nose. 'It's okay boy,' I whispered, knowing full well my voice did not sound okay. Uncertain of what to do, I continued to grip Wilbur's collar, as I stayed frozen in that position for some time. As if the adrenaline had settled into my joints, it was with some effort I straightened.

Swallowing, I glanced around. I decided to pile the drop sheets together against the back wall, furthest away from the glass of the French doors. Self-consciously I sat in the middle of them, motioning for Wilbur to join me.

I was drenched to the skin, however at least the dusty old drop sheets were dry, and so was Wilbur. After fidgeting around for some time, I eventually wrapped one of them around me, as we sat huddled waiting for Phil's return.

'He'll be back soon,' I said reassuringly, unsure if I was speaking to Wilbur or telling myself.

The side door was still slightly ajar and I hoped that nothing would come in, certainly nothing of the slithery kind. Every now and then, I shone the torch over the floor near the door, keeping up a monologue with Wilbur, who now seemed more than happy snuggled next to me. I could not recall the last time Brisbane had had a storm such as this, and I wondered at the devastation first light would bring.

Periodically, my hand went to my neck as I felt the beginning of a spasm. In between, I scrunched at my sodden curls, knowing I looked like something the cat had dragged in.

As the storm continued to rage, I noticed my hands were

balled into fists, and the muscles in my jaw were taut, doing nothing to help the extreme tension in my neck. Beside me, Wilbur's ears twitched at every sound. I attempted to stretch my neck first one way, then the other. Stretching the pain-free side first as Chang had shown me how to do. One, two, three times, and now the taut side. *'Argh!'*

The wait felt interminable, and then suddenly, the door was flung completely open and Phil dashed in, taking both Wilbur and I by fright. Wilbur raced to him, while from my position on the floor, I quickly shone the torch over him, making sure it was indeed him. With a hand, he half shielded his face, blocking the light.

Taking in the tear in the sleeve of his now muddy T-shirt, I jumped up, shocked. 'Are you okay?'

Sluicing his hands over his face and down his body, he nodded. 'I slipped down the embankment.'

'Are you hurt?' Limping over to him, I held the beam of light steady on his arm.

Glancing over his shoulder at his tricep, he examined it for a few seconds, touching it tentatively. 'Just a bit of bark off. I'll survive.' And then he looked down at me and I felt his breath on my face. Realising I was closer than I meant to be, I stepped back. Although I knew he couldn't see me in the dark, feeling transparent, I instantly crossed an arm in front of myself. The torch beam fell on my naked feet.

It appeared Phil summed up the situation before he spoke again. 'I guess we'll have to wait here until it dies down a bit. It's a bloody nightmare out there.' He stalked over to the French doors, hands on his hips, and stood staring out into the black night.

Staying where I was, I said not a word. I watched as he removed his T-shirt and rung it out, spreading it on the ladder rung.

My breath caught as I took in the outline of his well-built arms and chest. I stood mesmerised, as he turned back to the windows once again.

Finally, I asked, 'Are the chickens all right?' My voice was a tad high.

'They'll be okay.' He didn't look back at me, but continued to survey the storm. 'The old tarp Brownie uses to pile the leaves on was down near the side fence. After I turned the coop, I draped it across... and then I fell down the embankment,' he added with an air of derision, shooting me a brief look.

'You were lucky you didn't fall into the river,' I told him with some concern.

He turned back to me. 'You were right about the river. It's broken its banks down in the right hand corner. They've let some water out of the Wivenhoe Dam upstream, which is not exactly helping.'

I noticed he was examining his grazed tricep again.

'Let me have a look,' I offered. 'Oh... you're bleeding.'

'It's only surface.' However, he used the corner of his T-shirt to blot the wound before spreading it back over the ladder rung.

The entire time, I stood like a stuffed dummy, holding the torch, watching. I recognised the rugged, manly fragrance that I had come to know as his - musk, sandalwood, lavender and birch.

Finally, he turned to me, his face unreadable in the dark, and waited.

'Oh...' I said letting out a breath, unaware I had been holding it. 'I was sitting over here waiting.' And I flashed the beam over to my nest of drop-sheets, where Wilbur had returned and flopped onto. 'I guess I'll just sit there again, while we wait.' *Yes, wise thinking Peach!*

Turning the torch off, I busied myself on the ground wrapping a sheet around me, before once again I noticed the outline of Phil as he stood at the French doors gazing into the mayhem. Jean clad legs apart and hands firmly placed low on the hips, in my former life I would have called it "powerful pose". Now, I just watched. Really what else was there for me to do? Neither of us spoke.

After what appeared to be an eternity, he turned, hands still bracing his hips and looked my way. In the dark, my hand on Wilbur's head, I looked back, wondering what to say next. I felt very small in my nest, and sitting still, I was glad he couldn't read my face.

Finally, he said one word. 'So?'

Raising my brows, I leant forward attempting to catch his voice over the drumming on the roof. 'Sorry?'

Exhaling heavily, he repeated. 'So Peach, I've noticed an air of annoyance about you lately that comes and goes, relating to me.' Without appearing to take his eyes off me, he sat on the concrete floor opposite, his back upright, legs bent, hands clasped loosely on his knees, and waited.

Hmmm… he appeared to be taking the upper hand… again. Placing my hands together, I put them under my chin, and then pulled them away. What was I thinking? I just needed to be direct. However, right at that moment, Wilbur stood up and walked over to Phil and dropped at his feet. Although it was dark, I gave him the evil eye. *Bloody turncoat!*

Clearing my throat, I straightened my back. 'I'm not annoyed Phil… I'm… I don't know anything about you.' There I went again, sounding prissy. What the heck was wrong with me? I changed my tone, attempting to sound more businesslike. 'It's odd having someone around your home, who you know nothing of. Nothing!' Thought I'd just throw that extra *nothing* in for good measure.

I saw that he could barely hear me as he tuned his head slightly to catch my words. Scrunching up one of the sheets, I pushed it to one side. 'Here sit on this. It's more comfortable than the cold concrete.' I wasn't sure if he had heard, however he must have understood, as he came and sat against the wall nearby. Wilbur, going with the flow, moved to a position between us, placing his head on Phil's knee. *Off to the sausage factory with you,* I vibed!

Before I could repeat myself Phil began to speak. Although his voice was low, I heard the three words succinctly. 'My wife died.'

My head snapped back, and instantly my hand went to my neck, I could not contain a tiny wince. 'What…?' Glancing at Phil in the dark, merely a metre away, I was aware he no longer looked at me, but appeared to be staring at his hands.

'Two years ago.' He paused for a few moments as if to gather his emotions. 'She had an aneurism after the birth of our daughter, Sophia. She stood, said she felt faint and then hit the floor.' He stopped speaking.

To say I was stunned was an understatement. I shuddered, swallowing hard against the lump in my throat that literally ached for him.

He continued, and I strained my ears to hear his lowered tone. 'I knew she wasn't just fainting. I knew it was more.' Once again he paused, and then exhaled wearily, as if the mere mention of it exhausted him. 'We were in Melbourne and both our families in Brisbane. Katrine had begun a blog when she first found out she was pregnant, so our families could follow it. The last posting was before we left for the hospital saying: *This is it guys!* The next posting came from me as her funeral notice. I'm still not sure I knew what hit me.

'I continued to blog, thinking that is what Katrine would have wanted. After a while, through my oblivion, I realised people were reading it, and more than once. Then things started coming. In one day 24 things were left on my doorstep. I wasn't sure how they knew my address, but clothes, toys, money, beer… lots of beer came.' His tone was rueful. 'The beer I needed, the money I didn't. Hell it wouldn't bring my wife back. I know they were trying to help, but I felt embarrassed, so I began a trust for people in a similar situation to me, but far needier. It helped my grief to be in some way useful. It was as if the busier my mind was, the less time I had to think about what had happened in my life. I was meant to be the strong one, so I carried on as if nothing had changed. I did not take the time to grieve properly for her.

'However, I could not escape it. Ten months ago, I had a break down. For Sophia's sake, I had to come up here to be with family. I told myself we were coming for just a moment, a break, a few months with family support to allow me to catch my breath. It would be a time when I would gain control of my emotions, catch up on some sleep, find out who I was once again. Plus it was only fair to Katrine's parents. They had lost their only daughter, and although they were back and forth to Melbourne, they were missing out on their granddaughter.'

'Oh…' was as much as I managed to come up with.

He shrugged. 'One of the hardest things to do was leave Melbourne. What if Katrine came back and couldn't find us? What if it was some mistake? Just a nightmare. One I could wake up from. I began to see her everywhere. Or I was convinced it was her, but then she'd turn around and it would be someone else. I frequented all of her favourite places. I so much wanted her to see Sophia.' And then his voice was much quieter, and once again I had to strain to hear him. 'But of course she was never coming back.'

He took a huge breath and then once again exhaled audibly. 'So... I am here for now, however in a couple of months it will be time to return to Melbourne.' In the dark, he turned to me. 'Is there anything else you'd like to know?'

Feeling intrusive, I swallowed. 'No... no of course not.' I spoke gently. 'Phil... I am so sorry. I don't know what to say...' Absentmindedly, I rubbed at my neck. We both sat in silence for some time and then I said. 'It must be so hard...'

'Tell me about it. One day I had this full head of dark hair, the next I had this huge patch of grey at the front. I took the clippers to it and got rid of the lot.' He ran a hand over his closely shaven head.

'You're lucky it suits you.'

I felt, more than saw, him give a shrug. 'It seems easier and appears to suit the life I now live.'

I wondered if he wore it as badge of mourning. 'I mean it... it suits you.'

'Hmmm...' he shrugged. 'Katrine would have been a stricter parent than me, you know. She was going to be the authoritarian, and I was going to be the one who let our children play with sticks and eat leaves. Now, I have to think about how she would want Sophia to be raised. So I have become the authoritarian, but I still let her play with sticks and eat leaves.' He gave a brief chuckle, which lightened the mood. 'Most days, I'd be happy to dress her in jeans, but I know that Katrine would have liked to have dressed her in matching panties and ribbons. So I take the time. And Mum helps out as well.'

I smiled. 'So that is why your time is precious, why you

come and go, and the way you are always checking your watch?'

His hand made a rasping sound as he rubbed at the growth on his jaw. 'Hmmm… something like that. Katrine's death has been difficult for her parents, as you can well imagine. I promised them while we were in Brisbane they could see Sophia as much as they wished, so some days are easier than others. But other days, I want to be there for everything. I know she has my mother, but under the circumstances…'

'And on top of that you work with the boys as well?'

'I have a connection with them because I have experienced some of what they are going through. I was lucky though, as there was always something ticking in the back of my head saying, "there is more".' His voice had fallen into a relaxed state. And it was strange, I too was beginning to feel oddly relaxed even under the circumstances. Although, every now and then my neck made itself known to me, not letting me forget… although I would keenly have loved too. However, with the sound of the storm outside drowning out the rest of the world, I listened to Phil's voice, his tone somewhat comforting.

'A couple of years after my father died in a boating accident in Moreton Bay, I went off the rails. Poor Mum, she tried lecturing me, grounding me, and on one occasion when I punched the back door and put a hole in it, even taking a swing at me.' He gave a gentle laugh, and then sobered once more. 'I had this deep insecurity born from fear, and my way of dealing with it was anger. Anger is an expression that tells everyone to back off. The trouble is, before you know it, you're good at it.'

He was thoughtful for a minute, and quite frankly I was wondering who the heck this man was sitting beside me on the shed floor. He had gone from using the smallest amount of words to now telling me his life story.

'Anyway, I had two people in my corner, so to speak. My mother, who taught me about yoga and meditation, and hasn't ever had a conversation with me without telling me she loved me, and Frank Carmody, who paid my tuition at Toowoomba Grammar. Thank God, because it was the making of me. Most wayward boys do not get that opportunity. And then much later on, Frank stepped back in and mentored me. Funny thing, I always remember him telling me, if you're unhappy or if you're stressed, just grow something, it will save you.'

Knowing he couldn't see me didn't stop me raising my brows in surprise, not only that his life appeared to have come full circle, but also at his forthrightness. Not for the first time I thought to myself that the past has a funny way of weaving itself back into the present.

I turned towards Phil as he continued. 'My father taught me a lot too. Although he worked in the city, he was a man of the bush. Through him I learnt to love nature, the sounds of the forest, the birds, the smell of the wet earth and leaves...' He drifted off as if in memory.

I stayed silent, forcing myself to be still, waiting for him to continue.

'He was a keen fisherman.' I could hear the nostalgia in his voice. 'He taught me about patience, sitting, being quiet.' He gave an ironic laugh. 'Funny, but it was doing what he loved most that ended his life.' He gave a shake of his head as if he still couldn't understand it.

Before I could speak, he went on. 'Anyway, when I first returned to Brisbane with Sophia, I seemed to do nothing but be with Sophia and my mother, and once a week when my in-laws had Sophia, I ventured up the boys. I wasn't much good to anyone though. I struggled with myself, because I was meant to be showing the boys guidance, when all I could do was doubt everything I believed in.' His hand went to his bicep. In the dark, it appeared as if his fingers were tracing the letters.

'That's why you had the tattoo.' I said quietly.

He turned to me. 'Hmmm… yes.'

The way he answered made me wonder if he had forgotten I was there at all.

'What's wrong with your neck?' he asked.

Realising I had been clutching it, closing my eyes, I once again slowly stretched my neck first to one side then to the other. I grimaced. 'It's got a spasm.'

'Pinch it like this.' He held his hands up in the dark, to show me. 'Hold the pressure on though. The muscle needs to be released.'

I did as I was told, although it is rather hard when you have fingernails.

'Is that working?'

'Sort of,' I lied.

'Turn around,' he instructed, scooting himself a little closer. Sweeping my hair aside, I felt his firm fingers probe around my neck and shoulder. 'You're a bit bloody tight,' was all he said, his warm hands feeling strong and capable.

Helping, I pulled my drenched curls over to one side with one hand, resting the other on the floor to keep my balance. But then his vice-like fingers began to relentlessly squeeze at the muscle that ran from my shoulder up my neck. It hurt! Biting my lip, I had to stop myself from batting his hand away. The pain so excruciating I thought I may throw up.

'Hurts, I know,' was all he said.

'Kills,' was all I said, my voice high.

'Close your eyes and breathe,' he instructed gently, exhaling heavily as he did, as if guiding me to follow his breath. 'In through your nose,' he breathed, 'And taking it all the way into your belly. Most people only breathe in one sixth of their lung capacity.' Through the pain, I fell in with his breath, deep inhalation, long slow exhalation, over and over, and over again.

This went on for some time and although there was an obvious lessening of pain, Phil continued on. And I must say, I felt no need to stop him. It felt fantastic. Plus I could not deny, I was enjoying the intimacy.

We were both quiet, and I felt the situation to be quite surreal. After all it is not every day you have a man's hands upon you in a small shed, in the dark, whilst a storm rages on overhead. However, I continued to breathe and block out thoughts of anything other than those hands. Minutes went by.

And then from the warmth of his hands, I felt an energy pass between us. I *can't* explain it. It was like nothing I had felt before. It was the Qi that my yoga instructor always spoke of, always asking if we could feel it. Usually, I had nodded, but truly had no idea what the hell he was talking about it.

Right that moment I felt the Qi, the circulating life force, the flow of energy from Phil's hands to my shoulder and through my body. There was a feeling of deep bliss, of inspiration, of invigoration. The energy filled every part of me. I almost wanted to cry out *yes, yes, yes*, like in the movie *When Harry Met Sally*, but thought it a little odd under the circumstances.

And then his hands loosened. 'It has helped,' he said. I was unsure if this was a question or a statement, but I nodded. 'Good,' he said, his voice low and slow. 'Roll your shoulders. That's it.' And his hands slipped slightly lower and began kneading my taut shoulder muscles.

I exhaled audibly. And then the moan that I had been holding in check, slipped out. '*Hmmmm… that's great,*' I literally purred. Abruptly, feeling foolish, I pulled myself up short, opening my eyes wide.

Coughing, I rolled my shoulders once more, slightly pulling away. 'Great thank you.'

Instantly, he removed his hands and moved back over to where he had been seated earlier.

I felt a slight discomfort between us, as if we were on another footing and had no idea how to behave. Keen to continue the previous conversation, I asked, 'So, is life a little better?'

He appeared thoughtful for a few seconds. 'Yeah… it is.' His tone was lighter, more upbeat. 'This place has helped immensely. It has been my therapy.'

'But Phil… with everything you've just told me, I think it sounds like this has added far too much to your already full plate.'

'Not in the least.'

I stayed quiet while he searched around for the right words.

'In the beginning it was tracing a riding path I knew as a boy, and then it became more. That first day I stepped back inside the gates here, I felt the strong presence of my father, and I could not keep away. When I was young, he had given me a small plot of land in our back yard. I can't tell you how many times I redesigned it and rebuilt it. It was a gift. I have always found nature utterly inspiring and wonderful. After spending time here again, I hatched an idea that it could work for the boys as well. In hindsight, probably not one of my best ideas…'

'It was a great idea. That fight at the end threw me, and then you didn't come back…'

'Well yes, but I had told you that.' He had adopted a more relaxed pose now, slightly turned to me, one leg bent, the other flopped to the side, his arm draped across his knee.

'I know... I must have forgotten.' I picked at some invisible lint on the drop sheet.

'My mother had a small procedure and I needed to be around for Sophia.'

I looked up. 'You should have said.'

His eyes were upon me. 'I wasn't ready to.'

'Oh!' I changed the subject. 'Anyway you built the chicken coop,' I said lightly.

'I built the chicken coop,' he repeated, mocking my tone.

I laughed loudly, waking Wilbur from his slumber. His heavy tail went into overdrive, hitting my leg. I pushed it aside. 'I am sorry Phil. I was a bit of a cow, wasn't I?'

'Full blown heifer, I'd say,' he teased.

'What?' I said turning my neck, my hand shooting up to it instantly.

'Careful,' he reminded. 'I gather you've had quite a bit to contend with over the past year as well.'

'Well... nothing like you.'

'You're doing a great job here Peach. I can't tell you how much I'll miss it when I go. It has been a healing sanctuary for me.'

'It has for me too.'

After that, we were both contemplative for a bit, until Phil broke the silence, turning to me. 'I meant to tell you though how much young Matty talked about your vegetable garden after he helped you in the kitchen that day. In fact, it was enough to inspire us to build a kitchen garden for the school.'

'Really?'

'Yep. The school has a kitchen where the boys help to prepare lunch and then along with the staff sit and eat as a family, which I must say is a rarity for most of them. The food preparation and the simple meals ground them, allowing them to get on with the rest of the school program more effectively. The kitchen garden will add an entirely new level, give them some responsibility in their health and nutrition. Plus they will all be required to contribute, which is a good lesson about promoting respect.'

'I love the sound of that. Only the other day, I was reading about a study where a group of prisoners were given fish oil capsules and there was a marked improvement in behaviour.'

'Yes, yes I've heard of that as well.' He appeared well pleased that I knew of what he was talking about. 'Society accepts that food and health are linked, but manage to decouple that relationship when it comes to behaviour. Crazy!'

And then we both fell comfortably quiet, and I must say I felt no need to fill the void. Although I was moved by his story, I was enjoying sitting in the dark, swaddled in dusty old paint sheets, on the cold hard concrete, chatting with him. To say I missed intimacy was a major understatement. And that thing that had happened earlier with the Qi, well I dare say I needed to give that some thought.

I think he sensed it as well. I felt his gaze on me.

'I must say, I've noticed you're good under pressure.' And he gave a chuckle and shook his head. Although his tone had been light-hearted, it still annoyed me.

Shifting uncomfortably, I folded my arms. 'You've said that before. I do try Phil. This is all new to me.'

Surprisingly, he nodded. 'You *do* try. And you're doing… as Brownie would say… a *bloomin'* good job!'

I snorted. 'Why thank you sir.'

'Your face is a dead giveaway though.'

I scowled with a self-righteous air. 'What?'

'Even in the dark, I know the look you will be giving me.'

'What…?' I repeated, horrified. Now would be a good time for him to shut up! I think I preferred it when he was short on words.

'Lately, you've had that look on your face, as if you thought I may have been a criminal or something.'

Instantly, I sat upright. 'No I did not!' I lied, my voice now much louder than necessary, as the sound of the rain on the roof had begun to lessen.

'Yes, you did.' He laughed. 'And then when the chooks came you looked horrified. I thought you wanted them?'

'I did! Or I do! I didn't think they'd come for a while, and I'm meant to be going away for a long weekend in a few weeks. So I've either got to sort something out, or cancel on my friends, which I think they arranged for my benefit.'

'I'll feed the chooks,' he said matter-of-factly.

Although, I knew I needed to digest everything he had recently divulged, I knew that I could no longer take advantage of him. 'Truly you cannot do that. Lou might be able to come and stay,' and then I remembered she was looking after Dad's dogs while he was gone, 'or something,' I finished with.

Phil insisted. 'I'll do it! I may have to take some responsibility for jumping the gun with the chickens. Perhaps I wanted them more than you did. For a city joint, you're becoming very self-contained with the kitchen garden. I couldn't help but think fresh eggs would be a great drawcard for your B&B breakfasts.'

'I agree.'

'Oh you do, do you. That's nice for a change.' He laughed, crossing his legs at his ankles, and cradling the back of his head in his hands, his pose now extremely relaxed. 'So I guess there's no chance of finding some Indian Runner ducks to organically balance the earwig onslaught in the rose garden?'

'What?' I was flabbergasted. 'Indian Runner ducks? Earwigs?' One of my hands came down and smacked my leg. 'For God's sake Phil… my sister Lou was right, I'm turning into a farmer. Can we *please* see how the chooks go first?'

'Haha… I'm teasing,' he chuckled.

'Thank God for that.' I shook my head. 'Lou would never let me hear the end of it.'

'Bit like that is she?'

'Yes… constantly trying to…' And then I felt I was divulging far too much information. '… make me do stuff.' Could I have said that any better! Sighing heavily, I twisted and turned attempting to make myself more comfortable.

'Bit of a boss?'

'You could say that!' I lay down on my back, which surprisingly appeared far more comfy. In the dark, I looked at the ceiling. 'It's a role reversal for us. That was my job.' I was contemplative. 'Funny, but now I'm not too sure what my job is. My life has changed so much.'

'How so?'

I've always liked a man that asked questions. Mind you, this one had taken some time.

'It doesn't seem that long ago, I was one of the directors of our company, sat on the board of two others, mentored young women, all while I worked a 60 hour week in the corporate world. Now, I'm getting around in gumboots, spending my day brushing up on the old fashioned art of jam making and preserving. I'm embarrassed to say how ridiculous it is the pride that a good set on my marmalade brings,' my voice carried a twist of irony. 'Plus, I appear to know most plants by their botanical names now. *And* I have chickens…' I glanced at him in the dark, and I heard a slight chuckle, 'and I'm discussing Indian Running ducks and earwigs.'

I was on a roll and I couldn't stop myself. 'Right this moment, I am not only missing my Jimmy Choo slippers… God rest their souls… I am also missing my Prada heels. Can't remember the last time I wore them. Hello… who is this person?' Taking a breath, I was grateful I pulled up before I said that I hadn't had sex since the dark ages!

Phil let out the hugest laugh. Even though I was rolling my eyes at myself in derision, I couldn't help but laugh with him. It felt good.

'Runner!' he finally said, his voice filled with mirth.

I rolled to face him. 'What?'

'It's Runner ducks. You said running.'

'Runner, running, whatever! I can just see me running all over the place after them. Not yet okay!'

Phil let out a sniff of humour. 'In your Prada heels, I take it?'

'Yes… something like that…' I nearly called him a smart arse, but pulled up just in time. Perhaps the storm had sent me hysterical?

'You seem happy.' He was back to not using many words again, however there was now an apparent ease between us and I was enjoying it.

'Hmmm… I am. To be honest, I'm not sure who that other person was.' I was thoughtful. 'Perhaps, she was so busy attempting to please others, she forgot to please herself.'

'That's called life.'

I shrugged.

'Any changes?'

'One! Children. I look around me and see that this place would make a wonderful family home.' Suddenly I felt I'd been far too candid. I rushed on. 'However, it will also make a great B&B. So that's what it will be.'

I sensed him nodding.

I rolled back onto my back and we stayed there in companionable silence for some time. In my mind I was now contemplating what his body language was saying, so when he spoke he threw me.

'How do you want to do this?'

Flinching, I opened my eyes wide. 'Huh?' I asked. I have always been an eloquent speaker. Thoughts quickly flashed through my mind of: 'Perhaps you too may not have had sex since the dark ages as well. If you come a little closer, we could manage it. The concrete is hard, but so what!

And then he answered, shaming me to my core. 'It sounds like the rain has eased considerably. However you don't have any shoes.'

What the hell was wrong with me? 'No… I don't.' I was pensive for few seconds. 'I can wait until first light and then I'll be able to see where I'm treading.' And then I read his mind. 'And *no*, you are *not* carrying me.'

He laughed. 'It's becoming a habit.'

'I would hardly call once or twice a habit,' I said with some seriousness, but laughed all the same.

Getting up from his position on the floor, Phil poked his head outside to check the conditions. 'Rain may have eased off, but it looks like one hell of a cyclone went through!'

Stretching, I yawned. 'Without shoes, it's too far to make a run for it. I'm staying here until morning. I've got Wilbur.' I was enjoying my little cocoon on the floor, and if I was being totally truthful, that was not all I was enjoying.

Chapter 19

With a heavy heart, I folded my arms across my chest, and then thoughtfully tapped at my top lip with an index finger. I watched as Phil fired up the chainsaw, brandishing it like it was a sword. Within minutes he had felled the magnificent Manchurian pear tree, and before long it was reduced to a pile of woodchips.

A few months back, another storm, nowhere near as severe as the evening before, had come through mid-afternoon, and a huge branch from the same tree had split from its trunk and crashed across the driveway, just missing a work truck.

After consulting an arborist, Phil had taken off some of the smaller branches to reduce the weight, however we had been aware there was another somewhat dubious branch up higher in the tree.

And then last night's storm had hit, and another branch had come crashing down. It was lucky that there were not any cars parked beneath, or horror of all horrors, no one standing there at the time. It appeared only weeks ago, that I had stood in the same spot as I stood now, and admired the beauty of the arching branches, heavy with white blossom.

In its wake, the storm had left much damage across Brisbane, tearing up trees, closing roads, roofs off, flying debris, power cut to more than 30,000 homes, and forcing the rescue of dozens of people from flooded creeks and the river. New Farm had been lucky compared to most.

However, although there was a bevy of tradespeople swarming like bees over the site and into the house, my attention turned from the tree, back to my mother, who had been patiently waiting beside a small furniture truck, much further down the driveway, out of harm's way.

In her usual layered white, and trademark psychedelic scarf wrapped around her head, she looked rather elegant amongst the throng of tradies, as she purposely strode towards me.

'I'm sorry Bea, what did you say it was?' I asked, my brow furrowed, my face wearing a look of disbelief that she had chosen this moment. Under Bea's direction, the delivery truck had begun to back up the driveway, its reverse sensor beeping adding to the already riotous din, the chainsaw still the loudest.

'A daybed,' Bea repeated. With a proud look on her face, her bangles jangled as she waved a bejewelled hand at the driver to halt.

Scratching at my neck, I was still confused. 'I'm sorry... I don't follow?'

'Your studio Peach! Every artist needs somewhere to contemplate.' She turned her attention from me and called to the driver in his cab. 'Thank you driver, it will have to be carried the rest of the way.' She glanced around.

Frowning from the incessant noise, and I daresay from my mother as well, I followed her gaze, until it finally rested on Phil, who had just set the chainsaw on the ground, and now stood with his back to us, legs astride, hands on his hips, as he surveyed his handiwork for a few seconds. It was a pose I now found familiar. Picking up his stainless steel water bottle, he pushed his Akubra back on his head and drank thirstily, wiping his mouth on the back of his hand.

As he replaced the bottle back on the ground, Bea called to him. 'Excuse me... hello... gardener... can you help please?'

'Bea?' I murmured.

She turned to me. 'What darling, he doesn't mind. Do you?' she called. 'Now there's a good fellow.' With her head cocked on an angle, she played with a few tendrils of hair that had deliberately escaped her scarf, and fluttered her blue eyes.

'Bea!' I admonished. 'For goodness sake!'

My mother looked back at me, and gave me the once over, as if it was the first time in her life she had seen me. She bounced a hand under my newish shoulder length do. 'Darling, *I am loving* those curls, very youthful,' her voice was loud enough for all and sundry to hear. 'Dropping those few kilos is very flattering, but *why* on earth are you wearing gumboots? Hmmm? Truly you need to show your legs off more. I do *love* you in heels. You were always a heel's girl. And you do need more colour on your face. Did you try that Revlon fire engine red lipstick I recommended? Number 42 if I recall!' And before I could utter a sound, she turned from me. 'Careful now gentlemen.'

Rooted to the spot, with my hands at my sides, I blinked in disbelief, feeling my hands repeatedly clench and unclench. I was surprised you could not see the steam coming out of my ears. 'Mother... stop.' I put my hands up. 'Wait just a minute!'

Turning, Bea put an arm around me, steering me back over towards the front steps. My badly bruised foot chose that moment to remind me of last night's injury, not exactly helping my mood with my mother. She lowered her voice. 'Darling, Johnny and Lou have asked me to come and talk to you. I think they're rather concerned that after that debacle with Davis, it has turned you off men altogether. Lou didn't say it, but I got the distinct vibe that she was suggesting you may have switched teams and would find being a lesbian far more desirable.'

To say I spluttered was an understatement. In fact, I believe my nostrils may have flared. 'What...?'

However, Bea carried on as if I hadn't made a sound. 'God knows we've all dabbled once or twice, however I just do not get the feeling that you are one, and trust me, I have a good sense for that type of thing.'

'MOTHER!' I yelled, thinking she did not have much sense for anything else. Growing up I had to contend with the fact that Bea was never going to be a conventional mother. In recent years, I felt I had come to terms with her unique ways, however right at that moment… and then hurriedly I glanced around to see if Phil and the driver had overheard our exchange. Although he did not look my way, I was sure Phil was wearing a bemused expression.

'Oh do calm down darling.' Bea theatrically waved a hand in the air. 'You know I do not like to interfere, it just *had* to be said!' She slapped her hands together, to finalise the subject. 'But one last thing darling… I am not sure about those boots. As I said, I do love you in heels. Maybe something with a small kitten heel perhaps?' she glanced at my stony face before continuing. 'No? Well, it's not my style to chat to you about your personal life. However do something about it, to get your sister off all of our backs.'

Gobsmacked, for almost the first time in my life, I had nothing to say.

'Now, I'll leave your private life alone, but you will allow me to help with the studio, because that's what mothers do.' Clapping her hands, she walked back over to the truck, leaving a waft of *Youth Dew* in her tracks.

Why I was surprised was anyone's guess. When had my mother ever acted like a mother? *That's what mother's do!* Bloody hell… I could put a list together of the top one hundred things that mothers did… perhaps not Bea… but other mothers, and setting up an art studio would not be there.

My feet were glued to the spot, and I stood watching as a daybed made of lime washed rattan cane, with an off white calico mattress, and a jumble of cushions on top, were lifted from the truck. And then it hit me. Lou was *exactly* like my mother. Where their train of thought came from was beyond me. Blinking a few times, I shook my head.

'Careful now gentlemen. That's it. Oh you are strong boys.' Turning back to me, those perfect eyebrows raised, and fiddling with her hair, Bea called, 'Darling are you going to lead the way or am I supposed to guess?'

*

Her eyes narrowed, and with an air of authority, Bea studied the small room. 'You are right about the light in here Peach. I always thought you had my eye. I can see many wonderful creations taking place here.'

I had to admit the daybed was perfect. And I could see myself in contemplation, idling away the hours, the northern sun filtering through the French doors, with perhaps the entire property's most perfect view of the river. Although I must say that today it was no beauty. After the previous night's downpour and with the release of the water out of the dam, the river now looked like chocolate milk.

However, I softened towards my mother. 'It's great Bea, thanks.'

We returned back to the house, me with a slight limp. My mother riffled though her handbag. 'I want to give that lovely gardener ten dollars for his trouble.'

'Mum don't…. please… you'll offend him.'

'No one is offended by money darling. Trust me. Oh there's Lou, I'll bet she came to make sure I chatted to you. Tell her I did a good job and have sex as soon as you can.'

I closed my eyes, pretending she hadn't spoken. Perhaps if

I kept them closed long enough, she would be gone when I opened them.

*

'He wouldn't take it!'

'I told you that Bea… but you didn't listen,' I admonished, my head in the pantry, looking for a special herbal blend of tea I had purchased especially for her. Hurriedly, I closed the pantry door afraid Lou and my mother would see the jars of homemade jams, marmalade and pickles.

'Who wouldn't take it?' Lou asked, a pork-pie hat and a pair of Wayfarer sunglasses shading her face.

'The gardener, handyman or whatever,' Bea waved a hand behind her indicating somewhere outside.

'Don't call him that.' I frowned.

'What darling?'

'Well he's a… I don't quite know what he is… but he's more than a handy man. He's more like a foreman.'

'Who Farmer Joe?' Lou asked, finally removing the sunglasses. 'The gorgeous secretive one, with those mysterious dark eyes, luscious tanned skin, a body to die for, and who knows all of your secrets, and you know absolutely nothing at all about him? Ewww… very odd!'

'Thank you Lou. I do happen to know a little about him.'

'Since when?' Lou fired off, like a loaded gun. 'Yesterday you said he was still a mystery.'

'Since… last night!'

'LAST NIGHT,' Lou screamed. 'And I thought you were a LESBIAN.' Her voice was still loud. 'Good for you sis.'

I waved a hand at her to shut her up. 'Will you cut it out Lou?' I eyed her severely. 'He came by to let Wilbur out of the shed and we ended up talking.' I omitted the entire cosiness of the situation.

My mind turned to first thing that morning. Stifling a smile, I was reminded of the surprise I'd had when I awoke alone to find my gumboots sitting beside me, with one wet Jimmy Choo slipper placed beside them.

I was uncertain of when exactly Phil had left, as we had chatted for quite some time, and eventually I must have dozed off. Our conversation at some point had turned to favourite movies. There was an intimacy and contentment in talking freely about the things you love with someone of the opposite sex, lying in such close proximity.

'My all-time favourite is *The Way We Were* with Barbra Streisand and Robert Redford,' I had told him, my voice beginning to sound sleepy.

He had asked me what it was I liked about it.

Turning on my side, I had snuggled my hands under my face, and starring into the darkness of where he sat, explained. 'They fell in love and married despite the differences in their backgrounds and temperaments. And even though they divorced, the tragedy of it was that they both knew they would never love anyone as much as they loved each other. Pretty powerful.' I sighed. 'And then that scene when she asks him to stay until the baby comes. Oh my God… I howl every time. I could howl thinking about it.'

He chuckled. 'Ah please don't,' and I could hear the mirth in his voice. 'I think Wilbur's done enough of that for one night.'

I giggled, a sense of buoyancy overtaking me. But then I sighed. 'And Hubbell… Robert Redford,' I explained, 'was *so… damn… gorgeous*. And I really loved Barbra Streisand as Katie. Originally, my mother had the video and after I saw it the first time, I wore red nail polish for months attempting to copy Katie's innate style.'

Phil didn't say anything so I continued, rolling onto my back once again. 'I have watched that movie five million times.' I smiled into the darkness. 'But do you know, it was only recently as I watched the DVD once again, at the end of the movie, when they ran into each other years later in front of the Plaza Hotel in New York, and she does that thing where she sweeps his hair to one side with her fingers, and he asks after his daughter, that it finally dawned on me, that this is something he should know. I mean what type of father doesn't keep contact with his child? But, I guess it was the 1940s, and perhaps that was how it was back then.'

'And yet you still love it?'

'Yes I do.' I smiled to myself. 'Every single second of it! Even the music is so emotional, it makes me cry.' I had put a hand to my chest. 'That scene on the boat,' I explained, 'the beach, the bookshelves, the screening room. I love it! I love it all!' I had exhaled heavily. 'And yours?'

I had expected he'd give it some thought before answering, however he didn't even take a breath.

'Braveheart!'

'Really?' I had rolled back towards him. 'What did you like?'

I heard him stir around making himself comfortable. 'I like William Wallace's courage. It resonated with me. I understood how he felt when his father was killed. Loss, rage, responsibility, courage… I understand that.' I heard him exhale, but I kept quiet, enjoying his forthrightness. And then he took an audible breath. 'Yep… only too well it seems.'

Without him having to say another word, I had remembered all too clearly William Wallace's wife dying as well. We were both quiet then. But then I had a thought. I turned to him.

'But it was a love story as well, wasn't it?'

'It was.'

'Hmmm... I do remember liking that movie.' In the dark, I nodded my head. 'Good choice.'

'Why thank you Ma'am.' We both lightly laughed, before he asked, 'How's your neck feeling now?'

I shrugged sleepily. 'Bit sore.'

For a while we continued to chat, although I kept expecting him to say he had to leave. And then we had a few silences where I felt, and imagined he must have as well, that there was no need to fill. The company was more than enough. It must have been during one of those silences when I dozed off, although not before I had asked him what he had done for a living before coming to Brisbane.

'Much the same as here,' he had said, locking his hand in front of himself and stretching. He gave a huge yawn. 'I'm part of a landscape team.'

'Oh...' I imitated his yawn. 'So you *do* do this for a living?' I said with an element of surprise, although I was unsure why.

He had yawned once more. 'Amongst other things.'

Without giving me time to think further, he had shrugged and changed the subject. It made me wonder if he moved from one thing to another, and that was how he had gained knowledge about so many things.

After waking, I had gingerly stuck my head out the door to survey the scene in front of me. Blinking a few times against the brightness of the day, I swear it looked like a mini tornado had gone through, with branches down, and trees stripped bare. Actually make that not so mini. However, upon further investigation, still dressed in my now not so white silk pyjamas, teamed beautifully with gumboots, I realised that the bottom garden had not fared too badly. The river had left quite a muddy residue where it had encroached upon the land, with one small area of the garden now flattened. A huge clean-up was required but no major damage.

I had pulled the tarpaulin from the chook house. 'Morning Ladies! You had quite a welcome last night didn't you?' Picking up the contraption, I wheeled it about until it was facing north, feeling quite capable, and marvelling at my strength. Who would have thought, was all I could think. You pay a personal trainer three times a week, or you do plain simple hard work and receive greater benefits. The incongruity of the situation was not lost on me.

I called to Wilbur, who was busy fossicking away over on the northern boundary. 'Come on boy, you must be starving, and I need coffee and a shower.' As he followed me up to the house, I could not help but ask, 'So did you see Phil leave, or were you sleeping as soundly as me?'

The dog made a small noise and cocked his head to the side.

I stopped and regarded him. 'I know you're frustrated you can't talk. But not as frustrated as I am. Can you try harder please? There's so much you could tell me.' I peered into his eyes. 'Try Wilbur, try!'

His face carried a worried air, and he gave a little whine, which to my trained ears… not… sounded very much like… *I'm trying*.

Laughing, I patted the top of his head. 'It's okay boy. I'm teasing you.'

It appeared I had no sooner breakfasted and showered when from outside I heard Phil speaking to Wilbur. 'What a mess boy!'

I don't know why but I felt a little sheepish. The thing was we had now crossed a line. He was more than someone who simply worked for me. You cannot, I repeat cannot, spend the better part of the night, laying on the floor of a shed, in the dark, him extremely close by... without a shirt I might add... me in transparent pyjamas... sharing important information about your life, without feeling like you're on new territory with that person.

To cover any uncertainties I had, I'd popped my head out of the bedroom window, called hello and given him a cheery wave.

'Did you sleep well?' he had asked, looking up, both hands on his hips. Even from where I was, I could see a smile playing about his lips, and I must say we were both pretty lively for two people who'd had very little sleep.

'Better than I have in years,' I'd called back. Hands low on his hips, he had thrown his head back and laughed.

'Forget the Egyptian cotton sheets and the Heavenly bed, in fact I don't know why I bothered to buy this house, all I really needed was a shed, and a few dusty drop sheets.'

'So... you're discovering you're a woman of simple tastes.'

'Hmmm... I wouldn't go that far,' I told him, flashing my eyes, aware there was a bit of flirting going on.

'Ah hang on... I forgot about those Prada heels.'

'Shame on you!'

He had laughed again. 'And your neck?'

'Like a brand new one!' Showing off I turned it from side to side, and then gave a small grimace as it pulled a little. 'Well almost brand new.'

*

But right then Lou's insistent voice broke into my thoughts. 'And?' Lou insisted, her voice still loud with excitement.

'And nothing.' I shushed. 'Keep your voice down. The poor man's wife died a couple of years ago. Leave him alone.'

'Well… I can't think of anyone more perfect. He's probably hanging out for it. You'd be doing him a favour.'

Reaching for the mugs on a top shelf, I spun around to face her, my eyebrows raised. 'You'll have to forgive me Lou if I was expecting more than doing someone a favour.'

'Yes Lou,' Bea admonished, busy rifling through her bag. 'Good looking though he is, your sister can do far better than a handyman.' And then she looked up, waving a small package in the air, her face literally beaming. 'I thought I'd put this in here. It's for you Peach.' Looking very pleased with herself, she pushed it across the bench to me.

'What is it?' I asked, picking the bag up, opening it and holding it to my nose.

'Damiana tea,' Bea explained.

'Oh… thanks Bea.'

Putting her hand out, Lou took it from me, opened the bag and inhaled. 'Hmmm… smells odd,' she said, inhaling once more. Squinting, she began to read the label. 'I love it,' she shrieked. 'It says if you drink this tea you will be happy, healthy and horny.'

To say I was dumbfounded was an understatement. Before a word could pass my lips, Lou was shrieking once more.

'Make me some. Make me some. I'll drink it!'

I could not help myself. Snatching the packet from her, I took a small swipe across her head. 'You!' I said. 'You don't bloody need any!' Opening the pantry door, I threw it in and closed the door as quickly as I could. 'I am making coffee!' I stated.

*

'Tell me what you are wearing Peach?' Lou asked.

With the phone tucked under my neck, I fastened my earrings. 'My red Leona Edmiston wrap dress.'

'Ah nice.' Lou paused. 'It shows your boobs off beautifully. Make sure you wear it nice and low.'

Glancing down, I pulled the neckline of my dress higher.

'Which shoes?' she inquired.

'Nude Mui Mui heels.'

'Hmmm... nice touch. Wear that Betsy Johnson cuff you bought in the States.'

Rifling around in the jewellery drawer, I pulled out the cuff and slipped it on, looking at myself in the full length mirror.

'How does it look?' Lou asked.

'Perfect,' I lied, taking it off and closing the drawer.

'Now make sure you introduce yourself to everyone.'

My voice carried an acerbic tone to it, 'Oh that's a great tip Lou. Thank you. I may never have thought of that myself.'

'Smart arse. I'm just excited for you. I feel like my child is going out on her first date, even if there are going to be five other people. Plus, I'm a little concerned your dating skills are not up to par.'

Exhaling heavily, I rolled my eyes at the phone.

'Now make sure you call me the minute you get in.'

'What if I don't come home tonight?' I teased.

'*Oh God...* I hadn't thought about that... *text me...*text me something and I'll know. Now don't talk too much about yourself... men like it if you ask about them. I hope you've had some of Bea's damiana tea. Maybe make a big...'

'Lou I'm hanging up now,' I said, as I cut her off.

*

From the car I could see a table set for six on the footpath. It was deserted. I exhaled and checked my watch. What was I doing here? I fumed to myself. *Bloody Lou!*

Pulling the visor down to see the mirror, I added a touch more lip gloss, wiped an imaginary smudge from under an eye, scrunched my curls, and busily examined my face for a new wrinkle. How had I suddenly gotten to 35 years of age?

I watched as a couple with a baby in a pram left the restaurant. I couldn't take my eyes off them, even watching from the rear view mirror as they disappeared behind the car. I had become fixated on couples with babies.

At 35 my fertility was halved. In five years' time, my chance of naturally falling pregnant was down to five per cent, such an uplifting thing to know.

The thought of adoption was not new to me either. I knew I did not have to give birth to a child to love it as my own, however the small amount of information I had, I knew being single meant I was an unlikely candidate.

And that was what I was doing here. Regardless of Lou, I wanted to believe in the fairy tale of happy ever after. I could not give up on it. What if the future father of my children was here at dinner tonight?

From the car, I saw a woman walk towards the restaurant. She looked nice, dark shoulder length wavy hair, a little bohemian in her dress, flat sandals, a colourful silk bag slung over her shoulder.

Despite butterflies doing cartwheels in my stomach, I checked my watch once again, and realised I had two choices. Either go in or go home. Years ago, when I had first turned 18 and begun clubbing with my girlfriends, our mantra had been, *go hard or go home*. Oh, how times had changed.

Stepping from the car, I once again pulled at the neckline of my dress, checking it was not too low. Surprisingly, I was nervous. Goodness, how many functions had I attended over the years, with literally thousands of people, and it would not have bothered me if I knew any. Tonight was different though.

My eyes swept around the restaurant. Just inside the door

was another table set for six, with four people already seated. With looks of expectation, three glanced my way. The fourth had his back to me. Hesitantly, my hand fiddling with the chain at my neck. I smiled and was grateful the bohemian woman smiled back. I felt myself exhale.

'Well…' I said, pulling a chair out, and then I stopped in my tracks. Seated beside me was a man I knew through the real estate industry, Mike Henry. Briefly, I closed my eyes. Anyone but Mike. Mind you, I could well imagine him thinking *anyone but me.*

He had an agency a block further south from ours and we had always shared a mutual amicability. But then one day a few years ago, I had run into him, and he had asked about a bracelet I was wearing. He had told me that the girl he was seeing was having a birthday the following week, and he was looking for a bracelet such as mine.

Two weeks later I saw him out to dinner with his girlfriend. I couldn't help myself but wish her a belated happy birthday. Her unmistakable look of bafflement told me instantly that I had it all wrong. Standing behind her, Mike ran a hand across his throat. The next day I called him to apologise. 'It wasn't your fault Peach. I am seeing a few people. Perhaps I should have mentioned that.'

Six months later, late one night, Davis, Marty and I were leaving Il Centro in the city when we passed his table. He attempted to introduce his colleague, a woman who had caused us no end of grief a few months earlier, when a real estate deal had been handled badly.

Unfortunately, Mike's introduction did not go well as my tongue had been loosened by the three glasses of red wine at dinner. I launched into a diatribe telling the women if she ever behaved that way again, I would report her for her unethical manner. Shortly after that evening, I found out Mike was engaged to her. Oops!

Now, I caught the look of complete discomfort that crossed his face. It felt like eons before either of us spoke.

'Mike… nice to see you.'

'And you Peach,' he said standing. 'It's been some time.'

Awkward introductions took place around the table. Annie, the bohemian woman took charge, appearing to be an old hand at it. Next to Mike was Maureen. Introducing herself as a librarian, *I really never would have picked it.* Not. She smiled shyly, and tucked her black mid-length hair behind one ear.

To my right was Brian, a butcher. Happy, open face, and a little porky, too many sausages he joked. Straight up, he asked if it was reasonable to only have two courses and water. Plus he had a two for one offer and wondered if anyone wanted to split it. It crossed my mind that he appeared much older than the 35 to 42 year age bracket, Lou had mentioned. For that matter so was Mike Henry. I would have sworn he was at least 45.

Annie worked at a vintage clothing store at Paddington, believed in love… me too I wanted to say, but refrained… had four cats and loved the internet.

And now it was my turn. 'Well hello everyone…'

At that moment our sixth person joined us, a glass of scotch in his hand already. It appeared he had been watching from the bar. I soon learnt his name was Paul.

Smiling at him, I continued, 'My name is Peach, I'm opening a B&B in the area.' I gestured towards Mike. 'And Mike and I have met previously in my former life in real estate.' There I'd said it. My plan had been to not even mention anything about my previous life, however I realised with Mike there I could not get away from it.

Expectantly, all eyes turned to Paul, perhaps in his mid-forties, tanned skin, close cut receding hair, causal shirt worn out with jeans. He only had to open his mouth for it to become apparent that he had been the first to arrive and had knocked back a couple at the bar, to put it politely.

*

Pulling the bed covers back, I glanced at the clock. I picked up my iPhone from my bedside table and texted Lou. 'Staying out', was all I sent and then promptly switched my phone off. Now that would give her something to think about.

*

Daylight streamed in through the open French doors onto the daybed. Pushing my magazines aside, I lazily got to my feet and switched off the kettle. I waited a couple of minutes for the water to be off boiling point before I poured it over the top of fresh mint leaves, into the prettiest French Limoges teapot. Instantly, the fragrance wafted up to me, and I inhaled it in. Briefly, I admired the prettiness of the teapot, and ran my finger over the shabby pink trailing roses, and little daisies.

The mint was running rampant in the kitchen garden, so Phil had wisely suggested I use it as a refreshing tea. It was fast becoming addictive, however to keep that plant in control, it would require me drinking dozens of pots of mint tea a day. As thirst quenching as it was, and as pretty as my new pot was, I thought not!

Mesmerised, I watched as the colour of the water mildly changed as it leeched from the leaves. Placing the floral lid on, I let it steep for a few minutes. I had found the teapot, along with two teacups and saucers, at a French auction house. All had the green Limoges stamp. Although not a set, they looked very pretty together. I poured the mint tea into one of the porcelain cups, admiring the pretty pattern of pink roses and green foliage. My index finger traced the gold scalloped edge. The mint tea ritual was one I was fast learning to enjoy. The naturalness of it was something Bea would have done. Once again, the thought crossed my mind, that there was more of Bea in me than I had been admitting.

Feeling the warmth emanating from the cup and saucer in my hands, I glanced around at the garden shed, my studio, feeling that this entire scene had remnants of when Lou and I had played cubbies as little girls. It gave me a good feeling and I smiled to myself.

Walking over to the open French doors, with a smug sense of satisfaction, I turned and surveyed the scene. Pressed against one wall was an antique white sideboard. On one end was a tiny crystal vase I had bought down from the house earlier, a small posy of mixed flowers picked along the way pinched into it.

Sitting neatly on a mirrored tray was the teapot, the remaining teacup, two small china canisters, one with coffee and one with tea, a small crystal sugar bowl, and a container of almonds. Taking inventory, I was once again reminded that the ants loved the crystal sugar bowl, and I realised I would have to bring down a sealable container, as lovely as the crystal was.

On the opposite wall was the French washed daybed, not leaving much space in between for my artworks, which at this point of time totalled six blank canvases, and not an ounce more of art paraphernalia. For the umpteenth time, I promised myself that I would eventually get to it, reminding myself that at the moment I was setting everything up to create the life I wanted. Once the entire house and garden were complete, I would have all the time in the world.

In an effort to be proactive as far as the studio went, I had made it my mission to monitor exactly how the light moved across the floor, as the sun passed through the day. There was something about this lovely little room that delighted me. I had hoped that what Bea had said about many wonderful creations taking place in it, was true.

Gently placing the fragile cup on the floor, with childlike glee, I flopped back on the day bed, pushing a couple of cushions under my head. With intense pleasure, I gazed at the river. Although some distance away, from the daybed, I felt as if I could stretch my hand out and trail my fingers in the water. With one hand absentmindedly playing with one of my curls, minutes passed as I listened to the gentle wake lapping at the shore, no longer the angry river it had been only days before. Although, every now and then, I couldn't help but notice the flotsam and jetsam sail past, which the river had stolen from the riverbanks much further upstream.

I could also see the havoc the storm had wrecked upon the garden, which would take some time to restore. Propping my chin on one hand, I watched as a mother duck and her babies, waddled across the grass and then jumped down the embankment. I wondered where they had sheltered last night.

Just outside the doors, three butterflies, oblivious to the storm's mess, fluttered in and out of the passionfruit vine and then over to a classical urn sitting atop a concrete plinth. And in the distance, I spotted the elusive Whitie crossing the garden as if he was the king of the jungle. Keen to keep the peace, I kept Whitie's whereabouts quiet from Wilbur, who noisily slumbered just outside the door.

Standing, I picked up my cup once more and leant against the door frame gazing at the view, allowing the morning sun to warm my face, noting how at this early hour, it bounced from the city skyscrapers across the river, like a giant mirror. Closing my eyes, I could not remember the last time I had felt this wonderful sense of peace. Breathing deeply, I felt my shoulders drop and relax.

Placing the cup down on the small step, I stepped out onto the grass and rolled my neck first one way and then the other, still feeling a slight twinge. I placed my arms above my head and stretched. Slowly rolling forward, one vertebrae at a time, I dropped until my hands touched the cool spongy grass. Bracing myself, I stepped my feet back and raised my hips in the air, positioning myself into the downward dog yoga pose. This position still difficult for me, I pressed my heels towards the ground attempting to stretch my calves.

The words of my yoga instructor from yesterday's class came to me. 'See what it feels like to be fully oxygenated.'

I'm trying, I thought to myself. *I'm trying*. But try as hard as I might, yoga did not come naturally to me. I was not as flexible as I would like, although I was fast becoming an avid believer in the benefits.

From my upside down position, I looked between my legs. Now that I had lost a few kilos, it did not go unnoticed by me, that although I would never be tall, my legs were really in perfect proportion to the rest of my body.

I was not sure I had ever felt this content with my body size and shape. It just showed what personal happiness did for you. Yes I loved, and will always love, the beautiful things in life. However, I was aware they truly only bought fleeting happiness. Although, I could not lie, my Lady Peeptoe killer shoes from Christian Louboutin, the ones with the six inch white patent leather heels with turquoise patent leather tops, still put the smile of lust on my face whenever I wore them. However, I was noticing more and more often lately, how my true happiness came from feeling contented, and at peace with myself.

With my head between my legs, and my face flushed crimson from the time I had spent in the inverted position, I was startled as Wilbur scrabbled to his feet and gave a woof of excitement. From my position, I glanced around and saw Phil bouncing down the stone steps some distance away. The moment he saw me he hesitated.

Instantly, I dropped to my knees. Legs apart and backside in the air was definitely not my best angle. I knew Lou would beg to differ. She would argue that it was every girl's best angle. Sheepishly swallowing a small smile, I gave him a wave before rearranging my magenta singlet top, as if being upside down was the most natural thing in the world.

'I didn't mean to intrude so early on this Sunday morning Peach. I was hoping to slip in and out without disturbing you.' My thoughts still on Lou, I swallowed once again at his last comment, thinking it just may disturb me, but not in an entirely unpleasant way. Refocusing, I noticed his lips were still moving.

'Being Sunday, I thought you'd still be asleep.' Placing his hands low on his hips, legs astride, eyes narrowed in thought, he looked across the big expanse of garden. 'I was wondering if after the damage of the storm it might be rather industrious to have those advanced trees delivered tomorrow. We might need to wait until we get this clean up under control. Thursday was damn hectic up top, so I didn't get a chance to thoroughly access the situation down here. And if I am going to put a halt on the trees, I'll need to ring them first up tomorrow morning.'

The advanced trees he spoke of were to be strategically placed to frame views from all aspects of the house.

With an authoritive air, he glanced around. 'I think I will cancel it until next week. We're going to have our hands full here.'

Nodding, I agreed. 'Whatever you think, Phil.' I was in a constant state of appreciation for his forward thinking. I didn't know what I was going to do once he left, and as usual, I pushed that thought from my mind.

He scratched his head. 'Just a thought... you might find if you straighten your arms a little more,' he demonstrated putting his arms out in front of himself, 'and ease your spine back, it will be far more comfortable.'

'Sorry?'

'Downward dog!'

'Oh of course. It's my calves. Too many years wearing heels.'

'Ah yes... those Prada heels.' And I saw a small upturn of the corners of his mouth.

'And the rest.' I smiled. 'By the way I've been making the mint tea you recommended.'

'You have? And?'

'Yes... it's good!' I turned and glanced back into the shed. 'Would you like a cup? The pot is still warm.'

'I don't want to disturb your Sunday, particularly...'

I cut him off, holding a hand up. 'You're not... unless you need to be back for Sophia?'

I saw his slight hesitation. 'No... no hurry.'

While I poured the tea, Phil plonked himself down on the front step of the shed, knees bent, arms resting loosely on them. I was reminded of how different he looked without his trademark akubra. Although I did note that the causal checked shorts and round neck fitted t-shirt gave him a look of a man with easy style. Plus the quality of his navy leather loafers did not escape me either.

Wilbur resettled himself at Phil's feet, a smile of contentment curling the corners of his black lips.

The sound of birdsong was loud in the air. Other than

that, the utter peace and quiet was complete bliss.

'It was too nice a morning to sleep in,' I said, by way of something to say, handing him the fine teacup which looked terribly dainty in his large hands. 'So I came down here.' I perched myself on the step beside him.

'There is no sleeping in with Sophia,' he smiled, sharing a rare glimpse of his life.

'How is she?' I asked, as if it was completely normal for me to do so, knowing how guarded he was of his privacy.

I caught a note of humour in his voice. 'I fear we are growing apart. I have discovered we have completely different taste in food, music and books.'

I chuckled, although before I could comment further, Phil changed the subject. 'So, no big plans for this weekend?'

I laughed. 'Me… big plans… this is it?' I waved my arms around. 'Actually I tell a lie. I went out on a hot date last night with three men. They could not resist me, had to fight them off with a stick.'

'Now that I'd like to see.' His laughter was unfeigned. It could not have come from politeness, because it came from his toes up. Looking sideways at him, I noticed how much I enjoyed hearing him laugh, as although more frequent these days, they had been few and far between.

It made me smile, I gave a snuff. 'Well it wasn't quite like that. It was one of those dinners for six.' I rested my chin on my hand.

'Oh?'

I exhaled heavily. 'Something my sister set up for me. She's hell bent on me finding a date for a Melbourne Cup function next month.' Frustrated, I shook my head and tutted.

He glanced sideways at me. 'I'm gathering there were no takers by the sound of your voice.'

'None! The ladies were lovely, however I had to remind myself I was not there to collect new girlfriends.' I laughed at the irony of it. 'Brian the butcher seemed like a nice man, but not my sort. One of the other men had had a little too much to drink before we arrived. He kept telling me he thought I looked like the type that would one day run my own business and be a boss. Apparently he had a way of *knowing these things*. He said if I listened to his advice, I too could be as successful as him.' I rolled my eyes and let out a breath. 'It was incredibly painful to say the least.'

Phil gave a small laugh. 'So, I'm gathering you didn't tell him about your business achievements?'

'You got it. I just wanted to tell him to go away, however under the circumstances it seemed impolite.' I wondered how much Phil actually knew of my work history, however was under no illusion Pete, the electrician, would have filled him in on every detail.

'And the third one?'

'Oh, Mike Henry, poor man. I knew him from my real estate days. I don't think he has been single long, and seeing me appeared to shake him up a bit. He left immediately after the main course.' And then I laughed, remembering something. 'Although, at one point he leant across to me and nodding at,' raising my brows, I drew inverted commas in the air, '"my mentor" he said, *someone definitely forgot to send him the memo.*' Rolling my eyes, I shook my head and then continued thoughtfully, 'My dear sister is right about one thing, although I am never going to admit it to her.'

With interest, Phil raised his brows in question.

'My flirting skills have well and truly atrophied.' Annoyed with myself, I shook my head in frustration, and began to trail one of my fingers along behind a track of ants.

Phil gave a laugh. 'You're funny, you know that.'

With mock seriousness, I glanced sideways enjoying his easy going conversation. 'That was not my intention.'

He laughed again. 'Do you miss your former life?' His forthrightness startled me.

For the briefest of seconds I wrinkled my brow, and then turned to him. 'Not one bit! And it astounds me that I don't. It was such a different life from this.'

'So you don't miss any of the accolades?'

'No.' I shook my head. 'None.'

'That's good.'

'Mmmm,' I nodded thoughtfully. 'These days I cannot imagine living any other way. The other day, I was going through some things, and I found papers from years ago. I had kept a collection of stories about gourmet farmers and their wonderful fresh produce. At that time, although I thought I was happy with my life, I was constantly seduced by visions of fat bulbs of purple garlic drying on country verandas, carrots being pulled from the ground covered in rich earth, free range chickens, and eggs gathered by children's tiny hands…'

Suddenly pausing, I felt I had said far too much. I gave my head a shake, before I continued. 'My grandfather used to say that the love of gardening is a seed that once sown, will never die. When I was quite young, we'd work together in his sprawling vegetable patch. I'd help pull weeds, plant seeds and seedlings, while he explained what we were doing and how important it was to regularly put your hands into the soil. He was right, and for many years I had forgotten how good it actually felt.

'Anyway, I may not be in the country but it feels like I am. And I know I am more on track than any other time in my life. Since coming here, fat tomatoes, golden skinned onions and enormous cabbages are as much objects of desire as the perfect shoe. Or almost,' I said with a laugh, catching the look of amusement on his face. I let out a breath. 'And you?' I asked attempting to change the subject. 'You said you put your life on hold to come here. Do you miss…?'

Just then my phone rang. Glancing at the screen, I pushed it away, deciding to ignore it. I saw Phil raise his eyebrows. 'My sister,' I explained, shaking my head. 'I'll let her wonder about last night a little longer.'

He gave a light hearted nod. 'By the way, which weekend is it you're heading away? I meant it when I said I'd feed the chickens.'

'It's next weekend. Are you sure?'

'Of course. I've picked up some Royal Rooster drinkers and feeders to attach to the coup. Their slimline, compact design will simplify things.'

'Royal Roosters sounds quite regal. Lucky chooks.' However, I was disappointed that other than Katrine, Phil had not commented on his former life. And not for the first time, I wondered if perhaps there was not much to comment on. Although he was a man of great knowledge, that did not mean he used it to his best advantage. There was a noticeable silence.

'My friends Thomas and Steve, I think you've met them coming and going occasionally, have invited me and another friend.' I explained, knowing he had not asked.

'That's the Steve you got in the marriage settlement?'

'Ahh so you remember?' And then I felt a twinge of discomfort, as I recollected telling Phil about Steve the day we had gone to the nursery and I had run into Davis and … *that woman.* On principal, I chose never to say her name.

'Yep,' was all he said. I decided then and there that he was a good listener.

And typically my style, I began to rabbit on. 'We're heading up to Clovelly Estate just outside of Montville. We'll all have the first night there and then another friend of theirs, Jules, is meeting us for the second night. Now hopefully that will keep Lou off my back for some time.' And then, I stopped abruptly. I was unsure why, but I felt as if I was always giving Phil far more information than required.

'How so?'

'Oh… she knew that years ago Jules had a mad crush on me.' Talk about giving away too much information. I attempted a joke. 'The man is only human after all.'

'Of course,' he said with humour. 'So… I take it Jules is not gay?'

'I bloody hope not, or it is not as flattering as I would have thought.'

Taking me by surprise, Phil let out a loud laugh, which made me laugh with him. And then he changed the subject. 'Have you ever heard of stingless bees?'

Resting my chin on my hand, I drily said, 'Yep, you mentioned them to me some time back.'

'I think they'd really compliment what you're doing here.'

'Okay… so my designer shoes may not be quite as important to me as they once were, but some things do not change. I'm telling you now, I would not look good in a bee keeper suit. Really not my style. I am not a trouser girl… and white loose fittings ones… not very flattering…'

He laughed again, shaking his head and giving a loud tut. 'The bees are *stingless*. You wouldn't have to wear a suit.'

'Ever?' I asked with mock seriousness.

'Ever!'

'Well that might change things.' Arms crossed, I cocked my head on the side. 'Hmmm and the reason you think I should have these bees Professor Hunter? I don't really see myself with a roadside stall selling honey.'

Once again, shaking his head with good humour at my cheeky comments, he rolled his eyes to the heavens before answering. 'Actually these bees don't make as much honey as their more exotic counterparts, however they are efficient and important pollinators of native plants and crops. And low maintenance,' he stressed as an afterthought. 'Do you realise that if all the bees in the world died then our crops would die off as well?' He didn't give me time to answer but continued on. 'They are a tiny, dark coloured bee. Just seems like the perfect addition to the paradise you're creating here.'

I let out a long slow breath. 'I'll give it some thought.' And then I narrowed my eyes. 'How do I get them here?'

'Pick them up in your car. Don't wind the windows down. They'll buzz around a bit but…' He caught the look on my face and laughed. 'I'm joking. They're harmless to humans, however they come in a log or a wooden box. I've done a bit of research. I'll give you the website if you like.'

'Hmmm…' I pondered.

'No pressure Peach. Just a thought.'

'Well thanks for thinking of it.' The man seemed to think of everything. And the more I thought about it, the more I liked the idea. It would be giving nature a hand. My beautiful garden was fast becoming a hobby farm.

Phil stood. 'I must be off. I'll put a hold on those trees for another week.'

'Sounds good.' Standing, I faced him.

He leant forward. 'You've got something,' he said, touching my hair. I stood still. 'It's a small twig,' he said by way of explanation. 'It's caught around one of your curls.'

I put my hand up, and tangled it all the more.

'Stand still,' he commanded, as if speaking to a child. Using two hands he fiddled with my hair, attempting to release the small wayward stick. In concentration, he bent his head closer almost touching his forehead to mine. Looking straight ahead at his chest, I inhaled him, instantly feeling my head spin. I gave an almost imperceptible sway. I could feel his breath. I knew that with little effort I could lean into this man, rest my head on his chest and listen to his heart. However, with my hands pulled up almost in prayer position, I stayed still. My fingers twitched as if wanting to reach out and touch him.

'Got it,' he said, stepping back.

I exhaled. 'Oh,' was all I said, and then I had no idea why I said it but I did. 'What am I going to do without you Phil? I mean…' I shook my head and glanced around, 'the garden. What is the garden going to do without you?'

With a lovely smile, he shrugged. 'I'm not sure what I am going to do without this place when I'm gone.' Leaning forward he picked a long stalk of grass and ran it through his fingers over and over, looking to the distance. He turned back to me. 'The truth is you won't need me Peach. I've got another month or so and by then the garden will be finished. Before I go, I'll help you find the right maintenance man to assist Brownie.'

I nodded. The earlier feeling I had, suddenly changed. He took a few steps and then turned back to me. 'You're funny, you know that.'

Without giving me a chance to respond, he turned. As I watched him head over the grassy area towards the stone steps, I replayed his words in my mind. *You won't need me Peach.*

But I will! I will! I realised I had come to rely upon this man who was still at times a complete stranger. And I was quite unsure exactly what that meant to me.

Chapter 20

'Would you consider giving me some?'

'Peach, *I don't know!*' Thomas wailed dramatically. '*Darling*, I'm flabbergasted. I've never thought about it.' I watched as he glanced at Steve to gauge his reaction.

Lounging back in the dining chair, cowboy boots crossed at his ankles, typical of Steve, he simply shrugged, placing his wine glass to his lips, taking another sip of his *pinot gris*. With a raise of his brow, he looked between the two of us, summing the situation up.

Thomas flopped back on the banquette, and folded his arms. 'Why are you only asking *me* for sperm?' He gave me a direct look. 'What about Steve?'

'I can't ask Steve, it's too close to… his brother.' I paused. 'Look I am just saying if in five years' time, when I am 40, if I haven't had a baby and there is no prospective man on the scene, would you help me out?' Crossing my legs, I took another sip of champagne.

As Thomas grimaced, I couldn't help but laugh. 'You only have to donate it sweetie, you don't have to put it there.'

Chin propped on his hand, Thomas pursed his lips while he thought some more. 'Can I think about it?'

'Of course you can.'

We were all quiet for a few minutes while the third course of Cameron Matthews's degustation was presented to us. Innovatively displayed upon a slate tile, three succulent juicy scallops, tender duck meat, and a puree of tangy mango, topped with crunchy cashews were placed in front of us. My mouth watering, and with a hand to my chest, I moaned with delight.

'There'll be none of that if I do!' Thomas groaned.

'Oh shut up!' I told him, laughing and shaking my head.

It was during the earlier course of Mooloolaba spanner crab with spring peas, pea shoots, lemon, leek and chervil that I had blurted out my proposal. It had nothing at all to do with the third glass of French champagne I was now on. I guess, I could not blame Thomas for being shocked.

'I can't help feeling that it would be providing an obligation forever.' Thomas placed a hand in the air. 'I'm not saying that's a bad thing. I… just… don't… know.'

'Hang on sweetie, although I have asked you, it is a decision for you and Steve to make together. I have given this a huge amount of thought, and I promise I won't expect any obligation from you. You can be involved as little or as much as you would like. But think about it, I could be artificially inseminated by donor sperm, and although I believe they provide the most miniscule details…'

Steve interrupted, this somehow catching his attention. 'How so?'

'The article said that my baby could know if its father has chest hair, or dimples, or even what shoe size he is.' I flashed my eyes. 'However, it's not enough for me to only know that he has good DNA and fast swimmers, I also want to know that he is a good person, a loving, caring, honourable person. Also my child will never get to hug him or even know his name until it is 18. Even then it will have to wade through miles of red tape to find him. Now, at the end of the day that may be the road I take.' I shrugged and glanced between the two men. 'I just wanted to put it out there to you first, and to give you heaps of thinking time.'

Thomas looked thoughtful for a minute, and with a knowing look proposed, 'You haven't ruled out Jules, have you? *He* could be your man in more ways than one. And he could put it there.'

'Oh good thinking Thom.' My tone held a sarcastic note. 'When he turns up tomorrow I could ask him! Let's think… Oh I know… do you have any sunscreen… and what about sperm. I may need some.'

'Bitch! You know he's always liked you.'

My laughter rang out. 'He's always liked *everyone*.' With a flash of my eyes, I cocked my head to the side. 'I'm just the one he hasn't had.'

'*Touché* babe!' Steve chimed in. His hand slapped at the table. 'Anyway enough about this sperm thing. What's the story with the B&B? What's taking so bloody long? I want three months prior to opening for the PR to do it justice. *Surely* you must have a date by now.' Typical Steve, he was never happy unless he was talking business, everything else was frivolous to him.

'I promise I'll give you three months. I guess we are getting closer. However, the last thing I need is pressure to open when the reality is, everything has taken much longer than I first expected. I am not opening until I have it perfect. With hospitality you get one chance. Guests are not going to return if they are unhappy because something isn't finished. As unusual as it sounds, I actually do have the luxury of time, and I love living there so much, I may just enjoy it for a few months once it is finished before I open it up to paying guests.'

Steve held his hands up. 'Okay, okay… just trying to help.' He drummed his fingers on the table. 'I still think you should come by the office in the next few weeks though to have a preliminary meeting. I've been thinking I'll put Trent and Rowena on your account. It's right up their alley. We need to achieve national coverage in print, on-line and radio. I want you blogging and I'd recommend a separate Facebook page, plus you'll Tweet.'

'Right,' I said, knowing he was, but wondering when I was going to find the time.

'Hey guys,' Thomas interrupted, 'do we have to talk business all bloody night? I want another slice of that fantastic homemade bread and freshly churned butter.'

'Oh my God, me too,' I moaned.

'Do not even think about it babe,' Steve commanded.

Quizzically, I looked at him. 'Why?'

'No you cannot have a jersey cow at New Farm. You will not be churning your own butter.'

*

I am not sure if it was possible, but I may have drunk my weight in champagne. My mouth was worse than bone dry, and I wondered if the thudding I could hear was my head, or actually someone at the door. Rolling over, with only one eye opened I firmly planted my feet on the floor, feeling around for the white towelling slippers. Giving up, barefoot I ambled across the carpet to the door, and flung it open. 'What?'

Surprisingly, after the amount of alcohol we consumed last night, Thomas looked relatively perky. 'You said we should all take a country walk before breakfast. You said the fresh air would do us good. You said…' Without a word, I pushed the door closed and leant against it. From the other side I heard, 'Honey, you've got two minutes before Steve changes his mind.'

I closed my eyes. 'Bugger!'

*

The three of us, rugged up against the early mountain chill, in relative silence headed up the curved driveway and turned right heading away from Montville. The mountainous air was crisp and fresh, the view of lush green paddocks across the Blackall Ranges and the deep blue Pacific Ocean on the horizon, heaven indeed. The area's eponymous wildlife was in full voice with the sounds of cockatoos, whipbirds, kookaburras and rainbow lorikeets serenading us as we trudged along.

Empowered by nature at its best, Thomas and I strode out, leaving Steve in our wake. Turning to check on him, I noticed the permanent frown he had set in place above his dark glasses. I simply shook my head at him and laughed affectionately.

However, 15 minutes into our walk, as I was about to suggest we leave the roadside and meander through the lush rainforest surrounds, Steve, with an acerbic tone to his voice, called from behind. 'Babe are you sure you can't just get scared of something so we can go back.'

Swinging around, Thomas shot him a haughty look, and then attempted to raise his botoxed brow. 'Hmmm… did we interrupt your beauty sleep Lovey?' And then I caught an almost imperceptible shake of Thomas's head as he continued to glare at Steve.

'I'll give you effing bloody beauty sleep...' Steve mumbled, still coming up the rear. I knew only too well the bantering between these two was their way of showing affection for one another. I decided then and there that after breakfast, I would leave them to themselves, and take a run down to Noosa for a swim.

All the same, after Steve's earlier comment I decided that for now perhaps sticking to the roadside was indeed the best option. Plus I could not help glance around for any sticks that looked like they may begin to move at any moment.

And then I had thought. On the way back from Noosa I just might go via the Eumundi Markets and the legendary Berkelouw bookstore. There was a special book I was after.

*

The north facing Noosa Main Beach with its year round gentle waves was always a popular spot for locals and tourists alike. That day was no different. With a high of 28 degrees, a brilliant indigo blue sky and not one cloud in sight, who wouldn't have wanted to be on that beach?

I pulled into the bustling surf club car park, guessing that as usual my search for a park would be futile. I watched the flotilla of four wheel drives in front of me jostling for positions. But then, as I was about to exit, I saw a slim space with a sign reading *Very Small Car Only!* It possibly should have read… Bambino's car space. Mentally, I thanked the powers that be, and gave Bambino's steering wheel a fond pat.

'You have a way of bringing me luck little one.'

Shaded by a giant pandanus palm, I stood on the boardwalk at the edge of the sand and with some enthusiasm surveyed the scene. Surprisingly, in the many times I had visited this beach in the past, I had never seen the tide out as far as it was that morning. To the far right, I noticed that there was enough sand exposed in front of the huge rocks on the headland, enabling beachgoers to walk all the way around to Little Cove Beach. In the past I had only gone there by the roadside boardwalk.

As Little Cove did not have parking nearby, it was generally a local's beach and did not attract the heavy crowds of Noosa's Main Beach.

Pulling a white cap down on my head, I set off across the warm sand towards the ocean's edge in nothing more than my new white swimmers. Happy to soak up some sun, I dropped my silk wrap on the sand. Further on, I saw the usual mid-morning crowd gathered around the familiar iconic quad bike of *Hey Bill*. For four decades this man had plied his trade up and down the beach, replenishing hot and thirsty beach goers with ice cream cones and cold drinks. I smiled at the trademark sight of his straw hat, and wondered if he would be recognisable without it.

As I passed, I watched as mothers handed their offspring drippy ice creams in a multitude of flavours and colours. For the first time I realised, the sight of those mothers and babies had not made me painfully yearn for what might have been. I pondered, unsure when this shift of consciousness had occured, thinking Emerald Green would be proud of me.

I deliberately turned my attention to the surfers beyond the headland, refusing to let anything bother me on this glorious day, noting the glorious morning sun sparkling on the water like millions of diamonds.

I continued on, enjoying the feel of the wet sand between my toes, the sun embracing my shoulders. Following the water all the way around to the charming secluded beach, I relished the gentle waves lapping at my ankles. Breathing it in, I realised how blissfully happy I was.

In the past, on my half dozen visits to Little Cove, I must have always come at high tide, when there was little sand left exposed on the beach. This morning it was the opposite, and I marvelled at what a beautiful private beach it was. I watched as a dozen beribboned, white Tiffany chairs were placed on the sand in preparation for a wedding. Right in front, someone had etched into the sand a huge heart that said *Frank loves Stella*. Ironically, it too added to my happiness. Love was always a good thing.

Playfully lolling in the shallow water, one hand allowing the wet sand to repeatedly sift through my fingers, I watched as four men attired in caramel coloured trousers, and pale green open necked shirts, worn loose, made their way down to the beach. I decided they must be the groom and groomsmen. A few well-dressed, although barefoot, guests began to saunter down. An elegantly dressed woman in a colourful caftan in blues and greens, handed out white parasols from a huge woven basket.

The longer I observed, the more parasols went up creating the prettiest picture. Lost in time, I stayed in the shallows hoping to catch a brief glimpse of the bride. At some point, I felt the intense warmth of the sun upon my back, and glanced up at it to gauge the time. At the same time, I noticed that although I was still sitting, the water now came up to just beneath my chin. The thought of walking in nothing else but my new swimmers back to my car via the roadside boardwalk, was not a welcome one. So, leaving my little slice of paradise and disappointed not to have seen more, I headed back the way I had come, keeping an eye on the tide, now having to skip in and out, and up and over the rocks, the gentle swell of the ocean gradually increasing.

As I neared the main beach, feeling carefree, I cut across the water on an angle, jumping the gentle waves as I did, feeling even more elated as I watched a school of whiting darting to and fro, in the crystal clear water. Finally, feeling safe that the tide could no longer catch me out, I dived under an oncoming wave.

Clear headed and refreshed, I waded and swam the rest of the way, pondering the lack of emotion I had shown earlier while watching the mothers with their babies and young children. Perhaps it was that now I was happy with me, living the life I wanted, I was happy to let my life unfold. All the wanting in the world was not going to bring it to me. Perhaps motherhood would elude me. Perhaps the higher powers had something else for me. At that moment it occurred to me, I may have passed another milestone.

For a brief moment, I tilted my head back, closed my eyes against the sun, held my hands out wide and said out aloud, 'I am ready for you to bring to me what you will.' And then, laughing to myself, glanced around to make sure no one thought I was a complete nutcase.

The colour of the ocean reminded me of the colour I had selected for the new pool tiles at home. The tilers should have been finishing off the last of the aqua glass mosaics today. Even though my original plan had been to simply repair the pool, the fact that there were so many broken turquoise tiles had made the exercise futile.

Phil and I had discussed the difficulty of finding a tile to match. He had also come up with the idea of the letters of Carmody House being picked out in a deeper colour on the bottom of the pool, which meant the pool was best tiled in something lighter than what it had been. He drew up sketches and then handed me a palate of tiles in blues and greens to select from.

And for the hundredth time, I thought how much I would miss him, would miss our talks, sometimes working side by side, often at those times saying nothing, just a companionable silence, both enjoying the tasks. I felt he had taught me much, had broadened my horizons and thought process when it came to the garden, and my way of living with nature. As if reading my mind, he had helped me to create the life that was more me than ever before. Because of that, I was happier with the person I had become, and I realised that finally I had grown into who I was meant to be.

I attempted to remind myself that people came into our lives for a reason. Not for the first time, I wondered if Mr Carmody had had a hand in bringing Phil to Carmody House, to recreate what had been. However, the job was almost completed. Plus as he had alluded to more than once, he had a life that he needed to return to. But what was that life?

I could not help but notice the thought of Phil leaving always left me with a feeling of hollowness. Perhaps it was that old *hanging on to something* that I had battled with as a child, and obviously still did now. I deliberately batted that thought away, not wanting to spoil my mood. However, the feeling kept returning.

Swooping my silk wrap up off the warm sand, I scrunched my saltwater hair, and taking long strides, headed up the beach towards the icy cold shower, now keen to visit the pretty town of Eumundi and the legendary markets, on my way back up to Montville.

Just under twenty minutes later, I entered the historic township and slowly cruised along the now bustling Memorial Drive, wondering why I had not come here more often, as it was only an hour's drive from Brisbane. Something I had to put on my "to do more often" list.

This otherwise sleepy town sprung to life each Saturday morning, transforming it into a vibrant mecca for shoppers from many kilometres away, looking for something different.

Today, I was having one of those days when everything flowed. No sooner had I thought of needing a car park when, directly opposite the markets, someone pulled out in front of the year round *All Things Christmas* store. As I climbed from Bambino, I couldn't help but glance into the cheery window of the Christmas shop and wonder what the next Christmas would have in store for me. It also reminded me that I had promised myself a new tree, a huge tree, to sit in front of the French doors in the library. I could imagine rounding the curve of the driveway at night and seeing the lights flickering from the window, welcoming me home.

Now dressed in tailored black shorts, a black ruffled sleeveless blouse and gold sandals, I slung an oversized soft leather bag over my shoulder, and dodging the market traffic, crossed the wide road. With my hair caught back in a long colourful scarf, worn like a large headband with the tails hanging down my back, I casually wandered under the canopies of towering heritage-listed fig trees. It was not hard to pick up the vibe of the slower pace here. Strolling along the shady walkways amongst stalls and quirky old buildings, the sights, sounds, smells, and tastes fascinated my senses. It was a joy to see how passionate these people were about their products.

I sampled a bit of this and a bit of that: olive oils, sauces and condiments, roasted macadamias coated in sugar and cinnamon, handmade organic sourdough bread, artisan cheeses, and Gympie Farm butter. Everywhere I looked there was literally a plethora of locally handmade. Their policy was: *make it, bake it, design it, sew it, or grow it'* They sold everything from delicately constructed craft, to organically green produce.

Weaving myself in and out, interested in everything, I surprised myself when I paused at a Palmist's stall. Intrigued, I read the poster through. *A map of your future, your business success, and romance. No two people have the same print. You are unique...*

My reading was interrupted by the palmist's serene voice. 'Good morning!'

'Oh… hello!' I glanced at the smiling woman perhaps in her late fifties, sitting behind a pink cloth covered table, her hands elegantly resting on the top. Returning her smile, for some reason I felt drawn to her. 'You're not busy?' I asked, an eyebrow cocked.

'Not at this particular moment.' She rested her chin on her

hands and smiled once again. 'Perhaps I am waiting for you.'

Laughing, I shrugged. 'Perhaps!' I was thoughtful for all of a few seconds, and then pulled out the chair opposite her and sat down. I placed my hands upon the table.

'So you are psychic?' she asked, as she glanced back up at my face.

I shrugged. This was not the first time this had been said to me, and I laughed to myself thinking the boys would probably call me *psycho* rather than psychic. And then a sobering thought hit me. If I was so bloody psychic *why oh why* had I not seen what was happening with Davis sooner? Perhaps I had not wanted to. And the next thought to cross my mind was that I was exactly where I was meant to be right this moment. Take that Emerald Green!

The palm reader continued, and I stopped my rambling thought process to pay attention.

'Hmmm... I see you are very much in charge of your own destiny!' she traced the 'M' on my right hand, and then continued. 'Loyal, strong willed, capable, listens to everyone.' She gave a grunt. 'They don't always listen to you though.' And then she smiled. 'Animals love you.' For a while she continued studying my palms, using a gold pen to trace lines. 'See here... this is interesting... you have two lifelines. You have been travelling along one, and have recently crossed to another one... hmmm... it's a good path.' Indicating with the pen, she explained, 'See how it's curved. It shows that you are passionate about life. And here,' she traced another line, 'your heart line is curved. You are a lover.'

Although I rolled my eyes at her comment, she had her head bent over my hand and went on. 'On your right hand your thumb sits straight, which means you are good at business. However on your left hand, your spiritual side, it's curved out.' Looking up at me, she smiled. 'Very good, it means you are listening to your heart.'

This time she caught the look of cynicism on my face. Taking both of my hands in hers, she asked, 'Can I say something that has nothing to do with the palms?'

Feeling the warm energy from her touch, slowly I nodded, my eyes on her face.

Although she took her time, when she spoke, her words were precise. 'Love shows up in different ways. You may miss it if you're waiting for it to present itself in a certain way.' She nodded her head at me, to see if I understood.

I narrowed my eyes. 'I'm…' I paused. 'I'm not sure I'm looking.'

'Really?' Shrugging, she gently released my hands. However, I could still feel her energy and although it was only seconds, I continued to sit quite still as if in a trance.

And then the spell was broken by a voice from behind. 'Excuse me, but how long does it take, and what does it cost?'

I caught the look on the palmist's face as if she was most amused that someone would interrupt another person's session so brazenly. However, with a pleasant tone she explained. 'It's $30 for fifteen minutes. It's all there on the poster.' She gave a gentle laugh. 'I should have printed it a little larger.'

Sliding the chair back, I stood. 'Thank you. That…' I searched for the correct words, 'that was nice.'

I turned to go however she called after me. 'Find yourself a rose quartz crystal. Wear it close to your body.' She saw the look of miscomprehension on my face. 'Its powerful love will resonate through your entire body, healing your chakras. Wherever you go it will vibrate love.' Slowly I nodded, and then turned.

With her words ringing in my ears, I wound my way around

the markets, enjoying the ambiance and layback vibe, eventually finding a small stall that sold crystals. My hand instantly went to a small rose quartz, approximately three centimetres in diameter. I weighed it in my hands, liking the smooth feel of it. After paying for it, I placed it in the pocket of my shorts.

I continued to roam, purchasing very little, other than a jar of mango and passionfruit jam, which of course made perfect sense with all of my own home made jam rowed up in my pantry at home, three cakes of lemongrass soap, and some odd long stick chewy thing for Wilbur. Eventually I wandered back across the road to the Berkalouw book store and browsed their phenomenal range of antiquarian books.

Taking a different route back up the mountain, through the quaint and pretty town of Palmwoods, I felt a hypnotic calmness had enveloped me, as my car appeared to know the wind of the road all by itself. The last six months of rain had rendered this area so intensely green and picturesque, my head turned from side to side, not wanting to miss one moment of the lush beauty, as my car pottered along under the speed limit.

Approaching the Montville turnoff on my left, I was surprised to find the road was closed, with a sign saying that due to heavy rain it had been washed away. Although I was unsure of where I would come out, I followed the detour sign, thinking the road was much like life. Just when you thought you were following a certain path, it suddenly closed, and you needed to find another to make it through.

The road became steep, appearing to be going straight up. I wondered if it was like my life line. My ears popped and I swallowed a couple of times. To the left of me, I eagerly waved at cattle grazing on lush green pastures. I wondered if any of them were responsible for the fantastic butter the evening before. Coming out through a rainforest canopy, I suddenly realised I had reached the top of the mountain. Slowing, I turned left and entered the main street of Montville, merely a couple of kilometres from Clovelly Estate.

I continued my leisurely drive, soaking up the true village charm, brimming with local craft shops, galleries and gift stores, the architecture a delightful blend of Tudor, Irish and English.

Although I'd had a wonderful day, it registered how much I missed Carmody House even though I had only left home merely 24 hours ago. I wondered how Wilbur had coped being on his own last night. I was quite sure he would have been pleased to see Phil today, and I imagined the welcome he would have had.

Within minutes, my car sailed through the unassuming gates of Clovelly Estate, and wound its way around the curved road leading to the car park, behind the delightful French inspired chateau.

As I alighted from the car, I reminded myself of the afternoon of indulgence ahead. Checking my watch, I had timed it perfectly to join the boys for afternoon tea on the terrace, under the sweeping arms of a huge jacaranda, overlooking the rolling lawns. Although I had a decadent massage booked, I had hoped for at least an hour by the pool with the new book I had just purchased from the Eumundi bookstore, *The Essential Ingredient-Love*. Although a novel, I felt I needed all the help I could get on this subject.

Plus, we had another ten course degustation this evening and of course Jules would be there. My step quickened.

*

'Every year I go somewhere I haven't been before,' Jules was saying over pre dinner drinks and canapés.

Listening intently, I was comfortably ensconced in the luscious overstuffed couch. I took a sip of my Negroni, Thomas's choice of aperitif this evening. I was fully aware that one can drink too many Negronis. Over the years I have tested this theory more than once, so I paced myself.

From the massage room earlier, to the backdrop of the occasional sharp call of a whip bird, I had heard the unmistakable sound of Jules's Porsche Turbo 911 heralding his arrival. He was, as always, one who loved to make an entrance. Unnecessarily, Jules had screeched to a halt on the gravel, and I can't deny I had felt a tiny flutter of excitement. Although, the thought that I hoped he did not park near Bambino kept creeping into my mind. And I didn't know why, but that thought troubled me.

Sneaking off to my room post massage, wrapped in a luxurious white robe, my hair looking like something the cat had dragged in, I decided a girl needed to look her best before being seen by the likes of gorgeous Jules.

I had waited until pre-dinner drinks to see him. Of course there was a small part of me that wondered if Jules Monroe still had that effect on me that he'd had years earlier. Although short of stature, Jules was huge on presence. And not only was the guy good looking and successful, he was also an incurable flirt. He had a way of looking at you like you were the only girl in the world. He used to tell me, that I was *the one*. I was under no illusion that it was easy for him to do so, as I was a married woman. However, I could not deny there had always been some thing between us.

Thomas and Jules had become friends at college while doing their hairdressing apprenticeships. Later, Jules had moved to Sydney, opened a bevy of salons, and generously attributed much of his success to the power of Steve's PR.

It had been some time since I had seen him. Years ago, Davis had told me he found the guy *bloody irritating* and if he saw him brazenly flirting with me one more time, he'd knock his block off.

Legs elegantly crossed, I smoothed the black velvet fabric of my dress, surreptitiously touching under my left breast, where the rose quartz crystal now was deeply ensconced in my bra, and then briefly admired my new mirror-heeled jewelled shoes, twisting my foot first one way, and then the other. My hand graced the curve of my calf, and I thought to myself that in my new life, although I had missed my heels, that was perhaps the only thing. The thought made me smile, as I realised that other than a few seconds earlier, it had been some time since I had even thought of Davis. He was fast becoming another lifetime ago.

Leaning forward, I placed my glass upon the huge French oak coffee table, stacked with a multitude of glossy travel and fashion books. Clovelly Estate certainly had a feeling of elegance and quiet luxury, much the same as how I wanted Carmody House to be. I snuggled back amidst the mass of plump cushions, enjoying the company of the three gorgeous males.

Jules continued to hold the floor. 'For years I had to force myself out of the salons. They had overtaken my life. Did I tell you I was in the south of France last month? Favourite destination of all time! Stayed at the *Colombe d'or* in *Saint Paul de Vence...*'

Although my mind had been wandering as I mentally took notes on the French provincial décor around me, my ears pricked at the mention of somewhere in Provence, and I tuned back in noticing not only how flawless Jules French accent was, but also how he managed to make everything about himself. Hmmm…

Wearing designer jeans, white shirt and suitably creased linen jacket, Jules was impeccably dressed in what would be described as formal cool.

For the umpteenth time that evening, his hand went to the impressive timepiece on his wrist, as if checking it was still there. Earlier, he had extolled the virtues of the new watch, the Breitling, a birthday present to himself, a necessity, as he was now having flying lessons. And actually, he did not call it a watch or a timepiece, but a *wrist instrument*.

'If I was married by this point I would have spent a squillion on an engagement ring,' and he flashed me a look. With good humour, I flashed my eyes back at him. He continued. 'As I'm not, I decided to spoil myself with this little beauty.'

Apparently, the US Air Force Thunderbirds, the British Red Arrows and the Japanese Blue Impulse all wore Breitlings. After 15 minutes, I was confident I would be able to spot a fake from ten paces as it was explained to us in such major detail. From that point on, I would always know the foremost six ways to pick a genuine. I listened attentively, as if this was something I may be questioned on later.

Sliding my aquamarine cocktail ring up and down on my finger, I wondered how Phil was going with Wilbur and the chickens, and I made a mental note of things I must mention to him. He would have appreciated Clovelly Estate.

Earlier, on my way back to my room from the pool, I had come across the chef, scrounging in the vegetable garden for chickweed to embellish one of his dishes on the menu that evening. It hadn't gone unnoticed by me, that the restaurant could have quite possibly been named after him. At 203 centimetres tall, his apron was indeed long, although I did not feel it prudent to mention it. Kindly, he had given me a tour of the herb and vegetable garden, as he continued to select ingredients for that night's degustation. He explained that he liked to play with produce from not only there, but also other local farms, dairies and the rainforest.

However I knew that Phil would have definitely enjoyed seeing the vegetable garden, although with some pride I had to admit, it was not as quite as large as Carmody House's.

Hoping I wasn't appearing rude, I cleared my thoughts, wiggling in my seat, attempting to bring myself back to the present and focus on the conversation at hand. Jules was still speaking. '... so they closed the Great Ocean Road for us for the first time in history. Can you imagine 200 Porsches following each other? Spectacular! Now I tell you that was a clear highlight...'

I glanced across at Thomas who was leaning forward and listening with rapt attention. And then Steve caught my eye. With one arm draped along the back of the couch, the other cradling a vodka and tonic as if it was an old friend, he surveyed the scene, enjoying his drink. With a sparkle in his eye, he gave me a knowing wink and held my gaze. I smiled, knowing he was thinking let Thomas have his fun. My heart warmed, and I was reminded of how much I loved this man.

Without moving his head, Steve's questioning eyes slowly went to Jules and then back to me. Almost imperceptibly, he raised his eyebrows. I had seen that look before, and I knew what he was asking. For the briefest of seconds I gave a thoughtful pause, and then I gave Steve a slight raise of my shoulders in question.

I thought of Lou's advice on the phone yesterday, as I had driven through the gates of Carmody House upon my arrival, her voice shrieking, 'For God's sake... just have sex!' At that point, I had pushed the red button on the phone cutting her off.

*

Jules, taking a break from giving us the details of skiing with the Italian Olympic ski team while in the Dolomites, held the small espresso cup up to one of his nostrils. With an index finger blocking one side, he inhaled deeply and somewhat audibly with the other. As if this was of the utmost importance, we all sat quietly watching this ritual, one we had witnessed many times over the years. Switching nostrils, he went through the procedure once more. Finally, there was a look of satisfaction on his face as he downed the strong brew in one gulp and then looked at all of us.

It went through my mind that I used to enjoy the fact that Jules was a connoisseur of the finer things in life, however it was fast becoming intensely annoying. For the first time, I realised he was a self-proclaimed expert on everything.

I couldn't help myself but turn the conversation to something that Jules may not be the expert on. 'I'm thinking of getting a hive of stingless bees for the garden at Carmody House.' Immediately, I could see that by the look on all three of their faces, this was not exactly riveting news.

'Bees... *really*... fascinating,' Jules said, slowly nodding his head while he looked at me. However, I could plainly see that it was not as he turned back to Thomas and continued on with his ski story. 'I'd actually met one of the team a couple of years ago in Lake Como. I was staying at the Villa D'Este.' He gave a low whistle. 'Now that's a place where you get a shitload of bang... for a shitload of bucks.'

Throwing his head back, he laughed at his own joke. 'Let me tell you...' he said this, as if we were attempting to stop him, 'Villa D'Este is the *ultimate* in luxury accommodation in Lake Como. Everyone who is everyone stays there. George's villa is not far...'

A small part of me wanted to ask, *George who?* However, I knew that it would only be irksome and small minded to do so. Knowing Jules, it was clear to me he meant no other than George Clooney, and wanted us to believe he was on first name basis with him.

*

Jules hands were everywhere. One minute they were groping at my breasts as if he was attempting to turn on twin faucets at the same time, and the next they were clumsily fumbling at the zipper at the back of my dress.

Putting my hands up, breathlessly I pushed him slightly away. 'Slow down Jules.' It had been so long since I'd had sex, but this was not how I'd pictured it. I think he'd had more to drink than I realised and I was beginning to wonder if this smooth man was all talk.

'Okay, sorry, sorry,' his voice, like the rest of him, was hurried.

'That's better.' Perched on the edge of the bed, I put a hand to my chest and took a breath. 'Let's talk for a minute.'

'We've been talking all night. What do you want to talk about?' he asked, beginning to run his hands through my hair.

I found myself almost shrugging uncomfortably, wishing he would leave my hair alone. I moved away ever so slightly. 'Did you know that if every bee died, all of our crops would disappear pretty damn quickly?'

'Ummm... no. But *baby who the hell cares?*' He flopped back against the bedhead, and then looked back at me. 'What's all this talk of bees and crap?' Leaning forward once again, his hands immediately went back to attempting to turn my breasts on as if they were now headlights.

It was a pivotal moment for me. I cared about the bees. *That was the thing.* I didn't know how much I cared until that moment. I grabbed at his hands and stilled them. 'Oh Jules, this is so hard, because it's not as if I don't feel the sexual energy between us,' and I faked a deep swooning breath, and placed a hand upon my chest, 'but that is because we've never slept together. I *like* that. If we sleep together, it may be gone, and I don't think I could live with that.' Standing, I walked to the door. With my hand on the doorknob, I turned back to him, a questioning look on my face. 'You really wouldn't want that, would you Jules?'

I could see the puzzlement on his face. He was unsure whether to nod or shake his head. His glassy eyes were wide as he racked his brain for the right answer, however I really didn't care. Closing the door behind me, I headed for my room.

*

Fully dressed, travel bag over one arm, red jewel encrusted flat shoes tucked up under the other, quietly as possible, I pulled the door closed after me. It gave a gentle click.

'You're up early,' a quiet voice said from behind me.

Hand to my chest in fright, I spun around to the adjacent small sitting room. 'For goodness sake Steve, you almost gave me a heart attack! What are you doing?' I asked, although by the large pot of coffee and laptop in front of him, it was perfectly obvious. A well-known insomniac, I could see he had been checking the stock market, even at this ridiculously early hour of the morning.

'Doing the walk of shame?' he asked, his voice still low, his head nodding towards my door.

'Huh? Hardly!' I wrinkled my brow. 'In case you didn't notice, that's *my* room.'

He gave me a knowing look.

'Jules is not in there. I swear.' Shrugging, I placed my bag on the floor, and perched on the arm of the sofa. It was not hard to miss that Steve was looking at me with a questioning look, waiting for me to say more.

Once again I shrugged and then gave a hollow laugh. 'After all of those years of flirting, I can tell you, there is *nothing* between us. Not a damn thing!' My hands cut through the air in finale. 'Well at least not on my behalf.' I attempted to be light hearted. 'But you know… I was always flattered. I think I'll keep him guessing. It might be more fun.'

Expressionless, Steve rested his chin on his hand and was looking at me, expecting more.

Turning, I glanced out of the French doors at the magnificence of the colour of the jacarandas at this early hour of the day. When I turned back, Steve was pouring coffee. Adding milk, he placed it on the table in front of me, and patted the sofa next to him.

Lowering myself onto the sofa, I stirred the coffee as if it was the utmost of importance, and then tapping the spoon on the rim of the cup, out of habit, I placed it in my mouth, before returning it to the saucer. With both hands I picked the cup up, drawing comfort from not only the warmth, but the intoxicating aroma as well. I paused before drinking, and hazarded a sideways glance at Steve. 'Do you think me crazy?' Taking a sip, I narrowed my eyes, and looked at his face, gauging his reaction.

With one arm draped casually along the back of the sofa, Steve shrugged. 'If you're not into him, you're not… plenty would be. To be honest… he's not for me either. Can't stand all that bloody twaddle…' and lowering his voice even more, he imitated Jules, 'I radioed the control tower for clearance and they said india, alpha, juliet, romeo blah, blah, blah.' And then he gave a quiet laugh. 'Sometimes in meetings I tell him to cut the bullshit and get to the point.'

Although I exhaled relieved, I could not help but smile, correcting him. 'I don't think there was any romeo, I think it was just india, alpha, julia.'

'*Whatever!*' He looked at me, and I watched while one of his hands tapped at the back of the wheat coloured linen sofa, and then he commanded, 'I'm getting a vibe that something else is going on with you though?' His eyes narrowed, searching out the truth.

Slowly, I shook my head, attempting to come up with something. Scratching at some imaginary thing on my leg, I said, 'He's not into bees,' as if this spectacular piece of information explained everything.

Tilting his head, Steve looked at me for what appears to be minutes. When he spoke, he articulated every word clearly. 'This may come as a shock Peach, and I hate to be the one to break it to you… but many wouldn't be.' His face was deadpan.

Slowly I nodded, knowingly. 'But *I am*, and now I know that, I cannot not be.'

'I *seeeee*,' he said, dragging it out, head turned slightly to the side giving a small nod. By the look on his face, I could see clearly that he did not.

I shrugged once more, as if that explained it all.

I saw him watching my face before he spoke. 'But there's more to this, isn't there?' and he leant into me.

I threw my hands in the air, having trouble keeping my voice low. I whispered with intensity. 'He'd *hate* Bambino.'

Steve gave a snuff. 'Boo bloody-hoo!' He looked amused and bamboozled all at the same time. 'How about I buy you an ice-cream Peach?'

Shaking my head in exasperation at him, it was my turn to splutter. 'What?'

'You sound like a child!' And he did his best to imitate me, *'He doesn't like my toy car, blah, blah, blah!'*

'No, no, no… you don't get it. Part of his attraction was to my former success, the status symbol of the black BMW I drove, not the cute little Fiat, driving it just because for the first time in my life, I have done something because it is *fun.* I can tell you now, Jules Monroe would never do that unless it was a Ferrari. He doesn't get that simple things bring me so much pleasure. I don't blame him. It's only been the last year that I've gotten it.' Folding my arms, I shook my head. 'Jules belongs to my former life. Steve,' I spoke with vehemence, 'I *cannot* go back.'

We eyed each other. And then after what appeared to be the longest of silences, he almost whispered. 'I get it.'

I visibly exhaled, my shoulders dropped. 'Thank you. Good lord, I've wondered if I was going insane.' I almost felt exhausted by our talk, and was grateful that I could perk myself up with the strong hit of caffeine Steve was known for.

'But there is something else isn't there?' Not happy to leave it there, Steve pushed.

'What now?' I asked, with a hint of annoyance, glancing at him over the top of the coffee cup.

Once again, he drummed his fingers on the sofa. 'There's something else going on in your pretty little head and I want to know what it is?' He folded his arms, giving me a determined look.

I frowned, my exasperation returning. 'Look, I really don't know what you mean.'

Leaning towards me, his thumb smoothed my forehead. 'For goodness sake, don't let Thomas see you do that, he'll have you botoxed in no time at all. And I think you *do* know what I mean. I watched you all through dinner last night. And

I heard you loud and clear. In fact, I have heard you loud and clear all weekend. Come on Peach... spill?'

For the longest time, I said nothing, but continued to sip my coffee, the words the palmist said to me going over and over in my mind. In fact, I had thought of nothing but those words since yesterday. *Love shows up in different ways. You may miss it if you're waiting for it to present itself in a certain way.*

'I've been thinking,' I shook my head, and then sounding desperate asked, 'What if I'm looking in the wrong place Steve? What if what I have been looking for has been in front of me the entire time and I have missed it, and... I'm... oh I don't know...?'

Resting his chin on his hand, he eyed me, and asked, 'Such as?'

'Such as someone who likes stingless bees and runner ducks and chooks and kitchen gardens... and... and smiles at my cute car...'

Steve interrupted, looking down his nose quizzically at me, 'Excuse me... runner ducks?'

With a wave of my hand, I dismissed his question. 'The thing is, I don't need a man to keep me or even contribute to my lifestyle.'

He flashed his eyes. 'True... you never have.' He opened his hands wide. 'Not sure I understand though...'

'Is it enough?' I asked, without giving him a chance to speak. 'I mean... I'm just thinking... what if...' I swallowed, '... the person I meet has all of the qualities I admire, but perhaps not much in the way of financial assets?' And without waiting for his retort, I continued, 'The old me would have felt that was important, but... I mean, I have enough for both of us. Does that make it wrong?' Once again, I did not let him answer. 'He has many, many,' I stressed, '... other qualities he would bring to the relationship. Qualities, I now know I require. Qualities that are on the list Thomas made me make.' Scratching the top of my head, I furrowed my brow. 'So what am I waiting for Steve… you tell me?' And then I rushed on, answering my own question. 'Him to leave… that's what I'm waiting for.'

I looked at Steve to see if he had understood. Finally I saw he was nodding, and a small smile played around his lips, and his hands gave a gentle slow clap.

'Thank you,' I whispered in earnest.

'It's been a pleasure,' he said with mock sincerity, and then cocked his head to the side. 'Honey… in case you haven't noticed, you *aint* a spring chicken no more. We reach an age when we know what we want. Perhaps you've been lying to yourself, but you have been waxing on about this guy forever. At any rate, stop wasting time and have some bloody fun will you.' And then he kissed my cheek. 'I'm going back to bed. Thomas likes me there when he opens his eyes. You get out of here before everyone wakes up. I'll come up with some excuse.' Standing, he headed for the hallway and then turned back. 'Go get 'im tiger!'

Chapter 21

It did not matter how many times I came up Carmody House's long curved driveway, there was always a sense of wonderment and delight. A sense of being home that I had never felt anywhere else before. The fact that I was caretaker of this tapestry of intense horticulture still enthralled me.

And, returning from Montville earlier than expected, my spirits had heightened even more so and I was buzzing with a palpable feeling of a mere possibility or, if I must admit it, a damn strong one. A possibility that once it had taken up residence in my mind, had refused to budge.

I could not deny though that there was also another thought, one that disturbed me, one I knew that would require time to properly mull over, perhaps even a session with Emerald Green. Once I had begun rehashing the conversation I'd had earlier with Steve, when I had said that *I didn't need a man to look after me*, and when he answered *you never have had*, I recalled a look, so fleeting, and a change to his tone, so minute, I could have imagined it... I don't think I imagined it... I knew my instincts were telling me something. That acknowledgement alone would have received accolades from Emerald Green.

Garaging Bambino, I glanced around looking for my usual welcoming party. Strangely enough, Wilbur was nowhere to be seen.

Placing the strap of my LV monogramed travel bag over one shoulder, I tucked my handbag under the other arm, and from the back seat removed two bags of groceries, and my purchases from Eumundi. Although Bambino's rear seats could be folded when required, there were times when cargo space was indeed limited. Arms full, I nudged the car door closed with my hip, at the same time feeling a thud as something dense hit my foot. Glancing down, I noticed the rose quartz on the ground. Redistributing my bags, I reached down and once again pushed it into my bra for safekeeping.

Hearing the familiar crunch of gravel from outside, a smile graced my lips at the sound of four paws racing towards the garage.

'Ah there you are boy,' I said, as Wilbur buoyantly greeted me, as if I had been gone for years. His welcome always the same even if I had returned after merely minutes. 'I've got a treatie for you. A long stick chewy thing,' I told him, balancing everything precariously, and using my knee to gently nudge him hello. 'I wondered where you were. Did you have a good weekend without me? Were the chooks well behaved? Hope Whitie wasn't too bossy. Cats can be like that you know.' As if in understanding Wilbur cocked his head, a serious look on his face. 'Guess I don't have to tell you that. And I've been thinking… we're going to get bees. But I don't want you to worry. They're the stingless kind. Phil was telling me…' and then I paused, as once again I heard the sound of someone on the gravel outside.

Giving the groceries a little jig, to better balance my full arms, I peered around the side of the garage. It took some seconds for it to register that a tiny blonde fairy was standing under a huge green umbrella. Blinking in disbelief, I shook my head, looking once again. It was definitely a fairy, although it was not an umbrella, but one of the huge leaves of the Monstera Deliciose plant she stood in front of.

At first glance, I took in the pink tutu, pink tights and fairy wings. Dumbfounded, I took a second look. The tights were snagged and the odd leaf was stuck to the tulle of the tutu, but more surprising was the fact she was wearing glasses.

It was possibly only seconds, but I was still blinking at the incredulity of the situation, when she finally spoke, startling me. 'Puppy,' I thought she said.

'Oh… hello.' I took a few steps closer, and placing my bags on the ground, bent down, studying her. 'Where on earth have you come from darling?'

'Puppy,' she repeated, stretching her small upturned hand out to Wilbur.

The deep crease in her palm did not go unnoticed by me. And then I took in her short neck, flat face, and upturned eyes behind her glasses, making her condition obvious. I crouched closer to her, putting a hand out.

But at that moment I heard Phil's anguished voice calling. With fright, I spun around as I heard him frantically yell, '*Sophia, Sophia!*'

Wilbur alarmed as well, began to bark. In an instant, I saw the look of fear on the tiny girl's face as she backed away from him.

'Darling, darling,' I cooed, as I hastily picked her up, placing her on my hip, feeling her little nappy padded bottom. 'Come on, I think we might need to find Daddy.' I may have sounded calm, however, I could feel my heart pounding. It seemed odd that he had made no mention.

I repeated the words of comfort to her, as with Wilbur at my side, we quickly took the path down the side of the house. 'We find Daddy, yes.' And I watched as her small mouth repeated the word daddy with some difficulty, her tiny chubby hand grabbing the fabric of my dress, and clasping tightly, her huge brown eyes looking up at mine with such utter trust and innocence. Feeling an overwhelming urge to protect her, I placed a hand behind her head, cradling it to my shoulder.

'You little sweetie.'

A little breathless at the top of the stone steps, I paused. In the distance, I could see Phil frenziedly running along the river's edge.

'PHIL, PHIL,' I yelled. 'SHE'S HERE!' In his desperation, he appeared not to have heard me. I watched as suddenly he kicked off his shoes, and scrabbled down the river bank, slipping and sliding as he went. Holding Sophia tightly, I hurriedly made my way down the stairs and began to run across the broad expanse of grass towards him, calling his name loudly as I went. 'PHIL ... PHIL'... SHE'S HERE. SHE'S NOT IN THE RIVER. PHIL ... STOP!'

Suddenly he turned, and even from that distance, I did not miss the sheer desperation on his tortured face. One minute he was looking at us incredulously, and then next he was gone as he lost his footing on a slimy rock. Continuing to run towards him, I winced, knowing he would have hurt himself. And then just as quick he was on his feet, clambering over the last few rocks, leaping onto the land and running towards us, wet and muddy. Blood was dripping down his shin.

Before I could say a word he was snatching Sophia from my arms, holding her tightly, his eyes closed as he squeezed her to him. 'Oh my God, oh my God, oh my God...' he kept saying, his voice trembling. His tone was scaring me, and I could only imagine what it was doing to Sophia. She wriggled, attempting to be set free. But he held on.

'Na, na, na, na ...' she wailed, pushing her little chubby hand against him.

My heart was pounding, a trembling hand went to my mouth, and I realised I had never seen a man so anguished. Still holding Sophia tight, Phil turned away but not before I saw a tear run down his face.

Tentatively, I put a hand out towards them. 'It's okay Phil.' I repeated the words a few more times. Stepping forward, I gently put my arms around the two of them, rubbing their backs, attempting to calm them. Breathing deeply, Phil bent his head and dropped his chin onto the top of my head.

'Thank you,' was all he said.

We stayed that way for what appeared to be minutes. Finally, he lifted his head and spoke, his voice muffled. 'My God... I thought I had lost her too.' He exhaled once again. 'Thank you Peach.' One of his arms loosened from Sophia and went around me. I felt him kiss the top of my head. I stayed where I was not daring to breathe.

Sophia continued to squirm, strongly pushing away. 'Na, na, na...'

'Come on,' I coaxed, keeping my voice as calm as possible. 'Let's move away from here so you can put her down. Come up to the house.' With a hand lightly resting on his back, I guided them the entire way, thinking how life can change in an instant. Wilbur, sensing something was up, ran ahead, as if leading the way. I noticed from time to time my hand went to the crystal in my bra, and I found it comforting.

As we neared the house, Phil spoke. He was slightly more composed, but only just, his voice still in shock. 'I cannot believe that happened. I *cannot* believe I took my eyes off her for one minute. I mean... what if...'

'Shhh,' I urged. 'Things just... happen.' I watched as he shook his head.

'Come on,' I said, taking charge, knowing that he probably needed some time before he drove home. 'Inside.'

'We really should go,' he said, his voice uncertain.

'Just come in,' I said with an air of authority. Collecting my bags from the garage, I unlocked the front door, and began to head up the stairs to my bedroom. I glanced back at them. 'This way. You can wash Sophia off up here.' I watched as he gave it some thought, looking at Sophia's fairy costume, now covered in black slime from his hands. Swallowing, he nodded and then followed.

Crossing the white painted floorboards in my bedroom towards the open plan bathroom, I perched on the edge of the white claw foot bath and ran the water. Without saying a word, I opened a drawer in the vanity and found Lakshmi's and Bob's rubber ducky and bath wash. I gave a generous squirt under the running water. Within seconds the beautiful fragrance of soothing camomile, lavender and mandarin permeated the room.

Walking across to the huge dome shaped window behind the bath, I swept back the voluminous white sheer curtain, revealing the most perfect view of the back garden, across the river and of the city. Turning, I observed not only Phil, but Sophia as well, glancing around.

'Pwitty,' Sophia said in her baby voice, reaching out to my canopied bed. Ensconced in a myriad of silk and velvety textured fabrics, the bed had only recently arrived, after being meticulously repainted and waxed. Even though Sophia was safely in his arms, Phil pulled her away from the luxurious linens, as if she might grubby them with her little hands, even from a distance.

From a 1940s china cabinet which I had fashioned into a linen cupboard, and painted white, I took two white fluffy towels. 'Right,' I said, turning to them once again, explaining clearly. 'Sophia goes in the bath. And here's a first aid kit for you. That shin looks nasty.' I placed the small box marked with a huge red cross, upon the mantle of the imposing marble fireplace, away from little hands. 'I've got some things of

Lakshmi's and Bob's somewhere here.'

From the bottom drawer of my dresser I unearthed a disposable nappy of Bob's, along with a clean pink shirt of Lakshmi's, left behind after one of our gardening days. I knew the T-shirt would be too big, but I didn't have anything else suitable.

Pausing for a brief moment, I watched from the ornate antique mirror above the cupboard, as Phil lovingly undressed Sophia before sitting her in the bath. Sophia's hands instantly reaching for the rubber ducky.

'Kak kak,' she said.

'Yes darling, quack, quack,' Phil repeated, touching her blonde head tenderly. He picked up her clothes, and then just stood, watching her, as if afraid she might disappear.

I placed the nappy and t-shirt on the end of the upholstered French linen bench running across the bottom of the bed. I spoke to Phil's back. 'I'll leave these clothes here for Sophia while I see if I can sponge her fairy costume.'

'Huh?' He turned. 'Oh sorry.' And he shook his head as if to clear it. 'Thanks… Peach.'

I reached for her clothes, but he looked at me blankly.

Raising my eyebrows, I smiled. 'The costume Phil?'

'Yeah… sorry… I'm a bit out of it. Look don't worry, I'll take it home.' His eyes still looked dazed. We both turned back to Sophie. Her little hands were reaching for the soft squeezy toys. I noticed the inwards turn of the little fingers on each hand.

'She's okay Phil,' I said to him reassuringly, resting my hand on his arm. And then I reached for her costume. 'At least let me put some dynamo on it, so it does not stain.'

I was halfway out of the room before I heard him. 'I wanted to show her the chooks.'

I stopped in my tracks, and turned. 'Of course.'

'The only thing I can think is that she followed Wilbur,' he said by way of explanation, his voice still not his own. 'One minute she was there and the next she was gone. In my panic, I must have run in the other direction looking for her.' He ran a hand across his shorn hair.

'Children are quick and resilient,' I said with a smile, and then I walked over and looked out the window down towards the river. I was thoughtful. 'It's time I fenced that river. It seems incongruous that there are swimming pool fencing laws but you can have an entire river unfenced on the same property. I've wondered more than once about it with Bob and Lakshmi. I never want to wonder about it again. Decision made.' I dusted my hands off, briefly reminding myself of my mother.

At the doorway I turned to speak. Phil had his back to me, but he had removed his shirt, baring his wide muscular naked shoulders and slim waist. Swallowing, I stood for all of three seconds, and then continued down the stairs. On each tread I repeated the same thing... *oh my God, oh my God, oh my God...* My heart getting an excellent workout once again.

At the bottom, I looked at Wilbur, opening my eyes wide and clenching my hands in front of me. 'Oh my God,' I whispered to him. The poor boy looked confused. I knew he wanted to know why I whispering and *oh my God-ding!*

My feet did double time, and in the kitchen I flicked the switch on the kettle for tea. Somehow coffee seemed too social. With two hands upon the bench, I stood quite still thinking, and then an idea struck me.

From the bottom kitchen drawer, I took my apron, quickly tying the pink gingham checked fabric, embellished with red cherries, behind my neck and back. Taking the scissors from the top drawer, I hurried along the small hallway, through the laundry and out into the kitchen garden. For a few seconds I surveyed the scene, then quick as a flash, I snipped parsley, thyme, basil, garlic chives and a really good handful of spinach, all gathered in my apron. As I turned to go, I remembered the mint tea, and snipped a few stalks from the rampant herb.

Returning to the kitchen, I placed a heavy based non-stick pan over the gas flame, and turned the switch on the oven grill to high. From the wire basket on the kitchen bench, I took four of the girls' lovely porcelain-like eggs, and rapidly whisked them, adding a splosh of cream. In the hot pan, I quickly sautéed the spinach, added the herbs and then poured the eggs over. I watched as the frittata began to set around the edges, and then pushed pieces of feta in to the hot mix.

I thought of Bob and how much he loved feta and hoped Sophia was the same. Lou's two were finicky eaters, although no matter what I put in my frittata they appeared to like. I kept my fingers crossed Sophia might as well.

Thank goodness Phil was taking a while upstairs, as it gave me time to get organised, placing the frittata in the oven under the grill, and taking Bob's highchair out of the pantry and placing it at the table.

For a moment, I stood to survey the scene, then with my hands working rapidly, I took a couple of juicy red heirloom tomatoes from the large platter I kept upon the kitchen bench, placed them on the huge wooden chopping board, sliced them and layered them with bocconcini from the fridge, topping each piece with a fresh basil leaf.

From the pantry, I grabbed my favourite Joseph's olive oil and drizzled it liberally. The rhythm of the chopping and preparation of the food had eased the tension I had felt only minutes earlier.

Wilbur had flopped on the floor near the table, his head on

his paws, his eyes following me.

'Well what do you think? Stressful hey?' I shook my head, and lowered my voice. 'But what a cutie!' Wilbur and I eyed each other for a few moments. 'Don't look at me like that. I meant Sophia. But, are you wondering why he didn't tell us? Hmmm…' I was thoughtful as I set the table, taking one of Bob's Peter Rabbit plates from the pantry.

By the aroma wafting from the oven, I knew that the top of the frittata was now browned nicely. Removing it, I placed a plate on top and flipped it, repeating once again until it was right side up. With pride, I placed it in the middle of the table, returning to the kitchen sink to wash the sharp knife.

I held the knife under the running water, my eyes looking out the window but not seeing a thing, while I thought of how it had felt standing so close to Phil, even at a time like that. He was a man with such *strong* physicality. And the sight of him half naked… My face flushed.

Phil's voice startled me from behind. 'I'd been reading…'

I spun around feeling as if he could have read my thoughts. Wilbur scuffled to his feet, his tail in overdrive.

'I'm sorry…?' I said smiling, shaking my head in incomprehension.

Phil looked a little more himself. Sophia was on his hip. Lakshmi's t-shirt long and loose, fitting her as a dress. She was without doubt a divinely beautiful child, her glasses only enhancing how extremely cute she was. Small for her age, she was chubby and luscious, and there was an innocence in that face that reached out and grabbed at my heart. I felt like I wanted to put my hands out to her and take her in my arms, and snuggle her to me. Although, by the way Phil was holding her, I was unsure if he actually planned to ever let her go. Standing there I struggled to take my eyes off her.

'I'd been reading last night that adding a clove of garlic to the chooks drinking water keeps it free from parasites. I was doing that when Madame here strolled off.' He kissed the top of Sophia's blonde head.

I tutted and smiled, attempting to lessen the seriousness of the situation. 'I've made mint tea. Sit.' And I indicated the highchair pulled up to the table, before I turned back to drying the knife. 'As it's near lunch time, I thought you guys might be hungry so I've made a frittata. Sophia can have eggs, can't she? There's spinach and herbs as well.' I didn't wait for Phil's answer, I continued, 'Bob likes when I add feta, so I thought…'

'It's fine Peach… Sophia eats like other children her age.'

'Yes of course, I just didn't know…'

'That she has Down Syndrome?' he said, turning and looking directly at me, his tone carrying just a hint of something I could not put my finger on.

I paused and met his direct gaze. 'No,' I said, dragging the word out. 'I actually meant I did not know what she liked to eat. I do know some children can be allergic to eggs.' I placed the Peter Rabbit plate with warm frittata cut into small wedges, the way I did for Bob, onto the table in front of the highchair, and then uncomfortably, I glanced away from him, and brushed a few stray curls from my face.

'I'm sorry that came out wrong.' He locked both of his hands on top of his head, looking sheepish. 'Sometimes I'm overly sensitive,' he spoke quietly. 'Look thank you… it's been a rough morning.' He exhaled heavily.

'You could say that,' I stated firmly.

'You've been fantastic. A pillar of calm in a storm.'

'Surprises you hey?'

He gave a brief light hearted snuff, and folded his arms.

'Well, you are a woman who is full of surprises.'

'I don't panic at everything you know,' I said with a flash of my eyes.

'No of course not... only snakes and storms and chooks...'

I held a hand up. '*Touché*! Okay, okay!'

'What does surprise me is *my* panic when it comes to my daughter.' He pulled a chair out and slid into it. It must have hurt to sit as I caught the wince on his face. Turning, he pulled the highchair closer, handing Sophia another piece of frittata. 'Ta,' he said to her.

'Taaaa,' she repeated, reaching for it and pushing it into her mouth.

Lovingly, he touched the top of her head. 'Good girl.'

We both watched as Sophia dropped a piece of frittata onto the floor, much to the delight of Wilbur, who sloppily hoovered it in a second.

I scrabbled through the bag of goodies I had purchased at the markets. 'Here it is,' I waved the chewy stick in the air. 'Wilbur you come with me. You can have this nice tasty treaty outside.' I had never approved of dogs eating scraps off the kitchen floor. However, right that moment Wilbur wore the look of a dog who thought he might miss out on some very tasty titbits, and was not prepared to leave.

I attempted to entice him by running one of my hands up and down the longish stick. 'Look Wilbur, very, very nice.' And then I made motions of eating the stick myself. 'Really tasty! Mmmm.' Grasping the dog by the collar, I led him out.

Returning to the kitchen, I slid into the chair opposite Phil.

Wrapping both of his hands around the mug, his eyes on the food, he appeared grateful, however there was also the slightest look of amusement on his face, no doubt at my cajoling of Wilbur.

'This looks really good Peach. You didn't have to go to so much trouble.'

'No trouble. The girls laid the eggs and the rest, except for the feta, is out of the kitchen garden you have put so much time and effort into. You might as well occasionally reap the rewards.'

'We already have been.'

I shrugged, knowing he meant the pesto and jams I had sent home to his mother.

I watched as he took the first mouthful. I saw a look of pleasure cross his face. Mouth full, he nodded at me.

I too began to eat, so his words took me by surprise.

'We didn't know,' he said, looking at me.

'Sorry?'

'We didn't know before she was born. In fact, I didn't know until she was four months old. When I look back at earlier photos, I can see it now, but at the time I didn't. At four months she developed an infection which required hospitalisation. While she was there, a sharp young doctor noticed her sandal toe.' He must have seen the look of miscomprehension on my face as he explained, 'The gap between her toes. He suggested they run tests for the extra chromosome 21.' He took a mouthful of the hot tea.

I eyed him as both of my hands wrapped around my mug, feeling the warmth. 'I can only imagine how tough that must have been considering your circumstances.'

He exhaled, but before he could answer, Sophia was reaching a hand out. 'Moorw.'

'For four months I had been walking around with the shock of losing Katrine, and at the same time caring for a baby. When the tests came back, I really had no time to think about how I felt. My first priority was to think about what

Sophia needed. When something like that happens, there's an automatic instinct to love these special children even more, if that's possible. Sophia became a part of me. It was hard to see where I finished and she began, if you know what I mean.'

I nodded, thinking this guy just kept surprising me.

'But we were lucky.' He caught the look on my face, and rushed on to explain. 'She doesn't have the congenital heart defect that often accompanies Downs. Generally, that is the number one indicator.'

'Oh… that's good.'

Phil nodded, slowly. 'Her milestones are a little slower, and her physical and cognitive developments are behind, however her social skills are fine. She loves dancing, singing, music. Don't you angel,' he said, ruffling her head once again, and handing her another piece of the frittata.

'So Katrine didn't have the tests during her pregnancy?' I asked, attempting to tear my eyes away from Sophia.

'She did! Actually, the ten week one did come back with an irregularity, which of course caused major concern. However, when she had the 18 week test, all appeared fine, so we hung onto that.' And then he answered my next question. 'But no, she didn't have an amniocentesis. Katrine was five years older than me. We discussed the pros and cons of having the test. However she desperately wanted children, and was concerned about the amniocentesis carrying a small risk of complication, which she had heard could result in the baby's death. I remember her telling me that something like one in every 200-400 mothers miscarry as a result, and she was not prepared to take that chance. She said that if something was wrong, she would hardly terminate the pregnancy, and that the test would cause her more worry than it was worth.'

I nodded, understanding. 'And what did you think?'

He appeared nonchalant. 'I guess I must have agreed at the time.'

'And now...'

He shrugged. 'It wouldn't have changed a thing, except we...' he hesitated, 'I... could have been more prepared.' And then his tone changed. 'I am not going to deny, there weren't a few odd moments when I wondered why the universe had chosen to give me this child, and take my wife. It seemed unfair for Sophia not to have a mother. But I have reconciled that. I think Sophia was given to me, because I could make her my priority. I could take care of her. She's the main reasons we're heading home to Melbourne soon. Before she was born Katrine had already picked out a kindergarten for her. They have a place coming up for her. It's most important for Sophia's development for her to integrate with other children. And,' he shrugged, 'I want to think that some of Katrine's dreams for her can come true.' He let out a huge sigh. 'So that's it. Sophia's my life. She always will be. It's the two of us against the world, isn't it chicken.' And he tickled her toes, while laughingly, she pulled her foot away.

'Of course,' I nodded slowly, watching how good he was with her. Although I could see what he was saying, there was a certain kind of flatness in me. A tiny bit of me wanted to ask if there was any chance he had seen a relationship with me as a possibility. But of course I could not. What on earth had I been thinking? I had allowed myself to become attracted to someone who I had consistently told myself I knew so little about. So now I knew. There was no room for me. My hand ever so lightly touched under my breast where the crystal nestled in my bra.

*

'Thanks for everything Peach. I'll return the t-shirt during the week.' Phil had wiped Sophia's hands on the washcloth I handed him, and was now removing her from the highchair.

As I walked them to the door, Sophia reached for me. Laughing, I took her. 'You are such a pretty girl. You can come anytime.' Squeezing her tight to me, I knew that would not happen, they were leaving soon.

Sophia pressed her little face closer, and I kissed her chubby cheeks.

'Gen,' she said to me, her chocolate eyes peering from behind the glasses.

'Again… why of course.' I laughed and kissed her once more.

'Gen,' she repeated. I laughed and gave her three more kisses.

Phil laughed as well. 'No more miss. Come on,' and he took her from me. Wilbur, grateful that the front door had been opened, ran inside to join us, dropping the half chewed stick at my feet.

'Yuk Wilbur, take this very delicious morsel outside.' I bent over, and between two fingers, delicately picked it up and flung it out into the garden, at the same time dislodging the rose quartz from between my breasts. It fell to the floor with a small thud, but then continued to bounce away from me, as I cupped my hands keen to catch it. One the fourth bounce I had luck, closing one hand securely around the smooth crystal.

I caught Phil's questioning look, however decided not to bother with an explanation. Really what could I say? Although I did not miss the flash of amusement that crossed his face. Of late, I felt like I was a constant source of hilarity for the man.

'Well thanks again,' he said as Sophia put her arms out to me. And then the strangest thing happened. Phil leant to kiss me. In the surprise of it, I turned my head, and he kissed my cheek. No doubt that was his intention, although, in that split second, I felt he was going to kiss me on the lips.

It was only a peck, a gracious *well thank you for having us kiss*. But I could tell by the look on his face that the kiss had happened without him thinking. And I cannot deny it had *me* thinking.

My mind was still whirling as I watched them leave. Phil hadn't gone very far when he turned back. His brow furrowed and I could see there was something he wanted to say. 'I am presuming you are wondering why I didn't tell you about Sophia's disability.'

I was wondering about a lot of things, and right that exact instant it was not that. 'Umm,' I shook my head, and opened my hands wide. 'No...' but I could tell my voice was not very convincing.

'I did tell you I had a daughter Sophia.'

I nodded slowly.

'Well although she has a disability, that is not who she *is*. She is Sophia Hunter.' I could see he was wondering if I understood.

I nodded slowly. 'Of course.' I smiled. 'Come again Sophia Hunter.'

*

Well that's that, I thought as I closed the door. He has no room for anyone other than Sophia. It didn't appear he would even welcome the idea of a relationship.

Sighing heavily, I eyed the frittata and bunches of fresh herbs still lying on the kitchen bench. Right this second, the last thing I needed or wanted was green. Riffling thought my handbag, I grabbed my car keys.

'You coming?' was all I said to Wilbur, who looked up at me. He wore that look of, *Oh no... what now?* I have often wondered if having a mistress was different for him than having a master. Did the poor dog feel he had to calibrate my moods? Did he wonder if it was *that time of the month again?* Or think to himself… *goddamn it woman, can you just be quiet for a few minutes… blah, blah, bloody blah!*

With him at my side trotting quick smart to keep up, I marched out of the house towards the garage. Only later upon my return would I realise I had left the front door wide open. Opening Bambino's door, I didn't have to say a word. Tail between his legs, Wilbur jumped in. With a measure of difficulty, he dove between the two front seats, ducking his head as if he was unsure of what might happen. Climbing in, I looked back at him. He returned my look.

I was a woman on a mission. I drove to the Spar supermarket in Brunswick Street. It seemed Wilbur knew to wait in the car as he made no fuss to get out. I did not notice his eyes watching me, as I crossed the car park, nor the small worried whimper he made.

Sunglasses on, I almost wished I also had a wig. I felt if someone had stopped to talk to me, my answer would be: *My name is Peach and I am an ice-creamoholic. It has been ten months since my last ice-cream binge and although I am about to fall off the wagon, tomorrow is another day.*

Entering the store I did not remove my glasses. There was no dawdling required. On a direct route, I made for the large ice-cream fridge along the left hand side of the store, towards the back. Serious bliss-out was required, and tall order though it was, Ben and Jerry's Funky Monkey was the ice-cream to do it.

Taking the once familiar carton from the fridge, I lingered briefly. My dark glasses made it a trifle hard to read the other cartons. Without entirely removing them, I raised them slightly and peered from underneath.

The trouble was, I was uncertain if the banana ice-cream with fudge chunks and walnuts would be enough on its own, on this particular day. I daresay a backup would be required. I pulled out the Chocolate Chip Cookie Dough. But then my eyes settled on the New York Super Fudge Chunk. I'd never seen that flavour before. Must be a newbie. Chocolate ice-cream with fudge chunks, pecans, walnuts and chocolate coated almonds. Yep… that would do it.

On my way back to the car, I dialled *Call Connect* and asked them put me through to the local Blockbuster store. 'I'll be there in two minutes,' I told them.

*

Just over three hours later, I stood and stretched my arms above my head, peering into the ice-cream tubs at the now liquefied remains. The movie so riveting from start to finish, I had not wanted to steal a second away to put them in the freezer. Retrieving the DVD from the player, I placed it back in its case.

Silently, I sat back on the couch and studied William Wallace's… aka a bulked up Mel Gibson's… face on the cover. Many years ago I had seen the movie *Braveheart*. At that time I had thought it horrifically gory. The brutally violent end had haunted me for weeks.

This time, I found the moving love story made all the gore worthwhile. Although a commoner, William Wallace was a powerful, capable leader, earning respect through his words and deeds. It was plain to see why it was Phil's favourite movie, and why it resonated for him as it did. Scarred by the death of his father, enraged by the death of his wife. Hmmm. And then the French actress Sophie Marceau came into it as the beautiful Princess Isabelle. Thoughtfully, I tapped my upper lip with an index finger.

I did not know how long I sat, but finally I got up, and went to the dresser. I knew exactly where to find my DVD of *The Way We Were*. Before I put it into the player, I filled a glass with cold water from the kitchen, my throat dry from too much ice-cream. Spying the box of tissues on the kitchen bench, I carried them with me on my way back to the couch. Before I made it there, I almost tripped on my handbag, so tunnel visioned was I earlier, I had left it tossed on the floor. As I picked it up, I spotted the Cadbury Marvellous Creations filled with crunchie and jelly bits, I had also bought earlier from the supermarket. I will say one word… addictive!

Snuggling back on the couch, I held the remote towards the television, and pressed play, just as I heard the house phone ring. I let it go to the answering machine. Within seconds, my mobile trilled. That too, I let go to the message bank. I nestled back, peeled the foil wrapper back on the chocolate, broke the first piece off and placed it in my mouth.

*

'Honey, you home?' a voice called, from the front door.

'I'm in the library Thom,' I called back, my voice teary. I gave a hefty sniff. 'I'm watching my favourite movie.'

Thomas propped himself in the doorway, in his hand he held my blow dryer.

'Goodness did I leave that behind? Hadn't even realised.' I glanced back at the television. 'This is the part where she asks him to stay with her until the baby comes… it gets me every time.' My voice broke up. I blew my nose. 'Pull up a chair.'

'Can't, got to run. Steve's in the car, Sunday night dinner at the Dragons, remember?' His eyes were on the screen as well.

'Okay well say hi… or whatever… to Dorothy.' Of late I had stopped good naturedly chastising Thomas when he called my ex-mother-in-law a dragon. It was no longer my business.

In any case, I could not tear my eyes away from the screen. I was waiting for the scene where Barbra Streisand looked terribly elegant, sitting up in bed after having the baby, no indication of the ordeal she had just endured, looking more like she had just left the hair salon.

'Call you tomorrow,' Thomas threw over his shoulder as he began to leave.

'Okay, well thanks.' I stayed where I was. 'Hey,' I called to his retreating back. 'Did you see Wilbur on your way in?' I suddenly realised that the one-dog-greeting-party had been extremely quiet.

'Yep, he's on the front lawn. He's chewing on that bull's dick thing.'

I smiled. 'Okay thanks.' However within two seconds, I practically levitated off the lounge, my rise was that quick. Was that what that thing was? Yuk! Trust Thomas to put it so succinctly. Any wonder Phil had look so amused at my antics. I must have looked like a complete pervert, running my hand up and down, pretending to put it in my mouth. I raced to the front door. 'Wilbur,' I called. 'Wilbur there's a good boy. Give that… *disgusting*… thingy to me. Come on Wilbur… Come on…'

Chapter 22

It was late in the day and the shadows had well and truly begun to lengthen when Phil decided to organise an informal game of bocce among the tradesmen. Shouts went up as Pete threw the first chrome ball. Up next was Brownie, his chest puffed out, almost unrecognizable in his fawn slacks, and blue and white checked, short sleeve shirt, instead of the navy overalls as was his usual uniform.

Wilbur, thrilled to be a part of the end of construction party, barked with excitement, while a myriad of small children ran helter skelter in delight as they watched their parents. With extreme satisfaction, I knew that this was exactly what the gardens of Carmody House were made for.

Finally, just as the sky was darkening, Phil sought me out. It didn't take much. All afternoon I had found myself watching him, marvelling at the way his custom-fitted white shirt fitted so snugly across his firm chest and well-shaped pecs. Even noticing once or twice, okay maybe three or four times, the way the white elastic on the band of his jockeys showed above his jeans when he playfully hoisted Sophia in the air, almost mesmerising me. I won't say how the flash of bare skin above them made me feel.

'I'm afraid she's tired,' he explained, his voice low, Sophia's little blonde head resting against his chest, her magnified dark eyes drowsy. My eyes were drawn to where one of her small chubby hands clutched at the placket of his white shirt.

'I guess it's time I took her and Mum home.' He glanced around at the handful of party guests beginning to pack up in the last of the light. 'Thanks for having us. Mum's had a blast chatting to everyone. Think the old place brings back fond memories.'

The end of construction party had been timed to coincide with Phil's last Sunday in Brisbane.

White cloth covered round tables dotted the lawn under the huge arms of the sweeping jacaranda. Nature helped to set the decorative touches by raining the blue mauve blossoms onto the white cloths, even delightfully settling in among the cerise coloured peonies I had massed in square glass vases. Peonies were a favourite of mine and because they were only available for four weeks of the year, I had been unable to resist using them.

After the heat of the day, it was refreshing when a cool breeze wafted, enveloping us in the fragrance of the nearby gardenia hedge. A flash of lightning out to the west caught my eye. I was grateful the promised storm had held off so far.

'Of course,' I nodded stroking Sophia's back, thinking her sleepy eyes looked so damn cute in those glasses. I too, kept my voice low. 'She seemed to have a good time with the other children. Poor little darling is worn out.' My hand touched Phil's firm forearm. 'I really appreciated your help this afternoon.' We had made quite the team, him taking over the role as host, offering drinks, refreshing glasses, making sure everyone was comfortable. A role that appeared to come naturally to him.

He looked down at me, his smile lazy, always impressing me with his beautiful white teeth. 'I enjoyed it.' He scratched at the back of his neck. 'I *really* enjoyed it.'

Folding my arms across my chest, I glanced around at the last of the guests. 'You know I'm going to miss this lot. I almost didn't want the renovations to come to an end.'

He gave a slow nod and exhaled. 'I know what you mean. But Peach,' and his voice dropped even lower as Sophia's eyes finally closed, 'if I know you, there will always be some new creation you'll be working on, some new thing happening. It won't be the end.' As I had become accustomed, he spoke as if he knew this for certain.

Leaning back against a table, wistfully, I gave a half-hearted shrug and a small smile, looking up at him. Returning my smile, he didn't look away. With his back to the remaining guests, and our voices low, there was a certain intimacy in our pose. Inhaling his warm masculinity, I noticed my breathing had become shallower, and I watched as his hand softly patted Sophia's back as he gently began to sway back and forth. 'The up side is that you won't have to bake all of those cupcakes every day for everyone's morning tea.'

Laughing softly, I found myself mirroring him, swaying from side to side, keeping time. 'What 1092 of them every day?' I cocked my head and flashed my eyes at him, knowing full well there was a touch of flirtiness in the way I spoke. 'You know I liked doing them.'

Although he gave a flash of his eyes in return, I almost had to struggle to hear him. 'I know you did. But,' and he paused, 'I guess all good things must come to an end.'

Once again he was speaking as if predicting the future. I couldn't help myself, I eyed him directly. My tone might have been soft but it was direct. 'Why?' There, I'd said it.

It was strange to see him at a loss for words. For days, I kept picturing that before he left we would talk, but right this moment I realised it was never going to happen. This man was going to go out of my life as quickly as he had come into it.

We looked at each other for some time, but neither of us spoke, no mean feat for him, but quite a one for me. I had the feeling there was something he wanted to say, although nothing came out.

Steve's words of being 90 and wondering *what if* came to

mind. And so I ploughed on. 'Phil, if there's anything I can do to help with Sophia… financially…' I stumbled around for the right words, even using my hands to help, 'or… or whatever.' There I went again, my eloquence surprising even me. 'I mean, if it means you can stay in Brisbane… at Carmody House… well I… I would be extremely grateful.'

His chocolate deep set eyes softened, crinkling in the corners. 'Peach,' was all he said, although I could hear the emotion in his voice. I watched as he gave an ever so slight shake of his head.

I didn't realise that my hand was pressed to my lips, until he reached for it, squeezing, not saying anything. I guessed there was nothing to say. Or if there was, he couldn't think of it.

I glanced down at my hand still clasped in his. His touch felt warm and strong and comforting. He was such a capable man, at the same time so gentle and caring with Sophia. There was much to admire about him. And I could not help but think that if his hand felt so damn good, I could only imagine how those arms must have felt. He smiled at me, and I wondered if he had similar thoughts.

And then he said the most surprising thing. His voice was low. 'I do see you Peach Avanel.' *No one* had ever said that to me, and at that moment it became the most important thing I had ever heard. I wanted to ask, *but do you? Do you really?* I was transfixed and could not look away from him.

There was an unexpected breeze on my face, ruffling my hair. The energy around me changed, and suddenly I felt as if we were the only two people left at the party. As if by magnetic force, I was drawn closer to him and I went to lean in, just as I heard his mother's voice come from behind him. 'I found her jacket.'

Gently, Phil gave my hand three squeezes before letting go, and then turned to his mother. With some difficulty, I dragged my eyes from his face to Gloria's.

'Peach, thank you for your lovely invitation, the garden is a credit to you. And as for the house, Frank would be thrilled.' With my heart still thudding in my chest, I noted Gloria's casual use of Mr Carmody's name. At the same time, all three of us turned to look back up at the house. With the lights ablaze it could not have been showcased any more magnificently. Although Pete had driven me crazy coming at all sorts of strange hours, he had done the most remarkable job with the lighting.

It was as if Phil had read my mind. 'Great job Pete,' he lifted his voice just a little, as he directed his comment to the other man, who stood on the other side of the hedge, encouraging his three girls from the pool, amidst complaints that it was too soon to leave.

'Pleasure working with you Phil. Any time man, any time…'

Stepping closer to the hedge, Phil put his free hand out to shake Pete's. I watched as the two men stood chatting in low voices for a few minutes.

'It saved him, you know.' Still in some sort of oblivion, I was surprised by Gloria's comment. Ignoring the fact that I had not said a word, she continued. 'I do not know what greater powers led him here, but thank God it did.' She glanced up at the heavens. 'I believe Frank had a hand in this. He was always looking out for Phil. And my dear, I am most grateful to you. My son is a new man.' She flashed her brown eyes at me.

Reaching out I took one of her slender hands in mine. 'Gloria… I am the one that is grateful. I would never have achieved this without Phil. He was an integral part of this entire project.' I could not help but add, 'I will miss him.' I glanced away, my hands now clasped firmly together in front of me.

'I can see that,' was all she said, pushing a wayward soft silver strand of hair behind one ear. Although she was nearing 70, she was an extremely stylish lady. In a white well cut linen shirt, and jeans belted at the waist with a soft calfskin silver tie, her trim arms were embellished with silver bracelets and her hands silver rings. I could see where Phil had gotten his olive skin tone and dark chocolate eyes.

I walked with them as far as the pool gate, where as with all the other guests, I played tag with Wilbur, and he continued on, escorting them as far as the front gate.

From where I stood, I watched as they began up the path and then Phil turned. For a few seconds, we shared a glance, and then slowly I raised a hand in farewell. His hands full with the now asleep Sophia, a slow smile spread across his face and he nodded before he turned and walked on.

*

Well, that was that. I blinked a couple of times, a horrible feeling settling in my stomach. Picking up a discarded wet Miss Kitty towel, I gently spread it across a sunlounge to dry. No doubt there would be tears when someone realised it was missing. Briefly, I perched on the end of the sunlounge, crossed my legs, watching as the sun finally slipped away, chased by a perfectly round full moon.

I was reminded of my first night here, seeing that same full moon. Even though I knew how much my life had been enriched since then, I could not help but feel as if a light had now gone out. I wondered how I would wake each day, and get used to the fact that Phil was not going to turn up. I tried to fathom the reason he had come into my life. Was it to give me hope that there were other guys out there like him, and one day I might find one? Or was it just to restore Carmody House and the gardens? Who *bloody* knew?

I don't know how long I sat, however finally I shook myself, glancing around, noticing that at this time of evening, the aquamarine pool appeared almost glass-like, reflecting not only the surrounding trees but also the festive paper lanterns strung above. The tea light candles I had so carefully hung from branches that morning, now gently illuminating the area.

Earlier that afternoon, as I had readied myself for the party, I had felt pretty and flirty in my new slip dress, the silk fabric luxurious on my skin, and the tangerine colour enhancing my healthy glow from working outdoors.

Looking around with wistful thoughts, I stood and slowly made my way out of the pool gate, down the stone steps and across the freshly mown lawn towards the garden shed. My bejewelled sandals confidently stepping as the glow from the full moon lit the way. Attempting to turn my mind to other things, I silently thanked the brilliance of Mr Carmody's vision and his wisdom in creating extensive vistas from every part of the garden. It was such a delight.

As another flash of lightning lit up the western sky, I was reminded of the night of the big storm, and how dangerous it had been, the grass strewn with debris. I also remembered being in the garden shed with Phil. It felt like eons ago.

Turning, I glanced back the way I had come. The pool area and surrounding garden was still lit up with an air of festivity. The smooth, lush sound of Michael Buble wafted across the grass reaching me.

Deliberately, I turned my thoughts to the party, batting away thoughts of Phil, thoughts that did me no good at all. Harveys in James Street had done a remarkable job with the catering. Now that Montgomery's had new owners, it just wasn't the same. When I had called Harvey's chef and explained that I wanted to use some of the fantastic produce from my kitchen garden, he was only too happy to see what he could work into the menu.

I had been thrilled when I had seen what they had done with my juicy heirloom tomatoes, sweet basil, peppery watercress and beautifully tipped asparagus. Mixed with my own salty preserved lemons and goat's cheese, it was a creation made in heaven.

My celery had been tossed with Roquefort, frilly leaves and white anchovies. Two months ago, Phil had suggested that we wrap every celery plant in newspaper, and tie each one firmly with twine. Even though quite a few small slugs and snails had enjoyed the protection of the newspaper, once washed, the celery was now the whitest, crispiest, crunchiest I had ever seen.

As for the famed Asian chicken salad Harveys was so well known for, I had proudly supplied the coriander and mint, but had certainly not parted with one of my girls for it.

Earlier, as each dish had been displayed, a sense of pride like I had never felt before had come over me. I remembered words Phil had spoken upon first seeing my kitchen garden. *'Growing food is such a basic human instinct,'* he had said. *'It's hardly surprising we feel good eating produce when it has come from our own garden.'*

There were a few other basic human instincts as well, however I attempted not to think of them. Of late, it appeared that I was constantly thinking of things Phil had said.

Still endeavouring to distract myself, I was reminded that Grant, one of the wait staff, had kindly placed the leftovers in the kitchen fridge. Although the thought should have given me a measure of pleasure, I could not deny the hollow feeling in my gut that had been plaguing me for weeks now. Once again I batted it away, as without knowing quite why, I continued on towards my studio on the south fence. That sense of pride I had felt earlier for my produce had now faded into nothing. Why was I even thinking about it? Disappointment like a leaden cloak, weighed heavily.

Earlier this afternoon I had opened the French doors to the small room, lighting vanilla and musk candles, plumping new navy and white scatter cushions in tickings, florals and patterns, and placing a cashmere throw rug over the arm of the daybed, making it inviting for guests who may have roamed this way to have a closer view of the river.

The huge silver pressed mirror on the back wall was a recent acquisition. And perhaps an overkill for this small area, however the reflection of the garden and river so perfect, I could not help myself. An old stainless steel trunk with chocolate leather trim sat in place of a coffee table. On it was a huge shallow copper dish filled with a mass of greenery straight from the garden, a stack of glossy gardening books, and a large silver chalice chilling opened bottles of wine. Up to date, I had not created any major masterpieces of artwork, or any minor ones, however I knew when the time was right I would begin.

Glancing around, I noticed a couple of the cushions had dents where bottoms must have been. Instead of plumping them and blowing out the candles, I topped up my wine glass, sat back on the daybed, crossed my legs, and staring into the flickering flame of one of the candles, pondered. I knew I should have been excited that Carmody House was now ready for a new beginning, however I was feeling the end of something, and there was a heaviness in me I could not shake.

And then the powerful voice of Witney Huston's album *I'm*

Your Baby Tonight floated all the way across the garden to me. One thought crossed my mind. *I wish!*

The sound of the river lapping at the banks beckoned me outside. For a second I gave a slight shiver as I felt the temperature drop. With my back to the house, I watched the lightning flicker in the western sky as if crafted by a fireworks expert.

Coming down from up at the pool, Whitney took her song to new limits, and feeling the music, I began to sway to her voice. I heard Wilbur's tell-taled four pawed approach.

'I'm here boy,' I softly called. Within seconds he placed his wet nose in my hand. Absentmindedly, with my eyes still on the city lights, I ruffled his head, the feeling of him bringing me comfort. 'It's just us now. The two of us. You... and... me.'

I glanced down at him, his head was cocked to the side as if taking in every word. 'Do you ever become frustrated because you can't answer me? Or do you simply wish I would not ask you so many questions. Hmmm, which is it?'

In answer he gave a small whine. Smiling, I ruffled his head. 'Perhaps we should open the B&B a bit sooner. What do you think? Yes, I know I was dawdling. Truth be known, I was enjoying the whole renovation part. Admit it... you were too? Plus... you liked Phil as well. Come on, I know you did?'

I nudged him with my leg. I took another sip of wine and went on with my dancing. 'Do you like dancing Wilbur? You should try it sometime. It can be very freeing!' With the moonlight and the beautiful city lights as the backdrop, the breeze cool on my face, and the feel of the fabric of my silk dress lovely against my skin, I gave myself over to the music, every now and then chatting with my four legged companion.

'Wilbur, have you ever heard the saying: dance as if no one is watching, love like you've never been hurt, sing like nobody's listening, and live like heaven on earth? Hmm… have you? Cause that's how I feel tonight. Don't worry, I won't put you through my singing, but you can watch me dance.'

And then Whitney began to sing *I Will Always Love you*. 'Oh *please*,' I spluttered. 'Do you have to tonight Whitney?' They were not the words I wanted to hear. I wiped a lone tear from my cheek.

The trouble was that every single time I watched *The Bodyguard*, I could not help but want Frank Farmer to end up with Rachel. I had reconciled that if that happened then there would never have been any wonderful song. But *please* not tonight.

Giving a small woof, Wilbur looked back at something, and then made a small sound at the back of his throat.

I flapped a hand at him. 'Ignore Whitie Wilbur. I tell you, at this time of night you will not win with that cat.' I ruffled his furry head, and continued to seductively dance around, the couple of glasses of alcohol I had imbued encouraging me to be more limber than usual. 'Thank you for being such a good host tonight, accompanying our guests up to the gate. We make a good pair Wilbur.' I took another sip of wine, tricky to do while dancing. 'Phil was a great help as well. The three of us made a really good team. Did you notice?'

However, I could tell Wilbur was distracted and not paying attention to me. Even though I knew I was waffling, it was a bit of a blow to have the dog think so too.

And then the thought hit me, Phil was definitely a Frank Farmer sort of guy.

Chapter 23

Only ten minutes by car from Carmody House, Eagle Farm racetrack was the closest thing Brisbane had to Flemington. On Melbourne Cup day, half of Brisbane flocked to Eagle Farm to celebrate Australia's most prestigious race day. And just like Melbourne, fashion was always the centrepiece off the track.

From the back seat of the yellow cab, I once again pulled my makeup mirror from my bag, and with a shaky hand re-applied my lipstick. Butterflies in my stomach, I reminded myself that the thundering hooves, the roar of the punters at the sideline, the subtle scent of spring blossoms in the air, and the hive of activity in the bookies ring had always been an exciting day for me. And even though I had fallen off the face of the earth and missed the last two, this one would be a fun day, exactly as Lou had repeatedly promised.

*

My eyes flashed around the decadent marquee shrouded in metre upon metre of custom died gold silk. Setting the opulent scene, strategically placed oversized antique gilded urns were massed with a stunning array of burgundy flowers, lush dark green foliage and huge black feathers. However, the *piece de résistance* had to be the spectacular nineteenth century French floral chandelier hanging from the ceiling. My kind of thing.

Stunning… but I had seen it all before and while once upon a time it would have impressed me, now I found it hard to raise enthusiasm.

The Melbourne Cup invitation had read vintage luxury. For most, it certainly did not disappoint. I gave myself a stern talking to, telling myself to pick my act up. What the bloody hell was wrong with me? No, don't answer that. God knew I needed to direct my thoughts elsewhere than where they had been the past 24 hours.

Exhaling heavily, I paused at a huge antique gilded mirror, and adjusted the fascinator Lou had created, not giving me a single excuse not to attend. Huge cabbage roses were massed together and sat to one side on my part. They gave me borrowed height, but did not overshadow, something large hats had a habit of doing to me. Once I had worn a wonderful black hat with a huge brim covered in hot pink ostrich feathers. It was only later when I saw myself in the social column, that I was reminded of a brightly coloured mushroom. Fashion *faux pas*, we have all had them.

I must say though, it was not hard to swirl and twirl a little as I walked in my very high nude patent shoes, enjoying the feel of my Juli Grbac silk skirt, patterned in a myriad of lavender, blush and rose blooms, worn with a panelled blush toned shell top, showing off my new slender, jewel encrusted satin tied waist and lovely golden tan. My designer friend Juli, fully aware of what had gone down with Davis, begged if she could design me something with wow factor, applauding my new measurements.

I caught a couple of surreptitious whispers behind hands and I hoped that they were commenting on my outfit, and not wondering if I had climbed out from under a rock as I had been gone from the social scene for some time. Designer outfit or not, I feared the latter was probably closer to the truth.

With my purple clutch tucked under one arm, the other nursing a champagne flute, Marty, Lou and I roamed out the front of the marquee to the fence line of the racetrack. Loudly we barracked for our horses, every now and then re-entering the marquee, keen to watch the huge plasma screens covering live events direct from Flemington Racetrack.

Marty was doing his best to teach Lou that she required more than a fondness for the colour of the horse in making her decision. The interplay between these two bought a smile to my face, and a great sense of satisfaction of how things should be. I held the belief that they were not ready to be a couple until this time, as Lakshmi and Bob had to exist in the world.

Marty was explaining that before Lou made her selection, a better criterion would be to study the name, form and staying ability. However, Lou would have none of it.

'It's no use,' she said flippantly, putting a hand up to her blonde tresses, steadying the cherry coloured birdcage she had fashioned as a top hat, only *she* could get away with. Teamed simply with a high necked, cut away shouldered, cherry coloured dress, I thought my sister looked terribly elegant, and that Marty was obviously agreeing with her.

'I'm only into the white ones,' she said. Perched on a stool, I watched as she gave Marty a flat measured look, as if to say *this is me, take it or leave it*, jiggling her foot in invitation to him.

Laughing out aloud, Marty kissed her nose as if he found her absolutely enchanting, and then with mock frustration, threw his hands in the air and strode back into the marquee to place a bet at the tote.

I could not deny they were not fun to be around, and with their individual flair and height, certainly made a striking couple. It went through my mind that perhaps I was glad Lou and Marty had been so persistent.

However every now and then realisation hit and I felt a lurch in my stomach. It had been two days. Two days since

Phil had left. Change your thoughts, change your thoughts, I ordered my mind.

Giving an almost imperceptible shake of my head I turned back to the track and took a sizable gulp of champagne. I decided then and there that champagne was, and will always be, a good idea. And I'll say it again, nude heels were my best friend, something I required right that moment. But I knew the mood I was in, I needed to take it easy.

I cast my eyes around one more time, focusing on nothing in particular, least of all the myriad of spectacular hats and beautiful dresses.

'He's not coming,' Lou told me, her voice knowing.

'*Huh?*' I spun back to her, concerned she could read my thoughts.

'Don't think I haven't noticed you continuously glancing around.'

'I'm checking out the hats.'

'Sure! I told you that Davis won't be here and I'm quite sure he won't be.'

Even though I gave her a quick nod, I had to question myself what, or who it was, I was searching for.

*

I am not going to deny that I'd had a nice day. Nice day period. There comes a time when the wisest thing to do would be to leave while you're on top. I missed that opportunity.

Unfortunately Lou's excuse of picking the kids up, didn't work for me. We'd almost had a stand up row when I insisted on being the one to collect Lakshmi and Bob from school and kindy. But for some reason it did not wash well with Lou, and Marty left with her.

For a day that had begun with beautiful people looking their best, somehow I had ended up with the same people, who by this late stage of the day, had totally trashed themselves. There was a lesson in that. *For me!* The lyrics of Kenny Roger's song, *The Gambler*, one of Johnny's favourites, kept careening through my mind at a great rate of knots.

The line of 'K*now when to walk away, know when to run* part', was entirely too appropriate, and I should have heeded my thoughts.

However some hours earlier, Steve, who had been partying next door in the Mercedes marquee, had given me a stern reminder of the power of PR and networking, and how Carmody House as a luxury B&B would require… blah, blah, blah! Somewhere in there I had rolled my eyes at him.

It was those moments which nearly turned me off the entire project. There was also no escaping the fact, that as much as my business head totally appreciated and acknowledged exactly what he was saying, it was simply that today I felt like I had stepped back into a time warp where everyone was still doing the same old, same old.

When I had said that to Steve, his eyes had narrowed and he had responded with a snappy tone. 'Babe, that's called life. What do you want them all to do, become farmers?'

'Don't be ridiculous,' I had retorted, miffed at his tone. 'You know that's not what I meant.' However, I guess the fact was these people were the old crowd I had partied with. And that bought up uncomfortable memories, ones I never wanted to think of again.

My present life was a *lifetime* away. As the day went on, I found myself sighing a lot. I kept wondering if there was something wrong with all of these people, or if there was something wrong with me. As much as I wanted it to be them, I guess the percentages spoke for themselves, and I chastised myself.

For an extremely long twenty minutes, I had been engaged

in a conversation with a woman called Sue who owned a recruitment company, the name of which escaped me. I may rephrase that, I believe I was listening and she was talking, although my eyes kept going to the structured big shouldered black jacket, fastened far too tightly across her oversized breasts, making her look more overweight than she actually was. Although, I did like her straw coloured netted skirt. I too had tried that very skirt on. Luckily, I had not bought it and worn it today.

Over the years, because of the fact Sue and I shared some mutual acquaintances, our paths had crossed. However I had never warmed to her. I found her brash and insensitive, and right this moment I couldn't help but remember our very last encounter a few years ago at a fund raising afternoon tea.

In some mad panic, she had asked if I could move my car as I was blocking the drive and she had to leave early. Confused, because I had distinctly remembered parking out on the street, I followed her to the front door, where she proceeded to point to a white Toyota Seca which had certainly seen better days.

I remembered frowning and saying slowly, 'Sue... that's not my car. That's mine over there, the black BWM with ADDRESS2 on the number plate.' In a flash, I watched as her face, and then her manner changed, insisting that we catch up later in the week for coffee, and not to forget her if I needed any help with staff recruitment, pressing her card into my hand.

I recall blushing at her behaviour, feeling that just because she now knew I drove a nice car, it changed her opinion of me, and she wanted to be better friends. It left me with such an uncomfortable feeling, that I knew I would not be catching up with her at any time.

And, after twenty minutes of watching her mouth move, I realised that my opinion of her at that time, was no different to now.

'… so Peach,' she was saying, breaking into my thoughts, 'I looked around for you earlier, but you must have been at that table at the back for the single girls?'

Blinking slowly, I watched as she downed half a glass of champagne in one hit, and then leant closer to me than necessary, her alcohol fuelled breath wafting over me.

Dumbfounded at her lack of diplomacy, my mouth practically dropped open, while I attempted to explain, at the same time wondering why the heck I even bothered. 'Actually… I was with Marty and Lou at Sherrie Storer's table…'

However, she cut in. 'Yeah I was stuck on the big business table with all couples. But you know, you've got to take advantage when you can.' She raised her glass in cheers before lifting it to her oversized lips once again.

I felt my hand clench around the stem of my own champagne flute, too astonished to respond to her rudeness.

'You and I used to be so much alike Peach,' Sue espoused in a singsong voice.

Not bloody likely, I wished to say, however refrained. Although she must have mistaken my wide-eyed look for interest, waving her arms around, sloshing her drink, and taking no notice as I used a napkin to blot the liquid off my Mulberry clutch.

'Successful, hardworking businesswomen. We've done it all, won every award, but let me tell you… there is nothing better than coming home to your husband and children.' She shook her head. 'Nothing better!'

Closing my eyes at her complete lack of sensitivity, I slid off the barstool, placed my own glass on the table, mumbled a few words of farewell, and made my way across the room through the sea of vibrant colour and movement of the ladies dresses and hats. That had done it for me, it was high time I called it quits.

My mind still elsewhere, I was startled to hear a familiar voice from behind call my name.

As clumsy arms encircled me, I grabbed at my fascinator, as a familiar scent I would never forget, overwhelmed me. My jaw gave an involuntary clench.

'Davis… let go.' Annoyed, I pushed against him, as he hung on. 'What the hell are you doing? Get off me. You reek of alcohol.'

'Frenchy don't! I just need a hug,' he slurred, pulling me closer, catching me off balance. Even though I had my clutch in my hand, I put both of my arms around him to steady myself. Annoyed, once again one hand went up to secure my fascinator, and then I stood still waiting for him to come to his senses. Funny, but I didn't even feel anger towards him anymore. Even this close, I felt… nothing!

My tone was dry. 'Are you done?' I gave a weary exhalation.

'Just one minute more.'

Briefly, I indulged him. 'Right, minute's up.' Patting him on the back with my clutch, I pushed at him with my other hand. Surreptitiously I glanced around, imagining we were making quite a spectacle. I lowered my voice. 'What is going on Davis? Where's your partner in crime? I'd prefer to avoid her if you don't mind.' Pursing my lips, I folded my arms in front of me, attempting to make a space between us, although not really succeeding.

Finally, he released his hold on me. His voice was not very happy. 'She's not here.' He ran a finger around his shirt collar as if it was too tight, and then awkwardly propped himself on a bar stool. With some level of surprise, I noticed how flabby he had become around the jaw line. Two things went through my mind, the fact that it was only recent, and the fact that it was unbecoming.

He felt around in his pockets, unearthing his car keys, placing them noisily on the marble bar top. In a split second, I recalled the dozens and dozens of times he had done that very thing before, usually asking me to put them in my handbag. With his eyes on his drink, he startled me when he spoke. 'She... she lost the baby.'

For a few seconds I was quiet, digesting this information. I felt around for a feeling, but there was nothing there. I gave a half-hearted shrug, my arms still folded in front of me. 'I'm sorry,' I said, my voice flat.

He threw back the last of his scotch, and then heavily banged the glass back down, his eyes on it. 'Yeah well it's been a bloody nightmare.'

I raised my brows, my voice matter of fact. 'I am sure it has. That's what happens when someone loses a baby Davis.'

His voice was gruff. 'No... I mean the entire bloody thing. Her in particular! She's the nightmare! Falling pregnant like that.' He rolled his eyes in exasperation, and clumsily ran his hands through his hair. 'And then pretending it was an accident. I knew it was no accident.' Briefly, he covered his face with his hands.

What a perfect thing for my ex-husband to discuss with me, his mistress falling pregnant to him, like I had no idea how it was done. Hurriedly, I batted away images that attempted to flood my mind. I let out a long slow breath. To say my tone was cynical was an understatement. 'What on earth would you like me to say?'

He glanced at me with a hangdog look. The middle finger

on his right hand repeatedly rimmed the edge of his empty glass. 'You don't have to say a word. I had it coming. I know, I know, I know. Practically every man and his dog have told me.'

I raised my eyebrows once more. 'Not every man and his dog.' After all, I could sick Wilbur onto him. Wilbur would not like him. I know!

Davis leant across the bar. 'Another Scotch,' he called to the barman, and then looked back at me. I shook my head. Turning, he held one finger up.

But when he turned back to me, his tone was accusing, and the look on his face was pure nasty. 'You didn't waste any time did you?' His voice was thick with alcohol and I struggled to understand him, as he accused, 'I mean always playing the wounded party, when in fact you met PK a couple of years ago. After all, how do I know,' and he poked himself in the chest, before he pointed at me, 'that *you* weren't seeing him all that time?'

Rolling my eyes in exasperation, I snapped. 'Look, I've got no idea what you're talking about, nor do I care. You've had more than enough to drink.' My hands cut through the air. 'It's high time you went home.' And then a thought hit me, and it was refreshing. 'Actually Davis, I don't have to do this. I don't have to do anything with you ever again.'

As I turned to walk away, he took my arm, his eyes narrowed. 'It's not like you to play dumb with me Peach. I wondered that day at the nursery where I had seen your boyfriend. I mean there was something different about him, his hair or something, but then it came to me who he actually was. PK Hunter!'

Screwing my face up, I shook my head. 'PK Hunter? Do you mean Phil Hunter?'

'*Yes*... I mean Phil or PK or whatever you *bloodywell* call him. He was a part of that consortium we had the meeting with for that Hastings Street development you were so keen on. Did you think I was so stupid, I would have forgotten him? The guy was sold as,' and he drew inverted commas in the air, 'one of Australia's top landscape architects, and he was sinking most of the dough into it? Don't know what happened cause it never went ahead.'

My voice was not only impatient, but also weary. 'Davis… I don't know what you're talking about. You're obviously mixed up. And you've had far too much to drink.'

'Oh for God's sake Peach, stop treating me like a fool. He might have had more hair, but I know it was him. There was that cocktail party at Urbane, and then later we had a meeting in Red PR's boardroom. Ring Fleur, she'll tell you!'

I wracked my brain for information to decipher what the heck he was talking about. My voice was slow while I recalled. 'I didn't go to that cocktail party, but I *was* at that meeting at Red PR's, and *he* sure as heck was not there. You've got it wrong.'

His voice was still accusing. 'I am telling you, I haven't.' I watched his face while he thought for a few seconds. 'He *was* at the cocktail party but he might not have been at the meeting.' He mumbled something I couldn't understand, and then a look of astonishment crossed his face. '*What…* you didn't know?' He gave a cynical laugh, as one of his hands slapped down hard on the bar. 'You're kidding me? This is priceless!'

I was exasperated. 'For goodness sake, it's not the same *person* Davis.' I shook my head. 'You're confused… and drunk… or both.'

'Am I?' He peered at me. 'Then how did you come up with the money to buy that property you live in? Don't think I haven't been wondering about that.'

'*What...* you think Phil had something to do with it? Think again. I'm telling you, he is not who you think he is.'

'Then Google him.' He spat out, giving an ironic laugh, before he downed half his drink in one gulp, slamming his glass back down on the marble bar top once again, sloshing the other half. 'I'm telling you, it's him.'

I felt the colour drain from my face. *Google him?* Why hadn't I already done that? But before I could give it further thought, Davis continued, his head bent over his drink, his voice so muffled, I had to strain to make out what he was saying.

'He wrote those books.'

I was beyond irritated by now. '*Which books?*'

'Those gardening books, the ones we had on the coffee table.' His head shot up and his voice took on an accusing tone, one I was unused to. 'Whatever happened to them? I suppose you got those *too*?'

My mind went into overdrive. I knew the books he was talking about. 'Davis, I took *nothing* from the apartment.' My tone was extremely succinct. 'If they are missing, I'd talk to *the nightmare!* My mind was racing, however I could not think as Davis kept talking.

'He's some kind of a philanthropist.'

'What?'

'He opened up that troubled boy's school, somewhere down the coast.'

I swallowed. 'Up the coast.' I knew my voice was small.

He slurred, 'Up, down... I don't care...'

'I'm going Davis. I can't talk to you now.' Flustered, I went to walk away, but before I did, I still had the peace of mind to reach out and place a hand over the top of his car keys, pocketing them in my handbag. Old habits die hard. He appeared to be on a destructive path. I had spent years looking after this man, and it was no different now. I knew I would find his car in the member's car park.

*

'I just need to do something before I get your dinner,' I hurriedly explained to Wilbur, my heels loud on the timber floor as I rushed down the hallway, plonking myself in front of the computer. Hurriedly, I prised off my entirely too high shoes which after a day standing in them, had felt as if they were glued to my feet. My feet cried out in thanks, although my brain barely registered this.

Damn the computer, whenever I was in a hurry it took forever. Keeping my eyes on the screen, I removed my fascinator, tossing it from where I was onto the couch, and began to take out all the bobby pins securing my hair. Putting both hands up, I ran them through my hair over and over, relieving the tension in my scalp, until my curls stood on end and I looked like a crazy woman. I glanced at Wilbur. Pulling his head back, he gave me a funny look, and then made a noise in the back of his throat.

'If you think I look like a wild person, then go find Whitie.' My tone was accusing, my hands poised over the keyboard. 'He'll fix you up.' That shushed him. He lay at my feet, head between his paws and said not another word, every now and then eyeing me strangely.

I had to type his name three times as my nervous fingers kept hitting the wrong keys. My heart thumped once, as if it would cease to beat forever. Then it began to race, its normal rhythm abandoned.

There they were, article after article on *PK Hunter*, and picture after picture. I squeezed the mouse tight in my right hand. I saw what Davis had been talking about. There was Phil only a couple of years ago, huge white smile, cleanly shaven, full head of thick dark hair, and not so many lines around his eyes. In stylish clothes, he wore his success well. It was like looking at another person, perhaps a relative of his, but not him. It was weird.

Pulling my hand away, I placed it to my mouth and sat still for the longest time. My head spun, as if the world was off balance.

Tentatively, I reached my right hand out, and once again touched the mouse, slowly scrolling down.

And then I saw it... *of course* why wouldn't it be? Briefly, I closed my eyes at the absurdness of the situation. *Fields of Dreams!* The name of the boys' school was the same as his Melbourne landscaping company. Of course I knew the name of the school, as it was where I had deposited his wages each week. I gave an acerbic laugh. *How ironic!* It was also the name of his first book.

Fields of Dreams, I saw the title now. And... that book, along with two of his others, had sat on our coffee table at the warehouse. The day I had left, I had even placed the little crystal bird on top of them. Those books had been about the only bloody thing I was allowed to have out on display. Davis didn't mind them because one of them had been personally signed by the author that night at the cocktail party, the one I had been unable to attend because of other work commitments. Davis used to brag about the book, telling our guests that the author was a friend of ours.

Without reading a word more, I sat back in my seat. I had *never* put two and two together. After all, why would I have? My middle finger taped at my top lip, while my mind raced.

Why, why, why? Why was everything such a secret? I thought of the end of construction party and how I had offered financial support for Sophia's education, if they wished to stay in Brisbane.

Even then, he'd said nothing. Not one single bloody word! Feeling like a fool, I blushed at the thought. I remembered the look on his face, and how he had put a finger to my lips and shushed me, closing his eyes and giving an almost imperceptible shake of his head. What the *hell* was he thinking? Was this some game he had been playing?

And all that time, I thought he had to return to Melbourne for Sophia, but it was also to resume his old life. A life he didn't wish to tell me about. It was as if this man was two people. I felt such a fool. *A bloody fool!*

The last couple of days, hoping against hope, I had wished and *dreamed* that before he left in the morning, he would ring or come by. Anything! But not one single word. I had even deliberately told him where I was spending Melbourne Cup. Just in case. Talk about humiliating. Folding my arms, I dropped my head and then closed my eyes.

It was 11.55pm by the time I pushed my chair away from the computer. I had read every editorial. The three successes he'd had at the Chelsea Flower show in London, even more at the Melbourne International Flower and Garden Show, the Premier's Sustainability Award, the design and construct of a resort in Hawaii, an entire island somewhere in Fiji, a former property of his in the Yarra Valley, the opening of the Fields of Dreams boys' school, accolade after accolade, until suddenly nothing.

The website appeared to still be current with photos of recent projects, just nothing more on him. And he was still listed as the director of the company, although I noticed there was also a general manager, Morag Newton, who I gathered must have taken over during his sabbatical, as someone needed to direct the thirty odd staff that had been mentioned.

Climbing the stairs to my bedroom, I lay on the silk coverlet still fully clothed. A tiredness I had never felt before washed over me. My mind kept going to the four pictures I had seen of Katrine. Tall, dark hair cut in an angular bob with a short blunt fringe, pale skin, red lips, striking in an arty way.

Shaking my head, all I could think was that the entire thing was… odd, odd, *odd!*

Chapter 24

In the kitchen, sunlight streamed in through every window, and I could already smell the warmth in the air. Christmas was fast approaching. Long days and good growing weather meant there was always plenty to do in the garden, and once again I made a mental list of chores which I had been lagging behind on.

Weeks ago, keen to make batches of tomato sauce to freeze, I had been impatient with the tomato crop when they were late to yield. But now as they sat luscious, plump and beautiful on the kitchen bench, piled on a white platter with fluted edges, I wasn't sure I wanted to destroy the masterpiece. I could decide later.

The climbing yellow beans had been delightful, even if it meant tearing down the enchanting sweet peas from the trellis which was needed as a support for the beans. It had been a ritual to pick small amounts, instantly steam them for a few minutes, and serve drizzled with extra virgin olive oil.

The zucchinis were loving the heat. Earlier I had picked a handful of the wide opened male flowers and placed them in the fridge, wrapped in damp paper towels, waiting for later that evening when the boys came by. The plan had been to dip them in a whisked egg and panko crumbs ready for a quick fry in olive oil. I sort of wished I hadn't rhapsodized so much about them, as right at that moment, the very thought of cooking them sounded rather like a chore.

To the side of the sink a bundle of cucumbers waited to be turned into bread and butter cucumbers. To Johnny's delight, I had promised him I would make them. Funny thing, but it seemed to me the older a man got the more he liked his pickles. Although I had intended on pickling the radishes, I actually wondered if I would ever eat them. It made me realise I really only needed to grow what I loved most. I didn't have to have an abundance of everything.

As if on automatic pilot, I rinsed my plate and mug, wiped the toast crumbs off the kitchen bench, folded the blue and white checked tea towel, and neatly hung it over the handle of the oven door, adjusting it until it hung evenly.

Lazily, from his position on the kitchen mat, Wilbur opened one eye and gave a sideways four legged stretch, along with a lazy groan. I stepped over him.

With my index finger, I poked at some purple cloves of garlic in a small china bowl. Earlier I had set them aside to take down to place in the chook's water to help keep them free from parasites, another one of Phil's suggestions. Normally, I would have let the girls out by now, leaving them free to roam.

However this morning, I found myself procrastinating, standing with one hand resting on the window sill looking over the back garden, my eyes searching. Silly as it was, I could not help myself. It was only after Phil had left that I had realised this was something I had done nearly every day, ever since he had begun coming to Carmody House, if not from this window then from the one in my bedroom.

Folding my arms against my chest, I gave a snort of derision. Absentmindedly, I played with one of my curls, twirling it around and around my finger. In the six weeks and five days since he had left I had wondered what greater powers had led him to Carmody House. With one finger tapping my upper lip, once again I wondered if Mr Carmody had sent him to rescue me, to help restore the garden to its former glory. I *had* to think that there was some purpose he had come and gone from my life with such impact. There just had to be.

Although I knew he would never be returning, there was some part of my brain that continued to expect to see him. I could be researching something for the garden, or talking to someone, or simply reading a newspaper, and I would think to myself, I must check that with Phil. And then I would have to remind myself that Phil was no more. That realisation was consistently met with a heavy feeling. One I did not like.

I thought of the numerous times over the past ten months when I had unexpectedly come across him in the garden. I thought of his deep set dark eyes, his sensual lips, alluring smile. And I thought of the sheer physicality of him. I drove myself crazy with thoughts of that.

I almost smiled at those thoughts, but caught myself in time when I thought of the life he had deliberately withheld from me. Once again my cheeks burned, and a feeling of embarrassment washed over me. I wished to God I did not feel that way, but I did!

There were moments when I wanted to turn back time. I wanted Phil to be who I thought he was. I wanted to hope that the old Phil would return, knowing the new one never could. I can't say how much time was wasted as I indulged this fantasy, but then the realisation that I knew my wishing was futile would jolt me back to reality. The world didn't work that way. *If only!*

With the small bowl of garlic in one hand, I went to the front door, pushed my feet into my gumboots, and weaved my way down to the chooks, Wilbur, as always, at my side. I deliberately batted away the thought that now my days at Carmody House seemed a little empty. *What was wrong with me?* It was a stupid thought. After all, there was much to do in this beautiful place.

Deliberately, I turned my thoughts to the herbaceous border in the kitchen garden and what a delight it had become. Instantly, I thought of how pleased Phil would be if he could see the flourishing bushes of rosemary, basil and mint, and the blue green leaves of sage and thyme. From the very beginning he had understood what I had been trying to achieve. Sharing it with him had intensified the pleasure a thousand fold.

Now, other than me, who cared if the capsicum bushes produced glorious fruit, or if the basil was magnificently laden? I could just imagine Lou's response if I discussed my broad bean crop with her. Would Steve care how many apples my Jonathan tree produced? What about Thomas? Perhaps as he enjoyed my homemade marmalade, he may take an interest in the fact that my one cumquat tree appeared to produce fruit all year round. Somehow I doubted it. My parents still shook their heads, as if having a daughter who grew stuff was an odd thing. I sighed. I guess I still had Brownie. He was interested.

I ricocheted between being grumpy and discontent, and telling Wilbur it was high time this B&B opened.

Right now, it was the latter. 'I have a meeting with Steve later today,' I told the dog, forcing my voice to sound more cheerful than I felt. 'It's time I stopped procrastinating and came up with a date for the opening of this place. What are your thoughts?'

With his head cocked to the side, the dog looked at me as if to say, *why do you keep asking me such questions. How would I know? Huh… how?*

*

As I set the chooks free, I wondered if they missed Phil. I speculated on what chooks actually thought about. Sometimes as I watched one of them standing on one leg, I imagined them practicing yoga, and I'd ask if Phil had taught them tree pose.

They hadn't been as much work as I had envisioned, and

had settled in straight away, wasting no time in getting the hang of their state-of-the-art chicken coop Phil had built, skittering up and down the ladder, hopping in and out of the peep hole.

Most afternoons they even put themselves away. I got a real kick out of watching. Daisy, usually last in, would take a look around as if to say, *well that's it, we're all in.*

I roamed down to the river, stopping to slip my boots off, wanting to feel the cool grass on my bare feet. From the corner of my eye, I glimpsed Wilbur chasing Whitie. For once, I left them to it. As per usual, Whitie leapt up onto the neighbouring fence, sitting with his eyes closed against the sun as if the cat didn't have a worry in the world, a slow smile spreading across his face, as he tormented his nemesis. And as per usual, Wilbur took great delight in repeatedly barking at the cat.

Continuing on, as if in a trance, I found a spot riverside, and in the broken shade of a gum tree sat, as if I had nothing more pressing to do.

The great old tree leaned out so far over the river forming a canopy of shade on the water. The carolling of a magpie from above broke free. My resident family of ducks scurried away from me, sliding down the bank, and slipping into the water with relative ease. From a nearby branch, a huge praying mantis swayed on its twig, swivelling its angular head to peer at me with bulbous sinister eyes. Butterflies with yellow thoraxes, and with big red spots flitted in and out. For all I knew they could have been the rare Richmond Birdwing butterflies that Phil had spoken of.

With perfect equal intensity of feeling, my thoughts rebounded from wanting to see Phil again, to wanting to forget all about him. I wished it to be six months down the track, so I could be over him. Maybe twelve months would be a better bet. Two years, perhaps.

*

Lou narrowed her eyes at me. 'What do you mean?' Our family had gathered together at Dad's and Patrice's for an early Christmas celebration. Surreptitiously, I had motioned for Lou to meet me around the side of the house. 'You seemed okay a few minutes ago.'

I kept my voice low. 'The smell of that lamb is making me sick. Didn't you notice how strong it was? I had to come outside.' Grimacing, I wrinkled my brow. 'I really do not want to offend Patrice… can you make something up?' With one hand to my stomach and the other up to my mouth, I almost gagged.

Lou chastised me, fiercely whispering, 'She only made it because you keep saying it's your favourite.' Over the past five years, Patrice had worked hard gaining our love. Generally she was a hopeless cook, although she had happened upon a lamb recipe, cooked with rosemary, cider and honey. Such a rarity for her to make something so delicious, I had pronounced it a winner and begged her to make it every time we came. Yes, I *did* like it, perhaps not as much as she had thought, although it certainly spared us some of her other culinary creations. I hadn't the heart to break it to her, but marshmallow salad was not actually a salad!

Swallowing, my mouth dry, I nodded. 'I know… but I have to go Lou. I need to lie down.'

'Was it what they said earlier?'

I knew exactly what she was talking about and while it certainly did not please me, I cannot say it had made me sick to my stomach. I gave a weary exhale. '*No*, it's got nothing to do with that. But I must say it is bloody offensive when a family trip is planned and a hotel booked out, and I am told I can share a room with old Aunt Honey, and that we'd be good company for each other. *What?* I am 36 years of age. I like my privacy. I don't want to feel penalised that I don't have a partner. I can also afford my own room. I don't want it to be said to me, "Oh well if you don't share with Aunt Honey, perhaps Lakshmi and Bob can go in with her, and you can have a fold out bed in with Lou and Marty. Or we could even put one in the communal lounge."' I shook my head in frustration, my eyes reflecting the horror I felt. 'I do love Aunt Honey but surely we are not of the same ilk. It's really made me feel brilliant about my life, I can tell you.'

'I don't think Dad meant anything.'

'Yeah... I know, I know. Look... I just have to go okay.'

Her face carried a look of worry. 'What's going on Peach?'

I sighed heavily. 'I don't know. I'm exhausted all the time lately. I'm probably just burnt out. These last twelve months have been huge and I have worked like a woman possessed. Now it's coming to an end, I think my body is giving out on me.' At least I hoped it was that and not a relapse of chronic fatigue, which I had suffered during my first year of university. It had become so severe, each day saw me sleeping for three or four hours. My studies had been deferred for some months.

'Yeah, you were not yourself last week when I dropped the kids off.' Her brow furrowed.

'I think that was just the smell of that white sliced bread you bought over for their lunch. It made me feel ill.' Just talking about it now, made me feel worse than ever, and I put a hand to my mouth. Never before had I noticed that packaged bread had such a strong odour, one that did not agree with me. It must be that now I had begun to make my own spelt bread, which Lou's children were not particularly fond of, that I smelt the preservatives and additives in the packaged bread.

Once again I swallowed, almost gagging. 'Lou, do you mind...?'

Lou put her hands out. 'Just go... I'll explain. Are we still on for breakfast at your place on Sunday morning?'

'Yes... of course,' I murmured turning to leave, however before I could go any further, I leant over the railing and threw up in the garden.

'Peach, you really are unwell. Marty or I will drive you.'

My face was clammy, and with the back of my hand I patted at my mouth. 'No, no, no... it comes and goes. I need to lie down. I'm exhausted. That's all it is.'

'You're sure?' Lou's eyes bored into mine.

'Yes... go back in... they'll be wondering what happened to us. Tell Dad and Patrice I'm sorry and I'll call them tomorrow.'

'Okay well don't worry about that weekend away. We'll sort something out.'

Unable to speak, I waved a hand over my shoulder.

In my car, I wondered something. Was there such a thing as being lovesick?

Twenty minutes later, dressed in comfy pyjamas, and feet slipper clad, I Googled the words *symptoms of lovesick*. Three words came up first. *Fevered, pale or depleted*. I was certainly pale and depleted. Not sure if I was fevered. Although, before I threw up earlier I had felt hot and clammy. Maybe I was fevered.

There were two more symptoms, *dry mouthed and clammy hands*. Right... there's the clammy thing. Apparently the body's nervous system goes haywire sending too much moisture to the hands and too little to the mouth. Hmm... not sure about the hands but the back of my neck had felt clammy at times, and my face.

Ah here we go... feeling *unfocused and being tired.* There was absolutely no doubt that of late those two words summed me up pretty well.

I clicked on another site... *empty feeling, ache in the heart, and obsessive checking.* Yep, yep and... no. Well I didn't call looking at Fields of Dreams's website almost daily obsessive. I was just coming to terms with who Phil... PK Hunter is... was. And maybe occasionally it was more than once a day. But it was still hardly obsessive. Was it?

With both hands wrapped around a mug of tea, I sat there going from site to site, every now and then munching on a gingernut biscuit. And then I read that if you understand what is happening to you, you can deal with the symptoms easier. It also said that unrequited love was certainly something that could make a person forlorn and depressed. I decided to read no further. After all, it was rather unflattering to know that fact, and I hardly needed reminding my love was unrequited. However, at least I knew what was wrong with me.

Getting to my feet, I called to Wilbur who was in the library. Ever since the Christmas tree had gone up, each evening he'd take up a spot right in front of it. He even appeared to have the uncanny knack of knowing which gift was his. When I would call him for bed, he'd bring his present to me. Each time I would say the same thing 'Not yet boy, put it back,' astounded that he had picked the right one.

However as I called him again, I realised for the first time that the damn chew toy had an odour about it. Any wonder he knew it was his.

Wearily, I turned the lights off and climbed the stairs. My bed beckoned. Tomorrow would be a better day.

*

With one eye barely opened, I glanced at the clock on my

bedside table. 'Good lord, they'll all be here shortly,' I mumbled to myself, heavily flinging back the covers, and sleepily wiggling my way to the side of the bed.

With my legs over the side, I gave thanks that I had done most of the prep for the Christmas breakfast yesterday, making up the bircher muesli, stewing stone fruits and preparing a smoked salmon and asparagus strata. Stratas were always better made the night before to allow the bread to soak up the eggy mixture.

However, right this minute I would have done anything to lie in bed for a little longer. Who was I kidding; the rest of the day would have done me.

Legs still over the side, I lay back down for a minute before I realised the urgency of my bladder could wait no longer. Perched upon the toilet, I honestly felt as if someone had glued my eyelids shut, and for a few minutes I sat there pants around my ankles, eyes closed.

Groggily, I made my way down the stairs, and in my state of oblivion got the fright of my life when someone rapped at the door just as I was passing.

'*Jesus Lou*, what the hell are you doing here this early?' I asked, a hand to my thumping chest. I wrapped my nightgown closer around myself.

'Merry Christmas to you as well dear sis,' she said kissing my cheek. I glanced behind her, expecting the children. I turned to her in question, noticing a glimpse of a black bra under her white singlet top.

'Dad bought them swings,' she said, as if that explained everything, pushing her way past me, heading towards the kitchen.

I looked at her retreating back for what seemed like forever, blinked a couple of times and then followed her. 'So,'

I frowned, my voice was still full of sleep, 'you've left them home alone on the swings?'

'No silly. I've been up with them since the crack of dawn and then Mitch called to see if he could pick them up earlier.' She gave a nonchalant shrug. 'So I decided not to hang around waiting for Marty. He's going to meet me here in an hour.' She glanced at her watch. 'You did say eight thirty didn't you?'

'Mmmm.' Flicking the switch on the kettle, I still didn't follow Lou's train of thought regarding the swings, but let it go. With my arms wrapped around myself, and as if it was of the utmost importance, I stood watching the kettle boil, as the steam began to come out of the spout in little curls.

At the sound of Lou's voice, I turned to see her splayed across the sofa, long legs in the air. 'I hate not having the kids Christmas day.'

'Hmmm,' I sympathised, the effort of talking, more than I could bear. I had always been a morning person, but of late if I didn't have to get up to feed those chooks, I would have laid there forever. It was high time I stopped feeling melancholic and sorry for myself. *Get on with it Peach*, I said under my breath.

'Is it just us and the boys?'

I turned. 'Uh-huh.' I took two cups down from the shelf. 'Tea?'

'Sure.' She narrowed her eyes, looking at me. 'Not firing up the coffee machine? Why tea?'

I shrugged. 'It settles my stomach.' I busied myself for a few minuted, still not ready to make conversation. With two hands, I removed the heavy tray of strata from the fridge, and placed it on the bench. After deliberating for a matter of seconds, I glanced at Lou.

Still reclining on the sofa, she held the latest edition of

Gourmet Traveller up to her face. Surreptitiously, I opened a canister in the pantry and placed a lone gingernut biscuit on the saucer beside my tea. Although it appeared an odd thing to have so early in the day, lately something as simple as that appeared to ease how I felt, and I just did not feel like discussing my health once again with Lou.

'Okay, when the oven reaches 180 degrees, can you slip the strata in,' I asked, indicating the baking dish. 'I'll go up and get ready,' my voice carried more energy than I felt.

However by the time I had made it up the stairs, I felt the need to sit on the upholstered bench at the end of my bed. Nursing my tea, tentatively I sipped at it, taking small bites from the biscuit. The very thought of that chronic fatigue incident years earlier, sent shivers up my spine, and I hoped against hope I was not relapsing. I remembered that no matter how much will I had, my body had a mind all of its own.

Thirty minutes later, after ditching the clingy red jersey dress I had planned to wear, and opting in favour of comfort, I pulled from my wardrobe a Noba White Label short silk caftan, deep V at the neck, and ruffled at the hem. Pushing my fringe to one side, I secured it with a Chelsea De Luca clip, and draped a blue and silver stoned necklace from Lily G around my neck. Peering in the mirror, I applied a final coat of mascara and a generous slick of lip gloss. With my fingers, I fluffed my curls. Feeling a little more energised, I made my way down the stairs, this time to find Steve and Thomas at the door. Talk about timing!

'Darling, darling merry Christmas,' Thomas gushed, amongst kisses. 'My God your tits look big in that.'

I raised my brows, giving him a flat measured look. 'And merry Christmas to you my friend.' I looked down the front of myself. 'Yes now that you mention it, these breasts do have a life of their own.'

*

'What is this?' Baffled, I looked at Lou, knowing very well what the pink and white box was that she had tossed onto my kitchen bench. How many times had I used that *First Response* pregnancy test, cursing the damn things, throwing them in the bin, so many negative outcomes?

Lou's face was deadpan. It matched her voice. 'It's a personal alarm system!' Looking at me, she blinked a few times, but then upped the amps. 'What the hell do you think it is? A bloody pregnancy test…'

I cut her off. 'You think you're pregnant?' I asked, knowing I would have to weigh this bit of news up, unsure how it would affect me emotionally. However, I couldn't believe she had produced it now. Steve had just walked outside, and was sitting on the front steps speaking on his phone. Although I could hear his intent voice, I doubted he would be long. Plus Thomas had taken a quick run to the shops and his return was imminent.

'Not me Honey… you!'

'What? Lou do not be ridiculous!'

I watched as she determinably folded her arms. I had seen that pose many a time on her. No matter what happened from this point on, you could never win.

'I want you to humour me…'

Still I tried, cutting her off. 'Lou!'

She was nonchalant. 'Hey if there's nothing to worry about, why are you getting your knickers in a knot?' We stared at each other, now my arms folded across my chest as well. I had no answer, however my heart had begun to thump.

Lou used her bossy voice. 'Come on… into the bathroom.'

'For goodness sake Lou!'

I watched as my brat of a sister headed towards the bathroom. And then I heard her voice once again, this time much louder. 'Peach get in here. I am not going to give up.'

Arms folded, I leant against the doorframe, while she began to read aloud from the side panel of the box. I snatched it from her, and used my puritanical voice. 'Lou... you are being silly!'

She ignored my attitude. 'You have to pee on the end for five seconds. Take the cap off first and don't wet the entire thing.'

Out of patience, I explained. 'Lou I have used these things before you know.'

She flashed me a look. 'However, you don't appear to have the smarts to use one now, do you?'

I could not help but think what a smart arse she was.

'Now if you want me to leave the room, you'll do as I say. If not, I'll stay in here until you do,' she challenged me. 'Your choice?'

Pushing her out the door, I slammed it behind her and turned the lock. For a few minutes I sat on the closed toilet seat, a million thoughts running through my mind.

And then Lou called again. 'I'm waiting!'

*

'My God... does Jules know?' Lou shrieked. I could easily see that although she had guessed as much, she was still completely flabbergasted, and I could hardly blame her. I felt the exact same way myself. From across the kitchen bench, she rested her chin on her hand, her eyes boring into mine demanding an answer.

My hands firmly clenched in front of me, I swallowed, grimaced and rapidly shook my head. 'It's... it's not Jules.'

Shaking her head, Lou wore a look of disbelief. 'It's not Jules! I thought you said you and Jules…'

I cut her off, splaying my hands across the bench. 'Noooo… you just expected we did and… and I did nothing to correct you.' I glanced across at Steve for support.

Lou followed my eyes, and then her own eyes very nearly popped out of her head. 'Oh for Christ bloody sake… not Davis?'

'Goodness no… what do you take me for?' And then I glanced once again at Steve, my voice small, 'Sorry.' He shrugged and shook his head, nonchalantly. I was glad he was feeling calm, because I sure as heck was not.

Lou's badgering continued, her voice rising to the occasion, her eyes opening wide. 'You had sex with one of the guys at the dinner for six?'

'No, no, no…' Covering my face with my hands, I took a deep breath.

Lou rushed on, her probing incessant. 'Something happened after we left you at the Melbourne Cup function?'

'Noooo!'

'Well it was not the bloody Immaculate Conception, you know!' And then Lou looked at Steve, her tone accusing, 'You know something!'

Once again he shrugged and then he came across and stood behind me. His hands went to my shoulders and he began to massage gently. 'Peach?' was all he said, prompting me.

I placed my right hand up to my shoulder and clasped one of his, the touch reassuring. I was still in shock myself. The longest pause went by and finally I whispered, 'Phil,' as if I could barely believe it myself.

'PHIL,' Lou yelled. 'PHIL WHO?' Watching her face, I could see when the penny dropped. 'You mean Phil the gardener?'

I corrected her, 'Phil, the award winning landscape architect, author, benefactor, entrepreneur…'

Shaking her head, this time she cut me off, her brow wrinkled, her tone confused. 'Do I know this guy?'

'It's the same bloody Phil,' I told her, suddenly feeling exhausted. The pressure of Steve's hands stopped as if finally I had said something that unsettled him. He walked around and sat beside Lou. I read the look of confusion on his face. His eyes questioned me.

I sighed loudly, glancing between the two of them. 'I know, I know… I only found out who he was after he had left, and I felt like such a fool so I didn't say anything to anyone.' I shrugged with exhaustion.

God knew that was not the only thing I felt a fool over. There was something else I had not shared with anyone. My mind turned back to the end of construction party and later that evening, when I had roamed down to the river. Mournful and lost I had been dancing on my own, as usual Wilbur my only companion. Embedded in my memory forever, I would never forget that night.

Chapter 25

I remembered every detail of *that* night distinctly. With the sound of Whitney Houston coming down from the pool, I had pirouetted rather ungracefully, messily spilling the wine I held in my hand. Giving a small woof, Wilbur looked back at something, and then made a small sound at the back of his throat.

I flapped a hand at him. 'Ignore Whitie Wilbur. I tell you, at this time of night you will not win with that cat.' I ruffled his furry head, and continued to seductively dance around, the couple of glasses of alcohol I had imbued encouraging me to be more limber than usual. 'Thank you for being such a good host tonight, accompanying our guests up to the gate. We make a good pair Wilbur.' I took another sip of wine, tricky to do while dancing. 'Phil was a great help as well. The three of us made a really good team. Did you notice?'

However, I could tell Wilbur was distracted and paying no attention to me. Even though I knew I was waffling, it was a bit of a blow to have the dog think so too.

And then the thought hit me, Phil was definitely a Frank Farmer sort of guy. However Wilbur gave a couple of woofs.

'Shhh Wilbur.' Still dancing, I spun to see if I could spot the blessed cat, stumbling as I did. 'Ooooops!'

In an instant, I came to a direct halt, the wine sloshing over my hand. I could feel the thudding of my heart, and the warmth as blood flooded my face. I swallowed hard, and gave my drenched hand a flick.

In the shadows nearby stood Phil, feet casually crossed at the ankles, one arm out leaning against a tree. He wore a look of amusement, and I was uncertain if it was because of my dancing, or what I had been saying about him to Wilbur, that he was a Frank Farmer sort of guy. My face continued to blush.

Quietly, I stood looking at him for some seconds, a million thoughts rampaging through my mind, my heart still racing. I said nothing and watched him, however he did not speak.

In a split second, I made a decision. Over my shoulder, I hurled my wine glass into the bushes. It may not have been my best decision, as I flinched at the sound of breaking glass, sobering instantly. I caught the mildly startled but somewhat entertained look on Phil's face as he crossed his arms, regarding me. I could see he was attempting to keep a straight face.

In turn, biting at the inside of my lower lip, I continued to regard him. The moment he went into the powerful stance I had become accustomed to, legs astride, hands low on his hips, it created a magnetic force I had no control over. Without taking my eyes from his, I walked towards him, stopping only centimetres away, close enough to hear his breath. I could not tear my eyes away from his. Seconds ticked by.

My own breath shallow, I stood silent, my heart pounding in my ears.

And then I felt his hands firm on my arms, his touch branding me. Our eyes still locked, my breath became faster. I simply stood. And then he pulled me to him, his strong arms wrapping around me. I let out a mixture of a sigh and moan all in one, as I melted into him, my head going to his chest, my arms reaching around him, feeling his warmth, the very beauty of his body, inhaling his clean masculine scent. His chin rested on my head. Never in my life had I felt so protected and safe. I could have stayed in that cocoon forever.

There was a dawning on me that I *loved* this man. I *truly loved* this man. And I don't think I knew how much until that moment.

Minutes went by and we stayed that way, recognising what we had become to each other. There was such power in his touch that in those few minutes it had become my life force, and I knew I could never live without it.

I wanted to *beg* him not to go. Pulling away slightly, I looked up at him, my eyes searching his. As I was about to open my mouth to speak, he slowly brushed his thumb down between my eyes, and over the bridge of my nose, pausing at my lips. Every part of my body began to vibrate.

Closing my eyes, I put both of my hands around his strong, capable hand and held it firmly to my lips, continuing to breathe him in. As if unable to help himself, he bent down and fastened his pulsating lips over mine. For moments we did not move, as if we were drawing breath from each other, and would not survive if we parted.

The intensity of the moment so potent, I felt myself swooning. As his tongue slowly introduced itself to mine, I could not contain a whimper. He was *the* most delicious tasting thing my mouth had ever had the pleasure of sampling. A feeling of euphoria radiated out from my spine, my skin tingling with a million tiny bubbles of desire.

One of his powerful hands claimed my lower back, gently pulling me towards him, as if we could possibly become closer than what we were. My body arched in a way no amount of yoga could have prepared it for. At that moment, if I could have climbed inside of him, I would have.

His other hand sought out one of mine, the pad of his thumb caressing my palm. Unable to contain myself, I moaned once again. Lifting my hand, he pressed his lips to my palm, before he moved onto every finger. His eyes did not leave my face.

Our trembling fingertips touched, creating such a force of

energy that spoke volumes, without us having to say a word. The eroticness of that alone, so pleasurable, I could have happily died from it.

I didn't know how long we would have stood there, or what other way it may have played out, however, as had happened since I first arrived at Carmody House, nature played a hand. In a theatrical burst, the sky lit up and within seconds a huge surge of thunder cracked overhead, startling us. The trees around us swayed as a westerly gale swept through, madly whipping my hair around my face. In a split second the first rain drops fell. One second later they were pelting.

Although, it was *me* who grabbed Phil's hand to lead him to the garden shed, *he* pulled me to him in a protective embrace, as we ran the short distance, not the first time we had found shelter in this special place.

Sinking back onto the daybed, I kicked off my sandals and loosened the ties on my dress, watching as his eyes never left mine. He leant over me, and I saw raindrops on his cheeks. Reaching up, I kissed them away.

His mouth hungrily finding mine, I unbuttoned his shirt. Kneeling astride me on the bed, he tossed his shirt behind him. Once again we eyed each other, snapshots of moments that would be indelible on my brain forever. Reaching up, our eyes locked, I began to unbutton his jeans, my fingers touching the white elastic band of his jockeys, firm around his hips. The sensitive tips of my fingers brushed at the dark down that trailed from his navel.

And then he exhaled heavily, letting out a breath. His hands steadied mine, and he spoke for the first time, his voice low, almost a whisper. 'I don't have a…'

I struggled to hear him over the din the rain was making on the roof. However I got the gist. Swallowing, I thought quickly of the box of condoms Lou had placed in the drawer of my bedside table. In case of an emergency, she had said.

It took a micro second for me to say, 'It's okay. I know I don't have anything.' Blood tests had been one of the first things I had done once I had found out about the affair.

'Same,' he whispered. I looked at him, and knew right that moment that even if he had some sort of insidious disease, I would have happily died alongside him, something I would have chastised my girlfriends a million times over for thinking.

I placed my hands either side of his face and pulled him to me. Never in my life had I felt so cherished and loved. Once again, I saw his cheeks were wet and it came to me, that it was not the rain.

*

I stirred. The sun was perhaps only minutes off rising but the birds were already up, the chatter of their twittering rousing me. Swallowing, I blinked a few times, bringing my mind up to speed. Realising I was alone did nothing to deter the smile that escaped my lips as a feeling of deliciousness washed over me. Placing a hand to my bruised lips, I stifled a small giggle.

Furtively, as if I needed confirmation, I glanced under the cashmere blanket at my naked body, and then smugly pulled it snug around me once again. For a few minutes, I lay very still, one hand to my still smiling mouth, my eyes darting at nothing in particular.

Going up on one elbow, I looked around the small room. Although the French doors were closed, I was able to make out a small posy of flowers on the mat. Opening my eyes wide, I beamed. I wondered where he was. I hoped he hadn't left. I found my dress and underwear on the floor, and shimmied into them, blushing but smiling all the same, as I noticed a tenderness in certain parts of my body. My hands rapidly fluffed at my hair.

Tentatively, from the doorway, I eagerly took a look outside at the breaking dawn, my hands nervously pressed to my belly. The smell of the overnight rain beckoned like perfume. Walking back over to the daybed, I slipped my sandals on. I picked up the posy from the mat, and slowly made my way across the wet grass towards the pool. Perhaps he was there, attempting to freshen up. I felt a pang of disappointment when I realised he was not. With a smile on my face, I kept looking around as if he might materialise at any moment.

Sitting on the edge of a chair, for some time I stared at nothing in particular, etching every detail from the evening before into my memory bank. *As if I would forget?*

Above the background symphony of bird calls, a kookaburra's laugh shook me from my reverie. Perched close by on the pool fence, we eyed each other. He was close enough for me to see the mottled blue on his wings, and the stripes on his brown eyes. And then he opened his massive beak and once again loudly cackled before taking flight in a flurry of wings. I wondered if he was letting me know more rain was to be coming, or if indeed, he was laughing at me.

And then I glanced around, for the first time taking in the remnants of last night's party.

I didn't wish to, however it finally registered that I needed to stack the chairs, as the hire company would be picking them up along with the tables later that morning. With one hand, I brushed the rain water from one of the seats, noting that the lanterns strung across the pool looked rather bedraggled and sad after last night's storm.

I knew I was doing that thing where I busied my mind, attempting to save it from something I did not want to know.

But sometimes you can't put it off any longer, and as I

glanced around, it finally registered. My eyes flickered to the sun lounge where I had draped the Miss Kitty towel the evening before. Then just as quickly, I glanced away before I looked back once again. The Miss Kitty towel was no more. It was gone.

For a few seconds I had the thought that perhaps last night's storm had blown it from its moorings, although my searching eyes told me differently.

With the colourful posy still clutched in my hand, I lowered myself onto the chair that I had so recently swept the puddle of rain from, tightly crossing my legs. Sitting extremely still, I felt my heartbeat quicken, becoming loud in my ears. I placed a hand to my mouth. My eyes stared at the turquoise pool, watching as a goanna, with an attitude of ownership, took an early morning dip, its tail propelling him forward, prehistoric in its movement. Once to the other side, his clawed feet scrabbled at the coping tile as he adroitly escaped onto the tile surround where he happily basked in the early morning sun, all done as if this was his norm, his pool.

Why was my heart pounding? Why did I feel a sense of embarrassment? *Why?* I scratched at my neck, a sudden feeling of foolishness washing over me. *Oh my God...* he had come back for the towel. *He had not come back for me.*

I had walked towards him. I had taken his hand and pulled him towards the garden shed. He had said 'he didn't have a...' *Of course he didn't have a condom.* He had returned for Sophia's towel and I had seduced him. Quite possibly he could have meant, he didn't have a blue clue what he was doing there with me!

And then I glanced at the posy. Then why did he leave this? For the longest time, unable to move, I sat, and then slowly I made my way back up to the house.

I could not deny the fallout of my divorce had left me scarred. Insecurity raising its head when I least expected it. It would not matter how successful I was in any other part of my life, the fact that my husband had chosen someone who he thought was better than me, someone he had placed before me in our marriage, had placed me last. It was not as if I could get the silver or bronze. In a marriage there are no second places, only winners or losers. These were the thoughts that traversed through my brain as I climbed the stone steps.

Pick me, I wanted to yell. *Pick me.* I wanted the gold. I wanted the first place. And I knew I did not mean Davis!

Chapter 26

Bringing me out of my stupor and back to the present moment, I glanced at Lou as she rested her hand on mine. 'Well Peach I certainly don't understand why Phil was incognito, but surely this is good? Yes?'

Biting my lower lip, I had to search my mind before answering. 'Well...' I swallowed, 'This is good...' Tentatively, I placed a hand on my ever so slightly bulging belly, and then I gave a nervous laugh. 'I cannot believe it.' One of my hands went to my chest. I spoke slowly so I could work it out as I went. 'I think... no... I know the baby part is good,' I tapped my hand on the bench. 'It's great... it's fantastic... it's... unbelievable.' My smile growing bigger by the second, I felt the elation rising up in me, and it was so rapid, I had to take a few deep breaths, as I was completely overwhelmed. 'But the Phil part...' I shrugged, 'it's odd, to say the least.' I shook my head. 'I have gone over it in my mind five thousand times, and it doesn't make any sense. 'Why lie? Why?'

'Who's lying?' Thomas walked in, appearing oblivious to the charged emotion in the room, tipping a white plastic bag full of chocolates across the bench in front of us. 'I go out to get treaties for movie time because you don't have a stash here, or a cupcake in what is normally cupcake heaven, and when I get back you all have faces like someone's murdered someone.' He cocked an already arched brow at us. 'Something happened I need to know?' One by one he looked between us. 'What?'

There was dead silence, but then Lou caved. 'No one's murdered anyone Thomas.' And then she spat it out. 'Peach has just found out she's pregnant to the gardener.'

'*This* Peach?'

'No…' Lou's acerbic tone returned. 'The bloody Peach on *The Bold and The Beautiful.*'

Glancing around at the blackened flat-screen on the wall, Thomas narrowed his eyes. 'I've never seen a Peach on that show. Which one is she?'

'Bloooody hell,' Steve muttered under his breath, looking at the floor with exasperation.

Lou wasn't much better. 'Of course you haven't you numbnut.' Lou had such a way with words. 'OUR Peach is pregnant!'

Quick as a flash, he looked at me, his eyes wide. 'To Daniel Day Lewis?' he asked with absolute astonishment.

Finally losing his cool, Steve's hand came down hard and smacked the bench. 'Who the *fuck* is Daniel Day Lewis?'

Briefly, I closed my eyes. 'Can everyone please settle down? *You* may be in shock, but my shock has overshot the Richter scale. And Steve,' I scratched the side of my face, 'he means Phil.'

Thomas looked at me, his tone was soft and he was beaming. 'Oh my goodness… Peachy… that's wonderful… you're going to be a mummy! Good for you honey! It's what you've always wanted.'

I looked at him and right that second was so grateful he was my friend, my family. My shoulders slackened and I took a deep breath, exhaling noisily. 'Oh Thom… thank you. I guess I am.' I placed one trembling hand to my chest, and the other went to my tummy. *I am going to be a mummy.* How long had I wanted to feel this way? And then I began to cry.

The three of them crowded around me, giving hugs and offering words of comfort. Overwhelmed, I pushed them away. 'I'm okay,' I stressed. 'Shocked, but okay. I can't believe this has happened.' And then once again another surge of emotion overrode me and the tears began.

An hour later found us lolling in different positions on the tobacco coloured leather chesterfields in the library. Chocolate wrappers littered the carpet beside us, coffee mugs had been well drained. The movies selected earlier, now a forgotten pile on the coffee table, life's current events far more riveting.

Lou's feet rested on Marty's lap. He had only arrived ten minutes prior and his face still wore the look of utter shock ours had worn earlier. I watched as his hands intimately massaged the instep of one of Lou's feet. 'A little higher,' she moaned. And then she turned to me, her voice lazy. 'So tell me again... how far along do you think you are?'

I exhaled, my fingers lazily combing through Wilbur's fur. 'Well... as I said before, I guess I must be about eleven weeks.'

'Bloody hell! And you had no idea?'

'I've already told you a dozen times, no... none. I *just* didn't expect it.' I attempted to explain. 'Think about how long Davis and I were trying with no luck. Because of that, and the fact of my age and the stats... believe me, I know them well.' I sighed. 'At 36, I have a fifty five per cent chance of falling pregnant over a one year period. Anyway, with those odds and my history, I got it into my head that falling pregnant was not going to be an easy thing for me...'

'Yeah but you did have assistance... Phil,' Thomas chimed in. 'Lucky, lucky girl. I'm as envious as hell.'

Sitting up in a hurry, Steve chided, his tone sharp, 'Hellooo does he realise I am actually in the room?' We all laughed at the two of them, shaking our heads. I was glad the attention was off me even for a few seconds. They wanted answers, ones I needed to think about.

'Those odds aren't too bad Peach,' Marty silent until now, added.

My voice was small. 'Yes... but I guess I did not expect it to happen that one and only time.'

'So what happened...?' Typical Lou, she had to know the nitty gritty. 'I mean with those stats and using condoms, what are the chances?' She sat up and faced me.

I sank further back into the cushions around me, feeling rather small. My voice was lower still. 'We didn't use anything.' I felt all eyes flash towards me as if I had committed the worst possible crime. Russian roulette was what I might have called it myself.

'Nothing!' Lou said, her tone incredulous, her eyebrows nearly leaping off her face. 'You mean nothing, *nothing*?'

'Nothing,' I replied, avoiding hers and everybody else's eyes.

'Do you realise this means you have slept with at least the last ten women he has slept with? And *you're* the sensible one... if this was *me*, I know what *you'd* say.'

I had absolutely not one single excuse. I could hardly tell them that the way I felt that night, if he'd had a terminal disease I would have been happy to die with him. Irrational, stupid and dangerous were some of the words that came to mind. But then again, if it was so stupid, would I be sitting here now pregnant, with a very wanted tiny person, all of my own, growing inside of me. And there was that glow again, one I had never felt until now. *Hello baby!*

However, the ever persistent Lou interrupted my thoughts. 'I *even* bought you a box of condoms before you went out on that dinner for six, just in case. And do you know what you said? You said,' and she did a wonderful imitation of me, when I was doing my prissy tone, *I think I can organise my own thank you very much.* In fact you were quite curt to me. What happened to those ones?'

Before I had a chance to answer, Marty cut in. 'Yes, but that's hardly the point right now, is it Lou? By the looks of things Peach is quite happy for this to have happened.'

'Yes, but it could have been a different story,' Lou admonished, arms folded across her chest.

'But it's not Lou. This is what it is,' Marty gently chided. Grateful to him, I gave him a small smile. In return he winked. I had always been able to rely on him to back me up, and I was glad to see that had not changed. And I could not deny, that there was a small part of me that registered that Lou was enjoying the fact that I was not the perfect sister for a change.

'I'll be back in a minute.' Stepping over Wilbur, I excused myself as I made my way to the bathroom, now fully understanding this sudden urge to pee all the time.

Panties around my ankles, I stayed sitting on the on the toilet much longer than was necessary, grateful for the peace. In the last hour, I'd had not one moment to myself to think.

With everyone talking about Phil, it had created a ceaseless current of *Phil quotes* and *Phil images* cursing through my mind. From the time he had left, I had mourned his lack of presence, and the life I'd had for the past ten months. A life, where I had woken each morning with glee and enthusiasm for the day, quite oblivious to the fact that it was centred on sharing it with someone so likeminded, and someone that I had been gradually falling in love with. But that was all a lie, a sham… and it had left me feeling like nothing more than a… I hate to say it… *loser*… one of those desperate women who make things up in their minds.

But then this… *a baby!* And the glow came again. *My own baby!* Maybe Phil was never meant to be in my life for long. Maybe he was just meant to give me this gift. This truly beautiful gift. One I would sacrifice everything for.

Standing in front of the mirror side on, I held my dress up and examined my stomach, a tiny podge, the type that could have easily been one too many cupcakes. The cutest little tiny podge ever. Well, it certainly explained my over enthusiastic breasts, that was for sure. Hand to my mouth, I shook my head, thinking I could not believe it.

A hammering on the door startled me. 'Peach, you okay?' It was Steve.

'Yes lovey.' I opened the door.

'I've been sent to get you,' he explained, leaning up against the wall opposite, his demeanour quite calm. I could well imagine the talk that must have gone on when I had left the room. With a flick of his head, he suggested, 'Come for a walk.'

Glad for a reprieve from the ceaseless questioning, I followed him down the hallway, stopping only to slide my feet into shoes at the door. Wilbur hearing the click of the lock, raced to join us. 'Back soon,' Steve called, quickly pulling the front door closed behind us, not giving anyone a chance to respond.

I put a hand up to shade my face from the sudden glare. At this time of year I would have expected no less, however everything appeared brighter than what it had been of late, colours more intense, the leaves greener, and flowers almost carrying a neon hue. My eyes zeroed in on fat bees drowsy with pollen, their buzz a wonderful symphony to my ears. A myriad of different coloured butterflies danced daintily across flower beds. Wherever I looked beauty greeted me. The thought that perhaps of late, I had been looking at life through sepia coloured glasses, crossed my mind.

I caught up to Steve. In tune with each other, we strolled the garden, walking in silence for some time before eventually we found ourselves in the walled garden with its deliciously perfumed hedge. With some surprise, I glanced around at the Fairy Magnolia Blushes Phil had planted some time back. Although the pretty lilac-pink flowers had blossomed *en masse* in early spring, it had amazed me that they had continued to flower profusely for months on end, their fragrant heads at least six centimetres in diameter. And today they offered no less, as if in celebration, showcasing themselves in all their beauty. Their large glossy dark green leaves creating the perfect backdrop for such pretty flowers.

My thoughts turned to the day at the nursery when Phil and I had gone to select the Fairy Magnolias. The day I had run into Davis and… Felicity … hmmm when did that name become a little easier to say… and witnessed the fact she was pregnant, carrying his child. Although a nightmare for me at the time, it had turned out to be a pivotal moment, a mark in the sand. It had freed me to move forward with my life, a life I had created with the best of me.

But who could have guessed that life would turn around so quickly from that point, and I would end up the one pregnant? *Me… pregnant… a baby of my own… unbelievable…* and there was that beautiful glow once again, and I found myself overwhelmed, placing a shaky hand to my mouth covering my smile.

We sat for some time, saying nothing. I appreciated Steve was giving me time out from the others to sort my thoughts.

'The Fairy Magnolia Blushes are doing well,' eventually I said, as though looking for something to say.

Propped on the teak bench, legs out in front, arms folded, Steve nodded. 'So you're happy babe?'

I nodded, and once again placed a trembling hand to my beaming mouth. 'Rather bamboozled but I'm happy… yes I am.'

'Right, well I want to know what your plans are for the B&B? We're about to send out media releases you realise?' Typical of Steve, he was always wearing his business head.

I sighed and propped myself next to him, tapping my top lip with my forefinger. 'Gosh I don't know.' I folded my arms across my chest. 'I mean… I haven't had time to give this thought.' And then I turned to him, my voice rising. 'Good lord Steve, what am I going to do? I can't open a B&B and have a new baby crying. That would be welcoming.'

'I'll get the team to put a hold on the releases for a few weeks, that will give you time to think.' He paused.

'Good thinking, thanks.' I sat back, crossed my legs and glanced around once again.

'Can I ask you something babe?'

I looked at him, wondering what was to come next. His eyes narrowed. 'Did you ever really plan on opening a B&B?'

I was taken aback by his question. 'What a strange thing to ask me. Of course I did!' Standing, I began to walk around the enclosed garden, searching for an answer to his question. I spun back to him. 'What else was I going to do here for goodness sake?'

'The thing is Peach, for quite some time, you have been saying one thing but acting another. Do you realise that?' His voice was matter of fact.

I flashed him a look. 'I really don't know what you mean, because I *always* saw Carmody House filled with people. That has always been my plan.'

'Perhaps they'll be your people. You'll make them.' And then he stood. 'Come on, the others will be wondering where we are.' He began to head back, and for a few seconds I watched his retreating back, pondering exactly what he was saying. I shook my head to clear it, and then followed him, taking my time.

*

By the time I went inside, Steve was already ensconced back in the library. One boot clad foot resting on his knee, and arms, with biceps most men would envy, spread along the back of the lounge. It struck me that if you didn't know him, it would take time to work out that this man was gay. He carried a very strong aura of masculinity about him. He was talking to Marty who was leaning forward, hands together, outlining some business proposal.

I went in search of Thomas and Lou. I found them in the kitchen, my laptop was open. They caught my look as I raised my brows in question.

'We've Googled him!' they spoke in unison, then looked at each other and began laughing like two naughty children. I was glad *they* found this amusing.

Pretending to fan herself with her hand, Lou quipped, 'Phew baby… if only we had known who he was.'

Leaning between them, I closed the laptop. 'That's enough for now.'

'Hey…' Thomas was entirely put out, '… what do you think God made Google for?' With folded arms, he leant back against the cupboards and looked at me. 'I cannot believe it took you so long to Google him?'

Before I could answer, Lou cut in. 'What a catch! Ooh baby!'

'I'll say! Actually I have always said,' Thomas told us with a knowing look on his face. I could not help but think that Thomas was entirely different to Steve. You would know he was gay upon the first second of meeting him. In fact he once told me, he knew the moment he was born. I didn't doubt that.

Thomas lowered his voice in a conspiratorial way. His eyes glanced towards the library where Steve was, 'Personally… I found your gardener *very* attractive.'

'It seems you weren't the only one,' Lou laughed, looking at me. 'Mind you sis, I actually said that to you a few times and you fobbed me off. I stand by my earlier statement… *what a catch!*'

My words when I spoke them were precise. 'He is not a catch Lou. He's an enigma, a paradox, a conundrum, an oxymoron… do you get it?' My eyes bored into her.

Lou's face wore a puzzled look. 'Ah no…' She shook her head.

'Me neither!' Thomas chimed in.

I stared back at the two of them, my voice was firm. 'He was someone who was passing through. He left me a gift. It's completely welcome, but that's as far as it goes.' I looked at them for understanding.

'That's a bit harsh!' Thomas told me, wearing a look of offence.

'You want to hear something harsh. Here it is… the guy is a liar!'

'Oh!' Looking taken aback, Thomas pouted and opened his eyes wide.

'Well he didn't exactly lie, did he?' Lou asked. 'Wasn't it more the fact he omitted stuff?'

'Listen, if you remember correctly I was married to a guy who omitted stuff. I *aint doin* it again!' I stared them down. Both wore looks of confusion as if they were Phil's strongest allies. My voice softened. 'Look the guy is not interested in me, and I sure as hell do not know who the heck *he* is.'

'But it's all there,' Lou pointed to the laptop, her reasoning so simple.

I looked at her, taking my time in answering. 'I can understand why he didn't say anything in the beginning. It makes sense. His wife had died, he needed to get away. This,' I waved my hands around me towards the garden, 'was all serendipitous. I understand that too… but at the end… he said *nothing*… not a word… not one *single* word… *oh come on.*' I looked between them. Lou stood with one hand on her hip, attempting to think up something to say. Thomas still leant against the cupboards, arms crossed, lips pursed, he too struggling for a thought. My voice softened. 'Look guys… after what happened on that night I have had to realise that the man was not interested in *me.*'

'That may be the case, but you still need to tell him about the baby,' from behind me, Steve's voice rang out loud and clear.

I turned to see Steve and Marty both standing in the doorway. At some stage my voice must have been raised and they had come to see what was going on. I attempted to speak but stopped, my brain feeling more bewildered than ever. Pulling a stool out, I perched on the edge of it, resting my head in my hands. For the longest time no one made a sound. I felt Lou place her arm around me. I looked up.

'There's been a lot to take in today. I am still coming to terms that…' and then my voice raced spilling out the next few words, '… I-am-going-to-have-a-baby. Phew! If you don't mind, I think I'll sleep on the telling Phil part.' I noticed each one nodding their heads in agreement.

'Well I think we should open a bottle of champagne in celebration,' Steve offered.

I gave a weary smile. 'Sounds great… but in case you haven't noticed, I am pregnant, and therefore not drinking!' I watched as their smiles faded. And then I laughed. 'But if I know you lot, that's hardly going to stop you.'

'You're right as usual!' Thomas quipped, 'However, as you are with child, nothing but sparkling water for you my dear.'

Chapter 27

Every time the thought crossed my mind that I was actually having a baby, a feeling of intense elation rose up in me, and I could feel myself literally beaming and, all 157 centimeters of me, standing much taller, perhaps even reaching 158 for the first time without heels. However, every time I thought of telling Phil, it died down again, and I would bend forward and nervously clutch my stomach. I ricocheted... baby and Phil... Phil and baby!

Standing at the top of the bedroom stairs, I peered into the little room opposite, imagining how I would furnish it, but most of all, imagining a little part of me, dressed in a white towelling grow-suit, standing in its cot, calling out in the early morning, and my heart would melt. To then sitting at the bottom of the stairs, imagining saying the actual words to Phil, and my heart would sink. I didn't even want to imagine it.

I tried to convince myself that he had been sent to Carmody House for a purpose, and the baby was that purpose. And then I would go back to dreaming about the baby, and my spirits would rise once again. In between, I made plenty of bathroom trips, and occasionally felt ill or exhausted, sometimes both at the same time, although now I understood why.

It was no surprise when at ten past ten Lou dropped by. I'd been watching the clock since ten on the dot, expecting her and her one hundred questions any minute. It was one of those times, when I wished I had never given her the code to the front gate, or any family member for that matter.

'So where are you off to?' I asked from my perch at the top of the stairs, attempting to waylay the baby talk for as long as possible.

She peered up at me. 'I've got a shoot at *Blow* hair salon.'

'Hmmm... *Blow* hey? Well, I wouldn't tell Thomas if I was you. He's so competitive, and *Blow*'s been getting a huge amount of press lately.'

'Actually Thomas put me onto them. Seems he knows the owner. Have you *seen* that guy? What a hotie! He's enough to make me change hairdressers, wrath from Thomas or not!'

I shook my head at her. She may have been maturing of late, but Lou would always be Lou.

'It's great you've got plenty of work on.' I was still buying time. After all, what could I tell her? I didn't have answers myself.

Perching a couple of steps lower than me, she wrapped her arms around her legs and looked up. 'Peach...' I noticed the change in her tone, and her brow furrowed. 'Don't be annoyed with me for asking... but I can't figure out how you weren't aware you were pregnant when you are this far along?'

I didn't blame her for asking. I exhaled heavily. 'I've been wondering the same thing myself.' I tapped my top lip with my index finger as I thought. 'I've definitely had two periods, although when I think about it, they were fairly light. I guess because I have been feeling so poorly, I didn't think much of it.'

Looking perplexed, Lou raised her brows. 'Hmmm... I've heard of women still getting their period when they're pregnant.'

'Odd isn't it. In the past when I have heard of someone not knowing they were pregnant, I've wondered what planet they were on. But Lou the truth is I didn't!' We continued to stare at each other. 'In any case, we shouldn't jump the gun, I've got another six days to go before I'm twelve weeks, and I daresay a visit to the doctors would be wise, amongst a million other things.'

'Okay… well there is something else.' And she leant towards me, her voice lowered. 'I need details.'

'Huh?'

'Details of that night.' Meaning business, she folded her arms across her chest. 'Tell me everything. Spare me nothing.'

'Lou…' I pointed to the front door. 'Go… now!'

*

Back at the top of the stairs, I once again peered into the tiny room. I had always wondered what I would use this room for. It appears to have been waiting just for this. Needing to clear my head, I went down the stairs, and this time instead of sitting at the bottom wondering what Phil would say, I put my gumboots on and went into the garden, wandering for some time, until I found myself down at the garden shed.

Lost in thought, I perched on the day bed, looking out but not seeing. And then I noticed a vision of white, dreamily crossing the lawn.

'Bea… what are you doing here?' No sooner were the words out of my mouth, when I realised Lou must have had a hand in this. I could not deny she was finally enjoying being the holier than though sister.

Surprising me, Bea opened her arms to me. I felt her press her lips to my forehead and she smoothed my hair away from my face. For a moment I felt like a small child, Bea's touch comforting. The thought that it was never too late to be the parent a child wanted crossed my mind.

Exhaling, I pulled away and looked at my mother.

'So?' was all she said, her face a little wistful, her sparkly blue eyes searching mine.

Shrugging, I walked over to the French doors. My back to her, I glanced out over the garden towards the river. 'You were right when you said you could imagine wonderful creations taking place here Mum. Not quite what you meant though, was it?' I turned in time to see her smile and raise her perfectly pencilled brows.

'Who knows what I meant?' Her voice was kind, and I was indeed grateful.

Uncertain of what to say, I folded my arms and studied the blank canvases still stacked against one wall. 'I haven't even begun to paint yet.'

'You've got all the time in the world, however *mon cherie* it does appear you are going to be fairly busy for some time.' Of late it had become apparent that Bea had begun to slip French words into her vocabulary. It more than likely had to do with the fact that ever since our trip to Papa's chateau in Provence, she had now decided to divide her time between there and here. Her reasoning was, that as in her youth, she found the light for painting far more beautiful. However something she had recently said, made me wonder if perhaps Provence also held a romantic interest.

Perching herself elegantly on the daybed, her back upright, she crossed her legs and patted the place beside her, encouraging me to sit. 'I take it this is what you want?'

Without saying a word, I nodded.

'*Parfait!* And you've told him?'

I could see Lou had wasted no time filling her in on who *he* was. 'I'm giving thought to it.'

'Well whatever you decide, your father and I will be here.' Strong words for Bea, as I knew she was leaving for Provence the very next day.

However I was more surprised that Johnny knew. 'Dad knows already?'

'Yes, we spoke this morning. He said to tell you he'll pop by later, and that he would be *abso-bloody-lutely* supportive.'

We both gave a half-hearted laugh, fondly shaking our heads. Bea continued, 'This is *your* time Peach.'

I was grateful for the simplicity of her words, and not a barrage of questions, which thankfully had never been her style, unlike Lou's. We were both quiet for a while with our own thoughts, until I broke the silence. 'I keep thinking of how young you were when you found out you were having me all on your own in France. You didn't even have any family support, and let's face it, you'd hardly known Papa a long time.'

Her face softened and her lips turned up. 'You do not have to be with someone long to know they're your soul mate. Whatever happened after that, I knew you had a good father in Alexandre, and I felt the same with Johnny. You cannot give a child more than that.' And then she slipped the next question in perfectly. 'You will tell him, *non?*'

Shrugging, I shook my head, confused, my voice was almost a whisper. 'I don't know.'

'Is he not a good father already?'

Boy, Lou really did a good job on filling her in on every detail. 'Yes... that's not it. The thing is, the guy is not interested in me. I had thought he was, but I was obviously wrong. That's it.' My tone had become matter-of-fact. 'Nothing else to say.'

Bea stood, making a move to leave. 'Perhaps when the time is right?'

'Perhaps Mother.'

'Meanwhile it is good news.'

*

'Don't get up honey-bun.' Through the sound of my relaxation yogic music I heard Johnny's voice.

From my position on the rug in the library, I lazily lifted one corner of the cold eye compress. After my chat with my mother earlier, Johnny's presence had not surprised me. From the time I had woken, I knew I would be in for a slew of visitors, all the ones with the code to the gate that is.

'Sorry Dad. I didn't hear you,' I explained as I rose to a seated position. I watched as he gave a brief look around, his eyes settling on the oil burner, from where peppermint, lemongrass and eucalyptus essential oils permeated the air.

'Mmmm' He smiled, plonking himself on the chesterfield. 'Smells like a massage parlour lovey.'

Surprised, I cocked my head and narrowed my eyes. 'Ummm… Dad, do you mean a day spa?'

He shrugged. 'Same thing!'

'Uh…' I gave a small chuckle, 'no they're not.' It was at that moment, where I saw how wide the gulf between Bea and Johnny actually was. Both had a different understanding of life, a different ethos, and a different way they wished to live. Bea would probably always be an enigma to him. And in turn, she probably required someone who understood her idiosyncrasies. It came to me that she probably did well to stay with him as long as she did.

Johnny broke into my thoughts. 'You know Peachy, it may look like it, but I don't have all the answers. I know I don't have to tell you that you can spend far too much of your life wishing for stuff that may never happen: wanting the perfect family, and all the traditions, and expectations that go along with it. But when all is said and done, that isn't what's important. It's the people you hold in your heart, that's what's most important. So you hold onto your baby. You hold on tight. It's your little family. Okay?'

I nodded at him, wondering where he was going with this.

'When your mum and I got together, I always thought I got two for the price of one.' His emotionally charged voice was not hard to miss. He kissed the top of my head. Both of us were unable to speak for the longest time.

'I told myself I would be the best father…'

'And you have been…' I eyed him, wondering what was to come.

'And then Lou came along and I had both of you. I was one lucky man.' I watched as Johnny stood and began to wander, picking things up, putting them down again, not really looking at them. 'Just before we found out your mum was having Lou, your mum was talking about returning to France. At the time, she seemed to think she may be happier there. When she found out she was pregnant, all of that changed. And I am glad it did. Your mum and I were never meant to run the full course, but we both were meant to have you two girls. That was not up to anyone else to decide but us.' He looked at me to see if I understood. 'When your… when Alexandre came back into the picture, I was worried he'd hurt you, and I wanted to knock his bloody block off. But he was your father and that was that. I never denied you that Peach. You always had to know where you came from.'

Slowly, I nodded, 'I know that Dad. But by then *you* were my dad.'

'Sure, I know. But you can't deny people who they really are, no matter how much you love them, want to protect them or even if you are afraid of losing them…'

'Dad…' He was such a good man, I felt myself choke up, tears being so readily available these days.

He stuck his hands in his front pockets, and I could see this was really raw for him. 'I'm just saying that people have a right to know. As your dad, it's my job to tell you this stuff, okay?'

This time I rested my chin on one hand, and with fatigue like I had never experienced, slowly nodded.

Once again Johnny kissed the top of my head, and told me

he loved me. He attempted to press fifty dollars into my hand. 'Buy the baby something will you, a little pressie from me.' I knew it futile to argue.

As he began towards the front door, I called to him. 'Dad!'

He turned, a look of expectation written across his face.

'You are the best dad ever.'

'Thanks Honey.' There had not been one word of *ab-so-bloody-lutely* mentioned, so I knew he had chosen his words carefully, words I knew required my careful consideration.

*

'I haven't told anyone this before, but a few years ago, I got a call from a seventeen year old boy. He said I was his father.'

In a microsecond, I halted mid-stir of the vegetable soup I was cooking. In absolute miscomprehension, I looked at Steve. 'What?' Could this day get any stranger? I sighed, turned the gas down and then perched myself on a stool, ready to hear an explanation.

He snuffed. 'Bit of a surprise isn't it?' Still dumbfounded, I stared at him, as he propped himself on the arm of the sofa. 'I didn't come out until after I had left school.' He shrugged. 'When I was in year 11, a group of us went to New Zealand with the local rugby club. A mate and I hooked up with a couple of older girls. I was always a solid build so I guess I looked older. My mate went off with one girl and under duress, I went with the other.' He shrugged. 'What can I say? It was brief, foreign and wrong, and at the time, left me in absolutely no doubt of where my future lay. I came back to Australia and that was it. Until that phone call…'

Brows furrowed, I couldn't help but interrupt. 'Why didn't she try to track you down at the time?' One of my fingers made its way between my brows and began to massage the tension away.

'The fact I was sixteen and she was twenty two at the time, what was she going to do? Take my pocket money off me? It was a ten second thing. I could barely remember what she looked like.'

I was still confused, and scratched my forehead. 'Why don't I know this?'

'Because in the end, I wasn't his dad. I was not the right blood type.' He sighed.

My body gave a voluntary collapse back on the stool. 'Oh!'

'Yep, but do you know what I remember most about that time? It was the fact that in the end I was actually disappointed. I had begun to like what I knew about the kid, and I had the chance of being his old man. Had I been, I would have been let down to have missed so many years of his life.'

I was pensive for a while. 'I don't think I have ever asked if you and Thomas wanted to have children. I'm sorry Steve. That was selfish of me.'

Steve folded his arms, and looked away from me. 'Thomas and I have *never* discussed it?'

'What? How could you not? Particularly after that story.'

He glanced back at me. His eyes direct. 'Look Peach, I've been a rugby player, and I sure as heck do not want my son on that field while his poof parents stand on the sideline. I wouldn't do it to him.'

'Yeah but that's *you*... what about Thom?'

'It has never come up and I sure as heck am not bringing it up.'

'It's *never* come up?'

'I don't think Thom would want to hear my answer.'

'So you do think he'd like a baby?'

He shrugged. 'He might. But I stand firmly by my belief.'

'But you guys would make great parents. You both have

so much love.' I could see by the look on Steve's face that the subject was now closed. In any case, I was well beyond exhausted. I narrowed my eyes. 'Thank you for sharing that with me. But why now?'

'The baby's father always deserves to know. It's the right thing.'

My legs crossed, I wrapped them even further around me, and folded my arms. Looking at the ground, wearily I nodded.

*

Once again left to our own devices, I glanced down at Wilbur who was pretending to slumber at my feet. Feeling my eyes upon him, he hazarded a glance, opening only one eye in question.

'In the last ten hours you have heard everyone's opinions, so now I am expecting you to summarise and give me an honest answer based on the facts.'

The poor dog opened his other eye in fright, and then closed both of them just as quickly. His brief look read *Don't drag me into it! I'm just the dog!*

*

Blearily, I squinted at the clock on the bedside table. 'Marty! Hello. No… you didn't wake me,' I lied, my words thick with sleep. By the looks of things, I had only been asleep for thirty minutes. 'I was tired.' And then I attempted a joke. 'A lot has being going on in the last few days in case you haven't noticed.' I gave in to a yawn. 'What's up love?' Briefly, I listened to my loyal friend on the other end of the phone.

'You what… Oh thank you. I needed to hear that. Thanks Lovey… speak tomorrow.'

I placed the phone back in its holder. One sentence… that's all he said. *I am extremely happy for you. I will support all of your decisions.* Actually that was two sentences, but they were short.

Lying on my back in the dark, I pulled the sheet up around my chin, staring at the ceiling. A hand rested low on my belly. *Hello little baby!* Apparently at eleven weeks my baby would already be five centimetres. *Five centimetres.* With me no more the wiser, the little darling had begun to grow.

In the dark, I reached for the rose quartz crystal on my bedside, clutching the cool smooth stone in one hand, keen to surround the baby with as much love as humanly possible. *Can you feel it,* I asked, as my heart radiated a direct white light down to my abdomen.

Yawning, I rolled on my side, keen for the following morning's visit to the obstetrician. I had been lucky and gotten in on a cancellation.

Chapter 28

Small, cramped and cluttered, *Café Bouquiniste* consisted of one tiny room, two bay window seats, a few ad-libbed tables, and a coffee machine. The bohemian cafe embraced New Farm's free spirited milieu, with its mismatched furniture, overflowing bookshelves and crammed with curiosities. I loved it! The complete opposite of New Farm's buzzy café culture, there was something about the cosy quaint charm of the café, which somehow reminded me of Nan's and Pop's home in Tasmania.

Not far from home, it was the place where during the renovations, on the days when one thousand questions were being asked of me, I could briefly escape to. Fortified by not only the coffee, but the peace and quiet, I would return all the better for it.

That morning, in need of a cosy environment, I had deliberately suggested the eccentric café for breakfast to Lou, Marty, Thomas and Steve. We had no sooner taken up residence at the only four seater table, dragging an extra chair up for Steve, who was still to join us, when the bearded barista greeted me. 'Hey Peach, your regular today?'

Knowing full well Lou thought me a recluse these days, I delighted in the look of surprise she shot me. Ignoring her, I called the young barista by name. 'Perfect Jackson. Plus…' with no need to look at the menu, I revelled in taking ownership of the little café. 'I think I'll have the *Bouqui Breakie* as well this morning. I was going to have the savoury mince, but hmmm no… the *Bouqui Breakie* always wins.'

Surreptitiously, and with a certain amount of smugness, I caught all three with bafflement written right across their faces, glancing at me in wonder. Keen to show that they did not know *absolutely* everything about me, I continued on. 'I hope Meredith still has some of that raspberry yogurt cake that I love?'

Leaving the others to peruse the small menu, my right hand felt around for the rose quartz crystal I had earlier placed in one of my pockets. Weighing it in my hand, I began to jiggle it. The evening before, out of curiosity, I had Googled 'healing properties of rose quartz crystals'. Four words leapt off the page at me... *Fertility, conception, pregnancy and childbirth! UN...BELIEVABLE!* Who on earth, would have possibly thought?

Returning it to the safely of my pocket, I zoned back in to the conversation at the table. My intention had been to wait until everyone was present, although before I knew it, I burst out, my voice louder than necessary. 'Okay...' I said, giving a small cough to clear my throat. Lou, Marty and Thomas stopped talking, and turned to me, their eyes questioning. As if laying down a deck of cards, I placed my splayed hands upon the table in front of me, and spoke precisely. 'I have decided to go to Melbourne.'

I was now sixteen weeks pregnant, and if you looked closely enough it was clear to see my belly was beginning to look like a baby bump, rather than a food paunch.

As if by mutual agreement, all four had all stoped badgering me a couple of weeks earlier, and were allowing me to come to my own decision regarding Phil. I guess the fact I had paid Emerald Green another visit pleased them.

There was dead silence and then Thomas jumped in, clapping his hands. 'You're going to tell Phil. Good decision Sweetie!'

Lou pulled out her iPhone and was scrolling through her diary. 'What about this Friday? Mitch will have the kids, and we can all stay the weekend.' She turned to Marty. 'We don't have anything on do we?'

Before Marty could answer, Thomas cut in. 'I'll have to check with Steve, but we could come down on the Friday night. I could do with a Saturday off, can't remember the last one I had.'

I shook my head, and placed my joined hands between my thighs, sitting up straight. Although my voice was quiet, it was firm. 'Sorry guys. Please don't think me ungrateful but… I have to do this myself.' I glanced between each of them, gauging the look on their faces. Before anyone could say a word, the front door was flung open, letting in the noise of the traffic in busy Merthyr Road, before being closed again, locking us back into our cosy world. With a brief glance around, Steve slid into the chair next to Thomas.

Thomas wasted no time. 'She's going to tell him,' his voice carried an air of authority, as if he been responsible for my decision.

With a curt nod of his head, Steve responded, his voice matter-of-fact, 'Fair enough!' And then he winked at me.

And all I could think was I hoped I *had* made the right decision.

*

From across the road, I took in the signage, discreetly etched on the not so discreet, oxidised copper, oversized double doors, *Fields of Dreams Landscapers, Designers and Planners*. As if it would give me more of an insight into Phil, I stood there examining the contemporary two story building.

A lusciously green two-metre-wide verdant living wall took precedence over the signage, running up the entire left hand side of the building and across the top, softening the exterior, and instantly giving a feeling of coolness.

To the right, on a slightly lower level, was a glassed in pod, which I took to be a boardroom, as from where I stood, I was able to see people beginning to gather around a large timber table. My eyes scanned, searching for Phil, and I felt my heart rate quicken even more so. However, as I watched, I was taken aback when suddenly the clear glass turned opaque, and I could see no more.

Procrastinating, I exhaled heavily, and scratched the back of my neck. I felt there was no right way to do this, and I did hope that I had made the correct choice in coming to see him. At the time of making my decision, I sensed that seeing him in person, as the real PK Hunter would make it easier. He would not be the person I wanted him to be, and it would simply be the courteous thing to do. I was uncertain of what that would mean, however at least I could move forward without thinking of it again, knowing I had done the right thing.

For some odd reason my mind turned to *The Way We Were*. I knew damn well I would not be asking Phil to stay with me until the baby was born, like Barbra Streisand had done with Robert Redford, nor would I be smoothing his hair across his forehead… for many reasons, although the fact that his hair was too damn short was a good one. However, I could envision that scene where years later, I run into Phil and he asks how *she* is, and if my husband is a good father to *her*. Mind you, I look pretty damn good in that scene as well. And then I snorted. I might just have a boy and that would throw everything into disarray! I had to stop romanticising. It was what it was, and that was it!

Deliberating long enough, I removed the almost chewed off finger nail from my lips, took a deep breath, and ran my hand over my empire styled dress. A dull silver background, embellished with huge tea-rose coloured cabbage roses on, the round necked dress, along with the fitted bodice that ended just below my breasts before flaring out, gave away nothing, except the fact that my breasts were indeed rather luscious.

Shoulders squared, I crossed the road, briefly catching sight of myself in a window. I stood a little taller, and touched the small silk rose that was attached to a clip, securing my fringe to the side. I hoped it wasn't too much. When Thomas had dropped me at the airport, he had told me I looked very pretty. I guess that was the look you'd want when you are about to tell someone he is the father of your unborn child.

But then I chastised myself. What did it matter how I looked? I had only one purpose, and then I'd be gone. End of story!

Out of habit, I fluffed at my curls. Tentatively, I pushed one of the large copper doors opened. My heart in my mouth, I entered a reception area. Edgy in design, it had a certain minimalism about it. Seated at a glass desk was a young woman frantically manning phones. Behind her, laser-cut copper screens divided a large area into work stations.

The girl on the phone gave me a friendly glance of greeting, motioning for me to take a seat.

Briefly, I looked around at the low white seats that looked like hard marshmallows, with dents in them for bottoms to sit upon. As there were already five other people waiting, I took the last available marshmallow closest to the desk. Surprisingly, it was more comfortable than what it had looked.

Crossing my legs, I couldn't help but take note of my Miss Dior blush-toned patent peeptoes. That morning… who am I kidding, I planned it a week ago… it had been a pleasure to unearth my lovely old friends and team them with my pretty dress.

And then the thought crossed my mind that, no doubt, I

did indeed look very different to the other people waiting. All were dressed in black, sporting varying degrees of edgy haircuts, and no, they were not clutching dusty-rose Mark Jacobs handbags, with a pink quartz crystal secreted in the pocket, they carried portfolios. No doubt they were there for a job interview. By the way a couple of them repeatedly glanced at their watches, I had no doubt the interviews were running late.

Once again, I wondered how this was going to work. *What was* my plan again? What if Phil came out of his office and saw me, but had to interview all of these people first? Or he could see me, but could only spare three minutes? Maybe I would have to wait half the day? Maybe I should have phoned first? Maybe I should have set up an appointment? Maybe a lot of things!

Before the receptionist could finish her call, another line began to ring. Glancing around at us, she raised her eyes to the heavens, mouthed an apology before quickly finishing, and taking the next call.

And then the copper door was flung open. A woman in her late thirties breezily entered. It wasn't hard for me to recognise her as the general manager, Morag Freeman. I had seen her picture on the website. After all… I had glanced at it once or twice! I almost raised a hand in greeting, before reminding myself that I actually did not know her.

'I'm here,' she appeared to announce to all and sundry. She stopped at the desk waiting for the younger woman to finish on the phone.

'Thank God you are here!' The younger woman spoke with some relief. 'Did PK say what was wrong with her?'

'Infected sinuses, poor little love.' Although they both spoke in hushed tones, because of my close proximity, I could still make out what they were saying.

'Hasn't she had that before?'

Morag frowned thoughtfully, tucking a long strand of dead-straight blonde hair behind one ear. 'Hmmm I think so... PK said it can be common because of her tiny passages. Anyway, sounds like the poor little love will be discharged later today.' She leant across the younger woman peering at the computer screen. 'PK said he'll work from home for the next few days. So cancel everything for him today. I've got a 3.30 free so if you can reschedule them, I can see the guys from the Cairns project then. If they want to speak to PK directly, we can conference call him. Hopefully they'll understand.'

'Frank called from the school. Said he couldn't get onto PK. I think there's an issue with one of the boys. I explained the situation and he said not to bother him. What do you think?'

Morag put a hand on her hip, and her tone carried an air of annoyance. 'What I think is that there is always going to be dramas up at that school. So *what's* new?' Her brows shot skyward. 'However... as with everything, PK likes to keep on top of it. Best send him an email and he can decide. You know what he's like.' And then she frowned. 'I hope he's available later in the week for the Moroney meeting. He *cannot* miss that one. And this thing in Fiji... it's a big deal. It's been on hold long enough.'

'Don't think there are enough hours in the day as far as the boss is concerned. When do you think he sleeps?'

'Didn't you know... he doesn't! That's why we get all those emails at all hours of the night.' She attempted to walk away but swung back. 'I've just remembered, the photographer from Belle will want to shoot those stills. Ring her... say whatever you have to. Buy PK some time.'

Listening to these two discuss PK, sounded like another

person entirely from the Phil I had known. For the life of me, I was having trouble putting the two of them together.

I glanced back up at them once again as another man appeared from behind. 'Morag, is he coming or not?' His tone was impatient. 'I thought we were having a team meeting to discuss the Collins Street project.' And then he turned around to speak to a younger man scurrying behind. 'Duffy can you get the drawings of the vertical garden off my desk? And also ask Sue if she has the plant schedule PK requested. He's been all over this one like a man possessed.'

'Sophia's been in hospital overnight. Sinus's again,' Morag explained to him.

'Oops…' was all he said, but his face said a lot more. He spun on his heels but then equally as quickly, turned back. 'Will he make the presentation on Thursday?'

'Fingers crossed.'

Shaking his head, he began to walk away. It was not hard to hear him mutter. 'Something's got to give…'

Morag called after him, 'Wait up Patrick, I'm coming.' And then she gave a surreptitious glance around, lowered her voice once more. I couldn't make out what she was saying.

The younger woman turned to all of us waiting. 'I am sorry but we are going to have to reschedule your interviews. We have your numbers and I guarantee each of you will be called in the next few days. I am sorry to have wasted your time.'

For a few brief seconds, I sat there thinking I should speak up and let her know I was there on another matter, but what was she going to do. Phil… or should I say PK… was not there anyway, and nor would he be back for few days.

What was the universe telling me?

I walked outside, and hailed a taxi. 'Airport please driver!'

Chapter 29

For months I had spent my days gloriously wandering the garden, talking to the baby about all I saw. Although Wilbur was never far from my side, he appeared relieved I had found someone else to confide in. Usually the wandering was done with a pair of gardening gloves and secateurs. In the midst of this wandering, a branch was snipped, a cutting taken, or the odd weed pulled.

I pondered the ease of how in recent times things had happened in my life, all without me trying to steer it. In my former life, I had lived by appointments, the day consisting of one billion and one decisions, each appearing to be of the utmost of importance.

But here at Carmody House, I watched as each season changed and bought with it an awakening of the garden, where there was always something precious growing. It bought an awareness to me, and I appeared to fall in sync with it, and without a whisper of ambition, my belly grew overnight like the bulbs. The simplicity of it nurtured me.

*

Ten metres away, I watched as a huge Bluetongue lizard briefly appeared. One of the garden regulars, I had christened him Barry. Although, I must say, it did take some time for me not to run in fright every time I saw him, and for Wilbur not to bail him up, delighted he had found a new friend to play with.

Well used to him now, with an air of nonchalance, Wilbur and I both watched him, me flopped on the grass in the dappled shade from the leafy tree overhead, Wilbur a short distance away, grabbing some vitamin D.

I had been down to the hen house giving the chooks their

weekly treat of sardines to encourage their shiny coats. As per usual the small fish had been scoffed with gusto. Like so many of the ideas Phil had implemented, the chooks had been another success.

When they had first come, I had devoured every book I could get my hands on relating to chooks. However, lately my reading material was of the baby kind. Although another chook book had arrived only a few weeks ago, I had absolutely no memory of ordering it. Must have been my mummy-brain. Anyway that was my excuse and I was sticking to it. I had placed it in the library, and unlike me, had not even opened one page. It could wait for another time.

Books aside, I received great enjoyment collecting the girl's freshly laid eggs each morning, only to be outdone by the satisfaction I got from using them to cook a simple breakfast or lunch. My favourite recipe at the moment, and one I just could not get enough of... must have been the protein the baby required... was eggs cooked in a rich tomato sauce which was laced heavily with handfuls of fresh herbs from my garden.

A bit pooped, this afternoon I'd put the girls away a little earlier and on the way back to the house I had stopped to sit a while. The Braxton Hicks had been coming strong and fast all day. However, in the last hour the tightening had intensified. One of my hands went to my rock hard stomach and gently rubbed in a circular motion.

The baby's due date was three weeks off, and I guess that this was how it was going to be until then. Once the discomfort had eased, I ran my fingers over Wilbur's head. He bought me such comfort.

'You're a good friend,' I told him, fondling his ears. 'You're going to love this baby, another member of our little family.'

Wilbur lowered his head onto his paws, his dark eyes looking concerned. After all, what did he know about babies? I reassured him we were both in the same boat.

Other than the initial emotions and extreme exhaustion, vomiting here, palpitations there, and constant nausea, all during the first trimester, I had well and truly blossomed while my body housed the formation of a little human being. My breasts had more than blossomed as well.

Spring was not long off and today I had felt the change in the weather, dressing in a blue and white paisley flowing sundress with cut away shoulders and thin straps. I wore a white cotton fitted t-shirt underneath. A girl still had to look her best, although at the present moment the t-shirt had riden up and now sat uncomfortably bunched around the top of my belly. Through the fabric of my dress I pulled at it, easing it down, noticing that the baby was now a lot lower than it had been.

A little backside pushed itself against my hand. Lovingly, I cupped my hand around it, smiling to myself. What are you I wondered, a pink one or a blue one?

With both hands, I adjusted my bra under my breasts, knowing they would love nothing better than to escape. There was not one ounce of room between them and my large belly.

Glancing around the garden, I pictured my child growing up at Carmody House, and what a lucky life it would have, a life full of love and happiness. Although I had not wanted to find out the sex of the baby, I was becoming keener and keener to meet the little person who had already begun to keep me up at night.

I felt around in my pocket for my iPhone. I had promised Thomas, my birthing partner, I would carry it everywhere for the next few weeks.

When I had attended the first pre-natal class, I couldn't help but notice I was the only one on my own. It was challenging. Although I was financially stable, the implications of raising a child alone were confronting.

Afterwards, on the phone, Thomas kindly reminded me of the conversation I'd had with him at Clovelly Estate about donor sperm. *Touché,* was all I had to say to him, showing that you never really know how you feel about something until it happens.

Thomas may not have donated the sperm as we had discussed, however you would have thought he had after that conversation, by the way he threw himself into my pregnancy, attending the following pre-natal classes with me. Both Steve and Thomas became my rocks.

Only last week, I had asked them if they would be the baby's godparents. It came as no surprise when Thomas's eyes had welled with emotion, but when I saw Steve do the same, even though he had pretended otherwise, I became emotional as well.

Right from the beginning, Thomas had nicknamed the baby Apricot. When I had enquired why, he said because it was a bit like a small Peach. Steve stirred the pot by calling the baby Sugar Plum. I gathered they were expecting a girl.

A few weeks earlier, as we had toured the birthing suites, once again, I was most grateful Thomas was with me. He must have sensed my trepidation, as suddenly from behind, I felt his fingers squeezing mine and heard him muttering, 'Good God girl, I think we need to deck this place out, make it a bit more welcoming for little Miss Apricot to come into the world. I'm heading into New Farm Editions to get some of those French candles. I'm calling Leahn the minute we leave here. And one of those elegant rugs from The Rug Establishment.' He elegantly crossed his arms and placed his index finger on his nose as he thought. 'The Diva Audrey would do the trick! Plus a bloody chandelier would not go astray… after all that's the thing that has gotten most people in this predicament…'

I flashed him a questioning look, cutting him off.

He whispered loudly into my ear, 'Ah… may I remind you… swinging from a chandelier can occasionally lead to touring a birthing suite,' and without pausing for breath, he continued, 'and we could add some warmth with a new paint colour. What about that latte colour you used…'

Before he could finish we were both given a silencing look by the nursing sister, as she displayed the spa area. 'And gentlemen, please remember to bring board-shorts as you will probably end up in the shower or spa with your partners. We're not really interested in seeing your naked bits if you don't mind.'

There was some good-natured twittering however I caught Thomas's look, knowing it was fast becoming far more than he had bargained for. I whispered to him, 'You can change your mind you know.'

'Not bloody likely honeybun. I said I will be here and I will.'

However, I did not miss a slight tremble as he raised a perfectly manicured hand to his mouth and chewed on a fingernail.

We left the hospital with another couple who we had attended pre-natal classes with, Charmaine and Leon. I fell into step with Charmaine, while the two men chatted from behind.

Charmaine could not help herself. 'Your partner is such a darling. I just love the way he notices all the details. Not a week has gone by that he has not commented on my maternity wardrobe and then just before, I heard him talking about the décor. I wish Leon was more like that.'

'Oh honey… he's gay. He's great with detail.'

It was only later in the car as I relayed the conversation to Thomas, and wondered at her look, that I realised I hadn't bothered to explain that he was my birthing partner and not my life partner. We laughed all the way home and I was reminded of what a huge bonding experience this had turned into for us, and although I had never bought it up with him, I knew it was the closest he would get to having a baby of his own.

But now, although the grass was a nice spot to be enjoying the last of the afternoon sun, I could not seem to get up. My back had begun to ache, not that that was a new thing, however it was far more intense than what it had been in the past. I reminded myself that it was all part of the pleasures of getting closer to meeting my child.

To take my mind away from the discomfort I was feeling, I began to pull out clover flowers, running them through my fingers, while Wilbur snuggled himself up to me. He appeared a bit sooky of late, keeping close to me as if knowing things might be about to change.

Another Braxton Hicks took over me and my back pain intensified. 'Bloody hell Wilbur,' I breathed, sitting in a crossed leg position and arching my back, jutting my breasts out. That helped. In an attempt to distract myself, I began to count the clover flowers, thinking by the time I'd finished counting, the tightening would be over and I would be able stand up and head up to the house. It must have been the way I had been sitting earlier that had disagreed with the baby.

… eight, I ran a clover through my fingers, nine, ah almost gone, ten, that's better. With the sun on my face, I closed my eyes and sighed deeply, and then I felt Wilbur scrabbling next to me, hastily jumping to his feet, at the same time making a noise that could only be described as a squeal of pure joy.

He could not have sounded any happier than if Mr Carmody had come back to life. I spun around, and then instantly put a hand to my stomach as it lurched.

We said nothing, just looked at each other. My heart was hammering in my chest and I had to stop myself crying out.

Immaculately dressed in single breasted deconstructed jacket that looked to me as if it was a cashmere blend, and God knew how I loved cashmere. His shirt was a very up to the minute black and white chevron print, worn with designer jeans. In my quick appraisal, I did not miss the crocodile skin brogues, nor the well groomed three day growth on his jaw. But mostly, I did not miss his full head of luxurious hair, the grey, his badge of honour, nowhere to be seen.

As I looked at him, I realised I was more than likely seeing the real Phil Hunter for the very first time, savvy and successful. Or should I say, I was seeing PK Hunter.

He looked exactly as if he was modelling for Giorgio Armani. In fact, he could not possibly have looked any better than if he had just stepped out of the Robb Report, advertising a private jet, or a watch worth a squillion bucks. Eight months on, he was better looking than I even remembered. And I had to admit, hair really suited him.

The thought flashed through my mind that I may not be looking my absolute best at this particular time. Without knowing why, a trembling hand went to my hair, and I wound a curl around a finger, my eyes locked on his.

'Hey boy!' With his eyes on me, Phil ruffled Wilbur's head. The dog let out another squeal and then joyfully looked back at me, as if to say, *I told you he'd be back.*

When Phil spoke, his voice was quiet. 'Peach,' was all he said.

I gave a slight raise of my brows in acknowledgment and

turned up the edges of my mouth. I stayed silent, not trusting myself to speak, although I did hope that Wilbur got the vibe I was sending, as he deliriously smiled, happily wagging his tail. *Bloody defector!*

And then I said the most stupid thing I could have, my voice small. 'I got the stingless bees, you know.' Swallowing, I continued to look at him, while he digested this piece of information, the elephant in the room notwithstanding.

I watched as he exhaled heavily. 'Just tell me?' He did not have to say more, I knew he was not asking about the bees.

Expressionless, I swallowed and then nodded.

His eyebrows shot high and he ran his hands through his hair. 'Jesus Peach! Were you *ever* going to let me know?'

I licked my lips, not thinking it would have happened like this. Neither of us said anything until finally I spoke. 'I came to see you at your offices in Melbourne some months back.' And then my voice had a certain edge to it. 'I didn't come to ask anything of you, but I felt you deserved to know…'

He cut me off, his voice terse. 'I'm sorry, I think I would have remembered that.'

I let out a huge breath, and gave him a pointed look. 'Can I finish?'

He opened his hands in a helpless manner, but said nothing.

My voice was flat. 'You weren't there. Apparently Sophia was in hospital with a sinus infection, your office was going crazy, the phone was ringing off the hook, people were waiting for interviews, meetings were being rescheduled, and there was a drama with one of the boys at Field of Dreams. It was crazy. In the ten minutes I sat there, I realised I could not burden you with one more thing, so I came home.'

At that he appeared to visibly sag, closing his eyes and exhaling heavily. I waited.

He placed his hands low on his hips. 'I cannot believe you Peach!' He shook his head. 'What on earth made you think it would have been a burden?'

'Hello!' my tone was indignant, and in a micro second switched to acerbic. 'Ummm... could it have been the fact that you hid who you were from me? Perhaps that was it? I am not sure of your reasoning Phil... but it sure as hell did not help. It was not as if you had wanted to include me in your life, much less share anything about it!'

Even though I glared at him, I noticed how uncomfortable he appeared.

He stuffed his hands into his front pockets. 'Look it wasn't like that...'

I snapped, 'Really... you tell me what it was like.' I knew my voice was loud, and even though I wanted to stand up, it seemed far too much effort and would have involved some rather indelicate manoeuvring.

However, my place on the grass did not deter me from continuing. 'My entire life was bared open to you, and *you* gave me crumbs. How hard do you think it was for me to come to see you in Melbourne in the first place, not to mention then leave without telling you? But *stupid* me,' and I began to poke myself in the chest, 'thought that perhaps *you* deserved to know.' And then my voice softened, and I glanced away. 'Actually, mostly I wanted you to know that Sophia would have a sibling.' And then my voice was quieter still. 'But I didn't want anything from you. If you didn't want to share your life before, you certainly would not wish to now. This is my choice, my responsibility and I am glad of it.' Protectively, I rested my hands either side of my belly.

Locking both of his hands together on his head in a pose I remembered well, he visibly exhaled through his lips. We were both quiet. Really I had nothing more to say, although I could see his mind ticking over as he appeared to be searching for the words.

He began to pace, and then turned back to me. 'I'm not sure I can explain how I was when I first came here...'

Wearily, I interrupted. 'I get that Phil...'

He cut me off. 'Let me explain?'

Giving a half shrug, half nod, I folded my arms on top of my belly waiting, once again my back beginning to ache, no doubt due to the position I was in.

He took his time. 'It's a funny thing when you realise that no matter how successful you are in business, no matter how much money you have you...' he exhaled and closed his eyes briefly, '... you *cannot* save the life of your wife or fix the disability your child has. No amount of money can do that.' He paused, and I waited as I could see he was thinking.

'Before Katrine died, I thought I knew who I was. I was PK Hunter, the strong one, the one she and other people relied upon, the one who could always make everything better. Well guess what... that changed! And I could not go back. I had to learn pretty damn quick who the hell I was. The only thing I knew for certain was, that no matter what, I was Sophia's father. Beyond that, nothing else mattered. I contemplated walking away from my business, but like it or lump it, I had created this huge well-oiled machine that needed to keep going, as I was responsible for a great many staff.'

Placing his hands back on his hips, he looked away for a few seconds and then turned back to me. 'I mean... what do you say to all those loyal people? *Look I'm closing. Go find another job.* As rough a time as I was having, I could not do that to them. I needed some time away to think, and find out who I really was. Luckily, my key people stepped up, but it was only ever meant to be short term. As it was, it went on much longer than I originally planned.

'When I first came here, it was as if I had escaped my life and the tragedy that had unfolded. There was no PK and the expectation of what came with that. My mother and Katrine's parents have always called me Phil, so I was simply that. I've got to tell you I liked being Phil again, and the simplicity and anonymity of it. And I liked working with my hands once more. Nature is very healing. I know I don't have to tell you, that the larger your business becomes, you find yourself doing less and less of what you really love, and more and more juggling the other stuff you could well and truly leave behind.

'Anyway, this place became *my* sanctuary. *I was* being selfish. But I needed to, so I could work out who I was and how to be the best father to Sophia. That and my sanity was all that mattered. There was even a period of time I was on anti-depressants, something that did not sit well with me. How could PK Hunter be on medication such as that? How could *he* not cope?

'But do not think for one minute, as time went on, I did not think about telling you many times about my life. What could I say? *Oh look, just so you know, I'm extremely successful and have a very comfortable life,* to put it mildly. That stuff meant *nothing* to me anymore. It was just stuff, it certainly is not who I am.'

Biting my lower lip, I shrugged, uncertain of what to say.

'That night after the party when I came back, I knew I needed to tell you more, but one thing led to another.'

For some reason that hit a nerve, and I couldn't help but be sarcastic. Flashing my eyes, I folded my arms and with a huff said, 'Well I am *sorry!*'

'Well I am *not* okay!' and he glared at me.

'Well… what did you decide, that you'd say nothing? Good move! God Phil, I feel like such an idiot suggesting I help financially with Sophia. That must have given you a laugh, considering your circumstances.'

It was not hard to hear the frustration in his raised voice. 'It was not like that.' And then he resumed his normal tone, although it was tinged with weariness. 'A few months before I returned to Melbourne, I was offered a buyout, but there were conditions, one of them is that I stay on for a twelve month period during the changeover. It could not have come at a better time, but I had to make sure it would work for all of my staff. I owed them that. Plus, I'm not one to talk of deals until they are definite. It's just the way I am.'

I nearly blurted out that he was generally not one to talk about much at all, but held my tongue.

'And when I left Brisbane it was far from being definite. There were things happening but I had to make certain of them.' He propped himself on the low stone wall. 'I did come to see you, you know, that Melbourne Cup day, the day before we left for Melbourne. I wanted to ask you to give me some time. I came by the house thinking I would catch you before you left for the track. Instead I ran into Pete. He told me that you were at the hairdressers having some do…' pulling a face, he placed his hands around the back of his head indicating something.

I narrowed my eyes. 'Chignon?' I was trying to figure out what he was getting at.

'Whatever! Anyway amongst everything else he told me, he mentioned that Davis and…' he paused, '… whatever her name was, had lost the baby, and were no longer together.'

Blandly, I shrugged, still wondering where this was leading.

'At the time it meant nothing to me. Just more of Pete's

bloody gossip. But then I decided to go out to the track, and find you. It was late in the day. I thought I might be able to pick you up and take you for a drive and talk,' he paused and exhaled heavily. 'But when I got there, I saw you and Davis embracing...'

I couldn't help myself, interrupting, '*He* had *his* arms around me...'

Before I could continue Phil cut in. 'If I remember clearly, it certainly looked like it was reciprocal. I saw your arms go around him, twice in fact. And look, I am not an idiot, I knew you still had feelings for him, and I was in no position to interrupt. I was there to lay my cards on the table and ask for time, while you were hugging your husband. So,' he shrugged, glancing away, 'I walked away.'

I shook my head. Arching my back, I began to massage it down low with one hand. 'Phil it was nothing other than Davis being a drunken pest. I spoke with him for two annoying minutes and I have not seen him since.'

'Bloody hell!' He stood and began to pace and then swung around to me. I could tell he was frustrated. 'I did come back the next morning you know. His car was out front.' He gave me a questioning look.

'Yes,' I nodded. 'It was. He was in no condition to drive. I had taken his keys, bought it home here and left it out front. The next day, I put the keys in the letterbox, texted him to tell him, and went out, hoping never to set eyes upon him again.' Frowning, I emphasised, 'I have not one ounce of feeling left for him. Nothing!'

'Then *why* couldn't you have just told me about the baby?'

'I've already said,' my voice was indignant and loud. '*You* could have called *me*? I mean to say... I never heard another word from you.'

He turned his back on me. Exasperated, I let out a sigh.

He swung back. 'Yes I could have... I tried, but under the circumstances... plus there was more than I bargained for waiting for me in Melbourne.'

'Oh *really!*' Suddenly I felt angry. 'What *else* could there be Phil? Who else could you be responsible for? Actually right this moment I am beginning to feel sorry for Katrine. Did you ever fit *her* in?' And then I caught the look on his face. I put a hand to my mouth. 'God I'm sorry. That was a rotten thing to say.'

He didn't speak for the longest time. I watched as his shoulders went up and down while he appeared to struggle to take in air. I could not believe I had been such a heinous cow. 'Look... I am sorry.' My voice was soft, and for some reason I felt my bottom lip quiver. 'I know you owe me nothing.' I guess I just hated feeling like I was so bottom of the list. Or if I was honest, I guess I didn't even make the list. *Bloody* lists!'

'Peach... when I first came here I was oblivious to everything, but as time went on... I could not resist the attraction I had for you.' He scratched at his head, as if he could not believe what he was saying. 'It was what kept me coming here each day when I should have returned to Melbourne much sooner. Yes, in the beginning it was because of my father and Mr Carmody, but pretty damn soon I realised I could not keep away because of *you*.'

At that point, I was uncertain if he had seen the look of surprise on my face. For months, I had been telling myself that it had been one sided, I had concocted something, I was not important enough, he thought of me as nothing more than a one night stand, a booty call as Lou would say. However, I had to stop my mind from rambling and listen to what he was saying.

'... but I was in a tricky situation. The responsibilities that go with Sophia are humungous. How do you ask someone to buy into that? It is a lifetime commitment.'

'Maybe they want to.' My voice was small and I saw his eyes soften. He gave a slight shrug. I continued, 'I mean she is rather adorable.'

His nodded. 'She is indeed.' He paused. 'Look, just so you know, the next morning after that night here, I went to see Katrine's parents. I told them I had been thinking about seeing someone. I *know* it sounds crazy, but I felt like I needed their permission. It was really hard for them, but they wished me luck, said Katrine would have wanted it, and that Sophia deserved a proper family. Regardless of what they said, I knew it hurt them.' Briefly, he closed his eyes. 'And then I spoke to my mother. She was quiet for the longest time and then she began to cry. She said that she had been worried that because of my commitment to Sophia, I would shut myself off to love. She was almost right!'

He scratched at his head. 'But then I didn't know what to think when I saw you and Davis. Plus I was uncertain of what exactly I had to offer.'

All I could think to myself was that I would have taken him with nothing more than Sophia. They were enough as they were.

'Anyway the first thing I did when I returned to Melbourne was to pack up Katrine's things. I know you don't believe me, but I *was* ready to move forward.' He was quiet for a few seconds and I let him be so.

'One night I was going through this box of cards and letters and things. She used to call it her *Love Stash*! It had photos, concert tickets, birthday cards, Christmas tags, some things from her childhood. It was like going through her life. Anyway…' He glanced away and I had to struggle to hear him. '… I came across a few letters tied together. It wasn't hard to see they were love letters. Thought it would give me a laugh. Something from before she had known me, maybe even from her teenage years. But…' I saw him swallow, 'it didn't take long to realise they were written in the year before she fell pregnant with Sophia.'

'Oh!' Horrified, I put a hand to my mouth, my face telling it all.

He nodded his head. 'Oh alright! Pretty bloody hard to take. I can't tell you what went through my mind. I felt like a raging bull. I wanted to kill someone.' By the way he ran his hands through his hair, it appeared he still did.

I realised my hand was still at my mouth, the shock of it hard to comprehend, my mind going into overdrive.

He read my thoughts. 'I know what you're thinking. I wondered the same bloody thing. It drove me insane. Was I really Sophia's father?' And then he said something that endeared him to me all the more, his voice soft and pleading. 'I could not have borne it if I wasn't.'

Finally I had something to say. I kept my voice gentle. 'Look Phil, I don't know if this helps, but in reality Johnny is my step-father. But *he* is my father. Fullstop!' And then I thought of something else. 'But Sophia looks just like you. Those huge brown eyes…'

He gave me a look. 'He has brown eyes too!'

Once again, my hand went back to my mouth, and my eyes nearly popped out of my head. 'You know him?'

'I didn't but I do now. I had to find him. I had to know more.'

'And do you…?'

He cut me off. 'I know enough.' He paused. 'There was a

restaurant Katrine used to frequent. She used them to cater for quite a few of our functions. I went there once or twice, but that was it. I sort of remembered this smooth Italian guy that owned it, swarthy sort, always trying to charm the ladies. A bit in your face type. Probably around my age.'

My voice was almost a whisper. 'It was him?'

'*No*,' he shook his head. 'I *thought* it was him. It *was* his father! They shared the same name. '

'What?' I practically yelled. 'How old was *he*?'

Putting out his hands, he shook his head, appearing exhausted. 'I don't know… mid-sixties or something. I must say extremely flattering for me. Anyway he ran front of house. I guess Katrine had a bit to do with him, you could say! Plus it made sense about the long-hand letters. I mean who does that these days, but I guess it would be normal for someone his age.'

Narrowing my eyes, I just had to ask. 'Well… did he look good for his age or what?'

Phil shrugged. 'He might have a couple of years ago, but… he looked old to me. If I racked my brain I have this slight memory of him being a big guy, olive complexion, well dressed, charming I guess. Katrine might have been five years older than me, but it made no sense to me, whatsoever.' And then it was as if he wanted to dismiss it. 'I don't know.' His voice then softened. 'I just could not get it. And the frustrating thing is, I cannot ask her.

'I read those letters *over and over,* and I thought back to that time. I remembered her asking more from me, but me being far too preoccupied with my business and other people. Who needed what? How could I help this person, that organisation? I think she felt she came last. I am not sure she really loved him, but she sure as heck loved his attention. I gathered by one letter that she had finished it.' He looked up to the heavens. 'I'm grateful for that small mercy. But it appeared...' he coughed and looked away, scratching at his neck. 'I think he really loved her.'

'Did you speak to him, ask him anything?'

'Speak to him. I wanted to kill him. I introduced myself, said I thought he had known my late wife. I will never forget that look on his face. By the look of him, he had suffered. He said he had heard we'd had a baby. How was she?'

I had run out of things to say. I had described this guy as a non-talker but my God when he told you something, he bloody told you!

'Well?'

Phil knew what I was asking. He shrugged. 'I don't believe so. All I do know is, he wasn't really interested in my answer. Moved on to something else immediately. But it doesn't matter. I *know* it really doesn't matter. Sophia's mine. She will always be. If I thought for one minute he could help her more than I could, I might reconsider, but he is an old man, what does he have to offer? Regardless, she was born into my family, I am her father.'

'And look... you probably are biologically as well.'

'I have given that thought. And by the dates on the letters, I have come to the conclusion that I am.'

I nodded slowly, suddenly feeling like I had a knife in my back, it was aching so much.

'Now, I know that all of that may sound lame to you, but there has been a lot of shit happening in the last eight months, if you'll forgive me for saying so.'

For a few minutes both of us were silent. I watched as he walked over to the edge of the terrace, his usual pose, hands on his hips, legs astride, gazing into the distance. When he turned, I had to strain my ears to hear him.

'A few months ago, my mother told me she had seen you at the shops and that you were pregnant. To be honest, I was blown away, so I didn't ask any details. For some reason, I had presumed by the way she spoke you weren't very far along. And of course, I had gotten it into my head that you and Davis were back together. I knew how much you wanted a baby Peach, and for that part I was happy for you.' And then his face changed, and I felt his voice accusing. 'But I must say *he* is a complete and utter dickhead. I will never see what you saw in him.'

'I agree!' I said forcefully, unused to hearing Phil speak that way.

'Well at least there's something we agree on. I thought it that first time I had a meeting with him regarding that Noosa project…'

I cut in, my eyes narrowing. 'So… I don't understand this. You knew who I was right from the start? Was this… was this some kind of set-up… or something?'

'Of course not!' he was indignant. 'No, I did not know who you were. Remember I was in another world at that time. I had never met you. It was all coincidental. If you recall, I was not looking for work. I was attempting to recover. And I had a history with this place.'

I nodded, knowing what he said to be true. 'Well… I guess I now know you do not just simply volunteer up at the boys' school, but you are the patron. Do you still visit them?' My voice was flat and my mouth dry, but I just had to know if he had been coming to Brisbane regularly.

'Yes, I do. Look Peach, I had thought of ringing or coming by, but *what* was there to say?'

And then something dawned on me. 'But you came today?'

'I did! It was timing. Or the universe organised it,' and he glanced up to the heavens. 'Or Mr Carmody. Or Pete.'

'Pete?'

He nodded. 'I organised for him to do some electrical work at Mum's. I happened to be in Brisbane for a meeting, and called back into her place to pick up Sophia. You know what Pete is like. He was waffling on about one thing and another, before he went on to say that he thought you were due soon. That stopped me in my tracks. However, I made some comment about how I hoped you were happy with Davis. He looked at me like I had two heads, and said as far as he knew the baby had nothing to do with Davis. In fact, and he seemed perplexed by this, because it appeared he had no bloody idea who the father was, some mystical man as far as he was concerned.' He looked at me. 'In that moment, I knew. I think my mother knew as well. She handed me the car keys and just said *go*.'

We were both quiet. I curled my legs under me, attempting to find some comfort.

Running both of his hands through his hair, he then stood with his hands locked at the back of his neck. 'Peach, I don't know what to say.'

A hot sweat had broken out on my upper lip. I dabbed at it. I could see Phil watching me as suddenly I made a small noise and my eyes opened wide. For a moment I was completely still and then frantically I felt around for the phone in my pocket.

His brow furrowed. 'What are you doing?'

I didn't look at him. 'I have to call Thomas.' I swallowed.

'Now?' his voice was incredulous.

I nodded swiftly. 'Yes!' I looked at him directly. 'He's my birth partner. My water has just broken.'

I could tell I had shocked him by the way he held his hand to his forehead. 'Oh my God! Are you sure?'

Dry mouthed, I nodded. 'This conversation has been riveting Phil, but I've got other things to do.'

'Pea…'

I put a slightly trembling hand up. 'Please don't Phil. I get that you have a million responsibilities. I am certainly not trying to make myself another one because…' And I stopped. What I wanted to say out loud, I continued in my head… *Because the man that I want, makes me a priority, does not just fit me in between things.*

'Are you okay? What… what do you want to do?' There was an air of franticness about him, and he was almost pacing, as once again he repeated himself. 'What do you want to do? We'll get you to the hospital. We must be at the hospital.'

Our earlier conversation had drained me. What I wanted to do was cry. I was in unchartered waters in more ways than one. The baby was three weeks early. I had just spent the past eight months feeling extremely alone. Plus in my mind I had gone over many different scenarios telling Phil about his child, however it had never played out like this. And to top it off, my pretty dress was now wet and sticking to me.

Before I had a chance to think further, a contraction took over, engulfing my entire being. *Eeeek*… so they *were* a billion times worse than a Braxton Hicks! My face screwed up in pain, I doubled over, my hands protectively under my heavy belly. I attempted the yogic breathing I had been studying, focusing on the breath not the pain. I had to centre myself and shut out everything to get through it.

Finally, I opened my eyes and saw the complete fear in Phil's eyes as he leant over me. He appeared agitated and not what I would have expected from someone always so in control. 'Peach what's the plan? I've got to get you to the hospital... um what... what do you want me to do?' He was totally rattled and I realised the only other time I had seen him like this, was the day he thought he had lost Sophia.

And then it hit me. His wife had died immediately after giving birth to Sophia. Not a great memory for him, or a great thought for me just as that moment, I might add. Touching the back of my neck, I felt clammy and slightly lightheaded. With serious effort, I attempted to pull myself together, but then quick as a flash I leant forward and vomited right next to his very expensive looking crocodile brogues.

I felt Phil's hands gently pull my hair away from my face, and was reminded that this was not the first time he had done so.

Sitting back, I didn't look at him, but fumbled once again for my phone, my voice was small. 'I have to call Thomas. We have it all organised.' My trembling fingers attempted to push the direct dial number for him.

'Here let me do it,' his voice was kind. He took the phone from me, dialled, and held it to his ear. Standing upright he was glancing around, although I could tell he wasn't seeing anything. Over and over he kept exhaling heavily through his mouth. I wanted to tell him that that was *my* job. Instead I motioned for him to give the phone to me. Shaking his head, he began to speak, and finally I sensed an element of control in him.

'It's not Peach, Thomas. It's Phil Hunter!' Pulling the phone away he looked at the screen for a second and then put it back to his ear. 'Hello... right... well Peach's waters have broken.' There was few seconds silence before he spoke again. 'Yes... we do have a situation here ... Three weeks early? Bring me up to speed as quickly as you can...' Once again he listened. 'I'll...' turning away from me, he paused, placing a hand on his head. I recognised that thinking pose of his. He glanced at his watch. 'You're going to hit peak hour traffic. It'll save time if I drive Peach to the hospital and you meet her there.' He listened once again. 'Right, you call her doctor.'

Although I was agitated, there appeared nothing for me to say, this entire situation completely surreal. I could feel the nervousness of Phil's hand when he placed it under my elbow as if to escort me. As surreptitiously as I could, I pulled my wet dress away from my legs and bottom and began to slowly walk, wishing I had not been right at the bottom of the garden at a time like this.

Phil guided me as if I was hard of seeing and had never treaded this path before. 'We're coming up to a few steps here. That's it, one, two, three, four, five. Right you're on the top one now. Okay we're heading over the flagstones, the blue garden is on the right. The two large urns are coming up…' Out of nowhere he asked, 'So you're not due for another three weeks?'

I shook my head. 'No,' was all I said.

'You've been well?'

'Yep.' My voice was small and I didn't look at him.

'And do you know if the baby is a boy or a girl?'

I shook my head again, not bothering to talk.

'Names? You must have picked out some names?'

I realised he was distracting me, although before I had time to respond, another contraction took hold. Pulling my arm away I halted, placing both hands over my belly, I closed my eyes and took long slow steady breaths. At one point I gave just the tiniest of whimpers.

Phil attempted to be reassuring. 'You're doing fine. That's great. Long and slow… breathe… that's it.' His breath fell in with mine, and helped me to keep pace. And although he kept repeating words of calm, I began to feel it was to calm himself. However, then his tone changed, and there was a sense of urgency. 'We've got to get you to the hospital, now.'

I put a trembling hand up, my throat dry. I swallowed, and found myself reassuring him. 'It's okay Phil, I'll be fine. I know what to do.' I attempted a few steps, but faulted a little. He put an arm around me and I glanced up at him.

Although his dark eyes were kind, by the pallor of his skin, I could tell this was raw for him, so I told myself to man up, which seemed an odd expression at that time. I also told myself that I could do this, that for the longest time I had been waiting to meet my beautiful baby.

'Lean on me,' he instructed, his voice comforting. I didn't need to be asked twice, grateful to feel the strength of him, and momentarily pondering on something he had said earlier. *Had* Mr Carmody sent him there today, of all days?

When I had woken that morning, I had absolutely no idea I would be bringing my baby into the world that day, but perhaps Mr Carmody had known. A bit like finding this house, from the moment I had stepped through the gates, life had appeared serendipitous.

Slowly, without talking, we continued. As we approached a low stone fence, I pulled away from him. There was a tremor in my voice. 'I just need to sit for a minute. My legs are wobbly.'

Before more could be said, he carefully swooped me up and carried me, his stride determined.

For heaven's sake, not this again. 'Phil, I'm the weight of a whale for goodness sake.'

'Be quiet,' was all he said, for the first time sounding like the old him. With Wilbur at his heels, he carried me up the side and around to the front of the house. Although he was unwavering, I knew it had to be of great effort. And how could

I not be concerned about his cashmere jacket? Cashmere and amniotic fluid… hmmm… not a great combination.

What a bloody nightmare! The pep talk I had given myself a few minutes earlier faded. With my head resting against his firm chest, I shed a few silent tears. Maybe they were humiliation, I don't know.

As he placed me on my feet, he asked. 'Do you have a bag ready?'

I nodded, 'Yes,' and attempted a surreptitious sniff, and a quick wipe of the end of my nose. 'Just inside the front door.'

Under instruction from Thomas, I had packed my monogramed duffle bag last week, including my relaxation CDs and aromatherapy, and placed it in the entry as he had insisted so we could grab it in a hurry. I think he was better prepared than I was, proudly telling me he had already packed a small bag for himself with the required board shorts.

Turning to Phil, I explained. 'I need to have a shower and put something else on.'

However, I saw him glance at his watch, actually it was a huge timepiece, and I was reminded of the millions of times he had done so in the past.

'Am I keeping you?' I asked, somewhat annoyed, my brow furrowed.

'What? Of course not… I am just concerned that we'll hit peak hour traffic if you do.'

Grimacing, I placed a hand on my belly. 'I have to have a clean dress.'

'Huh?'

Frowning, I pulled the wet fabric away from me as I walked inside. As I reached the front door, suddenly I bent forward letting out a small wail, and then grabbed at the door frame. In a second Phil was behind me, helping me over to the steps.

For some reason, instead of sitting, I went onto all fours. 'My back,' I moaned, grabbing at my lower back, feeling as if there was a hot poker pushed into it, the pain running down through the back of my legs as well. It flashed through my mind the horror stories I had heard regarding back labour. Along with everything else I was feeling, a sensation of dread washed over me.

In distress, it was a relief when I felt Phil's hands upon my back. 'Does this help?' his voice was intense.

'Hhhhh,' I whimpered, grateful for anything. From those first few contractions it now appeared to be just one long one, the pain fading a little every so often. I once again began my rhythmical breathing, making a loud whooshing sound on the exhalation. I could hear Phil breathing with me. As the pain began to subside, it left me flopped on the steps, attempting to catch my breath. Phil leant over me, and I looked up into his worried eyes.

One of his hands gently smoothed my hair away from my damp forehead. His voice was kind. 'We've got to go Peach. I want you at the hospital. Come on... *please.*'

Seeing the concern on his face, I nodded. 'Can *you* get me a dress?'

His face looked puzzled. 'Uh sure,' and he scratched at his head, before he took off up the stairs. At the top he turned. 'Where... which one?'

'Umm...' I waved my hand. 'Look in my wardrobe for an orange Thurley. It's got a fitted bodice, and tiny covered buttons down the front...'

Before I could add more detail he had disappeared. From the bottom step I could hear him muttering and then he called out, 'Got it,' before he rushed back down the stairs, taking two at a time, pushing the dress into my hands.

I held the skimpy, silky, slip dress out in front of me, and almost wailed. 'This isn't it. This is my tangerine Lisa Ho.'

He exhaled heavily, running a hand through his hair, attempting to stay calm, although failing dismally. 'Oh for God's sake Peach, won't it do?'

'No,' I cried. 'It won't fit.' I thought I might cry and my lips trembled. The burning thought that it was the dress I was wearing the night my baby was conceived did not escape me. I wondered if he remembered.

When he spoke his voice was very precise. 'I am sorry Peach but we do not have time for this. You are going as you are.' He sounded determined. 'The traffic is getting heavier by the second. I'll bring my car up the drive.' Hurriedly he looked around at the hall table where I had always kept my car keys. I knew he was looking for the remote clicker for the driveway gates. Without saying anything, I handed it to him.

Feeling like a bedraggled mess, I felt myself visibly sag, however did not have it in me to argue. I could not help but think this was such an odd experience. I was with someone who on one hand I trusted implicitly, and on the other I totally did not.

I watched his retreating back, my red patient Louis handbag over his shoulder, the monogramed duffel in his hand.

My mind was ticking over. Having Phil here at this moment had thrown me into complete disarray, and nothing was going as planned. However, I knew it was high time to pull myself together. Whatever we needed to say could wait until after this baby was born. Over and over I repeated the words Emerald Green had taught me, *I'll handle it! I'll handle it!*

When I found out I was having a baby as a single mother, I had once again returned to visit the green eyed therapist. It didn't matter what fearful scenario I came up with for having this baby on my own, she just kept telling me that *I'd handle it*. Once again, she insisted that each morning I journal three pages to create positive affirmations, and to allay my fears.

Repeating my mantra just now, with some difficulty, I slowly walked to the laundry to get a towel, my left hand clutching at the wall to keep myself steady, my right hand jammed into my lower back.

A pale pink Chinese silk kimono caught my eye. On a hanger over the knob of the door handle, I had placed it there yesterday to dry, keen to pack it in my case for the hospital. Leaning against the washing machine, I hoisted my somewhat wet blue paisley dress over my head and put it into the laundry tub. Over the top of my T-shirt, I wrapped the pretty robe, tying the soft sash in a bow above my huge bump. And then I felt the pain radiating from my spine and move out towards my sides. For the next 45 seconds or so, I clutched the washing machine. On my own now, I groaned out loud finding the noise actually helpful.

Once it had lessened, I weakly fumbled about in the clean washing basket amongst a few errant pegs and the delicate's laundry bag, for a pair of panties. Not a one. *Bugger! Why* couldn't there be that one pair, which for whatever reason had been left there time and time again, just like the wayward sport's sock that somehow had lost its partner, and been living in the basket for some months. But then from under the sock I noticed the tiniest bit of cream lace. It was the smallest of small, totally inappropriate G-string that had definitely not been worn since pre-pregnancy days. Exhaling heavily, I shook my head with frustration.

With effort, I stripped off my sodden white Bond's maternity bikini briefs, and then pulled the robe closely around me. I toyed with the thought of going commando. It was not exactly my cup of tea, particularly in this situation, so once again I reached for the tiny gee and then rather indelicately manoeuvred it on. Although I could not see it, I knew by the discomfort, it had to be barely covering a thing. There is only one way you can wear these blessed things, and yet it definitely felt like it was in the wrong place.

I let out a frustrated moan. I had a baby pushing its way out my *fanwoi* and a teeny tiny piece of lace pushing against it. That made *so* much sense. *Why* had I refused to buy those maternity high top boy leg britches, thinking they looked unattractive? Right now, I couldn't think of anything else that would bring comfort and support.

Tutting loudly, my face long, I glanced at Wilbur. 'Do not say a word, unless there is some chance you could run upstairs, go to my dresser, in the top drawer are my big girl panties...' and then I took in his face and I knew he was saying... *Lordy here she goes again!*

I patted his head. 'You're a good boy,' I told him, as with a towel under my arm, I waddled to the front steps just as Phil reversed the red Holden ute.

He appeared to be on the phone, although hung up almost instantly. He had removed his jacket, and literally ran around to the passenger side, swinging the door wide open. 'You've changed,' was all he said, taking the towel from me and spreading it on the seat.

I turned back to Wilbur, my voice attempting to be normal. 'Okay you're in charge no matter what Whitie says. And keep those chooks in line too will you. The bees will do their own thing, so don't worry about them. Lou and Marty will check on you, and Brownie will be about...'

But Phil cut me off. 'Peach, come on...'

With effort, I climbed into the car, giving Wilbur a

half-hearted wave. 'Wish me luck boy,' I called to him.

Very gingerly, Phil pulled the seatbelt out… and out… and leant across me and did it up. It went through my mind that he smelt nice, and familiar, and that was a comforting thought. But then I noticed that he gave his head a slow shake. 'What?' I asked, but he was walking, no I will rephrase that, almost running, back around to the driver's side. Another memory came to me of that day at the nursery when Phil's chivalrous actions saved me. That day he had helped me into the car and done the seat belt up around me, just as he had now.

At full speed as if we were attempting to gain pole position at Bathurst, we swept out of the driveway and turned left. I glanced over at him and then without knowing why, my tone cold, said, 'So you didn't bring the Ferrari today?'

With a look of bafflement plastered across his face, he glanced at me. 'I don't have a Ferrari.'

With attitude, I shrugged. 'Well the games up on this one. For someone like you, it would hardly be your standard drive car.'

I saw him lick his lips, as if thinking before he spoke. 'If you must know, it was my father's.' His tone was a little terse. 'He'd bought it only six months before he died. It was the first new car that man had ever had. It was his pride and joy. Mum couldn't part with it. Up until I began to use it at your place, it had sat under Mum's house, up on blocks, covered by a tarp. I used to have a mechanic turn it over every few months or so, and keep a check on it. I *kinda* thought it might mean something to Dad for me to use it at Carmody House, a place he loved.' Turning, he gave me a flat measured look, and then quirked his brows.

'Oh…' I slowly nodded, feeling chastised. I wondered what his father might have thought about it being used to take me to the hospital.

And then I caught Phil shaking his head again, before he gave an audible breath. He briefly glanced out his side window.

'What?' I asked.

He turned to me, brow furrowed. Although his tone was kind, his words were direct. 'What do you mean what?' However he didn't wait for me to reply. 'I don't have the words Peach. I'm not sure what to say. I'm...' He drifted off and then coughed, glancing back to me once more. 'You've been well?'

It appeared like such a formal question, I was taken by surprise. 'Under the circumstances, yes very well thank you.' My God, I sounded as formal as he did.

'You look good.' His voice may have been calm, but his driving wasn't.

I kept my eyes on the road, my hands clutched together around my belly. 'Thank you.'

'And you don't know what you're having?' he asked once again, as if attempting to make conversation with a stranger.

'No.'

There was silence between us and then finally he spoke, his voice soft. 'I'm sorry I wasn't here for you Peach. I'm even sorrier that you felt you couldn't tell me. I'm trying to understand that. But what I do understand is that it must have been hard on your own.'

I didn't say a word, just gave a half shrug, half nod.

When he spoke next he startled me. 'What the hell... will you look at this traffic!'

There did appear to be an unusual amount of traffic even for this time of day. Placing my hands on the vinyl dash, I arched my back thinking that the pain was just relentless, and at times felt literally as if I was going to be pulled apart.

I caught Phil glancing at me, his face worried. 'Just hang on. I'll get you there as quickly as I can.' Even in my state I could pick up the stress in his voice. I closed my eyes briefly, only to open them in fright when I heard him cursing, his fingers tapping on the steering wheel with impatience.

'*Bloody hell!* We'll take the second entrance onto the Story Bridge, it should be quicker.' And in a flurry of blasting horns, he accelerated, changed lanes, and weaved in and out of other cars. I realised at this point it was him with his hand on the horn.

'It's okay, it's okay Phil,' I said, my voice breathless.

He looked at me directly, his words succinct. 'No… no it's not okay Peach!'

He must have seen the look on my face, because he put a hand out and briefly touched my knee. 'How are you doing?' However, he then frowned and turned back to the traffic.

I just nodded, blowing out through my mouth. Right, I thought, the only thing I have to think of is bringing my baby into the world. *Nothing else. Do not think of one more thing. Breathe, that's it…*

And then it hit me! My face blushed, and I cursed Thomas. I was booked in for a wax at his salon next week. I was meant to go two weeks ago, but Thomas had convinced me that I should wait another week so I looked smart during the delivery. *My God*, I looked like a hairy beast. A hairy beast with a teeny tiny G-string on!

I saw Phil glance over at me. 'I can see how worried you are Peach, but it will be fine.' And then he repeated succinctly, 'It will be fine.' Once again, I felt he was reassuring himself more than me. I had no doubt the delivery would be fine. Or I bloody hoped so, although this back labour thing was a piece of extremely bad luck. I reminded myself that women gave birth every day of the week. I could not believe that I had let the hairy beast part worry me, allowing another emotion to enter my already frazzled state. I closed my eyes, the humiliation burning.

Then Phil began to curse and I decided between the two of us, there was a lot of swearing going on. However, when I opened my eyes, I let out a few expletives as well. All the lanes of the Story Bridge were closed with a barricade blocking cars from entering. Police were directing the traffic back around onto Bowen Terrace, down a side street, where it would once again join Brunswick Street, and then detour via the city and the South East Freeway. You did not have to be Einstein to work out that at this time of day it would take forever.

Before I could say a word, Phil pulled the car to the left, went up over the curb and screeched to a halt. He jumped out of the car, slamming the door behind him. With a hand to my mouth, I watched as he dodged traffic and ran across the road to speak to one of the policemen.

I noticed that if I tilted my pelvis forwards it took the pressure off my back ever so slightly, and gave me a minute ounce of comfort. Although I did have to be mindful not to let the robe fall open. So while waiting, to keep my mind occupied, I began to count as I tilted my pelvis, taking long slow breaths. *What the heck was taking Phil so long?*

I craned my neck around to see his arms wildly gesturing. I could tell by the look on the police officer's face that at first he was annoyed, although within seconds his attitude appeared to have changed. Barking off a command to another officer, he quickly accompanied Phil back to the car.

I was not sure if it was what Phil had said or the look on my face as I beseeched him, mid-tilt, hands splayed either side of my huge belly, however within seconds he was on his radio, stopping traffic and waving us out, his hands wildly motioning for Phil to do a U-turn. Phil drove up to the barricade and impatiently idled forward until it was moved for him. The officer indicated for Phil to put his window down.

He spoke with urgency. 'The other end knows you're coming, but proceed with caution, the jumper is about half way across. Now don't you worry about that, you just concentrate on getting your wife to the hospital safely.' He gave me a nod, and tapped the side of the car twice.

My hands on my belly, I glanced at Phil, as he slowly accelerated. There was an eerie feeling as we crossed the bridge I had been crossing my entire life, although now all lanes were empty.

Phil's hands appeared to be gripping the wheel. 'Some poor guy's making a point by holding Brisbane to ransom over custody of his child. Apparently he's up here on the left and been threatening to jump.'

A policeman stood on the side, waving us through.

My head turned watching him. 'What did you say to the officer back there?' I could feel the pain building once again around my spine, so I pushed my hands into the seat and tilted.

'I told him you'd never make the long trip around. I'm not sure if he believed me at first, as he asked if it was at all possible for you to go across on the Sydney Street ferry and he'd have an ambulance waiting for you. I told him no you bloody-well could not cross on the ferry as it would take too much time, and if he didn't let us though the baby would born on the side of the road. The minute he saw you, he knew it was no joke.' And then he shot me a concerned look. 'Does that help what you're doing?'

'Mmmm...' I nodded, biting my bottom lip, once again

unable to speak, the pain in my back intensifying. I ground my fists into my lower back attempting to relive the agony. At one point through my pain haze, I noticed Phil was taking long breathes in through his nose and exhaling them slowly through is mouth, as if encouraging me to do so.

We exited the bridge and headed up along River Terrace, normally a car park at this time of day, however due to the diverted traffic, I saw we had a clear run.

My phone rang startling us. With one eye on the road, as if it was a completely normal thing for him to do, Phil fumbled around in my red patient Louis, answering it. I could hear Thomas's high pitched voice rapid fire to Phil. Phil listened intently. 'Yes I know … I spoke to them and they let us through. Let me think.' He tapped on the steering wheel, thoughtfully. 'If you go across the Sydney Street ferry can someone pick you up or can you jump in a cab… You're *where?* With the phone tucked under his neck, he pulled back the cuff on his sleeve and checked his watch. By the way he did it, something triggered a faded memory in me, although I was unsure of what.

However, before I could think further, he continued speaking to Thomas. 'Okay, if you're bumper to bumper in the city, when you can, head towards the riverside and get the small ferry across to Kangaroo Point…' and then his voice was firm. 'Let me tell you, there will be no problem Thomas, I will stay with her… Yep… now stop worrying and go. We'll see you when we see you.'

'Isn't he going to make it?' I asked, my voice small.

Phil nodded, stating firmly, 'He will make it. I think we should turn right here and go via Lower River Terrace, okay?'

Although I gave a nod, I felt unable to speak. Sitting back, I clasped my hands together. I needed Thomas. He knew what to do.

Phil glanced over at me. 'It's okay Peach. I will stay with you.'
I shot him a panicked look.

'I am not going to leave you on your own *okay*.'

Although plenty came to mind, I had to work overtime to say nothing. I continued to look straight ahead.

His voice was kind. 'Would you like me to call your mother or Lou to come in?'

I shook my head. Number one that had not been the plan, and number two, it was hardly Bea's style, let alone the fact she was actually in Provence. And as far as Lou went, with the bridge closed it would take hours for her to arrive. My mind ticked over hoping that Thomas would make it.

The phone rang again. It was Thomas. Phil handed it to me.

Thomas's voice was quiet but emotional. 'Hey babe, I'm doing my best to get there. If you think I'm going to let Miss Apricot come into this world without me, you've got another bloody thing coming. You okay?'

I nodded as if he could see me. My voice wavered. 'Mmmm... this is it Thom. I really need you, please do your best.' From the corner of my eye, I saw Phil look at me.

Thomas kept speaking to me. 'Are you nervous Lovey? Cause I'm as nervous as hell. And I tell you what, I'll be bloody peeved if I don't get to at least prance around in those new board shorts I bought especially for the occasion, so nothing will keep me away, *nothing!*'

I gave a weak half-hearted laugh.

'That's my girl. Put Phil back on will you.' Quietly, I handed the phone back over.

I heard Phil repeating. 'Track four first... yep... and clary sage, lavender and geranium in the oil burner. Got it! It's all in her bag?' There was the longest pause while Thomas spoke, and then Phil answered, 'She'll be fine mate. I won't leave her…'

With that we screeched to a halt out the front of the Mater Mothers. Phil ran around and opened the door and helped me out, me doing my utmost best to keep the kimono closed.

Phil placed his right arm around me, his left holding my bags, as we slowly walked up the long walkway, past the decorative laser cut steel panels. Although I had visited girlfriends and their new bubs many times at this hospital before, at that moment I could not help but wonder *why oh why*, they had made the walkway so damn long, as it took every ounce of strength I had to make it all the way to the front doors. As we entered the reception, with overwhelming relief, I pointed Phil in the direction of the delivery suites.

'Excuse me, Mum, Dad you have to register first,' a friendly voice called across the void.

Damn! Thomas would have known this. We made our way across the room, but my face once again began to show signs of pain. Out of nowhere a wheelchair materialised, and I gratefully collapsed into it, once again riding the wild wave of agony.

Although too absorbed in my own journey, somewhere in the back of my mind I realised that although the reception area was not busy, across the void on a pair of sofas, a few people huddled together, no doubt playing the waiting game. Knowing that, was the only thing that kept a lid on my behaviour, because if wailing would have helped then believe you me, I would have done so.

The receptionist spoke to Phil. 'Okay Dad, now if we can just get some details off you…'

I interrupted, my voice not my own. 'My birth partner is stuck in traffic, but he should be here soon.'

'Oh I'm sorry, I thought you were the dad,' she said to Phil.

'I am,' he said, giving a curt nod.

The receptionist kept a straight face. No doubt she had heard it all before. She began to ask what felt like 20 questions. I knew that they were questions she had to ask, however I was having contractions so quickly I was struggling to comprehend what she was asking, and suddenly, uncharacteristically, I just wanted to tell her to *shut up*. Where the *heck* was Thomas?

As if reading my mind, Phil pulled the sleeve up on his chevron patterned shirt, and glanced at his watch. How many times had I seen him do that very thing, but today I immediately knew what was the different. The watch he wore. It was a Breitling, exactly like the one Jules wore when we were up at Clovelly. The one he had extolled the virtues of in such depth, I could sit a quiz on it and get every answer correct. But the biggest fact of all was that it was a watch that pilots wore.

I wrinkled my brow as if it could be further wrinkled. 'Phil… do you have a plane?' breathlessly I asked, and then gritted my teeth, whimpering through the pain.

'What?' he bent closer to me, his face a mask of bafflement. 'Do I have pain?'

'*No!*' I snapped. 'Not pain, *plane*! Are you a pilot as well?'

Even at time like that, I could see I had unnerved him, although his voice was calm. 'Yes… I have a twin engine. Why? What on earth has that got to do with anything?'

I threw my head back. *Oh for God's sake!* I had that feeling like, when at a certain time of the month, Davis would annoy the heck out of me, and I'd snap at him, generally for good reason mind you. But what would always make it worse, was if he mentioned that it must be *that* time of the month again. I swear during those times, if I'd had a gun, I could have quite possibly used it. Well it was like that, but multiplied by a thousand. Make that a million. A billion actually!

'Effing bloody hell!' I moaned through gritted teeth. 'Something else I didn't know about you.' My voice became raised, and my hands gripped the arms of the wheelchair. 'You're a *bloody* pilot. Anything else you might want to mention?'

From the desk above, I heard the voice of the receptionist. 'Okay… it looks like Mum is already in the transition stage.'

How dare she? That woman should be hung for sedition. Off with her head!

She continued with the last of the questions. *Don't mind me*, I wanted to yell. *After all I am just the one having a baby!* After what appeared to be hours but could have been seconds, I pulled at Phil's jacket. 'Phil… Phil… please just tell her… just tell her… I need an epidural *now*.' My voice had grown to a shriek. Within seconds the intensity of the pain had increased and I had reached a point where it was impossible for me not to scream the room down, strangers sitting opposite or not. I did not miss the terror on Phil's face.

Everything from that point felt like a blur and before I knew it I was in the delivery suite, and all I could think of, was that it was imperative for me to remove my bra, the *bloody thing* was strangling me, and I had to get rid of that *skimpy thing* between my legs. I might as well have worn a piece of ribbon for all the good it did. Although… I may have been insisting a little too loudly. Thank God Phil had been sent to move the car. I glared at the mid-wife, as I attempted with no avail to pull my t-shirt back on, who was attempting for me to do otherwise. Why was everyone being so *bloody effing* difficult?

Another contraction began and before I could think further, I had this overwhelming urge to go to the toilet. The sheet clutched to me, I tried to get up from the bed, only to have the mid-wife attempt to restrain my protesting body.

'Where are you going?'

'Please, I desperately need to go to the toilet. Like, I *really* need to go to the toilet,' I stressed making weird eyes at her.

'No, you don't,' she attempted to reassure me.

'But I do… I do…' and then this involuntary urge came upon me to push, and I was so embarrassed that I was going to go to the toilet then and there.

However, I caught the look on the midwife's face as she hurriedly examined me, only for her to loudly pronounce, 'Baby's head on view, head on view.' Medical staff materialised from everywhere.

Somewhere during that brief time, Phil had crept back into the room, and was quietly standing by my head. As I turned to the side, I blinked a couple of times as he looked to me to be a cardboard cut-out. I wanted to tell him that no matter what happened he must remain at the top end of the bed, but before I could say anything, he explained that he had spoken to my doctor, and like Thomas, she was doing her absolute best to make it.

'Right, well I want the epidural *now*,' I insisted to the mid-wife, for some crazy reason thinking it would buy me time.

'It's too late for that Peach,' I was informed, as once again she examined me. 'You're good to go.'

It felt like the baby was pushing its way out of my lower vertebrae, and I was fully aware that powerful drugs would be my preferred choice, however by the look on the mid-wife's face, the boat had well and truly sailed for that.

'Please a heat pack?' I breathed, desperate for just one lousy heat pack. Surely it would be some help.

'No time for that love,' I was informed as she patted my leg, the very one, she had just instructed Phil he would need to hold in the air, as I madly scrabbled to pull the sheet around me for modestly. She clapped her hands together. 'This baby is coming now.'

Sensing my trepidation, Phil leant in close to me and gently wiped my forehead with a cool wash cloth. He gripped my hand and looked into my eyes. 'You *can* do this Peach. I *know* you can.'

I felt my chin quiver, and a lone tear made its way down my cheek. 'This is too quick,' I whispered. Where were the hours of labouring? We hadn't had time to play my relaxation music, much less burn the aromatherapy. I swallowed, my mouth dry. Phil continued to stroke my forehead, gently pushing my hair back.

I *wanted* Thomas. As if reading my mind, Phil dialled Thomas's number and put it on speaker, holding it close to me.

'Mate, she's ready now. It's all happening rather fast, I'm afraid. Talk to her, she can hear you, she's just not up to conversation.'

In typical Thomas fashion, he dramatically proclaimed. 'Well Honey you know it's always been a mystery to me how you are going to push something that large out of your cha-cha, but if anyone can do it, you can.' With the weakest of smiles, I gave a snuff of derision, knowing Thomas was doing his best to make me smile. Although by the look on Phil's face, and the way he gave a startled blink, I gathered it surprised him.

But then I heard Thomas choke up, 'Phil has promised to look after you until I get there. It wasn't how we planned it Lovely. *Fucking traffic!* You just push that little Apricot right out, okay! When you think about it, she doesn't have too far to come!'

'Have to go mate,' Phil told him.

He took my hand and with some emotion squeezed it. I

hadn't realised how much I needed that touch, and I squeezed back. It was as if that simple gesture instantly sent me a message of strength and comfort. His eyes on mine, he gave a firm nod. 'You ready?' he asked, his voice kind

Biting my lip, I nodded, grateful to him.

'Good girl.'

And then the business started and a sense of calmness washed over me. My earlier angst strangely disappeared as quickly as it had come. With one foot bracing Phil's hip and the other on the mid-wife's, it was a complete relief to push, and I knew I could do it. The following contractions were nowhere near as bad as what the last few had been, and I felt as if I was making good progress. Phil leant into me and counted me through each push to ten, and continued to encourage. And it was funny but I didn't notice any pain associated with the contractions at all, just the contracting sensation. Within a few pushes my baby slipped into the world effortlessly.

I was exhausted, yet elated and so at peace with myself.

'Oh my God, it's a boy! It's a boy! Peach, it's a boy! ' Phil kept repeating. 'A boy, a little fellow, a mighty little guy.' I could feel the overflow of emotion between us, as my baby boy was placed on my chest. In an instant, all the pain was worth every second. Still in shock at the speed of the birth, I hugged him to me, my hands trembling. 'Hi baby,' I said, my voice high. 'Mummy is here, it's okay. I am so excited, cause I am going to love you so much.'

I glanced at Phil's face, which was leaning over us, a hand gently cradling the baby's head, a look on his face beyond elation. 'Hi mate.' Huge tears washed down his cheeks.

And then I watched as he turned, rested his elbows up against the wall, and with his bent head, silently sobbed. After a few minutes he turned back to us, pinched the end of his nose, and letting out a huge breath, smiled. 'Well,' he swallowed, and blinked a few times, and then laughed, attempting to cover his emotions. 'That wasn't exactly what I expected today.'

Chapter 30

As I looked into my baby's huge brown eyes, I realised that he had been sent here to teach me everything.

'Christopher,' I said, my voice thick. 'His name is Christopher.'

Leaning over me, unable to tear his eyes away from the baby, Phil nodded, a smile forming about his lips.

With one hand clasping Christopher's bunny rug covered body to my chest, as if in slow motion, I put the other up to my face and wiped my dry lips. I felt one of Phil's thumbs caress my forehead. The touch was comforting.

I closed my eyes, while one of the mid-wives fiddled around on the lower part of the bed, and then slowly I bought my hand down to cradle Christopher's head. My hand landed upon Phil's. Feeling sheepish, recent activity aside, I moved my hand away.

Without warning, I began to shake with uncontrollable tremors, my teeth rattling in my head. With fright, I clasped Christopher closer to me.

'Bit of shock there Mum?' Her voice matter-of-fact, one of the mid-wives patted me on the leg.

Phil's neck snapped back between her and me, his voice urgent. 'What's happening?'

'Here, t… t… take the baby,' I said to him, mid chatter, my hands trembling.

Speaking as if it was all in a day's work, the mid-wife's tone was calm. 'A bit of an adrenaline surge, plus her hormones have dropped, and…'

Before she could finish, Phil loudly interrupted her, anxiety written right across his face, his tone terse. 'Do something!'

'It's okay Dad, we'll get some blankets.' She left the room, her stride more casual than one would have expected.

Phil cradling Christopher to his shoulder, rapid fired to the remaining mid-wife, 'Maybe we need a doctor!'

Busy filling out paperwork, she raised her head. 'This can be quite…' Before more could be said, the other mid-wife returned with two blankets from the warming cabinet.

'Are you sure she doesn't need any more than that?' Phil's concern was evident.

She continued to tuck them around me. 'It's quite common, nothing to worry about. Now come on little man we've got to take some measurements.' Taking Christopher from Phil, she placed him in the perspex crib and began writing.

Phil pushed the blanket close around my neck. 'That better?' His tone was kind as he began to rub his hands up and down my arms over the top of the blanket.

I nodded, beginning to feel a little calmer, but still unable to stop my teeth from chattering.

He leant down to me, murmuring, 'Needs a bomb under her that one.'

My dry lips attempted a smile. My wavering voice whispered, 'It's okay Phil. I imagine this is all in a day's work for them. They can't panic every time something small happens.'

He nodded. 'I know, it's just that…' And he drifted off, looking away. It wasn't hard to imagine what he was thinking.

*

Still in the delivery suite, one of the mid-wives covered the phone with her hand, 'Your brothers are outside.'

I knew it had to be Thomas and Steve.

'Can they come in?'

Phil was holding Christopher, leaning over me, when we heard their muffled whispers from the door. He turned to them.

Thomas gasped and let out a sob, a hand to his chest. 'Oh my God!' Steve pulled him to him, and I saw his adam's apple go up and down as he swallowed hard. They gathered around Phil, and I noticed one of Thomas's hands rested on Phil's back.

Thomas looked over at me, making eyes. 'Peachy,' he cooed. 'You clever, clever girl.' And then he turned his attention back to Christopher. 'So... we have a little boy. Look Steve we have a little boy. I always knew it was a boy.' And with that he promptly began to cry.

'You finally made it,' was all I said, my voice still small.

He waved a hand at me, wiped at his nose and sniffed. 'Yes, Steve saved the day. He picked me up on the Harley and we hightailed it here as quick as we could. But I'll *never* forgive myself for not being here. *Never!* He gave a theatrical sniff, and then just as quickly moved on. 'I've heard of quick deliveries, but honey you take the cake.'

'You only missed it by a few minutes. And you beat the doctor!'

'Oh!' and I watched as he pursed his lips. And then he came and leant over me, lowering his voice, but still within earshot of Steve. 'I bet he's young, gorgeous and handsome, just like Dr McSteamy from Grey's Anatomy?'

'Ah no!' I summoned up a small laugh. 'Young, gorgeous and pretty! You've met her.'

'Hello, I am here you know.' Steve's voice was heard.

*

It was late on day three and I was impatiently waiting for the doctor to see me before I could be discharged. She had been held up by an emergency caesarean. I was hopeful she would come soon, as I felt I would be far more comfortable, plus have less interruptions, at home. It had been arranged that Phil would drive us. Although that had originally been Thomas's job, the fact that Phil was leaving for Melbourne the next day, made me consider it the right thing to do. We really hadn't managed to talk about anything at all other than Christopher in the last few days, and there appeared to be an unspoken agreement between us that we would wait until I went home before we did.

I was feeling a little teary, and could not get my feelings under control, even though one of the nurses had explained that due to the rapid decline of hormones, it was perfectly normal on day three to have the baby blues.

With one of my hands lightly resting on my sleeping baby, I was sitting on the bed, looking at him, as if he was a complete miracle, and the first child ever to be born. Tears welled yet again. I wondered how on earth I was going to live, now that my heart was on the outside of my body in another living breathing human being. A sense of protectiveness like I had never felt, washed over me. I thought I had loved Lakshmi and Bob as intensely as possible, but this was an entirely different level.

During, and immediately after labour, I had been on a phenomenal high. I remembered once reading an article that said the hormone oxytocin was released at this time and had the ability to make all new mothers think that their baby was the best looking baby to ever be born. When I looked at Christopher, I knew it was not the oxytocin, as he was in fact the best looking baby ever to grace this earth.

During the two pm feed that morning, I could not take my eyes off his little face, studying every nook and cranny. His mouth working hard upon my breast, he briefly pulled away and looked up at me as if to say, *Oh... you're my mum!* And that was when the feeling of overwhelming protectiveness began, and had been rapidly intensifying all day, along with the size of my extremely engorged breasts, which felt like they began up under my armpits.

I thought of mothers who sent their sons off to Afghanistan, and wondered how that was even possible. My eyes filled, and once again tears began to run down my cheeks. What if he wanted to join the army, what if he grew up and wanted to live in another country, got married, had children and never came back? What if he didn't like me? Or I wasn't a good mum? Or we fell on hard times? What if… I let out a sob and brushed at my cheeks.

'Peach… are you okay?' Marty hovered in the doorway.

I put a hand out to him, sniffed and smiled. 'No honey.' I blew my nose on a tissue. 'If you thought I was melodramatic before, you *aint* seen nothing yet? I'm already visualising the day he leaves home and doesn't need me anymore.'

Marty laughed. 'You crack me up Peach. Only you would think that.' He gave me a hug, and then glanced at my packed bag waiting beside the door. 'So what's all this, are you going home?'

I nodded. 'Just waiting for the doctor to see us and then Phil's taking us.' I didn't miss the look that crossed Marty's face. 'What?' I asked. 'What's that face for?'

Folding his arms, he looked lost for words. 'No reason.' However, I could tell by the tone of his voice that there was a reason. I kept looking at him, waiting for him to say something.

Placing his hands in his front pockets of his trousers, he stood looking out the window. 'So what's going to happen with Phil? I mean have you guys talked or anything?'

'Not yet.' I exhaled, feeling exhausted after my recent emotional bout. 'Look, I really don't know. In hindsight, having him here when Christopher was born was a godsend.' I shrugged. 'So who knows…?' I drifted off.

He spun around to me, his tone terse. 'Well you know… this guy has got to be honest with you.'

Silently, I nodded, wondering why he had attitude, especially when I was already feeling sensitive.

'He's got to come clean with everything.' The ferocity of his tone astounded me.

'Of course Marty. I'm not even sure…'

He cut me off. 'Yeah well, I just think you have to know everything.' We looked at each other for the longest time.

And then I was direct. 'Such as?' And the way I looked at him, he knew he was not going to get off the hook.

He turned back to the window, his voice was small. 'A few minutes ago, I stood behind him down in reception waiting for the lift, but he was on the phone and didn't notice me. I heard him talking to someone.' Turning around, he levelled a look at me. 'Sounded like stuff you'd say to a girlfriend.' He stuffed his hands back in his pockets once more, and shrugged. 'But I *dunno*. I could be wrong. The lift came, I got in and he stayed in reception talking.'

Although my heart thudded, my face stayed put. I felt as if someone had snuffed something out in me. I sat still for the longest time, and then I shrugged, knowing Marty would have been waiting for an answer. 'Oh well if he has, he has,' I lied.

For the next ten minutes, Marty and I leant over the crib and extolled the virtues of baby Christopher, however I could not stop my heart from hammering.

When it was time for him to leave, I could see him lingering. I knew he wanted to say more, so before he could, I did. 'You did the right thing.'

'After last time…'

I put a hand up and cut him off, not wanting to go there. 'Marty, I don't want to hold you up now, but do you think you could come back later and pick us up?'

He nodded. 'Sure thing. Call me after the doctor has been.'

Fully dressed, I lay back upon the bed, my hands joined on my stomach, and looked at the ceiling, for what felt like the longest time. Engorged breasts aside, it was as if my body had been run over by a steam roller, repeatedly, I felt so flat.

For the last few days, I had been play acting happy families. Phil's mother had come to the hospital bringing Sophia to meet her new baby brother. I had been under an intense new regime of feeding Christopher, burping Christopher, changing Christopher, and *oohing* and *aahing* over every part of Christopher. In between, family and friends had visited and flowers had arrived. Phil had sent the most incredible gift box from Edible Blooms. Made from fresh fruit, it had been artfully designed and carved to look like a huge box of flowers, so large I was not only sharing it with my visitors, but the nursing staff as well. The Belgium chocolate coated strawberries were the favourite, hands down.

*

'Knock, knock!'

Hearing Phil's voice, I sat up, putting my legs over the side of the bed.

'The doctor been yet?' he asked, his voice light hearted.

I shook my head. 'I have to ask you something?'

'Sure,' he was chipper. 'Ask away?' He sat in the visitor's chair, leaning towards me, his hands joined in front of him, his face smiling.

'Are you in a relationship?'

I saw the instant change on his face and an almost impeccable shake of his head, as he pulled back. He stood. 'No.' His voice was firm.

I narrowed my eyes, and gave him a look that demanded more. He began to pace. Although I had absolutely no right, I felt sick.

'I have been seeing someone for the past six weeks or so, but we are not in a relationship.'

Without meaning to, I placed a hand to my mouth, and then nodded, too afraid to speak in case my voice gave me away. I cleared my throat, and attempted to be matter of fact, but it was the last thing I felt. 'Oh okay.' I couldn't stop my head from nodding as if it was trying to convince my brain that this was perfectly acceptable.

'Look… she is someone I recently met and we have been taking it slowly…'

I put hand up to stop him. 'You… you don't have to explain anything to me. I get it.' I turned away, and for something to do, I reached for the glass of water on the bedside table, took a sip, and willed my taut throat to help me out and swallow.

However, he began to explain. 'I'm going to…'

I became agitated and cut him off. 'Can you go please? Marty's coming back to pick us up. I think that's best.'

'Will you let me explain?' he demanded.

'There's nothing to explain here.' I almost gave a laugh of hysteria. 'Please go.' I turned away.

*

From the hospital bed, I watched the sky darken and the city lights come alive. The doctor had come and gone and Marty was going to be back soon to take us home. I had almost reneged and stayed another night, although knew I would feel better in my own surroundings.

It was the fact that yet again, Phil had omitted an extremely vital piece of information. He had told me about speaking to his in-laws, asking for their acceptance of him being with someone else, and how emotional that all was; he'd told me about the *Love Stash* and the secret love letters and confronting the older guy; worrying he may not have been Sophia's father; the responsibility he felt for his staff; and working through some sort of agreement for a buyout, which I hadn't fully understood. However, he had *omitted* he was seeing someone.

Closing my eyes, my cheeks burned with embarrassment. I felt a fool. I wasn't angry with him. I was angry with myself. How clear does something have to be for me to get it?

Christopher gave a little meow like a kitten. One arm escaped his muslin wrap, and slowly went up in the air as if doing a contented stretch. He gave another squeak and arched his back. A rumble escaped his nappy. I picked him up and held him close, inhaling his precious baby scent. 'You're all I need. You and me, we're a family. Just us two… and Wilbur. You'll love Wilbur.'

*

Aside from the four hourly night feeds, which let's face it, by the time you changed a baby, fed and burped them, there was only three hours until the next feed, I had slept relatively well, conking out the minute my head hit the feather pillow each time. The huge roller coaster of emotions I had gone through the last few days rendering me practically unconscious. At one point, as I blindly felt around on the floor for my slippers, I realised I had actually worn them to bed three hours earlier.

Due to the depth of sleep I went into, I had wheeled Christopher's crib into my room from the small room across the landing, and placed it right up against my bed, concerned that I would not hear him. However, almost immediately, I realised that the moment Christopher opened his mouth and gave the smallest of sounds, I would sit up in bed as if a Harley Davidson had been revved beside my head.

I had not given one ounce of thought to Phil and the person he was seeing. *Well...* I tell a lie... I had given it thought, however immediately pushed it from my mind each time, reminding myself that Christopher was the sole reason Phil had come into my life, and it was *nothing* more than that. To have expected more would have been ludicrous. I could not do it to myself.

*

Bea was not due to return from Provence for another two weeks. As Christopher had not been due for three weeks, she had planned her return for the week before his birth. In typical Bea style, upon hearing about his premature arrival, she had told me that there was no point in her returning any sooner, as it would give me time to settle him in, and that young mothers of today had it all sorted.

I wanted to remind her I was actually not a young mother, and that I wouldn't have minded a bit of sorting from her, however it was futile to expect the free spirited Bea to be the traditional doting grandma. I remembered back to both Lakshmi's and Bob's births and recalled that it had been me who had taken time from work that first week to assist. Johnny's wife Patrice, had been helpful by providing some dinners, which took great effort as we all knew cooking did not come naturally to her. And, if I remembered correctly, Mitch's mum was not too bad either.

However, I can still distinctly remember Bea sitting on the couch in Lou and Mitch's tiny one bedroom unit, saying that she didn't want to hold Lakshmi, she preferred to gaze upon her. That may have been all well and good, however a crying baby needs pacifying. And then Patrice had walked in bearing a Tupperware dish containing a frozen sausage casserole, and Bea's comment had been... *oh... are we supposed to bring food?* By the time Bob arrived she was more hands on... a tad!

So it was not as if I expected any more than that from my mother. Bea was Bea and that was that.

However, I was most grateful Lou was dropping the children off to their dad's, and coming by. I needed a shower, and it appeared as if the smallest of mundane tasks were now a complete ordeal. I began to wonder how I would ever look respectable again, and that perhaps pyjamas may become my new wardrobe. I thought back to Emerald Green's comment about when my life changed, my wardrobe might as well. I gave a snort of derision.

*

Lou had come and gone, doing two loads of washing and allowing me the luxury of a hot shower, while she made me tea and toast.

Around lunch time, Steve, arrived with an esky full of gourmet dinners for one, courtesy of his housekeeper, under instruction from him.

Watching as he loaded them into my freezer, I held Christopher up to my shoulder, and rubbed his little back in time to a Burt Bacharach CD playing in the background.

'By the time he's ten he'll know all of these songs,' I bragged.

'By the time he's ten he'll be gay if you keep that up,' Steve quipped. Leaning against the fridge, he eyed me. 'Did Phil come by this morning?'

I turned from him, and with one hand picked up the dishcloth and wiped out the sink, Christopher still over my shoulder. 'Uh-huh!'

With the dishcloth still in hand, I continued now on the kitchen bench, and it seemed like minutes went by while neither of us said anything. Finally, I glanced at Steve. 'What?'

He cocked his head to one side. 'What's going on with you two?'

'Nothing.' My tone clipped, I shook my head. 'Not one thing. He's got a girlfriend.'

My mind returned to this morning and Phil's brief visit. Possibly he would have stayed longer, however I had seen no need to drag it out.

Lou had just left when he had arrived. His mother had kindly sent me some pea and ham soup.

It was just after feed time, so I had handed Christopher to Phil to burp. Phil appeared to have the touch as a tiny milky gurgle was heard. Proudly, he had smiled at me over the top of Christopher's head. Watching my tiny son, it wasn't hard to smile at Phil in return, although silently I chastised my heart for feeling warmth.

Quietly, I had motioned for Phil to follow me upstairs, so he could place Christopher back in his crib. Earlier I had returned it to the nursery.

With some pride, I noticed Phil's eye's sweeping around the small room, taking in the tiffany blue colour scheme and the softly textured white bunny decals. Truth be known, those bunnies had been waiting for soft pink ribbons to go around their necks. It was certainly not an unwelcome surprise for them to stay as they were. Pride of place in the corner sat Chester, my old rocking horse from when I was a small child.

Lost in time, Chester had sat up in the manhole at Johnny's house, stumbled upon only when he'd had his ceiling insulated some time back. Unbeknown to me, Johnny had been working on the rocking horse for some months, restoring the paintwork, giving it a new mane and having a lovely little bridle made. I had plaited that mane one million times, before Lou tragically took the scissors to it. Ready to surprise me upon our arrival home, Johnny had bought Chester over while I was still in hospital.

With one hand cradling his head, Phil gently lowered the tiny body into the crib. 'He's a lucky, lucky little boy Peach.' I nodded, hoping my brows didn't raise one single millimetre, giving away my thoughts. Although Christopher was well wrapped in a bunny rug, I pulled the white crocheted blanket up around him, tucking him in snuggly. He was so perfect, my heart swelled.

We both stood quietly for some time leaning over the bassinet, gazing at our slumbering child, every now and then one of us gently stroking some part of him as if we could not believe he was real. I reminded myself that I felt that way even though I'd had six months to get used to the idea, however, Phil had only had days.

It was not hard to feel a certain palpable feeling in the air of something wonderful, a certain type of bliss.

I don't know how long we stood, but I can say, as per usual, whenever I was around Phil he oozed a sense of comfort. It was with some effort that I reminded myself to protect my heart. I used to think that if you followed your heart you couldn't go wrong. At some point I had changed that to, if I protected my heart I could not go wrong. I knew I had to be resolute. I searched for a positive between us, and came up with the fact, that regardless of who we were to each other, we would always be Christopher's family. That resonated well with me.

Eventually I gave myself a shake, and signalled to Phil to follow me out to the landing. I knew time was getting on, and he and Sophia had a plane to catch. As I descended the stairs, I kept my voice low, so as not to disturb Christopher. However now I had to keep a lid on other feelings that were attempting to escape, feelings of something wonderful being over.

With effort, I injected warmth into my voice, hoping I didn't sound false, but hearing a clipped tone to my voice as I spoke. 'Please call whenever you and Sophia are in town. I'd like her to get to know her brother.' I knew I was making it more about Sophia's relationship with Christopher, than Phil's. 'And please tell your mother she will always be welcome.'

As we reached the bottom of the stairs, Phil placed a piece of paper on the entry console. 'Here are all of my contact details. You'll have no trouble getting me anytime.'

I glanced at the paper although did not touch it. 'Is there a best time to call?'

'No... whenever.'

'I wouldn't want to upset your girlfriend.' There I'd said it, the bitch in me finally escaping.

Phil exhaled heavily, and scratched at this head, looking sheepish. 'Peach... she's not exactly my girlfriend...'

I cut him off, an odd smile on my face. 'Does she know about Christopher yet?'

I could see this flustered him. 'Not entirely.'

'Ah-huh,' and then the bitch was joined by its acerbic sister. 'Not entirely. Funny answer. What... she knows partly?'

He closed his eyes briefly. 'I'm not sure about you, but it's an odd thing to find out on the phone. I cannot deny that she hasn't sensed something's going on. I feel the very least I can do is to tell her in person.'

My fake smile continued. 'Yes... good thinking... it's the least you can do. She deserves that.' I wondered what I deserved, however felt it prudent to shut the hell up at that point. With everything I could muster, and I must say, it was not without huge effort, I drew on my nicer side. 'Well Phil, thank you for all of the support you have given the last few days.' At least I did mean this, although I did have to stop myself extending my hand as if we had just completed a business transaction.

'I'll call tonight?'

'Whatever,' my tone was flippant, even if my heart wasn't. I'd be manning those calls, it wouldn't pay to get too familiar.

*

Steve's voice cut into my thoughts. 'I asked if they were serious.'

'What do you mean *are they serious?* I snapped, and then lowered my voice. 'You sound like Phil!'

'Well I'm just saying, he didn't have to be sitting around single waiting for you, did he?'

Because of the fact I was holding Christopher, and only that, I tried incredibly hard to keep my voice agreeable, although I am not saying it was not tinged with sarcasm. 'No Steve, I didn't expect him to be single for the rest of his bloody life. It's just that he didn't say anything about it.'

'From what I can gather, you have been rather busy since he arrived. Exactly *when* would you have liked him to have told you? In between contractions?'

Although Steve was always a straightshooter, I was completely flabbergasted by his tone. I shook my head and did a double take. 'I feel as if I am speaking to Phil.' I narrowed my eyes. 'What's going on here? Have you been speaking to him?'

Steve appeared to take some time before he answered. Widening my eyes, I put a hand up. 'Hang on,' my tone may have sounded amused, but it sure as heck was not, 'let me put Christopher down in his crib. I am not going to have this riveting conversation in front of him.'

On the way back down the stairs I could hear the sounds of Steve using the coffee machine. Walking back into the kitchen, I ignored him and busied myself plugging the baby monitor in. Even though I could feel his eyes upon me, for a few minutes I continued to fiddle with the buttons, at one point loudly turning on *Twinkle, Twinkle Little Star*, or was that *Baa Baa Black Sheep*? I had never noticed that they had the same tune before. Tutting loudly with annoyance, I peered at the monitor.

'Here let me,' Steve said from behind. Within seconds the image of Christopher soundly sleeping appeared. For a few seconds it irked me that men were so bloody good at this type of thing. 'It's this button here,' was all he said, before returning to the coffee machine.

'Hmmm,' I said. As if I was the visitor, I walked around to the other side of the kitchen bench, pulled out a stool, and forgetting about the sensitivity of my stitches, plonked myself down. Discreetly I winced, before letting out the hugest breath through my mouth. I decided I'd let Steve do the talking. For the longest time, chin propped on hand, I looked at him while he expertly whirled the machine.

Finally, when we both had a coffee in hand, and there was nothing left to distract him, he spoke. 'He called me.' Looking away, he placed his mug to his lips and drank as if that was the end of the subject.

'And?'

'Apparently he's moving back up here shortly, but meanwhile he asked me to look out for you. He explained that he had been sort of seeing someone however it was nothing serious, and that he had seen no reason to tell you…'

Cutting him off, I snapped. 'What? See what I mean!'

'Settle down tiger! He saw no reason to tell you, because

obviously he's putting an end to it.'

Folding my arms, I seethed, more at Steve, than anyone else. No, allow me to amend that... at *bloody men* in general. What was this? A boys' club? 'It's sort of not the point is it? The guy is *great* at omitting stuff.' I clenched my jaw. 'It just makes me wild.'

'Listen honey, I know you've been burned in the past, but at some point you have to give someone a go.'

I raised my voice. 'What go? What is wrong with everyone? There's no *go* here! He's not exactly interested. All I ask is, if he wishes to have Christopher in his life, he is honest. Is that too much?'

Steve placed his hands up. 'Okay, okay. Calm down.' He looked thoughtful for a few minutes, giving me time to fume to myself. I hated it when someone told me to calm down... I always wanted to respond with... *oh thank you for that wonderful piece of advice. I'll do just that!*

Steve interrupted my internal rant. 'Yeah well you know, I understand where the guy is coming from. I don't exactly like being on my own either. And Phil was for a while. If Thomas left tomorrow or something happened to him, I couldn't be on my own. It's just the way I am. Don't get all hysterical because the guy thought you were back with Davis and having his baby. Mind you, when he sent the scarecrow and stuff, the ball was in your court, you could have thanked him or something.'

Taken back, I wrinkled my brow, rapid firing, 'What do you mean?' However before he could talk, I began to work it out. 'The kitchen garden scarecrow? I remember coming home from that first pre-natal class, and Brownie saying that he had signed for a large parcel which had arrived from a nursery down south. If I remember correctly, I was feeling a little flat so I asked him to unpack it.' I narrowed my eyes. 'There was nothing in it to indicate that it was from Phil, although Brownie and I discussed that perhaps he had ordered it before he left and it had taken some time to come.' I spoke quietly then. 'It is a lovely scarecrow.' And then I glanced at Steve. 'Why did he send it?'

'He said he didn't want to come straight out and ask if you were with Davis. And that he hoped you would respond. But he heard nothing.'

'What… he thought I was a mind reader as well did he? It wasn't as if I was meant to know who *he* was. That was sheer arse I found that out.'

'He said there was a card in the box, asking if he could call in next time he was in Brisbane.'

'There was no card.'

'And he said he sent a cookbook or something. I didn't follow…'

I screwed my face up. 'I think I would know if he sent a cookbook. I mean why in the hell would he? That's crazy.'

Steve stood to rinse his mug. 'I dunno. I'm just telling you what he said. Honey I gotta go. Late for a meeting now.' He kissed the side of my cheek, grabbed his jacket and with his determined stride took off down the hallway, his boots loud on the timber floor, before he must have had the same thought as me, and treaded a little lighter. I heard the front door click.

I stayed where I was, my mind whirling in thought. There was *no* cookbook. Of that I was certain. *Cookbook, cookbook, cookbook?* Hmmm…

And then I jumped from the stool and headed towards the library. My fingers glanced across the poultry books, quickly removing one. The title jumped out at me. *Chookbook!* The one I couldn't remember ordering, thinking I had pregnancy brain. My trembling fingers opened it. My heart gave a loud thump at his handwriting, before I thought it may stop altogether.

Dear Peach,
Saw this book and thought of you. How are the girls?
Warmest regards Phil

Chapter 31

Christopher was almost three weeks old and this was the second time Gloria had come for morning tea. Except for when I fed him, Christopher had not left her arms. It appeared she could not get enough, her eyes studying every feature of his.

'Would you like to take him up to the nursery and settle him for his sleep,' I asked, watching as her face lit with pure joy.

'Oh may I?'

'I'd love you to,' I assured her, picking up the coffee cups. 'But I warn you, he will need changing and it may not be pleasant.'

She beamed. 'Well lucky me then.' Glowing with pride, she carefully placed him over her shoulder, and with one hand behind his head and the other under his little bottom, she made her way up the stairs, talking to him the entire time.

Wilbur stood watching, after a second he flopped back down, his face turned to the wall. It appeared he was ignoring Christopher. I think he felt usurped by him, wondering what on earth all the fuss was about and when would this little alien leave us to our former lives.

'Come here boy.' I patted my leg.

Standing, Wilbur looked at me, but stayed where he was. I read his confused face to mean, *do you mean me? Are you sure?*

I laughed. 'Come on silly billy.' I ruffled his fur and my hands framed his face. His dark eyes appeared to be grateful for the attention. It pulled at my heartstrings and I felt mean that perhaps I had been ignoring him. 'Oh poor you. I know things are a bit different around here. But you'll love him in time. He'll turn out to be your best friend. I promise. Meanwhile we'll try to come up with something just for you and me to do. Okay?'

I stayed where I was for a few minutes giving Wilbur plenty of love. My mind turned to Gloria upstairs. It was important to me that Christopher knew both sides of his family. Phil had been back and forth a couple of times, however I had been fairly business like with him. On his last trip he told me he was returning to live in Brisbane permanently this week, and had taken a lease on ground floor apartment at Cutter's Landing, walking distance to Gloria's and not too far from Carmody House. I had shrugged, thinking that whatever he did, really did not concern me.

However, I think it was only then, I actually realised that, that time Pete had told me he had seen Phil working in a garden up on Tenerife hill, he was referring to Gloria's home, where Phil had lived. At the time, I had thought Phil must have been working there. It was moments like those when the penny dropped, that I felt ridiculous for not putting two and two together sooner.

I gave Wilbur a couple of friendly heavy pats, fluffed the cushions, and straightened some magazines, looking longingly at the Country Style, thinking it may be years before I was able to take the time to read again. Wiping the kitchen bench, I dried my hands on the hand towel. Out of habit, I reached across and switched on the baby monitor. Once again I examined and then folded the beautiful Marquise baby clothes Gloria had come bearing. She had similar taste to me in baby clothes, preferring babies to look like babies and not be wearing harsh denim within a few weeks of their little lives.

Bea, the person who always wore white, seemed to select brightly hued tie-died caps, with corduroy overalls, and boldly striped jumpers. I was waiting for a Rastafarian cap to arrive next!

'Some things never change,' Gloria had told me when earlier I had held up the soft cotton sleeveless suit. Her voice was filled with pride. 'They look *exactly* like the ones Phillip wore when he was that age. Considering the label is at least 80 years old, I was thrilled to see they have continued to make the same beautiful styles with such lovely quality.'

'They are beautiful, and these singlets are perfect.' My hands had smoothed over the embroidered trains embellishing them. 'You bought gifts last time as well Gloria. You're far too generous.'

Gloria had sat back and elegantly crossed her legs, placing her hands in her lap. 'Allow me. This is such a lovely time.' And then she lowered her voice and a sadness washed over her. 'Unfortunately, it was not the same when Sophia was born. It is terribly hard to be excited about a baby when her mummy has just died. We were all in *such* shock, there was numbness… but… we had to pull ourselves together and get on with it for her sake, and for Phillip's.'

That conversation was still on my mind as I heard Gloria singing to Christopher on the monitor. Glancing over to it, I smiled as they came in and out of range. My heart warmed for Christopher. He deserved a full family around him. I was hopeful he would grow up knowing Sophia. I could put whatever private feelings I had aside and be magnanimous regarding Phil. For goodness sake, we were both adults.

And then I heard Christopher gurgle. I laughed. Of late he had begun to find his voice. How cute!

Unable to keep away, I picked up the new clothes and tiptoed up the stairs, so as not to disturb. From the doorway, I happily watched as Gloria proudly held him up to the mirror, her voice animated. 'Who's this? Who is this lovely boy? This is Christopher, Sophia's little brother, and our beautiful, beautiful surprise. Now here's a little secret.' She placed him on the change table and began to change his nappy. As she leant over him, her voice dropped to a loud whisper. 'I sort of thought you might be ours the day I saw your mummy at the shops.'

Startled, I felt like I was eavesdropping, however before I could speak, Gloria continued. 'Yes I did. I just hoped and prayed you were. But how could I say anything, cause your daddy…'

Deliberately, I gave a soft clearing of my throat. Gloria turned to me, her hands clutching both of Christopher's.

I smiled and raised my brows, my voice soft. 'How's he going?'

'We were just having a little chat before I put him down.' With that, she lifted him from the change table and placed him into the crib, rewrapping the muslin wrap firmly around him. 'I was telling him…' and then she changed the tone of her voice as once again she spoke to the baby, 'That your daddy's not much of a talker. No he's not. He's good at many other things. But sharing information isn't one of them. He keeps his cards close to his chest. It's just the way he is.'

As if loath to let go, one of her hands gently kept contact with Christopher, while she turned to me. She shook her head. 'Sometimes he used to drive me crazy. Even as a little boy, we'd come home from a function and I'd say to him that next time he might need to speak up a bit more. His response was always the same. With an astounded look on his face, he'd say, "But I was listening Mum."' Gloria tutted loudly. 'How do you argue with that? I daresay we could all do to listen a bit more.'

I leant against the doorway, my arms folded, hoping Gloria

was not going to divulge information I did not want to hear, but at the same time, hoping that she did.

'His father was the same. Getting details out of the two of them was like getting blood out of a stone. But...' and she gave a chuckle, 'get them in the right mood and you can't shut them up.'

I knew exactly what she meant. Wanting to know more about the other side of Christopher's family, I couldn't help but ask, 'It must have been hard for you, losing your husband so young?'

She gave a grim smile and slowly nodded. 'Of course! Missing him, the loneliness, raising Phillip on my own, it was hard. Stan and I had married late. Like you, I was 35 when Phillip was born. However in those days that was quite old. As much as we might have wanted it, there were no more children. Hard on Phillip more than anything. As if he doesn't have enough going on, he always feels responsible for me. Calls me every single day.' Her face lit up. 'But, if he'd had siblings they could have shared that responsibility.' And then she was thoughtful for a few seconds.

'There were days when I prayed that Stan knew of Phillip's successes, but there were days when I prayed that he did not know of his despairs. How awful would that be to know you couldn't be with your child to console, but could only watch from afar? So some days, I just didn't pray at all. And other days I got angry at Stan for leaving us. A million times I asked *why* he had to go fishing that particular day. *Why?* What would have happened if he'd gone the next day?'

And then as if too serious, she lightened her tone. 'Anyway, after Stan went I was lucky that Frank Carmody took such an interest. It seemed whenever I had problems with Phillip he stepped in. I was most grateful. He was a good man.'

Not for the first time, I caught something in her eyes when she spoke of Mr Carmody. I walked over to the crib. 'Gloria… I hope you don't mind me asking, but was there… did you and Frank…'

'Heavens no! No it was nothing like that.' However, I watched as a smile played about her lips. She lowered herself onto the white cane rocking chair, once again placing her hands in her lap in her ladylike manner. She didn't look at me but her face wore a wistful look and her voice changed, now more of a conspiratorial tone to it. 'You know there could have been. He *was* a large strapping man, a fair bit older, but a good looking type…'

I smiled to myself, thinking poor old Mr Carmody's looks had well and truly faded by the time I had met him. But how nice to think he had been good looking at some point.

'… Frank would have been keen, but I'd had my marriage to Stan. I didn't see myself marrying again.' And then she laughed. 'To tell the truth, Frank probably didn't want marriage either, but I wasn't *that* type. I had my boy.' Shrugging, she smiled at me. 'In hindsight, I may have done it differently. In fact, I probably should have.'

'How so?'

'Hmmm… I don't know. Well… no one really wants to be on their own do they? It would have been nice to share the things Phillip did with someone. And it would have been nice for Phillip to have a stepdad, someone who could do all that manly stuff with him. But look, I'm not complaining. Phillip's turned out fine. He's a wonderful son. It's just you want to know you've given them every chance, don't you?'

Slowly I nodded, watching as she walked back over to the crib, placing a comforting hand once again on Christopher, patting his little back, her eyes adoringly watching him. 'They are so precious aren't they? I'm afraid that feeling doesn't change no matter how old they get to be.' She looked at me, before she glanced away. 'There'll be times you'll feel as if he is misunderstood by someone, and you'll want to call that person and say, "My son is a good boy. It wasn't what he meant. Give him another chance." But he'll be an adult and you'll have to hold your tongue. My goodness the amount of times, I have wanted to do that on Phillip's behalf...' Her voice faded for a moment before she continued.

'I've always thought that it's a good thing we don't have a crystal ball. How could we bear it if we knew? If I had known what Phillip would have had to endure when he lost Katrine, I think it would have killed me. It nearly did. As his mother, if I could have taken that pain, I would have. Many a time I asked the good Lord why. It was hard for me not to question my faith at the time. *After all* I had lost Stan. It was unfair. Why did Phillip have to lose his dad so young, and then his wife? Damn cruel. But this I know... it's how it is meant to be.' She gave a smile, lightening the moment. 'Phillip is such a good father to Sophia. No doubt more so because of Katrine's death.'

And then I noticed she appeared to be choosing her words. 'We don't know what's around the corner, so we should just remember to love as much as we can. In my maturity, I realise all a person ever needs is someone to love, a dream, and something to do. If you've got that, you've got it all.' She caught sight of my thoughtful face.

'Goodness I'm getting a bit heavy here aren't I?' She waved a hand at me. 'Don't tell Phillip, he might ban me.'

I laughed, lightening the moment. 'No chance of that. What we talk about on your visits is our business.' My hands reached for the crystal handles on the white dresser. Delicately, I placed the little clothes in the drawer, my hands smoothing the fabric far longer than was necessary. Something had been triggered in my brain and I was uncertain of exactly what it was.

*

Arms folded, my tone determined, I asked, 'Come on now Fred give over, what's your story?' For the twentieth time in the past few weeks, I studied the scarecrow. I did remember the day he arrived, although I probably wasn't as excited as I should have been. I guess I now felt neglectful.

As I examined him, I realised that whoever had made him had done a wonderful job.

Standing an impressive six feet tall, and mounted on solid bamboo, he was attired in navy overalls, similar to the ones Brownie wore each day, with a red and yellow light-weight checked shirt that blustered in the breeze, a red bowtie, and an old brown hat covered in metallic silver nuts and bolts which glistened in the sunlight. He featured long corn hands, feet and hair, designed to blow in the wind and to deter even the bravest of birds.

To keep the birds guessing, Brownie took it upon himself to move Fred around on a constant basis.

I guess if Phil told Steve he had sent him as a gift, then he had. But what I wondered was, how he expected me to know the scarecrow was from him? Was I meant to ask that man one hundred questions on the off chance I may get some information about *something*? He had told me he was not one to talk of things until they had happened. I begged to differ... he was also not one to talk of things full stop. However, I was not one to be ungrateful, and if he had sent it, I would have liked to have known, so I could have at least thanked him.

Fred's position of late was in the raised garden bed amongst the cabbages and beetroots. Climbing in amidst them, better to scrutinize the scarecrow, I had a sudden vision of the snake saga, and hiding out in that same garden bed, at that time amongst the pumpkins. My mind turned to what a lifesaver Phil had been, however just as quickly I pushed it away.

Reaching up, I touched Fred's hat which had begun to fade a little. I wondered how often I would have to redress him in new clothes, the old becoming faded and tatty. I tucked his shirt in, and then pulled it back out again, knowing it was far more purposeful if the tails were free to flap in the wind. My hands smoothed the front pockets of Fred's overalls, noticing the stitching a little frayed. However I decided that may have been the initial intention. One pocket had some stiffening in to keep it in shape, the other did not feel as if it did. I ran three fingertips around the edge of the firmer pocket feeling the piece of cardboard. I could always cut another piece for the other side.

Using my fingers to estimate the size, I decided it would be easier to use the other piece as a template. As I pulled it out, I felt my heart give a lurch. Yes, it was a piece of cardboard although not as I had had thought. Somewhat water logged and faded, it appeared to be a small floristry card, dirty white with a tiny posy in the corner. The minute writing by this point was blurred and well faded. Squinting, I held it on an angle, attempting to make the inscription out. With major effort, the only words I could read were: *Dear Peach.... my friend Jake... kitchen garden. X Phil a*nd then a phone number which was impossible to decipher.

Hmmm. Two things came to mind. One I had been calling the poor guy Fred when his name was really Jake. And two, what exactly had Phil wanted me to do?

No... *I am sorry,* although this was a generous deed, it was far *too* cryptic for my liking. Once again, I was not a mind reader.

With much mulling over, I could not work out if Phil's diverse behaviour was wrong or odd, or… I simply did not know!

Chapter 32

Even to my ears, I could hear that the tone of my voice sounded as if I was conducting a business meeting. But then again, I guess I was. 'Well Phil, obviously I will not be opening the B&B at this point.'

Placing my coffee cup back in the saucer, without giving Phil a chance to settle Christopher, I automatically reached for him as he began to squirm fretfully in Phil's arms. Placing him to my shoulder, I stood and began to pat his back, all the while giving a little jig and a sway, a move perfected by me over the past few weeks.

'You seem to have the knack.' Phil watched as Christopher appeared to immediately fall back into his slumber.

Without looking at him, quick as a flash I responded with that tone again. 'I think it's called being a mother.' As it came out of my mouth, I wished I could have taken it back. Surely this man must think me a right bitch. In this instance, it had not been my intention. I was only too aware that in Phil's case he had been mother and father to Sophia. I attempted to soften things. 'It's just that I'm with him all the time.'

Christopher fussed once again, and I jigged and swayed a little more vigorously, calming him. That morning, the little darling had woken earlier than usual and fretted until I had fed him. He had continued this twice more before the next two feeds, so by the time we met with Phil and Sophia, we were well and truly out of our routine. All I could think about was keeping him settled until we arrived back home to the privacy of Carmody House. I had absolutely no intention of feeding him in front of Phil.

I was also a touch frazzled because during the last feed I

had noticed I appeared to have less milk than usual. After referring to my bible, *Babywise,* I realised that this was normal when a baby had a growth spurt and upped their feeds. Apparently, I would have more milk the next day to keep up with him. Fingers crossed, as earlier Christopher had appeared frustrated and pulled at my breasts hungrily.

Still standing, and doing my little jig, I poured myself another glass of water, keen to keep my fluids up.

A couple of weeks ago, wanting to show Christopher off, I had begun heading out on marathon walks, discovering all sorts of things in the area I called home. With Christopher tucked up snuggly in his pram, and with Wilbur's lead tightly in my hand, we had begun our journeys.

Only the week before, as we had walked along the Teneriffe boardwalk, I had come across a stainless steel sculpture, done in the most intricate detail of a sheep called, of all things, *Gloria.* I had chuckled, wondering if Phil's mother knew that this Gloria stood here. Her home up on the hill probably overlooked it. This Gloria stood about six feet tall, wore a wonderful hat and had a Gucci handbag over her arm. Positioned close to the old wool press, she had been commissioned by the council to represent the history of the wool trade in the area. In the background stood the original wool stores, now, sought after apartment living.

I couldn't remember seeing Gloria before, although that came as no great surprise. In the last twenty months or so, it was not as if I had been keen to do anything unless it involved Carmody House.

We had also begun visiting the New Farm dog park. I had explained to Wilbur that it was now time for us to be more social. We had closeted ourselves away enough. 'You might meet friends. Maybe you'll find yourself a poodle girlfriend. What do you think? Would you like a white poodle?' The poor dog had looked at me with some concern. I read his face to say... *A poodle! Do I even like poodles?*

I laughed at him. 'You'll love a poodle. We'll pick a pretty one.' My words did not lessen the concern he showed. However the dog park did. With Christopher in his pram, I sat on the park bench under the arms of a massive Moreton Bay fig and watched as Wilbur ran and sniffed every dog in cooee. He didn't fall in love with a white poodle but he did spend that first afternoon playing with a caramel Kavoodle called Gussy. Wilbur's smile was priceless. Hmmm... I had never thought of dogs as gay, however like humans I guess there was a distinct possibility.

Our little outings reminded me there was much to discover, and I couldn't wait for Christopher to be old enough for me to share it. *But*, there was something else as well. Something far more important. On these walks, I spoke to other mothers. It was as if suddenly becoming a mum, made others more inclusive. From a total stranger there'd be that chitchat... *How old is he? Is he waking at night? He likes his dummy! Do you like the Bugaboo pram? Love the yellow Bugaboo Bee. Good for boys or girls. We had the red one last time, might get the Bee next time...* and on and on.

It made me feel as if I belonged. I was part of *that* club, the one I had so desperately wanted to be included in, although had given up hope of ever belonging. *I was normal.* I had a family. It may have looked different to other people's families, as one of us was a canine... but it was still *my* family.

Yesterday, as I had walked through New Farm Park, past the playground, I waved to a woman I had spoken to the week before. Each week she bought her grandson there to play. She told me that people often asked if she was babysitting. Her response was that it was their playdate. I liked her attitude. However I didn't stop. As if on a mission, I continued on. At the entrance to the Powerhouse, I noticed the posters for the outdoor Moonlight Cinema.

'Might be quite a while before we attend those my darling,' I told Christopher, thinking he just might be my hot date for quite a few years to come.

In front of us, I could not help but notice a little family, heading in the same direction as us. With one hand the father pushed the pram with the baby in, with the other he hung onto one of the toddler's hands. The mother held the other hand. Between them they repeatedly counted to three and then swung the toddler in the air. The tiny child squealed with delight. 'More,' the little fellow repeated.

Although I smiled at them, it did not go unnoticed by me, that Christopher would never have that. I shrugged. I felt I had come to terms with it.

Leaving the main path, I cut down towards the river, and around the back of the Powerhouse. It had been a couple of years since I had bothered to come this way. Memories of crazy Sunday afternoon drinks with Davis and Marty, along with whichever girl he was dating at that time, flooded in. It had always appeared as if half of Brisbane was there. There was excessive wine, great tapas, loud music and plenty of loud people. At the time it had been fun and I can't say they were unpleasant memories. In fact, sometimes of late, a memory surfaced, and it reminded me there were many good times. Great times in fact.

I had confided this to Emerald Green. She had used the onion analogy, where letting go didn't come all at once but like an onion, gradually another layer was shed. I wondered how many more layers had to be shed although didn't ask.

Those memories of old drew me along the riverfront, and before I knew it I had come to the restaurant *Watt*. It certainly had been some time. On that particular weekday, the sun-drenched terrace was scattered with people chitchatting over coffee. Children played upon the impressive sculpture of five huge letters that formed the word FLOOD. It had been erected to commemorate the Brisbane '74 floods, neatly marking the waterline. Who knew that children would love it so much?

I stood for a few minutes watching, thinking it a relaxed and inviting place for coffee, somewhat different to the craziness of the former Sunday afternoon sessions. But then suddenly Christopher squirmed, reminding me of feed time. I decided I would return later in the week and sit for a while.

Later that afternoon, taking me by surprise, Phil had called, and suggested we meet the following day. Strangely, he asked if he could take us to lunch. I suggested coffee and asked that he bring Sophia, treating it as his time with Christopher.

*

My mind returned to the question Phil had asked regarding my plans with Carmody House. As if there had been no break in conversation, my tone continued its briskness. 'Christopher will not be a baby forever, so in time, I believe Carmody House would make a wonderful wedding venue.' Sitting, I crossed my legs, wrapping them tightly around each other. If I had analysed my own body language, as I had a habit of doing to others, I would have thought myself in a protective mode.

Phil leant forward, his tone direct, his eyes slightly narrowed. 'And is that the line of business you would like to pursue now?'

Feeling as if I was conducting a meeting with my bank manager, I sat quite upright, knowing that if I had not been holding Christopher and had been sitting behind a desk, my hands would have been joined upon it.

'Yes and no. Although I am in a fine position now, it would be preferable if in the future Carmody House was financially viable. I always saw it as a place filled with people. And weddings are happy occasions…' I spoke as if this would be a revelation to him, '… and I do think Mr Carmody would like that.' Was that a condescending tone to my voice? Perhaps!

Phil stretched his legs out, placing his elbows wide on the arms of the chair. It did not escape me he was taking up as much space as possible, and was perhaps far more relaxed than I was. It also did not escape me that he continued to have one eye on Sophia the entire time. And then he leapt to his feet, giving me a fright, dived across the three metres where Sophia had slipped. In a second he righted her, brushed her off, and removed her glasses before wiping her tears with a tissue he pulled from his pocket. He kissed her knee and returned to his seat.

My heart was still in my mouth. 'Is she okay?'

'Yup!' was all he said, his eyes still upon her. I noticed he appeared to allow her to do what most children her age did, even though it took more effort and created much stress. And then he turned his attention to me. 'So… no regrets about the B&B then?'

Unfortunately, the scare Sophia gave, had not encouraged my voice to thaw, and I could not help that slight tilt of my head. 'Not a one. It was always a business deal, but somehow I think I've gotten a much better deal.' Finally, my voice gave an inkling of warmth at the thought of Christopher. At the same time I felt his weight become a little heavier in my arms, as he drifted into a deeper slumber.

Keeping him up to my shoulder, I lowered my head, inhaling his blissful scent. If I'd had my way, I would have held him in my arms all day. However my bible said a baby with a routine was a happier baby. Although, I was still not past the novelty of simply holding him because I loved the feel and touch of him. Minutes, possibly hours, had been wasted as I had stared at his face, unable to look away, unable to get enough.

I caught Phil watching us, before he asked, 'I want to ask you something?' He paused. 'Peach, what do *you* want, because you've never really said clearly what *you want?*'

His question hit a raw nerve, and I felt an unjust amount of anger rise. Buying time against answering, and belying the way I felt, I gently placed Christopher in the Bugaboo, spending an inordinate amount of time tucking the navy bunny rug embellished with white stars around him.

For God's sake, Phil sounded like Steve. What the bloody hell did he mean what did I want? What does every woman want!

Concerned the wrong words might escape, with tightly pursed lips I glanced at him. I knew my eyebrows were sky high and I desperately tried to lower them, sick to death of my face being so *bloody* readable. Why couldn't I be one of those people who kept their cards close to their chest, and mulled it over in private?

I must have then looked like I was frowning because Phil appeared to think I wasn't following. He began to repeat himself. Even though I was anxious my words may be construed as desperate, I couldn't help myself but jump in, keen to stop him repeating the question.

So as to not waken my sleeping baby, I kept my tone deliberately softened, however each word was enunciated precisely. 'Phil… in my marriage, I lost who I was. I lived someone else's dream. That is no one else's fault but mine. But… in the last couple of years, I have worked really hard to find out exactly who I am.'

I actually thought he had already gleaned that from me, and I was not sure why the heck I had to spell it out. 'The old me would have lived someone else's life. Would have overlooked the odd untruth. Would have smoothed things over. But I am *no longer* happy to live someone else's dream. I cannot overlook it when someone...' I felt around for the right word, before I looked at him directly, *'omits stuff!* I *cannot* do it again. I have to be me. I am worth more.' I caught him nodding his head, but I didn't stop. 'And Carmody House is my home. That is where I want to raise Christopher. That is the place that bought out the best of who I am. I will always be eternally grateful to Mr Carmody for that. And I cannot lie... I am not sure if I can ever compromise again.'

For the longest time, I looked at him, and neither of us spoke. I remembered years ago, a therapist on television, in attempting to get a few laughs, explained the difference between men and women's brains. Apparently, women's brains had all of these compartments. When a man said something, a woman instantly went to the right compartment, got the info and fired back a response. Okay, so sometimes it wasn't always the right compartment, but the point was, they always had an answer. Men on the other hand, only had a few compartments, and some of them were empty. If a woman spoke, the man would first of all be unsure which compartment to go to, then when he did, there was a good chance it would be bare. He'd come up with nothing. *This was one of those times.*

In his sleep, Christopher gave the tiniest of meows and stretched, one of his little arms, escaping from his wrap. Busying myself, I tucked his arm back in and pulled the bunny rug closer around. I had dressed him in one of the Marquis suits courtesy of Gloria, thinking it nice for Phil to see what his mother had bought for his son. I hadn't actually said anything about it yet. However, at that moment, the suit bought memories of the words Gloria had voiced. My over-active imagination imagined Christopher as a man. Something softened in my heart. I thought of him standing in front of a woman trying to make right. I would not want that woman to be cruel to him. I would want her to give him a chance, just like Gloria had not so surreptitiously asked me to do.

Before I could say anything, the waiter placed the bill on the table. I watched while Phil read it, and then stood. He reached around to his back pocket, and took out his wallet. He pulled out a note and with an air of authority slid it into the folder, snapping it closed. Turning, he held it up. The waiter returned to collect it.

I watched all of this. Not one detail escaping me. I realised I'd had a baby to a man, whom I had never seen pay for anything, much less a coffee. I had never seen his wallet. Funny thing! I had never seen him socially. The list of what I had never seen began to grow in my mind. It created an odd feeling.

I coughed. 'Phil, please do not think me ungrateful for all you did at Carmody House. At the time, I was most appreciative that you appeared to share my dream. In fact…' I paused, '… you actually made me feel as if it was a life you loved.' I frowned, the incongruity of it all too much. 'But of course, I am not delusional. You have another life,' as much as I tried, I could not help the slight change in my voice, 'a secret high-flying life. And while I am happy for you to have whatever role you wish to with Christopher, I do not wish to live between two worlds.' Instantly I could have bitten my tongue. After all he was hardly asking me to.

He opened his palms wide. 'Neither do I!' His voice was firm.

'I'm not asking you to,' I said, my voice soft.

I would have had to lie, if I said there was not an element of disappointment, or more than even an element, however, I was not entirely surprised. Although I may have wished differently, I'd had many months to come to terms with who he was. I shrugged and voiced my thoughts. 'Well there you have it.'

His hands ran up and down the arm of the chair, giving him an air of uncertainly, and then he opened his palms. 'I want you to give me a chance Peach.'

'I've already said I'd not deny you your son. I promise you will not need to hold Brisbane to ransom and attempt to jump off the Story Bridge.' I glanced over to where Sophia was now busy attempting to pull herself up on one of the letter O's of the sculpture to no avail. I looked back at him. 'I have told you, you and Sophia can visit him whenever you like. And your mother as well. My door will always be open to her.'

'But I want you to give *me* a chance.'

While this should have filled me with joy, it somehow didn't. I knew I was scared of him only wanting me because of Christopher, and I knew I deserved so much more. Also, I did not want a part time partner. I wanted someone who wanted to share my life. I was quiet for the longest time.

'I'm not sure how this works Phil?'

'I've already told you, I am lightening my load, so I can return to Brisbane. I don't know what I was thinking when I took Sophia back to Melbourne for school. I was following an old dream, but let's face it, dreams change. She was always going to be better off up here with my mother and Katrine's parents. I should never have taken her away from their love.'

I nodded in agreement, however I hardly wanted someone to be with me, simply because it was now more convenient.

He looked at me, his eyes searched mine. 'There was a time I could not see my future, but now I cannot see it without you Peach.'

I was quiet. I had no idea how to answer. I found myself biting my lower lip. I glanced across the river, my eyes skimming the luxurious riverside homes. Finally I focused on a building site, thinking. To his credit, Phil gave me time. Funny that at a time like that I actually noticed the name of the construction company. The huge banner was draped across the entire second floor. Only able to see the last few letters of the name, I narrowed my eyes to read them… O…V…E Properties! Blinking, I caught my breath. *What?* Oh My God! Was this some crazy sign? Unable to believe my eyes, I leant to the right to read the entire thing. G… R… O… O… V… E Properties. I gave a light snuff.

Finally, I spoke. 'You may ask me out.' Even to me, my words sounded starched, prim as a paper collar.

His voice sounded surprised. 'Ask you *out?*'

'And we'll date.' I caught his slow blink of astonishment.

'Right… of course.' But I could see by the look of total incomprehension written across his face, that he did not understand.

I shrugged, knowing I was on uncertain territory. 'Phil, this is not a normal situation.' My hands waved around me. 'In case you haven't noticed, we appear to have done some things in reverse. And the fact remains, I *really* don't know you.'

'I think you do.' His tone sounded determined, he sat back. He folded his arms. 'But if it is the fact I come as a package, just say the word and I'll leave you be.' He eyes flicked to Sophia.

Annoyed, I felt myself frowning. My voice rapid fired back. 'Um have you noticed I too come as a package these days?'

'My package is a little bit more hard work.'

'That remains to be seen. Your package would be an honour to take on.' I glanced over to Sophia. Her blonde piggy tails were tied with scarlet coloured ribbons to match the strawberries embellished on her yellow dress. I wondered if Gloria had had a hand in this, or if Phil dressed her this way. 'It's more than that. It runs deeper. Trust me when I tell you I do not even have to think twice about Sophia.'

My eyes returned to her once again. She now sat atop of the O laughing gleefully at what she had accomplished. I couldn't help but smile. Turning back, I looked at Phil squarely. And then I exhaled heavily. 'I know you're a good man Phil. And I'm trying to get my head around who you are now. But let's face it, a relationship based on a lie is not exactly a good way to start...' I drifted off. 'And... there are things I'd like to know... things like... like which political party you vote...'

Before I could say more he laughed loudly and placed his hands low on his hips, a look I now found irresistible. Shaking his head, he looked at me with sheer disbelief. Quickly, I placed a finger to my lips, glancing at Christopher. He did not stir.

I had no intention of explaining myself. However, I had a theory that I could only fall in love with someone who voted the same way I did. Call me odd. And plenty have.

Anyway, I rushed on, 'I don't know if you read aloud in bed, or read silently but move your lips? Leave the toilet seat up? Eat with your mouth open? Favourite travel destination? What type of education you would expect for Christopher...' On a roll, finally I paused and put a hand up. 'I think you know what I mean.' I shook my head grasping at straws.

'*What do I know about you?*' I eyed him and we were both quiet for a minute. I took it he was thinking, checking for a compartment with something in.

And then he let out a huge breath. 'So you want to know more about me.' He narrowed his eyes. 'Right… here goes. I do read in bed, but not aloud. I like biographies, and I don't *think* I move my lips, although now that you've mentioned it, I will have to check. My mother has done a fairly good job, and I consider myself house trained. However, I'll try to keep my manners in check…'

Cutting him off, I waved a hand at him. 'You know what I mean.'

With a look of mirth on his face, he continued. 'I think you already know education is pretty damn important to me, or I would *never* have begun the Field of Dreams School.' He flashed me a look, and I took it that he would have loved to have called me a smarty pants. I knew I had a certain guise about me, as if I was interviewing him for a job, but I just couldn't help myself. I would have liked a clipboard to put ticks or crosses beside the questions.

He folded his arms, drawing himself up his full height. 'Now as for the deal breaker…' His voice carried a sense of fun, however I kept my face straight, surreptitiously crossing my fingers that we were both on the same page politically, so to speak. 'You might notice I have a little lady with me,' affectionately he glanced at Sophia, 'so I have had to remedy my ways, and therefore do put the toilet seat down. Does that one score huge brownie points?'

Annoyed, I huffed, and glanced to the heavens. He gave a quick laugh and shook his head as if in frustration and sheer disbelief this was the angle I was taking.

I knew I wasn't making it easy for him.

And then he placed one of his elbows on the arm of the chair and rested his chin upon it. It surprised me when he continued, as if keen to actually answer. 'In the last few weeks, I have realised the thought of more children fills me with nothing but delight.' I watched as he glanced at Christopher, his face filled with joy at the sleeping bundle, and then back across to Sophia, before he turned his attention to me. 'And although I haven't been in the position to do so in the last few years, I do like to travel.'

'Favourite city?' I rapid fired, sounding like the host of a TV show.

'Huh?'

'I want to know your favourite city?'

'Is this a test? If I get it wrong, am I'm out?'

'*No*, I just want to know.' What I didn't say was that favourite cities tell you a lot about people.

'Venice! Is that okay with you?'

I had rested my chin on my hand, and with my lips pursed, I gave a non-committal, 'Hmmm.'

I saw the look of amazement cross his face and he muttered something inaudible before he said, 'I can see I am going to have work real damn hard here.' As if settling in, he leant back in his chair, his legs stretched out towards me.

'Well that will hardly hurt you, you barely spoke for most of your time at Carmody House.' I knew I sounded difficult. I was reminded of that John Wayne movie where he shot off a gun around someone's feet telling them to *dance, goddamn it, dance.* I wanted to say, *talk, goddamn it, talk*, without the gun of course. Or maybe not!

I watched his face. His eyes moved to the right as if recalling information. 'Mostly I like to sit in a piazza, drink coffee, read a book and then just wander about, getting lost.' He shrugged. 'It's the best way to find out-of-the way restaurants and galleries. My favourite place for coffee, *Trattoria da Romano*. Best risotto, *alla Madonna*. Favourite dish of all time, *Al Covo* has the hands-down best soft shell crab.'

I didn't know if he was simply reeling off these places as if off a list, or was trying to impress me, however I could not deny his Italian accent was flawless and rather attractive. But then again, as I spoke absolutely not one word of Italian, how was I to know? Regardless, I could hear in his voice he was enjoying talking about his favourite city.

'Close to the heart of Venice are these beautiful gardens, the *Giardini della Biennale,* with huge trees and a calm atmosphere.' His voice began to warm to the theme. 'They're the main drag for the Biennale art festival which I used to go to every two years, although, I haven't been of late.' He took a breath, and then smiled. 'Also... Harry's Bar is *my* bar.' He said this with a sense of pride and ownership. 'I think of it like a headquarters, somewhere to end up most afternoons, best time to avoid the crowds. They have this fantastic tasting *croque-monsieur*, a pricie toasted sandwich that I continue to return for.' He took a deliberate pause. 'And I've got to say their peach Bellinis are pretty damn delicious.' He flashed me a look at the mention of my name. My heart gave a thump.

'And *then* there's a little island *Isola di San Francesco del Deserto*, which has this monastery where I have been known to spend a few days...' And once again, I was reminded that when this man warms to a theme he really does, exactly how his mother had said. With rapt attention, I watched his face as he continued.

'I guess it's not for everyone, however it really appeals to me because it's sweet and meditative. In the past it has always been a place where I can get off the conveyor belt, if you know what I mean. I love the architecture and complete solitude. It's quite a contrast to the chaos and fun of Venice.' He looked back at me, his voice developed an intimacy. 'I can't say I don't love discovering new places as well. Places where you feel there are moments you can't recreate. You're somewhere special, you have a great meal, and it is a moment, a sense of connection to the place you're in, a beautiful memory, it can change your life.'

I had become mesmerised by the way he spoke, the thought of discovering new places with him, terribly seductive. I said nothing, too intent on staring at him.

And then I caught him looking at me, appearing aware of the effect he had on me. His head cocked to the side, his eyes dancing, he asked, 'Can you give me an indication of whether or not I'm giving the correct answers here?' Moving his chair so it was alongside mine, his low voice began to tease. 'Does a low score allow me a little peck like this?' Surprisingly, he leant across and kissed me gently on the lips. 'Or does a high score, allow me a much longer lingering kiss, such as this.'

My seditious voice was breathless. 'Ummm, I'm thinking it was an *extremely* high score.' I couldn't help but glance around wondering if we were creating quite a scene, however no one appeared to be looking our way. He kissed me again and my hands reached out and touched his warm body. Not caring who the heck was watching now, I let my head drop back, and my mouth opened to his. All I wanted was to be close to him, didn't he know that, didn't I know that.

But he pulled away. 'What do I get if I answer the political question correctly?'

'Oh I'd say that one gets bonus points.' However, before more could be said, from the pram beside us, a wail began. Turning, we both looked with awe at the child we had created.

I felt one of Phil's hands rest in the middle of my back. It felt wonderful.

'You've done an amazing job Peach.'

Not wanting to spoil the moment, I turned back to him, my face showing a grimace. 'I'm afraid I am going to have to take him home to feed him.'

'Can you feed him here?'

I shrugged, thinking I would prefer to take him home. 'We walked, so he'll be in fine form by the time we get there.'

'We'll drop you.' He stood and gathered Sophia, taking her by the hand. I didn't say anything but was wondering how that was going to be possible, as Christopher required a capsule.

As we walked around the side of the restaurant, Sophia reached for one of my hands. '*Wun, twoooo, fibe,*' her little voice suggested. I heard Phil laugh as we both lifted her off the ground. My face beamed.

'You did the hard part without me,' Phil said wistfully, his eyes on the little man's face.

I shrugged nonchalantly. What was there to say? I've no doubt the hard part was ahead of us. And the thought that he had not answered that last question lingered in my mind for all of three seconds.

Chapter 33

The November day had dawned with a relentless downpour. By mid-morning the sun had made a watery appearance, and frail looking daffodils tentatively raised their battered heads, only to be drenched again by eleven. However, by the stroke of noon, the rain clouds had totally disappeared and the sun emerged to illuminate the garden, so perfect for our first Thanksgiving luncheon.

My kitchen was filled with so many wonderfully tempting aromas, my mouth was watering. As I stole a glance out the kitchen window, I noticed that the sky was now the perfect shade of blue, and there was not a cloud to be seen.

With a huge sense of satisfaction, I glanced at the wire basket filled with fresh eggs from the girls, gracing its place on the kitchen bench. Through the open door of the pantry, I glimpsed the rows of my home-made condiments. On the shelf beneath, wrapped in a black and white checked tea towel, a golden brown loaf of freshly baked spelt bread leant its fragrance as well.

Sophia, dressed in a lemon check ruffled dress, sat on her haunches at the table colouring in, her short fingers gripping the pencil, her little head bent low, her glasses pushed up her nose. Her effort was slow but unusually precise for someone her age. Pleasingly, her fine motor skills appeared perfect. To enhance her concentration further, her small pink tongue was pushed to the corner of her mouth, slightly protruding.

Under her chair lolled Wilbur, her constant companion, and smart as to where the snacks might fall. Arthritis had slowed him, although he was well contented, and loved with his family around him. His favourite time of day was early in the morning when he accompanied me to the hen house to help collect the eggs.

With Christopher on my hip, I watched as, with oven mitted hands, my husband lifted the weighty turkey from the oven, placing it on the kitchen bench beside the pumpkin pecan pies, cooling on wire racks. Turning, he took Christopher from my arms. 'What do you think?' he asked.

With some trepidation, we both peered at the blackened cheesecloth the bird was wrapped in, before I began to carefully peel it back. 'Sue said the orange juice would do that to the cheesecloth but not to worry.' As the beautiful golden skin of the turkey was revealed, I let out the breath I was holding. As with many things in the last couple of years, cooking a turkey was a first for me.

My friend Sue was an American food and travel journalist whom I had met many years before when I had attended the PR conference with Steve in Paris. Sue and I had hung out doing the spousal tours. Later we had continued our friendship through Facebook. For years I had followed her family's Thanksgiving feasts. Finally, I was able to copy her turkey recipe.

'Well done,' said Phil from behind. His arms went around me, and he gently patted my once again growing belly. Hairs stood up on the back of my neck as I felt his lips upon it. One of his hands brushed at my backside. 'You have a floury handprint on the seat of your shorts,' he laughed. These days I appeared to be covered in either baby food, milk, or some thing or another I was bottling. If I was not in the garden, I was in the kitchen, both places heaven for me.

'Do you want me to put Christopher down for his sleep?' he asked.

However before they could leave, I took Christopher from

his arms and kissed the chubby bracelets of his wrists, his collagen filled thighs, and his soft spongy brown cheeks. Cheeks I gently pinched with my fingers, reminding myself not to squeeze too hard even though my fingers itched to. Holding him in the air, I blew a raspberry onto the warm sponge of his fat little belly. The kitchen was filled with his squeals of delight, a sound I can never get enough of.

'Careful honey, he's getting too heavy for you to do that,' warned Phil, reaching for him.

'Never, I'll be doing it when I am an old woman!' However, at the sound of his daddy's voice, Christopher reached out his fat little chubby hands, wiggled his fingers and squealed some more. I delivered him back to his father.

Turning, I watched as my gorgeous husband left the room, our fifteen month old over his shoulder. As he passed Sophia, Phil affectionately touched the top of her head. Without flinching she continued on with her task. Phil was such a natural, loving, hands-on father with both Sophia and Christopher, it literally took my breath away every day.

Lifting his head, Wilbur watched Phil until he could no longer see him. Contented all was well, he dropped his head back between his paws, sleepily closing his eyes. Once again I was reminded that I had much to be thankful for.

Stretching to reach a huge oval serving platter in the pantry, my rounded belly pressed against a shelf, and my thoughts instantly turned to the growing baby boy inside of me. Smiling, I pondered how my life had changed in such a short time.

With a sense of satisfaction, I placed the platter upon the kitchen bench, covered the turkey with foil and slid the sweet potatoes back in the oven. Glancing at the clock, I still had 30 minutes before the first guests arrived.

Still aproned, nursing a glass of berry punch, I roamed

through the house, noticing each room appeared to have some sort of baby and small child accoutrements. Although I shook my head, my heart was overwhelmed.

As I walked towards the front door, I was reminded of what I had seen that morning. I had come down a little earlier than usual to begin the Thanksgiving preparation. Halfway down the stairs, I had stopped in my tracks in awe, when I had seen the letters of Carmody House reflecting in a myriad of rainbow colours on one of the hallway walls. The early morning sun was in the perfect position behind the leadlight window above the front door. It lasted simply seconds, not giving me time to rouse Phil to see the miracle.

I had wondered if Mr Carmody was sending me a message this Thanksgiving Day. Often, I had hoped that he knew how grateful I was. I now believe he did. My fingers traced the invisible letters upon the wall.

I pondered how synchronicity was always working, moving the pieces around, while all the while our ego believed we were in charge.

Giving my head a shake, I strolled out to the front veranda where a long white clothed table has been laid with beautiful white china and sparkling glassware for eighteen. My hand went to one of the centrepieces to straighten a wayward yellow rose. I had hollowed out three of my home grown pumpkins to use as vases and filled them with masses of roses, daffodils and calla lilies in colours of yellows and oranges.

On either side of them were five square glass vases filled with cranberries. Candles had been placed in the middle of each. Off to the side was a small round table where a large wicker basket was stacked high with parting gifts of my own homemade pumpkin relish. As like the first day I had seen the kitchen garden, the pumpkins continued to flourish. The labels on the jars were marked *Carmody House Produce.* Proudly, each lid had been covered with a square of orange gingham fabric and tied with twine.

I adjusted Christopher's highchair. It was beside my place setting at one end of the table. Reaching across I straightened Henri's place card, and with a smile, shook my head at the thought of my mother. Henri was finally coming to Australia. No not to visit me, it was my mother he was smitten with. Hopefully now that they were a couple, we might expect to see a little more of him, although Bea was spending more and more time at the chateau. And surprise, surprise, Henri was finally divorcing his wife. Wonders would never cease.

When Bea had explained that Henri was coming to visit and would be with us for Thanksgiving, I had hurried along to make sure Bea had told Henri I was now a married woman.

She had looked at me over the top of her reading glasses. 'He is coming to see me.'

I cannot say how delighted I was. How wonderful for my mother.

My eyes settled on Mr John Scott's place card, which I had put on the other side of my mother, knowing full well she would entertain Mr Carmody's lawyer. Steve and Thomas were respectively seated on the other side of him. Our angel, Sophia, had Phil's mother, Gloria, next to her.

There had been a bit of deliberation in this, as I wanted Gloria opposite John Scott so they could talk. Although she was ten years older than him, she was an extremely attractive woman. I hadn't told Phil of my scheming, as I was still attempting to work out if perhaps Mr John Scott batted for the other team.

On the other side of Sophia, Lakshmi and Bob had Lou and Marty beside them. I had laid the table for Dad and Patrice, and was hopeful they would make it. When I had phoned to invite them, Dad's response had been, 'Abso-bloody-lutely Peachy, but we may be late honey.'

I could not be more thrilled that Emerald Green was joining us. Forever, I would be grateful for her help in leading me on from my old life, readying me to embrace my new one. Plus I was keen to meet her partner Georgia.

I felt no bitterness for what had gone before. During the time of my first marriage I had been mostly happy, and although I was following Davis's dream, that had been my choice. The skills I had learnt during that time stood me in good stead and led me right to the point I was at.

There were rare moments when I thought of Davis, although it was mostly with concern. Steve and Thomas were mindful to keep his antics from me, however occasionally I heard of him through friends. It was not the most flattering for him. My wish for him was that he sorted out his life and lived it with integrity, returning to being the honourable man I once knew him to be. Unfortunately, these days that did not appear to be the case. Davis's strength laid in the powerhouse team he, Marty and I made up.

My thoughts almost never turned to her… but when they did, I pushed them out of my mind instantly. Although she was the type of woman other women needed to be warned about, it would be a waste of my precious life to spend one more second giving thought to her.

I cannot say I was so charitable when a friend felt the need to share that Felicity had confided how sorry she had felt for me being married to Davis for so long. I wondered at what point she actually gave me thought, while she was screwing my husband and stealing my life, or when he dumped her.

However, these days I saw that her coming back into my

life was all part of the journey I was meant to have experienced, painful though it was. There was no denying she had been the catalyst, or else how would I have ended up sitting on the front steps of Carmody House right that very moment? And how would I have ever worked out all the things that brought me joy?

My thoughts went to that day when I had come in through the front gate with Marty. The magic seducing me. One glimpse of the enchanted garden and I had fallen in love. I remembered knowing that I was going to live at Carmody House. I just didn't know how it was going to come about.

With effort, I shook myself out of my reverie, knowing it would not be long before our guests arrived, and that I should rouse myself. Without hearing his approach, I felt Phil's legs touching my back. He placed his hands on my shoulders and gave a squeeze. 'What *ya* thinking?' Smiling with contentment, I felt him press his lips to the top of my head.

Reaching around with my left arm, I held him close. Standing, I kissed him, winding my arms around him. 'Hmmm… just thinking how much I love you.'

He pulled away, looking down at me. '*Really?* Even when I annoy you, like I did this morning, when I woke Christopher?'

'Hmmm… that I'll have to think about,' I said with mock seriousness, flashing him a cheeky look, and chastising him by giving him a tiny whack on the arm. I cannot deny his passion for politics and yelling at the television when he did not agree, sometimes aggravated me. But only sometimes. The thing was that as luck would have it, he had turned out to have the same political beliefs as me. I would have been up the creek if that had been the straw to break the camel's back, putting an end to my theory. Only difference between us, was that I was not as vociferous as him. 'Well… I guess I am fast learning that when you are passionate about something, *you are passionate!*'

He kissed the end of my nose. 'I'll tell you one thing… I'm damn passionate about you!'

'Mmmm I know,' I said a little boldly.

*

Amid lots of good natured jesting, one by one, the various members of our hotchpotch family claimed their seats around the bounteous table, laden with beautiful food, some traditional, some from the kitchen garden.

Brightly hued marinated grilled capsicums lent their brilliant colour to the festivities. Small, young fresh zucchinis tossed with olive oil, grilled and scattered with finely chopped garlic and torn basil and mint, drizzled with Joseph's olive oil, were proudly piled high on a platter. Next to them, darkly coloured eggplants were stuffed with mint, garlic, parmesan and breadcrumbs. As per usual, I was proud to share my bounty with my loved ones.

A huge platter of crispy roasted potatoes along with the *piece de resistance*, the turkey, had been placed in front of Phil at the other end of the table.

With baby Christopher still on my lap, I asked our guests to join hands and take a quiet minute of gratitude. Opening my eyes, my heart warmed as I saw happy faces everywhere. Emerald Green and her lovely partner Georgia were thrilled to be included as our family. I caught Lou flashing her eyes at Marty, as his thumb caressed her hand. My eyes settled on Henri, and I was reminded of when Bea had told me he was very much like my papa, although a somewhat younger version. Gratitude rose in my chest and I said a silent thank you to Alexandre. Without him, none of this would have been possible. Emotions surged and briefly I felt tears prick.

Swallowing, I kissed the top of Christopher's blonde head, and for the thousandth time thought that there was no better smell in the world.

Righting the back of Christopher's singlet, I watched as Phil pulled the mammoth turkey platter closer to him. As he picked up the huge carving knife, something caught my eye. Immediately I was covered in goose bumps. I called Phil's name. By the tone of my voice, he instantly halted, following my gaze. Coming across the gravel drive were Miriam and Keith, Sophia's other grandparents.

Nervously, I stood, depositing a gurgling Christopher onto the lap of a surprised Thomas. My hands hurriedly untied the floral apron strings from around my neck and waist.

They had come. Like all of the past invitations, a note of inability had been sent. They had been slow to acknowledge me, and I had understood. I knew having Christopher so soon had been hard for them.

There was quiet at the table, and I watched as Phil greeted them with affection. In an instant Sophia was in Keith's arms. Uncertain of what to do, I stood at my chair. Phil motioned for me to come forward. With his hand on my back he introduced me. They embraced me warmly, the emotion palpable, a lump forming in my throat. They had lost their child, however because of Sophia, we were to be forever united as a family.

Nervously, Miriam pushed a china plate wrapped in a tea towel into my hands. Inside was an apple teacake, still warm and fragrant from the oven.

'I didn't know what to make,' she said. 'Thanksgiving is new to us.'

Keith interrupted, 'She was panicking and carrying on, and I said *just make the bloody thing*.' I could tell he was being brusque to cover his feelings. I smiled at this big bear of a man, knowing straight away that he and Johnny were going to hit it off enormously.

I turned as Marty came from inside carrying two more chairs. For a few moments there was chaos as introductions were made, everyone moved slightly around the table, two more place settings were laid, and our new family members were seated. Baby Christopher was being passed around from lap to lap like the fat happy plaything he was, before with a great sense of satisfaction, I scooped him up and deposited his wriggling body into the highchair, securing him with the belt.

Keith spoke and I glanced at him, noticing his eyes were shining, and he was looking at me. 'What more can a man ask for, than to share Thanksgiving with his granddaughter and her family and a good bit of turkey? Hey Soph?'

Now with everyone assembled, I glanced around at all of the faces, and with a strong sense of peace in my heart, I realised that families were tricky things. Some we were born into, some we inherited. All we loved.

*

The garden, bathed in a unique golden light in that magic hour before sunset, was extraordinary. It heralded the end of a perfect day, instantly setting the pace to slow, and easing the mind. As the sun slipped lower, everywhere I looked there was something beautiful and different. The spectacular scenery, the river, open spaces, wattle birds, bush turkeys, rosellas and blue wrens all contributed to my sense of wellbeing.

It was my true Garden of Eden and it was a relief to be where I belonged, a place that transcended time.

For someone who used to have lengthy lists of goals and dreams to achieve, I now realised there were, as Gloria had pointed out, only three things in life that a person needed to be happy. Someone to love, a dream, and something to do.

In the last of the light, my eyes did not miss a praying mantis swaying on its twig, swivelling its angular head to peer at me with wonderful sinister eyes. Peering back, I marvelled that once upon a time, there was much I would not have seen.

Gazing at Christopher sleeping soundly in his pram, a muslin wrap lightly covering him, a shock of blonde hair showing, I sighed with contentment. He was beautiful, just beautiful!

Although I could not hear what was being said, I heard Sophia's laughter as she sat with her father on the front steps. As per usual, Wilbur was with them.

The next day we were to be heading to our beachside home at Pottsville. Phil wanted the children to learn how to surf from a young age.

There had been a period of time, I imagined that in the business circles I had previously mixed in, whenever my name came up, it would have ended with, 'You know Davis left her for someone at work, a girl who had been her childhood friend, *just* when she was trying to have a baby.' There was something healing for them now to say, 'Oh she's remarried. With a couple of kids and another on the way. Couldn't be happier!'

Somebody once said when you lose love from one person and then find another to love, it's not profit and loss, one arriving doesn't cancel the other out. But it sure changes your story to a happy one.

Sometimes you have to leave your home to find it.

With a deep sense of gratitude about how lucky and blessed I was, I briefly placed a hand on the butterfly stirrings in my belly, before I rose from under the wisteria laden pergola, released the break on the pram, and together with Christopher headed to the steps to gather my family in for the evening. Carmody House beckoned.

Acknowledgements

To my dear mother Annette Monger who set me on my journey when she first began my collection of Enid Blyton books. My favourites, *The Magic Faraway Tree* and *The Enchanted Wood* have special places in my heart. Who knew one day they would inspire me when writing *Love Is the Answer*.

And of course how could I grow up with world renowned landscape designer Don Monger as my father, without having a creative mind and a passion for beautiful rooms, inside and out. Perfect to set the backdrop for this novel.

My sincerest thanks go to my editor Julie Capaldo from Brolga Publishing, who loves my characters as I do and treats them as the real people they have become to me. Your words of encouragement spur me on. Your time and effort does not go unappreciated. Thank you for believing in me Julie.

To my childhood bestie, Joanne Mulford. After listening to everything I have had to say since I was seven, you then take on the huge task of casting your eyes over another 191,000 words of mine. You, more than anyone, know how much I have to say. I love you darling girl.

I am most grateful to Fleur's amazing team at Red Public Relations. Thank you ladies for your polish, expertise and hard work.

To the readers of *The Essential Ingredient – Love* your wonderful words of encouragement, emails, cards, letters and friend requests on Facebook have been nothing short of delightful and a major source of joy to me.

To my family, what a team. You are loved. My wonderful Chris, my beautiful Fleur, my darling Nick, my lovely Genevieve and my little men, Hunter and Boston. You nourish my soul and enrich me daily.

And finally to Chilli Montgomery. I will always be grateful to you for the experiences you gave me, bringing so many wonderful new friends into my life, and opening the doors you have. You were an experience I would have hated to have missed.

Testimonials

Dear Tracy,

I really wanted to contact you to let you know how much I loved reading your book. From beginning to end it was like listening to the story of a friend of a friend, laughing one minute, a blubbering mess the next, and being totally engrossed from page one. Having lived in Brisbane my whole life, I felt connected to the story, especially since I used to work in the Fortitude Valley/New Farm area, often frequenting some of the cafes/bars/places of interest mentioned in the book. I loved, loved, loved the foodie aspect, and enjoyed the elegance of Paris entwined into the storyline.

The biggest thing I got out of reading it however, was how I needed to cherish and love my husband more - that was quite insightful for me. Reading of the special relationship between Chilli and her husband reminded me of my relationship with my husband, and I realised that I had forgotten the importance of showing him that love. Needless to say that he has profited from me reading your book too :-)

Thank you so much for taking the time to write what is for me, one of the best novels I've read in a long time. As soon as I finished that final page I just wanted to start reading it again. Unfortunately I've passed it on to someone else in my book club. She too is enjoying it immensely - she keeps sending me text messages. I've also been told that it will become a book club initiation read for our book club.

So thank you very much again for adding this to the literary world. I wish you all the very best for your future endeavours, including your next book (which I very much look forward to reading).

Kindest Regards,
Natasha Rudd
A fan of Tracy Madden - Author

*

Oh my god Tracy, am nearly finished your book - essential ingredient - love, I can't put it down - I love it.

Everything about it is so, I guess, real to people like me. I am a 48 year old woman with two adult children, happily married for 26 years, going through all of Chilli's life moments and meeting someone new, the love of just simple things in life like the food we have and the love of a special person, of course the beach etc makes this one of the best books I have ever read.

Like I said I haven't finished yet and will be keen to see what the ending has in store for me. I will be sorry to finally take this book back to the library, like I will miss it I suppose, how strange, never really felt like this about a book before.

Thank you for a truly lovely book.
Joanne

*

Hi Tracy,

Its Joanne here, I wrote you an email a week or so ago, and thank you for your reply. I mentioned at the time I was reading your book and was not quiet finished, well unfortunately I finished it last night, oooooohhhhhhhhh.

I have to say I woke up this morning and thought I wonder how Chilli, Jeff and family are going, how strange, they became part of my day, I will miss them. I have never said that about a book I have read in my life, and I have read many over the years.

I truly will miss them and their travelling, of course always enjoying what they were eating every day, the beach house I can still picture.

I am taking the book back to the library today, and guess what Tracy, I don't want to let that book go down the chute, hahaha, have you heard of anything so bizarre. I can't believe it had that much of an impact on me.

Anyway, thank you again for a truly lovely book, like I said I will miss Chilli and Jeff, looking forward to your next book, you did a fantastic job.

Best Wishes
Joanne

*

Hi Tracy

Your book is FANTASTIC. I cried on the train (or maybe my Mascara was in my eyes) that was on the way to work reading about the wedding. Then on the way home this evening my Mascara stung my eyes reading about Rob. Hated being at work today as I wanted to sit in a comfy chair and finish the book.

GREAT first book, CONGRATULATIONS and hope there are more of them locked inside of you.

Kind regards
Jane

*

Dear Tracy,

I am so glad you handed me the opportunity to read your book, whilst browsing at Angus and Robertson in Carindale.

It was a wonderful read, full of such heartfelt emotion,

beautiful food, wonderful locations and yes, it made me yearn for all that you promised on the cover.

What a fantastic first book by a great Australian author. Thank you so much.

Kind Regards
Tanya

*

Dear Tracy

I had the pleasure of meeting you in Brisbane's Borders Bookstore at your signing earlier this month.

I just wanted to let you know that your 'The Essential Ingredient - Love' is the first work of fiction I've enjoyed in a long, long time. Somewhere amidst a mountain of science and management literature, I misplaced my love of losing myself in a good novel but rediscovered it last Sunday - while reading your book from cover to cover in one sitting.

Chilli - what an amazing heroine. She literally leapt off the pages and into my heart - making me laugh, curse, sigh, and ball my eyes out (now that's an understatement).

What an experience. What a book. Thank you!
Jane

*

Hi Tracy

I have just finished your book The Essential Ingredient Love... and I loved it such a lovely book to read... makes one want to cook beautiful food and live and love well xx Looking forward to your next book well done! X Vanessa

*

Dear Tracy

Hello to you, Well Tracy your book was so amazing I have recommended it so many times, it had a profound effect on me in many levels, I do thank you so. I have made brownies and I eat rocky road ice cream delicious, and I have looked up the Dello Mano website, amazing. You have a wonderful gift kindest regards to you

Janet x

www.tracymadden.com.au

About the author

Tracy Madden is a best-selling Australian fiction author living in the Brisbane riverside suburb of New Farm. She has been married to her childhood sweetheart Chris for 35 years and has two children, the powerful and beautiful Fleur, and the strong, silent achiever Nick. She is grandmother, 'Gracy', to Hunter and Baby Boston Bear.

In addition to being a successful novelist, Tracy is also a talented interior decorator, having brought colour and style into the homes of her clients across the country for the last 20 years.

With an enormous passion for her family and food, Tracy feels the two are intrinsically linked. If she cannot be found on her zebra print Louis chair, closeted away in her office surrounded by all of the things she loves while creating characters, Tracy will be in the kitchen, cooking up a storm, feeding her family, and creating the love.

The very mention of the word Paris brings a smile to her face as for most of her life she has endured a love affair with the city of lights.

Following the international success of her debut novel, 'The Essential Ingredient – Love', is Tracy's latest offering, 'Love is the Answer'.

Also by Tracy Madden

The Essential Ingredient—Love
9781921596612 • $24.99

Warning... this novel will leave you with a passion for the finest of food ...and the love of your life!

The Essential Ingredient—Love

TRACY MADDEN

With her passion for love and food, Chilli Montgomery is at a stage in her life when it seems life itself could not get much better… a happy marriage to her childhood sweetheart, and a successful business with her son in their restaurant. However, all is not as it seems and Chilli is unprepared for what this next chapter of her life brings. In minutes, the world she once knew is shattered and nothing will ever be the same again. Not even her infatuation and adoration of food.

Set against the backdrop of many phenomenal Queensland locations, with Paris weaving its magic in and out, on this gastronomic journey of indulgence you will enjoy every meal with the Montgomerys and be touched by their tears and laughter as they become a part of your life.

ORDER

LOVE IS THE ANSWER

Tracy Madden

		Qty
ISBN 9781922175304		
RRP	AU$24.99	.....
Postage within Australia	AU$5.00	.....
	TOTAL* $_____	

★ All prices include GST

Name:...

Address: ....

....

Phone:..

Email: ....

Payment: ❏ Money Order ❏ Cheque ❏ MasterCard ❏ Visa

Cardholders Name:..

Credit Card Number: ....

Signature:...

Expiry Date: ....

Allow 7 days for delivery.

Payment to: Marzocco Consultancy (ABN 14 067 257 390)
PO Box 12544
A'Beckett Street, Melbourne, 8006
Victoria, Australia
admin@brolgapublishing.com.au

BE PUBLISHED

Publish through a successful publisher.
Brolga Publishing is represented through:
- **National** book trade distribution, including sales, marketing & distribution through **Macmillan Australia**.
- **International** book trade distribution to
    - The United Kingdom
    - North America
    - Sales representation in South East Asia
- **Worldwide e-Book distribution**

For details and inquiries, contact:
Brolga Publishing Pty Ltd
PO Box 12544
A'Beckett St VIC 8006

Phone: 0414 608 494
markzocchi@brolgapublishing.com.au
ABN: 46 063 962 443
(Email for a catalogue request)